THE ICE QUEEN

ALSO BY NELE NEUHAUS

Snow White Must Die

Bad Wolf

THE ICE QUEEN

NELE NEUHAUS

TRANSLATED BY STEVEN T. MURRAY

MINOTAUR BOOKS ✠ NEW YORK

THE ICE QUEEN. Copyright © 2009 by Nele Neuhaus.
English translation copyright © 2014 by Steven T. Murray. All rights reserved.
Printed in the United States of America. For information, address
St. Martin's Press, 175 Fifth Avenue, New York, N.Y. 10010.

www.minotaurbooks.com

Designed by Omar Chapa

The Library of Congress Cataloging-in-Publication Data is available upon request.

ISBN 978-0-312-60426-4 (hardcover)
ISBN 978-1-4668-3691-4 (e-book)

Minotaur books may be purchased for educational, business, or promotional use.
For information on bulk purchases, please contact the Macmillan Corporate and
Premium Sales Department at 1-800-221-7945, extension 5442, or write
to specialmarkets@macmillan.com.

First published in Germany under the title *Tiefe Wunden* by List Taschenbuch,
an imprint of Ullstein Buchverlage GmbH, Berlin.

First U.S. Edition: January 2015

10 9 8 7 6 5 4 3 2 1

For Anne

THE ICE QUEEN

Prologue

No one in his family could understand his decision to spend the twilight of his life in Germany; he certainly couldn't, either. All of a sudden he had felt that he didn't want to die in this country, which had been so good to him for more than sixty years. He longed to read German newspapers and to have the sound of the German language in his ears. David Goldberg had not left Germany voluntarily. At the time, in 1945, it had been a matter of life and death, and he had made the best out of losing his homeland. But now there was nothing left to keep him in America. He had bought the house near Frankfurt almost twenty years ago, shortly after Sarah's death, so that he wouldn't have to stay in anonymous hotels when his numerous business or social obligations took him to Germany.

Goldberg gave a deep sigh and looked out the big picture windows at the Taunus hills, bathed in a golden light by the setting sun. He could hardly remember Sarah's face. The sixty-plus years he had spent in the States often seemed erased from his memory, and he had a hard time even recalling the names of his grandchildren. But his memories of the years before he went to America, which he hadn't thought about in a long time, were that much sharper. Sometimes when he woke up from a brief nap, it took him a few minutes to realize where he was. Then he would look with contempt at his gnarled, trembling old-man hands, the scaly skin covered with age spots. Getting old was no picnic—what nonsense to think otherwise. At least fate had spared him from becoming a slobbering, helpless vegetable, like so many of his friends and acquaintances who hadn't been fortunate enough to be carried off in time by a heart attack. He had a solid constitution, which kept astounding his doctors, and he seemed immune to most signs of old age—thanks to the iron discipline with which he had mastered every challenge in his life. He had never let himself go, and even today he paid attention to correct attire and the proper appearance. Goldberg shuddered at the thought of his last unpleasant visit to an old folks' home. He was repelled by the sight of the aged people shuffling along the corridors in bathrobes and slippers, their hair wild and their eyes empty, like ghosts from another world, or simply sitting around forlornly. Most of them were younger than he was, and yet he wouldn't for a moment have stood for being lumped into the same category with them.

"Mr. Goldberg?"

He gave a start and turned his head. The housekeeper, whose name and presence he forgot from time to time, was standing in the doorway. What was her name? Elvira, Edith . . . it didn't matter. His family had insisted that he not live alone, and had hired this woman for him. Goldberg had rejected five applicants. He didn't want to live under the same roof with a Pole or an Asian, and looks did matter to him. He had liked her at once: big, blond, forceful. She was German, with degrees in home economics and nursing. Covering all the bases, Goldberg's eldest son, Sal, had said. He was undoubtedly paying this woman a princely salary, because she put up with his quirks and disposed of the traces of his increasing frailty without ever batting an eye. She came over to his easy chair and scrutinized him. Goldberg returned her stare. She had makeup on, and the neckline of her blouse revealed the roundness of her breasts, which sometimes appeared in his dreams. Where could she be going? Did she have a boyfriend she met on her evenings off? She was no more than forty and very attractive. But he wasn't going to ask her. He didn't want to be on familiar terms with her.

"Is it all right if I go now?" Her voice had a slight hint of impatience. "Do you have everything you need? I've prepared your supper and your pills, and—"

Goldberg cut her off with a wave of his hand. Sometimes she treated him like a mentally disabled child.

"Just go," he snapped. "I'll be fine."

"I'll be here tomorrow morning at seven-thirty."

He didn't doubt it. German punctuality.

"I've already pressed your dark suit for tomorrow, and the shirt, too."

"Yes, all right. Thank you."

"Should I turn on the security alarm?"

"No, I'll do it later. Just go. And have fun."

"Thank you." She sounded surprised. He had never before told her to have fun. Goldberg heard the heels of her shoes clack across the marble floor of the foyer; then the heavy front door closed. The sun had vanished behind the hills of the Taunus, and it was twilight. He stared out the window with a somber expression. Outside, millions of young people were heading off on dates, seeking carefree amusement. Once he had been one of them: a good-looking man, well-off, influential, admired. At Elvira's age, he had wasted no thoughts on the old men who sat shivering with aching bones in their easy chairs, a woolen blanket over arthritic knees, waiting for the last great event in their lives: death. He could hardly comprehend how time had caught up with him. Now he, too, was one of those old fossils, a remnant of the dim past, whose friends, acquaintances, and companions had long since left him behind. There were three people left in this world with whom he could speak about the old days, people who remembered him when he'd been young and strong.

The sound of the doorbell tore him out of his reverie. Was it already eight-thirty? Probably. She was always on time, just like the housekeeper. Goldberg got up from his chair with a muted groan. She had wanted to speak with him urgently again before the birthday party, in private. It was hard to believe that she was already eighty-five, the one little. He crossed the living room and hall with stiff steps, casting a glance in the mirror next to the door, reaching both hands up to smooth back his still quite full head of white hair. Even though he knew that she would be arguing with him, he still looked forward to seeing her. Always. She was the most important reason why he had come back to Germany. With a smile, he opened the front door.

Saturday, April 28

Oliver von Bodenstein took the saucepan of hot milk off the burner, stirred in two spoonfuls of cocoa powder, and poured the steaming mixture into a pitcher. As long as Cosima was breast-feeding, she did without her beloved coffee, and he occasionally showed solidarity with her. Besides, a cup of hot chocolate was nothing to be scoffed at. His eyes met those of Rosalie, and he grinned when he saw the critical expression on his nineteen-year-old daughter's face.

"That's got to be at least two thousand calories," she said, wrinkling her nose. "How can you!"

"Now you see what sacrifices we make for our children's sake," he replied.

"I certainly wouldn't do without my coffee," she said, demonstratively taking a sip from her cup.

"Just you wait." Oliver took two mugs from the cupboard and set them on a tray next to the pitcher of cocoa. Cosima had gone back to bed because the baby had roused her at 5:00 A.M. Her whole life had changed completely since the birth of Sophia Gabriela last December. The first shock at the news that he and Cosima were going to be parents again had brought a sense of happy anticipation, which then gave way to apprehension. Lorenz and Rosalie were twenty-three and nineteen, respectively, grown up and done with school. How would it be to start over again? Could he and Cosima even do it? Would the child be healthy? Bodenstein's secret concerns had proved groundless. Cosima had continued to work until the day before the delivery, and the reassuring results from a test of her amniotic fluid had been confirmed when Sophia was born: The baby was perfect in every way. And now, after scarcely four months,

Cosima was going to the office every day, taking the baby with her in a carrier. Actually, Oliver mused, it was all much easier than it had been with Lorenz and Rosalie. Sure, he and Cosima had been younger then and more energetic, but they hadn't had much money and lived in a small apartment. At the time, he had also sensed that Cosima was depressed about having to give up her job as a TV reporter, which she loved.

"Why are you up so early anyway?" he asked his eldest daughter. "It's Saturday."

"I have to be at the castle at nine," Rosalie replied. "We have a gigantic event today. A champagne reception and then a six-course dinner for thirty-five people. We're giving a party for one of Grandma's friends who is celebrating her eighty-fifth birthday."

"Aha."

After finishing her exams last summer, instead of going to university, Rosalie had decided to serve an apprenticeship as a cook at the elegant restaurant owned by Oliver's brother Quentin and his wife, Marie-Louise. To her parents' surprise, Rosalie was full of enthusiasm about the job. She never complained about the barbaric working hours or her strict and choleric boss. Cosima suspected that it was this very boss, the temperamental star chef Jean-Yves St. Clair, who was the real reason behind Rosalie's choice of work.

"They've changed the menu, the wine list, and the number of guests at least ten times." Rosalie put her coffee cup in the dishwasher. "I'm anxious to know whether they've come up with any more changes."

The telephone rang. At 8:30 on a Saturday morning, that seldom boded well. Rosalie picked it up and soon returned to the kitchen with the cordless phone. "For you, Dad," she said, holding the phone out to him and then leaving with a brief wave. Oliver sighed. He supposed nothing was going to come of his planned walk in the Taunus and a pleasant dinner with Cosima and Sophia. His fears were confirmed when he heard the tense voice of Detective Inspector Pia Kirchhoff.

"We've got a body. I know I'm on call today, but maybe you should take a brief look, boss. The man was a big shot, and an American."

It was sounding a lot like a ruined weekend.

"Where?" Bodenstein asked curtly.

"It's not far. Kelkheim. The address is Drosselweg Thirty-nine a. David Goldberg. His housekeeper found him at around seven-thirty this morning."

Bodenstein promised to hurry, then took Cosima her hot chocolate and broke the bad news to her.

"Dead bodies should be banned on weekends," Cosima murmured with a big yawn. Oliver smiled. Not once in their twenty-four years of marriage had his wife ever reacted with anger or displeasure when he suddenly had to leave, ruining their plans for the day. She sat up straight and grabbed the cup. "Thanks. Where do you have to go?"

Oliver took a shirt from the wardrobe. "Over to Drosselweg. I could actually walk. The man is named Goldberg, an American. Pia Kirchhoff is afraid it might get complicated."

"Goldberg," Cosima said with a frown. "I've heard that name recently, but I can't remember where."

"Apparently he's some big shot." Oliver decided on a tie with a blue pattern and slipped on a jacket.

"Oh yes, now I remember," said Cosima. "It was Mrs. Schönermark at the flower shop. Her husband delivers fresh flowers to Goldberg every other day. Six months ago, he moved here for good. Before that, he stayed at the house only occasionally, whenever he was visiting Germany. She said she'd heard he was once an adviser to President Reagan."

"Then he must have been an elderly man." Oliver leaned over and kissed his wife on the cheek. In his mind, he was already imagining what awaited him. Every time he was called to some location where a body had been found, this mixture of heart-pounding anxiety and trepidation came over him. It disappeared only after he had seen the body.

"Yes, he was pretty old." Cosima sipped absentmindedly at her chocolate, now lukewarm. "But there was something else. . . ."

Besides himself and the priest with his two sleepy altar boys, the only people who had showed up for Mass at St. Leonhard were a few old ladies, driven so early to church either by fear of the approaching end or the prospect of another desolate, lonely day. They sat scattered throughout the front third of the nave on the hard wooden pews and listened to the droning voice of the priest,

who occasionally stifled a surreptitious yawn. Marcus Nowak knelt in the last
row, staring blankly into space. The accident had led him to this church in
the middle of Frankfurt. No one knew him here, and he had secretly hoped
that the comforting ritual of the holy Mass would restore his spiritual equilibrium, but it had not. Quite the opposite. How could he have expected it to,
when he hadn't been to church in years? He imagined that everyone could see
what he'd done the night before. It wasn't one of those sins that could be ab-
solved in the confessional or atoned for by saying ten Our Fathers. He wasn't
worthy to sit here hoping for God's forgiveness, because his repentance was
not genuine. The blood rose to his face and he closed his eyes when he thought
about how much he had enjoyed it, how much of a rush it had given him, how
happy it had made him. He could still see the man's face before him, the way
he had looked at him, and finally had knelt down before him. My God. How
could he have done that? He rested his forehead on his folded hands and felt
a tear run down his unshaven cheek as he realized the full implication. His
life would never be the same again. He bit his lip, opened his eyes, and looked
at his hands with a trace of repugnance. He couldn't wash away this guilt
in a thousand years. But the worst thing was, he would do it again as soon
as a suitable opportunity presented itself. If his wife, his children, or his
parents ever found out, they would never forgive him. He heaved such an
abysmally deep sigh that two of the old ladies in the front rows turned
around to look at him. He hurried to lower his head again and cursed his
faith, which made him a captive of his acquired moral standards. But no matter how he twisted and turned it, there was no excuse as long as he did not
sincerely repent of his action. Without repentance, there was no atonement,
no forgiveness.

The old man was on his knees on the mirrorlike marble floor in the entry hall
of the house, barely ten feet from the front door. His upper body was slumped
forward and to the left, his head lying in a pool of blood. Bodenstein didn't
want to imagine how his face looked, or what was left of it. The fatal bullet
had entered the back of his head, and the small dark hole seemed remarkably
inconspicuous. The exit of the bullet, however, had caused considerable damage. Blood and brain matter were sprayed all over the room, sticking to the

subtle pattern of the silk wallpaper, to the door frame, the paintings, and the big Venetian mirror next to the front door.

"Hello, boss." Pia Kirchhoff stepped out of the doorway at the end of the entry hall. She had been a member of the K-11 team at the Regional Criminal Police in Hofheim for about two years. Although she was usually a real morning person, today she looked as if she'd overslept.

Bodenstein had a hunch why, but he stifled a remark and nodded to her.

Their colleagues from the evidence team arrived, took one look at the body from the front door, and stepped outside to put on white disposable overalls and booties.

"Superintendent!" called one of the men, and Bodenstein turned to the door.

"There's a cell phone lying here." With his gloved right hand, the officer fished out a phone from the flower bed next to the front door.

"Bag it," said Bodenstein. "Maybe we'll get lucky and it belongs to the perp."

He turned around. A sunbeam coming in the doorway struck the big mirror and lit it up for a moment. Bodenstein stopped short.

"Did you see this?" he asked his colleague.

"What is it?" Pia Kirchhoff came closer. She had plaited her blond hair into two braids and wasn't even wearing eye makeup, a sure sign that she'd been in a hurry this morning. Bodenstein pointed to the mirror. In the middle of the blood spatter, a number had been scrawled. Pia squinted and scrutinized the five figures.

"One one six four five. What could that mean?"

"I don't have the foggiest idea," Bodenstein admitted, tiptoeing past the corpse so as not to disturb any evidence. He didn't go into the kitchen right away, but he looked into the rooms off the entry hall and the foyer. The house was a bungalow, but bigger than it looked from the outside. The decor was old-fashioned—heavy furniture in the late-nineteenth-century style, walnut and oak, with carved details. In the living room, there were faded Persian area rugs on top of the beige carpet.

"He must have had a visitor." Pia pointed to the coffee table in front of the couch. Two wineglasses and a bottle of red wine stood on the marble surface, and next to them was a small white porcelain dish containing olive pits. "The front door wasn't damaged, and from the first cursory examination, there were no signs of a break-in. Maybe he offered his murderer something to drink."

Bodenstein went over to the low coffee table, bent down, and squinted to read the label on the wine bottle.

"Unbelievable." He reached for the bottle but remembered just in time that he wasn't wearing gloves.

"What is it?" asked Pia Kirchhoff. Bodenstein straightened up.

"It's a 1993 Château Pétrus," he replied with a reverent look at the unprepossessing green bottle, so sought after in the world of wine, with the red type in the middle of the label. "This one bottle costs about as much as a small car."

"Incomprehensible."

Bodenstein didn't know whether his colleague was referring to the crazy people who would pay that much money for a bottle of wine or to the fact that the murder victim, shortly before his death—and perhaps in the company of his murderer—had partaken of such a noble vintage.

"What do we know about the deceased?" he asked after determining that the bottle was only half-empty. He felt genuine regret at the thought that the rest would have to be poured down the drain before the bottle was sent to the lab.

"Goldberg had been living here since last October," said Pia. "He was born in Germany, but he spent over sixty years in the United States, and he must have been quite an important man there. The housekeeper thinks his family was very well-to-do."

"Did he live alone? He was pretty old, after all."

"Ninety-two. But quite physically active. The housekeeper has an apartment in the basement. She has two nights off, on the Sabbath and another evening of her choosing."

"Goldberg was Jewish?" Bodenstein glanced around the living room until he caught sight of a bronze seven-armed candelabra on a sideboard. The candles in the menorah had not yet been lit. They went into the kitchen. In contrast to the rest of the house, it was bright and modern.

"This is Eva Ströbel," Pia said, introducing her boss to the woman sitting at the kitchen table, who now stood up. "Mr. Goldberg's housekeeper."

She was tall, and despite her flat shoes, she hardly had to raise her head to look Bodenstein right in the eye. He extended his hand and scrutinized the woman's pale face. Her shock was clearly visible. Eva Ströbel told them that she had been hired seven months ago by Sal Goldberg, the victim's son, to be his father's housekeeper. Since then, she had lived in the basement apartment and taken care of the old gentleman and the household. Goldberg had still been very independent, mentally alert, and extremely disciplined. He set great store by a regular daily routine and three meals a day, and he hardly ever left the house. Her relationship with Goldberg had been formal but good.

"Did he have frequent visitors?" Pia asked.

"Only occasionally," Eva Ströbel replied. "Once a month, his son comes from America and stays for two or three days. He also had friends come to visit now and then, but mostly in the evenings. I can't tell you any of their names, because he never introduced me to his guests."

"Was he expecting a visitor last night, as well? On the table in the living room, there are two glasses and a bottle of red wine."

"Then somebody must have been here," said the housekeeper. "I didn't buy any wine, and there's none in the house."

"Could you tell if anything was missing?"

"I haven't checked yet. When I came in and . . . and saw Mr. Goldberg lying there, I called the police and waited by the front door." She made a vague motion with her hand. "I mean, there was blood all over the place. It was obvious that there was nothing I could do to help him."

"You did precisely the right thing." Bodenstein gave her a kindly smile. "Don't worry about it. What time did you leave the house last night?"

"Around eight. I fixed dinner for him and set out his pills."

"And what time did you return?" Pia asked.

"This morning just before seven. Mr. Goldberg appreciated punctuality."

Bodenstein nodded. Then he remembered the numbers on the mirror.

"Does the number one one six four five mean anything to you?" he asked.

The housekeeper gave him a quizzical look and shook her head.

Bodenstein heard voices in the hall. He turned to the door and saw that

Dr. Henning Kirchhoff had arrived. Kirchhoff was the acting head of the Institute of Forensic Medicine in Frankfurt and the ex-husband of his colleague Pia Kirchhoff. When he used to be with K-11 in Frankfurt, Bodenstein had enjoyed working with Henning Kirchhoff. The man was an eminent authority in his field, a brilliant scientist with a professional work ethic bordering on obsession, in addition to being one of the few specialists in Germany in the field of forensic anthropology. If it came to light that Goldberg had at one time been an important personage, public and political interest would put considerably more pressure on K-11. So much the better that a noted specialist like Kirchhoff would be doing the postmortem examination and autopsy. Because Bodenstein would rely on the autopsy, no matter how obvious the cause of death might seem.

Bodenstein heard Pia's voice behind him. "Hello, Henning. Thanks for agreeing to come."

"Your wish is my command." Kirchhoff squatted down next to Goldberg's body and examined it closely. "So the old guy survived the war and Auschwitz, only to be executed in his own house. Unbelievable."

"Did you know him?" Pia seemed surprised.

"Not personally." Kirchhoff looked up. "But he was highly regarded in Frankfurt, and not only in the Jewish community. If I remember correctly, he was an important man in Washington and an adviser to the White House for decades, as well as being a member of the National Security Council. He was involved in the defense industry. He also did a great deal for the reconciliation between Germany and Israel."

Bodenstein heard Pia ask skeptically, "How do you know that? Did you do a quick Google search on him so you could impress us?"

Kirchhoff got up and gave her an offended look.

"No. I read it somewhere and filed it away."

Pia accepted that. Her ex-husband had a photographic memory and his IQ was far above average. In interpersonal relationships, however, he possessed some striking flaws; he was both a cynic and a misanthrope.

The ME stepped aside so that the officer from the evidence team could shoot the necessary photos of the crime scene. Pia directed his attention to the numbers on the mirror.

"Hmm." Kirchhoff inspected the five numbers up close.

"What could that possibly mean?" Pia asked. "The killer must have written them, don't you think?"

"I presume so," said Kirchhoff. "Somebody wrote it in blood when it was still fresh. But what the numbers mean—no idea. Take the mirror and have it checked by the lab."

He turned back to the corpse. "Ah yes, Bodenstein," he said lightly. "I'm waiting for your query about the time of death."

"Usually I don't ask before ten minutes have passed," Bodenstein replied drily. "Despite my high regard for you, I don't consider you clairvoyant."

"As a nonbinding estimate, I'd say that death occurred at twenty past eleven."

Bodenstein and Pia exchanged a baffled look.

"The glass on his wristwatch is shattered"—Kirchhoff pointed to the dead man's left wrist—"and the watch has stopped. It's going to cause quite a stir when people find out that Goldberg was shot."

Bodenstein found that a fairly restrained statement. He also was not thrilled by the prospect that a discussion of anti-Semitism might deflect the focus of the investigation in the mind of the public.

The occasions when Thomas Ritter felt like a bastard always passed quickly. The end actually did justify the means. Still, Marleen believed it was pure coincidence that had led him on that November day into the bistro in the Goethe Passage where she always ate lunch. The second time they had run into each other "by chance" was in front of the office of the physical therapist on Eschersheimer Landstrasse, where she always exercised at 7:30 in the evening in order to regain the muscle strength she'd lost. He had actually resigned himself to a long courtship, but everything went astoundingly fast. He had invited Marleen to dinner at Erno's Bistro, although it was way more than he could afford and had taken a worrisome bite out of his publisher's generous advance. He gently inquired as to how much she knew about his present situation. To his relief, she had absolutely no idea and was only glad to have run into an old friend. She had always been a loner; the loss of her lower leg and the prosthesis had made her even more reserved.

After the champagne, he had ordered a fantastic 1994 Pomerol Château L'Eglise Clinet, which cost about as much as he owed his landlord. He skillfully induced her to talk about herself. Most women like to talk about themselves, and so did lonely Marleen. He learned about her job as archivist for a large German bank and about her boundless disappointment when she found out that her husband had fathered two children with another woman during their marriage. After two more glasses of red wine, Marleen had lost all her inhibitions. If she'd had any idea how much her body language was betraying her, she undoubtedly would have been ashamed. She was starving for love, for attention and tenderness, and by the time the dessert came, which she scarcely touched, he knew that he would get her into bed that night. He waited patiently for her to make a move, and an hour later it happened. Her breathless whispered confession that she'd fallen in love with him fifteen years earlier did not surprise him. During that period in which he had gone in and out of the Kaltensee house, he had seen her often enough. She was her grandmother's favorite, and he had paid her compliments that she never heard from anyone else. By doing that back then, he had already won her heart, as if he'd known that one day it might prove useful. When he saw her tastefully decorated apartment—sixteen hundred square feet in an Art Nouveau building of classic design, with ornamental plaster ceilings and parquet floors in the ritzy Westend of Frankfurt—he became painfully aware of what he had lost because the Kaltensee family had chosen to ostracize him. He had sworn to recover everything that had been taken from him, and a great deal more in the bargain.

All that had been only six months ago.

Thomas Ritter had planned his revenge with farsightedness and patience, and now the seed was sprouting. He turned over on his back and stretched. He heard the toilet in the bathroom flush for the third time in a row. Marleen suffered from severe morning sickness, but for the rest of the day she felt fine, which meant that so far no one had noticed her pregnancy.

"Are you all right, darling?" he called, suppressing a smug grin. For a woman with her sharp intelligence, she had been surprisingly easy to dupe. She had no idea that after their first night of love he'd replaced her birth-control pills with ineffective placebos. After about three months, he'd found her sitting at the kitchen table when he came home, her face swollen and ugly, with proof of the positive pregnancy test lying in front of her. It had been like hitting all six numbers in the lottery, plus the power ball. Just the thought of how *she* would go wild when *she* found out that *he* was the one who had gotten her beloved crown princess pregnant had been the purest aphrodisiac for him. He'd taken Marleen in his arms, acting at first a bit baffled at how in the world this could have happened but then utterly enthusiastic, and he'd ended up fucking her on the kitchen table.

Marleen came out of the bathroom now, pale but smiling. She crept under the covers and snuggled up to him. Although the smell of vomit prickled his nose, he pulled her closer. "Are you sure that you want to do it?"

"Of course," she replied seriously. "If it doesn't bother you to marry a Kaltensee."

It was obvious that she hadn't yet spoken about him and her condition with anyone in her family. What a good girl! The day after tomorrow, on Monday at a quarter to ten, they had an appointment at the registry office at city hall. By no later than ten o'clock, he would be an official member of the family that he hated with all his heart. Oh, how he was looking forward to meeting *her* as Marleen's lawfully wedded husband! He could feel himself getting an erection from his favorite fantasy. Marleen noticed and giggled.

"We have to hurry," she whispered, "In an hour, I have to be at Grandma's house and—"

He sealed her lips with a kiss. To hell with Grandma! Soon, soon, soon it would be time; the day of vengeance was near at hand. But they would announce it officially only when Marleen had a seriously fat belly.

"I love you," he whispered without a hint of a guilty conscience. "I'm crazy about you."

Dr. Vera Kaltensee, flanked by her sons Elard and Siegbert, was sitting in the place of honor at the center of the sumptuously laid table in the great hall of Schloss Bodenstein, wishing that this birthday would finally be over. Naturally, the entire family had accepted her invitation without exception, but it meant little to her, because the two men in whose company she would have liked to celebrate this birthday were not present. And for this, she had only herself to blame. Just yesterday, she had argued over a trifle with one of them—how childish that he chose to hold it against her and hadn't come today—while the other she had banished from her life a year ago. Her disappointment over Thomas Ritter's devious behavior after eighteen years of trusting collaboration still hurt like an open wound. Vera didn't want to admit it, but in moments of self-reflection she sensed that this pain had the quality of genuine lovesickness. Embarrassing at her age, and yet it was true. For eighteen long years, Thomas had been her closest confidant, her secretary, her Dear Abby, her friend, but, unfortunately, never her lover. Vera wouldn't have missed any of the men in her life nearly as much as that little traitor. Over the course of her long life, she'd come to the conclusion that the saying "Everyone is replaceable" was wrong. No one was easily replaced, and certainly not Thomas. Only seldom did Vera permit herself a look back. Today, on her eighty-fifth birthday, it seemed perfectly legitimate to recall at least in passing all those who had ultimately left her in the lurch. She had parted from some companions with a light heart, while it had been more difficult with others. She gave a deep sigh.

"Are you all right, Mother?" asked Siegbert, her second eldest, who was seated to her left, instantly concerned. "You've hardly touched your food."

"I'm fine." Vera nodded and forced herself to give him a reassuring smile. "Don't worry about me, my boy."

Siegbert was always so attentive to her welfare and eager for her praise. Sometimes she couldn't help feeling almost sorry for him. Vera turned her head for a brief glance at her eldest. Elard seemed distant, as he had so often lately, and was clearly not following the conversation around the table. Once again, he had not slept at home the night before. Vera had gotten wind of the rumor that he was having an affair with the talented Japanese painter who was currently being sponsored by the foundation. The woman was in her mid-twenties, almost forty years younger than Elard. But in contrast to plump, cheerful Siegbert, who had not had a hair left on his head by the time he was twenty-five, the years had been kind to Elard. At sixty-three, he almost looked better than ever. No wonder that women of any age kept flocking to him! He fancied himself a gentleman of the old school, eloquent, cultivated, and pleasantly laconic. It was unthinkable to imagine Elard in bathing trunks at the beach. Even in the heat of summer, he preferred to dress all in black, and this attractive combination of nonchalance and melancholy had for decades made him the object of desire for all female creatures in his vicinity. Herta, his wife, had resigned herself to it early on and had accepted without complaint that she would never be able to have a man like Elard all to herself. She had died a few years ago. But Vera knew that things looked quite different behind the handsome facade that her eldest son presented to the world. And for a while now, she had thought she could discern a change in him, an unease that she had never noticed in him before.

She toyed absently with the string of pearls she wore around her neck and let her gaze move on. To the left of Elard sat Jutta, her daughter. She was fifteen years younger than Siegbert, a latecomer and actually not planned. Ambitious and determined as she was, she reminded Vera of herself. After an apprenticeship at a bank, Jutta had studied economics and law, and twelve years ago, she had gone into politics. For the past eight years, she'd held a seat in the state parliament of Hesse, and had also become a party chairwoman. In all probability, she would run in the state elections next year as the top female candidate of her party. Her long-term plan was to win the position of prime minister for Hesse and enter national politics. Vera had no doubt that she would succeed. The Kaltensee name would help her chances considerably.

Yes, Vera could truly count herself lucky with her life and her family. Her three children had all made their way in the world. If only this matter with Thomas hadn't surfaced. As far back as she could remember, Vera Kaltensee had acted prudently and played her cards right. She had kept her emotions under control and made important decisions with a cool head. Always. Until now. She hadn't foreseen the consequences and had acted rashly out of anger, wounded pride, and panic. Vera reached for her glass and took a sip of water. A feeling of menace had pursued her ever since that day when she had severed all ties with Thomas Ritter; it hovered over her like a shadow that could not be chased away.

She had always succeeded in circumventing dangerous precipices in her life with farsightedness and courage. She had mastered crises, solved problems, and successfully averted attacks, but now she felt vulnerable and alone.

All of a sudden, the huge responsibility for her life's work, for the company and the family, no longer seemed to her a pleasure, but, rather, a burden that made it hard for her to breathe. Was it merely her age slowly closing in on her? How many years did she have left before her strength deserted her and control inevitably slipped away?

Her eyes swept over her guests, all those happy, carefree, smiling faces; she heard the buzz of voices, the clatter of silverware and plates as if from a great distance. Vera looked at Anita, her dear friend from her youth, who, unfortunately, could no longer go out except in a wheelchair. It was incredible how fragile the resolute Anita, so hungry for life, had become. To Vera, it seemed only yesterday that they had gone to dancing school together, and later to the League of German Girls, like almost all the girls had in the Third Reich. Now Anita sat huddled in her wheelchair like a delicate, pale ghost. Her once-shiny dark brown hair was now nothing but white down. Anita was one of the last of Vera's friends and companions from her youth; most of them were already pushing up daisies. It was no fun getting old, deteriorating and watching her friends die off one after the other.

Gentle sunlight on the leaves, cooing doves. The lake as blue as the endless sky above the dark forests. The smell of summer, of freedom. Young faces excitedly following the regatta with sparkling eyes. The boys in their white sweaters shoot across the finish line first in their boat. They beam with pride, waving. Vera can see him. He has the tiller in his hand, he's the captain. Her heart is pounding in her throat as he leaps with a lithe motion onto the quay wall. Here I am, she thinks, waving with both arms; look at me! At first, she thinks he's smiling at her, so she calls out congratulations to him and holds out her arms. Her heart takes a leap; then he comes straight toward her, smiling, radiant. The disappointment pierces her like a knife when she realizes that his smile is not for her but for Vicky. Jealousy chokes her throat. He hugs the other girl, puts his arm around her shoulder, and vanishes with her into the crowd that is wildly cheering him and his crew. Vera notices the tears in her eyes, the bottomless emptiness inside of her. This insult, this rejection in front of everyone else, is more than she can bear. She turns away, quickens her step. Disappointment turns to fury, to hate. She balls her fists, running down the sandy path along the shore of the lake—she has to get away, away!

Shocked, Vera gave a start. Where did these thoughts suddenly come from, these unwanted memories? With an effort she sneaked a look at her wristwatch. She didn't want to appear ungrateful, but all the commotion, the stuffy air, and the din of voices had made her feel quite dazed. She forced herself to bring her attention back to the here and now, the way she had done for sixty years. In her life, there had always been a "forward," no nostalgic looking back at the past. For this reason, she had never let herself be used by any group of exiles or cultural association of citizens expelled from the eastern regions of the Reich after the war. The baroness of Zeydlitz-Lauenburg had vanished for good on the day of her wedding to Eugen Kaltensee. The former East Prussian she had once been never reappeared. And that was as it should be. That part of her life was over and done with.

Siegbert rapped on his glass with his knife, and the hum of conversation stopped; the children were sent to their places.

"What is it?" Vera asked her son in confusion.

"You wanted to make a brief speech before the main course, Mother," he reminded her.

"Ah, yes." Vera smiled apologetically, "I was just thinking about something else."

She cleared her throat and got up from her chair. It had taken her a couple of hours to compose the speech, but now Vera put aside her notes.

"I'm happy that you all have come here to celebrate this day with me," she said in a firm voice, looking around the room. "On a day like this, most people take a look back at their lives. But I would like to spare you the reminiscences of an old woman; you all know everything there is to know about me anyway."

As expected, there was a brief surge of laughter. But before Vera could go on, the door opened. A man entered and stood discreetly at the back of the room. Without her glasses, Vera couldn't tell who it was. To her dismay, she broke out in a cold sweat and her knees felt wobbly. Could that be Thomas? Did he really have the nerve to show up here today?

"Is something wrong, Mother?" asked Siegbert softly.

She shook her head emphatically and quickly reached for her glass. "It's so lovely to have you all here with me today!" she said. At the same time, she racked her brain about what to do if that man really was Thomas. "Cheers!"

"Three cheers for Mama!" Jutta called out, raising her glass. "Happy birthday!"

They all raised their glasses and gave the guest of honor three cheers, while the man came over to stand next to Siegbert and cleared his throat. Her heart pounding, Vera turned her head. It was the manager of Schloss Bodenstein, not Thomas! She was relieved and disappointed simultaneously, and annoyed by the intensity of her emotions. The French doors of the great hall opened, and the waiters of the Schlosshotel marched in to serve the main course.

"Excuse me for disturbing you," Vera heard the man say softly to her son. "I have a message for you."

"Thank you." Siegbert took the note and unfolded it. Vera saw the blood drain from his face.

"What is it?" she asked in alarm. "What does it say?"

Siegbert looked up.

"A message from Uncle Jossi's housekeeper." His voice was toneless. "I'm so sorry, Mother. Especially today. Uncle Jossi is dead."

Chief Commissioner Dr. Heinrich Nierhoff was not content to summon Bodenstein to his office in order to emphasize his authority as usual. Instead, he went into the conference room of K-11, where Chief Detective Inspector Kai Ostermann and Detective Assistant Kathrin Fachinger were preparing for a hastily scheduled meeting. After Pia Kirchhoff had called everyone that morning, they canceled their plans for the weekend and came in to K-11. On the still-empty whiteboard in the big conference room, Fachinger had printed GOLDBERG in her neat handwriting, and next to it the mysterious number 11645.

"What's up, Bodenstein?" asked Nierhoff. At first glance, the leader of the Regional Criminal Unit seemed unremarkable; a stocky man in his mid-fifties, graying at the temples, a small mustache, and bland facial features. But this first impression was deceptive. Nierhoff was extremely ambitious and possessed a sure political instinct. For months, rumors had been flying that sooner or later he would be exchanging his chief's position in the Regional Criminal

Unit for the county manager post in Darmstadt. Bodenstein invited his boss into his office and informed him tersely of the murder of David Goldberg. Nierhoff listened in silence and said nothing when Bodenstein was done. At the police station, it was well known that the chief commissioner loved the limelight and enjoyed holding press conferences in the grand manner. Ever since the media circus surrounding the suicide of Chief District Attorney Hardenbach two years before, no one of such prominence had been murdered in the Main-Taunus district. Bodenstein, who had actually expected that Nierhoff would be excited at the prospect of a storm of clicking digital cameras, was a bit surprised by his boss's restrained reaction.

"This could turn into a tricky situation." The noncommittal amiable expression that Commissioner Nierhoff normally wore had vanished, and the crafty tactician now came to the fore. "An American citizen of the Jewish faith and a survivor of the Holocaust executed with a shot to the back of the head. For the time being, we should keep the press and the public out of it."

Bodenstein nodded in agreement.

"I expect you to conduct the investigation with the utmost tact. No screwups," he said, to Bodenstein's annoyance. Since K-11 had been moved to Hofheim, Bodenstein couldn't recall a single investigative screwup on his watch.

"What about the housekeeper?" Nierhoff asked.

"What about her?" Bodenstein didn't quite understand. "She found the body this morning and was still in shock."

"Maybe she has something to do with it. Goldberg was quite wealthy."

Bodenstein's anger grew. "For a registered nurse, there are probably less obvious opportunities than shooting someone in the back of the head," he noted with light sarcasm. Nierhoff had been concentrating on his career for the past twenty-five years and hadn't taken part in an actual investigation that whole time. Yet he still felt obliged to offer his opinion. His eyes darted here and there as he pondered and weighed the pros and cons that might emerge from this case.

"Goldberg was a very prominent man," he said at last in a low voice. "We'll have to proceed with the utmost caution. Send your people home, and make sure there are no leaks."

Bodenstein didn't quite know what to make of this strategy. In an investigation, the first seventy-two hours were crucial. Evidence grows cold very fast, and witnesses' memories grow fainter the more time passes. But of course Nierhoff was afraid of precisely what Dr. Kirchhoff had prophesied this morning: negative publicity for his office and an abundance of diplomatic red tape. Politically, it might be a sensible decision, but Bodenstein didn't see it that way. He was an investigator; he wanted to find the murderer and arrest him. An old man advanced in years, who had experienced abominable things in Germany, had been murdered in cold blood in his own house. It went completely against Bodenstein's perception of good police work to waste valuable time for tactical reasons. Secretly, he was angry that he had even bothered to include Nierhoff. At any rate, Nierhoff knew the head of his department better than Bodenstein imagined.

"Don't even think about it, Bodenstein." Nierhoff's voice sounded like a warning. "High-handed behavior could have a very unfavorable influence on your career. You probably don't want to spend the rest of your life in Hofheim running after murderers and bank robbers."

"Why not? That's the reason I became a policeman in the first place," said Bodenstein, irritated by Nierhoff's implied threat and the almost contemptuous dismissal of his work.

With his next words, the chief commissioner made matters worse, even if they were meant to be conciliatory. "A man with your experience and your talents should assume responsibility and hold a leading position, Bodenstein, even if it's uncomfortable. Because that's precisely what it is, I can tell you that."

Bodenstein was trying hard to keep his composure. "In my opinion, the best people belong in the field," he said, his tone bordering on insubordination, "and not behind some desk, wasting their time on political squabbling."

The commissioner raised his eyebrows and seemed to be pondering whether this remark was meant as an insult or not.

"Sometimes I ask myself whether it was a mistake for me to mention your name at the interior ministry with regard to deciding on my successor," he said coolly. "It seems to me that you're totally lacking in ambition."

That left Bodenstein speechless for a couple of seconds, but he was able to exercise his iron self-control; he'd had plenty of practice concealing his emotions behind a neutral expression.

"Don't make a mistake now, Bodenstein," said Nierhoff, turning toward the door. "I hope we understand each other."

Bodenstein forced himself to give a polite nod and waited until the door closed behind Nierhoff. Then he grabbed his cell phone, called Pia Kirchhoff, and sent her straight to the pathology lab in Frankfurt. He had no intention of canceling the autopsy that had already been approved, no matter how Nierhoff might react. Before he set off for Frankfurt himself, he stopped by the conference room. Ostermann, Fachinger, and the DIs who had showed up in the meantime, Frank Behnke and Andreas Hasse, all looked at him expectantly.

"You can all go home," he said curtly. "I'll see you on Monday. If anything changes, I'll let you know."

Then he turned and left before any of his astonished colleagues could ask a question.

Robert Watkowiak finished his beer and wiped his mouth with the back of his hand. He had to take a piss, but he didn't feel like walking past the rowdy idiots who'd been playing darts beside the door to the john for the past hour. Only the day before yesterday, those guys had stupidly harassed him, trying to start a fight over Robert's regular seat at the bar. He glanced over at the dartboard. It wasn't that he couldn't deal with them; he just wasn't in the mood for an argument.

"I'll have another." He shoved the empty glass across the sticky bar. It was 3:30. By now, they were all crowded together, dressed to the nines, guzzling champagne and acting as though they were overjoyed to be allowed to take part in celebrating the old snake's birthday. What a bunch of phonies! Actually, none of them had much use for the others, but on such occasions they acted like one big happy family. Of course they hadn't invited *him*. Even if they had, he wouldn't have gone. In his daydreams, he'd smugly pictured throwing the invitation at her feet with scorn and sneering at her shocked and horrified face. It was only yesterday that he had realized they had denied him that satisfaction by not inviting him at all.

The bartender shoved a freshly tapped pilsner over to him and added another tick to his beer mat. Robert reached for the glass and noticed angrily that his hand was shaking. Shit! He didn't give a fuck about the whole lot of them. They'd always treated him like dirt and made him feel that he didn't really belong in their crowd because he was an unwanted bastard. They would whisper about him behind their hands, sending him meaningful looks and shaking their heads. What self-righteous, archconservative assholes! Robert, the loser. Had his driver's license revoked again for drunk driving. The third time? No, the fourth time! Now he'll probably get sent back to the joint. Serves him right. He had all the advantages in the world, that guy, and he never made anything of himself. Robert grabbed his glass and watched his knuckles turn white. That's how his hands would look if he put them around her wrinkled chicken neck and squeezed till her eyes popped out of her head.

He took a big gulp of beer. The first one was always the best. The cold liquid ran down his esophagus, and he imagined it flowing with a hiss over those smoldering lumps of envy and bitterness inside him. Who was it that claimed hate was cold? A quarter to four. Damn it, he had to go to the john. He fished a cigarette out of the pack and lit it. Kurti would show up eventually. He had promised him last night. At least he'd been able to pay him back what he owed, after he leaned on Uncle Jossi a little. He was his godfather, after all, and that ought to count for something.

"One more?" the bartender asked in a businesslike tone. He nodded and looked in the mirror on the wall behind the bar. The sight of his slovenly appearance, the greasy hair falling to his shoulders, the glassy eyes, and the beard stubble threw him instantly into a rage. Ever since that fight with the asshole in the Frankfurt-Höchst train station, he was missing another tooth. It made him look like a thug. The next beer arrived. The sixth one today. He was gradually reaching operating temperature. Should he convince Kurti to drive him over to Schloss Bodenstein? Just the thought of how they would all stare when he sauntered in, climbed up on the table, and calmly emptied his bladder made him grin. He'd seen somebody do that in a movie once, and he thought it was cool.

"Could I borrow your cell for a minute?" he asked the bartender, noticing that he was having trouble speaking clearly.

"Use your own," she replied pertly, pulling another beer without looking at him. But unfortunately, he no longer had it. What a bummer. It must have fallen out of his pocket somewhere.

"I lost it," he slurred. "Don't give me that look. Come on."

"No way." Then she moved past him and, carrying a full tray, went over to the guys at the dartboard. Looking in the mirror, he saw the door open. Kurti. Finally.

"Hey, man." Kurti slapped him on the shoulder and sat down on the bar stool next to him.

"Order whatever you want; I'm buying," said Robert magnanimously. The dough from Uncle Jossi would last for a couple of days; then he'd have to look around for a new source, and he already had a good idea. He hadn't visited his dear Uncle Herrmann in quite a while. Maybe he should let Kurti in on his plans. Robert twisted his face into an evil smile. He was damn well going to get what he was entitled to.

In Henning Kirchhoff's office, Bodenstein was searching through the contents of a carton that Pia had taken from Goldberg's house and brought to the Institute of Forensic Medicine. The two used glasses and the wine bottle were already on their way to the lab, as well as the mirror, all the fingerprints, and everything else the evidence techs had collected. Meanwhile, downstairs in the basement of the institute, Dr. Kirchhoff was performing the autopsy on the body of David Josua Goldberg in the presence of Pia Kirchhoff and an assistant district attorney who looked like a second-year law student. Bodenstein scanned a few thank-you letters from various individuals and institutions that Goldberg had sponsored and supported financially. Then he glanced at several photos in silver frames and some newspaper articles that had been carefully clipped out and meticulously mounted. A taxi receipt from January, a worn little book in Hebrew. Not much. Apparently, Goldberg had kept the majority of his belongings elsewhere. Among all the things that must have had some meaning for their original owner, only an appointment diary was of any interest to Bodenstein. Goldberg exhibited amazingly clear penmanship for someone of his advanced age, with no shaky or wobbly letters. Bodenstein turned to the previous week, in which there were notes for each day. He was disappointed by what he found: nothing but names that were almost all abbreviated. Only on today's date was a full name written: *Vera 85*. Despite the meager results, Bodenstein took the appointment diary to the copier in the administrative office of the institute and began copying all the pages since January. Just as he reached the last week of Goldberg's life, his cell phone buzzed.

"Boss." Pia Kirchhoff's voice sounded a little broken up because of the less than optimal reception in the basement of the institute. "You've got to come down here. Henning has discovered something strange."

"I have no explanation for this. Absolutely none. But it's quite clear. Utterly unequivocal," said Dr. Henning Kirchhoff, shaking his head as Bodenstein stepped into the autopsy room. The ME had lost all his professional composure and cynicism. Even his assistant and Pia seemed stunned, and the assistant DA was nervously chewing on his lower lip.

"What did you find?" Bodenstein asked.

"Something unbelievable." Kirchhoff motioned him closer to the table and handed him a magnifying glass. "I noticed something on the inside of his upper left arm, a tattoo. I could hardly see it because of the livor mortis on his arm. He was found lying on his left side."

"Everybody who was in Auschwitz had a tattoo," Bodenstein replied.

"But not one like this." Kirchhoff pointed at Goldberg's arm. Bodenstein closed one eye and examined the spot he was pointing to through the magnifying glass.

"It looks like . . . hmm . . . like two letters. Old Gothic letters. An . . . *A* and a *B,* if I'm not mistaken."

"You're right," said Kirchhoff, taking the magnifying glass from him.

"What does it mean?" Bodenstein asked.

"I'll resign if it turns out I'm wrong," Kirchhoff replied. "It's incredible, because Goldberg was a Jew."

Bodenstein didn't understand what was agitating the ME.

"Don't keep me on tenterhooks," he said impatiently. "What's so extraordinary about a tattoo?"

Kirchhoff peered at Bodenstein over the tops of his half-moon glasses.

"This," he said, lowering his voice to a conspiratorial whisper, "is a blood-type tattoo, like the members of the Waffen-SS had. Twenty centimeters above the elbow on the inside of the upper left arm. Because this tattoo was a clear identifying mark, many former SS men tried to get rid of it after the war. This man did, too."

He took a deep breath and began to circle the autopsy table.

"Normally," Kirchhoff expounded, as if in a first-semester lecture in the auditorium, "tattoos are made by inserting a needle into the center layer of the skin, the dermis. In this case, the color has penetrated into the subcutis. Superficially, only a bluish scar was visible, but now, after the epidermis had been removed, the tattoo can again be seen clearly. Blood type AB."

Bodenstein stared at Goldberg's corpse, which lay with its chest opened on the dissection table. He hardly dared think what Kirchhoff's incredible revelation might mean or what consequences it might have.

"If you didn't know who this was on your table," he said slowly, "what would you surmise?"

Kirchhoff stopped in his tracks.

"That the man in his younger days must have been a member of the SS. And probably from the very beginning. Later, the tattoos were done in roman letters, not in Old German script."

"Couldn't it be a matter of some other harmless tattoo that over the years somehow . . . hmm . . . changed?" Bodenstein asked, although he had no real faith in this theory. Kirchhoff almost never made a mistake; at least Bodenstein couldn't remember a single occasion when the pathologist had had to revise his opinion.

"No. Especially not in this location." Kirchhoff wasn't offended by Bodenstein's skepticism. He was just as aware of the implications of his discovery as everyone else present. "I've seen this sort of tattoo on the table before, once in South America and several times here in Germany. For me, there is no doubt."

It was 5:30 when Pia opened the front door to her house and took off her muddy shoes on the enclosed porch. She had fed the horses and dogs in record time and was in a hurry to get into the bathroom to take a shower and wash her hair. Unlike her boss, she wasn't upset about Nierhoff's instructions not to start any investigations in the Goldberg case. She had been afraid that she might have to cancel her date with Christoph tonight, and that was the last thing she wanted to do. She had been separated from Henning for a year and a half now. The earnings from her stock portfolio had made it possible for her to buy the Birkenhof farm in Unterliederbach, and return to her profession in the criminal police. The icing on the cake was without a doubt Christoph Sander. They'd met ten months ago at a homicide scene at the Opel Zoo in Kronberg. The glance from his dark brown eyes had struck like a bolt of lightning. She was so used to finding a rational explanation for everything in her life that she was deeply confused by the attraction that this man had exerted on her at first sight. For the past eight months, she and Christoph had been . . . well, what were they? Lovers? Friends? A couple? He often spent the night with her. She went in and out of his house and got along well with his three grown daughters, but they hadn't really shared much daily life yet. She still found it exciting just to look at him, be with him, and sleep with him.

Pia caught her reflection in the mirror, foolishly grinning. She turned on the shower and waited impatiently for the water to get warm. Christoph was mercurial and passionate in everything he did. Even though he was sometimes impatient and quick-tempered, he was never hurtful. Not like Henning, who was a real connoisseur when it came to poking around in open wounds. After sixteen years at the side of an introverted genius like Henning, who could effortlessly go for days without saying a word, who didn't like pets, children, or spontaneity, Pia was constantly fascinated by Christoph's straightforward nature. Since she'd gotten to know him, she had developed a whole new self-confidence. He loved her the way she was, even bleary-eyed and without makeup, in stable gear and rubber boots; he wasn't bothered by a pimple or a couple of extra pounds on her ribs. And besides that, he possessed truly remarkable qualities as a lover, which, unbelievably enough, he had withheld from any other woman in the fifteen years since his wife had died. Pia still got palpitations when she recalled that evening in the deserted zoo, when he had confessed that he was attracted to her.

Tonight would be the first time she would be going out with him to a public function. There was going to be a gala reception at the Frankfurt Zoo as a benefit for the construction of the new ape house. All week long, Pia had been thinking about what to wear. The few clothes that had made the transition from her marriage to Henning into her new life were all size ten and, to her horror, no longer fit her properly. She had no desire to suck in her stomach all evening, full of anxiety that some seam or zipper might burst the next time she made a careless move. That's why she'd squandered two evenings and a Saturday morning in the Main-Taunus shopping center and at the Zeil galleria in downtown Frankfurt looking for a suitable dress. But it was obvious that the stores were all geared to anorexic women. She had searched for a salesperson her own age who might have some sympathy for her problem areas, but to no avail: All the employees seemed to be exotic beauties who had hardly outgrown their teenage years and wore size double zero. They viewed with indifference or even pity her attempts to squeeze herself into various evening attire, sweating in cramped dressing rooms. She had found something at H&M, only to learn, to her chagrin, that she was in the maternity department. At last she'd had enough, and knowing that Christoph liked her the way she was, she'd decided on a little black dress in size fourteen. She'd rewarded herself for all the sweat-inducing fittings with a supersized meal at McDonald's, including a McFlurry with M&M's on top for dessert.

When Bodenstein got home that evening, he found that his family had gone out, and only the dog was there to give him an enthusiastic welcome. Had Cosima told him that she was going out? On the kitchen table he found a note. *Discussion about New Guinea at the Merlin. Took Sophia along. See you later.* Bodenstein sighed. In the past year, Cosima had had to give up a long-planned film expedition to the rain forests of New Guinea because of her pregnancy. He had secretly hoped that after Sophia was born she wouldn't be interested in adventurous trips anymore, but obviously he'd been mistaken. He found cheese and an opened bottle of '98 Château La Tour Blanche in the fridge. He made himself an open-faced sandwich, poured himself a glass of red wine, and went into his workroom, followed by his eternally hungry dog. Ostermann could probably have found the information he needed from the Internet ten times faster, but Bodenstein wanted to follow Nierhoff's instructions and not involve any colleagues in his investigation of David Goldberg.

Bodenstein opened his laptop, inserted a CD by Sol Gabetta, the Argentine-French cellist, and sipped at his wine, which was still a little too cold. As he listened to the sounds of Tchaikovsky and Chopin, he clicked through dozens of Web sites, going through newspaper archives and jotting down anything worth knowing about the man who had been shot to death last night.

David Goldberg had been born in 1915 in Angerburg, in what was then East Prussia, the son of the grocery wholesaler Samuel Goldberg and his wife, Rebecca. He graduated from secondary school in 1933, and then all traces of him vanished until the year 1947. In a brief biography, it was mentioned that after the liberation of Auschwitz in 1945, he had emigrated via Sweden and then England to the United States. In New York, he had married Sarah Weinstein, the daughter of a respected banker of German extraction.

But Goldberg had not joined the banking firm. Instead, he'd made his career with the American defense giant, Lockheed Martin. By 1959, he was already director of strategic planning. As a member of the board of the powerful National Rifle Association, he'd been one of the most important gun lobbyists in Washington, and several presidents had held him in high esteem as an adviser. Despite all the atrocities that his family had suffered under the Third Reich, he had always felt strong ties to Germany and cultivated numerous close contacts, especially in Frankfurt.

Bodenstein sighed and leaned back in his chair. Who could possibly have a reason for fatally shooting a ninety-two-year-old man?

He ruled out robbery as a motive. The housekeeper had not noticed anything missing, and besides, Goldberg had kept no really valuable items in his house. The surveillance system in the house was out of order, and the answering machine that had come with the telephone seemed never to have been used.

At the zoo reception, the usual Frankfurt mixture of the old moneyed aristocracy and the brash nouveau riche had assembled, interspersed with celebrities from television, sports, and the demimonde who had generously contributed to giving the apes a new roof over their heads. The superb caterers had made sure that nothing was lacking for the discriminating palates of the guests, and the champagne flowed in rivers. On Christoph's arm, Pia made her way through the crowd. In her little black dress, she felt acceptably attired. She had also found a flat iron in one of the many moving boxes not yet unpacked and had used it to coax her unruly locks into a proper hairdo. Then she spent a good half hour on her makeup to create the effect that she wasn't wearing any at all. Christoph, who knew her only in jeans and a ponytail, was deeply impressed.

"My God," he'd said when she opened the front door. "Who are you? And what are you doing in Pia's house?"

Then he took her in his arms and kissed her long and tenderly—while taking care not to ruin her look. As a single father of three teenage daughters, he was well schooled in how to deal with female creatures and made astonishingly few mistakes. For example, he knew what catastrophic effect a single offhand remark about a girl's figure, hairdo, or clothing could have; very wisely, he refrained from commenting. His compliments tonight were not tactical, but sincere. Pia felt more attractive under his appreciative gaze than any of those skinny twenty-year-olds.

"I hardly know anyone here," Christoph whispered to her. "Who are all these people? What do they have to do with the zoo?"

"This is Frankfurt high society, and those who think they need to belong to it," Pia explained. "In any case, they're going to leave a pile of money here, and that's no doubt the whole point and purpose of the function. Over there by the table in the corner are some of the truly rich and powerful of the city."

As if on cue, at that instant one of the women at the table craned her neck and waved at Pia. She had to be forty, and with her tiny figure she could effortlessly find a suitable dress in any boutique in town. Pia gave her a friendly smile and waved back. Then she took a closer look.

"I'm impressed." Christoph grinned in amusement. "The rich and powerful know you. Who's that?"

"I don't believe it." Pia let go of Christoph's arm. The petite dark-haired woman made her way through the crowd and stopped in front of them.

"Püppi!" the woman cried, and threw her arms wide, grinning.

"Frosch! Is that really you? What are you doing in Frankfurt?" Pia asked, then she gave the woman a big hug. Many years ago, Miriam Horowitz had been Pia's best friend. Together they had lived through some wild and fun times, but then they'd lost touch.

"Nobody's called me Frosch in years," the woman said with a laugh. "Man, is this ever a surprise!"

The two women looked each other up and down, curious and overjoyed. Pia could see that her friend had hardly changed—except for a few wrinkles here and there.

"Christoph, this is Miriam, my best friend from school," said Pia, remembering her manners. "Miri, this is Christoph Sander."

"Pleased to meet you." Miriam extended her hand to him and smiled. They chatted for a while; then Christoph left the two alone and went to join some of his colleagues.

When Elard Kaltensee woke up, he felt completely bewildered, and it took him a few seconds to figure out where he was. He hated falling asleep in the afternoon; it threw off his biorhythms, but it was the only chance he had to catch up on his sleep. His throat hurt, and he had a terrible taste in his mouth. For years, he'd rarely had any dreams, and when he did, he couldn't remember them. But a while back he'd started having ghastly, oppressive nightmares that he could avoid only by taking sleeping pills. His daily dose of lorazepam was now up to two milligrams, and if he forgot to take the pills even once, then the nightmares descended on him—vague, inexplicable memories of fear, of voices and bloodcurdling laughter, which left him bathed in sweat and jolted him awake, his heart racing. Sometimes the nightmares would cast a shadow over the whole next day. Dazed, Elard sat down and massaged his throbbing temples. Maybe everything would get better when he could finally go back to his daily agenda. He was relieved that with the family celebration the last of the countless official, semiofficial, and private festivities in honor of his mother's eighty-fifth birthday were finally over. Naturally, the rest of the family had expected that he would take care of everything, simply because he, too, lived at Mühlenhof, and in their eyes he had little else to do. Only now did it dawn on him what had happened. The news of Goldberg's death had put an abrupt end to the celebration at Schloss Bodenstein.

Elard Kaltensee smiled bitterly and swung his legs over the edge of the bed. Goldberg had enjoyed a remarkable ninety-two summers, the old son of a bitch. No one could claim that he'd been yanked out of the middle of his life. Elard tottered into the bathroom, undressed, and stepped in front of the mirror. He gave himself a critical look. Even at sixty-three, he was in pretty good shape. No potbelly, no spare tire, no baggy turkey neck. He let the tub fill up, tossed in a handful of bath salts, and lowered himself with a sigh into the fragrant hot water. Goldberg's death didn't shock him; actually, he was glad that it had brought the celebration to an early conclusion. He had immediately complied with his mother's request to drive her home. When Siegbert and Jutta had shown up only seconds later at Mühlenhof, he had taken the opportunity to withdraw discreetly. He badly needed some peace and quiet so he could contemplate the events of the past day.

Elard Kaltensee closed his eyes and rewound his thoughts back to last night, seeing with a pounding heart the sequence of the events that were equally rousing and frightening unfold before his inner eye like a clip from a video. Over and over again. How could things have gone so far? All his life, he'd had to wrestle with difficulties of both a private and professional nature, but this seriously threatened to derail him. He was filled with concern because he simply didn't understand what was going on inside him. He was losing control, and there was nobody he could talk to about his dilemma. How was he supposed to live with this secret? What would his mother, his sons, his daughters-in-law say if it ever came out? The door flew open. Elard gave a start in alarm and covered his nakedness with both hands.

"Good Lord, Mother," he said angrily. "Can't you ever knock?"

Then he noticed Vera's devastated expression.

"Jossi didn't just die," she gasped, sinking down on the bench next to the bathtub. "He was *shot*!"

"Oh no. I'm so sorry." Elard couldn't come up with anything but this hackneyed phrase. Vera stared at him for a moment.

"How heartless you are," she whispered in a trembling voice. Then she buried her face in her hands and began to sob quietly.

"Come on, we have to drink a toast to finding each other again!" Miriam pulled Pia toward the bar and ordered two glasses of champagne.

"Since when are you back in Frankfurt?" Pia asked. "The last I heard, you were living in Warsaw. That's what your mother told me a couple of years ago when I ran into her."

"Paris, Oxford, Warsaw, Washington, Tel Aviv, Berlin, Frankfurt," Miriam rattled off with a laugh. "In every city, I met the love of my life and left him again. I guess I'm just not suited for a steady relationship. But tell me about yourself. What are you doing, anyway? Job, husband, kids?"

"After three semesters of studying law, I joined the police force," said Pia.

"You're kidding!" Miriam's eyes widened. "How come?"

Pia hesitated. She still found it hard to talk about, even if Christoph thought it was the only way to work through the trauma she'd endured. For almost twenty years, she hadn't told anyone about the worst experience of her life, not even Henning. She didn't want to keep being reminded of her weakness or fear. But Miriam was more capable of empathy than Pia had thought, and all at once she turned serious. "What happened?"

"It was the summer after I graduated," Pia said. "I met a man in France. He was nice. It was a summer flirtation. We had fun. After vacation, it was over for me, but, unfortunately, not for him. He started following me, terrorizing me with letters and phone calls. He stalked me everywhere. And then he broke into my apartment and raped me."

Her voice was calm, but Miriam seemed to sense how much it cost Pia to talk about the matter so calmly and with apparent nonchalance.

"Oh my God," she said softly, taking Pia's hand. "That's just horrible."

"Yes, it was." Pia gave a wry smile. "Somehow I must have thought that as a police officer I wouldn't be so vulnerable. Now I'm in the Kripo, the criminal police, in the homicide division."

"So what else have you done to deal with it?" Miriam asked.

Pia understood what she meant. "Nothing." She shrugged. Now that she'd begun talking, it seemed surprisingly easy to tell Miriam about the chapter in her life that had previously been taboo. "I never even told my husband. Somehow I thought I'd get over it soon enough."

"And that didn't happen. . . ."

"Oh yes, it did. For a while, I did pretty well. But then last year, the whole thing finally caught up with me."

She gave Miriam the short version of the two murder cases from the previous summer, and the investigations, during which she had met Christoph and confronted her past.

"Christoph wants to persuade me to sponsor a self-help group for rape victims," she said after a pause. "But I don't really know if I should."

"Of course you should! No question," Miriam insisted. "A trauma like that could destroy a woman's whole life. Believe me, I know what I'm talking about. When I worked in Wiesbaden at the Fritz Bauer Institute and the Center Against Expulsions, I heard about the terrible fates of women in the eastern provinces after World War Two. The things these women lived through were unspeakable. And most of them never talked about what happened to them. It destroyed them emotionally."

Pia was watching her friend attentively. Miriam had changed a lot. There was no trace of the carefree, superficial girl from a privileged family. Twenty years was a long time.

"What sort of institute is it that you work for?" she inquired.

"It's a center for studying and documenting the history and effect of the Holocaust, connected to the university," Miriam explained. "I give lectures there, organize exhibitions, and so on. Pretty crazy, don't you think? Earlier, I always thought I'd own a disco or compete in show jumping." Miriam giggled. "Can you imagine how shocked our teachers would be if they knew we'd both turned out to be so respectable?"

"Especially since they always prophesied that someday we'd both wind up in the gutter, at the very least," Pia said with a grin. She ordered two more glasses of champagne.

"What's the deal with Christoph?" Miriam asked. "Is it serious?"

"I think so," replied Pia.

"He must really be in love." Miriam winked at her and leaned forward. "He can't take his eyes off you."

Pia instantly felt the butterflies in her stomach again. The champagne arrived, and they clinked glasses one more time. Pia told her about Birkenhof and her animals.

"Where are you living now?" she inquired. "Here in Frankfurt?"

Miriam nodded. "Yes. In my grandmother's house."

For someone who didn't know Miriam's family background, that would not have sounded impressive, but Pia knew better. Miriam's grandmother Charlotte Horowitz was the grande dame of the cream of Frankfurt society. Her "house" was a magnificent old villa on a gigantic estate in the Holzhausen district, which brought tears of avarice to the eyes of every real estate speculator. A thought suddenly occurred to Pia.

"Tell me, Miri," she said to her friend, "does the name David Josua Goldberg mean anything to you?"

Miriam gave her a puzzled look.

"Of course it does," she said. "Jossi Goldberg is one of Oma's oldest friends. His family has supported projects in the Jewish community in Frankfurt for decades. Why do you ask?"

"Just because," Pia said evasively as she saw the curiosity in her friend's eyes. "At the moment, I can't say any more."

"Police business?"

"Something like that. I'm sorry."

"No biggie." Miriam raised her glass again and smiled. "To our reunion after such a long time. I'm so happy!"

"Me, too." Pia grinned. "If you want, come and visit me. We could go for a ride, the way we used to."

Christoph came over to them at the cocktail table. The nonchalance with which he put his arm around Pia's waist made her heart leap with joy. Henning had never done anything like that. He regarded tender touches in public as a "tasteless display of a primitive pride of ownership" and awkwardly avoided them. Pia didn't share his opinion. The three of them drank another round of champagne, and then another. Pia told the story of her outing to the maternity-wear department at H&M, and they laughed so hard, they cried. It was half past midnight before she knew it, and Pia said she hadn't had such a relaxing and fun time in ages. Henning would have wanted to go home by ten o'clock, or else return to the institute. Or he would have become engrossed in some important conversation in a corner of the room, having automatically excluded her. This time, it was different. In Pia's secret rating system, Christoph had scored ten out of ten in the category of "going out."

They were still laughing when they left the zoo reception hall and made their way back to the car, walking hand in hand. Pia knew that she couldn't be happier than she was at that moment.

Bodenstein gave a start when Cosima appeared in the doorway to his workroom.

"Hi," he said. "So, how did your discussion go?"

Cosima came closer and bent down. "Extremely constructive." She smiled and kissed him on the cheek. "Don't worry, I don't personally intend to go climbing through the jungle. But I did manage to land Wilfried Dechent as expedition leader."

"I've been asking myself whether you planned to take Sophia along or whether I had to apply for a leave of absence," he said, concealing his relief. "What time is it anyway?"

"Twelve-thirty." She leaned forward and looked at the screen of his laptop. "What are you doing?"

"I'm looking for information on the man who was shot."

"And?" she asked. "Did you find anything?"

"Not a lot." Oliver gave her a brief rundown of what he'd found out about Goldberg. He liked talking to Cosima. She had a sharp mind and enough distance from his cases to help him make the leaps when he could no longer see the forest for the trees during prolonged investigations. When he told her about the result of the autopsy, her eyes opened wide in astonishment."

"I don't believe it," she said emphatically. "That could never, ever be true."

"I saw it with my own eyes," he replied. "And Kirchhoff has never been wrong. At first sight, there was nothing to indicate that Goldberg might have had a sinister past. But in over sixty years, he could have hushed up a lot of things. His appointment book told me nothing, a few first names and abbreviations, that's it. But under today's date, there was a name and a number."

He yawned and rubbed the back of his neck. "Vera and the number eighty-five. Sounds like some sort of password. My Hotmail password, for instance, is Cosi—"

"Vera eight-five?" Cosima interrupted him and straightened up. "This morning, something dawned on me when you mentioned Goldberg's name." She tapped the side of her nose and frowned.

"Oh yeah? What was it?"

"Vera. Vera Kaltensee. Today she celebrated her eighty-fifth birthday at Quentin and Marie-Louise's place. Rosalie told me about it. Even my mother was invited."

Oliver felt his fatigue abruptly vanish. *Vera 85.* Vera Kaltensee, eighty-fifth birthday. So that was the explanation for the cryptic note in the dead man's diary. Naturally, he knew who Vera Kaltensee was. She had received numerous honors and awards for her philanthropic efforts, but also for her magnanimous social and cultural involvement. But what did this woman of irreproachable reputation have to do with a former SS officer? If connected to this man, her name would lend even greater shock value to the case, which was something that Bodenstein would have preferred to avoid.

"Kirchhoff must have made a mistake," Cosima said straight out. "Vera would never in her life be friends with a former Nazi, especially since she lost everything because of the Nazis: her family, her homeland, the castle in East Prussia . . ."

"Maybe she didn't know," Oliver responded. "Goldberg had built up the perfect cover story. If someone hadn't shot him, and if he hadn't landed on Kirchhoff's autopsy table, he would have taken his secret to the grave."

Cosima was chewing pensively on her lower lip. "My God, this is really awful!"

"Above all, it's really awful for my career, as Nierhoff let me know today in no uncertain terms," said Oliver with a hint of sarcasm.

"What do you mean?"

He repeated what Nierhoff had said in his office.

Cosima raised her eyebrows in astonishment. "I had no idea that he wanted to leave Hofheim."

"He does, and there've been a lot of rumors going around the station about it." Oliver turned off the desk lamp. "Nierhoff is probably afraid of diplomatic complications. With a case like this, he isn't going to win any kudos, and he knows it."

"But he can't just prohibit the investigations. That's obstruction of justice!"

"No, it's not," Oliver said, putting his arm around Cosima's shoulder. "It's just politics. But the hell with it. Let's go to bed; tomorrow's another day. Maybe our little princess will let us get some sleep."

Sunday, April 29

Chief Commissioner Nierhoff was worried—extremely so. Early Sunday morning, he got an unpleasant call from a high-ranking official in the National Criminal Police, who had given him strict orders to cease all investigations in the Goldberg case, effective immediately. Nierhoff wasn't keen on bringing himself and his office under the spotlight of criticism because of political intrigues that might easily arise from the murder case, but he was also not happy about the way they had treated him. He called Bodenstein into his office and told the superintendent of the investigative team in confidence what had happened.

"Salomon Goldberg arrived this morning on the first flight from New York," he said. "He demanded the immediate surrender of his father's mortal remains."

"From you?" Bodenstein asked, astounded.

"No." Nierhoff shook his head indignantly. "Goldberg brought backup: two people from the CIA and the U.S. general consul all showed up at the office of the President of police. Of course he had no idea what it was all about, so he contacted the Interior Ministry and the NCP."

The interior minister had dealt with the matter personally. Everyone convened at the Institute of Forensic Medicine: Nierhoff; a state secretary from the Interior Ministry; the Frankfurt police president; Professor Thomas Kronlage, head of the institute; two officers from the NCP; Salomon Goldberg, accompanied by the influential chairman of the Frankfurt Jewish community; the American general consul; and the CIA agents. A state of diplomatic emergency was in effect; the demands of the Americans were unambiguous. They wanted Goldberg's body without delay. From a legal standpoint, of course, no one from the delegation of German and American authorities had the right to interfere in an ongoing homicide investigation, but the interior minister had no interest in a scandal, especially not six months before the election. Barely two hours after Salomon Goldberg showed up, the case was in the hands of the NCP.

"I don't understand anything anymore," Nierhoff concluded in consternation. He had been pacing around his office but now stopped in front of Bodenstein. "What's going on?"

Bodenstein had only one explanation for this unusual action on a Sunday morning at the crack of dawn: "At the autopsy yesterday, a tattoo was observed on the inside of Goldberg's upper left arm that indicated he was formerly in the SS."

Nierhoff froze, and his mouth almost fell open.

"But . . . but . . . that's ridiculous," he countered. "Goldberg was a survivor of the Holocaust. He was in Auschwitz and lost his whole family."

"At least that was his cover story." Bodenstein leaned back and crossed his legs. "But I have complete faith in Dr. Kirchhoff's opinion. And it would explain why Goldberg's son showed up with a whole entourage less than twenty-four hours after we discovered his father's body. He wanted to prevent further investigations. Either the younger Goldberg or someone else has connections and an interest in making the mortal remains of his father disappear as quickly as possible. Goldberg's secret had to stay secret. But we were faster."

Nierhoff took a deep breath, then sat down behind his desk.

"Okay, I agree that you're right," he said after a moment. "But how could Goldberg's son mobilize all these people so fast?"

"He knows the right people in the right places. You know how these things work."

Nierhoff gave Bodenstein a skeptical look. "Did you inform the next of kin yesterday?"

"No. I presume Goldberg's housekeeper did that."

"They want the autopsy report." Nierhoff nervously rubbed his chin. Inside him the policeman was struggling with the politician. "Can you imagine what might come of this, Bodenstein?"

"Yes, I can," he said with a nod. Nierhoff jumped up and resumed silently pacing back and forth in his office.

"What am I supposed to do now?" he finally mused out loud. "I'll be fired if that detail gets out to the public. Not to mention what the press will do with it if anything leaks out!"

Bodenstein grimaced at this self-pitying utterance. Apparently, solving a homicide case didn't interest his boss in the slightest.

"It's not a matter of the public," he replied. "Since nobody's interested in shouting that particular detail from the rooftops, nothing is going to happen."

"That's easy for you to say. . . . What's the deal with the autopsy report?"

"You're going to run it through the shredder."

Nierhoff went over to the window, his hands clasped behind his back, and stared outside for a moment. Then he turned abruptly.

"I've given my word that for our part no further investigations will be conducted in the Goldberg case," he said in a lowered voice. "I trust that you will comply."

"That goes without saying," Bodenstein replied. He didn't care who the chief commissioner had given his word to, but it didn't take any particularly clairvoyant abilities to know what that meant. On directions from on high, Goldberg's murder was to be swept under the rug.

Monday, April 30

"I could have danced all night! I could have danced all night! . . ."

It was just past seven when Bodenstein stopped short in the doorway of the conference room, watching his colleague, who was warbling away and dancing with an imaginary partner between the table and the flip chart. He cleared his throat. "Was your zoo director nice to you? You seem to be in a great mood."

"I feel fantastic!" Pia Kirchhoff did one last pirouette, then dropped her arms and gave the hint of a bow with a big grin. "And he's always nice to me. Shall I get you some coffee, boss?"

"Did something happen?" Bodenstein raised his eyebrows. "Are you trying to get me to sign off on a vacation?"

"My God, how suspicious you are. No, I'm just in a good mood," Pia replied. "Saturday night, I ran into an old friend who used to know Goldberg, and—"

"Goldberg is ancient history," Bodenstein said, interrupting her. "I'll tell you why later. Would you be so kind as to call in the rest of the team?"

A little later, everyone at K-11 in Hofheim was sitting around the conference table, listening in amazement to Bodenstein's curt announcement that the Goldberg case had been dropped. Detective Inspector Andreas Hasse— who today was wearing a golden yellow shirt and an argyle sweater vest with corduroy pants instead of his usual brown suit—showed no emotion upon hearing the news. He had no spirit whatsoever, and although he was only in his mid-fifties, for years he'd been counting the days to his retirement. Even Behnke just went on indifferently chewing his gum, obviously lost in thought. Since there was nothing urgent pending, Bodenstein had agreed that his team would help out their colleagues in K-10 in investigating an eastern European auto-theft gang that had been making trouble in the Rhein-Main area for months. Ostermann and Pia Kirchhoff were to concentrate on an unsolved carjacking. Bodenstein waited until he was alone with the two to relate the details of what he knew about Goldberg's past and the strange events of Sunday morning, which had led to K-11 being taken off the Goldberg case.

"So that means we're really out of it?" Ostermann asked in disbelief.

Bodenstein nodded. "Officially, yes. Neither the Americans nor the NCP show any interest in solving the case, and Nierhoff is simply relieved to have the matter off his back."

"What about the lab evaluation of the evidence that was collected?" Pia asked.

"I wouldn't be surprised if they've forgotten all about it," Bodenstein replied. "Ostermann, get in touch with the crime lab right away and do some snooping around. If they've already got test results back, go to Wiesbaden and pick them up in person."

Ostermann nodded.

"The housekeeper told me that Goldberg had a visit on Thursday afternoon from a bald man and a dark-haired woman," Pia said. "On Tuesday, a man she didn't know was there in the early evening as she was getting ready to leave. He had parked his car right in front of the gate, a sports car with Frankfurt plates."

"Well, that's something anyway. Anything else?"

"Yes," said Pia, looking through her notes. "Twice last week, fresh flowers were delivered to Goldberg. On Wednesday, they weren't brought by the florist as usual, but by a rather unkempt man in his early forties. The housekeeper let him in. The man went straight up to Goldberg and spoke to him in a familiar way, as if they knew each other. She couldn't hear the conversation because the man had closed the door to the living room, but this visit apparently left the old man quite upset. He ordered the housekeeper to take delivery of the flowers at the front door from now on and not let anyone into the house."

"Good." Bodenstein nodded. "I'm still wondering what those numbers on the mirror meant."

"Could be a phone number," Ostermann opined. "Or the number of a locker, a password, a Swiss bank account, or a membership number—"

Kirchhoff interrupted him. "A membership number! If the motive for the murder was actually something in Goldberg's past, the one one six four five might have been his membership number in the SS."

"Goldberg was ninety-two," Ostermann mused. "Somebody who knew his number from back then would have to be almost that old, too."

"Not necessarily," said Bodenstein pensively. "It would be enough to know about Goldberg's past."

He recalled cases of murderers who had left obvious messages at the scene or on their victims as macabre calling cards. Perps who were playing a little game with the police to show off their intelligence and cunning. Could that be what was going on here? Was the number on the mirror in Goldberg's hallway a sign? If so, what did it mean? Was it a reference to something? Or was it meant to deliberately mislead them? Like his colleagues, Bodenstein couldn't see any rhyme or reason to it, and he was afraid that the murder of David Josua Goldberg would remain unsolved.

•   •   •

Marcus Nowak was sitting at his desk in his small office and carefully sorting the documents that he needed for the consultation the day after tomorrow. Finally, there seemed to be some movement in the project in which he had invested so much time. Recently, the city of Frankfurt had repurchased the Technical Courthouse, which was supposed to be torn down in the course of an extensive urban-renewal project in the Old Town. As early as two years ago, the Frankfurt city council had debated vigorously over what sort of architecture should be commissioned to replace the ugly concrete monstrosity. Renovation was planned for parts of the Old Town between the cathedral and Römerberg Square. Seven of the half-timbered structures of historical significance that had been destroyed during the war were supposed to be reconstructed, making them as true to the originals as possible. For a gifted but still mostly unknown restorer like Marcus Nowak, a commission like this meant more than merely an incredible professional challenge and full employment for his firm for years to come. He was being offered a once-in-a-lifetime chance to make his name known far and wide, because the ambitious project would undoubtedly attract a lot of attention.

His cell phone rang, tearing him from his ruminations. He searched for it under the piles of plans, sketches, tables, and photos, and his heart beat faster when he recognized the number on the display. He'd been waiting for this call, longingly and yet with a terribly guilty conscience. He hesitated a moment. He had actually made Tina a firm promise to go to the soccer field where the Fischbach Sports Club had set up a tent, as they did each year, hosting a big dance to celebrate the first of May. Nowak paused as he looked at his cell and bit his lip, but the temptation was too strong.

"Damn," he muttered softly, and took the call.

He hadn't touched a drop of alcohol all day; well, only a little. He'd washed down the two Prozacs an hour ago with a gulp of vodka; nobody would smell it. He'd promised Kurti not to drink, and now he was feeling good and his head was clear as glass. His hands weren't shaking. Robert Watkowiak grinned at himself in the mirror. What a difference a decent haircut and a respectable outfit made. His dear Uncle Herrmann was a real German bureaucrat and set great store by a clean, proper appearance. So it was better to show up at his office dressed neatly and clean-shaven, without booze on his breath or blood-shot eyes. Sure, he would get the money no matter what, but it seemed better to present his request politely.

It was pure chance that he had happened upon the dark secret of the old man—the secret that he assiduously concealed from the whole world—and since then they had been the best of friends. He wondered what Uncle Jossi and his stepmother would say when they found out what dear Uncle Herrmann was doing in his basement. Watkowiak chortled and turned away from the mirror. He wasn't so stupid that he'd ever tell them, because then his source of income would dry up for good. He just hoped the old bugger would live a long time! He rubbed a cloth over his black patent-leather shoes, which he'd bought specially for the occasion, along with the gray suit, the shirt, and tie. He'd spent almost half of Uncle Jossi's money on the clothes, but his investment was sure to pay off. In a splendid mood, Watkowiak set off shortly before eight o'clock. Kurti had said he'd pick him up at the train station at eight on the dot.

Auguste Nowak was sitting on the wooden bench behind her little house, enjoying the evening calm and the fragrant scent of the nearby woods. Although the weather forecast had predicted a marked drop in temperature along with rain, the air was mild, and the first stars were appearing in the cloudless evening sky. In the rhododendron bush, two blackbirds were squabbling, and a dove was cooing on the roof. It was already quarter past ten, and everyone in the family was having fun up at the soccer field, dancing to welcome the first of May. Except for Marcus, her grandson, who was still sitting at his desk. But they didn't see that—all those jealous people who'd been bad-mouthing the young man ever since his company had become successful. None of them was prepared to work sixteen hours a day, with no weekends and no vacation.

Auguste Nowak clasped her hands in her lap and crossed her ankles. If she stopped to think about it, she'd never had it so good in her whole long life full of work and worries. Her husband, Helmut, had been irreparably trau-matized by the war, had never held a job longer than four weeks, and had hardly set foot out the front door in the last twenty years of his life. Two years ago, he had died. Auguste had then given in to the urgings of their son and moved into the little house on the company property in Fischbach. After Helmut's death, she could no longer endure living in the village in Sauerland. Finally she had her peace and quiet. She no longer had to put up with a TV that was always on and the infirmities of her husband, for whom, in the best moments of their marriage, she had felt only indifference. Auguste heard the clatter of the garden gate, turned her head, and smiled in delight when she recognized her grandson.

"Hello, Oma," said Marcus. "Am I bothering you?"

"You never bother me," Auguste Nowak replied. "Would you like something to eat? I have some goulash and noodles in the fridge."

"No thanks."

He didn't look good. He seemed stressed-out, and for weeks she'd had the impression that something was weighing on him.

"Come here and sit with me." Auguste patted the cushion next to her, but he remained standing. She watched the play of emotions on his face. She could still read him like a book.

"The others are at the May Day dance," she said. "Why don't you go over there, too?"

"I will. I'm on my way up to the soccer field now. I just wanted to—" He broke off, pondered for a moment, and then looked mutely at the floor.

"What's the matter, hmm?" Auguste asked. "Does it have something to do with the company? Are you in a financial bind?"

He shook his head, and when he finally raised his head to look at her, his gaze cut her to the quick. The expression of torment and despair in his brown eyes made her heart ache. He hesitated a moment longer, then sat down next to her on the bench and heaved a deep sigh.

Auguste loved the boy as if he were her own child. Maybe it was because his parents had always been busy with work and the company and had never had time for their youngest son; that's why he had spent large parts of his childhood with her. But maybe it was also because he was so like her older brother Ulrich, who was incredibly good with his hands, a true artist. He could have gone far if the war hadn't thwarted his plans and ruined all his dreams. He fell in France in June 1944, three days before his twenty-third birthday. In appearance, Marcus also reminded her a lot of her beloved brother. He had the same fine, expressive facial features, the smooth dark blond hair that was always falling into his dark eyes, and a beautiful mouth with full lips. But although he was only thirty-four, deep furrows of worry were etched on his face, and he often seemed to Auguste like a boy who had been forced to take on the burdens of a grown man much too soon. Suddenly, Marcus laid his head in her lap, the way he'd always done as a little boy when he needed consolation. Auguste stroked his hair and hummed softly to herself.

"I've done something really, really bad, Oma," he said in a strained voice. "And I'm going to go to hell for it."

She could feel him shudder. The sun had disappeared behind the hills of the Taunus and it was getting cool. After a while, he began to speak, faltering at first, then more and more rapidly, obviously glad to be able to share with someone at last the dark secret that was weighing on his soul.

After her grandson left, Auguste Nowak remained sitting in the dark for a while, thinking. His confession had shaken her, although not so much for moral reasons. In this family of small-minded people, Marcus was as out of place as a kingfisher among crows, and he had married a woman who couldn't muster the slightest understanding for an artist like him. Auguste had been skeptical and concerned that the marriage might not be in her grandson's best interest, but she had never asked him about it.

He visited her every day, telling her about his worries both great and small, about new assignments, about successes and setbacks; in short, about everything that concerned him. Things that a man should actually be discussing with his wife. Even Auguste was not very fond of the family; although they lived under one roof, they were bound not by affection or respect, but by mere convenience. For Auguste, they had remained strangers who said nothing when they spoke and were steadfastly determined to maintain the facade of harmonious family life.

After Marcus had left for the athletic field half an hour later, she went in the house, tied a scarf around her head, grabbed her dark windbreaker and a flashlight, and took the key to Marcus's office from its hook. Although he kept telling her not to, she cleaned his office regularly. She hated to be idle, and work kept a person young. Her eyes fell on the mirror next to the front door. Auguste Nowak knew what the years had done to her face, yet she was sometimes surprised to see the wrinkles, her mouth caving in because of missing teeth, and the heavy-hooded eyelids. Almost eighty-five, she thought. Unbelievable that she could be old so soon! To be honest, she never felt any older than fifty. She was tough and strong and a lot more agile than many thirty-year-olds. At sixty, she had gotten her driver's license, and at seventy, she'd taken her first vacation. She found joy in small things and never quarreled with her fate. Besides, she still had something she needed to do, something of immense importance. Death, which she had looked in the eye for the first time over sixty years ago, would have to be patient until she had put everything in order. Auguste winked at her reflection in the mirror and left the house. She crossed the courtyard, opened the door to the office building, and went into Marcus's office, which was in the annex to the workshop that he'd had built in the meadow down the hill from Auguste's little cottage a few years back. The clock above the desk said 11:30. She would have to hurry if she didn't want anyone to know about her little outing.

He could hear the throbbing bass of the music as soon as he walked across the jammed parking lot. The DJ was playing all the silly pop hits back to back, and the people were drunker than Marcus Nowak would have believed possible at this hour. A few kids, including his own, were playing soccer on the grass, and about three hundred people were crammed into the festival tent. Most of the adults had withdrawn to the bar at the clubhouse. Marcus was sickened by the sight of the two obviously tipsy men from the board of directors who were leering at the young girls.

"Hey, Nowak!" A hand slapped him on the back, and somebody breathed foul schnapps fumes in his face. "I can't believe you're here!"

"Hi, Stefan," replied Marcus. "Have you seen Tina?"

"Nope, sorry. But come on over to our table and have a cold one with us, man."

The man grabbed his arm as he followed reluctantly through the sweating, boisterous crowd in the rear of the festival tent.

"Hey, people!" Stefan yelled. "Look who I brought!"

Everybody turned to look at them, yelling and smirking. He was looking into familiar faces with glassy eyes, which told him the alcohol had already been flowing freely. Earlier, he'd been one of them: They were buddies from school or sports, guys from the annual fair, and had played their way from the junior league in soccer up to the first-string team. They had served with the volunteer fire department and partied at a lot of celebrations like this one. He'd known them all since they were kids, but suddenly they seemed like strangers. They shoved together to make room for him. He sat down, determined to grin and bear it. Somebody stuck a glass of May wine in his hand and gave a toast, so he drank. When had he stopped enjoying this sort of thing? Why didn't he have as much fun as his old pals with simple pleasures like this? While the others downed their drinks within five minutes, he was still holding his glass of May wine. At that moment, he felt his cell vibrating in his pants pocket. He pulled out the phone, and his heart skipped a beat when he saw who had sent him a text. The contents made his face turn crimson.

"Hey, Marcus, I wanna give you some advice, as a good friend," Chris Wiethölter babbled in his ear. He was one of the coaches he used to play on the team with. "Heiko is really hot for Tina. You'd better keep an eye on them."

"Right, thanks. I will," he replied absently. How was he going to answer the text message? Ignore it? Shut off his phone and get drunk with his old pals? He sat on the bench as if paralyzed, holding the glass with the May wine, which was now lukewarm. He just couldn't think straight.

"I just mean . . . between friends, you know," Wiethölter muttered, then chugged the last of his beer and belched.

"You're right." Nowak stood up. "I'm going to go look for her."

"Yeah, do that, man. . . ."

Tina would never start anything with Heiko Schmidt or any other guy, and if she did, he didn't give a shit, but he took the opportunity to get out of there. He made his way through the crowd of sweaty bodies, nodding to people here and there, and hoped he didn't run into his wife or any of her girlfriends. When had he realized that he didn't love Tina anymore? He couldn't figure out what had changed. It had to be something he'd done, because Tina was the same as always. She was content with the life they shared, but it had suddenly gotten too confining for him. He slipped unnoticed out of the tent and took the shortcut through the club bar. Too late he realized his mistake. His father was sitting with his friends at the bar, as he did almost every evening.

"Hey, Marcus!" Manfred Nowak wiped the beer foam off his mustache with the back of his hand. "Come on over here!"

Marcus Nowak felt his stomach turn over, but he obeyed. He could see that his father was already sloshed, so he steeled himself. A glance at the clock on the wall told him that it was 11:30.

"A *weizen* beer for my son!" his father bellowed. Then he turned to the other older men, who were still clad in track outfits and running shoes, even though they'd had their modest success in sports decades ago.

"My son is a real big shot now. He's rebuilding the Old Town of Frankfurt, house by house! I bet you're all surprised, right?"

Manfred Nowak slapped Marcus on the back, but his eyes held neither recognition nor pride, only scorn. He kept on mocking him, and Marcus didn't say a word, which merely egged his father on. The men were smirking. They knew all about the bankruptcy of Nowak's construction company, and Marcus's refusal to take over the firm, because in a little town like Fischbach, nothing was ever secret, especially not such a grandiose failure. The bartender set the *weizen* beer on the bar, but Marcus didn't touch it.

"Cheers!" yelled his father, raising his glass. Everybody drank but Marcus.

"What's the matter? You're not too stuck-up to drink with us, are you?"

Marcus Nowak saw the drunken anger in his father's eyes.

"I don't feel like listening to any more of your stupid pronouncements," he said. "Talk to your friends, if you want. Maybe one of them will believe you."

His father tried to release his pent-up fury by slapping his youngest son's face, as he'd done so often in the past. But the alcohol slowed down his reflexes, and Marcus easily avoided the blow. He looked on without sympathy as his father lost his balance and crashed to the floor, along with the bar stool. Then he escaped before his old man could get back on his feet. At the door of the clubhouse, he caught his breath and hurried across the parking lot. He got into the car and peeled out of the lot. Not two hundred yards farther on, the police stopped him.

"So," said the first officer, shining his flashlight in Marcus's face, "finished celebrating May Day at the dance?"

The cop sounded nasty. Marcus recognized his voice. Siggi Nitschke had played on the first-string team in the Ruppertshain club when Marcus had been the top goal scorer for years in the circuit league.

"Hello, Siggi," he said.

"Well, lookee here. It's Nowak. The big *entrepreneur.* Driver's license and registration, please."

"I don't have them with me."

"Now, isn't that a shame," Nitschke mocked him. "Then please exit the vehicle."

Marcus sighed and obeyed. Nitschke had never been able to stand him, mainly because he'd always been a step below Marcus as a soccer player. For Nitschke, pulling him over for a traffic violation must be like having a field day, he realized. Marcus submitted without protest to being treated like a felon. They made him blow into the Breathalyzer and were clearly pissed off when zero popped up on the display.

"Drugs?" Nitschke wasn't going to let him off that easy. "Been smoking anything? Or snorting it?"

"Nonsense," replied Marcus, who didn't want any trouble. "I've never done anything like that, and you know it, Nitschke."

"Don't get so familiar. I'm on duty. *Officer* Nitschke to you, understand?"

"Oh, let him go, Siggi," said his colleague in a low voice. Officer Nitschke gave Marcus a fierce stare, wracking his brain to think up something he could run him in for. In his whole life, he'd never get another chance like this.

"Present your driver's license and registration to my colleagues at the station in Kelkheim no later than ten in the morning," he said at last. "Now get your ass out of here. You were lucky."

Without a word, Marcus got into his car, started it up, put on his seat belt, and drove off. All his good intentions were gone. He grabbed his cell and texted a brief reply: ON THE WAY. SEE YOU SOON.

Tuesday, May 1

Bodenstein drummed his fingers impatiently on the steering wheel. The body of a man had been discovered in Eppenhain, but the only road that led to the remote district of Kelkheim had been blocked off by police. The contestants in the "Round the Henninger Tower" bicycle race were struggling for the second time this morning up the steep hill from Schlossborn to Ruppertshain. Hundreds of spectators lined the sidewalks and waited in front of big video screens at the sharp curve at Zauberberg. Finally, the first riders came into view. The advance guard zoomed past like a magenta cloud, followed closely by the main field in all colors of the rainbow. In between, next to them, and close behind them came the supply vehicles, and in the air circled the helicopters from Hesse TV, which was broadcasting the whole event live.

"I can't imagine that this is a healthy sport," Pia Kirchhoff said from the passenger seat. "They're riding right in the middle of the exhaust from the escort vehicles."

"Sports kill," said Bodenstein, to whom competitive athletes were almost as suspect as religious fanatics.

"Cycling, at least. Especially for men. I read recently somewhere that men who ride bikes often become impotent," said Pia, adding without segue, "By the way, our colleague Behnke rides with the amateurs. At least the one-hundred-kilometer hill section."

"How am I supposed to take what you just said? Have you got inside information about the state of Behnke's health that you're keeping from me?" Bodenstein couldn't refrain from an amused grin. The relationship between Kirchhoff and Behnke was still not smooth sailing, even though the open animosity had gradually evolved to collegial acceptance since last summer. Pia suddenly realized what she'd just said.

"For God's sake, no." She gave an embarrassed laugh. "The road's clear now."

Nobody who got to know Detective Superintendent Oliver von Bodenstein would have guessed how crazy he was about any sort of gossip. Pia's boss, who always dressed in a suit and tie, outwardly gave the impression of a man in full command of every situation—someone who ignored the private lives of other people with aristocratic courtesy. But that impression was deceptive. In reality, his curiosity was virtually insatiable and his memory shockingly good. Maybe it was the combination of these two characteristics that made Bodenstein the brilliant detective he undoubtedly was.

"Please don't tell Behnke about this," Pia said. "He might misunderstand it entirely."

"I'll have to give that some thought," replied Bodenstein with a smirk, steering his BMW in the direction of Eppenhain.

Marcus Nowak waited in the car until his family had left the house and driven off; first his parents, then his brother with his family, and finally Tina with the children. He knew them all so well—they would drive over to watch the bicycle race and be gone quite a while, and that was fine with him. They never missed the race, even if they'd been partying until the wee hours—it was important to keep up appearances. This morning, he had already run twelve kilometers, his usual course along the Reis to the Bodenstein estate, up to Ruppertshain, and through the woods in a big loop all the way back. Normally running relaxed Marcus and cleared his head, but today he hadn't been able to escape the sting of conscience and strong feelings of guilt. He had done it again, even though he was well aware that he would roast in deepest hell. He got out of his car, opened the front door of his house, and ran straight upstairs to his apartment. For a moment, he stood in the middle of the living room with his arms hanging limply at his sides. Everything looked the same as always in the early morning: The breakfast table had not been cleared off yet, and toys were scattered all over. The sight of this familiar and normal scene brought tears to his eyes. This was no longer his world, and it never would be again! Where had this dark urge come from, this desire for the forbidden? Tina, the kids, friends and family—why did he want to put all that at risk? Didn't it mean anything to him anymore?

He went into the bathroom and was shocked to see his sunken cheeks and bloodshot eyes in the mirror. Was there any way back for him, if no one found out about what he'd done? Did he even *want* to go back? He undressed, got in the shower, and turned on the water. Cold. Ice-cold. He had to be punished. He gasped through his clenched teeth as the icy spray hit his sweaty skin. He couldn't prevent the images from last night from crashing in on him. The way he had stood in front of him and looked at him, astounded— no, horrified! Without turning his eyes away, he'd then slowly knelt down before him, turned his back, and, trembling, waited for him to ... Sobbing convulsively, he put his hands over his face.

"Marcus?"

He gave a start when he saw the figure of his grandmother through the wet shower door. He hurriedly turned off the water and slung the towel he'd hung over the glass door around his hips.

"What's the matter?" asked Auguste Nowak with concern. "Don't you feel well?"

He stepped out of the shower and met her searching look.

"I didn't want to do it again," he blurted out in despair. "Really, Oma, but ... but I ..."

He stopped, searching in vain for an explanation. The old woman took him in her arms. At first, he resisted her embrace, but then he leaned against her, inhaling her familiar smell.

"Why do I do these things?" he whispered, filled with despair. "I just don't know what's wrong with me. Maybe I'm not normal."

She took his face in her calloused hands and gave him a worried look from her surprisingly youthful eyes.

"Stop tormenting yourself, my boy," she said softly.

"But I just don't understand myself anymore," he said in a strained voice. "And if anybody finds out, then—"

"How would anyone find out? Nobody saw you there, did they?" She sounded like a coconspirator.

"I . . . I don't think so." He shook his head. How could his grandmother possibly understand what he'd done?

"Well then." She let him go. "Now get some clothes on. And then come downstairs and I'll make you some hot chocolate and a good breakfast. I'm sure you haven't had anything to eat."

Against his will, Marcus Nowak had to laugh. That was his grandmother's standard remedy: Food always helps. As he watched her go, he actually did feel a little better.

Herrmann Schneider's house was a typical but run-down hipped-roof bungalow located right at the edge of the woods, surrounded by a large, rather untidy yard. Schneider's body had been discovered by a person who did community work for the Maltese Relief Service and came to check on the old man every morning. Oliver von Bodenstein and Pia Kirchhoff experienced a gruesome déjà vu. The man was on his knees on the tile floor in the foyer of his house, and the fatal bullet had entered through the back of his skull. It looked like an execution, the same as with David Goldberg.

"The deceased is Herrmann Schneider, born March second, 1921, in Wuppertal." The young female officer who was the first on the scene with her partner had already done the preliminary research. "After his wife's death a few years ago, he lived here alone. Home care came by three times a day, and he received Meals on Wheels."

"Have you questioned the neighbors already?"

"Of course." The efficient policewoman shot Bodenstein a somewhat annoyed glance. As in other areas of life, animosities also existed within the police force. The cops on the beat thought that the Kripo detectives considered themselves superior and looked down on them, and basically they were right.

"The woman who lives next door saw two men visit Schneider around eight-thirty last night. They left a little after eleven, making quite a ruckus."

"So someone was targeting pensioners," her colleague remarked. "For the second time in a week."

Bodenstein ignored the flippant remark.

"Any signs of forced entry?"

"At first glance, no. Looks like he let his murderer in the front door. And nothing seems to have been disturbed in the house," the officer replied.

"Thank you," said Bodenstein. "Good work."

He and Pia pulled on latex gloves and bent over the corpse of the old man. In the dim light of a forty-watt ceiling lamp, they both saw simultaneously that the apparent repetition of events was no accident: In the blood spatter on the floral-patterned rug someone had written five numbers: 11645.

Bodenstein looked at his colleague. He said firmly, "I'm not going to allow this case to be taken away from me."

At that moment, the medical examiner arrived. Pia recognized him. It was the gnome who had done the autopsy on the body of Isabel Kerstner a year and a half ago. She turned a grimace into a tight smile.

"Out of the way," he grumbled rudely. Either that was his personality or he still bore a grudge. Back then, Bodenstein had given him a piece of his mind regarding his indifference.

"Be careful not to destroy any evidence," Bodenstein said with equal lack of courtesy and got a dirty look in reply. He motioned for Pia to follow him into the kitchen.

"Who called this guy?" he asked in a low voice.

"Must have been our colleagues who were the first responders," she said. Her gaze fixed on a bulletin board hanging next to the kitchen table. She moved closer and removed a card of handmade paper that was pinned among the receipts, recipes, and a couple of postcards. *Invitation,* it said. Pia opened it and gave a surprised whistle. "Take a look at this!" She handed the invitation to her boss.

Pia ascertained from a look around that the bungalow from the early seventies combined all the stylistic tastelessness of that era in its old-fashioned furnishings. Rustic oak veneer in the living room, vapid landscape pictures on the walls that gave no hint of the preferences of the man who'd lived there. The floral pattern on the wall tiles in the kitchen hurt her eyes, and the guest toilet was done in a dusty rose color. Pia entered the sparsely furnished bedroom. On the nightstand beside Schneider's bed stood a couple of medicine bottles, and next to them an open book. A well-worn copy of

Marion, Countess Dönhoff's *Names That No One Mentions: People and History of East Prussia.*

"And?" Bodenstein asked. "Find anything?"

"Zip." Pia shrugged. "No workroom, not even a desk."

As the body of Herrmann Schneider was being transported to the forensics lab, the evidence techs packed up their tools. Even the ME had left after taking the rectal temperature of the corpse and estimating the time of death at about 1:00 A.M.

"Maybe he had an office in the basement," Bodenstein said. "Let's go downstairs and look."

Pia followed her boss to the basement. Behind the first door was a room with a modern oil furnace. In the room next to it, carefully labeled cartons stood on shelves; on the opposite wall were wine bottles stored in wooden crates. Bodenstein looked more closely at the wine bottles and gave an appreciative whistle.

"He had a small fortune stored here."

Pia was already at the next door. She turned on the light and stopped short in astonishment.

"Boss!" she called. "You've got to see this!"

"What is it?" Bodenstein appeared behind her in the doorway.

"Looks like a screening room." Pia studied the walls covered in dark red velvet, the fifteen comfortable plush easy chairs arranged in three rows, and the closed black curtain at the other end of the surprisingly large space. By the wall next to the door stood an old-fashioned film projector.

"Let's see what kind of movies the old boy watched in his quiet little chamber." Bodenstein stepped up to the projector, in which a reel of film was threaded, and pressed a couple of random buttons. Pia tried the switch plate next to the door, and suddenly the curtain parted. Both of them gave a start when gunfire and martial music resounded from hidden loudspeakers. They stared at the screen. Tanks rolled across a snowy landscape; in flickering black and white, the grinning faces of young soldiers crouched at antiaircraft cannons and machine guns. Airplanes flew across the gray sky.

"Newsreels," Pia said in astonishment. "Here in his private theater he watched newsreels? How sick is that?"

"He was young back then." Bodenstein, who had feared they would find an archive of porn films, merely shrugged. "Maybe he just liked to remember those days."

He looked through the vast number of meticulously labeled reels of film stored on shelves and discovered countless episodes of the weekly German *Wochenschau* newsreel from the years 1933 to 1945: movies of Goebbels's speeches at the Sport Palace, films of the National Socialist Party national conventions in Nürnberg, Leni Riefenstahl's *Triumph of the Will, Storm Over Mont Blanc,* and other rarities that a collector would pay a fortune for. Bodenstein switched off the projector.

"He probably watched these movies with his visitors." Pia pointed to three used glasses, two empty wine bottles, and an overflowing ashtray, all on a little table between the first two rows of seats. She carefully picked up a glass and inspected it closely. Her suspicion was confirmed: The dregs at the bottom of the glass had not yet dried. Bodenstein went out to summon the officers from the evidence team to the basement; then he followed Pia into the next room. Its furnishings left him momentarily speechless.

"For heaven's sake," Pia blurted out in disgust. "Is this a movie set?"

The windowless room, which seemed even lower than it really was because of the fake wooden beams on the ceiling and the maroon carpet, was dominated by a massive desk of dark mahogany. Floor-to-ceiling bookshelves, document cabinets, a heavy safe, on the walls a swastika banner and several framed photos of Adolf Hitler and other Nazi big shots. In contrast to the upper part of the house, which seemed impersonal and almost unlived in, the legacy and evidence from a long life were abundantly present here. Pia looked closely at one of the photos and shuddered.

"This one has a personal inscription from Hitler. I feel like I'm in the bunker under the Reich Chancellery."

"Look around on the desk. If we're going to find a lead, it would be here."

"*Jawohl, mein Führer!*" Pia stood at attention.

"Quit joking around." Bodenstein looked around the overcrowded, gloomy room, which was exerting a claustrophobic effect on him. Pia Kirchhoff's comparison to a bunker was not that far-fetched. As she sat down at the desk and opened one drawer after another with her fingertips, Bodenstein took files and photo albums at random from the shelves and paged through them.

"My God, what's all this?" Kröger, from the evidence team, stepped inside the room.

"Creepy, isn't it?" Pia glanced up. "Could you please pack up all this stuff after you take pictures of the room? I don't want to stay in this place any longer than necessary."

"We're going to need a truck for all this." Kröger looked less than enthusiastic and grimaced. Pia came upon carefully filed account withdrawals from various banks in the second drawer from the top. Herrmann Schneider had received a sizable pension, but in addition there were regular payments of five thousand euros a month from a Swiss bank. The current balance in these accounts stood at 172,000 euros.

"Boss," Pia said. "Somebody was transferring five thousand euros a month to him. KMF. I wonder what that stands for?" She handed Bodenstein one of the printouts.

"War Ministry Frankfurt," Kröger guessed.

"My Führer's account," his colleague joked. Bodenstein felt the uneasiness inside him growing stronger, because the connection could no longer be ignored. The invitation upstairs in the kitchen, payments from the KMF, the ominous numbers that the perp had left behind at both crime scenes. It was high time they paid a visit to a very respected lady, even if it might be just a coincidence.

"KMF means Kaltensee Machine Factory," he told Pia in a low voice. "Schneider knew Vera Kaltensee. Just as Goldberg did."

"She obviously had very refined friends," Pia replied.

"But we don't know whether they were really her friends," Bodenstein remarked. "Vera Kaltensee enjoys an irreproachable reputation, and there is absolutely no doubt about her integrity."

"Goldberg's reputation was also irreproachable," said Pia, unconvinced.

"What are you trying to say?"

"That not everything is what it seems at first glance."

Bodenstein looked pensively at the account payments.

"I'm afraid there are still thousands of people in Germany who sympathized with the Nazis in their youth, or even were Nazis themselves," he said. "But all this was over sixty years ago."

"That doesn't justify anything," Pia retorted, getting up. "And this Schneider was no mere sympathizer. He was a full-blooded Nazi. Just take a look around."

"But we can't automatically conclude that Vera Kaltensee knew about the Nazi past of two of her friends," said Bodenstein with a big sigh. A gloomy premonition filled him. No matter how impeccable Vera Kaltensee's reputation might be, as soon as the press connected her with this offensive muck, some of it was bound to rub off on her.

At the parking lot in Königstein, he got off the bus and strolled down the pedestrian street. It was a good feeling to have money. Robert Watkowiak contentedly observed his reflection in the shop windows and decided the first thing he'd do with Uncle Herrmann's dough was have his teeth fixed. With the new haircut and the suit, he no longer stood out in a crowd; none of the passersby turned to look at him and shake their heads. That was an even better feeling. To be honest, he was sick and tired of the life he'd been more or less forced into. He needed a bed, a shower, and the comfort he had been used to in the past, and he hated having to shack up with Moni. Yesterday, she'd probably thought he was going to beg for a place to crash at her place again, but she was wrong on that score. Even though she was no more than a lying slut who let herself be fucked by anybody for money, she thought she was something special. Sure, she wasn't bad-looking, but as soon as she opened her mouth, it was obvious that she was just a low-class chick, especially if she'd been drinking. A couple of weeks ago, she'd provoked him so much in front of his pals at the Brake Light bar that he'd had to belt her one. Then she'd finally shut her trap. After that, he'd hit her whenever he felt like it, sometimes for no reason at all. He liked the feeling of having power over somebody.

Robert Watkowiak turned toward the spa park and walked past the Villa Borgnis in the direction of the town hall. For a while now, he'd been using the abandoned house next to the lotto shop as an occasional place to crash. The owner put up with his presence and didn't say a word. Sure, it was full of dust and filth, but it had electricity and the toilet and shower worked—better by far than sleeping under a bridge.

With a sigh, he sank onto the mattress in the top-floor room, pulled off his shoes, and fished a can of beer out of his backpack. He finished it off in a few gulps, giving a loud burp. Then he reached into his backpack again and smiled as his fingers touched the cool metal. The old man hadn't noticed that he'd stolen it. The pistol had to be worth a fortune. Genuine weapons from World War II were traded for insane prices. And there were freaks who would gladly fork over double or triple the price for guns that had actually been used to kill someone. Robert took out the pistol and studied it thoughtfully. He simply hadn't been able to resist. Somehow he had the feeling that things were slowly going to improve for him. Tomorrow, he could cash the checks. And go to the dentist. Or the day after. Tonight, he was going to stop by the Brake Light one more time. Maybe that guy would be there who dealt in military shit.

In Fischbach, Bodenstein turned right at the intersection and took the B455 toward Eppstein. He'd decided to talk to Vera Kaltensee right away, before his boss could stop him with some tactical excuse. As he drove, he thought about the woman, who was undoubtedly one of the foremost personalities in the region and whose presence enhanced any occasion. Vera Kaltensee had been born baroness of Zeydlitz-Lauenburg. With only a suitcase in one hand and a baby on her arm, she had fled from East Prussia to the West. There, she had soon married the Hofheim entrepreneur Eugen Kaltensee, and together they had built the Kaltensee Machine Factory into a worldwide concern. After the death of her husband, she had taken over running the business and at the same time was tirelessly engaged in various charitable organizations. As a generous donor and fund-raiser, she had garnered the very highest esteem, and not only in Germany. Through the Eugen Kaltensee Foundation, she promoted the arts and cultural events and worked for the preservation of the environment and historical sites. She also supported the needy with numerous social projects, most of which she herself had initiated.

The "Mühlenhof," as the grand residence of the Kaltensees was called, was tucked away in the valley between Eppstein and Lorsbach. It lay behind thick hedges and a high black iron fence with golden spikes on top. Bodenstein turned into the drive; the double entrance gate stood wide open. In the rear area of the parklike grounds stood the manor house, and to its left was the historic mill.

"Oh! I'm jealous," Pia exclaimed at the sight of the deep green lawns, perfectly clipped bushes, and carefully designed flower beds. "How do they get it to look like this?"

"With an army of gardeners," Bodenstein replied drily. "And I don't think any critters are allowed to run across the grass."

Pia grinned at this allusion. At her home in Birkenhof, some animal was always where it wasn't supposed to be: the dogs in the duck pond, the horses in the garden, the ducks and geese on a reconnaissance mission through the house. The last time her chickens had escaped, Pia had spent a whole afternoon removing the greenish deposits they'd left in all the rooms. Good thing that Christoph wasn't very finicky about things like that.

Bodenstein parked the car near the steps of the manor house. As they got out and looked around, a man came around the corner of the building. He had gray hair and melancholy Saint Bernard eyes in a long, narrow face. Obviously, this was the gardener, because he was wearing green overalls and held rose clippers in his hand.

"May I help you?" He eyed them suspiciously. Bodenstein pulled out his police ID.

"We're from the criminal police in Hofheim and would like to speak with Mrs. Kaltensee."

"I see." He took his time fumbling with a pair of reading glasses, which he had retrieved from the breast pocket of his overalls, and carefully studied Bodenstein's identification. A polite smile then suffused his face. "The craziest things happen if I don't close the gate immediately. A lot of people think this is a hotel or a golf club."

"I'm not surprised," said Pia, glancing at the beds of blooming shrubs and rosebushes and the artistic boxwood topiary. "That's what it looks like."

"Do you like it?" The man was clearly flattered.

"Oh yes!" Pia nodded. "Do you do all the work yourself?"

"My son helps out occasionally," he admitted modestly, although he was enjoying Pia's attention.

"Tell me, where can we find Mrs. Kaltensee?" Bodenstein interjected before his colleague got involved in a technical discussion of lawn fertilizer or the care of roses.

"Oh, of course." The man gave an apologetic smile. "I'll tell her you're here. What did you say your name was?"

Bodenstein handed the gardener his business card, and the man left, heading for the front door.

"Compared to the grounds, the house seems rather shabby," said Pia. From up close, the building didn't look quite as manorlike and magnificent as it had from a distance. The blotchy plaster was in disrepair and had started to flake off; in many places, the brickwork was visible.

"The house isn't as significant historically as the rest of the structures here," Bodenstein explained. The estate is best known for the mill, which was mentioned in documents in the thirteenth century, if I remember correctly. Until the early twentieth century, it belonged to the Stolberg-Werningerode family, who also owned the Eppstein Fortress, until they donated it to the city of Eppstein in 1929. A cousin of the Wernigerodes married a daughter from the house of Zeydlitz, and that's how the estate came into the possession of the Kaltensees."

Pia stared at her boss in amazement.

"What is it?" he asked.

"How do you know all that? And what do the Wernige what's their names and Zeydlitz have to do with the Kaltensees?"

"Vera Kaltensee was born into the Zeydlitz-Lauenburg family," Bodenstein informed his colleague. "I'd forgotten to tell you that. The rest is common knowledge if you know anything about local history."

"Ah, naturally." Pia nodded. "Among the blue bloods, you probably learn that sort of fundamental detail by heart, along with the Gotha directory of German nobility."

"Do I detect a note of sarcasm in your voice?" Bodenstein asked with a grin.

"Good Lord, no!" Pia raised both hands. "Ah, the mistress herself will soon come rushing to greet us. How should I address her? With a formal curtsy?"

"You're impossible, Ms. Kirchhoff."

Marleen Ritter, née Kaltensee, looked at the simple gold band on the ring finger of her right hand and smiled. She still felt dizzy from the swift tempo of the enormous positive changes that had occurred in her life over the past weeks and months. After the divorce from Marco, she had been convinced that she'd live alone for the rest of her days. She'd inherited her stocky figure from her father; a more important deterrent for any potential suitor was the amputated lower part of one leg. But not for Thomas Ritter! He had known her since childhood and had lived through the whole drama with her: the forbidden liaison with Robert, the serious accident, the horrible crash that had shaken the whole family to the core. Thomas had visited her in the hospital and driven her to doctor's appointments and to physical therapy when her parents didn't have the time. He had always found consoling and encouraging words to say to the unhappy fat girl she had become. Yes, she had undoubtedly fallen in love with him back then.

When she had run into him last November, it had seemed to her like a sign from God. He had not looked good, almost appearing a bit down-at-the-heels, but he had been as obliging and charming as ever. He had never said a single bad word about her Omi, although he would have had every reason to hate her. Marleen didn't know exactly what had led to the break between Thomas and her grandmother after eighteen years. In the family, there were only whispered speculations about what might have been the cause, but it hurt her a great deal, because Thomas was a special man. It was because of her grandmother and her connections that he no longer had the ghost of a chance of finding a decent job in Frankfurt that was worthy of his talents.

Why hadn't he simply left town and tried to start over somewhere else? Instead, he'd kept his head above water through his efforts as a freelance journalist. His tiny apartment in Frankfurt-Niederrad was a depressing hole. She had urged him to move in with her, but he told her he didn't want to be beholden to her. She was very moved by that. She didn't care that Thomas hardly owned more than the shirt on his back. It wasn't his fault. She loved him from the bottom of her heart; she loved being with him, sleeping with him. And she was looking forward to the baby they were going to have. Marleen had no doubts that she would manage to bring about a reconciliation between Thomas and her grandmother. After all, Vera had never denied her anything. Her cell phone rang with the special ringtone reserved for Thomas. He called her at least ten times a day to ask how she was doing.

"How are you, sweetheart?" he asked. "What are you two up to?"

Marleen smiled at the allusion to the baby in her belly.

"We're lazing around on the couch," she replied. "I'm reading a little. What are you doing?"

A newspaper city room never closed, not even on holidays. Thomas had volunteered to go in on May Day to help out his colleagues, who wanted time off to be with their families and kids. Marleen found it typical of Thomas. He was always so considerate and unselfish.

"I still have to wait for two things that are pending." He sighed. "I'm really sorry I had to leave you alone all day today, but at least I'll have the weekend off."

"Don't worry about me. I'm doing fine."

They talked for a while longer, and then Thomas had to go. Marleen looked blissfully at the ring on her finger. Then she leaned back, closed her eyes, and thought about how much happiness she'd had with this man.

Dr. Vera Kaltensee was waiting for them in the entry hall, an elegant woman with snow-white hair and alert light blue eyes in a suntanned face, in which a long life had etched a network of deep furrows. She stood ramrod-straight, and the only concession to her age was a cane with a silver knob.

"Come in." Her smile was sincere, and her deep voice quavered a bit. "My dear Moormann told me that you'd like to speak with me about an important matter."

"Yes, that's right." Bodenstein held out his hand and returned her smile. "Oliver von Bodenstein, from Kripo Hofheim. My colleague, Pia Kirchhoff."

"So you're the talented son-in-law of my dear friend Gabriela," she said, scrutinizing him. "She always speaks of you with the greatest respect. I hope my present on the birth of your little daughter met with approval?"

"But of course. Thank you so much." For the life of him, Bodenstein couldn't recall any present from Vera Kaltensee when Sophia was born, but he assumed that Cosima had acknowledged it appropriately with a thank-you note.

"Good day, Ms. Kirchhoff," Dr. Vera Kaltensee said, turning to Pia and taking her hand. "I'm very pleased to meet you."

She leaned forward a bit.

"I've never met such a pretty policewoman. What lovely blue eyes you have, my dear!"

Pia, who usually reacted suspiciously to such compliments, actually felt flattered and gave an embarrassed laugh. She'd expected to be looked down on by this prominent and extremely rich woman, or ignored entirely. So she was pleasantly surprised at how normal and unpretentious Vera Kaltensee seemed.

"But please do come in." The old lady took Pia's arm as though they were old friends and led her into a salon whose walls were covered with Flemish tapestries. In front of the massive marble fireplace stood three easy chairs and a coffee table, which, in spite of their plain appearance, were probably worth more than all the furniture Pia had at Birkenhof. Vera Kaltensee showed her to an easy chair.

"Please have a seat," she said kindly. "May I offer you coffee or some refreshment?"

Bodenstein declined politely. "No thanks." It was easier to announce a person's death while standing than while drinking a cup of coffee.

"All right, then. What brings you here? It's not a purely courtesy call, I suppose?" Vera Kaltensee was still smiling, but an anxious look appeared in her eyes.

"Unfortunately, no," Bodenstein admitted.

The smile vanished from the old woman's face. All at once, she seemed helpless, in a touching sort of way. She sat down in one of the easy chairs and stared at Bodenstein expectantly, like a schoolgirl looking up at her teacher.

"This morning, we were called to the scene where the body of Herrmann Schneider had been found. In his house, we found indications that he knew you; that's why we're here."

"Goodness gracious," Vera Kaltensee whispered in shock, her face as pale as chalk. She dropped her cane, and the fingers of her right hand closed around the medallion on her necklace. "How did he ... I mean ... what ... what happened?"

"He was shot to death in his house." Bodenstein picked up the cane and tried to hand it to her, but she ignored his gesture. "We presume that it was the same perpetrator who killed David Goldberg."

"Oh no." Vera Kaltensee stifled a sigh and pressed a hand to her mouth. Tears came to her eyes and ran down her wrinkled cheeks. Pia gave her boss a reproachful look, to which he responded by briefly raising his eyebrows. She knelt down in front of Vera Kaltensee and put her hand sympathetically on the old woman's.

"I'm so sorry," she said softly. "Shall I get you a glass of water?"

Vera Kaltensee struggled to compose herself and smiled through her tears.

"Thank you, my dear," she whispered. "That would be very kind of you. There's probably a carafe over there on the sideboard."

Pia got up. She found various spirits and upside-down glasses on the sideboard. Vera Kaltensee smiled gratefully when Pia handed her a glass of water, and she took a sip.

"May we ask you a few questions, or would you rather we postpone it to some other time?" Pia asked.

"No, no. It's all ... Now is fine." Vera Kaltensee conjured an apple blossom white handkerchief from the pocket of her knit cashmere jacket, dabbed at her eyes, and blew her nose. "It's just such a shock to get news like this. Herrmann is ... I mean, he was ... such a good, close friend of our family for so many years. And for him to die in such a dreadful way ..."

Again her eyes filled with tears.

"In Mr. Schneider's house, we found an invitation to your birthday party," said Pia. "And there were also regular payments from KMF to his account in a Swiss bank."

Vera Kaltensee nodded. She had composed herself now and spoke in a soft yet firm voice.

"Herrmann was an old friend of my late husband," she explained. "After he retired, he was a consultant to our Swiss subsidiary, KMF Suisse. Herrmann was previously a financial officer, so his knowledge and advice were quite valuable."

"What do you know about Mr. Schneider and his past?" Bodenstein asked. He was still holding the cane in his hand.

"Professional or private?"

"Both, preferably. We're looking for someone who had a reason to kill Mr. Schneider."

"I really have no idea." Vera Kaltensee shook her head emphatically. "He was such a sweet man. After his wife died, he lived all alone in that house of his, although his health was not good. But he refused to move to a retirement home."

Pia could imagine why. There he couldn't have watched the old Nazi newsreels or hung an autographed photo of Adolf Hitler on the wall. But she said nothing.

"How long have you known Mr. Schneider?"

"A long time. As I said, he was a very good friend of Eugen, my late husband."

"Did he also know Mr. Goldberg?"

"Yes, of course." Vera Kaltensee seemed a bit annoyed. "Why do you ask?"

"We found the same number at both crime scenes," said Bodenstein. "One one six four five. It was written in the victims' blood and might indicate some connection between the two crimes."

Vera Kaltensee did not reply immediately. Her hands gripped the armrests of her chair. For a fraction of a second, an expression flitted across her face that surprised Pia.

"One one six four five?" the old woman repeated pensively. "What's that supposed to mean?"

Before Bodenstein could say anything, a man came into the salon. He was tall and thin, almost gaunt. With his suit, silk scarf, three-day growth of beard, and shoulder-length salt-and-pepper hair, he looked like an aging actor. In amazement, he looked from Bodenstein to Pia and finally at Vera. Pia was sure she knew him from somewhere.

"I didn't know you had visitors, Mother," he said, and made as if to leave. "Please excuse the interruption."

"Don't go!" Vera Kaltensee's voice was sharp, but she was smiling when she turned to Bodenstein and Pia. "This is Elard, my eldest son. He lives here with me."

Then she looked again at her son.

"Elard, this is Detective Superintendent von Bodenstein from the Kripo in Hofheim, Gabriela's son-in-law. And this is his colleague . . . Please forgive me, I didn't catch your name."

Before Pia could say a word, Elard Kaltensee spoke up. His smoky voice had a pleasant, melodious sound.

"Ms. Kirchhoff." He astonished her with his phenomenal memory for names. "It's been quite a while since we last met. How is your husband?"

Professor Elard Kaltensee, Pia thought. Of course she knew him. He was an art historian and for many years had been the dean of his department at the university in Frankfurt. As acting head of the Institute of Forensic Medicine, her ex-husband, Henning, also belonged to the faculty of the university, so she had occasionally attended functions at which Elard Kaltensee had also been present. Pia remembered hearing a rumor that he was a ladies' man and had a preference for young female artists. He had to be over sixty now, she realized, but he was still attractive, albeit in a somewhat dissipated way.

"Thank you for asking." Pia omitted mentioning that she and Henning had divorced two months ago. "He's doing fine."

"Herrmann has been murdered," Vera Kaltensee remarked. Her voice was quavering again. "That's why the police are here."

"Oh no," said Elard Kaltensee, raising his eyebrows. "When did it happen?"

"Late last night or in the early-morning hours today," said Bodenstein. "He was shot in the foyer of his house."

"That's terrible." Professor Kaltensee received the news without any visible emotion, and Pia wondered whether he might know something about Schneider's Nazi past. But she could hardly ask. Not here and not now.

"Your mother has already told us that Mr. Schneider was a good friend of your late father," said Bodenstein. Pia noticed the glance that Elard Kaltensee cast at his mother. She thought she noticed a trace of amusement in his expression.

"That's right," he replied.

"We're assuming there's a connection with the murder of David Goldberg," Bodenstein went on. "At both scenes, we found a number that presents us with a riddle. Someone had written 'one one six four five' using the victims' blood."

Vera Kaltensee uttered a choking sound.

"One one six four five?" her son repeated thoughtfully. "That could—"

"Oh, it's so horrible! This is all too much for me!" Vera Kaltensee burst out, covering her eyes with her right hand. Her narrow shoulders shook, and she began sobbing. In sympathy, Bodenstein took her left hand and said softly that they could continue the conversation later. Pia, however, was not watching her, but her son. Elard Kaltensee made no move to console his mother, whose sobs had grown louder. Instead, he went to the sideboard and calmly poured himself a cognac. His face was completely unmoved, but his eyes revealed what Pia could only describe as contempt.

His heart was pounding, and he stepped back a bit when he heard the footsteps on the other side of the door. Then the front door swung open. The sight of Katharina took his breath away once more. She was wearing a pink linen dress and a white jacket, her gleaming black hair falling in great locks over her shoulders, her long legs suntanned.

"Hello, sweetheart. How are you?" Thomas Ritter forced himself to smile and went over to her. She coolly looked him up and down.

"*Sweetheart*," she repeated derisively, "are you trying to make fun of me?"

As beautiful as she was, she could also be so rude. But that was part of her appeal. Alarmed, Ritter wondered if Katharina could have found out about him and Marleen; he rejected that notion. For weeks, she'd been either at the publishing house in Zürich or on Mallorca, so she couldn't possibly know.

"Come in." She turned around and he followed her through the sprawling penthouse and all the way out onto the terrace. The thought went through his head that Katharina would probably be royally amused if she found out what he'd done. When it came to the Kaltensee family, they shared a strong desire for revenge. But he wasn't quite comfortable with the idea of laughing with Katharina about Marleen.

"So," Katharina said, stopping and not offering him a chair, "how far along are you? My boss is starting to get impatient."

Ritter hesitated.

"I'm still not happy with the first few chapters," he admitted. "It's almost as if Vera appeared out of thin air in Frankfurt in 1945. There are no earlier photos, no family documents—nothing at all. Right now, the whole manuscript reads like any old celebrity bio."

"But you told me you had a really hot source!" Katharina Ehrmann frowned, annoyed. "Why do I have the feeling that you're trying to stall?"

"I'm not," replied Ritter gloomily. "I'm really not. But Elard keeps avoiding me and pretends not to be available."

The radiant blue sky arced over the Old Town in Königstein, but Ritter had no interest in the spectacular view from Katharina's penthouse terrace, a scape extending from the ruins of the fortress on one side to the Villa Andreae on the other.

"Your source is Elard?" Katharina shook her head. "You should have told me that earlier."

"What good would that have done? Do you think he'd rather talk to you than to me?"

Katharina Ehrmann scrutinized him.

"Whatever," she said at last. "Just make use of what I told you. That should be enough ammunition."

Ritter nodded and bit his lower lip.

"I still have a small problem," he said in embarrassment.

"How much do you need?" Katharina Ehrmann asked, her face stony.

Ritter hesitated, then sighed. "Five thousand would fill the biggest holes."

"You'll get the money, but under one condition."

"And what's that?"

Katharina Ehrmann gave him a sardonic smile. "You're going to finish writing the book in the next three weeks. It has to come out by early September, when my bosom friend Jutta plans to be nominated as the top candidate."

Three weeks! Thomas Ritter stepped over to the parapet of the terrace. How the hell had he wound up in this shitty situation? His life had been in good shape until he'd lost his common sense in an attack of megalomania. When he'd told Katharina about his idea of writing a tell-all biography of Vera, he hadn't imagined what enthusiasm this plan would trigger in the former best friend of Jutta Kaltensee.

Katharina had never forgiven Jutta for the ice-cold way in which she'd been dumped; she was hungry for revenge, although it wasn't really necessary. Her brief marriage to the Swiss publisher Beat Ehrmann had been more than profitable for her in terms of finances. Old Ehrmann, in a grandiose overestimation of his physical prowess a mere two years after their wedding, had suffered a heart attack between the thighs of his best editor, and Katharina had inherited everything: his fortune, his possessions, his publishing company. But the insult she'd suffered from Jutta's jealous intrigue was obviously still festering. Katharina had made Thomas Ritter's mouth water at the prospect of the millions he could earn from writing a scandalous biography about one of the most famous women in modern Germany. Subsequently, he had lost everything that had ever meant anything to him: his job, his reputation, his future. Because Vera had found out about his little project and thrown him out. Since then, he'd been a social pariah, living more or less off of Katharina's money, working at a job that he deeply despised. He found himself unable to escape this situation. His secret marriage to Marleen, which in his blind vindictiveness had seemed like such a brilliant idea, had proved to be merely another trap. He just didn't know anymore what he could say to whom.

Katharina stepped up beside him. "Every day I have to think up new excuses for why you haven't delivered that damned manuscript," she said in a sharp tone that he hadn't heard before. "They want to see some results, since we've been shoving money up your ass for months now."

"You'll have the complete manuscript in three weeks," Thomas hurriedly promised her. "I have to do some rewrites on the beginning, because I didn't find out what I'd hoped to discover. But the thing with Eugen Kaltensee is explosive enough."

"I hope so, for your sake." Katharina Ehrmann tilted her head. "And for mine. Even though it's my publishing company, I'm accountable to my business partners."

Ritter managed a guileless smile. He was very aware of his looks and his charm. Experience had taught him that he possessed something that made women fall at his feet. The lovely Katharina was no exception.

"Come on, darling." He leaned on the parapet and stretched out his arms. "Let's leave business till later. I've missed you."

She remained aloof for a few more moments, then let down her guard and even smiled.

"It's a matter of millions," she reminded him in a softer voice. "Our legal team has found a way to get around the interim injunction regarding publishing the book in Switzerland."

Ritter let his lips drift down to her slim neck and sensed a growing desire in his groin as she now urgently pressed against him. After the boring, tepid sex with Marleen, he was getting excited at the thought of Katharina's violent abandon and the way she could push him to his sexual limits.

"Besides," she murmured, undoing her belt, "I'm going to talk to Elard myself. He never could refuse me anything."

"Did you notice the way she reacted when she heard that number?" Pia asked as they drove from Mühlenhof to the station in Hofheim. She'd been fretting about what she thought she'd seen for just an instant on the face of Vera Kaltensee. Anxiety? Hatred? Shock? "And the way she spoke to her son was so . . . imperious."

"I didn't notice a thing." Bodenstein shook his head. "And even if she did have a strange reaction, it's quite understandable. We had just told her that an old friend of the family had been shot. How do you happen to know the son, by the way?"

Pia explained. "The news of Schneider's death seemed to leave him cold," she added. "He didn't look particularly shocked."

"And what do you make of that?"

"Not a thing." She shrugged. "At most, that he didn't especially like either Schneider or Goldberg. But he didn't have a single consoling word for his mother, either."

"Maybe he thought she was getting enough sympathetic support," Bodenstein teased her, raising an eyebrow and laughing. "I was afraid you were going to break out in tears, too."

"I know. It was really unprofessional of me," Pia admitted remorsefully. She was angry that she'd been taken in so easily by the old woman. Normally, she managed to keep enough distance to observe someone's tears without pity. "Sobbing white-haired grandmas must be my Achilles' heel."

"Now, now." Bodenstein gave her an amused sidelong glance. "I used to think your Achilles' heel was emotionally unstable young men from good families who were suspected of murder."

Pia got the reference to Lukas van den Berg from a previous case, but her memory was as least as good as Bodenstein's.

"People who live in glass houses shouldn't throw stones, boss," she countered with a grin. "Now that we're speaking of weaknesses: I have a vivid memory of a lady veterinarian and her pretty daughter, who—"

"That's enough of that," Bodenstein said, interrupting her. "You really have no sense of humor."

"You don't, either."

The car phone buzzed. It was Ostermann, who told them that the permission for the autopsy on Schneider's body had been received. He also had interesting news from the forensics lab in Wiesbaden. Their colleagues from the National Criminal Police, in their zeal to hush things up, had actually forgotten about the evidence that had been sent to the lab for analysis.

"The cell phone that was found in the flower bed next to Goldberg's front door belongs to a Robert Watkowiak," said Ostermann. "He's on the books, with mug shots and fingerprints and everything. An old acquaintance whose ambition seems to be to break every paragraph in the criminal law books. He's been missing a homicide in his collection. Otherwise, he's got everything on his rap sheet: burglary, assault and battery, robbery, repeated violations of the narcotics laws, driving without a license, having his license suspended several times for DUI, attempted rape, and so on."

"Then have him brought down to the station," said Bodenstein.

"It's not that easy. He's had no permanent address since he got out of the joint six months ago."

"And his last address? What was that?"

"That's where it gets interesting," said Ostermann. "He's still listed as living at Mühlenhof with the Kaltensee family."

"Are you kidding me?" Pia was stunned.

"Maybe because he was an illegitimate child of old Kaltensee," Ostermann replied, elucidating the situation.

Pia glanced at Bodenstein. Could it be a coincidence that the name Kaltensee had turned up again? Her cell played its ringtone. Pia didn't recognize the number on the display, but she took the call.

"Hello, Pia, it's me," said her friend Miriam. "Am I interrupting anything?"

"Nope, you're not," said Pia. "What's up?"

"Did you already know on Saturday night that Goldberg was dead?"

"Yes," Pia said. "But I couldn't say anything to you."

"Oh God. Who would shoot an old man like him?"

"That's a good question, and we don't have the answer yet," Pia replied. "Unfortunately, they've taken us off the case. Goldberg's son showed up the next day with reinforcements from the American consulate and the Interior Ministry and took his father's body away. We were pretty surprised about that."

"Ah well, it's probably because you're not familiar with our burial rites," said Miriam after a brief pause. "Sal, Goldberg's son, is an Orthodox Jew. According to Jewish ritual, the deceased has to be buried the same day if at all possible."

"Aha." Pia looked at Bodenstein, who had finished talking with Ostermann, and put her finger to her lips. "So was he buried right away?"

"Yes. First thing on Monday. At the Jewish cemetery in Frankfurt. Anyway, after they sit shiva for seven days, an official funeral service will be held."

"*Shiva?*" Pia asked, clueless. She knew the word only from the name of a Hindu god.

"*Shiva* is Hebrew and means 'seven,'" Miriam explained. "Shiva is the seven-day period of mourning that follows a burial. Sal Goldberg and his family will be staying in Frankfurt for that."

Suddenly, Pia had a brilliant idea.

"Where are you now?" she asked her friend.

"At home," said Miriam. "Why?"

"Would you have time to meet me? I have to tell you something."

Elard Kaltensee stood at the window on the second floor of his mother's big house and watched his brother's car come rushing through the gate and stop at the front door. With a bitter smile, he turned away from the window. Vera had put everything in motion to keep the situation in check, because things were heating up, and Elard himself was not entirely innocent. Of course, he didn't know the meaning of those numbers, but he suspected that his mother did know. She had skillfully avoided further questions from the police with her utterly atypical crying fit; it was her way of immediately taking the reins in her own hands. The Kripo officers had barely left before Vera had called Siegbert, who had, naturally, dropped everything to come to his mama's rescue. Elard took off his shoes and hung his jacket on the clothes rack.

Why had the policewoman, Dr. Kirchhoff's wife, given him such an odd look? With a sigh, he sat down on the edge of the bed, buried his face in his hands, and tried to remember every detail of the conversation. Had he said anything wrong or acted suspiciously? Did the detective suspect him? And if so, why? He felt terrible. Another car drove up and parked. Naturally, Vera had also sent for Jutta. Now it wouldn't be long before they called him downstairs to a family meeting. He realized now that he'd been incautious and had made a big mistake. The thought of what could happen if they found out sent a stabbing pain into his chest. But it was no use to hide. He had to go on living as usual and act as if he were completely clueless. He gave a start when his cell suddenly rang much too loudly. To his surprise, it was Katharina Ehrmann, Jutta's best friend.

"Hello, Elard," said Katharina, sounding upbeat. "How are things?"

"Katharina!" said Elard more nonchalantly than he felt. "I haven't heard from you in ages. To what do I owe the honor of your call?"

He'd always been very fond of Katharina, occasionally running into her at cultural events in Frankfurt or at other social functions.

"I guess I'll just have to be blunt," she said. "I need your help. Could we meet somewhere?"

The urgent undertone in her voice exacerbated the sense of foreboding he had inside.

"It's a little awkward at the moment," Elard replied evasively. "We're in the middle of a family crisis."

"Old Goldberg was shot. I heard about it."

"Oh yes?" Elard wondered how she could have heard, since the murder of Uncle Jossi had been successfully kept out of the papers. But maybe Jutta had told her about it.

"Perhaps you know that Thomas is writing a book about your mother," Katharina went on. Elard didn't say a word to that, but the foreboding increased. Naturally, he knew about this crackpot book idea, which had already caused plenty of anger within the family ranks. He would have preferred simply to end the call, but that wouldn't do any good. Katharina Ehrmann was known for her persistence. She would never leave him alone until she got what she wanted.

"I'm sure you've heard what Siegbert did about it."

"Yes, I have. Why are you interested?"

"Because the book is coming out from my publishing house."

This news left Elard momentarily speechless.

"Does Jutta know this?" he asked at last.

Katharina laughed loudly. "No idea, but I can't worry about that. For me it's all about business. A biography of your mother is worth millions. At any rate, we want to publish the book in time for the book fair in October, but we're still missing some background info. I assume you could help us out with that."

Elard froze. His mouth suddenly went dry as dust, and his hands were sweating.

"I don't know what you mean," he replied in a hoarse voice. How could Katharina know about it? From Ritter? And if he had told her, who else had he told? Damn, if he'd known what all the repercussions would be, he would have kept out of the whole business.

"You know exactly what I mean." Katharina's voice turned a few degrees cooler. "Come on now, Elard. Nobody is going to find out that you helped us. At least think about it. You can call me anytime."

"I've got to go." He disconnected without saying good-bye. His heart was racing and he felt sick to his stomach. He made a great effort to gather his thoughts. Ritter must have told Katharina everything, although he had sworn up and down to keep his mouth shut. He heard footsteps in the hall outside the door, the brisk clacking of high heels that only Jutta wore. It was too late to escape the house unnoticed. Years too late.

Pia and Miriam met in a bistro on Schillerstrasse that had been touted as the latest hot spot on the Frankfurt foodie scene since it opened two months ago. She ordered the specialty of the house: a fat-free grilled burger made with meat from contented cows raised in the Rhön hills. Miriam could barely contain her curiosity, so Pia got right to the point.

"Listen, Miri. Everything we talk about now is strictly confidential. You really can't mention it to anybody, or I'll be in the biggest trouble of the century."

"I won't say a word, cross my heart. Promise."

"Good." Pia leaned forward and lowered her voice. "How well did you know Goldberg?"

"I met him a few times. As far back as I can remember, he always came to visit us whenever he was in Frankfurt," Miriam went on after thinking it over. "Oma was very close with Sarah, his wife, and through her also with him. Have you got any idea who murdered him?"

"No," Pia admitted. "But it's not our case anymore. And to be honest, I don't think that it had anything to do with Jewish burial rites when Goldberg's son showed up with the American general consul and people from the NCP, the CIA, and the Interior Ministry in tow."

"The CIA? NCP? You can't be serious!" exclaimed Miriam.

"It's true. They took the investigation out of our hands. And we also suspect that we know the real reason for that. Goldberg had a pretty murky past, and there's no way his son or his friends would want that secret to come out."

"So tell me," Miriam said, pressing her. "What sort of secret? I heard that he had made some questionable deals in the past, but that's true for lots of people. Did he shoot Kennedy or something?"

"No," said Pia, shaking her head. "He was a member of the SS."

Miriam stared at her and then broke into incredulous laughter.

"Don't joke about stuff like that," she said. "Now tell me the truth."

"That *is* the truth. During the autopsy, they discovered a blood-group tattoo on his upper left arm that was worn only by members of the SS. There is absolutely no doubt."

The laughter vanished from Miriam's face.

"The tattoo is a fact," Pia said soberly. "At some point, he apparently tried to have it removed. But in the deep layer of the skin, it was clearly visible, blood group AB. That was his blood type."

"Okay, but that just can't be. Honestly, Pia!" Miriam shook her head. "Oma has known him for sixty years; everyone here knows him. He donated a ton of money to Jewish institutions and did a lot for reconciliation between Germans and Jews. It can't be possible that he was ever a *Nazi*."

"And what if it's true?" Pia argued. "What if he really wasn't the person he was pretending to be?"

Miriam stared at her in silence and chewed on her lower lip.

"You can help me," Pia went on. "At the institute where you work, you must have access to records and documents about the Jewish population in East Prussia. You could find out more about his past."

She looked at her friend and could definitely see the wheels turning in her mind. The possibility that a man like David Goldberg could have had such an incredible secret and managed to preserve it for decades was so monstrous that Miriam first had to get used to the idea.

"This morning, the body of a man by the name of Herrmann Schneider was discovered," Pia said softly. "He was murdered in his house, exactly like Goldberg, shot in the back of the head. He was past eighty and lived alone. His workroom in the basement looks like Hitler's office in the Reich Chancellery, with a swastika flag and a personally signed picture of the

Führer—very creepy, I have to tell you. And we found out that this Schneider was a friend of Vera Kaltensee, just like Goldberg."

"Vera Kaltensee?" Miriam's eyes went wide. "I know all about her! She has supported the Center Against Displacement for years. Everybody knows how much she hated Hitler and the Third Reich. She won't stand for anyone accusing her of making friends with former Nazis."

"We don't want to do that, either," Pia said, trying to calm her down. "No one is claiming that she knew anything about Goldberg's or Schneider's past. But the three did know one another very well for a long time."

"Insanity," muttered Miriam. "Total insanity!"

"Next to both bodies we found a number that the murderer wrote with the blood of the victims. One one six four five," Pia continued. "We don't know what it means, but it proves that Goldberg and Schneider were shot by one and the same person. Somehow I have a feeling that the motive for the murders can be found in the past of the two men. That's why I wanted to ask you for help."

Miriam didn't shift her gaze from Pia's face. Her eyes were gleaming with excitement, and her cheeks were flushed.

"It could be a date," she said after a while. "The sixteenth of January, 1945."

Pia felt the adrenaline shoot through her body, and she straightened up with a start. Of course! Why hadn't they thought of that themselves? Member number, account or telephone number, all of it nonsense! But what could have happened on January 16, 1945? And where? And how was it connected to Schneider and Goldberg? But above all: Who might have known about it?

"How can we find out more about this?" asked Pia. "Goldberg came from East Prussia, just like Vera Kaltensee; Schneider was from the Ruhr. Maybe there are still archives that could give us a lead."

Miriam nodded. "There must be. The most important archive for East Prussia is the Secret State Archives in Berlin, and many old German documents can be found in online databases. There's also Registry Office Number One in Berlin, where all the registry documents that could be saved from East Prussia are stored, especially about the Jewish population, because in 1939, a rather detailed census was taken."

"Okay, that might really be important," Pia said, enthused over the idea. "How do you get in to see it?"

"It should be no problem for the police," Miriam told her. Then it occurred to Pia that there was indeed a problem.

"But officially we're not allowed to investigate Goldberg's murder," she said, sounding disappointed. "And I can't really ask my boss at the moment to give me permission to go to Berlin."

"I could do it," Miriam suggested. "I don't have much to do right now. The project I've been working on for the past few months is over."

"Would you really? That would be great."

Miriam grinned but then turned serious.

"I'll do it to prove that Goldberg was never a Nazi," she said, taking Pia's hand.

"As far as I'm concerned, that's fine." Pia smiled. "The main thing is to find out what this date could signify. I'll run your theory past my boss."

Wednesday, May 2

Detective Frank Behnke was in a bad mood. The euphoria of the day before, when he'd achieved an excellent eleventh-place finish in the "Round the Henninger Tower" bicycle race, had long since dissipated. The grayness of everyday life had reclaimed him, and it coincided with a new homicide investigation. He had been hoping this lull in activity would last a little longer so that he could knock off work on time. His colleagues had thrown themselves into the case with zeal, as if they were glad finally to put in some overtime hours and work straight through the weekends. Fachinger and Ostermann had no family, while the boss had a wife who took care of everything. Hasse's wife was happy when her husband was out of the house, and Kirchhoff seemed to be past the first phase of ardent infatuation with her new guy and once again keen to make a name for herself. None of them had the slightest inkling of what sort of problems hounded him. Whenever he left the office on time in the evening, he had to put up with people looking askance at him.

Behnke got behind the wheel of the shabby patrol car and waited with the motor running until Kirchhoff finally showed up and climbed in. He could have taken care of the matter himself, but the boss had insisted that she come along. Robert Watkowiak's fingerprints had been found on a glass in the basement of the murdered Herrmann Schneider, and his cell phone had been found lying next to Goldberg's front door. It couldn't be a coincidence, and that's why Bodenstein wanted to talk to the guy. Ostermann had asked around and found out that for the past few months Watkowiak had been living with a woman in an apartment in Niederhöchstadt.

Behnke hid behind his sunglasses, not saying a word as they drove through Bad Soden and Schwalbach toward Rotdornweg in Niederhöchstadt. Pia also made no attempt to start a conversation. The ugly high rises seemed like foreign bodies in the midst of all the single-family dwellings and row houses with manicured lawns. At this time of day, most of the parking spots were vacant, with the residents of the houses at work. Or at the welfare office, Behnke thought bitterly. No doubt the majority of these people lived off the government, especially those who were immigrants. They made up an overwhelming share of the renters, as it was easy to see from the nameplates next to the doorbells.

"M. Krämer," said Pia, pointing at one of the labels, "this is where he supposedly lives."

Robert Watkowiak was dozing. Last night had gone pretty well. Moni hadn't been mad at him, and around 1:30 they'd staggered back to her place. He'd spent all his cash, of course, and the guy hadn't contacted him about the pistol, but he would run right out and cash the three checks from Uncle Herrmann.

"Hey, take a look at this." Moni came into the bedroom and held out her cell phone. "Yesterday, I got a really crazy text. Any idea what it means?"

Robert blinked, still not fully awake, and tried to make out what it said on the display: SWEETHEART, WE'RE RICH! GOT RID OF THE OTHER OLD GUY, TOO. LET'S HEAD SOUTH!

He couldn't make head nor tail of the message, either. He shrugged and closed his eyes again while Moni wondered out loud who could have sent her such a message and why. His temples were throbbing and he had a nasty taste in his mouth, and her shrill voice was getting on his last nerve.

"Then call the fuck back if you want to know who wrote it," he muttered. "I need to snooze awhile."

"No way." She tugged on his blanket. "You've got to be out of here by ten."

"Got another visitor coming, eh?" He really didn't give a shit how she made her money, but it pissed him off that he had to sit around somewhere waiting until the "visitor" left. This morning, he didn't feel like getting up at all.

"I need the bread," she said. "And I'm not getting anything out of you."

The doorbell rang and the dogs started barking. Moni mercilessly pulled up the shades.

"Now get your ass out of that bed," she hissed, and left the room.

Behnke pressed the doorbell again and was surprised when a voice said hello from the scratchy speaker. Dogs were barking in the background.

"This is the police," said Behnke. "We want to talk to Robert Watkowiak."

"He's not here," said the woman's voice.

"Please buzz us in anyway."

It took a while before the door buzzed and they could enter the building. Each floor had a different smell, none of them particularly pleasant. Monika Krämer's apartment was on the sixth floor, at the end of a dark hallway. The ceiling light was evidently out. Behnke rang the bell, and the flimsy, scratched door opened. A dark-haired woman gave them a suspicious look. She was holding two tiny dogs in one arm; her other hand held a cigarette. Behind her, the TV was blaring.

"Robert isn't here," she said after looking at Behnke's ID. "I haven't seen him in ages."

Behnke pushed past her and took a look around. The two-room apartment was cheaply but tastefully furnished. A nice-looking white couch, and an Indian wooden chest that served as a coffee table. On the walls were pictures with Mediterranean motifs, the kind you could buy for a couple of euros at a discount store, and in one corner stood a big potted palm. A colorful rug was on the laminate-wood floor.

"Are you Mr. Watkowiak's girlfriend?" Pia asked the woman, who was in her late twenties at most. She had used a dark eyebrow pencil to draw exaggerated arches over her excessively plucked eyebrows, which gave her face a skeptical look. Her arms and legs were hardly thicker than a twelve-year-old's, but she had remarkably large breasts, which she displayed in a low-cut blouse, with no sign of false modesty.

"Girlfriend? No," replied the woman. "He crashes here once in a while, that's all."

"And where is he now?"

She shrugged and lit another menthol cigarette. She put the trembling dogs down on the snow-white couch. Behnke went into the next room. A double bed, a wardrobe with mirrored doors, and a dresser with lots of drawers. Both sides of the bed had been slept in. Behnke put his hand on the sheet. It was still warm.

"What time did you get up?" he asked, turning to Monika Krämer, who was standing in the doorway with her arms crossed, not taking her eyes off him.

"What's all this about?" She reacted with the aggressiveness of someone caught in the act.

"Just answer my question." Behnke could feel himself about to lose his temper. The woman was pissing him off.

"An hour or so ago. How do I know?"

"And who slept on the other side of the bed? The sheets are still warm."

Pia put on latex gloves and opened one door of the wardrobe.

"Hey!" Ms. Krämer yelled. "You can't do that without a search warrant!"

"So, you have experience with this sort of thing." Behnke looked her up and down. With her tight jeans skirt and the cheap patent-leather boots with the run-over heels, she would have fit in on any street corner around the train station.

"Keep your mitts off my dresser!" Monika Krämer hollered at Pia, blocking her way. At that moment, Behnke noticed a movement in the front room. For a fraction of a second, he glimpsed the profile of a man; then the front door slammed.

"Shit!" he said, wanting to run after the man, but Monika Krämer put a leg out and tripped him. He stumbled, slammed his head against the door frame, and crashed into a bunch of empty bottles standing by the door. One bottle broke, and a shard pierced his forearm. With a bound, he was back on his feet, but the slut attacked him like a fury. All the anger that had been building up inside him since early morning finally exploded. The force of the slap flung the skinny girl against the wall. He slapped her again, then grabbed her and twisted her arm behind her back. She resisted with astounding strength, kicked him in the shin and spat in his face. The whole time, she was cussing him out in obscene language he hadn't heard since he used to be on the vice squad in the Frankfurt red-light district.

He would have beaten the shit out of her if Pia hadn't intervened and torn him away from her. The whole commotion was accompanied by hysterical barking from the two little mutts. Breathing hard, Behnke straightened up and looked at the gash on his right forearm, which was bleeding profusely.

"Who was the man that just ran out of here?" Pia asked the woman, who had sat down with her back to the wall. Blood was running out of her nose. "Was that Robert Watkowiak?"

"I'm not telling you fucking pigs a thing!" she snarled, fending off the panic-stricken little dogs, which were trying to climb into her lap. "I'm going to report you! I know a few lawyers!"

"Listen here, Ms. Krämer," said Pia in a surprisingly calm voice. "We're looking for Robert Watkowiak in connection with a homicide. You're not doing him or yourself any favors if you keep on lying. Not to mention that you attacked my colleague, which will look very bad to a judge. Your lawyers would tell you the same thing."

The woman thought it over for a moment. She seemed to comprehend the seriousness of her situation and finally admitted that it was Watkowiak who had run out of the apartment.

"He was on the balcony. He's got nothing to do with any murder."

"Aha. So why did he run away?"

"Because he doesn't like cops."

"Do you know where Mr. Watkowiak was on Monday evening?"

"No idea. He just showed up here late last night."

"And last Friday night? Where was he then?"

"Dunno. I'm not his baby-sitter."

"Good." Pia nodded. "Thanks for your help. In your own interest, it would be best if you called us if he shows up here again."

She handed Ms. Krämer her business card, which the woman tucked into her bra without looking at it.

Pia drove Behnke to the hospital and waited by the emergency room while they sewed up the deep gash in his arm and the cut on his forehead with a few stitches. She was leaning on the fender of the unmarked police car and smoking a cigarette when her colleague came out of the revolving door with a gloomy expression, a Band-Aid on his forehead and a dazzling white bandage around his right arm.

"Well?" she asked.

"They put me on sick leave," he replied without looking at her. He got into the passenger seat and put on his sunglasses. Pia rolled her eyes as she ground out her cigarette with her foot. For the past couple of weeks, Behnke had once again been completely unbearable. During the short drive to the station, he didn't say a word, and Pia wondered whether she should tell Bodenstein about his blowup. She didn't want to be a snitch, but even though Behnke was known for his irascible temperament, losing it in Monika Krämer's apartment had surprised her. A police officer needed to be able to tolerate provocations and control himself. When they reached the parking lot at the station, Behnke got out without a word of thanks.

"I'm going home" was all he said, gathering his service weapon, shoulder holster, and leather jacket from the backseat. He pulled the medical release from the hospital out of the back pocket of his jeans and held it out to Pia. "Could you give this to Bodenstein?"

"If I were you, I'd go in and tell him what happened in person." Pia took the piece of paper. "And it would probably be better if you wrote up the report yourself."

"You do it," he grumbled. "You were there, too."

He turned and went to his car, which was parked in the public lot. Pia was fuming as she watched him go. What Behnke did really shouldn't bother her, but she was fed up with his grumpy behavior and the nonchalant way he had of getting his colleagues to do his work lately. Still, she didn't want any bad blood in the team. Bodenstein was an easygoing boss who seldom wielded his authority with an iron hand, but she was sure he would have wanted to hear from Behnke himself how he'd sustained his injuries.

"Frank!" Pia called out, getting out of the car. "Wait up!"

He turned around reluctantly and stopped.

"What's the matter with you?" Pia asked her colleague.

"You were there," he replied.

"No, that's not what I mean." Pia shook her head. "Something is going on with you. You've been in such a bad mood lately. Is there anything I can do to help?"

"Nothing's going on with me," he snapped. "Everything's fine."

"I don't believe you. Is it something with your family?"

Inside him, an iron shutter seemed to roll down. His expression said, That's enough, no further.

"My private life is nobody's business," he shot back.

Pia felt she'd done her duty as a good colleague, and she shrugged. Behnke had always been a stubborn guy. Nothing had changed on that score.

"If you ever want to talk, you know how to get hold of me," she called after him. Then he tore off his sunglasses and came storming toward her. For a moment, Pia thought he was going to give her the same treatment he'd given Monika Krämer.

"Why the hell do you women always have to play Mother Teresa and butt in where you're not wanted? Does it make you feel better, or what?" he berated her.

"Are you kidding?" Pia was mad. "I want to help you because you're my colleague and because I can tell something is wrong. But if you don't need my help, then do whatever you want!"

She slammed the car door and left him standing there. She and Frank Behnke were never going to be friends.

Thomas Ritter lay in the hot bathwater with his eyes closed, feeling his aching muscles slowly relax. He wasn't used to this sort of exertion anymore, and to be honest, he no longer cared much for it. Katharina's aggressive sexuality, which used to drive him crazy with desire, had lost its allure. And he was surprised at how guilty he'd felt when he'd gone over to Marleen's place later in the evening. He was deeply ashamed of his afternoon activities when faced with her innocent warmth. At the same time, he'd been furious. She was a Kaltensee, an enemy. He'd come on to her specifically to get back at Vera and humiliate her; his affection was merely feigned and part of the plan. Once he achieved his goal, he would kick both Vera and Marleen in the ass. That was what he'd imagined during those many sleepless nights on the rickety sofa bed in the shabby apartment. But suddenly emotions had become involved, emotions that he hadn't anticipated.

After his wife had filed for divorce and his social decline became obvious, he had sworn never to trust a woman again. His relationship with Katharina Ehrmann was based on business. She was the publisher who was paying him to write the life story of Vera Kaltensee—and quite well, too. He was her preferred lover whenever she was in Frankfurt. What she did when he was out of reach didn't really matter. Ritter heaved a sigh. He had maneuvered himself into a really shitty position. If Katharina found out about Marleen, he might lose his meal ticket. If Marleen found out about his breach of trust and all the lies he had told her, she would never forgive him, and he would inevitably lose both her and the baby. No matter which way he turned, he was in a bind. The phone rang. Ritter opened his eyes and fumbled to pick it up.

Katharina's voice sounded in his ear. "It's me. Did you hear? Old Schneider was murdered, too."

"What? When?" Ritter shot up, and the water sloshed over the edge of the tub onto the parquet floor of the bathroom.

"Late Monday night or early Tuesday morning. He was shot, just like Goldberg."

"How do you know this?"

"I just know."

"Who would want to shoot that old fart?" Ritter was trying to keep his tone indifferent as he got out of the tub and gazed at the mess he'd made.

"No idea," said Katharina. "My first suspicion was you, to be honest. You visited him and Goldberg recently, didn't you?"

Ritter was speechless for a moment. He went ice-cold. How could Katharina know that?

"What bullshit," he said with an effort, hoping that his voice sounded amused. "Why would I do something like that?"

"To shut them up?" Katharina suggested. "You were putting a lot of pressure on both of them."

Ritter could feel his heart pounding in his throat. He hadn't told anyone about these visits, nobody at all. Katharina was hard to read, and she never showed her cards. Ritter hadn't been able to tell which side she was really on, and occasionally he had a bad feeling that for Katharina he was no more than a tool to accomplish her own revenge on the Kaltensee family.

"I didn't put pressure on anybody," he replied, sounding cool now. "Unlike you, my dear. You were at Goldberg's, and it was because of those stupid company shares that you've all been fighting over for eons. Maybe you were at Herrmann's, too, watching a few movies and putting away a bottle of Bordeaux with him. I know you'd do anything to get even with the Kaltensees."

"Let's drop it," said Katharina calmly after a brief pause. "The police have Robert in their sights, by the way. I wouldn't be surprised if he did it; he's always hard up for cash. But for now, just keep writing. Maybe we'll get another chapter out of this, all about the current adventures of the dear Kaltensee family."

Ritter put down his cell next to the washbasin, grabbed a couple of towels, and cleaned up the bathwater before it could damage the parquet floor. In his head, all the information was swirling around. Goldberg, that repulsive old creep, shot to death. Schneider also shot dead. He knew that Elard had hated both old men deeply, for different reasons. Robert was always in need of money, and Siegbert was undoubtedly after the damn company shares. But was either of them capable of committing a murder, or even two? The answer was unequivocal: yes. Ritter had to laugh. All he had to do was sit back comfortably and wait.

"Time is on my side," he sang to himself, but he had no idea how wrong he was.

•   •   •

Monika Krämer was still shaking all over as she tried to stop the nosebleed with a wet towel and ice cubes. That arrogant, ugly piece of shit cop had really hurt her. Too bad he hadn't cut his throat falling into the pile of bottles! She gazed at her face in the bathroom mirror. Cautiously, she touched her nose, but it didn't seem to be broken. And it was all because of Robert. That idiot must have really pulled some number he'd never told her about. She'd seen the gun in his backpack; he claimed he'd found it. Murder, the cops had said. Now the shit was really going to hit the fan! Monika Krämer had absolutely no desire to have the cops on her back, and that was why she was going to throw Robert out once and for all. But the real reason was that he got on her nerves. It was getting harder and harder to get rid of him, but she had such a hard time saying no. She always felt sorry for him and kept bringing him home, although she'd sworn to herself a dozen times not to do it again. He never had any money and was jealous on top of it.

She went into the bedroom and stuffed the used bedclothes in the wardrobe. From the chest under the bed she took out the silk sheets she used when she had a "visitor." Two years ago, she'd started putting classified ads in the paper. The text, which read "Manu, 19, very discreet—tasty, no taboos," appealed to many men, and once they showed up, they didn't care that her name wasn't really Manu or that she wasn't nineteen. Some of them came regularly: a bus driver, a couple of pensioners, the mailman, and the teller from the bank during his lunch hour. She charged thirty euros for the standard services, fifty for French, and one hundred for extras, which nobody had yet requested. Together with the welfare check, she was able to make a decent living, put away a little every month, and treat herself to something once in a while. Another two or three years and she could realize her dream: to buy a small house on a lake in Canada. That's why she was studying English on the side.

The doorbell rang. She glanced at the clock in the kitchen. Quarter to ten. Her Wednesday-morning regular customer was punctual. He was with the sanitation department and spent his breakfast break with her once a week. Like today. The fifty euros were easy money; he never stayed more than fifteen minutes.

Only five minutes after he left, there was a knock at her door. It could only be Robert, because Monika wasn't expecting anyone else until noon. What was he thinking, showing up here again? The cops were probably downstairs in their car waiting for him. Furious, she marched to the door and tore it open.

"What the heck—" she began, then stopped when she saw a gray-haired stranger standing in front of her.

"Hello," said the man. He had a mustache, was wearing old-fashioned glasses with tinted lenses, and clearly belonged in the category of "tolerable." Not a sweaty fatso with hair on his back, not a dirty slob who hadn't showered in a week, and not a guy who would try to haggle over the price afterward.

"Come in," she said, turning around. As she passed the mirror next to the front door, she glanced at herself. She didn't look nineteen anymore, but maybe twenty-three. Anyway, no one had left disappointed.

"It's right this way." Monika Krämer pointed toward the bedroom. The man was still standing in the doorway, and she noticed he was wearing gloves. Her heart began to pound. Was the guy some sort of pervert?

"You won't need rubber gloves," she joked. Suddenly, she had an uneasy feeling.

"Where's Robert?" he asked.

Shit! Was he a cop, too?

"I have no idea," she replied. "I already told that to the other damn cop."

Without taking his eyes off her, he reached behind and turned the key in the lock. Suddenly, she was scared. He wasn't from the police. Who had Robert gotten mixed up with now? Did he owe somebody money?

"You must know where he hangs out when he's not here with you," said the stranger. Monika thought fast and decided that Robert wasn't worth getting herself involved in any trouble.

"Sometimes he crashes in an abandoned house in Königstein," she said. "In the Old Town, at the end of the pedestrian zone. Could be he's there now, hiding out from the cops. They're looking for him."

"Okay." The man nodded and gave her an appraising look. "Thanks."

He looked kind of sad with the mustache and the thick glasses. A little like the guy from the bank. Monika Krämer relaxed and smiled. Maybe she could make some money out of the situation.

"How about it?" She smiled coquettishly. "For a twenty, I'll blow you."

The man came closer, until he was standing right in front of her. The expression on his face was calm, almost indifferent. He made a quick movement with his right hand, and Monika Krämer felt a burning pain in her neck. She grabbed reflexively at her throat and gazed incredulously at the blood on her hands. It took a couple of seconds before she realized it was her own. Her mouth filled with a warm coppery-tasting fluid, and she felt the pricking of real panic at the back of her neck. What was happening? What had she done to this guy? She backed away from him but tripped over one of her dogs and lost her balance. There was blood everywhere. Her blood.

"Please, please don't," she croaked, raising her arms protectively in front of her body when she saw the knife in his hand. The dogs were barking like crazy. She punched and kicked in all directions, desperately defending herself with strength bolstered by the fear of death.

It was no real surprise to anyone at K-11 that when Dr. Kirchhoff performed the autopsy on the corpse of Herrmann Schneider, he found the same blood-type tattoo as he'd seen earlier on Goldberg's arm. What *was* surprising was that Schneider, on the day before his body was discovered, had written a cashier's check for ten thousand euros, which Robert Watkowiak tried to cash at around 11:30 this morning at the Taunus Savings & Loan branch in Schwalbach. The bank employees had refused to honor the unusually large amount and called the police. The man could be seen on the tapes from the surveillance camera trained on the tellers, and a warrant had been issued for his arrest. When he noticed that there was a problem, Watkowiak had fled the bank and left the check behind. A little while later, he showed up at the Nassau Savings Bank in Schwalbach and tried his luck with a cashier's check for over five thousand euros, again without success. Bodenstein had both checks lying in front of him on his desk. A graphological report would determine whether Schneider's signature was authentic. At any rate, the circumstantial evidence against Watkowiak was overwhelming, since his fingerprints had been found at both murder scenes.

There was a knock at the door, and Pia Kirchhoff came in.

"One of Schneider's neighbors called," she announced. "He says that the night Schneider was murdered, he saw a suspicious vehicle parked in Schneider's driveway around twelve-thirty, when he stepped out to take his dog for a late walk. It was a light-colored station wagon with a company name on the side. When he returned fifteen minutes later, the car was gone, and the lights were off in the house."

"Did he get the license plate number?"

"A local number. It was dark and the car was about sixty feet away. At first, he thought it might be the vehicle used by the home care for the elderly. But then he noticed the company logo."

"Watkowiak wasn't alone at Schneider's. We know that because of multiple sets of fingerprints on the glasses and the statement from the neighbor. The other guy may have been driving a company car and then came back later."

"Unfortunately, the fingerprint database didn't spit out any names but Watkowiak's. And the DNA results are going to take a while."

"Then we have to find Watkowiak. Behnke will have to drive out to that woman's apartment again and ask her what bars her lodger usually frequents."

Bodenstein noticed his colleague hesitate and gave her a quizzical look.

"Uh, Frank went home," Pia said. "He's on sick leave."

"How come?" Bodenstein seemed astounded at Behnke's behavior. He'd worked with this man for more than ten years. When Bodenstein moved from Frankfurt to Hofheim and took over leadership of the newly formed K-11 at the Regional Criminal Unit, Behnke was the only one from his team who had gone with him.

"I thought he'd called you," said Pia cautiously. "Ms. Krämer tried to stop Behnke from following Watkowiak. He fell on a broken bottle and cut himself on the arm and forehead."

"Ah" was all Bodenstein said. "Then our colleagues from Eschborn will have to cover all the bars in the area and talk to the proprietors."

Pia waited for Bodenstein to ask more questions, but he didn't go any deeper into Behnke's behavior. Instead, he stood up and grabbed his jacket.

"We're going back out to Mühlenhof and talk to Vera Kaltensee. I'd like to know what she can tell us about Watkowiak. Maybe she knows where he might be."

•   •   •

The big gate to the estate stood open, but a man in a dark uniform who was wearing an earpiece motioned for them to stop and roll down the window. Another uniformed man was standing nearby. Pia showed him her ID and said that she wanted to speak with Vera Kaltensee.

"Just a moment." The security guard stood in front of the car and spoke into a microphone that he was wearing on his lapel. After a moment, he nodded, stepped aside, and signaled to Pia that she could drive on. Three cars were parked near the manor house, and a clone of the first guard stopped them there. Another ID check, another inquiry.

"What's going on?" Pia muttered. "This is pure harassment."

She had fully intended to show absolutely no emotion in her next conversation with Vera Kaltensee, even if the old lady were writhing on the floor in fits of sobbing. The next inspection took place at the front door of the house, and Pia was starting to get mad.

"What's the point of this whole circus?" she turned and asked the gray-haired man who was escorting her and Bodenstein into the house. He was the same one who'd stopped them the day before. Moormann was his name, if Pia's memory served her correctly. Today, he was wearing a dark turtleneck and black jeans.

"There was an attempted break-in. Last night," he said with an anxious expression. "That's why the security precautions have been beefed up. Mrs. Kaltensee is often all alone in the house."

Pia remembered how afraid she had been in her own house after the break-in last summer. She could understand Vera Kaltensee's anxiety. The old lady was still worth millions and fairly well known. She might be hoarding art treasures and jewelry of inestimable value, which would always prove a temptation for art thieves and burglars.

"Please wait here." Moormann stopped at a different door than he had the day before. Agitated, muffled voices were coming from the room, but they stopped when Moormann knocked on the door. He stepped inside and closed the door behind him. With an indifferent expression, Bodenstein sat down in an easy chair upholstered in dusty brocade. Pia looked around the big foyer curiously. The sunlight falling through three Gothic stained-glass windows over the parapet of the stairs limned colorful patterns on the black-and-white marble floor. Dark, gold-framed portraits hung on the wall next to three unusual hunting trophies: a huge stuffed moose's head, a bear's head, and a gigantic rack of stag's antlers. Upon closer inspection, Pia saw once again that the big house was not particularly well kept. The floor was scuffed, the wallpaper faded. Cobwebs marred the animal heads, and there were rungs missing in the wooden banister. Everything seemed slightly dilapidated, which lent the house a sort of morbid charm, as if time had stopped sixty years ago.

Suddenly, the door opened, and a man of about forty in a suit and tie came out of the room that Moormann had entered. The man did not appear to be in a good mood, but he nodded politely to Pia and Bodenstein before leaving through the front door. It was about another three minutes before two more men came out, one of whom Pia recognized. Dr. Manuel Rosenblatt was a noted Frankfurt attorney who was often engaged by big-time industrial bosses when they got into difficulties. Moormann appeared in the open doorway. Bodenstein stood up.

"Dr. Kaltensee will see you now," he said.

"Thank you," said Pia, following her boss into a large room with oppressive dark wood paneling that extended nearly fifteen feet to the plaster decorations on the ceiling. At the rear of the room was a marble fireplace as big as a garage door; in the center stood a massive table of the same dark wood as the wainscoting, with ten uncomfortable-looking chairs. Vera Kaltensee was sitting ramrod-straight at the head of the table, which was covered with documents and open file folders. Although pale and visibly distraught, she managed to preserve her dignity.

"Ms. Kirchhoff. My dear Mr. Bodenstein. What can I do for you?"

Bodenstein behaved courteously and decorously, like very old-school aristocracy. All that was missing was for him to kiss her hand.

"Mr. Moormann just told us that there was an attempted break-in here yesterday." His voice sounded concerned. "Why didn't you call me, Mrs. Kaltensee?"

"Oh, I didn't want to bother you with such a petty matter." Vera Kaltensee shook her head. Her voice sounded uncertain. "You must have enough to do already."

"What, exactly, happened?"

"It's not worth mentioning. My son has sent over some people from his company's security team." She gave a shaky smile. "Now I'm feeling a bit safer."

A stocky man who looked to be in his sixties entered the room. Vera Kaltensee introduced him as her younger son, Siegbert, the managing director of KMF. Siegbert Kaltensee, with his pink piglet face, flabby cheeks, and bald pate, seemed friendly and affable compared to his gaunt and aristocratic brother, Elard. Smiling, he shook hands, first with Kirchhoff, then Bodenstein, before taking up a position behind his mother's chair. His gray suit and snow-white shirt with the conservative patterned tie fit him so well that they must have been custom-tailored. Siegbert Kaltensee seemed to place great value on making an understated impression, in his behavior as well as his attire.

"We won't take up much of your time," said Bodenstein. "But we're on the hunt for Robert Watkowiak. There are indications that he was at both crime scenes."

"Robert?" Vera Kaltensee opened her eyes wide in consternation. "You can't think he had anything to do with . . . *that*?"

"We don't really know," Bodenstein admitted. "It's an early lead. But we'd like to talk with him. Earlier today, my colleagues went to the apartment where he's staying at present, and he fled before they could speak to him."

"He's still registered with the police as residing here at Mühlenhof," Pia added.

"I didn't want to slam the last door in his face," said Vera Kaltensee. "The boy has caused me no end of trouble ever since he first set foot in this house."

Bodenstein nodded. "I know all about his arrest record." Siegbert Kaltensee said nothing. His alert gaze shifted back and forth between Bodenstein and Kirchhoff.

"You know," said Vera Kaltensee with a deep sigh, "for years Eugen, my late husband, never told me about Robert's existence. The poor boy grew up in his mother's care in the most impoverished conditions, until she finally drank herself to death. He was already twelve when Eugen came out with the truth about his illegitimate son. After I recovered from the shock of his infidelity, I insisted that Robert come to live with us. It wasn't his fault, after all. But I'm afraid that by then it was too late for him."

Siegbert Kaltensee put his hand on his mother's shoulder, and she clasped it. A gesture of intimacy and affection.

"Robert was obstinate even as a child," she went on. "I never succeeded in getting close to him, though I tried everything. When he was fourteen, he was caught shoplifting for the first time. And that was the start of his ignominious career."

She looked up with a sad expression.

"My children say that I was too protective of him, and maybe it would have set him straight if he'd landed in jail earlier. But I felt such sympathy for that boy."

"Do you think he's capable of killing someone?" Pia asked.

Vera Kaltensee thought it over for a moment as her son remained silent in a show of polite restraint.

"I wish I could say no with complete confidence," she responded at last. "Robert has disappointed us so often. He was last here about two years ago. He wanted money, as usual. Siegbert had to throw him out."

Pia saw that Vera Kaltensee had tears in her eyes, but this time she was prepared and able to observe the old lady with dispassionate interest.

Siegbert Kaltensee now spoke up. His high-pitched voice contrasted oddly with his powerful aura. "We really did give Robert every opportunity, but he was never interested. He was always begging Mother for money, and he kept stealing like a raven. Mother was too good-natured to put him in his place, but eventually I'd had enough. I threatened to report him for trespassing if he ever dared set foot in this house again."

"Did he know Mr. Goldberg and Mr. Schneider?" Pia asked.

Siegbert Kaltensee nodded. "Of course. He knew them both well."

"Do you think it's possible that he asked them for money?"

Vera Kaltensee grimaced, as if she found the thought highly unpleasant.

"I know that he used to put the touch on them both regularly." Siegbert Kaltensee laughed, a curt snort with no humor. "He really has no scruples."

"Oh, Siegbert, you're so unfair." Vera Kaltensee shook her head. "I blame myself for listening to you. I should have taken responsibility and kept

Robert within reach. Then he wouldn't have come up with all these stupid ideas."

"We've been over this a thousand times, Mother," Siegbert Kaltensee replied patiently. "Robert is forty-four years old. How long do you think you could have protected him from himself? And he never wanted your help; he just wanted your money."

"What stupid ideas did Robert come up with?" Bodenstein asked before Siegbert Kaltensee and his mother became sidetracked further by the discussion they'd obviously had many times before.

Vera Kaltensee gave a stiff smile. "You know his record," she said. "Robert isn't vicious by nature. He's simply too gullible and always gets mixed up with the wrong people."

Pia observed how Siegbert Kaltensee raised his eyebrows in mute resignation at these words. He was probably thinking the same thing she was. She'd heard this very same statement from relatives so many times. Other people were always to blame when a son, daughter, husband, or partner became a criminal. It was so easy to palm off the responsibility on bad influences in order to justify one's own failure. Vera Kaltensee was no exception. Bodenstein asked her to call him if Robert Watkowiak got in touch with her.

Robert Watkowiak was marching along the paved footpath from Kelkheim to Fischbach in a foul mood. He was grumbling and cursing Herrmann Schneider with every swearword he knew. Most of all, it made him furious that he'd let that old shithead trick him. The checks were as good as cash, he'd said, regretfully showing him his empty wallet. No way! The uptight bastard at the bank had made a gigantic fuss about it, phoning around, probably to the cops. So he decided he'd better split. But now he didn't have a cell phone or enough dough for the bus and had to hoof it. A few hours ago, he'd just taken off, without thinking about where he was going. The scare this morning when the cops showed up at Moni's place had sobered him up quick, and the walk in the fresh air made him realize the seriousness of his position: He'd reached the end of the line. He was hungry, thirsty, and had no roof over his head. He couldn't show up at Kurti's, since his grandmother had already called him names and thrown him out, and he no longer had any other friends. The only possibility he still had was Vera. He had to wait for a chance to talk to her alone. He knew how he could get into Mühlenhof unnoticed, and he was familiar with every inch of that house. Once he was face-to-face with her, he would calmly explain what kind of dilemma he was in financially. Maybe she would give him something voluntarily. If not, he'd pull out his gun and hold it to her head. But it wouldn't go that far.

Actually, it wasn't Vera who had told him he was forbidden to enter the house. It had been Siegbert, that fat, arrogant pig. Siegbert had never been able to stand him, especially not after the accident, when he was blamed for the whole thing. Marleen had actually been behind the wheel, but nobody would believe him, because she was only fourteen at the time and such a sweet, well-behaved girl. It had been her idea to take Uncle Elard's Porsche on a joyride. She'd stolen the key and taken off. He had only gotten in the car to keep her from doing anything stupid. But of course the family assumed he'd been driving in order to impress the girl.

Robert Watkowiak trotted past the Aral gas station and crossed the street. If he got a move on, he could be at Mühlenhof in an hour. Suddenly, a loud honk from a car horn shook him out of his dismal thoughts. A black Mercedes pulled up next to him. The driver lowered the window on the passenger side and leaned over.

"Hey, Robert! Can I take you somewhere?" he asked. "Come on, hop in."

Robert hesitated for a moment, then shrugged. Anything was better than walking.

"Those damn dogs have been barking all day. I've had a million complaints," moaned the super of the apartment building on Rotdornweg as he rode the tiny elevator up to the top floor with Bodenstein and Kirchhoff. "But often they're not home all day long and just let the dogs bark and shit all over the apartment."

Ostermann had convinced the judge in charge that it was a dangerous situation and in no time he had a search warrant for Monika Krämer's apartment.

The elevator stopped with a lurch. The super opened the scratched and filthy door and kept on blathering. "Hardly any decent people living in this

building. Most of them can't even speak German, but the welfare office pays
their rent. On top of that, they're snotty. I should really be making twice as
much for all the hassle I have to put up with."

Pia rolled her eyes. In front of the door at the end of the dim hall waited
two uniforms, three evidence techs, and a man from a locksmith shop. Bodenstein knocked loudly on the apartment door.

"Police!" he yelled. "Open up!"

No reaction. The super pushed his way forward and hammered on the
wood panel.

"Open the door, and quick!" he shouted. "I know you're in there, you
deadbeats!"

"Okay, just take it easy," said Bodenstein, planting his hand on the man's
shoulder.

"That's the only language they understand," the super grumbled. The
door of the apartment across the hall opened a crack and closed again.
The police were obviously not unexpected visitors in this building.

"Open the door," said Bodenstein to the super, who nodded eagerly.
He tried the pass key, but with no luck.

The locksmith had the cylinder lock out in a few seconds, but the door
still wouldn't budge. "They probably blocked the door with something," he
said, stepping back. Two uniformed officers put all their weight against the
plywood door and finally got it to open. The dogs were barking like crazy.

"Shit," muttered one of the uniforms when he saw what had been blocking the door. On the floor lay the lifeless and blood-smeared body of the ten-
ant, Monika Krämer.

"I think I'm going to throw up," the officer gasped, and shoved past Pia
into the corridor. Without a word, Pia pulled on latex gloves and bent over
the body of the young woman, who lay with her knees pulled up, facing the
door. Rigor mortis had not yet set in. Pia grabbed the woman by the shoulder
and turned her over on her back. In all her years of service with the Kripo,
she'd seen plenty of horrible sights, but the brutality with which someone
had mutilated the young woman's body truly shocked her. Someone had slit
Monika Krämer open from throat to pubis, right through her panties. Her
entrails had poured out of her open belly.

"Oh God," Pia heard her boss say in a choked voice behind her. She gave him a quick look. Bodenstein could stand most things, but right now he was as white as a sheet. She turned back to the corpse and saw what had shaken Bodenstein so much. Her stomach clenched and she fought against the rising nausea. The killer hadn't been content to kill the woman; he had also gouged out her eyes.

"Let me drive, boss." Pia held out her hand, and Bodenstein gave her the car keys without argument. They had finished their work in the apartment and spoken with all the neighbors on that floor and on the floor below. Several had heard a violent argument and dull thuds around ten o'clock that morning, but they all agreed that loud physical fights in Monika Krämer's apartment were an almost daily occurrence. Had Watkowiak returned to the apartment after Pia and Behnke had left? Had he murdered the young woman in this bestial manner? She hadn't died instantly; despite her terrible wounds, she had managed to crawl to the door and tried to make it out to the corridor. Bodenstein rubbed his face with both hands. He looked worse than Pia had ever seen him.

"Sometimes I wish I'd become a forest ranger or a vacuum cleaner salesman," he said gloomily after they'd been driving for a while. "That girl was hardly older than Rosalie. I'm never going to get used to things like this."

Pia glanced over at him. She was tempted to pat her boss's hand or make some other consoling gesture, but she didn't. Although they'd been working together almost every day for the past two years, there was still a distance between them that held her back. Bodenstein was anything but a chummy guy, and he normally hid his emotions well. Sometimes Pia asked herself how he could stand it—the horrific images, the constant pressure, which he never seemed to need to vent by cursing or exploding in rage. She guessed that this superhuman self-control was the result of his strict upbringing. It was probably what people called "composure." Maintaining control at all costs and in any situation.

"Me, neither," she replied. She might outwardly give the impression that she was unmoved, but inside it was a different story. Even endless hours in the forensic lab had not inured her or made her impervious to the fates and tragedies of the people she encountered only as corpses. For good reason psychologists were brought in to counsel first responders at scenes of disasters, because the sight of mutilated corpses burned its way into their minds and could not be driven out. Like Pia, Bodenstein also sought refuge in routine.

"This text message on her cell," he said in a businesslike voice, "could prove that Watkowiak was actually behind the murders of Goldberg and Schneider."

The crime lab had found a text on Monika Krämer's cell phone, presumably from Robert Watkowiak, from yesterday at 1:34 P.M. It said: SWEETHEART, WE'RE RICH! GOT RID OF THE OTHER OLD GUY, TOO. LET'S HEAD SOUTH!

"If so, our homicides are solved," Pia replied without much conviction. "Watkowiak killed Goldberg and Schneider out of greed; they knew him well as the stepson of Vera Kaltensee and had no qualms about letting him in. Afterward, he killed Monika Krämer because she knew about what he'd done."

"What do you think?" Bodenstein asked. Pia thought it over for a moment. She wished that the solution to the three murders could be that simple, but somehow she doubted it.

"I don't know," she replied. "My gut tells me that there's more behind the whole thing."

The wet manure in the horse stalls was heavy as lead and the smell of ammonia took her breath away, but Pia ignored it, just as she did her aching back and the pain in her arms. She had to distract her thoughts somehow, and there was nothing better for that than hard physical labor. Plenty of her colleagues in a similar situation would seek forgetfulness in alcohol, and Pia could understand that. She doggedly shoveled one pitchforkful after another onto the manure spreader, which she had maneuvered right outside the stall until the prongs scraped over the shiny concrete floor. She scraped out the last of it with a shovel; then she stopped, out of breath, wiping the sweat from her brow with her sleeve.

She and Bodenstein had driven to the station and reported the murder to their colleagues. The manhunt for Robert Watkowiak had intensified; for a while, they were considering involving the public in the search with an appeal broadcast on the local radio station. Pia was just finishing up her work when her dogs, who had been following her movements attentively, jumped up and ran off, barking happily. Seconds later, the green pickup from the Opel Zoo pulled in next to the tractor, and Christoph climbed out. His expression was concerned as he strode toward Pia.

"Hey, sweetheart," he said softly, enclosing her firmly in his arms. Pia leaned against him and felt the tears well up in her eyes and spill down her cheeks. It was such a relief to be allowed to be weak for a moment. With Henning, she'd never dared.

"I'm glad you're here," she murmured.

"That bad?"

She felt him kissing her hair and nodded mutely. Christoph held her tight for a long time, stroking her back.

"You go take a nice hot bath," he said firmly. "I'll bring in the horses and feed them. And I brought us something to eat. Your favorite pizza."

"With extra tuna and anchovies?" Pia raised her head and smiled wanly. "You're a dear."

"I know." He winked at her and then kissed her. "And now go soak in that tub."

When she emerged from the bathroom half an hour later, her hair wet, wearing a terry-cloth robe, she still felt dirty inside in spite of the bath. The brutality of the murder was horrible enough. But the fact that she had spoken with the young woman only a couple of hours before made the whole situation so much worse. Had Monika Krämer died because the police had shown up at her apartment?

In the meantime, Christoph had fed the dogs, set the table in the kitchen, and opened a bottle of wine. The seductive aroma of pizza reminded Pia that she hadn't eaten all day.

"Do you want to talk about it?" Christoph asked when she sat down at the table and began eating her lukewarm pizza *al tonno* with her fingers. "Maybe it would do you good."

Pia looked at him. His sensitivity was incredible. Of course it would do her good to talk. To detach herself from it, she needed to share what she'd seen. That was really the only way to deal with the trauma.

"I've never seen anything so horrendous," she said with a sigh. Christoph poured her some more wine and listened closely as Pia objectively described what had happened that day. She told him about her morning visit to Monika Krämer's apartment, about Watkowiak fleeing, and about Behnke losing his temper.

"You know," she said, taking a sip of wine, "to a certain extent I can handle anything, no matter how terrible it might be. But the insane brutality, the cruel way that young woman was killed, was too much for me."

Pia ate the last piece of pizza and wiped her greasy fingers on a paper towel. She felt completely exhausted yet at the same time tense enough to burst. Christoph stood up to put the empty pizza boxes in the trash. Then he stepped behind Pia, put his hands on her shoulders, and began gently massaging her cramped neck muscles.

"The only redeeming factor is that it makes me even more determined to do my job." She closed her eyes. "I'm going to find the fucker who did this and get him locked up forever."

Christoph leaned over and kissed her cheek. "You really look all in," he said softly. "I'm so sorry that I have to leave you home alone—it's such bad timing."

Pia turned to face him. Tomorrow, he was flying to South Africa. The one-week trip to Capetown to attend the Conference of the World Association of Zoos and Aquariums, WAZA for short, had been planned for months. Pia already missed him with every fiber of her being.

"It's only for eight days." She was acting cooler than she actually felt. "And I can always call you."

"Be sure to call me if anything happens, okay?" Christoph pulled her close. "Promise?"

"Cross my heart." Pia flung her arms around his neck. "But you're still here now. And we should take advantage of that."

"You think?"

Instead of an answer, she gave him a kiss. She would have preferred never to let him go. Henning had often gone on trips, and sometimes she hadn't been able to reach him for days, but that had neither worried nor bothered her. With Christoph, it was different. Since the day they'd met, they hadn't been apart for longer than twenty-four hours. The mere thought of not being able to drop by the zoo to see him filled her with desolation.

He seemed to sense the urgent, feverish desire emanating from her body. This wasn't the first time she'd slept with him, but her heart was pounding hard enough to burst as she followed him to the bedroom and watched him strip off his clothes. She'd never known a man like Christoph—a man who demanded everything and gave everything, who permitted her no shameful withdrawal, no embarrassment, and no fake orgasm. Pia was practically addicted to the powerful way her body reacted to his. There would be time for tenderness later. Right now, she wanted nothing more than to sink into his embrace and forget the whole terrible day.

Thursday, May 3

Bodenstein felt absolutely exhausted when shortly before eight o'clock he dragged himself up the stairs to the office of K-11 on the second floor. The baby had cried for half the night. Cosima was considerate enough to move into the guest room, but he still got hardly any sleep. Then he'd been delayed by an accident on the B519 just before the off-ramp to Hofheim, wasting half an hour. And to top it off, Chief Commissioner Nierhoff came out of his office just as Bodenstein was climbing the last steps.

"Good morning, good morning." Nierhoff smiled affably, rubbing his hands. "Congratulations! That was fast work. Great job, Bodenstein."

He looked at his boss with annoyance, realizing that Nierhoff had been waiting for him to arrive. Bodenstein hated being ambushed like this, before he'd even taken a sip of his coffee.

"Good morning," he said. "What are you talking about?"

"We're going to the press right away with the news," Nierhoff continued undeterred. "I've already instructed our press secretary and all—"

"What are you going to the press with?" Bodenstein asked, interrupting the chief commissioner's flow of words. "Did I miss something?"

"The murders have been solved," Nierhoff replied, gloating. "You've found the perpetrator. So the case is off the table."

"Who says that?" asked Bodenstein, nodding to two colleagues passing by.

"Your colleague Fachinger," Nierhoff went on, "she told me that—"

"Hold on." Bodenstein didn't care if he sounded rude or not. "Yesterday, we found the body of an acquaintance of the man who was at the scene of both homicides, but so far we don't have a murder weapon or unequivocal proof that he actually committed the murders. We definitely haven't solved the cases."

"Why do you have to make everything so complicated, Bodenstein? The man killed out of greed; all the evidence points in that direction. And then he killed the woman because she knew too much. We'll catch him sooner or later, and then we'll get a confession." For Nierhoff, the case was crystal clear. "The press conference has been scheduled for eleven o'clock. I'd like you to be there."

Bodenstein couldn't understand it. The morning actually seemed to be proceeding even worse than it had begun.

"Eleven sharp downstairs in the big conference room." The chief commissioner wasn't entertaining any objections. "Afterward, I'd like to speak with you in my office." With that, he left with a smug smile on his face.

Bodenstein furiously tore open the door to the office that Hasse and Fachinger shared. Both of them were already at their desks. Hasse quickly pressed a key on his keyboard, but at the moment Bodenstein didn't care if he was surfing the Net again, searching for a suitable spot in southern climes for his retirement.

"Ms. Fachinger," Bodenstein said to his youngest colleague without bothering to offer a greeting, "come with me to my office."

As angry as he was, he didn't want to reprimand her in front of another colleague.

A moment later, she came into his office with an anxious expression and cautiously closed the door behind her. Bodenstein sat down behind his desk but didn't ask her to take a seat.

"Why did you tell the chief commissioner that we'd solved both homicide cases?" he asked sharply, scrutinizing his colleague. She was still young and very capable, but she lacked self-confidence, and she sometimes tended to make mistakes out of sheer eagerness.

"*Me?*" Kathrin Fachinger turned beet red. "But what was I supposed to tell him?"

"That's exactly what I'd like to know!"

"He . . . came into the conference room . . . last night," Fachinger stammered nervously. "He was looking for you and wanted to know how the investigation was going. I told him that you and Pia were in the apartment of a murder victim and that she was the girlfriend of the man who could be tied to both crime scenes."

Bodenstein looked at his colleague. His anger dissipated as rapidly as it had appeared.

"That's all I said," Fachinger insisted. "Really, boss. I swear it."

Bodenstein believed her. Nierhoff was in such a hurry to get this case cleared up that he'd put the pieces of the investigation together the way he wanted. It was outrageous—and strange.

"I believe you," said Bodenstein. "Please excuse my tone of voice, but I was pretty mad. Is Behnke here yet?"

"No." Fachinger looked uncomfortable. "He . . . he's on sick leave."

"Oh, right. And Ms. Kirchhoff?"

"She had to take her friend to the airport this morning; then she went straight over to forensics. The autopsy of Monika Krämer is due to start at eight."

"Have a bad night?" Dr. Henning Kirchhoff asked, greeting his ex-wife shortly after 8:00 A.M. in Autopsy Suite 2 of the Institute of Forensic Medicine. Pia glanced in the mirror over the washbasin. She thought she actually looked pretty good—considering she hadn't slept for half the night and had been bawling in her car ten minutes ago. Amid the chaos at the airport, her parting with Christoph had been far too brief. In Terminal B, two of his colleagues—one from Berlin and the other from Wuppertal—who were also headed for the congress in South Africa had been waiting for him. With a trace of jealousy, Pia had noticed that the colleague from Berlin was female, and fairly attractive. A last embrace, a quick farewell kiss, and he had vanished with the others into the crowded terminal. Pia had gazed after him, not prepared for the overwhelming feeling of emptiness.

"Do you remember my friend Miriam?" she asked Henning.

"Fortunately, Miss Horowitz and I met only once many years ago." He sounded rather bitter, and Pia remembered that Miriam had called Henning a "humorless Dr. Frankenstein," whereupon he had characterized her as a "silly party chick." Pia deliberated briefly whether to expound on Miriam's professional career, but she dropped the idea.

"Anyway," she said, "I ran into her recently. She works at the Fritz Bauer Institute."

"Her daddy probably got her the job." Once again, Henning showed his tendency to hold a grudge, but Pia ignored it.

"I asked her to make inquiries about Goldberg. At first, of course, she couldn't believe that he might have been a Nazi, but then she discovered documents in the institute's archive about Goldberg and his family. The Nazis were meticulous about documenting everything."

Henning's assistant, Ronnie Böhme, stepped up next to Pia, who was standing beside the table on which the washed and naked body of Monika Krämer lay. In these clinical surroundings, her death had lost all semblance of horror. Pia told them that Goldberg, his family, and all the Jewish residents of Angerburg had been deported in March 1942 to the Płaszów concentration camp. While Goldberg's family had perished there, he had survived, until the camp was cleared out in January 1945. All the prisoners were then taken to Auschwitz, where Goldberg was murdered in the gas chamber that same month.

Utter silence descended upon the autopsy suite. Pia looked at the two men expectantly.

"Well, and then what?" Henning asked in a condescending tone. "What's the big deal?"

"Don't you get it?" Pia was miffed by his reaction. "That's the proof that the guy you had on the table here was definitely not David Josua Goldberg."

"That's nuts." Henning shrugged, unimpressed. "So where's that DA? I can't stand people who show up late."

"Here she is," a female voice replied. "Good morning, everyone."

District Attorney Valerie Löblich strutted in with her head held high, nodding to Ronnie and ignoring Pia, who again registered with interest Henning's obvious discomfort.

"Good morning, Ms. Löblich," was all he said.

"Good morning, Dr. Kirchhoff," the DA replied coolly. The formality with which they greeted each other prompted Pia to grin. She recalled her last meeting with DA Löblich, which had taken place in the living room of Henning's apartment, a situation that could only be described as extremely compromising. At that time, both Valerie and Henning had been wearing considerably fewer clothes than today.

"We might as well get started." Kirchhoff avoided all eye contact with DA Löblich and Pia as he launched into frenetic activity. When Pia had caught them in the act, he had assured her that despite concerted efforts on the part of Löblich, that was the only time they'd slept together—she knew that the DA blamed her for that. Today, she stayed in the background while Henning performed the external postmortem examination, dictating his comments into the microphone attached to his lapel.

"Now she's picked up a judge," Ronnie whispered to Pia, nodding toward the DA, who, with arms crossed, stood right next to the autopsy table. Pia shrugged. She really couldn't have cared less. A slight ache in her thighs and back reminded her of the passionate night she'd just spent with Christoph, and she calculated when he would be landing in Capetown. He'd promised to send her a text as soon as he got there. Was he thinking about her? Pia's thoughts wandered off. She was hardly following what Henning was doing.

He extended the brutal cut that the murderer had inflicted on the girl, removed the individual organs, and then dissected the heart. Ronnie took samples from her stomach contents to the lab on the top floor. The whole time, nobody said a word, except for Henning, who was narrating his work in a low voice for the autopsy report.

"Pia!" he called out loudly. "Are you asleep?"

Rudely yanked from her reverie, she took a step forward. At the same time, the DA stepped closer to the table.

"You need to look for a knife with a hawkbill blade about four inches long," Kirchhoff told his ex-wife. "The perpetrator made the cut with a great deal of force and without hesitation. The blade injured the internal organs and left incision marks on the ribs."

"What's a hawkbill blade?" the DA asked.

"I'm not your private tutor. Do your own homework," Kirchhoff snapped, and Pia suddenly felt sorry for Valerie.

"A hawkbill blade is curved like a half-moon," she explained. "They're originally from Indonesia and were used by fishermen. Blades like that aren't suitable for cutting, but they are used exclusively as combat knives."

"Thank you." DA Löblich nodded to Pia.

"You can't buy a knife like that at the supermarket." Kirchhoff's mood had abruptly deteriorated. "The first time I saw knife wounds like this was in victims of the Kosovo Liberation Army."

"What about her eyes?" Pia was trying hard to remain objective, but she shuddered at the thought of how much the woman must have suffered before she died.

"What about them?" snapped her ex-husband irritably. "I haven't gotten that far yet."

Pia and the DA exchanged a meaningful glance, which did not escape Henning. He began examining the woman's abdomen, taking samples and muttering incomprehensibly to himself. Pia pitied the secretary who would have to type up the autopsy report. Twenty minutes later, Kirchhoff inspected the bluish lips of the dead woman with a magnifying glass, then thoroughly examined the oral cavity.

"What is it?" Valerie Löblich asked impatiently. "Don't keep us in suspense."

"Please be patient for a moment, dear District Attorney," Kirchhoff replied sharply. He grabbed a scalpel and dissected the esophagus and the larynx. Then with an expression of extreme concentration, he took several samples with cotton-tipped swabs and handed one after the other to his assistant. Finally, he picked up a UV lamp and shone it in the mouth and in the opened esophagus of the dead woman.

"Aha!" he said, straightening up. "Would you like to look, District Attorney?"

Valerie Löblich nodded eagerly and stepped to his side.

"You have to look very closely right here," said the pathologist. Pia had an idea what there was to see there, and she shook her head. Today, Henning was really taking things too far. Even Ronnie knew what was going on and, with effort, had to suppress a grin.

"I don't see anything," said the DA.

"Don't you notice the bluish shimmering areas?"

"I do." She raised her head and frowned. "Was she poisoned?"

"It depends. I can't tell at the moment whether the semen was poisoned or not." Kirchhoff smirked. "But we'll be able to determine it in the lab."

The blood rushed to the DA's face when she realized she'd been the victim of an inappropriate joke. "You know what, Henning? You're an asshole!" she hissed furiously. "The day when you'll be lying on this table yourself will come sooner than you think if you keep this up!"

She turned on her heel and marched out. Kirchhoff watched her go, then shrugged and looked at Pia.

"You heard it," he said with an innocent expression. "A blatant threat of murder. Oh well. Those DAs just don't have a sense of humor."

"That wasn't very nice of you," Pia replied. "Was she raped?"

"Who? Löblich?"

"Not funny at all, Henning," Pia said sharply. "Well?"

"My God!" he exclaimed with unusual vehemence after he made sure that his assistant wasn't in the room. "She's such a pain in the butt. She just won't leave me alone. She keeps calling and babbling all sorts of crazy stuff."

"Maybe you gave her cause for false hopes."

"You're the one who gave her cause for false hopes," he countered. "Since you forced me into a divorce."

"I think you're imagining things." Pia shook her head in astonishment. "But after your performance today, she's probably lost all interest in you."

"I should be so lucky. She'll probably be back here in an hour."

Pia scrutinized her ex-husband.

"I bet that you lied to me," she said.

"What do you mean?" he asked, feigning innocence.

"The little intermezzo last summer on the living room coffee table—that wasn't the only time you cheated on me. Am I right?"

Kirchhoff suddenly looked guilty. But before he could say anything, Ronnie came back into the autopsy suite, and Henning switched instantly to his professional tone of voice.

"She was not raped. But she had oral sex before she died," he explained. "Afterward, the other injuries were inflicted, and they were fatal. She bled to death."

"Monika Krämer bled to death from the deep wounds she suffered from a knife with a hawkbill blade," Pia reported to her colleagues an hour later in the conference room. "Traces of semen were found in her oral cavity and esophagus. Since we have Watkowiak's DNA in our computer, we should know in a matter of days whether the semen is his. We'll have to wait and see if the DNA of a third person is present in the traces, fibers, and hairs. Our colleagues in the crime lab are working at top speed."

Bodenstein cast a quick glance at Chief Commissioner Nierhoff and hoped that his boss realized how extremely thin the evidence was so far. Downstairs, all the reporters had gathered, waiting to hear Nierhoff brag about how fast the police had solved the murders of Goldberg and Schneider.

"The man got rid of the woman because he'd told her earlier about the murders he'd committed." Nierhoff got up. "Clear proof of his propensity to violence. Good work, colleagues. Bodenstein, remember that I want to see you at twelve o'clock in my office."

Then he left the room, hurrying to the press conference without insisting that Bodenstein accompany him. For a moment, no one spoke.

"I wonder what he's going to tell them downstairs," said Ostermann.

"No idea." Bodenstein had given up. "But at this point, a false report of progress won't do any harm."

"So you don't think Watkowiak murdered Goldberg and Schneider?" asked Fachinger hesitantly.

"No," Bodenstein replied. "He's a habitual criminal but not a murderer. I also don't think he killed Ms. Krämer."

Fachinger and Ostermann looked at their boss in astonishment.

"I'm afraid that a third individual is involved. But somebody doesn't want us to keep snooping around, so it's important to find a suspect fast and pin the murders of Goldberg and Schneider on that person instead."

"You're thinking that the murder of Monika Krämer could be a hired job?" Ostermann raised his eyebrows.

"I'm assuming something like that," said Bodenstein. "Given the professional MO and the use of a combat knife. The question is, Would Goldberg's family really go that far? After all, inside of twenty-four hours they had mobilized the NCP, the Interior Ministry, the American general consul, the Frankfurt president of police, and the CIA in order to prevent a certain fact from being made public. But we had already figured it out—namely, that the murdered Goldberg was anything but a Jewish survivor of the Holocaust." He gave his colleagues an urgent look. "One thing is clear: Somebody who has a lot to lose will stop at nothing. That's why we have to be very, very careful not to endanger any more innocent people while conducting this investigation."

"Then it may be a good thing that Nierhoff is announcing that we've found the perp," Ostermann opined, and Bodenstein nodded.

"Precisely. That's why I'm not trying to stop him. Whoever ordered the murder of Monika Krämer will think that he's safe."

"By the way, we found several old text messages on Watkowiak's cell phone," Pia said. "All in uppercase and lowercase, and not once did he call Monika "sweetheart." The texts we found weren't from him. Somebody bought a cell phone, probably a prepaid one, under a false name and sent the texts to Monika Krämer in order to divert suspicion and place it on Watkowiak."

Everyone understood the implications of this theory, and for a moment there was silence in the room. Watkowiak, with his lengthy rap sheet, was a highly plausible murder suspect.

"So who even knows that we're considering Watkowiak as the perp?" Fachinger asked. Bodenstein and Kirchhoff exchanged a quick glance. That was a good question. No, it was *the* question that had to be answered in the event Watkowiak was not the person who had first blinded and then literally butchered Monika Krämer.

"Vera Kaltensee and her son Siegbert know," said Pia, breaking the silence. She was thinking about the security men in the black uniforms at Mühlenhof. "And probably the rest of the Kaltensee family, as well."

Bodenstein disagreed with her. "I don't believe that Vera Kaltensee had anything to do with this. Something like that doesn't seem to fit her demeanor."

"Just because she's a big philanthropist doesn't mean she's an angel, too," Pia retorted. She was the only one who knew why her boss was trying to see the old woman in a good light. Due to his work, Bodenstein was familiar with all levels of society, from the dregs all the way to the upper class, and yet he was still inevitably tied to the class consciousness of his upbringing. His whole family belonged to the aristocracy, just as the former baroness of Zeydlitz-Lauenburg did.

"Is anyone interested in the lab results?" Ostermann patted the file folder lying in front of him.

"Of course." Bodenstein leaned forward. "Is there anything about the murder weapon?"

"Yes." Ostermann opened the folder. "It was definitely the same weapon. The ammunition is quite special: in both cases, a nine-by-nineteen-millimeter parabellum round, manufactured sometime between 1939 and 1942. The lab was able to determine this from the alloy, because it hasn't been used since then in this particular combination."

"So our killer uses a nine-millimeter weapon and ammunition from World War Two," Pia said. "Where would someone get hold of something like that?"

"You can order such things on the Internet," said Hasse. "Or get them at gun shows. I don't think it's as unusual as it seems."

"Okay, okay," said Bodenstein, cutting off the discussion. "What else have we got, Ostermann?"

"Schneider's signatures on the checks were genuine. And the graphologist says the mysterious number was printed by the same person. The DNA on the wineglass in Goldberg's living room belongs to a woman, but no match was found for the DNA or the fingerprints. The lipstick is nothing special—a common product by Maybelline—but besides the lipstick, traces of acyclovir were found."

"And what's that?" asked Fachinger.

"A medication that combats herpes, or cold sores, on the lips. It's one of the ingredients in Zovirax."

"Well, that's certainly news," Hasse grumbled. "The murderer was found guilty because of herpes. I can just imagine the headline."

Bodenstein couldn't help smiling, but his smile vanished with Pia's next words.

"Vera Kaltensee had a Band-Aid on her lip. Of course she'd put lipstick over it, but I noticed it. Remember, boss?"

Bodenstein frowned and gave Pia a dubious look.

"Possibly. But I couldn't swear to it."

At that moment, there was a knock on the door, and the chief commissioner's secretary stuck her head in.

"The chief commissioner is back from the press conference and is expecting you, Mr. Chief Inspector," she announced. "Urgently."

There was no question about what his assignment entailed. He absolutely had to locate the chest. Why was not an issue. He wasn't being paid to speculate about motives. He had never had scruples about following an order. That was his job. It took an hour and a half before Ritter finally left the ugly yellow-painted apartment house in which he'd been living since his fall from grace. The man watched with spiteful satisfaction as Ritter crossed the street to the S-Bahn stop at Schwarzwaldstrasse with a laptop case slung over his shoulder and a cell phone pressed to his ear. The days of being chauffeured around were over for this arrogant guy.

He waited until Ritter had vanished from sight; then he got out and went into the building. Ritter's apartment was on the fourth floor. It took the man exactly twenty-two seconds to breach the ridiculous safety devices on the apartment door. It was child's play. He pulled on some gloves and looked around. How would someone like Thomas Ritter, who was used to a life of luxury, feel in a dump like this? A room with a view of the building next door, a bathroom with a shower and toilet and no daylight, a tiny entryway, and a kitchen that made a mockery of the name. He opened the doors of the only wardrobe and worked his way systematically through stacks of clean and less clean clothes, underwear, socks, and shoes. Nothing. No sign of a chest or any reference to the family. The bed looked as if it hadn't been used in a while; it wasn't even made up. Next, he turned to the desk. There was no permanent Internet connection or any answering machine that might provide a clue. To his disappointment, he found only uninteresting junk on the desk, old newspapers and cheap porn magazines. He took one with him. Some inspirational reading for all the boring hours he spent waiting in the car couldn't do any harm.

Then he searched meticulously through the pile of handwritten notes and discovered that Ritter's prose had deteriorated considerably. He deciphered the words *rustling sheets*, *juicy pussies,* and *breathless cries of orgasm* and had to smirk. So he'd sunk this far, the Dr. Ritter who had previously written highbrow speeches. Now he wrote dull short stories with pornographic content. The man paged further. He stopped short when he saw on a yellow Post-it a hastily jotted name, a cell phone number, and a word that instantly electrified him. With his digital camera, he photographed the piece of paper and then covered it with the other documents. His visit to Ritter's apartment had not been a waste of time.

Katharina Ehrmann was standing in her slip and bra in her walk-in closet, trying to decide what to wear. She had never considered herself especially vain until after the sudden death of her husband. She had played the grieving widow and stopped using makeup for a while. Looking in the mirror had been a shock each time. A shock that she preferred to avoid, especially since she no longer had to live off the paltry salary of an office worker. Shortly before her fortieth birthday a couple of years ago, she had started taking measures to counteract her age. It started with hours at the fitness center, lymphatic drainage, and colonic cleansing. She had also opted for Botox treatments every three months and sinfully expensive wrinkle injections with collagen and hyaluronic acid. But it was worth it. She looked ten years younger than other women her age. Katharina smiled at her reflection in the mirror. A lot of wealthy people lived in Königstein, and discreet private clinics specializing in every sort of antiaging treatment were popping up like mushrooms.

But that wasn't why she had returned to the small town in the Taunus. The reason for her return was far more pragmatic. She didn't want to live in Frankfurt, but she needed a house close to the airport because she spent a lot of time in Zürich or at her finca on Mallorca. The purchase of the big house right in the middle of the Old Town in Königstein had been a triumph for her. It was only a couple of hundred yards from the hovel in which she had grown up as the daughter of a poor innkeeper. This was where the man who had driven her father into bankruptcy had lived. Now he was broke himself, and Katharina had acquired his house for a ludicrously cheap price. She smiled. What goes around comes around, she thought.

A shiver of anticipation ran down her spine as she thought about the day when Thomas Ritter had told her about his plan to write a biography of Vera Kaltensee. Overly confident about his own abilities, he had assumed that Vera would be enthusiastic about the idea, but the opposite had been the case. Vera hadn't shilly-shallied long. She had fired him without notice after eighteen years. At a chance meeting with Katharina, Ritter had complained bitterly about this injustice, and then Katharina saw her opportunity to get revenge on Vera and the whole Kaltensee family. Ritter had greedily pounced on her offer.

Now, a year and a half later, after Ritter had indeed received a high-five-figure advance, he hadn't put anything that even hinted at a best-seller on paper. Although Katharina occasionally slept with him, she had not let herself be fooled by his grandiose pronouncements and promises. After a sober analysis of what Ritter had turned in so far, she knew that his scribblings were miles away from the scandalous tell-all account that he had been promising her for months. The time had come to intervene.

As usual, she was well informed as far as the Kaltensee family went, because she maintained a friendly contact with Jutta, acting as though nothing had ever happened. Jutta, in her vanity, never doubted Katharina's sincerity. Through Ritter, Katharina knew about the circumstances that had led to his termination without notice. A highly informative conversation with Vera's not particularly loyal housekeeper had convinced her at last to contact Elard. She didn't know for sure how helpful Jutta's elder brother would be, but at least he had been present at the altercation last summer. As Katharina was still pondering this, her cell rang.

"Hello, Elard," she said. "You must be a mind reader."

Elard Kaltensee skipped the chitchat and got straight to the point.

"How do you picture the handover?" he asked.

"From what you said, I gather that you have something for me in exchange," replied Katharina. She was curious as to what Elard planned to offer her.

"I've got plenty," said Elard. "And I want to get rid of the stuff. So?"

"Let's meet at my place," Katharina suggested.

"No. I'll send over what I have by messenger. Tomorrow at noon."

"Agreed. Where?"

"I'll tell you then. Good-bye."

And he hung up. Katharina smiled contentedly. Everything was going like clockwork.

Bodenstein buttoned his jacket and knocked on the door to his boss's office before entering. To his surprise, he saw that Nierhoff had a redhead visiting. He was about to excuse himself, but the chief commissioner jumped up and came over. He seemed to be still under the intoxicating influence of what he regarded as a highly successful press conference.

"Come in, Bodenstein!" he exclaimed affably. "This may seem a bit unexpected, but I would like to introduce you to my successor."

Then the woman turned around, and Bodenstein froze. What had started out as a bad day now raced with the speed of an InterCity Express train to its absolute blackest depths.

"Hello, Oliver."

Her husky voice was unmistakable, as was the discomfort that her cool, calculating stare triggered inside him.

"Hello, Nicola." He hoped she hadn't noticed how his facial features had been derailed for a fraction of a second.

"What?" Nierhoff seemed disappointed. "You know each other?"

"We certainly do." Nicola Engel got up and extended her hand to Bodenstein, which he shook briefly. In his mind, a movie of gloomy memories was playing, and a glance in Nicola's eyes revealed that she hadn't forgotten, either.

"We were at the Police Academy together," she explained to the astonished chief commissioner.

"Aha" was all he said. "Please take a seat, Bodenstein."

Bodenstein complied. He tried to recall his last meeting with the woman who was going to be his boss from now on.

". . . had brought up your name several times," the voice of the chief commissioner resounded in his ears. "But the Interior Ministry suggested we bring in someone from outside the Regional Criminal Unit. As far as I know, you're not too keen on accepting a position to become the head of this office. Politics are not really your forte."

At these words, Bodenstein thought he noticed a mocking glint in Nicola's eyes, and at that moment everything came back to him. It had happened about ten years ago. She'd been bogged down in a hopeless investigation of a series of grisly murders in the red-light district, which still remained unsolved. The whole K-11 office in Frankfurt had been under tremendous pressure. A snitch whom she'd persuaded to infiltrate one of the rival gangs had apparently been exposed by another snitch and was then shot to death on the street in broad daylight.

Bodenstein was certain to this day that the betrayal could be traced back to a grave mistake that Nicola had made. At the time, she'd been the head of another department inside K-11. Nicola, ambitious and ruthless, had wanted to pin the failure on Bodenstein's people. The power struggle had finally ended with the direct intervention of the police president. Nicola had then transferred from Frankfurt to Würzburg and had subsequently risen to vice president of the police presidium of Lower Franconia. She was considered competent and incorruptible. Now she had been made commissioner, and as of June 1, she would be Bodenstein's new boss. He had absolutely no idea what to make of this.

"Dr. Engel has already left her position in Würzburg, and I will be familiarizing her with our work here," Nierhoff said, concluding his speech, although Bodenstein had caught only fragments of it. "I will be officially introducing her to the whole team on Monday."

He looked at his department head expectantly, but Bodenstein offered no comments and asked no questions.

"Is that it?" he finally said, getting up. "I have to get back to my meeting."
Nierhoff nodded in consternation.

"Our K-Eleven has just about wrapped up the investigations into two homicide cases," he explained to his successor proudly, probably hoping that Bodenstein would support his claim.

Nicola Engel also got up and again held out her hand to Bodenstein.

"I look forward to working with you," she said, but the look in her eyes belied this statement. From now on, a new wind would be blowing at the Regional Criminal Unit; that was clear to Bodenstein. It remained to be seen how much Dr. Nicola Engel would interfere with his work.

"So do I," he replied, shaking her hand.

The meeting with the architect and the contractors had gone well. After a year of planning, the work on the Idstein Witch Tower would start next week. Marcus Nowak was in good spirits when he entered his office in the early evening. It was always an exciting moment when a project reached the imminent construction stage and things really got going. He sat down at his desk, switched on his computer, and looked through the day's mail. Among all the bills, offers, ads, and catalogs there was an envelope made of recycled paper, which usually didn't bode well.

He tore open the envelope, scanned the contents, and gasped in disbelief. It was a summons from the Kelkheim police. They were accusing him of negligent bodily harm. This couldn't possibly be true. Hot rage boiled up inside him, and he furiously crumpled up the letter and flung it into the wastebasket. At that moment, the phone on his desk rang. Tina. She must have seen him going into his office from the kitchen window. Reluctantly, he picked up the receiver. As he'd expected, he had to justify why he wasn't going to the open-air concert at the Kelkheim pool. Tina simply wouldn't accept that he didn't feel like it. She was upset, and while she was rattling off the usual accusations in a whiny voice, Marcus's cell beeped.

"I'll go with you next time," he promised his wife without meaning it, and flipped open his cell. "Really. Don't be mad. . . ."

When he read the incoming text, a delighted expression flitted across his face. Tina was still bitching and begging as he typed an answer with the thumb of his right hand.

ALL CLEAR, he wrote. BE AT YOUR PLACE NO LATER THAN 12. HAVE TO TAKE CARE OF SOMETHING FIRST. SEE YOU THEN.

Anticipation raced through his body. He would do it again. Tonight. The feeling of guilt that had tormented him so much was now no more than a faint echo somewhere deep inside him.

Friday, May 4

"We ought to notify the police." The executive housekeeper, Parveen Multani, was seriously concerned. "Something must have happened to her. All her medications are there. Really, Mrs. Kohlhaas, I have a bad feeling about this."

At 7:30 this morning, she had found out that one of her residents was missing, and there was no explanation for it. Renate Kohlhaas, the director of the elegant senior residence Taunusblick, was angry. Why did something like this have to happen today of all days? At eleven o'clock, she expected a delegation from the American head office to pay a visit for quality-control purposes. She wouldn't dream of calling the police, because she knew precisely what a devastating impression the unexplained disappearance of a resident under her authority would make on the company management.

"Let me worry about it," she said to Parveen with a soothing smile. "Go do your job, and please don't mention this to anyone. I'm sure we'll find Mrs. Frings soon."

"But wouldn't it be better—" began Parveen Multani, but the director cut her off with a wave of her hand.

"I'll take care of the matter myself." She escorted the anxious woman to the door, sat down at her computer, and pulled up the master file for the missing resident. Anita Frings had been living at Taunusblick for almost fifteen years. She was eighty-eight and for some time had been largely confined to a wheelchair because of severe arthritis. Although she had no relatives who might make trouble, all the alarm bells in the director's head began to go off when she read the name of the person to be notified in case of illness or death. Real problems might develop if the old woman did not return unscathed to sit in her apartment on the fourth floor.

"That's all we need," she murmured, grabbing the telephone. She had about two hours to find Anita Frings. At this moment, the police would definitely be the wrong choice.

Bodenstein was standing with his arms crossed in front of the big whiteboard in the conference room of K-11. Three names were printed on the board: David Goldberg, Herrmann Schneider, and Monika Krämer. And despite the bulletins announced on the local radio station, to which he'd agreed yesterday, there was still no trace of Robert Watkowiak. His eyes followed the arrows and circles that Fachinger had drawn with the marker. There were a few similarities. For instance, Goldberg and Schneider had both had close relations with the Kaltensee family; they'd been killed with the same weapon; and in their younger days, they had belonged to the SS. But that didn't take him any further. Bodenstein sighed. It was enough to drive him crazy. Where should he start? What reason could he present for another talk with Vera Kaltensee? Since the investigation of Goldberg's murder had been officially taken away from him, he couldn't very well mention the lab results or the DNA traces on the wineglass. It was not certain that Watkowiak's girlfriend had been killed by the same person who had shot Goldberg and Schneider. There were no eyewitnesses, no fingerprints, no evidence—except from Robert Watkowiak. He seemed to be the ideal perp: He had left traces at all the crime scenes, he had known all of the victims, and he needed money badly. Maybe he'd murdered Goldberg because the old man had refused to come up with any cash; maybe he'd killed Schneider because the old man had threatened to turn him in, and Monika Krämer because she'd been a liability. At first glance, everything seemed to fit perfectly. Only the murder weapon was missing.

The door opened. Bodenstein was not particularly surprised to see his future boss.

"Hello, Dr. Engel," he said politely.

"I thought you would prefer formality." She scrutinized him, raising her eyebrows. "All right, then. Hello, Mr. von Bodenstein."

"You can skip the 'von.' What can I do for you?"

Dr. Nicola Engel looked past him at the board and frowned.

"I thought the Goldberg and Schneider cases were solved."

"I'm afraid not."

"Chief Commissioner Nierhoff told me that the evidence against the man who killed his girlfriend was overwhelming."

"Watkowiak left some traces behind, that's all," Bodenstein replied. "The fact that he may have been at the crime scenes does not automatically make him a murderer in my eyes."

"But that's what it said in the morning papers."

"Don't believe everything you read."

Bodenstein and Engel stared at each other. Then she looked away, crossed her arms, and leaned back against a table.

"So all of you let your superior go to the press conference with incorrect information," she said. "Is there some special reason for that, or is it the custom around here?"

Bodenstein didn't react to this provocation.

"The information was not incorrect," he replied. "But unfortunately, it's not always possible to slow down the chief commissioner, especially when he considers it essential to have a quick, successful resolution to an investigation."

"Oliver, as the future leader of this unit, I want to know what's going on. So, why was there a press conference yesterday if the cases have not yet been cleared up?" Her voice sounded sharp and reminded Bodenstein unpleasantly of another case and another place. Nevertheless, he didn't want to cave in to her, even if she was going to be his boss.

"Because Nierhoff wanted it that way and he refused to listen to me," he replied in the same sharp tone. His expression was calm, almost indifferent. For a couple of seconds, they stared at each other. She backpedaled, trying for a calm voice.

"So you don't accept that all three persons were killed by the same perp?"

Bodenstein ignored her placating approach. As an experienced detective, he was well versed in interrogation techniques and was not thrown off by her switching from aggression to conciliation.

"Goldberg and Schneider were killed by the same person. My theory is that somebody didn't want us continuing with our investigations, so they tried to direct our suspicions to Watkowiak. We haven't located him yet, but at this point it's pure speculation."

Nicola Engel stepped over to the whiteboard. "So why did they take you off the Goldberg case?"

She was petite and delicate, yet she could have an intimidating effect on people. Bodenstein wondered how his colleagues—especially Behnke—would get along with the new boss. Bodenstein knew her well enough to realize that Dr. Engel would not be satisfied with written reports as Nierhoff had been. She had always been a perfectionist with a blatant desire to maintain control. She wanted to be kept informed at all times, and she was good at sniffing out intrigues behind the scenes.

"Somebody who has a lot of influence in the right places is afraid that something may come to light that should be kept hidden."

"And what might that be?"

"The fact that Goldberg was not a Jewish survivor of the Holocaust, but a former member of the SS. A blood-type tattoo on his arm clearly attests to that fact. Before they took the body away from us, I was able to order an autopsy."

Nicola Engel offered no comment about this revelation. She walked around the table and stopped at the end.

"Have you told Cosima that I'm going to be your new boss?" she asked in a casual manner. Bodenstein was not surprised by the abrupt change of subject. He had anticipated being confronted with the past sooner or later.

"Yes," he replied.

"And? What did she say?"

For a moment, he was tempted to tell her the less than flattering truth, but it wouldn't be smart to make an enemy of Nicola.

She misconstrued his hesitation. "You haven't told her a thing," she said with a triumphant flash in her eyes. "I thought so. Cowardice was always your biggest weakness. You really haven't changed at all."

The strong emotions behind these words both stunned and alarmed him. Working with Nicola Engel wasn't going to be easy. Before he could contradict her erroneous assessment, Ostermann appeared at the door. He gave Dr. Engel a quick look, but when Bodenstein made no move to introduce him to the woman, he made do with a polite nod in her direction.

"It's urgent," he said to Bodenstein.

"I'll be right there."

"Don't let me detain you, Mr. Bodenstein." Nicola Engel smiled contentedly like the cat who caught the canary. "I'm sure we'll be seeing plenty of each other."

The old woman was covered in blood and stark naked. Someone had bound her wrists and stuffed a stocking in her mouth.

"Execution-style shooting," said the medical examiner summoned by his uniformed colleagues who were first on the scene. "Time of death was about ten hours ago."

He pointed to the woman's naked legs.

"She was also shot in both knees."

"Thank you." Bodenstein grimaced. The person who had murdered Goldberg and Schneider had struck a third time. There was no doubt about that, because the number 11645 had been printed in blood on the victim's naked back. And the killer hadn't bothered to bury the body; the pap had apparently felt it important that the woman be found quickly.

"This time, he moved his victim into the open." Pia pulled on latex gloves, squatted down, and examined the corpse thoroughly. "I wonder why."

"She lived in the Taunusblick retirement home," the uniformed sergeant told them. "Obviously, he didn't want to risk anyone hearing the shots."

"How do you know where she lived?" Pia asked in astonishment.

"It's on the wheelchair." He pointed to a bush a few yards away, where the wheelchair was visible. Bodenstein studied the body, which a person out walking his dog had discovered. He felt a mixture of sympathy and helpless anger as he imagined how the old woman must have suffered in the last minutes of her long life, the fear and humiliation she must have felt. It upset him to think about this murderer, who was getting more and more sadistic, running around loose. This time, the perp had even risked being seen by someone. Once again, Bodenstein was overcome by an irritating sense of powerlessness. He didn't have the faintest idea how to tackle the problem. In the meantime, there had been four murders in the course of a week.

"It almost looks like we're dealing with a serial killer," said Pia at that moment, which just made matters worse. "The press is going to tear us to pieces if this keeps up."

A uniformed officer ducked under the crime-scene tape and nodded a greeting to Bodenstein.

"There's no missing persons report," he told the superintendent. "The evidence team is on the way."

Bodenstein nodded. "Thank you. We're going over to this retirement home and ask some questions. Maybe they haven't noticed yet that the woman is missing."

A little later when they entered the spacious foyer, Pia was flabbergasted to see the shining marble floor and the Bordeaux red carpet runners. The only retirement home she'd been inside was the nursing home in which her grandmother had spent the last years of her life. She remembered the linoleum floors, wooden handrails along the walls, and the smell of urine and disinfectant. The Taunusblick, on the other hand, seemed like a grand hotel, with its long reception counter of polished mahogany, fresh flowers everywhere, signs printed with golden letters, and soft music playing in the background. The young receptionist beamed at them as she asked how she might be of help.

"We'd like to speak with the director," said Bodenstein, showing his Kripo badge. The young woman stopped smiling and reached for the telephone.

"I'll tell Ms. Kohlhaas at once. Just one moment, please."

"Health insurance would never pay for a place like this," Pia whispered to her boss. "It's crazy."

"The Taunusblick is very expensive," said Bodenstein. "There are people who buy their way in twenty years before they're ready to move here. An apartment costs a good three thousand euros a month."

Pia thought about her grandmother and felt a pang of guilt. The nursing home in which she'd had to spend the last three years of her life was filled with patients suffering from dementia and others who were totally disabled. That was where she'd ended up after a productive life in full possession of her mental faculties, because it was the only place the family could afford. Pia was ashamed because she had visited her Oma so seldom, but the sight of the old people sitting in their bathrobes with lost, empty expressions had depressed her terribly. The carelessly prepared food, the loss of individuality, the less than satisfactory care by surly and chronically overworked staff members who never had time for personal conversations—a life shouldn't have to end like that. The people who could afford to spend their sunset years at the Taunusblick had probably been privileged all their lives. An example of yet one more injustice.

Before Pia could express any of these thoughts to her boss, the director appeared in the hall. Renate Kohlhaas was a thin woman in her late forties. She wore stylish rectangular glasses and an elegant pantsuit, and her hair was cut in a smooth pageboy. Her clothes reeked of cigarette smoke and her smile seemed nervous.

"How may I help you?" she asked politely.

"About an hour ago, someone walking in the wooded grounds of the Eichwald discovered the body of an elderly woman," replied Bodenstein. "Nearby was a wheelchair from Taunusblick. We'd like to know whether the deceased might be a resident here."

Pia noticed a flash of shock in the eyes of the director.

"As a matter of fact, we are missing one female resident," she admitted after a brief pause. "I have just notified the police after we searched the whole complex without result."

"What is the name of the missing woman?" Kirchhoff asked.

"Anita Frings. What happened?"

"We assume that she was the victim of a violent crime," said Bodenstein vaguely. "Could you help us with the identification?"

"I'm sorry, but . . ." The director seemed to notice how odd her refusal must seem, and her voice trailed off. Her eyes darted here and there, and she was getting more nervous.

"Ah, Ms. Multani!" she shouted suddenly with obvious relief as she motioned to a woman just emerging from the elevator. "Ms. Multani is our executive housekeeper and also our liaison for all the residents. She'll be able to assist you further."

The sharp look that the director gave her subordinate did not escape Kirchhoff's attention. Then the director made a swift departure, heels clacking. Kirchhoff introduced herself and her boss and extended her hand to Ms. Multani. She was an Asian beauty with shiny black hair, snow-white teeth, and sad-looking velvety eyes. As far as the male residents were concerned, her appearance alone no doubt sweetened the late autumn of their lives. In her simple dark blue suit and white blouse, she looked like a flight attendant from Cathay Pacific.

"Have you found Mrs. Frings?" she asked in slightly accented German. "She's been missing since early this morning."

"Is that right? Then why didn't you call the police earlier?" Kirchhoff asked. The housekeeper gave her a bewildered look, then turned in the direction the director had taken.

"But . . . Ms. Kohlhaas said . . . I mean, she wanted to inform the police at seven-thirty this morning."

"Then she must have forgotten. Obviously, she had more important things on her mind."

Ms. Multani hesitated but remained loyal.

"Today we're having an important visit from the Taunusblick head office," she said, trying to excuse the behavior of her superior. "But I am at your disposal."

"Oh my God." The executive housekeeper covered her mouth with both hands at the sight of the body. "Yes, that's Mrs. Frings. How horrible!"

"Come with me." Bodenstein took the shocked woman gently by the elbow and led her back to the forest path. The sergeant in charge had been right: The perp had committed the murder in the woods because at the retirement home too many people would have heard the shots. Bodenstein and Kirchhoff followed Ms. Multani back to the Taunusblick and took the elevator to the fourth floor, where Anita Frings's apartment was located. They were attempting to reconstruct how the killer must have proceeded this time. How had he managed to get the frail old lady out of the building unnoticed?

"Do you have any sort of surveillance system here?" Kirchhoff asked. "Any cameras?"

"No," replied Ms. Multani after a brief pause. "Many residents would prefer that we did, but so far the administration has not made a decision one way or the other."

She told them that there had been a big function at the Taunusblick the evening before—an open-air theater performance on the grounds with a fireworks display afterward. The event had been attended by many outside guests and visitors.

"What time were the fireworks?" Kirchhoff asked.

"About a quarter past eleven," Ms. Multani replied. Bodenstein and Kirchhoff exchanged a glance. As far as the time was concerned, it fit. The perp had used the opportunity to take the old lady into the woods under cover of darkness and then fired three shots from his pistol during the fireworks.

"When did you notice that Mrs. Frings was missing?" Kirchhoff asked.

Ms. Multani stopped in front of an apartment door. "I didn't see her at breakfast," she said. "Mrs. Frings was always one of the first to arrive. Although she was confined to a wheelchair, she put great store by her independence. I called her apartment, and when she didn't answer, I went looking for her."

"About what time was that?" Kirchhoff asked.

"To be honest, I'm no longer quite sure." The housekeeper's face had lost all color. "It must have been around seven-thirty or eight. I looked for her everywhere and then informed the director."

Kirchhoff glanced at her watch. It was eleven o'clock now. The discovery of a dead body had been reported around ten. But what had gone on during the three hours since eight o'clock? It made no sense to keep questioning Ms. Multani. The woman was completely devastated. She opened the door to the apartment and let Bodenstein and Kirchhoff inside. Pia stopped in the doorway to the living room and looked around. Light-colored wall-to-wall carpeting with a Persian rug in the middle, a plush couch with lacy cushions, a recliner facing the TV, a massive living room cabinet, and a sideboard with decorative carvings.

"Something's wrong here," she heard the housekeeper saying behind her. She was pointing at the cabinet. "There were always photos on the shelf, and the framed pictures on the wall are missing, too. And she kept her photo albums and document binders in the bookcase. They're all gone. How could that happen? I was here just this morning, and everything was the same as usual."

Pia remembered how fast the Goldberg case had been taken out of their hands. Was somebody trying to hush up something here, too? But who could have heard about the old lady's death so quickly?

"Why do you think the director didn't call the police right away after she was told that a resident was missing?" Kirchhoff asked.

The housekeeper shrugged. "I assumed that she would do it. She told me that she—" She broke off, shaking her head helplessly.

"Have you had break-ins here before?"

Kirchhoff's question obviously made Ms. Multani uncomfortable.

"The Taunusblick is an open facility," she replied evasively. "Residents can come and go as they like. We have nothing against visitors, and our restaurants and events are open to the public. So strict supervision is difficult."

Pia understood. The luxury of freedom had its price. There could be no question of enforcing strict security measures, and the hotel-like character of the residence made it vulnerable to criminal elements. She resolved to make inquiries about any reported break-ins or thefts at Taunusblick.

On his cell phone, Bodenstein requested that the evidence response team come to the apartment. Then he and Kirchhoff, accompanied by Ms. Multani, took the elevator down to the ground floor. The executive housekeeper told them that Anita Frings had been a resident for fifteen years. "In the past, she sometimes visited friends and stayed with them overnight," she said. "But she hasn't been able to do that in a long time."

"Did she have friends here?" Kirchhoff asked.

"No, not really," replied Ms. Multani after thinking it over. "She was very reserved and preferred to keep to herself."

The elevator stopped with a slight jolt. In the foyer, they found the director talking to a group of businessmen. Renate Kohlhaas seemed less than pleased by another encounter with Kripo, but she excused herself and came over to Bodenstein and Kirchhoff.

"I'm sorry, but I have very little time," she said. "We have visitors from our external inspection team. Once a year, Taunusblick undergoes a quality assessment in order to maintain certification for the care and services that we offer here."

"We won't keep you long," Kirchhoff assured her. "The body that was discovered was that of your resident Anita Frings."

"Yes, I heard. It's horrible."

The director made an effort to display the appropriate sadness, but she was mostly irritated because the murder of one of her residents was going to cause so much trouble. She was probably concerned about damage to the image of their elegant retirement home if the details of the woman's death were made public. She led Bodenstein and Kirchhoff into a small room behind the reception desk.

"Is there something else I can do for you?"

"Why did you wait so long before notifying the police?" Kirchhoff asked.

Ms. Kohlhaas gave her an angry look. "I don't understand what you mean," she replied. "After Ms. Multani informed me that Mrs. Frings was missing, I called the police immediately."

"Your housekeeper told us that she reported Mrs. Frings missing between seven-thirty and eight," Bodenstein interjected. "But we were first informed about the body around ten o'clock."

"It was not seven-thirty or eight," the director countered. "Ms. Multani told me about Mrs. Frings at about nine-fifteen."

"Are you sure?" Kirchhoff was skeptical but couldn't explain why Ms. Kohlhaas might have delayed her call to the police by nearly two hours.

"Of course I'm sure," retorted the director.

"Have you informed Mrs. Frings's relatives?" Bodenstein asked. Ms. Kohlhaas hesitated for a couple of seconds.

"Mrs. Frings had no relatives," she said at last.

"No one at all?" asked Kirchhoff, digging deeper. "There must be some-one you would inform in the event of her death. An attorney or an acquain-tance."

"Naturally, I asked my secretary at once to look up the relevant telephone numbers," replied the director. "But there is no one. I'm sorry."

Pia let the subject drop.

"According to your housekeeper, there are various objects missing from Mrs. Frings's apartment," she went on. "Who could have stolen them?"

"That's impossible." Renate Kohlhaas was indignant. "No one would steal anything here."

"Who has a key to the residents' apartments?" Kirchhoff asked.

"The residents themselves, the executive housekeeper, possibly relatives," replied the director with obvious displeasure. "I hope you aren't insinuating anything about Ms. Multani. After all, she was the only one who knew that Mrs. Frings was missing."

"You knew it, too," replied Kirchhoff, unmoved. Renate Kohlhaas turned first red, then pale.

"I'll pretend I didn't hear that," she said icily. "Now if you'll excuse me, I have to take care of my visitors."

In the apartment belonging to Mrs. Frings, there were no longer any personal items that might give some clue about the life of this woman who had spent the last fifteen years within these four walls—no photos, no letters, no dia-ries. Bodenstein and Kirchhoff could make no sense of it. Who would be in-terested in the possessions of a woman who was eighty-eight years old?

"We ought to assume that Mrs. Frings knew Goldberg and Schneider," Bodenstein said. "This number or date means something that we don't yet understand. And it's probable that she also knew Vera Kaltensee."

"So why, if Anita Frings had been missing since early morning, did the director delay her call to the police?" Pia wondered out loud. "She's acting funny, and I don't think it's only because she has important visitors."

"What could she possibly gain from the death of Mrs. Frings?"

"A generous bequest to the retirement home?" Pia conjectured. "Maybe she had the apartment cleared out so that there would be no trace of potential heirs."

"But she couldn't have known whether Mrs. Frings was actually dead or not," Bodenstein countered.

They went to the director's office. A fat little woman on the far side of fifty sat enthroned in the anteroom. With her bleached-blond hairdo plastered with hair spray, she looked like a member of the bubbly Jacob Sisters pop group, but she turned out to be a regular Cerberus.

"I'm sorry," she intoned. "The director isn't in, and I'm not allowed to give you any information about a resident."

"Then call Ms. Kohlhaas and get permission," said Pia brusquely. Her patience had run out. "We don't have all day."

Unimpressed, the secretary scrutinized Pia over the top of her reading glasses, which were attached to an old-fashioned gold chain.

"We're having a visit from top management today," she replied coolly. "Ms. Kohlhaas is occupied elsewhere in the building. I can't reach her."

"When will she be back?"

"At about three o'clock." The secretary was intransigent. Bodenstein intervened with a winning smile.

"I know that we've come at an inconvenient time, since such important visitors are on-site," he said, attempting to appease the outer-office dragon. "But a resident was abducted last night and brutally murdered. We need the address or phone number of a relative in order to inform them of her death. If you help us, we won't have to bother Ms. Kohlhaas."

Bodenstein's courteous manner succeeded where Pia's gruff style had not. The old warhorse turned soft as butter.

"I can look up all the necessary information in Mrs. Frings's file," she chirped.

"That would be an immense help to us." Bodenstein winked at her. "And if you happen to have a recent photo of Mrs. Frings, we'll be on our way at once."

"You are so slimy," Pia murmured, and Bodenstein flashed her a surreptitious grin. The secretary typed away on her keyboard, and seconds later two pages slid out of the laser printer.

"There you are." She beamed at Bodenstein and handed him one of the sheets. "That should help you out."

"What's on the second page?" Kirchhoff asked.

"That's internal information," said the secretary regally. When Kirchhoff held out her hand, she performed a deft left-handed twist and with a smug smile fed the page into the shredder. "I have my instructions."

"And in an hour, I'll be back with a search warrant," said Pia furiously. Maybe it wouldn't be as desirable as it had first seemed to spend her golden years in this retirement home.

"The items are on the way," Elard announced. "Shortly after twelve at your parents' old house. Is that all right?"

Katharina glanced at her watch.

"Yes, perfect. Thanks a lot," she said. "I'll call Thomas now so that he can come over. Do you think we'll find anything useful?"

"I'm sure you will. Among other things, there are nine of Vera's diaries."

"Really? Then the rumor must be true."

"I'll be glad when I'm out of all this. So, I hope you'll—"

"Just a sec," said Katharina before Elard could finish his sentence. "Who do you think shot the two old guys?"

"It's now three," Elard informed her.

"Three?" Katharina straightened up.

"Oh, you haven't heard?" Elard sounded almost gleeful, as if he'd been given a chance to tell a funny anecdote. "Last night, our dear Anita was murdered. Execution-style. Like the other two."

"The news doesn't seem to be breaking your heart," Katharina replied.

"You're right. I couldn't stand any of them."

"Me, neither. But you know that already."

"Goldberg, Schneider, and dear Anita," said Elard dreamily. "Now the only one left is Vera."

His tone made Katharina sit up and take notice. Could it have been Elard who had shot his mother's three closest and oldest friends? He certainly had the motive. He'd always been treated as an outsider in the family, more tolerated than loved by his mother.

"Do you have any idea who could have done it?" she asked again.

"I'm afraid not," said Elard at once. "But I don't really care. Whoever did it, he should have done it thirty years ago."

By early afternoon, Pia had spoken with about twenty residents of the Taunusblick who, according to Ms. Multani, had been in close contact with Mrs. Frings, and also with some of the staff. All of it had produced less than satisfactory results, including the extract from the file that Bodenstein had begged for from the receptionist. Anita Frings had no children or grandchildren and seemed to have been torn from a life in which she had left behind no visible traces. It was depressing to think that no one would miss her and no relatives would mourn her death. A human life had simply been extinguished and was already forgotten. Her apartment at Taunusblick would be renovated and immediately rented to the next person on the waiting list. But Pia was determined to find out more about the old lady, and she wasn't going to let a pompous secretary and an uncooperative director stop her. She planted herself in the entry hall with a direct view of the door to the director's office, preparing to wait. After three-quarters of an hour, she was rewarded: The Cerberus apparently felt the call of nature and left the office without shutting the door.

Pia knew that the unauthorized confiscation of evidence was strictly against police regulations, but she didn't care. Making sure that she was not observed, she crossed the hall and entered the outer office. In a few steps, she was behind the desk and opening the shredder. The old witch hadn't destroyed very much today. Pia gathered the shredded paper from the bin and stuffed it under her T-shirt. In less than sixty seconds, she left the office, sauntered through the entry hall, and walked out the door. She proceeded along the edge of the woods to her car, which she had parked near the site where the body had been found.

When she opened the driver's door to her car and pulled out the prickly paper shreds from under her T-shirt, she realized that Christoph's place was just a couple of hundred yards away. He'd been gone for only twenty-four hours, but she missed him so much that it hurt. Pia was glad for the distraction that her work offered at the moment, so she didn't have time to worry about what Christoph might be doing with his evenings in South Africa. The buzz of her cell phone startled her out of her reverie. Although Bodenstein had admonished her many times not to talk on the phone while driving, she took the call.

"Pia, it's me, Miriam." Her friend sounded troubled. "Have you got a minute?"

"Yes, I do. Did something happen?"

"I don't know yet. Listen. I told Oma what I discovered at the institute and about my suspicion that Goldberg had altered his life story. She gave me a funny look; I thought at first she was mad at me, but then she asked me why I wanted to rummage around in Goldberg's past. I hope you're not angry that I told her."

"If it gives us a lead, of course not." Pia clamped the cell between her shoulder and chin so she could free her hand to shift gears.

"Well, Oma told me that she and Sarah, Goldberg's wife, had gone to school together in Berlin. They were very good friends. Sarah's family emigrated to the States in 1936, after Sarah had a bad experience with three drunken boys. Oma said that Sarah hadn't looked Jewish at all; she was big and blond, and all the boys were crazy about her. One evening, they were at the movies, and on the way home the three guys were rude to her. It would have turned out badly if a young SS man hadn't intervened. He escorted her home, and as thanks for rescuing her, Sarah gave him the medallion from her necklace. She met the man in secret a few more times, but then her family left Berlin. Eleven years later, she saw this medallion again—on a Jew named David Josua Goldberg, who was standing right in front of her in her father's bank in New York! Sarah recognized her former rescuer at once and married him not long after. Except for Oma, she never told anybody about her husband's true identity."

Pia listened to the story in silence and with growing incredulity. It was final proof of the great lie about the life of David Goldberg, a lie that over the decades had taken on enormous proportions.

"Can your Oma still remember his real name?" she asked excitedly.

"Vaguely," Miriam said. "Otto or Oskar, she thinks. But she knows that he was at the SS officers' school in Bad Tölz and a member of Adolf Hitler's personal bodyguard. I'm sure it's possible to find out more about something like that."

"Damn, Miri, you're a wonder." Pia grinned. "What else did your Oma tell you?"

"She never cared much for Goldberg," Miriam went on in a shaky voice. "But she had to swear to Sarah by all that was holy never to say a word. Sarah didn't want her sons to learn anything about their father's past."

"But evidently they did know about it," said Pia. "That must be the reason why his son appeared with such reinforcements the day after Goldberg died."

"Maybe it was for religious reasons," Miriam countered. "Or because Goldberg really did have the best-possible connections in the world. Oma remembers that he had several passports, and even during the coldest phase of the Cold War, he was able to travel freely throughout the Eastern Bloc." She paused. "Do you know what really shocks me about the whole thing?" she asked, then answered her own question. "Not the fact that he wasn't a Jew, but a former Nazi. Who knows how I would have acted in his situation? The will to survive is human nature. But what genuinely upsets me is that someone can keep a secret like that for sixty years . . ."

Until he landed on Henning Kirchhoff's dissection table, thought Pia, but she didn't say it out loud.

" . . . and that there was only one person in the whole world who knew the truth."

Pia certainly doubted that. There were at least two other people who knew the truth: the person who had killed Goldberg, Schneider, and Anita Frings, and the person who wanted to prevent the whole story from coming out.

Thomas Ritter took a drag of his cigarette and cast a sullen glance at the clock. Quarter past twelve. Katharina had called him and told him to be at the parking lot in front of the Luxemburg Castle in Königstein at eleven. Somebody would show up there and give him something. He'd been punctual and had been waiting now for a whole wasted hour, getting more and more annoyed. Ritter knew full well that the manuscript had weaknesses, but he was insulted by Katharina's comment that his work was of no commercial value. No scandalous revelations, no best-seller potential. Damn it! Now Katharina had promised to get hold of some new material, but he couldn't imagine what she could pull out of her hat on such short notice. Did she have proof that Eugen Kaltensee's fatal accident was murder after all? In any case, Katharina's sales manager was planning a first printing of 150,000 copies. The publishing house's marketing people were planning strategy, scheduling interviews with the biggest German magazines, and negotiating with a major tabloid about an exclusive prepublication excerpt. All of this was putting Ritter under enormous pressure.

He flicked his cigarette out the open window with the other butts he'd already smoked and met the punishing gaze of a grandmother dragging her old and infirm poodle behind her. An orange Mercedes flatbed truck turned into the parking lot and stopped. The driver got out and looked around, searching for something. Astonished, Ritter recognized Marcus Nowak, the contractor, who two years before had restored to its original condition the old mill on the Kaltensee estate of Mühlenhof, and as thanks had been slandered and duped. Because of him, a disagreement with Vera had resulted, which, in turn, had ruined Ritter's life overnight, turning him into an outcast. Nowak had spotted him and came over.

"Hello," he said, standing next to Ritter's car.

"What do you want?" Ritter gave him a suspicious look and made no move to get out of the car. He had no desire to be drawn into anything else by Nowak.

"I'm supposed to give you something," Nowak said, visibly nervous. "And I also know someone who can tell you more about Vera Kaltensee. Follow me in your car."

Ritter hesitated. He knew that Nowak was a victim of the Kaltensee family, just as he was, but he still didn't trust him. What did this man have to do with the information that Katharina had promised? He couldn't allow any mistakes, especially not now during this extremely sensitive phase of his plan. And yet he was curious. He took a deep breath and noticed that his hands were shaking. No big deal. He needed this material; Katharina had claimed it was sensational. Marleen wouldn't be home for a couple of hours yet, and he had nothing better to do. So having a conversation with this person whom Nowak knew couldn't hurt.

Bodenstein's sister-in-law Marie-Louise squinted as she looked at the fuzzy black-and-white photo that Renate Kohlhaas's secretary had provided.

"Who's this supposed to be?" she asked.

"Is it possible that this woman was at Vera Kaltensee's birthday party last Saturday?" Bodenstein asked. Pia had suggested the idea of questioning the staff of the Schlosshotel. She was firmly convinced that the murderer wasn't killing at random and that there was some connection between Anita Frings and Vera Kaltensee.

"I'm not sure," replied Marie-Louise. "Why do you want to know?"

"The woman was found dead this morning," he said, realizing his sister-in-law wouldn't give up until she found out what this was about.

"Then it could hardly have had anything to do with our food."

"Of course not. So, what do you think?"

Marie-Louise examined the photo again and shrugged. "If it's all right with you, I'll ask the serving staff," she said. "Come with me. Would you like a bite to eat?"

It was impossible for Bodenstein to refuse this tempting offer. When it came to food, he suffered from regularly recurring attacks of a shocking lack of discipline. He followed his sister-in-law eagerly into the huge restaurant kitchen, which was already buzzing with activity. It took several hours each day to prepare the extravagant culinary creations of Maître Jean-Yves St. Clair, but the result was sensational every time.

"Hello, Papa." In Bodenstein's opinion, Rosalie was standing much too close to the great chef, and her cheeks were much too flushed. St. Clair was not above chopping the vegetables himself. He looked up and grinned.

"Ah, Olivier! Is the Kripo now checking on gastronomy?"

More likely checking on thirty-five-year-old star chefs who turn the heads of nineteen-year-old apprentices, thought Bodenstein, but he said nothing. As far as he knew, St. Clair always behaved with complete propriety toward Rosalie—to her deep regret. Bodenstein chatted with the Frenchman and asked about Rosalie's progress. In the meantime, Marie-Louise had fixed up a plate of all sorts of delicacies, and as he munched on an unbelievable selection of lobster, sweetbreads, and blood sausage, she showed the photo to her staff.

"Yes, she was there on Saturday," a young woman from the serving staff reminded her. "The old woman in the wheelchair."

Rosalie also took a look at the picture. "That's right," she confirmed. "All you had to do was ask Oma; she sat right next to her."

"Oh, really?" Bodenstein took back the photo.

"Why are you asking about her?" Rosalie asked curiously.

"Rosalie! Do I have to wash all these vegetables by myself?" St. Clair roared from the depths of the kitchen, and the girl vanished like lightning. Bodenstein and his sister-in-law exchanged glances.

"Apprentice years are no picnic." Marie-Louise permitted herself an amused smile before she again frowned as she remembered something that she still had to do before the service really got going in an hour. Bodenstein thanked her for the snack and, much fortified, left the Schloss Bodenstein.

Professor Elard Kaltensee made excuses for his mother when Bodenstein appeared at Mühlenhof in the early evening. The news of the violent death of her friend had affected her so much that she'd accepted a sleeping pill from her doctor and was now asleep.

"But do come in." Kaltensee gave the impression he'd been just about to leave the house, yet he didn't seem in a hurry. "May I offer you something to drink?"

Bodenstein followed him into the salon and politely declined the offer of a drink. His gaze wandered to the windows. He could see armed security men patrolling in pairs.

"I see you've increased your security precautions considerably," he remarked. "Is there some reason for that?"

Elard Kaltensee poured himself a cognac and remained standing behind an easy chair, an absent expression on his face. The death of Anita Frings obviously had moved him as little as that of Goldberg or Schneider, but something was on his mind. The hand holding the cognac glass was shaking, and he looked bleary-eyed.

"My mother suffers from paranoia. Now she thinks that she'll be the next one lying in the front hall with a bullet in the back of her head. That's why my brother called out his troops."

Bodenstein was amazed at the cynicism audible in Kaltensee's voice.

"What can you tell me about Anita Frings?" he asked.

"Not much." Kaltensee's bloodshot eyes were pensive. "She was a childhood friend of my mother from East Prussia, and she lived in East Germany. Her husband died a few years after the Wall fell, and she moved into the Taunusblick."

"When was the last time you saw her?"

"On Saturday at my mother's birthday party. I'd never spoken with her all that much, so it would be an exaggeration to say that I knew her well."

Elard Kaltensee took a swallow of his cognac.

"Unfortunately, we have no idea which direction to take in our investigation of the murders of Schneider and Anita Frings," Bodenstein admitted. "It would be a great help if you could tell me more about your mother's friends. Who might have something to gain from the death of these three elderly individuals?"

"I really don't know," replied Kaltensee with polite disinterest.

"Goldberg and Schneider were killed with the same weapon," Bodenstein said. "The ammunition was vintage World War Two. And at all three murder scenes, the number one one six four five was left behind. We assume that it's a date, but we don't know why it's significant. What does the date January sixteenth, 1945, mean to you?"

Bodenstein observed the neutral expression of the man standing in front of him and waited in vain for some sign of emotion.

"On January sixteenth, 1945, Magdeburg was obliterated in an Allied bombing raid," said Kaltensee, now speaking as the historian he was. "On that day, Hitler left his secret headquarters in the Wetterau valley and moved with his staff to the bunker underneath the Reich Chancellery, which is where he would die."

He paused for a moment.

"In January 1945, my mother and I fled from East Prussia. Whether it was precisely on the sixteenth, I don't know."

"Do you remember that time?"

"Only vaguely. I have no vivid memories because I was so young. Sometimes I think that some of my memories are really the result of watching films and TV documentaries over the years."

"How old were you then, if I may ask?"

"You may." Kaltensee turned the now-empty glass in his hands. "I was born on August twenty-third, 1943."

"Then you could hardly remember much," said Bodenstein. "You were less than two years old."

"Strange, isn't it? Though I've been back to my old homeland several times since then. Maybe I'm just imagining it all."

Bodenstein wondered whether Elard Kaltensee knew about Goldberg's secret. He was having a hard time reading this man. Suddenly, he had an idea.

"Did you actually know your biological father?" he asked, and he couldn't miss the astonishment that flitted across Kaltensee's face.

"Why do you ask?"

"You can't be the son of Eugen Kaltensee."

"That's true. My mother never found it necessary to tell me the identity of my progenitor. I was adopted by my stepfather when I was five years old."

"What was your name before that?"

"Zeydlitz-Lauenburg. Like my mother. She wasn't married."

Somewhere in the house, a clock struck the hour with seven melodious chimes.

"Could Goldberg have been your father?" Bodenstein asked. Kaltensee managed a pained smile.

"For God's sake! What a horrible thought."

"Why?"

Elard Kaltensee turned to the sideboard and poured himself another cognac. "Goldberg couldn't stand me," he said. "And the feeling was mutual."

Bodenstein waited for him to go on, but he did not.

"How did your mother happen to know him?" he asked.

"He was probably from a nearby town. He went to secondary school with my mother's brother, after whom I was named."

"That's odd," said Bodenstein. "Then your mother must have known the truth."

"What do you mean?"

"That in reality Goldberg was not a Jew."

"Excuse me?" Kaltensee's surprise seemed genuine.

"During the autopsy, a blood-type tattoo was found on his upper left arm—a tattoo only members of the SS had."

Kaltensee stared at Bodenstein, and a vein was throbbing at his temple. "Which would have made it even worse, had he been my father," he said without a trace of a smile.

"We assume that this was the reason the Goldberg case was taken out of our hands," Bodenstein went on. "Somebody is interested in keeping Goldberg's true identity secret. But who?"

Elard Kaltensee didn't reply. The shadows under his bloodshot eyes seemed to have deepened; he looked quite ill. He sank down heavily into an easy chair and rubbed his face.

"Do you think that your mother knew Goldberg's secret?"

Kaltensee thought over this possibility for a moment.

"Who knows?" he said bitterly. "A woman who refuses to tell her son the identity of his biological father would certainly be capable of playing a role for sixty years."

Elard Kaltensee did not like his mother. But why, then, did he continue to live under the same roof with her? Was he hoping that one day she would disclose his true origin? Or was there more behind it? And if so, what?

"Schneider was in the SS, too," said Bodenstein. "The basement of his house is a regular Nazi museum. He also had the same type of tattoo."

Elard Kaltensee stared mutely into space, and Bodenstein would have given much more than a penny for his thoughts.

Pia spread out the paper from the retirement home's shredder on the kitchen table and got to work. She meticulously smoothed out one strip of paper after another, placing them next to one another, but the damned strips kept curling up under her fingers and stubbornly refused to reveal their secret. Pia felt herself starting to sweat. Patience had never been her strong point, and after a while she had to admit that what she was doing was pointless. She scratched her head as she considered how to make the work easier. Her eyes fell on her four dogs, then on the clock. It would be better if she took care of the dogs before she threw a fit and stuffed the whole pile of shredded paper into the trash can. Actually she'd planned to clean up the pile of dirty shoes, jackets, buckets, and horse halters on the porch this evening, but that would have to wait.

Pia marched to the stable, mucked out the stalls, and scattered fresh straw on the floor. Then she brought in the horses from the paddock. Soon it would be time to harvest the hay, if the weather didn't thwart her plans. And the grassy borders along her driveway hadn't been mowed in a long time. When she opened the door to the feed room, two cats appeared out of nowhere. They had decided a couple of months before to take up immediate residence at Birkenhof. The black tomcat jumped up on the shelf over the workbench where Pia mixed the feed. Before she could stop him, he'd knocked off a whole row of bottles and cans and then leaped down to find a new hiding place.

"You rascal!" she shouted after the cat. She bent down, and when she picked up the bottle of Mane 'n Tail spray, she had a bright idea. She hurried to feed the dogs, cats, chickens, and horses and then ran back into the house. She emptied the rest of the spray into the sink and filled the bottle with water. Then she placed the strips of paper on a kitchen towel, combed through them with her fingers, and sprayed them with water. Finally she covered them with another towel. Maybe her efforts would be fruitless, maybe not. But the antics of the director's secretary at Taunusblick had awakened her mistrust. She wondered if the woman had noticed that somebody had emptied the shredder. Pia giggled at the thought and went to look for her steam iron.

In the past, when she was married to Henning, everything had always been in its proper place, and the cabinets had all been neatly arranged. Here at Birkenhof, chance ruled. After two and a half years, Pia still hadn't unpacked some of her moving boxes. Something else always seemed to come up that required her attention. At last, she found the steam iron in the bedroom cabinet and set about ironing the damp paper strips. In the meantime, she ate a helping of microwaved veggie lasagna and a prepackaged salad, both of which gave only the illusion of vitamin-rich, healthy nutrition, but they were still better than a Turkish *döner* or junk food. Putting the strips back together demanded all the patience and fine motor skills that Pia possessed. She kept swearing at her clumsiness and shaky fingers, but at last she did it.

"Thank you, dear tomcat!" she murmured with a grin. The page contained sensitive medical information about Anita Frings, née Willumat, including her last address in Potsdam, before she moved into the Taunusblick. At first, Pia couldn't understand why the secretary hadn't simply handed over the page, but then she caught sight of a name. She glanced at the kitchen clock. Not too late to call Bodenstein.

Bodenstein's cell, which he had turned off, vibrated in the inner pocket of his jacket. He pulled it out and saw his colleague's name on the display. Elard Kaltensee was still sitting there mute, the empty cognac glass in his hand, staring into the middle distance.

"Yes?" Bodenstein answered in a low voice.

"Boss, I found out something." Pia Kirchhoff sounded excited. "Have you seen Vera Kaltensee yet?"

"I'm here right now."

"Ask her how she knew about Anita Frings's death and when she heard about it. I'm anxious to hear what she says. Vera Kaltensee is listed in Taunus-blick's computer as the person to be informed in an emergency. She was Anita Frings's legal guardian and also paid for her expenses at the home. Do you recall the housekeeper being surprised that nobody had informed us? I'm certain the director phoned Vera Kaltensee first to get instructions."

Bodenstein listened closely, wondering how Pia had learned all this.

"Maybe she wasn't allowed to tell us sooner because the Kaltensees wanted to get Mrs. Frings's apartment cleared out first for security reasons."

A car rolled by the window, then a second one. Tires crunched on the gravel.

"I have to go," Bodenstein said. "I'll call you back soon."

Seconds later, the door to the salon opened, and a tall dark-haired woman came in, followed by Siegbert Kaltensee. Elard Kaltensee remained in his easy chair, not even looking up.

"Good evening, Mr. Chief Detective Inspector." Siegbert Kaltensee held out his hand to Bodenstein, smiling briefly. "May I introduce my sister, Jutta?"

In the flesh, she seemed quite different from the tough politician that Bodenstein knew only from TV. More feminine, prettier, and, yes, unexpectedly sexy. Although she wasn't really his type of woman, he felt attracted to her at first sight. Before she could even extend her hand, Bodenstein had already undressed her with his eyes and imagined her naked. His indecent thoughts embarrassed him, and he almost blushed under the searching gaze from her blue eyes. She was also assessing him, and she seemed to like what she saw.

"My mother has told me a lot about you. I'm happy to finally meet you in person." She smiled earnestly, taking Bodenstein's hand and holding it a moment longer than necessary. "Even though the circumstances are sad."

"Actually, I'd like to speak with your mother briefly." Bodenstein made a concerted effort to suppress the internal upheaval that the sight of her had triggered in him. "But your brother told me that she is indisposed."

"Anita was Mama's oldest friend." Jutta Kaltensee released his hand and sighed, looking concerned. "The events of the past few days have really taken a toll on her. I'm getting seriously worried about her. Mama is no longer as robust as she might seem. Who would do such a thing?"

"In order to find out, I'm going to need your help," Bodenstein said. "Would you have a moment to answer a few questions for me?"

"Of course," said Siegbert and Jutta Kaltensee in unison. Quite unexpectedly, their brother Elard awoke from his state of listless brooding. He got up, set the empty glass on a little side table, and directed his bloodshot gaze at his siblings, who were both a head shorter than he was.

"Did you know that Goldberg and Schneider were in the SS?" Elard said.

Siegbert Kaltensee reacted with only a brief raise of his eyebrows, but Bodenstein thought he saw an expression of shock on his sister's face.

"Uncle Jossi a Nazi? Nonsense." She laughed incredulously and shook her head. "What are you talking about, Elard? You're not drunk, are you?"

"I haven't been more sober in years." Seething with hatred, Elard Kaltensee stared first at his sister, then at his brother. "Maybe that's why I'm so upset. I can stand this hypocritical family only when I'm drunk."

Jutta was obviously embarrassed by her elder brother's behavior. She gave Bodenstein an apologetic look and smiled.

"They both had blood-type tattoos, as was customary in the SS," Elard Kaltensee went on with a gloomy expression. "And the longer I think about it, the more sure I am that it's the truth. Especially Goldberg, who—"

"Is that true?" Jutta asked, looking at Bodenstein.

"Yes, it's true," he confirmed. "The tattoos were discovered during the autopsies."

"That just can't be!" She turned to her brother Siegbert, grabbing his hand as if seeking refuge with him. "I mean, with Herrmann it wouldn't surprise me, but never Uncle Jossi."

Elard Kaltensee opened his mouth to protest, but his brother beat him to it.

"Have you found Robert?" Siegbert asked.

"No, we haven't tracked him down yet." Following a vague hunch, Bodenstein didn't mention the brutal murder of Monika Krämer to the Kaltensees. He had noticed that Elard Kaltensee hadn't bothered to ask about Watkowiak.

"Oh, Mr. Kaltensee," he said, turning to the professor. "When and from whom did you learn of the death of Anita Frings?"

"My mother got a call this morning," replied Elard. "Around seven-thirty. Apparently, Anita had disappeared from her room. A couple of hours later, we got the news that she was dead."

Bodenstein was astounded by this honest answer. Either the professor didn't have enough presence of mind to lie or he was truly guileless. Maybe Pia Kirchhoff was mistaken and the Kaltensees had nothing whatsoever to do with the old lady's disappearance.

"How did your mother react?"

Elard Kaltensee's cell phone rang. He glanced at the display and his expression instantly livened up.

"Please excuse me," he said. "I have to go to the city. An important appointment."

And then he left without saying good-bye or shaking hands. Jutta watched him go with a shake of her head. "He goes for girls that are barely half his age—but they tend to wear him out," she remarked derisively. "After all, he's no longer the youngest guy in the room."

"Elard is going through an identity crisis at the moment," explained Siegbert Kaltensee. "Please forgive his behavior. Ever since he was made professor emeritus six months ago, he's fallen into a deep funk."

Bodenstein studied the siblings, who despite their age difference seemed to be very close. Siegbert Kaltensee was difficult to read. Attentive, almost excessively polite—and he gave no clue as to his real feelings about his older brother.

"When did you find out about Mrs. Frings's death?" asked Bodenstein.

"Elard called me about ten-thirty." Siegbert frowned at the memory. "I was in Stockholm on a business trip and caught the next plane home."

His sister sat down on a chair, took a pack of cigarettes out of the pocket of her blazer, lit one, and inhaled deeply.

"Bad habit." She winked at Bodenstein conspiratorially. "Just don't tell my voters about it. Or my mother."

"I promise." Bodenstein nodded and smiled at her. Siegbert Kaltensee poured himself a bourbon and also offered Bodenstein a drink, which he once again refused.

"Elard sent me a text message about it," said Jutta. "I was in a plenary session and had turned off my cell."

Bodenstein strolled over to a sideboard to look at a number of family photos in silver frames.

"Are there any suspects? Do you have any idea who could have committed the three murders?" Siegbert Kaltensee asked.

Bodenstein shook his head. "Unfortunately, we don't," he said. "You knew the three of them well. Who would gain from their deaths?"

"No one at all," Jutta Kaltensee said, puffing on her cigarette. "They've never harmed a living soul. Of course, I remember Uncle Jossi only as an old man, but he was always very nice to me. He never forgot to bring me a present," she mused with a smile.

"Do you remember that gaucho saddle, Berti?" she asked her brother. He made a face at the mention of his childhood nickname.

"I think I was eight or nine and could hardly lift the thing. But my pony had to bear it. . . ."

"You were ten," Siegbert Kaltensee said, correcting his younger sister with affection. "And I was the first to carry you through the living room wearing that saddle—not your pony."

"That's right. My big brother always did anything I wanted."

The emphasis was on the word *anything*. She exhaled cigarette smoke through her nose and gave Bodenstein a smile that conveyed more than idle curiosity. He suddenly felt hot.

"Occasionally," she added without taking her eyes off him, "I have that sort of effect on men."

"Jossi Goldberg was a very congenial and friendly person," Siegbert Kaltensee now commented as he went over to join his sister, holding a glass of bourbon in his hand. The two took turns speaking and gave a completely different picture of Goldberg and Schneider than Elard had done. Everything they said sounded quite natural, and yet Bodenstein felt like a spectator at a play.

"Herrmann and his wife were very dear people." Jutta Kaltensee stubbed out her cigarette in an ashtray. "Really. I liked them a lot. I first got to know Anita in the late eighties. I was very surprised that in his will my father had left her a share in the company. Unfortunately, I can't tell you much about her."

She stood up.

"Anita was our mother's oldest friend," Siegbert Kaltensee added. "They'd known each other since they were little girls, and they never lost contact, although Anita lived in East Germany until the Wall came down."

"I see." Bodenstein picked up one of the framed photos and looked at it thoughtfully.

"My parents' wedding photo." Jutta Kaltensee came up next to him and picked up another picture. "And here . . . Oh, Berti, did you know that Mama had framed this one?"

She grinned with amusement, and her brother smiled, too.

"That was after Elard graduated," he explained. "I hate that picture."

Bodenstein could see why. Elard Kaltensee was about eighteen in the photo. He was tall, slim, and good-looking in a dark sort of way. His younger brother seemed like a little round piglet in the picture, with sparse, colorless hair and fat cheeks.

"That's me on my seventeenth birthday." Jutta tapped on another picture and glanced at Bodenstein. "Slender and sylphlike. Mama dragged me to the doctor back then because she thought I was anorexic. Unfortunately, I have no proclivities in that direction."

She ran both hands over her hips and giggled. Bodenstein could find no fault with her curves. In astonishment, he realized that with this casual gesture she had succeeded in directing his attention to her body, as if she knew what he was imagining at the sight of her. Bodenstein was still wondering whether she'd done this on purpose as she pointed to another photo. Jutta and a young woman with black hair, both in their mid-twenties, were beaming at the camera. "My best friend, Katharina," she explained. "And that's Kati and me in Rome. Everybody called us 'the twins' because we were inseparable."

Bodenstein looked at the picture. Jutta's friend looked like a photo model. Next to her, the younger version of Jutta seemed like a gray mouse. Bodenstein tapped on another photo, which showed a youthful Jutta with a man of about the same age. "Who's that next to you?" he asked.

"Robert," replied Jutta. She was standing so close to Bodenstein that he could smell her perfume and a hint of cigarette smoke. "We're exactly the same age; I'm only a day older. That always bothered Mama a lot."

"Why?"

"Just think about it." She looked at him; her face was so close to his that he could make out the dark speckles in her blue eyes. "My father got her and another woman pregnant almost on the same day."

The candid mention of this highly intimate information embarrassed Bodenstein. Jutta seemed to notice and smiled suggestively.

"I'd be inclined to suspect Robert, by the way," Siegbert Kaltensee interjected. "I know that he was always trying to tap our mother and her friends for money, even after I told him he was banned from the house."

Jutta put back the framed pictures.

"He has totally let himself go," she said regretfully. "He doesn't even have a permanent place to live anymore, not since he got out of prison. It's sad that he's sunk so low; he really had all the opportunities in the world."

"When was the last time you spoke with him?" Bodenstein asked. The Kaltensees looked at each other before replying.

"It's been quite a while," Jutta finally said. "I think it was during my latest campaign. We had a stand on the pedestrian mall in Bad Soden, and all of a sudden he was standing in front of me. At first, I didn't recognize him."

"Didn't he ask you for money?" Siegbert Kaltensee gave a contemptuous snort. "All he ever talked about was money, money, money. I never saw him again after I threw him out. I think he realized that he wasn't going to get anything from me."

"They took the investigation in the Goldberg case away from us," Bodenstein said now. "And today, Mrs. Frings's apartment was cleaned out before we could have a look around."

The Kaltensee siblings stared at him, clearly baffled by the abrupt change of subject.

"Why would anyone clean out her apartment?" Siegbert asked.

"I have a feeling somebody is trying to block the investigation."

"Who would want to do that?"

"Well, that's the big question, isn't it? I don't know."

"Hmm," said Jutta, looking at him thoughtfully. "Anita wasn't rich, of course, but she did have some jewelry. Maybe it was somebody from the retirement home. Anita had no children, and they must have known that."

Bodenstein had briefly considered that idea himself. But that wouldn't explain why someone had cleared out everything except the furniture from the apartment.

Jutta continued her musings. "It can't be coincidence that all three were killed in the same way. Sure, Uncle Jossi had an eventful life, and there's no doubt that he made both friends and enemies. But Uncle Herrmann? Or Anita? I can't understand it."

"What has us puzzled is the number that the perpetrator left behind at all three murder scenes. One one six four five. It might refer to a date, or something else. But what?"

At that moment, the door opened. Jutta gave a start when Moormann appeared in the doorway.

"Can't you knock?" she chided the man.

"I beg your pardon." Moormann nodded politely to Bodenstein, but his horsey face remained expressionless. "Mrs. Kaltensee is feeling much worse. I just wanted to inform you before I call the emergency doctor."

"Thank you, Moormann," said Siegbert. "We'll be right up."

Moormann bowed every so slightly and then left.

"Please excuse me." Siegbert Kaltensee suddenly seemed very worried. He fished a business card out of his inside jacket pocket and handed it to Bodenstein. "If you have any more questions, call me."

"Of course. Please give your mother my wishes for a speedy recovery."

"Thank you. Are you coming, Jutta?"

"Yes, right away." She waited until her brother had left, then pulled out a cigarette from the pack with nervous fingers.

"Terrible, that Moormann." Her face was white and she took a deep breath. "Creeping all over soundlessly and scaring me half to death each time, that old spy."

Bodenstein was surprised. Jutta had grown up in this house and must have been used to the presence of discreet servants. Together, they walked through the foyer to the front door, where Jutta Kaltensee paused and looked around suspiciously.

"By the way, there's someone else you ought to talk to," she said in a low voice. "Thomas Ritter, my mother's former assistant. He's capable of anything."

Bodenstein was deep in thought as he returned to his car. Elard Kaltensee didn't like either his mother or his siblings, who both countered his dislike with an air of condescension. Then why did he continue to live at Mühlenhof? Siegbert and Jutta Kaltensee had been polite and helpful and had answered all of his questions without hesitation. But they, too, seemed surprisingly unaffected by the brutal murder of the three old people, whom they had supposedly held in high esteem. Bodenstein stopped next to his car. Something had bothered him during his conversation with the two Kaltensees, but what was it? Twilight was falling. With a hiss, the sprinklers started up, spraying the water that was responsible for the lush green of the extensive lawns. And then it dawned on him. It had been only a casual remark that Jutta Kaltensee had made, but it might turn out to be important.

Saturday, May 5

Bodenstein looked at the taped-together paper strips that Pia Kirchhoff had handed him and listened in disbelief to her explanation of how she had obtained this evidence. They were standing at the front door of his house. Inside, frantic activity reigned. In this phase of the investigations, he really couldn't permit himself a day off, but it would have led to a fairly serious family crisis if he had gone to the station on the day of his youngest daughter's christening.

"We definitely need to talk to Vera Kaltensee," Pia insisted. "She has to tell us more about the three victims. What if there are more murders?"

Bodenstein nodded. He remembered what Elard Kaltensee had said about his mother: "How she thinks that she'll be the next one lying in the front hall with a bullet in the back of her head."

"Besides, I'm convinced that she was the one who ordered Anita Frings's apartment to be cleared out," Pia said. "I'd really like to know why."

"Mrs. Frings probably had a secret, just as Goldberg and Schneider did," Bodenstein remarked. "But I'm afraid we'll have to forget about talking to her for the time being. I just spoke to her daughter on the phone, and she told me that the emergency doctor had Vera admitted to the hospital last night. She's in the locked psychiatric ward, suffering from a nervous breakdown."

"Bullshit. She's not the type to have a nervous breakdown." Pia shook her head. "She's going underground because things are getting too hot for her."

"I'm not so sure that Vera Kaltensee is behind the whole thing." Bodenstein scratched his head as he pondered the latest developments.

"Who else could it be?" Pia asked. "In Goldberg's case, it could have been his son, or maybe the CIA. Someone who didn't want the man's past to be made public. But this old woman? What secret could she possibly have been hiding?"

"We may be on the wrong track about the number referring to a date," he said. "Maybe the solution is much more banal than we assume. This number, for example, could also be a red herring that the perp left to confuse us. At any rate, Ostermann is going to have to find out more about KMF. Jutta

Kaltensee mentioned some shares that her father had signed over to Anita Frings."

Bodenstein had called Pia after his visit to Mühlenhof and briefly summarized the contradictory information he'd gleaned from the Kaltensee siblings about Goldberg and Schneider. He hadn't told her that Jutta had called him back late in the evening, because he didn't quite know what to make of that phone call.

"You think that it was about money?"

"In the broader sense. Perhaps." Bodenstein shrugged. "At the end of the conversation, Jutta Kaltensee suggested that I talk to her mother's former assistant. We ought to do that in any event, to get another angle on the Kaltensee family."

"Okay." Pia nodded. "I'll also look into Schneider's estate. Maybe I'll get lucky."

She was about to leave, when she remembered something else. From her pocket she took out a small gift-wrapped package and handed it to Bodenstein. "For Sophia," she said with a smile. "With best wishes from K-Eleven."

All morning long, Pia plowed through the mountains of files and documents that had been stored in Schneider's house for safekeeping. Ostermann used all means at his disposal to gather information about KMF, as Bodenstein had requested.

It was almost noon when Pia gave up in frustration.

"The guy had half the tax office archives in his basement," she said with a sigh. "I just have to ask why."

"Possibly these documents earned him the true allegiance of the Kaltensees and others," Ostermann conjectured.

"How do you mean? Extortion?"

"For example." Ostermann took off his glasses and pinched the bridge of his nose between thumb and forefinger. "Maybe he used the files to exert pressure. Just think of the payments from KMF to Schneider's Swiss bank account."

"I don't know." Pia was doubtful. "At any rate, I don't think these documents were the motive for the murder."

She closed a document binder with a bang and tossed it on the floor with a pile of others.

"Were you able to find out anything?"

"Quite a lot." Ostermann bit on the earpiece of his glasses as he rummaged in a pile of paper until he found the right page. "KMF is a group of companies with three thousand employees worldwide and representation in one hundred and sixty-nine countries. It encompasses about thirty corporations. The chairman of the board is Siegbert Kaltensee. The concern has equity of forty percent."

"And what do they do?"

"They make rolling mills for processing aluminum. The founder of the firm invented the first type of press for shaping aluminum into various thicknesses. Even today KMF holds the patent to this rolling press and the new developments that have come out of it. Well over a hundred in all. It seems to be a lucrative business."

He got up from his desk. "I'm hungry. Should I order us a couple of *döners*?"

"That would be great." Pia dived into the next box. Their colleagues from the evidence team had marked it "Cabinet Contents, Lower Left," and it contained several shoe boxes that were tied with cord. The first box held travel mementos; boarding cards for a cruise ship; postcards with pictures of exotic lands; a dance card; menus; invitations to christenings, weddings, birthdays, funerals; and other keepsakes that had no value to anyone but Schneider. The second shoe box contained neatly bundled handwritten letters. Pia unfolded one of them. It had been written on March 14, 1941. She laboriously deciphered the faded old-fashioned script. *Dear son, we hope and pray each day that you are well and that you will return to us in good health and in one piece. Here everything is as peaceful as always. Everything seems just the same, and you'd hardly believe there's a war on.* This was followed by news of friends and neighbors, and descriptions of daily occurrences that would have interested the recipient of the letter. The letter was signed *Mother.* Pia took letters from the stacks at random. Schneider's mother seemed to have been an avid letter writer. One letter was still in its envelope. *Käthe Kallweit, Steinort, Landkreis Angerburg* was the return address. Pia stared at the envelope, which was addressed to a Hans Kallweit. She was surprised to see that these letters weren't from Schneider's mother at all. But why had he saved them, carefully tying them up in bundles? A vague memory began stirring in her mind, but she couldn't pin it down. She read more of the letters. Ostermann came back, bringing her a *döner* with extra meat and feta. Pia put the food on the table without touching it. Ostermann started eating, and soon the whole conference room smelled like, a *döner* stand.

On June 26, 1941, Käthe Kallweit wrote to her son, *Herr Schlageter from the castle told your father that a whole wing had been requisitioned for Ribbentrop and his men. He said it has something to do with the construction site of the Askania at Görlitz.* Then a passage had been blacked out by the censor. *Your friend Oskar visited us and brought greetings from you. He says that he now has things to do in the area and will try to visit us regularly,* the letter continued.

Pia stopped. Vera Kaltensee had claimed that Schneider was an old friend of her late husband, but Elard Kaltensee had said only "That's right" and then gave his mother an odd look. And Miriam's Oma said she remembered that the phony Goldberg's name used to be Otto or Oskar.

"What sort of letters are they?" Ostermann asked, chewing his food. Pia picked up the last one she'd read.

"'Your friend Oskar visited us . . .'" she began reading aloud. Her heart was beating excitedly. Was she getting close to the secret?

"Herrmann Schneider saved bundles of about two hundred letters from a Käthe Kallweit from East Prussia, and I'm asking myself why," she said, rubbing the tip of her nose thoughtfully. "Supposedly he was born in Wuppertal and went to school there, but these letters came from East Prussia."

"So what's your theory?" Ostermann wiped his mouth with the back of his hand and rummaged in his drawer for a paper towel.

"That Schneider falsified his identity, too. The phony Goldberg's real name was Oskar, and he attended the SS Junker School in Bad Tölz." Pia looked up. "And this Oskar was, in turn, a friend of Hans Kallweit from Steinort in East Prussia, whose mother's correspondence we found in Herrmann Schneider's cabinet."

She pulled over her keyboard and mouse. She entered the key words on Google that she had found in the letters—*East Prussia* and *Steinort, Ribbentrop* and *Askania*—and found an extremely informative site about the former

East Prussia. For almost an hour, she delved into the history and geography of a lost region and realized to her shame how rudimentary her knowledge was of the recent past in Germany. The construction site of the Wolf's Lair, Hitler's headquarters in the East, had been given the cover name "Askania Chemical Works." No one in the general populace had any idea what was going on deep in the thick Masurian forests not far from the hamlet of Görlitz, near the town of Rastenburg. Foreign Minister von Ribbentrop had actually requisitioned a wing of Steinort Castle from the Lehndorff family for himself and his staff, starting in the summer of 1941, when Hitler moved into the Wolf's Lair. Käthe Kallweit from Steinort had apparently had some sort of connection to the castle—she might have worked there as a maid—and kept her son informed in her letters about the daily gossip and news. Pia gave an involuntary shudder at the idea of how the woman must have sat at her kitchen table a good sixty-five years earlier and written this letter to her son at the front. Pia jotted down a few key words and her information sources from the Internet, then grabbed her phone and dialed her friend Miriam's cell.

"How can I find information about fallen German soldiers?" she asked after a brief greeting.

"You can try the War Graves Commission," Miriam told her. "What, exactly, are you looking for? Oh, I have to warn you. This call could be expensive. I've been in Poland since last night."

"What? What are you doing there?"

"This Goldberg case has piqued my curiosity," Miriam admitted. "I thought I'd do a little research on-site."

For a moment, Pia was speechless.

"And where is that?" she asked at last.

"I'm in Wegorzewo," said Miriam, "formerly called Angerburg, on the Mauersee. The real Goldberg was born here. There are advantages to speaking Polish. The mayor himself has opened the city archives to me."

"You're out of your mind." Pia had to grin. "Well, good luck. And thanks for the tip."

She clicked through the Internet until she came to a Web site with the title worldwarvictims.de. It had a link to an online graves search. She entered the full name of the murdered Herrmann Schneider as well as his birth date and birthplace. She stared at the monitor as she waited. A few seconds later, she read with amazement that Herrmann Ludwig Schneider, born March 2, 1921, in Wuppertal, recipient of the Knight's Cross, first lieutenant and squadron captain of the Sixth Squadron of Fighter Group 400, fell in action on December 24, 1944, in an aerial battle at Hausen. He had flown a Focke-Wulf Fw 19 A-8, and his mortal remains were buried at the main cemetery in Wuppertal.

"That can't be true!" she exclaimed, and then told Ostermann what she had found. "The real Herrmann Schneider has been dead for fifty-two years."

"Herrmann Schneider is an ideal pseudonym. A common name." Ostermann frowned. "If I wanted to falsify my identity, then I would also seek out a name that was as ordinary as possible."

"Right." Pia nodded. "But how did our Schneider get hold of the data on the real Schneider?"

"Maybe they knew each other, were in the same unit. When our Schneider needed a new identity after the war, he remembered his friend, who had died in the meantime, and took his name."

"But what about the family of the real Schneider?"

"They had already buried their Schneider, so that settled the matter for them."

"But it was way too easy to figure out," said Pia, sounding dubious. "I found him in a few seconds."

"You have to put yourself back in time," replied Ostermann. "The war is over and chaos reigns. A man in civvies with no papers appears before the officials of the occupation forces and claims his name is Herrmann Schneider. Maybe he even got hold of the real Herrmann's military service book. Who knows? Sixty years ago, nobody could have imagined that it would be possible to find things in a few seconds by computer—things that previously required a detective and a lot of luck, in addition to a heap of money and large amounts of time. In that situation I would have taken the identity of somebody I knew something about, but only if it was absolutely necessary. And I would have made sure to stay out of the public eye. That's what our Schneider did. For his whole life, he was unobtrusiveness personified."

"Unbelievable." Pia made some notes. "Then we need to search for a Hans Kallweit from Steinort in East Prussia. Steinort is in the vicinity of Angerburg, where the real Goldberg came from. And if your theory is right, then the phony Goldberg—Oskar—could actually have known the real Goldberg before the war."

"Precisely." Ostermann cast a covetous glance at Pia's *döner* on the desk; it had gone cold. "Are you going to eat that?"

"No." Pia shook her head absently. "Be my guest."

Ostermann didn't have to be told twice. Pia was already back on the Web. Anita and Vera had been friends, as were the phony Schneider—Hans Kallweit—and the phony Goldberg—Oskar. Not three minutes later, she had a brief bio of Vera Kaltensee on her screen.

Born April 28, 1922, in Lauenburg am Dobensee, Angerburg district, she read. *Parents: Baron Heinrich Elard von Zeydlitz-Lauenburg and Baroness Hertha von Zeydlitz-Lauenburg, née von Pape. Siblings: Heinrich (1898–1917), Meinhard (1899–1917), Elard (1917, missing Jan. 1945). Fled in Jan. 1945; the rest of the family died in a Russian attack on the column of refugees trekking from Lauenburg.*

She clicked further to the informative East Prussian site, entered "Lauenburg," and found a reference to a tiny village named Doba on the Dobensee, near the ruins of the former castle of the Zeydlitz-Lauenburg family.

"Vera Kaltensee and Anita Frings came from the same corner of East Prussia as the phony Goldberg and the phony Schneider," Pia told her colleague. "If you ask me, all four of them must have known one another in the past."

"That could be," said Ostermann, leaning his elbows on the desk. He looked Pia in the eye. "But why did they make such a secret out of it?"

"Good question." Pia was nibbling at her ballpoint pen. She thought for a moment, then grabbed her cell and called Miriam again. Her friend picked up seconds later.

"Have you got something to write with?" Pia asked. "Since you're already doing research, keep an eye out for a Hans Kallweit from Steinort and an Anita Maria Willumat."

The Frankfurt Kunsthaus, one of the premier addresses for national and international contemporary art, was located in a historic town house right on Römerberg Square. Pia had to admit that her SUV was not very practical on a Saturday afternoon downtown. The parking garages around Römer and Hauptwache were all full, and finding a parking spot on the street for the bulky Nissan turned out to be hopeless. Finally, she gave up and drove right onto the big square in front of the Frankfurt city hall. It took less than a minute for two zealous female officers to show up and motion for her to drive off at once. Pia got out and showed the officers her ID and Kripo badge.

"Is that real?" asked one of them suspiciously, and Pia imagined her biting the badge to see whether it might be made of chocolate.

"Of course it's real," Pia said impatiently.

"You wouldn't believe the stuff people show us." The officer handed back her ID and badge. "If we confiscated it all, we could open our own museum."

"I won't be long, don't worry," Pia assured them, and headed for the Kunsthaus, which was always open on Saturday afternoon. Personally, she didn't care much for contemporary art so she was astounded to see how many people were crowded into the foyer, the exhibition rooms, and on the stairs. All to see the work of a Chilean sculptor and painter whose name Pia had never heard before. The café on the ground floor was also jammed. Pia looked around and felt like a real cultural philistine. None of the names of the artists in the brochures and flyers were even vaguely familiar, and she asked herself what on earth people saw in those blobs and slashes.

She asked the young woman at the information stand to inform Professor Kaltensee that she had arrived. As she waited, she leafed through a brochure that described the focus of the Frankfurt Kunsthaus. Besides the emphasis on so-called contemporary art in all its forms, the Eugen Kaltensee Foundation, which owned the property, also supported and promoted young and talented musicians and actors. On one of the upper floors, there was a concert hall as well as living quarters and work studios for artists in residence from Germany and abroad. Considering Professor Kaltensee's reputation, Pia suspected these were primarily young *female* artists whom the director of the Frankfurt Kunsthaus found to be particularly attractive. Just as she was thinking this, Pia saw Elard Kaltensee coming down the stairs. The man had made no real impression on her at Mühlenhof, but today he seemed completely transformed. He was dressed in black from head to toe, almost like a priest or magician—a somberly impressive figure, before whom the crowd parted respectfully.

"Hello, Ms. Kirchhoff." He stopped in front of her and held out his hand without smiling. "Please excuse me for making you wait."

"No problem. Thanks for finding time to see me on such short notice," Pia replied. Seen up close, Elard Kaltensee also looked exhausted today. There were dark shadows under his red-rimmed eyes, and a three-day growth of beard covered his sunken cheeks. Pia had the impression that he had put on a disguise to play a role that he no longer enjoyed.

"Come with me," he said, "and we'll go up to my residence."

She followed him curiously up the creaking stairs to the fifth floor. For years, the wildest rumors had been circulating through Frankfurt society about this residence on the top floor of the building. Apparently, plenty of decadent parties had taken place here. People whispered about orgiastic cocaine binges with prominent guests from the city's art and political scenes. Kaltensee opened a door and politely allowed Pia to enter first. At that moment, his cell phone rang.

"Please excuse me." He stayed on the landing. "I'll be right there."

A dim twilight reigned in the apartment. Pia looked around the huge room with its exposed ceiling beams and worn hardwood floorboards. In front of the windows that reached from floor to ceiling stood a cluttered desk made of dark mahogany. Stacks of books and catalogs covered every available inch of the surface. In one corner, the sooty maw of a fireplace gaped in front of a leather sofa group arranged around a low wooden coffee table. The walls, which seemed to be freshly painted, were bright white and bare except for two huge framed photographs. One depicted the rather attractive back view of a naked man, the other a close-up of someone's eyes, mouth, nose, and chin covered by splayed fingers.

Pia sauntered farther through the apartment. The scarred oak floor creaked under her feet. From the kitchen, a glass door led out onto a roof terrace. The bathroom was done all in white, with wet footprints still visible on the tiles. A used towel tossed next to the shower, a pair of jeans dropped carelessly on the floor, the smell of aftershave lingering in the room. Pia wondered whether she might have interrupted Elard Kaltensee in a bit of hanky-panky, because the jeans weren't the sort of thing he'd wear.

She couldn't resist the temptation to cast a curious glance into the next room, which was separated only by a heavy velvet curtain. She saw a wide, rumpled bed and a clothes rack. Every single item of clothing was black. A gilt figure of the Buddha served as the base for a glass table on which a bouquet of withered roses stood in a silver champagne cooler. The fragrance of the flowers hung heavy and sweet in the air. On the floor next to the bed stood an old-fashioned steamer trunk and a massive, many-armed bronze candelabra. The candles had burned down, leaving a fanciful pattern of wax on the wooden floor. Not quite the love nest Pia had expected. Her adrenaline level shot up involuntarily when she saw a pistol on the nightstand. Holding her breath, she ventured a step closer and leaned over the bed. Just as she was about to reach for the gun, she noticed a movement directly behind her. Startled, she lost her balance and suddenly found herself lying on the bed. Next to her stood Elard Kaltensee, scrutinizing her with a strange look in his eyes.

Marleen could smell that he'd been drinking, and he'd obviously had quite a lot. But before she could say a word, he took her face in his hands and planted a kiss on her lips with such passion that her knees got weak. His hands slipped underneath her blouse, undid her bra, and enveloped her breasts.

"Jesus, I'm crazy about you," Thomas Ritter said in a husky whisper. As he urged her toward the bed, her heart was pounding in her throat. With his eyes fixed on hers, he unzipped his pants and dropped them to the floor. Then he was on top of her, pressing her onto the bed with his whole weight. He thrust his pelvis against hers, and her body instantly responded to his demand, matching his need with her own. Arousal flowed through her body, and even though she had imagined the afternoon proceeding somewhat differently, she was starting to enjoy it. Marleen Ritter kicked off her shoes and wiggled with feverish impatience out of her jeans as they continued to kiss. Only then did she realize that today she'd put on a pair of panty hose, those love killers, but her husband didn't even seem to notice. She gasped for breath and closed her eyes as he entered her without a trace of tenderness. It didn't always have to be pure romance with candlelight and roses . . . .

•   •   •

"Disappointed?"

Elard Kaltensee went over to a small bar in the corner of the room and took two glasses from a shelf. Pia turned to him. She was glad that he'd handled the embarrassing situation a moment before without comment. He didn't seem to resent her indiscreet snooping around in his apartment. The old dueling pistol that he had pressed into her hand was a fine piece and probably very valuable to a collector. It was certainly not the weapon recently used to murder three people.

"Why would I be disappointed?" Pia retorted.

"I know the rumors that have been going around about this apartment," he replied, motioning her to take a seat on the leather sofa. "Would you like something to drink?"

"What are you having?"

"Diet Coke."

"That's fine for me, too."

He opened a small refrigerator, took out a bottle of Coke, and filled two glasses, setting them on the low coffee table. He sat down on a couch across from Pia.

"Did these legendary parties really happen?" Pia asked.

"There were quite a few parties, but never the sort of orgies that were rumored. The last one was in the late eighties," he said. "After that, it just got too exhausting. I'm actually rather bourgeois. I prefer to spend the evening with a glass of red wine in front of the TV and then go to bed at ten."

"I thought you lived at Mühlenhof," said Pia.

"Yes, I do. It became impossible to live here anymore." Elard Kaltensee studied his hands. "The whole Frankfurt art scene seemed to think it owned me and refused to stop besieging me. Eventually, I lost all desire to be part of this circus; I didn't want anything to do with these people who kept badgering me. From one day to the next, I found them revolting, these pompous, clueless art collectors, the so-called experts who buy as if possessed by whatever was just declared 'in,' paying horrendous sums. But even worse were the untalented wannabe artists who can't cope with ordinary life. I got sick of their puffed-up egos, their crazed worldview and confused understanding of art. They would jabber on for hours, even whole nights, trying to convince me that they and they alone were worthy of the foundation's grants and stipends. Out of a thousand, there's usually only one who is really worth sponsoring." He emitted a sound that was more of a snort than a laugh. "They probably assumed that I was keen on carrying on a discussion with them into the wee hours, but in contrast to these people, I had to show up at the university to give an eight o'clock lecture. That's why I moved to Mühlenhof three years ago."

For a moment, neither of them said a word. Kaltensee cleared his throat.

"But you came here to ask me about something," he said formally. "How can I help you?"

"It's about Herrmann Schneider." Pia opened her purse and took out a notebook. "We're sifting through his estate and have encountered some inconsistencies. Both Goldberg and Schneider seem to have adopted false identities after the war. Schneider isn't really from Wuppertal, but from Steinort, in East Prussia."

"Aha." If Kaltensee was surprised, he didn't show it.

"When your mother told us that Schneider was a friend of her late husband, you said that was right. But I had the feeling that you wanted to say something more."

Elard Kaltensee raised his eyebrows. "You're an astute observer."

"A basic prerequisite for my job," said Pia.

Kaltensee took another sip of his Coke. "In my family, there are many secrets," he said evasively. "My mother keeps quite a few things to herself. For example, to this day she has never told me the name of my biological father, or, as I sometimes suspect, my actual birth date."

"Why would she do that? What makes you think that?" Pia was surprised.

Kaltensee leaned forward, propping his elbows on his knees.

"I can remember things, places, and people I really shouldn't be able to remember. And it's not because I possess psychic abilities, but because I must have been a year older when we left East Prussia."

He rubbed his unshaven cheek as he stared into space. Pia said nothing, waiting for him to go on.

"For fifty years, I never thought much about my origins," he said after a while. "I had resigned myself to not having a father or a hometown. Many people of my generation share that experience. Fathers didn't come back from the war; families were torn apart and had to flee. My fate was not unique. But then one day, I got an invitation from our sister university in Krakow to attend a seminar. I didn't give it much thought but decided to go. One weekend, I took an excursion with a few colleagues to Olsztyn, formerly Allenstein, in order to view the newly opened university. Until that moment, I had felt like an ordinary tourist in Poland, but all of a sudden . . . I had the strange feeling that I'd seen this railroad bridge and this church before. I could even remember that it must have been wintertime. Without the slightest hesitation, I rented a car and drove east from Olsztyn. It was—"

He broke off, shook his head, and took a deep breath.

"If only I hadn't done that."

"Why?"

Elard Kaltensee stood up and went over to the window. When he spoke again, his voice sounded bitter.

"Up to that point, I was a relatively content man with two well-mannered children, occasional love affairs, and a job that was fulfilling. I thought I knew who I was and where I belonged. But after that trip, everything changed. I've had the feeling that with regard to important areas of my life, I'm totally fumbling in the dark. And yet I've never dared undertake a search in earnest. Now I think I was afraid of learning things that would destroy even more for me."

"Like what?" Pia asked. Kaltensee turned around to face her, and his expression of undisguised anguish caught her off guard. He was more fragile than was apparent on the surface.

"I assume that you know your parents and grandparents," he said. "You've surely heard the remark 'You must get that from your father,' or 'from your mother,' or 'from Oma or Opa.' Am I right?"

Pia nodded, taken aback by his sudden confiding tone.

"Well, I *never* heard it as a child. Why not? My first assumption was that my mother had probably been raped, like many women were back then. But that would have been no reason not to tell me anything about my origins. Then a much worse suspicion occurred to me. Maybe my father was a Nazi who had some sort of horrendous atrocities on his conscience. Had my mother been to bed with a guy in a black SS uniform who only an hour before had been torturing and executing innocent people?" Elard Kaltensee was talking himself into a fury, almost screaming, and Pia felt spooked when he stopped directly in front of her. Once before she'd been alone with a man who had turned out to be a psychopath. The facade of polite reserve crumbled; Kaltensee's eyes shone as if from a fever, and he balled his hands into fists.

"For me, there was no other reason for her silence. Can you begin to understand how this thought, this uncertainty about my origins, has tormented me day and night? The more I dwell on it, the more clearly I feel this . . . this darkness inside me, this compulsion to do things that a normal, well-balanced person would never do. And I ask myself, Why is this so? Where does this impulse come from, this sense of longing? Which gene do I have inside me? That of a mass murderer or that of a rapist? Would it be different if I had been raised in a real family, with a father and a mother who loved me with all my strengths and weaknesses? At last I know what I was missing. I feel this black, disastrous rift running through my whole life. They took away my roots and turned me into a coward who never dared ask any questions."

He wiped his mouth with the back of his hand and went back to the window. There he braced his hands on the windowsill and leaned his forehead on the pane. Pia didn't move or say a word. There was so much self-loathing, so much despair behind his every word.

"I *hate* them for doing this to me," he continued in a strained voice. "Sometimes I've hated them so much that I even wanted to kill them."

His final words put Pia on high alert. Kaltensee's behavior was beyond strange. Could he be mentally ill? What else would prompt someone to utter such openly murderous intentions to a police officer?

"Who are you talking about?" she asked. She'd noticed that he was speaking about "them." Kaltensee spun around and stared at her as if seeing her for the first time. There was something demented about the glassy look in his bloodshot eyes. What was she going to do if he suddenly jumped on her and tried to strangle her? She had foolishly left her service weapon at home in the cabinet, and nobody knew that she'd come here.

"About those who know," he replied huskily.

"And who is that?"

He went to the couch and sat down. Suddenly, he seemed to come to his senses; he laughed, as if nothing had happened.

"You haven't touched your Coke," he said, crossing his legs. "Would you like some ice cubes?"

Pia didn't take the bait.

"Who knows about it?" she insisted, although her heart was pounding hard, convinced as she was that a triple murderer was sitting across from her.

"It doesn't matter anymore," he replied calmly, almost cheerfully, and finished off his Diet Coke. "They're all dead now. Except for my mother."

Not until she was back sitting in her car did it occur to Pia that she'd forgotten to ask Kaltensee about his opinion on the ominous number and about Robert Watkowiak. She had always been proud of her excellent knowledge of human nature, but with Elard Kaltensee, she'd been totally wrong. She'd taken him for a cultivated, composed, and charming man who had things worked out in his own life and with the world. She hadn't been prepared for the unexpected delving into the somber depths of his conflicted soul. Pia didn't know what had scared her more: his violent outburst, the hate behind his words, or his abrupt switch to cheerful normality. "'Would you like some ice cubes?'" she muttered. "Unbelievable!"

She noticed with annoyance that her leg was trembling when she used the clutch. She lit a cigarette and turned onto the Alte Brücke, which spanned the Main River to Sachsenhausen. Gradually, she began to calm down. Viewed rationally, it was altogether conceivable that Elard Kaltensee had shot his mother's three friends because they hadn't wanted to tell him the truth about his origins and he blamed them for his unhappiness. After what she had just witnessed, it seemed conceivable that he could have killed them without giving it a second thought. Maybe he had first spoken with them calmly and objectively and then went ballistic when they refused to tell him anything. Anita Frings had known him well, and she probably hadn't objected when he took her out of the building in her wheelchair. And unsuspecting, Goldberg and Schneider had let him into their homes. The number 11645 must mean something to Elard Kaltensee as well as to the three people he'd murdered. Possibly it was the date they'd been forced to flee. The longer Pia ruminated about this, the more convincing this whole thing seemed to her.

She drove along the Oppenheimer Road at a walking pace in the direction of Schweizer Platz, staring pensively out the window. It had started to rain, and the wipers scraped across the windshield. On the passenger seat, her cell phone rang.

"Kirchhoff," she answered.

"We found Robert Watkowiak," her colleague Ostermann said. "But he's dead."

Marleen Ritter lay on her side, her head resting on her hand as she studied the face of her sleeping husband. She should have been mad at him: First, he hadn't called her in almost twenty-four hours; then he'd showed up reeking of booze and pounced on her without offering any explanation. But she simply couldn't stay mad at him, especially not now that he was home and snoring peacefully next to her in bed.

She tenderly looked at the etched contours of his profile and his thick, disheveled hair. She was once again amazed that this good-looking, intelligent, wonderful man had fallen in love with her. Thomas could have chosen any woman at all. Yet he had picked her, and that filled her with a warm, deep sense of happiness. In a few months, when the baby came, they would be a real family, and then her Oma would forgive Thomas everything—she was quite sure of it. Whatever had happened between Thomas and her grandmother was the only shadow clouding her happiness, but he was bound to do his utmost to patch things up, because he felt no animosity toward Vera. He moved in his sleep, and Marleen leaned over and pulled the blanket over his nakedness.

"Don't go." He reached out for her with his eyes closed. Marleen smiled. She cuddled up to him and stroked his unshaven cheek. He turned over on his side with a groan and put a heavy arm across her.

"I'm sorry I didn't call you," he mumbled. "But in the last twenty-four hours, I've learned so much that I'll probably have to rewrite my whole manuscript."

"What manuscript?" Marleen asked in astonishment. He was quiet for a while, then opened his eyes and looked at her.

"I haven't been completely honest with you," he admitted with a remorseful smile. "Maybe because I was ashamed. After Vera threw me out, it was pretty hard for me to get another job. So to make some money, I started writing novels."

Marleen smelled the stale alcohol on his breath.

"But there's nothing demeaning about doing that," she replied. When he smiled like that, he looked good enough to eat.

"Ah well." He sighed and scratched his ear in embarrassment. "What I'm writing won't get me the Nobel Prize in Literature. But I do earn six hundred euros per manuscript. I'm writing cheap novels. Romance novels. Broken hearts. You know."

For a moment, Marleen was speechless. But then she started to laugh.

"You're laughing at me," said Thomas, offended.

"Oh, nonsense!" She threw her arms around his waist and giggled. "I love trashy books. Maybe I've already read something you wrote."

"It's possible." He grinned. "Anyway, I use a pseudonym."

"Will you tell me what it is?"

"Only if you make me something delicious to eat. I'm dying of hunger."

"Can you take over, Pia?" asked Ostermann. "The boss is going to his daughter's christening today."

"Sure, no problem. Where do I have to go? Who found him?" Pia had put on her right-turn signal ages ago, but these twits behind her refused to let her in. Finally, a small gap opened up, and she stomped on the gas, forcing the guy behind her to brake, instantly followed by honking in response to her rude maneuver.

"You won't believe it: a real estate agent. He was showing his daughter's house to a couple, and there was Watkowiak, plunked down dead in a corner. Not a great way to sell a house."

"Very funny." After her experience with Elard Kaltensee, Pia was in no mood for jokes.

"The real estate agent said that the house had stood empty for years.

Watkowiak must have broken in to use it as a hideout. It's in Königstein Old Town. Hauptstrasse Seventy-five."

"I'm on my way."

When she passed the main train station, the traffic eased up. Pia slipped in a Robbie Williams CD, for which her colleagues had teased her mercilessly, and drove on the autobahn past the fairgrounds to the sounds of "Feel." Her musical taste was highly dependent on her mood. Except for jazz and rap, she liked almost everything, and her CD collection ranged from Abba through the Beatles, Madonna, Meat Loaf, and Shania Twain all the way to U2 and ZZ Top. Today she was in the mood for Robbie. At the Main-Taunus Center, she turned onto the B8, and fifteen minutes later she was in Königstein. She knew the narrow, winding streets of the Old Town from her school days, so there was no need to ask directions. As soon as she turned onto Kirchstrasse, she saw two patrol cars and an ambulance parked up the street. Number 75 was between a women's clothing boutique and a lotto store. The building had obviously been empty for years. With windows and doors nailed shut, peeling plaster, and a damaged roof, it had turned into an ugly eyesore in the heart of Königstein. The agent was still there, a suntanned man in his mid-thirties with a gel hairdo and patent-leather shoes—the very epitome of someone in the real estate profession. It had started to rain, so Pia pulled her gray hoodie over her head.

"I finally had somebody interested in the property, and now this!" he complained to Pia as if it were her fault. "The woman almost had a nervous breakdown when she saw the body."

"Maybe you should have checked out the place first," Pia chided the agent. "Who owns the house?"

"A woman client here in Königstein."

"I'd like her name and address," said Pia. "Or perhaps you'd like to inform your client yourself about the aborted showing of the house."

The agent heard the sarcasm in her voice and gave her a dark look. He pulled a BlackBerry out of his sports jacket, tapped on it for a moment, and then jotted down the name and address of the owner on the back of a business card. Pia put it in her pocket and looked around the inner courtyard. The property was bigger than it looked at first glance, and the back abutted the spa park. The sagging fence was a poor way to keep trespassers out. A uniformed colleague stood in front of the back door. Pia nodded to him and entered the building after getting rid of the real estate agent. The house looked no better inside than it did on the outside.

"Hello, Ms. Kirchhoff." The ME, whom Pia knew from other crime scenes, was packing his things. "At first glance, it looks like an inadvertent suicide. He probably has half a pharmacy inside him and at least one bottle of vodka."

He motioned behind him.

"Thanks." Pia went past him and said hello to the beat cops who were present. The room with the worn floor planks was pretty dark because of the shuttered windows—and completely empty. It smelled of urine, vomit, and decay. Pia felt the nausea start to rise at the sight of the dead man. He was sitting on the floor, leaning against the wall, and surrounded by bluebottle flies. His eyes and mouth were wide open. A whitish substance covered his chin and had dripped onto his shirt and dried, probably vomit. He was wearing dirty tennis socks, a blood-flecked white shirt, and black jeans. His shoes— brand-new, expensive-looking leather shoes—stood next to him. Thanks to the real estate agent, the body had been discovered before passersby could notice the stench of decay; otherwise, the time of death could have been determined only with the help of an entomologist. Pia's eyes swept across an impressive number of empty beer and vodka bottles lying next to the body. Beside them were an open backpack, medication packages, and a stack of banknotes. Something in this picture bothered her.

"How long has he been dead?" she asked, pulling on latex gloves.

"Rough estimate, about twenty-four hours," said the doctor. Pia calculated backward. If that was right, Watkowiak could easily have committed the murder of Anita Frings. Her colleagues from the evidence team came in, said hello to Pia, and waited for instructions.

"Incidentally, the blood on his shirt may not be his own," said the doctor behind her. "He has no external injuries on his body, as far as I can tell at the moment."

Pia nodded and tried to comprehend what had happened here. Sometime yesterday afternoon, Watkowiak had broken into the house, loaded down with a backpack, seven bottles of beer, three bottles of vodka, and a shopping bag full of medications. He had sat down on the floor, guzzled enormous quantities of liquor, and then took pills on top of it. As the effect of the alcohol and the antidepressants came on, he'd lost consciousness. But why were his eyes open? Why was he sitting upright against the wall instead of tipping over sideways?

She asked her colleagues to bring in more lights, then went through the other rooms in the house. On the second floor, she found signs that one room and the adjoining bathroom had been used occasionally. A mattress with dirty sheets lay on the floor in the corner, and there was a worn couch and a low table, even a small TV and refrigerator. Articles of clothing were hung over a chair, and in the bathroom were personal hygiene items and a few hand towels. On the ground floor, however, everything was covered with several years' worth of dust. Why had Watkowiak sat down on the bare floor to drink and not on the couch upstairs? Suddenly, Pia realized what had seemed so odd to her: The floor of the room in which Watkowiak's corpse lay was clean as a whistle! Watkowiak had hardly swept the floor himself before he doped himself up. When she returned to the room where they'd found the body, she saw a petite red-haired woman looking around curiously. In her elegant white linen suit and high-heeled pumps, she looked very out of place.

"Might I ask who you are and what you're looking for here?" Pia asked sternly. "This is a crime scene."

She didn't need any bystanders interfering with their work.

"I can certainly see that," replied the woman. "My name is Nicola Engel. I'm Chief Commissioner Nierhoff's successor."

Pia stared at her in astonishment. Nobody had told her about Nierhoff's successor.

"I see," she said a little more gruffly than was usually her style. "And why are you here? Just to tell me that?"

"No, to support you in your work." The red-haired woman gave her a charming smile. "I happened to hear that you were holding down the fort alone. And since at the moment I have nothing better to do, I thought I'd drop by and have a look."

"Could you show me some ID?" Pia was suspicious. She asked herself whether Bodenstein knew about a successor to the chief, or whether this was all some sort of crass trick by a daring reporter to get a look at a corpse. The woman's smile remained charming. She reached into her handbag and presented Pia with a police ID. "Commissioner Dr. Nicola Engel," Pia read. "Aschaffenburg Police Headquarters."

"All right, if you'd like to take a look around, be my guest." Pia handed her back the ID and forced a smile. "Oh, yes, I'm Pia Kirchhoff from K-11 at the Hofheim station. We've had a few tough days, so please excuse me for not being more polite."

"No problem." Dr. Engel was still smiling. "Please go back to what you were doing."

Pia nodded and turned back to the dead body. The photographer had taken pictures from every angle, also of the bottles, the shoes, and the backpack. The evidence techs began to bag up everything that might be of interest. Pia asked a colleague to turn the body over on its side. That proved to be rather difficult, because rigor mortis had already set in, but they managed it at last. Pia squatted down next to the body and inspected the back, backside, and palms of the dead man. All covered with dirt. That could only mean that somebody had cleaned the room *after* Watkowiak had been deposited there. It also meant that she might not be looking at a successful suicide. It might be murder. She didn't mention her suspicion to Dr. Engel. Instead, she searched the contents of the backpack, which seemed to confirm Nierhoff's theory of Watkowiak as a murderer. She found a knife with a hooked blade and a pistol. Were these the weapons used to kill Monika Krämer and the three old people? Pia rummaged further and found a gold chain with an old-fashioned medallion, a collection of silver coins, and a massive gold bangle. These valuables might have belonged to Anita Frings.

"Three thousand four hundred sixty euros," Dr. Engel announced, after counting the money. She slipped the bills inside a plastic bag that an officer handed to her. "What's that?"

"Looks like the knife used to kill Monika Krämer," Pia replied somberly. "And this might be the weapon used to shoot the three other victims. It's a Luger oh eight."

"Then this man could be the murderer you were searching for."

"It looks that way at least." Pia frowned as she pondered the scene.

"Do you have doubts?" asked Engel. She had put aside her amiable smile and seemed attentive and concentrated. "Why?"

"Because it seems too easy," said Pia. "And because something is fishy here."

Pia considered whether she ought to disturb her boss at his family celebration, then decided to give him a call. She didn't feel able to make polite small talk, so when Bodenstein's son picked up the phone, he passed Pia over to Oliver. She concisely told him about her visit to Elard Kaltensee, about the discovery of the body, and her doubts that Watkowiak had committed suicide.

"Where are you calling from?" he asked. Pia was afraid he was going to invite her to drop by for dinner.

"From my car," she said. She could hear loud laughter in the background, but it grew fainter, and then a door slammed and it was quieter.

"I've learned a couple of interesting things from my mother-in-law," Bodenstein told her. "She's known Vera Kaltensee for years, since they move in the same social circles. She was also at Vera's birthday party last Saturday, although they aren't exactly bosom buddies. But my mother-in-law's name is always an impressive addition to any guest list."

Pia knew that Cosima von Bodenstein's blood was even a bit bluer than that of her husband. Her paternal grandparents had known the last Kaiser personally, and her maternal grandfather had been an Italian prince with a claim to the throne.

"My mother-in-law had some rather negative things to say about Vera's late husband," Bodenstein went on. "Eugen Kaltensee made a fortune during the Third Reich supplying the Wehrmacht. Later, he was classified as a collaborator, but after 1945, he was soon back in business. He had transferred his money to a Swiss bank during the war, just as Vera's family had done. When he died in the early eighties, Elard Kaltensee was suspected of having killed his stepfather. The investigation fizzled out and his death was later judged an accident."

Pia shuddered involuntarily when she heard the name Elard Kaltensee.

"After an internal family dispute, Siegbert had to go to the States in 1963, where he attended a university. He didn't return until 1973 with his wife and daughter. He is the sole managing director of KMF. During her student years, Jutta Kaltensee allegedly had a lesbian relationship, which she ended by taking up with a man who worked for her mother, of all things."

"Have you found anything other than family gossip?" Pia asked with slight impatience. "I still have to get hold of the DA about the autopsy of Watkowiak's body."

"My mother-in-law didn't particularly like Goldberg and Schneider," Bodenstein went on, not offended. "She described Goldberg as an unpleasant, inconsiderate person. She called him a sleazy arms dealer and a pompous ass. Supposedly, he had several passports and could travel freely throughout the Eastern Bloc, even during the Cold War."

"Then she's in agreement with Elard Kaltensee on that score." Pia had reached the parking lot in front of the station and turned off the engine. She rolled down the window and lit one of her emergency cigarettes. She'd already smoked twelve of them today. "By the way, I've traced the real Schneider. He was a pilot in the Luftwaffe and died in aerial combat in 1944. Our Herrmann Schneider actually came from East Prussia, too; his real name was Hans Kallweit."

"Interesting." Bodenstein didn't seem very surprised. "My mother-in-law is firmly convinced that the four all knew one another from the old days. In later years, Vera used to call her friend Anita 'Mia,' and she would occasionally make remarks about folkloric events back home and indulge herself by reminiscing."

"Someone else must have known about this," Pia mused. "And I bet it was Elard Kaltensee. He could be our killer, because he obviously suffers a lot from not knowing his origins. Maybe he shot the three friends of his mother out of rage because they wouldn't tell him anything."

"That seems a bit far-fetched to me," said Bodenstein. "Anita Frings lived in East Germany. According to my mother-in-law, she and her husband both worked for the Stasi, the Ministry for State Security. The husband held a rather important position. And contrary to the claims of the director of Taunusblick, they had a son."

"Maybe he's already dead," Pia conjectured. Her cell phone vibrated. She glanced at the display: Miriam.

"I'm getting a call," she told her boss.

"From South Africa?"

"Excuse me?" Pia was confused for a moment.

"Isn't your zoo director in South Africa?"

"How do you know that?"

"Well, isn't he?"

"Yes. But he's not the one trying to reach me." Pia wasn't too surprised that her boss once again seemed so well informed.

"It's my friend Miriam, calling from Poland. She's sitting in the city archives in Wegorzewo, the former Angerburg, looking for traces of the real Goldberg and also the real Schneider. Maybe she's found something."

"What does your friend have to do with Goldberg?" Bodenstein asked. Pia explained the connection. Then she promised to attend the Watkowiak's autopsy if it was going to be held the next day, and ended the conversation so she could call Miriam back.

Sunday, May 6

The ringing of the telephone next to her bed jolted Pia out of a sound sleep. It was pitch-dark and stuffy in the room. She pressed the switch on the bedside lamp and fumbled for the receiver.

"Where are you?" her ex-husband grumbled in her ear. "We're waiting for you! You were the one who was in such a hurry for the autopsy results."

"Henning, my God," Pia muttered. "It's the middle of the night."

"It's quarter past nine," he informed her. "Hurry up, please."

He hung up. Pia squinted her eyes and looked at the alarm clock. He was right. Quarter past nine. She threw off the covers, jumped up, and staggered to the window. Last night, she must have pulled down the shades inadvertently, and that's why her bedroom was as dark as the inside of a coffin. A quick shower put some life into her, but she still felt like she'd been run over by a bus.

The DA had granted authorization for an immediate autopsy to be performed on the corpse of Robert Watkowiak, although not until Pia had more or less talked him into it. She'd argued that the medications the victim had taken, either deliberately or accidentally, would decompose and no longer be detectable if they waited too long. Henning had not been happy when Pia called, begging him to do the autopsy the next day. To top it all off, when she'd finally gotten home a little after 9:00 P.M., she'd discovered that her two yearlings had broken out of the paddock and were sampling the unripe apples in Elisabethenhof, the next town. After a sweaty chase, she'd managed to get the two prodigals back in the stable and then staggered into the house, totally exhausted. She'd found only a past-due container of yogurt and half a Camembert in the refrigerator. The only bright spot had been a call from Christoph before she collapsed into bed like a dead woman. And now she had overslept and might miss the start of the autopsy. One look in her dresser drawer told her that her supply of fresh underwear had dwindled to nothing, so she hurried to stuff some dirty clothes in the washing machine. No time for breakfast, and the horses would have to stay in their stalls until she came back from Frankfurt. Tough.

It was almost ten when Pia showed up at the autopsy and once again ran into Löblich, who was representing the DA's office. This time, the DA was wearing not a stylish suit, but jeans and an oversize T-shirt, which Pia easily identified as one of Henning's. It wasn't hard for Pia's exhausted psyche to connect the dots.

"Now we can finally get started" was Henning's only comment. All of a sudden, Pia felt like a stranger in this room where she and Henning had spent countless hours together. For the first time, she realized that there was no place for her in his life anymore. Sure, she was the one who had left him, and she had to accept it if he was now doing the same thing and looking for a new partner. Still, it gave her a shock that she wasn't prepared to handle in her present condition.

"Pardon me," she murmured. "I'll be right back."

"Stay here!" Henning snapped, but Pia fled from the autopsy suite into the next room. Dorit, the lab technician, who had agreed to some overtime hours in order to perform the stat analyses, had made coffee, as usual. Pia took a ceramic mug and poured herself some. It tasted bitter as gall. She set down the cup, closed her eyes, and rubbed her temples with her fingers to alleviate the pressure in her head. She'd seldom felt as worn-out and demoralized as she did this morning, which might also be due to the fact that she had gotten her period. To her annoyance, she felt tears burning behind her eyelids. If only Christoph were here so she'd have somebody to talk and laugh with. She pressed her palms on her eyes and fought back the rising tears.

"Is everything okay?" Henning's voice made her jump. She heard the door close behind him.

"Yes," she said without turning around. "It's just all been . . . a bit much the past few days."

"We could postpone the autopsy until this afternoon," he offered. So that he could go back to bed with Löblich while she sat around alone?

"No," she said curtly. "I'll be all right."

"Look at me." He sounded so sympathetic that the tears she had almost quelled now surged into her eyes. She shook her head mutely like a stubborn child. And then Henning did something he had never done in all the years they were married. He took her in his arms and held her tight. Pia stood stock-still. She didn't want to drop her guard with him, especially if she thought he might tell his lover about it.

"I can't stand it when you're unhappy," he said softly. "Why doesn't your zoo director take better care of you?"

"Because he's in South Africa," she murmured, allowing him to take her by the shoulders, turn her around, and lift her chin.

"Open your eyes," he commanded. She obeyed and saw, to her surprise, that he actually looked worried.

"The colts got out last night, and Neuville injured himself. I had to chase them all over the neighborhood for two hours," she whispered, as if that was the explanation for her pitiful condition. And then the tears started running down her face. Henning pulled her into his arms, stroking her back to console her.

"Your girlfriend will probably be mad if she sees us like this," Pia said, her voice muffled by the fabric of his green smock.

"She isn't my girlfriend," he replied. "You're not jealous, are you?"

"I have no right to be. But still."

He was silent for a moment, and when he spoke again, his voice sounded different.

"You know what?" he said softly. "Why don't we get this job done, and then you and I can go out and have a proper breakfast. And if you want, I'll go back to Birkenhof and take a look at Neuville."

The offer was clearly made in the spirit of friendship; it wasn't a crude attempt at a pass. Henning had been present last year at the birth of the colt, and he was a horse lover, like herself. The prospect of not having to spend the day alone was tempting, yet Pia resisted it. In reality, she didn't want Henning's sympathy, and it would be unfair to encourage him just because she was feeling shitty and lonesome. He didn't deserve that. She took a deep breath to clear her head.

"Thank you, Henning," she said, wiping off the tears with the back of her hand. "That's very kind of you. I'm happy that we still understand each other so well. But I have to get back to the office later."

That wasn't true, but it made her refusal sound less like a rejection.

"Okay." Henning let her go. She saw in his eyes an expression that was hard to interpret. "But first, have your coffee in peace. Take your time. I'll wait for you."

Pia nodded and asked herself whether he was aware of the double meaning of his words.

Monday, May 7

"Robert Watkowiak was murdered," Pia announced to her colleagues at the morning meeting in K-11. "The consumption of alcohol and pills did not occur voluntarily."

In front of her lay the preliminary autopsy report, which had pretty much surprised everyone yesterday, including herself. The stat analyses of blood and urine from the deceased indicated a high level of intoxication. The cause of death was doubtless the extreme concentration of tricyclic antidepressants in combination with a blood-alcohol level of 0.39 percent, which had led to cessation of breathing and circulation and subsequently to death. In addition, Henning had found hematomas and bruises on the head, shoulders, and wrists of the corpse. He suspected that Watkowiak had been bound and chained. Fine purpuric longitudinal tears in the tissue of the esophagus and traces of Vaseline had corroborated his suspicion that someone had administered the deadly cocktail to the man by means of a tube. Additional samples would be examined in the forensic laboratory in Wiesbaden, but Henning could conclusively state that death had resulted from the intervention of another, unknown individual.

"In addition, the site where the body was found was not the site of the crime." She passed around the photos taken by their colleagues from the evidence team. "Someone deliberately swept the floor so as not to leave any tracks. But it seems to have been an afterthought; it probably didn't occur to the perpetrator until after he'd laid Watkowiak down on the floor. The victim's clothes were full of dust."

"So now we have our fifth murder," said Bodenstein.

"And we have to start from scratch," Pia added despondently. She felt done in. The nightmares of the night before, in which Elard Kaltensee and a Luger 08 had played a frightening role, were still haunting her. "Although we really hadn't made much progress."

They agreed that whoever had murdered Goldberg, Schneider, and Frings was not the same person who had killed Monika Krämer. But to Pia's disappointment, no one seemed to share her suspicion that Elard Kaltensee might be the triple murderer. She had to admit that her reasons, which she had considered absolutely conclusive on Saturday, now sounded pretty far-fetched.

"But it seems crystal clear to me," said Behnke. He'd shown up promptly at seven o'clock and was now sitting grumpy and bleary-eyed at the table in the conference room. "Watkowiak shot the three old people because he needed money. He told Krämer about it, and when she threatened to spill the beans, he killed her."

"And then what?" asked Pia. "Who killed *him*?"

"No idea," Behnke admitted grouchily. Bodenstein got up and went to the whiteboard on the wall, which was now covered with writing from top to bottom, along with a series of crime-scene photos. He clasped his hands behind his back and studied the jumble of lines and circles.

"Erase all of this," he told Kathrin Fachinger. "We have to start over. Somewhere we missed something."

There was a knock at the door. A female duty officer came in.

"Here's some more work for you. We received a report of aggravated assault early this morning." She handed Bodenstein a thin folder. "The individual who was injured has several stab wounds to the upper body. He's in the hospital here in Hofheim."

"Great," Behnke grumbled. "As if we didn't have enough to do already with five homicides to investigate."

His whining did no good. K-11 was responsible for working the incident, no matter how many murders were waiting to be cleared up.

"I'm sorry," said the officer, not sounding particularly sympathetic, and left. Pia reached for the folder. They were not making any progress on the homicide cases, and they had to wait for the lab results, which could take days or even weeks. Bodenstein's strategy to keep the press out of the investigations for the time being had one serious drawback: There would be no tips, either absurd or helpful, coming in from the public that might give them a lead. Pia skimmed the report by the patrol that had responded to the anonymous 911 call at 2:48 A.M. and discovered the seriously injured man named Marcus Nowak in his totally trashed office.

"If nobody has any objections, I'll take this one." She wasn't especially keen on spending the whole day sitting at her desk with nothing to do, waiting for lab results—and being demoralized by Behnke's negative energy. She preferred to combat her own gloomy thoughts with activity.

An hour later, Pia spoke with the head of plastic surgery at the Hofheim Hospital. Dr. Heidrun van Dijk looked exhausted; she had dark rings under her eyes. Pia knew that the doctors who were on call over the weekend often had to put in inhuman seventy-two-hour shifts.

"I'm not allowed to tell you any details." The doctor pulled out Nowak's records. "Only this: It was no bar fight. The guys who beat him up knew what they were doing."

"How do you mean?"

"They didn't just beat him. His right hand was smashed. We operated last night, but we might still have to amputate."

"An act of revenge?" asked Pia, frowning.

"Torture, more likely." The doctor shrugged. "They were pros."

"Is he out of danger?" Pia asked.

"His condition is stable. He came through the operation well."

They walked down the hall and Dr. van Dijk stopped in front of a door. They could hear an outraged woman's voice coming from inside the room.

"—you doing at that time of night in the office? Where had you been? Say something!"

The voice broke off when the doctor opened the door and ushered Pia in. There was only one bed in the big bright room. On a chair next to the window sat an old lady; standing in front of her was a woman at least fifty years younger. Pia introduced herself.

"Christina Nowak," said the younger woman. Pia estimated she was in her mid-thirties. Under other circumstances, she might have been quite pretty, with classic features, shiny brown hair, and an athletic figure. But right now, she was pale and her eyes were red from crying.

"I need to speak with your husband," said Pia. "In private."

"Go ahead. And good luck." Christina Nowak was fighting back more tears. "He won't talk to me, at any rate."

"Could you please wait outside for a minute?"

Christina Nowak looked at her watch. "Actually, I have to get to work," she said uncertainly. "I'm a kindergarten teacher, and today we're taking a field trip to the Opel Zoo. The kids have been looking forward to it all week."

The mention of the Opel Zoo gave Pia a pang. Involuntarily, she asked herself what she would do if Christoph were lying seriously injured in a hospital bed and wouldn't speak to her.

"We can talk later." She took a business card out of her pocket and handed it to Christina Nowak, who glanced at it.

"You're a real estate agent?" she asked suspiciously. "You told me you were from Kripo."

Pia took the card from her hand and saw that it was the one the agent had given her on Saturday.

"Pardon me." She pulled out the correct card. "Could you come down to the station this afternoon around three?"

"Of course." Christina Nowak managed a shaky smile. She looked over at her silent husband once more, bit her lip, and left. The old lady, who hadn't said a word the whole time, followed her out. Now Pia turned to the injured man. Marcus Nowak lay on his back, an oxygen tube in his nose and an IV in his arm. His swollen face was disfigured by bruises. Over his left eye was a row of stitches; another row ran from his left ear almost to his chin. His right arm was in a splint; his torso and the damaged hand were covered with thick bandages. Pia sat down on the chair that the old woman had been sitting on and scooted a little closer to the bed.

"Hello, Mr. Nowak," she said. "My name is Pia Kirchhoff, from Hofheim Kripo. I won't bother you for long, but I have to know what happened last night. Do you remember the attack?"

With an effort, the man opened his eyes, his eyelids fluttering. He shook his head gingerly.

"Somebody hurt you badly." Pia leaned forward. "With a little less luck, you'd be lying in the morgue instead of here in bed."

Silence.

"Did you recognize anyone? Why were you attacked?"

"I . . . I can't remember a thing," Nowak muttered indistinctly.

That was always a good excuse. Pia suspected that the man remembered quite clearly who and why somebody had beaten him badly enough to put him in the hospital. Was he afraid? There could hardly be another reason for him to keep silent.

"I don't want to press charges," he said softly.

"That's not necessary," Pia replied. "Aggravated assault is a criminal offense and is automatically pursued by the district attorney's office. That's why it would be very helpful if you could remember something."

He didn't answer, just turned his head to the side.

"Think it over in peace and quiet." Pia stood up. "I'll drop by later. Get well soon."

•   •   •

It was nine o'clock when Chief Commissioner Nierhoff came rushing into Bodenstein's office with an ominous look on his face, and Nicola Engel was right behind him.

"What . . . the hell . . . is . . . this?!" Nierhoff flung the morning edition of the *Bild* tabloid onto Bodenstein's desk and tapped his finger on the half-page article on page three, as if trying to bore right through the paper. "I want an explanation, Bodenstein!"

BRUTAL MURDER OF PENSIONER crowed the bold headline. Without a word, Bodenstein took the paper and scanned the rest of the sensational details. *Four dead bodies in a week, and the police are at a loss, with no leads, offering only an obviously made-up story. Robert W., nephew of the well-known industrialist Vera Kaltensee and alleged murderer of pensioners David G. (92) and Herrmann S. (86), as well as his partner, Monika K. (26), is still at large. On Friday, the serial killer struck a fourth time, murdering the wheelchair-bound pensioner Anita F. (88) with a bullet to the back of the head. The police are groping in the dark and decline comment. The only similarity: All the victims were closely linked to Hofheim millionaire Vera Kaltensee, who now must fear for her life. . . .*

The letters blurred before his eyes, but Bodenstein forced himself to read to the end of the article. His temples were throbbing so badly that he could hardly think clearly. Who had given this distorted story to the press? He glanced up, straight into the gray eyes of Nicola Engel. She gave him a look filled with both mockery and anticipation. Had she leaked the story to the press in order to bring even more pressure to bear on him?

"I want to know how this story got into the papers!" Chief Commissioner Nierhoff accentuated each word; he was more furious than Bodenstein had ever seen him. Was he afraid of losing face in front of his successor, or of consequences from an entirely different source? He had accepted outside interference and demands for a cover-up in the Goldberg case all too willingly, never imagining that the murder would be followed by two more very similar deaths.

"I don't know," said Bodenstein. "You were the one who spoke to the journalists."

Nierhoff gasped for breath.

"I told the press something altogether different," he snarled. "And now I see that it wasn't true. I was counting on you."

Bodenstein cast a quick glance at Nicola Engel and wasn't surprised to see her looking rather smug. She was probably behind the whole thing.

"You didn't listen to me," Bodenstein replied, looking at his boss. "I was against the press conference, but you were so anxious to see the cases cleared up."

Nierhoff grabbed the paper. His face was red as a lobster.

"I shouldn't have trusted you with this, Bodenstein!" he exclaimed, waving the paper in front of his face. "I'm going to call the editor and find out where they got this information. And if you or your people are behind this, Bodenstein, then get ready for disciplinary action!"

He left his successor standing there and took the paper with him. Bodenstein was shaking with rage. The newspaper article was bad enough, but he was more angry about Nierhoff's unfair insinuation that he had gone behind his boss's back in an attempt to ridicule him in public.

"What now?" Nicola Engel asked. Her sympathetic query seemed to Bodenstein the height of hypocrisy. For a moment, he was tempted to throw her out of his office.

"If you think you can obstruct my investigations in this way," he told her, keeping his voice under control with an effort, "then I assure you it's going to backfire."

"What are you implying?" Nicola Engel said with an innocent smile.

"That you leaked this information to the press," he said. "I recall another instance when a rash decision to notify the press resulted in blowing a colleague's cover. And then that colleague was murdered."

He regretted the accusation the moment he uttered it. Back then, there had been no disciplinary action, no internal investigation, not even a memo. But Nicola was taken off the case overnight, and for Bodenstein that was confirmation enough. The smile on her face turned frosty.

"Be careful what you say," she replied softly. Bodenstein knew that he was venturing into dangerous terrain, but he was too insulted and furious to be reasonable. Besides, this case had already been tormenting him for far too long.

"I refuse to be intimidated by you, Nicola." He looked down at her from his full height of six two. "And I won't put up with you monitoring my colleagues without consulting me first. I know better than anyone else what you're capable of when you have a specific goal in mind. Don't forget how long we've known each other."

Unexpectedly, she retreated. All of a sudden, he felt the balance of power tipping in his favor, and apparently she noticed it, too. She turned abruptly and left his office without another word.

Nowak's grandmother got up from the plastic chair in the hospital waiting area as Pia Kirchhoff came through the door with the milk-glass panel. She looked about the same age as Vera Kaltensee—but what a difference between the well-groomed lady and this burly woman with short-clipped ice gray hair and work-worn hands that showed clear signs of arthritis. Without a doubt, Auguste Nowak had experienced a good deal in her long life.

"Let's sit down for a moment." Pia motioned toward a group of chairs by the window. "Thank you for waiting."

"I can't leave the boy alone, though," replied the old woman. There was a worried look on her lined face. Pia asked her for a few personal details and took notes. Auguste Nowak was the one who had called the police during the night. Her bedroom faced the courtyard, where the workshop and office of her grandson's company were located. Around two in the morning, she'd heard noises, got up, and looked out the window.

"I haven't been sleeping very well for years," the old woman explained. "When I looked out the window, I saw a light in Marcus's office, and the door to the courtyard was standing open. In front of the office was a dark-colored vehicle, a van. I had a bad feeling and went outside."

"That was a rather foolish thing to do," Pia remarked. "Weren't you afraid?"

The old woman made a dismissive gesture.

"I turned on the outside light from the hallway," she went on, "and when I went out the door, they were already getting in the van. There were three of them. They drove right at me, like they wanted to run me down, and then they hit one of the concrete planters that are placed there to protect the garden fence. I tried to see the license plate number, but they didn't have any on the van, those crooks."

"No license plate?" Pia, who had been taking notes, looked up in surprise. The old woman shook her head.

"What sort of work does your son do?"

"He's a contractor," Auguste Nowak replied. "He renovates and restores old buildings. His company has an excellent reputation, and he has plenty of work. But after becoming successful, he's not very popular anymore."

"Why is that?" Pia asked.

"How does that saying go?" the old woman snorted contemptuously. "You have to work for envy, but pity is free."

"Do you think that your grandson knew the men who attacked him last night?"

"No," said Auguste Nowak bitterly, shaking her head, "I don't think so. None of the people he knows would dare do anything like that."

Pia nodded.

"The doctor thinks his injuries resulted from some sort of torture," she said. "Why would anyone torture your grandson? Did he have something to hide? Had he been threatened recently?"

Auguste Nowak was listening attentively. She might be a simple woman, but she wasn't slow on the uptake.

"I don't know anything about that," she said evasively.

"Then who might know? His wife?"

"I hardly think so." She gave a bitter smile. "But you could ask her this afternoon when she gets home from work. She thinks her job is more important than her husband."

Pia noticed the sarcasm in her voice. It wasn't the first time she'd encountered a profoundly dysfunctional family behind a facade of normality. "And you really don't know whether your grandson is in any kind of trouble?"

"No, I'm sorry." The old woman shook her head regretfully. "If he were having problems with the company, he certainly would have told me."

Pia thanked Auguste Nowak and asked her to go down to the station later for an interview. She ordered an evidence team to go to Fischbach and search the premises of Marcus Nowak's company, and then she headed for the crime scene.

Marcus Nowak's company was located on the outskirts of Fischbach, on a street blocked to public traffic, which residents liked to use as a shortcut, especially at night. When Pia arrived at the site, she found Nowak's colleagues in a heated discussion in front of a building that apparently housed the offices.

Pia held up her ID. "Good morning. Pia Kirchhoff, Criminal Police." The buzz of voices ceased.

"What's going on here?" she asked. "Is there a problem?"

"You bet," said a young man in a checked wool shirt and blue work pants. "We can't get in, and we're already late. The boss's father told us that we had to wait until the police arrived."

He nodded toward a man who was striding across the courtyard.

"Well, the police are here now." Pia was pleased that dozens of people hadn't trampled through the crime scene before the evidence techs could do their work. "Your boss was attacked very early this morning. He's in the hospital and will probably be there for a while."

That left the men speechless for a moment.

"Lemme through here!" shouted a voice, and the men instantly obeyed. "*You're* the police?"

The man looked Pia up and down skeptically. He was big and powerfully built, with a healthy complexion and a neatly trimmed mustache under his bulbous nose. A patriarch used to being obeyed, who had a hard time accepting female authority.

"That's right." She showed him her ID. "And who are you?"

"Manfred Nowak. My son owns the company."

"Who'll be running the business while your son is on sick leave?" Pia asked. Nowak senior only shrugged.

"We know what we have to do," the young man put in. "We just need the tools and the keys to the van."

"Now back off just a minute," snapped Nowak senior.

"I will not!" retorted the young man hotly. "You probably think you can finally get back at Marcus! But you have absolutely nothing to say about it!"

Nowak senior turned red. He put his hands on his hips and was already opening his mouth for a fierce comeback.

"Everybody calm down!" said Pia. "Please open the door. Then I'd like to discuss with you and your family exactly what went on here earlier today."

Nowak senior gave her a hostile look, but he did what she asked.

"You're coming with us," she told the young man.

The office had been completely tossed. Document binders had been torn out of bookshelves; drawers and their contents had been dumped all over the floor; the computer monitor, printer, fax, and copier were all smashed; cabinets were standing open and had been ransacked.

"Holy shit," the foreman exclaimed.

"Where are the keys to the vehicle?" Pia asked him. He pointed to a key box to the left of the office door, and Pia allowed him to enter the room. When he had taken all the necessary keys, she followed him down a hall and through a heavy security door into the workshop. At first glance, everything seemed to be in order in here, but the young man uttered a suppressed curse.

"What is it?" Pia asked.

"The storeroom." The man pointed to a door that was wide open on the other side of the shop. A moment later, they were standing in the midst of a mess of tipped-over shelves and destroyed material.

"Did you mean it when you said that Manfred Nowak could finally get back at his son?" Pia asked Nowak's foreman.

"The old man is absolutely furious with Marcus," explained the young man with undisguised dislike. "He was really pissed that Marcus wouldn't take over the construction company and all the debts. I can understand it. The company was broke because everybody had their fingers in the till and had no clue about bookkeeping. But Marcus is cast in a different mold than the rest of them. He's really clever, and he knows what to do. It's a pleasure working with him."

"Does Mr. Nowak work with his son in the business?"

"No, he refused." The young man snorted disparagingly. "Just like Marcus's two older brothers. They'd rather go to the employment office."

"Strange that nobody from the family seems to have heard anything when Marcus was attacked," Pia said. "There must have been a hell of a racket."

"Maybe they didn't want to hear it." The young man didn't seem to think much of his boss's family. They left the storeroom and walked back through the workshop. Suddenly, the foreman stopped short.

"How's the boss doing, anyway?" he asked. "You just said he'd be in the hospital for a while. Is that right?"

"I'm no doctor," replied Pia, "but as I understand it, he's been seriously injured. He's in the Hofheim Hospital. Will you be able to get along without him?"

"For a few days, sure." The young man shrugged. "But Marcus has an important job coming up. He's the only one who knows anything about it. And at the end of this week, there's a big deadline."

The behavior of Marcus Nowak's family ranged from hostile to indifferent. No one thought of inviting Pia into the house, so the questioning took place outside the front door of the big house, which was situated right next door to the company. A stone's throw away stood a little cottage in the middle of a neat garden. Pia was told that Nowak's grandmother lived there. Manfred Nowak took it upon himself to answer every question that Pia asked, no matter to whom she was speaking. Unanimously, if apathetically, the others nodded to confirm each of his statements. Manfred's wife seemed careworn and prematurely aged. She avoided all eye contact and kept her narrow lips pressed together.

Marcus Nowak's brothers were around forty, both stout, somewhat awkward, and physically exact copies of their father. Yet they lacked his self-confidence. The older brother, who had the watery eyes of an alcoholic, also lived with his family in the big house next to the company grounds; the other brother lived two houses away. Pia now knew why they were at home at this time on a Monday morning and not at work. Neither of them admitted to noticing anything at the time of the attack; apparently, all the bedrooms faced the rear, toward the edge of the forest. Not until the ambulance and police arrived did they realize that something must have happened.

Unlike Auguste Nowak, her son immediately had several suspects in mind. Pia wrote down the names of a belligerent tavern owner and a colleague who had been fired, but she thought it would be useless to check them out. As the doctor at the hospital had remarked, the attack on Marcus Nowak was the work of professionals. Pia thanked the family for their help and went back to Nowak's office, where her colleagues from the evidence team had begun their work. The words of Auguste Nowak popped into her head: "You have to work for envy, but pity is free." How true.

When she returned to the station two hours later, Pia noticed at once that something must have happened. Her colleagues were sitting at their desks with tense expressions and hardly looked up.

"What's going on?" she asked. Ostermann briefly told her about the newspaper article and Bodenstein's reaction. After a vehement altercation with Nierhoff behind closed doors, the boss had flown into a fit of rage—which was so unlike him—and accused one colleague after another of leaking information to the press.

"I'm sure it wasn't any of us," said Ostermann. "By the way, the report from the interview with a Mrs. Auguste Nowak is on your desk. She was just here."

"Thanks." Pia put down her bag on the desk and glanced over the transcript that the duty officer had made. There was also a yellow Post-it stuck to her telephone with the message "Urgent: Call back!" and a phone number with the prefix 0048, the country code for Poland. Miriam. Both would have to wait. She went to Bodenstein's office. Just as she was about to knock, the door was flung open and Behnke stormed out with a face as pale as wax. Pia went in.

"What's the matter with him?" she asked. Bodenstein didn't answer. He didn't look like he was in a very good mood.

"What was all that about the hospital?" he asked.

"Marcus Nowak, a contractor from Fischbach," said Pia. "He was attacked by three men in his office and tortured. Unfortunately, he won't say a word about it, and no one in his family seems to have any idea who or what might be behind the attack."

"Pass it on to the colleagues in K-Ten." Bodenstein rummaged in a desk drawer. "We have enough to do."

"Hold on," Pia said. "I'm not finished. In Nowak's office, we found a summons from our colleagues in Kelkheim. He's being charged with inflicting negligent bodily harm upon Vera Kaltensee."

Bodenstein stopped what he was doing and looked up. His interest was instantly piqued.

"In the past few days, the Kaltensees' telephone number at Mühlenhof was dialed from Nowak's phone at least thirty times. Last night, he talked on the phone with our friend Elard for over half an hour. It could be a coincidence, but I find it odd that the name Kaltensee is popping up again."

"I agree." Bodenstein rubbed his chin in thought.

"Remember when they said the presence of the company security people at the estate was because they'd had a break-in?" Pia asked. "Maybe Nowak was behind it."

"We're damn well going to find out." Bodenstein grabbed the phone and punched in a number. "I've got an idea."

A good hour later, Bodenstein parked in front of the door of the estate of Countess Gabriela von Rothkirch in the Hardtwald area of Bad Homburg, probably the most exclusive residential area in the lower Taunus region. Behind high walls and thick hedges, the real high society lived in opulent villas set in parklike grounds of quite a few acres each. After Cosima and her siblings had all moved out and her husband had died, the countess lived alone in the magnificent eighteen-room villa. An old caretaker and his wife lived in the adjacent guest house. By now they were more like friends than employees. Bodenstein had a high regard for his mother-in-law. She led an astoundingly modest life, donating vast sums to various family foundations; unlike Vera Kaltensee, she did this discreetly and without a lot of fuss. Bodenstein led Pia around the house to the spacious garden. They found the countess in one of her three greenhouses, busily repotting tomato seedlings.

"Ah, there you are," she said with a smile. Bodenstein had to grin at the sight of his mother-in-law in faded jeans, a baggy knit jacket, and floppy hat.

"My God, Gabriela." He kissed her on both cheeks before he introduced her to Pia. "I had no idea that your interest in growing vegetables had assumed such alarming proportions. What do you do with all this stuff? You can't possibly eat everything yourself."

"What we don't eat we give to the Bad Homburg food bank," replied the countess. "So my hobby does some good at least. But tell me—what's going on?"

"Have you ever heard the name Marcus Nowak?" Pia asked.

"Nowak, Nowak." The countess stuck a knife into one of the sacks lying beside her on the workbench and ripped through the plastic. Rich black soil spilled onto the bench, and Pia involuntarily thought of Monika Krämer. She exchanged glances with her boss and knew that he'd made the same association. "Yes, of course! That's the young contractor who restored the old mill at Mühlenhof two years ago, after Vera won approval from the monuments preservation office."

"That's very interesting," said Bodenstein. "Something must have happened, because she lodged a complaint against him for inflicting negligent bodily harm."

"I heard about that," said the countess. "There was apparently an accident and Vera was injured."

"What happened?" Bodenstein opened his jacket and loosened his tie. In the greenhouse it was at least eighty-two degrees, with 90 percent humidity. Pia was jotting things down in her notebook.

"I don't remember exactly. Sorry." The countess set the plants she'd finished repotting on a board. "Vera doesn't like to talk about her failures. At any rate, after the episode, she fired her assistant, Dr. Ritter, and filed several lawsuits against Nowak."

"Who's Dr. Ritter?" Pia asked.

"Thomas Ritter was for years Vera's personal assistant and gofer," explained Gabriela von Rothkirch. "An intelligent, good-looking man. After she fired him without notice, Vera bad-mouthed him everywhere, so he can't find a job anywhere." She paused to giggle. "I always thought she had a thing for him. But my God, that boy was clever, and Vera is an old bag. This Nowak, by the way, is also a rather handsome guy. I've seen him two or three times."

"He *was* a handsome guy," said Pia, correcting her. "Earlier this morning, he was attacked and badly beaten. In the doctors' opinion, he was tortured. His right hand is so shattered that they might have to amputate."

"Good Lord!" The countess stopped her work, horrified. "That poor man!"

"We have to find out why Vera Kaltensee sued him."

"Then you'd probably better talk to Dr. Ritter. And to Elard. As far as I know, they were both present when it happened."

"Elard Kaltensee isn't likely to tell us anything negative about his mother," Bodenstein said, taking off his jacket. Sweat was running down his face.

"I wouldn't be so sure about that," replied the countess. "Elard and Vera aren't very fond of each other."

"Then why does he live under the same roof with her?"

"Probably because it's comfortable," Gabriela von Rothkirch speculated. "Elard is not a person who seizes the initiative. He's a brilliant art historian, and his opinion is highly regarded in the art world, but in real life he's rather inept—not a man of action like Siegbert. Elard likes to take the easiest path and remain good friends with everybody. If that doesn't work, then he evades the issue."

Pia had gotten the same impression of Elard Kaltensee. He was still her prime suspect.

"Do you think it's possible that Elard could have killed his mother's friends?" she asked, although Bodenstein rolled his eyes. But the countess gave Pia a solemn look.

"Elard is hard to read," she said. "I'm sure he's hiding something behind his polite facade. You have to keep in mind that he never had a father, no roots to speak of. That bothers him a lot, especially now that he's reached the age when he would finally realize that perhaps he'll never find out. And there's no doubt he could never stand Goldberg and Schneider."

Marcus Nowak had visitors when Bodenstein and Kirchhoff entered the hospital room an hour later. Pia recognized the young foreman from that morning. He was sitting on the chair next to his boss's bed, listening to him and avidly taking notes. After he promised to come back that evening and left, Bodenstein introduced himself to Nowak.

"What happened to you?" he asked with no preamble. "And don't tell me you can't remember. I won't accept it."

Nowak didn't seem particularly enthused to see Kripo again, so he did what he was good at: He kept his mouth shut. Bodenstein had sat down on the chair while Pia leaned against the windowsill with her notebook open. She looked at Nowak's badly beaten face. Last time, she hadn't noticed what a nice mouth he had. Full lips, straight white teeth, and finely chiseled facial features. Bodenstein's mother-in-law was right. Under normal circumstances, he must have been a rather good-looking man.

"Mr. Nowak," Bodenstein said, leaning forward, "do you think we're here for our own amusement? Or don't you care if the men who may have caused the possible loss of your right hand get off scot-free?"

Nowak closed his eyes and stubbornly said nothing.

"Why did Mrs. Kaltensee sue you for inflicting negligent bodily harm?" asked Pia. "Why did you try to call her about thirty times over the past few days?"

Silence.

"Could it be that the attack on you has something to do with the Kaltensee family?"

Pia noticed that Nowak balled his uninjured hand into a fist when she asked this question. Bingo! She took a second chair, set it on the other side of the bed, and sat down. It almost seemed a little unfair to put this man through the wringer after he'd been through such a horrible experience less than twenty-four hours ago. She knew only too well how terrible it was to be attacked inside your own four walls. Still . . . she had five murders to solve, and Marcus Nowak could have easily been the sixth dead body.

"Mr. Nowak." She spoke in a kindly tone. "We want to help you, really we do. This is about much more than the attack on you. Please look at me."

Nowak obeyed. The expression of vulnerability in his dark eyes moved Pia. There was something appealing about the man, although she didn't know him at all. Occasionally, she would feel great sympathy and understanding for a person into whose life she had suddenly had a glimpse through her investigations. But that wasn't good for maintaining the required objectivity. As she continued to ponder why she liked this man who so stubbornly refused to divulge anything, she recalled what had gone through her head that morning when she saw Nowak's vehicles. On the night of Schneider's murder, a witness had seen a vehicle with a company name on the side in the driveway of Schneider's house.

"Where were you on the night of April thirtieth?" she asked out of the blue. Nowak was as surprised by this question as Bodenstein was.

"I was at a dance for the May Day celebration. At the sports field in Fischbach."

His voice sounded a bit indistinct, which could have been because of the bruises and his split lower lip, but at least he'd said something.

"You weren't possibly in Eppenhain briefly after the dance?"

"No. What would I be doing there?"

"How long were you at this celebration? Where did you go afterward?"

"I don't know exactly. Stayed until one or one-thirty. Then I went home," said Nowak.

"And on the evening of May first? Were you perhaps at Mühlenhof with Mrs. Kaltensee?"

"No," said Nowak. "Why do you ask?"

"Did you go there to talk to Mrs. Kaltensee? Because she had filed a complaint against you. Or maybe because you wanted to intimidate Mrs. Kaltensee."

Finally, Nowak emerged from his shell.

"No!" he said emphatically. "I wasn't at Mühlenhof. And why would I want to intimidate Mrs. Kaltensee?"

"You tell me. We know that you restored the mill there. While you were doing that, there was an accident, and Mrs. Kaltensee obviously blames you for it. What's going on between you and her? What happened back then? Why did she sue you?"

It took a moment before Nowak came up with an answer.

"She went to the construction site and broke through the freshly laid clay floor, even though I warned her about it," he finally explained. "She blamed me for her accident, so she didn't pay my bill."

"To this day, Vera Kaltensee has never paid you for your work?" Pia asked. Nowak shrugged and stared at his healthy hand.

"How much does she owe you?" Pia asked.

"I don't know."

"Oh, come on now, Mr. Nowak. I'm sure you know the amount down to the cent. Don't give us that. So, how much money does Mrs. Kaltensee owe you for your work on the mill?"

Marcus Nowak retreated into his shell and remained silent.

"A call to our colleagues in Kelkheim is all it'll take for me to get access to the lawsuit files," she said. "So?"

Nowak thought about it a moment, then gave a sigh.

"A hundred and sixty thousand euros," he said reluctantly. "Plus interest."

"That's a lot of money. Can you afford to lose that much?"

"No, of course not. But I'll get the money."

"How are you going to do that?"

"I'll sue her for the payment."

It was quiet for a moment in the hospital room.

"Now I'm wondering," said Pia, "how far you would go to collect your money."

Silence. Bodenstein's look signaled her to continue.

"What did the men last night want from you?" Pia went on. "Why did they ransack your office and storeroom and torture you? What were they looking for?"

"Nowak pressed his lips together and looked away.

"The men were in a hurry to get out of there when your grandmother turned on the outside lights," said Pia. "They ran into a concrete flowerpot. Our colleagues retrieved traces of auto paint that are being analyzed in our lab right now. We're going to get those guys. But it would go a lot faster if you'd help us."

"I didn't recognize any of them," Nowak insisted. "They wore masks and they blindfolded me."

"What did they want from you?"

"Money," he said after a brief pause. "They were looking for a safe, but I don't have one."

It was a smooth lie. And Marcus Nowak knew that Pia had seen through it.

"All right." She got up. "If you don't want to tell us anything else, that's up to you. We've tried to help you. Maybe your wife can tell us more. She's on her way down to the station right now."

"What's my wife got to do with this?" Nowak sat up with an effort. The thought that the Criminal Police were going to talk to his wife seemed to make him uncomfortable.

"We'll find out soon." Pia gave him a brief smile. "Best of luck to you. And if you think of anything else, here's my card."

Bodenstein brooded on the way down to the lobby of the hospital. "Does he really not know, or is he just scared?"

"Neither," Pia said firmly. "He's hiding something from us; I can feel it. I'd hoped that—"

She broke off, grabbed her boss by the arm, and pulled him behind a pillar.

"What is it?"

"That man over there, the one with the bouquet," Pia whispered. "Isn't that Elard Kaltensee?"

Bodenstein squinted and looked across the lobby.

"Yes, that's him all right. What's he doing here?"

"I wonder if he's going to see Nowak," said Pia. "But if he is . . . why?"

"How could he even know that Nowak is here in the hospital?"

"If the Kaltensees are actually behind the attack, then he'd know for sure," Pia replied. "I had our guys check his outgoing calls—last night he phoned Nowak—perhaps to keep him there until the thugs showed up."

"Let's ask him." Bodenstein headed for the man. Elard Kaltensee was busy reading the signs and spun around in shock when Bodenstein addressed him. His face turned even paler.

"You're taking your mother some flowers." Bodenstein smiled amiably. "I'm sure she'll be happy with them. How's she doing?"

"My mother?" Kaltensee seemed distraught.

"Your brother told me that your mother is in the hospital," Bodenstein said. "You're going to see her, aren't you?"

N—no, I . . . I'm on the way to see . . . an acquaintance."

"Mr. Nowak?" asked Pia. Kaltensee hesitated a moment, then nodded.

"How do you know that he's in this hospital?" Pia asked suspiciously. In Bodenstein's presence, Elard Kaltensee was not nearly as sinister as he'd seemed Saturday afternoon.

"From his bookkeeper," said Kaltensee. "She called me this morning and told me what had happened. You must know that I arranged a big commission for Nowak in Frankfurt, the renovation project of the Old Town. In three days, an important deadline is coming up, and Nowak's people are afraid that their boss won't be allowed to leave the hospital in time."

That sounded believable. He seemed to be slowly recovering from the shock, and the color was coming back to his waxen face. He looked as though he hadn't slept since Saturday.

"Have you already talked to him?" Elard asked.

Bodenstein nodded. "Yes, we have."

"Well? How's he doing?"

Pia gave him a mistrustful look. Was it merely polite concern about the health of an acquaintance?

"They tortured him," she said. "His right hand was smashed so badly that it might have to be amputated."

"Tortured?" Kaltensee turned pale again. "Oh my God!"

"Yes, the man has very serious problems," Pia went on. "You must know that your mother still owes him a six-figure sum for the work on the mill."

"Pardon me?" Kaltensee's surprise was genuine. "That can't be!"

"Mr. Nowak told us that himself just now," said Bodenstein.

"But . . . but that can't be true." Kaltensee shook his head in bewilderment. "Why didn't he ever say anything about it? My God, what must he think of me?"

"How well do you know Mr. Nowak, actually?" Pia asked. Kaltensee didn't reply right away.

"Not that well," he replied guardedly. "When he was working at Mühlenhof, we talked a few times."

Pia waited for him to go on, but he did not.

"Shortly before he was attacked, you made a thirty-two-minute phone call to him," she said. "At one o'clock in the morning, mind you. An odd time to chat with a casual acquaintance, don't you think?"

For an instant, utter surprise was apparent on the face of the professor. The man had something to hide; that was obvious. His nerves were frayed. Pia had no doubt that he would break down in a real interrogation.

"We spoke about the renovation project," Kaltensee replied stiffly. "It's a very big undertaking."

"At one in the morning? I don't believe a word of it." Pia shook her head.

"Your mother has also begun legal action against Mr. Nowak for inflicting negligent bodily harm," Bodenstein put in. "She has filed three lawsuits against him."

Elard Kaltensee stared at Bodenstein in bewilderment.

"What's your point?" He seemed nervous but still didn't grasp what they were getting at. "What does all this have to do with me?"

"Don't you think that Mr. Nowak would have plenty of reasons to hate your family from the bottom of his heart?"

Kaltensee remained mute. Sweat was beading on his brow. It didn't look like he had a clear conscience.

"So we're asking ourselves," Bodenstein continued, "how far Mr. Nowak would be willing to go to get his money."

"What . . . what do you mean?" The conflict-averse professor was clearly overwhelmed by the situation.

"Did Marcus Nowak know Mr. Goldberg or Mr. Schneider? And maybe also Mrs. Frings? A car with a company name on the side, such as Nowak has in his fleet, was seen in Schneider's driveway at around twelve-thirty the night of his murder. Mr. Nowak has no real alibi for this time period, because he claims he was at home, alone."

"Around twelve-thirty?" Elard Kaltensee repeated.

"Nowak worked for quite a while at Mühlenhof," said Pia. "He knew the three victims and he also knew that they were close friends of your mothers. For them, a hundred and sixty thousand euros might not be a lot of money, but for Mr. Nowak it's a fortune. Maybe he thought he could put pressure on your mother if he killed her friends, one after the other, in order to underscore that he was serious."

Kaltensee stared at her as if she'd lost her mind. He shook his head vehemently.

"But that's utterly absurd. What are you thinking? Marcus Nowak is no killer. And none of that is a motive for murder."

"Revenge and fear for one's livelihood are very strong motives for murder," said Bodenstein. "Only a small percentage of murders are committed by hardened killers. Mostly, they're quite normal people who see no other way out."

"Marcus never shot anybody!" Kaltensee retorted with surprising vehemence. "I can't imagine how you came up with such a ridiculous idea!"

Marcus? The relationship between the two was probably quite a bit closer than Kaltensee would have them believe. Pia had an idea. She recalled the indifference with which he had reacted to the news of Herrmann Schneider's death a few days earlier. Was that because he already knew about it? Was it conceivable that Kaltensee—a well-to-do, influential man—had used Nowak by enticing him with a million-euro contract, and then demanded three murders in exchange?

"We're going to check out Nowak's alibi on the night of Schneider's murder," said Pia. "And we'll also ask him where he was when Goldberg and Mrs. Frings died."

"You're totally wrong, I can tell you that." Kaltensee's voice was shaky. Pia looked closely at the man. Even though he now had himself well under control, she couldn't ignore how agitated he seemed. Did he realize that she was on his trail?

Pia's cell rang just as she came out of the hospital.

"I've been trying to call you for an hour." Ostermann sounded reproachful.

"We were in the hospital." Pia paused while her boss kept walking. "There was no reception inside. What's up?"

"Listen to this: Marcus Nowak was stopped on April thirtieth at eleven-forty-five P.M. by a police patrol in Fischbach. He had no driver's license and no ID with him and was ordered to present both the next day to our colleagues in Kelkheim. As of today, he has not done so."

"That's interesting. Where exactly did the stop occur?" Pia heard her colleague typing on his keyboard.

"Grüner Weg, corner of Kelkheimer Strasse. He was driving a VW Passat that's registered to his company."

"Schneider was murdered around one o'clock in the morning," said Pia, thinking out loud. From Fischbach to Eppenhain by car takes around fifteen minutes. Thanks, Kai."

She put away her cell and went over to her boss, who was standing by his car and staring into space. Pia told him what she'd learned from Ostermann.

"So he was lying about where he was at the time of the crime," she concluded. "But why?"

"Why would he murder Schneider?" Bodenstein asked in turn.

"Maybe at Professor Kaltensee's instigation. He had brokered a huge construction contract for Nowak and maybe demanded a favor in return. Or maybe Nowak wanted to put pressure on Vera Kaltensee by murdering her best friends."

"Forget about Elard Kaltensee as the perp or instigator," said Bodenstein. His forbearing tone of voice suddenly made Pia furious.

"No, I will not!" she exclaimed. "This man has the strongest motive of all the people we've spoken to. You should have seen the way he acted at his apartment. He said he *hates* anyone who has prevented him from learning more about his origins. And when I asked him whom he was talking about, he said, 'those who know.' He would have preferred to kill them all. I didn't let up. I kept asking questions, and then he said, 'They're all dead now.' "

Bodenstein gave her a contemplative look over the roof of the car.

"Kaltensee is in his early sixties," Pia went on, somewhat calmer now. "He doesn't have much time to find out who his biological father was. He shot the three friends of his mother when they refused to tell him. Or else he incited Nowak to do it. And I'm sure that his mother is next on the list. He hates her, too."

"You don't have a single piece of evidence to back up your theory," said Bodenstein.

"Damn it!" Pia slammed her fist onto the roof of the car. She would have preferred to take her boss by his shoulders and shake him, because he refused to see the obvious. "I'm positive that Kaltensee has something to do with it. Why don't you go back in the hospital and ask him about his alibis for the times of the crimes. I'll bet he tells you that he was at home. Alone."

Instead of answering, Bodenstein tossed her the car keys.

"Send a patrol car to pick me up here in half an hour," he said, and went back into the hospital.

Christina Nowak was waiting in the foyer of the station and jumped up when Pia came in. She was very pale and visibly nervous.

"Hello, Mrs. Nowak." Pia extended her hand. "Please come with me."

She signaled the officer inside the glass partition to let her in. The door buzzed. At the same time, Pia's cell rang. It was Miriam.

"Are you at the office?" Her friend's voice sounded excited.

"Yep, just walked in."

"Then look at your e-mails. I scanned the items and sent them as attachments. And the archivist gave me a few tips. I'm talking to a couple of people and I'll call back later."

"Okay. I'll take a look right away. Thanks."

Pia stopped at the door to her office on the second floor.

"Would you please wait here for a moment? I'll be right back."

Christina Nowak nodded mutely and sat down on one of the plastic chairs in the hall. Ostermann was the only one of her colleagues in the office. Hasse had gone to Taunusblick to talk with the residents, Fachinger was searching for possible witnesses in the apartment building in Niederhöchstadt, and Behnke was doing the same in Königstein. Pia sat down at her desk and opened her e-mail program. Among the usual spam, which the police server's firewall was apparently powerless to stop, she found an e-mail with a Polish sender. She opened the attached documents and looked at one after the other.

"Wow," she murmured with a grin. Miriam had really done good work. In the city archives of Wegorzewo, she had found school photos from 1933 that showed the graduating class of the gymnasium in Angerburg. Also a newspaper article about the presentation ceremony for the winner of a sailing regatta, because back then Angerburg on the Mauersee was already a stronghold of water sports. David Goldberg was included in both photos, and he was mentioned several times in the paper: as regatta winner and son of Angerburg merchant Samuel Goldberg, who had endowed the prize. That was the genuine David Goldberg, who would die in Auschwitz in January 1945. He had curly dark hair and deep-set eyes. He was a slight young man, no taller than five seven. The man who was shot in his house in Kelkheim must have been six one in his younger days. Pia bent over the printout of a newspaper article from the *Angerburger Nachrichten* of July 22, 1933. The winning team of the sailboat with the proud name of *Prussian Honor* consisted of four young men, who were laughing happily into the camera: David Goldberg, Walter Endrikat, Elard von Zeydlitz-Lauenburg, and Theodor von Mannstein.

"Elard von Zeydlitz-Lauenburg," Pia muttered, enlarging the picture with a mouse click. That must have been Vera Kaltensee's brother, the one who had been missing since January 1945. The similarity between the youth barely sixteen years old in the photo from 1933 and his sixty-three-year-old nephew of the same first name was unmistakable. Pia printed out the file, then stood up and asked Christina Nowak to come into her office.

"Please excuse me for making you wait." Pia shut the door behind her. "May I offer you some coffee?"

"No, thank you." Christina Nowak sat down on the edge of a chair and set her purse on her knees.

"Unfortunately, your husband has had very little to say to me, so I'd like to hear a bit more from you about him and those closest to him."

Christina Nowak nodded calmly.

"Does your husband have any enemies?"

The pale woman shook her head. "Not that I know of."

"How are things in your family? The relationship between your husband and your father-in-law doesn't seem to be so good."

"There are always tensions in any family." With a distracted gesture, Mrs. Nowak pushed a strand of hair out of her face. "But my father-in-law would certainly never do anything to hurt Marcus or me and the kids."

"But he resents your husband for not expanding the construction company back then, right?"

"The company was my father-in-law's life work. The whole family worked there. Naturally, he and my brother-in-law hoped that Marcus would help them out of the crisis."

"And you? What did you think when your husband refused to do that and instead went into business for himself?"

Christina Nowak fidgeted on her chair.

"To be honest, I also wanted him to keep the company going. In retrospect, I admire him for not doing so. The whole family—including me—put a lot of pressure on him. Unfortunately, I'm not a very brave person. I was afraid that if Marcus wouldn't do it, we'd lose everything."

"And how are things now?" Pia asked. "Your father-in-law didn't seem very upset by the attack on your husband."

"There you're mistaken," Christina Nowak replied. "My father-in-law has become very proud of Marcus."

Pia doubted it. Manfred Nowak was obviously a man who worried a lot about his loss of influence and reputation. Yet she could understand that his daughter-in-law wouldn't want to say anything negative about her husband's parents, since they all lived under the same roof. Pia had often met women like Christina Nowak, who shut their eyes with all their might to reality, dreading any change in their lives, and clinging desperately to the belief that everything was fine.

"Do you have any idea why your husband was attacked and tortured?" Pia asked.

"Tortured?" Mrs. Nowak turned even paler and stared at Pia in disbelief.

"His right hand was smashed. The doctors still don't know whether it can be saved. Didn't you know that?"

"No . . . no," she admitted after a brief hesitation. "And I don't have any idea why anyone would *torture* my husband. He's a craftsman, not a . . . secret agent or anything."

"Then why did he lie to us?"

"Lie? What do you mean?"

Pia mentioned the fact that Nowak was pulled over by the police on the night of April 30. Christina Nowak looked away.

"Please don't play games with me," said Pia. "It's quite common for a man to have secrets from his wife."

Christina Nowak flushed but forced herself to stay calm.

"My husband has no secrets from me," she said stiffly. "He told me about being stopped by the police."

Pia pretended to write something down, because she knew it would rattle the woman.

"Where were you on the night of April thirtieth?"

"At the May dance at the sports field. My husband had a lot to do that evening and came to the party later."

"What time did he arrive? Before or after the police stopped him?"

Pia smiled blandly. She hadn't mentioned the time of the traffic stop.

"I . . . I didn't see him at all. But my father-in-law and a couple of my husband's friends told me he was there."

Pia dug deeper. "He was at the party and didn't talk to you? That's odd."

She noticed that she had touched a sore point. For a moment, it was totally quiet. Pia waited.

"It's not what you think." Christina Nowak leaned forward a little. "I know that my husband doesn't care much for the people in the sports club anymore, so I didn't urge him to go to the party. He was there briefly, talked to his father, and then drove home."

"Your husband was stopped by the police at eleven-forty-five P.M. Where did he go after that?"

"Straight home, I presume. I didn't get home till six, after cleaning up, and he was already out jogging. Like he does every morning."

"I see. Very well." Pia searched through the papers on her desk and said nothing. Christina Nowak got more and more nervous. Her eyes flitted here and there, and beads of sweat shone on her upper lip. Finally, she couldn't stand it any longer.

"Why do you keep asking me about that night?" she asked. "What does it have to do with the attack on my husband?"

"Does the name Kaltensee mean anything to you?" asked Pia instead of answering.

"Yes, of course." Christina Nowak nodded uncertainly. "Why?"

"Vera Kaltensee owes your husband a large amount of money. And she has also sued him for negligent bodily harm. We found a summons from the police in his office."

Christina Nowak bit her lower lip. Apparently, there were some things she didn't know about. From then on, she refused to answer any of Pia's questions. "Mrs. Nowak, please. I'm looking for a reason for the attack."

She raised her head and stared at Pia. Her fingers were gripping the handle of her purse so tightly that her knuckles had turned white. For a long moment, there was silence.

"Yes, my husband does have secrets from me!" she exclaimed suddenly. "I don't know why, but since he was in Poland the year before last and met Professor Kaltensee, he's completely changed."

"He was in Poland? Why?"

Christina Nowak paused, but then it poured out of her like lava from a volcano.

"He hasn't taken a vacation with me and the kids for ages, because he supposedly doesn't have time. But he can spend ten days with his grandmother and go off to Masuria. Sure, he has time for that. It may sound silly, but sometimes I get the feeling he's married to Auguste and not to me. And then this Kaltensee shows up. Professor Kaltensee this, Professor Kaltensee that. They're on the phone constantly, making some sort of plans that he won't tell me about. My father-in-law exploded when he found out that Marcus was working for the Kaltensees, of all people."

"Why is that?"

"The Kaltensees are to blame for my father-in-law having to declare bankruptcy," Christina Nowak explained, to Pia's astonishment. "He built the new office park in Hofheim for the Kaltensees' company. They accused him of bungling the job. There were umpteen specialist reports and the case went to court and then dragged on for years. Eventually, my father-in-law ran out of steam, and besides, it was a matter of seven million euros. Once they finally reached an agreement six years later, the company could no longer be saved."

"That's very interesting. So why did your husband agree to work for the Kaltensees again?" Pia asked. Christina Nowak shrugged.

"None of us understood it," she said bitterly. "My father-in-law kept warning Marcus. And now the whole thing is repeating: There's no money, nothing but trials, one report after another . . ." Her voice trailed off and she heaved a deep sigh. "My husband is literally obsessed with this Kaltensee. He pays no attention to me anymore. He wouldn't even notice if I moved out."

From her own experience, Pia could comprehend what was happening for this woman, but she didn't want to hear any details about the Nowaks' marital problems.

"I ran into Professor Kaltensee today at the hospital. He was on his way to visit your husband and seemed very worried," she said, hoping to coax Mrs. Nowak to say more. "Apparently, he didn't know that his mother still owed your husband money. Why didn't your husband tell him that if they're such good friends?"

"Friends? That's not what I would call it. Kaltensee is exploiting my husband, but Marcus simply doesn't get it," Mrs. Nowak replied angrily. "With him, everything still revolves around the job in Frankfurt. It's total insanity. The project is far too big for him—he's taking on more than he can handle. How is he going to get the job done with the few employees he has? Urban renewal of Frankfurt's Old Town—bah! This Kaltensee has put a flea in his ear. If he fails, we'll lose everything."

Bitterness and frustration colored her words. Was she jealous of the friendship between her husband and Professor Kaltensee? Was she afraid they were going to go broke? Or was it the fear of a woman who felt her small, seemingly safe world was coming apart at the seams and she was losing control? Pia rested her chin in her hand and studied the woman.

"You're not helping me," she said. "And I wonder why not. Do you really know so little about your husband? Or don't you care what has happened to him?"

Christina Nowak shook her head vehemently. "Of course I care," she replied in a trembling voice. "But what am I supposed to do? Marcus has hardly spoken to me in months. I have absolutely no idea who did this to him or why, because I don't know what sort of people he's dealing with. But one thing I do know for sure: The fight with the Kaltensees is not about any mistake that Marcus made. It's about some chest that disappeared while the work was going on. Marcus had several visits from Professor Kaltensee and Dr. Ritter, Vera Kaltensee's secretary. They sat in his office for hours discussing confidential matters. But that's all I know, I swear it."

Her eyes were shining with tears. "I'm really worried about my husband," she said with a helplessness that aroused involuntary sympathy in Pia. "I'm afraid for him and for our children because I don't know what he's gotten himself into or why he won't talk to me anymore."

She turned her face away and sobbed.

"Besides, I think that he . . . that he has someone else. He often drives off late at night and doesn't come home until the next morning."

She rummaged in her purse and avoided looking at Pia. Tears were running down her face. Pia handed her a Kleenex and waited patiently as Mrs. Nowak blew her nose.

"That means he might not have been home on the night of April thirtieth, am I right?" Pia asked softly.

Christina Nowak shrugged and nodded. When Pia thought she wouldn't learn anything else of interest, the woman dropped a bombshell.

"I . . . I saw him recently with a woman. In Königstein. I . . . I was in the pedestrian area, picking up some books for the kindergarten class at the bookstore. I saw his car parked across the street from the ice-cream parlor. Just as I was about to go over there, a woman came out of that run-down house next to the lotto store, and he got out of his car. I watched as they spoke to each other."

"When was that?" Pia asked, as if electrified. "What did the woman look like?"

"Tall, dark-haired, elegant," replied Christina Nowak, greatly distressed. "The way he looked at her . . . and she put her hand on his arm. . . ."

She gave a sob and the tears were flowing again.

"When did this happen?" Pia repeated.

"Last week," Mrs. Nowak whispered. "On Friday, about quarter to eleven. I . . . I thought at first it was about a new job, but then . . . then she got in the car with Marcus, and they drove off together."

•   •   •

As Pia went over to the conference room, she had the feeling they'd reached a breakthrough. She didn't enjoy putting people under so much pressure that they burst into tears, but sometimes the end justified the means. Bodenstein had called a meeting for four-thirty, but before Pia could tell him what she'd just learned, Dr. Engel came into the room. Hasse and Fachinger were already sitting at the table, and a little later Ostermann came in carrying two binders. Then Behnke showed up. Precisely at four-thirty, Bodenstein appeared.

"I see that all the members of K-Eleven are present." Nicola Engel sat down at the head of the table, where Bodenstein usually sat. He didn't say a word, just took a seat between Pia and Ostermann. "This seems a suitable occasion for me to introduce myself. My name is Nicola Engel, and starting June first, I'll be taking over from my colleague Nierhoff."

There was dead silence in the room. Naturally, every officer in the Regional Criminal Unit in Hofheim already knew who she was.

"I worked for many years as a detective myself," Engel went on, unperturbed by the lack of reaction. "The work of K-Eleven is especially dear to my heart, and that's why I'd like—unofficially—to collaborate with you on this case. It seems to me that additional help would do no harm."

Pia gave her boss a brief glance. Bodenstein didn't move a muscle. His thoughts seemed to be elsewhere. As the commissioner gave a speech about her career and her plans for the future of RCU Hofheim, Pia leaned over to him.

"And?" she said in a tense whisper.

"You were right," Bodenstein said softly. "Kaltensee has no alibis."

The commissioner beamed as she looked around the table, "So, I already know Chief Detective Inspector Bodenstein and Ms. Kirchhoff. I suggest the rest of you briefly introduce yourselves. Let's begin with my colleague on the right."

She looked at Behnke, who was sprawled on his chair and acted as if he hadn't heard her.

"Detective Behnke." Dr. Engel seemed to be enjoying the situation. "I'm waiting."

The tension in the room was palpable, like before a thunderstorm. Pia recalled how Behnke had stormed out of Bodenstein's office, his face pale as wax. Was his unusual behavior somehow connected to Dr. Engel? At K-11 in Frankfurt, Behnke had been Bodenstein's colleague, so he had to know Nicola Engel as well. But why was the new boss acting as if she didn't know him? As Pia was pondering this, Bodenstein spoke.

"Enough of this chitchat. We have a lot of work to do."

He quickly introduced his colleagues, then immediately shifted to giving a rundown of the latest developments. Pia decided to be patient and wait till the end to give her report. The pistol that she'd found in Watkowiak's backpack was not the weapon with which the three old people had been shot; forensics had clearly confirmed that. They hadn't made much progress at Taunusblick. The residents Hasse spoke with hadn't noticed anything that might be relevant to the case. Fachinger, however, had talked to a neighbor of Monika Krämer in Niederhöchstadt who said she'd seen an unfamiliar man in dark clothing in the stairwell at the time of the crime, and later by the trash cans in the courtyard. Behnke had found out some very interesting things in Königstein: The proprietor of the ice-cream parlor kitty-corner from the dilapidated house where Watkowiak's corpse was found had recognized the victim from his photo. He said that Watkowiak occasionally spent the night in that house. Also, last Friday he had noticed the van of a renovation firm with a very prominent N as its logo, parked for almost forty-five minutes in front of the house. And a few weeks ago, Watkowiak had sat at one of the tables in the back of the ice-cream shop, having an intense conversation with a man who drove a BMW convertible with Frankfurt plates. The car was parked right in front of the shop.

As the investigative team speculated what one of Nowak's vans had been doing in front of the house in Königstein, and who the unknown man in the ice-cream parlor could have been, Pia leafed through the Goldberg file, which was conspicuously thin.

"Listen to this," she said, interrupting the discussion. "Goldberg had a visit on the Thursday before he died from a man in a sports car with Frankfurt plates. That couldn't be a coincidence."

Bodenstein nodded appreciatively. Now Pia told everyone what she had learned half an hour ago from Christina Nowak.

"What was supposed to be in this chest?" asked Ostermann.

"I don't know. But at any rate, her husband is much better friends with Professor Kaltensee than he would have us believe. Kaltensee and a man named Dr. Ritter, who used to work for Vera Kaltensee, were in Nowak's office several times after the incident at the mill."

Pia took a deep breath.

"And here's the kicker. On Friday at about the time Watkowiak died just before noon, Nowak was at the building in Königstein where we found Watkowiak's body. He met a dark-haired woman there and later drove off with her. I heard this from his wife, who happened to see him."

There was silence in the room. With that, Marcus Nowak moved back up the list of prime suspects to a much higher position. Who was the dark-haired woman? What had Nowak been doing at the building? Could he be Watkowiak's killer? New riddles and inconsistencies emerged with each new development.

"We'll ask Vera Kaltensee about the chest," Bodenstein said at last. "But first we have to talk to this Dr. Ritter. He seems to know a lot. Ostermann, find out where the man lives. Hasse and Fachinger, continue following up on Mrs. Frings's murder. Tomorrow, go and interview more residents of Taunusblick, also the staff, the gardeners, the deliverymen. Somebody must have seen how the old lady was taken out of the building."

"It'll take the two of us weeks," Andreas Hasse complained. "There are over three hundred names on the list, and so far we've talked to only fifty-six people."

"I'll make sure you get some help." Bodenstein made a note and looked around the table. "Frank, tomorrow you get to work on the neighbors of Goldberg and Schneider one more time. Show them Nowak's company logo; you can probably print it from their Web site. Then go to the sports club in Fischbach and ask if anybody saw him there the night of April thirtieth."

Behnke nodded.

"That wraps it up for now. We'll meet tomorrow afternoon at the same time. Oh, Ms. Kirchhoff. The two of us will go and see Nowak again."

Pia nodded. Amid the scraping of chair legs on the linoleum floor, the meeting adjourned.

"And what have you planned for me, Oliver?" Pia heard Nicola Engel ask on their way out. The use of his first name surprised her, so she stopped in the hall behind the open door and pricked up her ears.

"What the heck are you doing here anyway?" Bodenstein's muted voice sounded angry. "What's the point of this stunt? I told you that I didn't want any disruptions while my team is working on these investigations."

"I'm interested in the case."

"That's a laugh. You're just looking for a chance to catch me making a mistake. I know that's what you're up to."

Pia held her breath. What was all this about? "You think you're more important than you are," snapped Engel in a condescending tone. "Why don't you just tell me to go to hell and to stay out of the investigations?"

Tensely, Pia waited for Bodenstein's reply. Unfortunately, a couple of colleagues came down the hall, talking loudly, and the door to the conference room closed from the inside.

"Shit," Pia muttered. She wanted to hear more, and resolved to ask Bodenstein quite casually how he happened to know Nicola Engel.

Tuesday, May 8

There were no security men to be seen when Bodenstein and Kirchhoff showed up at Mühlenhof early in the morning. The big gate stood wide open.

"I guess they're not worried anymore," said Pia. "Now that Watkowiak is dead and Nowak's in the hospital."

Bodenstein nodded absentmindedly. He hadn't said a word during the drive over. A wiry woman with a practical short haircut opened the door and informed them that none of the Kaltensees was at home. From one second to the next, Bodenstein seemed transformed. He put on his most charming smile and asked the woman whether she had a couple of minutes to answer a few questions. She did, and the conversation lasted much more than a few minutes. Pia was familiar with this tactic, and in such instances, she let her boss do all the talking. Even Anja Moormann couldn't resist his concerted charm offensive. She was the wife of Vera Kaltensee's factotum and had spent more than fifteen years in the service of "the mistress of the house," as she put it. This outmoded term elicited an amused smile from Pia. The Moormanns lived in a small house on the extensive grounds and enjoyed regular visits from their two grown sons and their families.

"Do you happen to know Mr. Nowak, too?" Bodenstein asked.

"Yes, of course." Anja Moormann nodded eagerly. Her skintight white T-shirt clearly showed her tiny breasts, and her freckled skin was taut across her bony collarbones. Pia guessed her age to be somewhere between forty and fifty.

"I always cooked for him and his people when they were working here. Mr. Nowak is a very nice man. And so good-looking." She emitted a giggle that did nothing for her appearance. Her upper lip seemed a bit too short, or maybe her front teeth were too big. She reminded Pia of a breathless bunny. "To this day, I can't understand why the mistress was so unfair to him."

Anja Moormann might not be the brightest bulb in the chandelier, but she was curious and talkative. Pia was convinced that not much happened at Mühlenhof without her knowing about it.

"Do you remember the day the accident happened?" she asked, trying to decide at the same time what the housekeeper's regional accent might be. Was she from Swabia? Saxony? The Saar?

"Oh yes. The professor and Mr. Nowak were standing in the courtyard in front of the mill, looking at some blueprints. I had just brought them some coffee, when the mistress and Dr. Ritter arrived. My husband had picked them up at the airport." Anja's memory was impeccable, and she was obviously enjoying being in the spotlight, since life had otherwise consigned her to the role of an extra. "The mistress jumped out of the car and flew into a rage when she saw the people in the mill. Mr. Nowak tried to hold her back, but she shoved him away and dashed straight inside and up the stairs. The new clay floor on the second level was still quite moist, and she crashed right through the floor, screaming at the top of her lungs."

"What was she looking for inside the mill?" asked Pia.

"It was about something in the attic," replied Anja Moormann. "At any rate, there was a lot of yelling, but Mr. Nowak just stood there, saying nothing. The mistress then dragged herself to the workshop, even though her arm was broken."

"Why to the workshop?" Pia interjected when Anja stopped for air. "What was in the attic?"

"Oh God, tons of old junk. The mistress never threw anything away. There were six trunks, stored there, all dusty and full of cobwebs. Nowak's people had brought everything, along with those steamer trunks, down to the workshop before they tore out the floor in the mill."

Anja Moormann crossed her arms, pensively pressing her thumbs into her impressive biceps.

"There was a trunk missing," she went on. "The mistress and her family were shouting at one another, and when Ritter got involved, that's when the mistress exploded. I can't repeat all the things they were yelling."

Anja shook her head at the memory.

"When the ambulance arrived, the mistress screamed that if the trunk wasn't back at the estate within twenty-four hours, then Ritter could look for another job."

"But what did he have to do with it?" Bodenstein asked. "He'd been abroad with the mis—with Mrs. Kaltensee, hadn't he?"

"That's right." Anja shrugged. "But somebody's head had to roll. She could hardly throw out the professor. So poor Nowak and Ritter had to take the blame. After eighteen years! She chased him off the estate in disgrace. Now he lives in a shabby studio apartment and doesn't even have a car. And all because of a dusty old steamer trunk!"

A vague memory suddenly stirred in Pia's mind, but she couldn't recall what it was about.

"Where are the trunks now?" she wanted to know.

"Still in the workshop."

"Could we look at them?"

Anja thought for a moment, then came to the conclusion that it didn't matter if she showed the trunks to the police. Bodenstein and Kirchhoff followed her around the house to the low farm buildings. The workshop had been meticulously cleaned up. On the walls above wooden workbenches hung a multitude of tools, whose outlines had been carefully drawn with black marker. Anja opened a door.

"There they are," she said. Bodenstein and Pia entered the adjoining room, a former cold-storage space, judging by the tiled walls and the pipe channel running along the ceiling. Five dusty steamer trunks stood in a row. All at once, it dawned on Pia where the sixth one was. Anja chattered on cheerfully, telling them about her last encounter with Marcus Nowak. Shortly before Christmas, he'd appeared at Mühlenhof, ostensibly to deliver a present. After he used this pretext to gain entry into the house, he headed straight for the great salon, where the mistress and her friends were holding their monthly 'homeland evening.'"

"Homeland evening?" Bodenstein asked.

"Yes." Anja Moormann nodded eagerly. "Once a month they met, Goldberg, Schneider, Frings, and the mistress. If the professor was away, they would meet here; otherwise, they met at Schneider's place."

Pia glanced at Bodenstein. That was certainly informative. But at the moment, they were interested in Nowak.

"I see. And what happened then?"

"Ah yes. Well." The housekeeper stopped in the middle of the workshop and scratched her head. "Mr. Nowak accused the mistress of owing him money. He said it very politely—I heard it myself—but the mistress laughed at him and gave him an earful, like—"

She broke off mid-sentence. Around the corner of the house glided the black Maybach limousine. The tires crunched on the newly raked gravel as the heavy vehicle drove right past them and stopped a few yards farther on. Pia thought she could make out someone sitting in the backseat behind the tinted windows, but the horse-faced Moormann, today in his proper chauffeur's uniform, got out alone, locked the car with the remote, and came over to them.

"The mistress is unfortunately still indisposed," he said, but Pia was sure that he was lying. She noticed the brief glance he exchanged with his wife. How must it feel to be a servant of the rich, to lie for them and keep so many secrets? Did the Moormanns hate their boss? After all, Anja hadn't displayed much loyalty in the way she had behaved.

"Then please give her my heartfelt greetings," said Bodenstein. "I'll call again tomorrow."

Moormann nodded. He and his wife remained standing in front of the door to the workshop and watched Bodenstein and Pia go.

"I know he's lying," Pia said quietly to her boss.

"Yes, I think so, too," said Bodenstein. "She's sitting in the car."

"Let's go open the door," Pia suggested. "Then she'll make a fool of herself."

Bodenstein shook his head.

"No," he said. "She's not going anywhere. Let her think we're a little dim-witted."

Dr. Thomas Ritter had proposed the Café Siesmayer in the Frankfurt Pal-mengarten as the site for their meeting, and Bodenstein assumed that he was ashamed of his apartment. Vera Kaltensee's former assistant was already seated at one of the tables in the smoking section of the café when they came in. He stubbed out his cigarette in the ashtray and jumped up as Bodenstein headed directly toward him. Pia guessed he was in his mid-forties. With an-gular, slightly asymmetrical facial features, a prominent nose, deep-set blue eyes, and thick, prematurely gray hair, he was not ugly, but not convention-ally handsome, either. Yet his face had something that might cause a woman to take a second look. He looked Pia up and down briefly, seemed to find her uninteresting, and turned to Bodenstein.

"Would you rather sit at a nonsmoking table?" he asked.

"No, this is fine." Bodenstein took a seat on the leather banquette and got straight to the point.

"Five members of your former employer's social circle have been murdered," he said. "In the course of the investigations, your name has come up several times. What can you tell us about the Kaltensee family?"

"Who do you want to know about?" Ritter raised his eyebrows and lit another cigarette. There were three butts in the ashtray already. "I was Vera Kaltensee's personal assistant for eighteen years. So naturally I know a great deal about her and her family."

The waitress arrived at the table, handed out menus, and had eyes only for Ritter. Bodenstein ordered a coffee, Pia a Diet Coke.

"Another latte macchiato?" the young woman asked. Ritter nodded casually and cast a quick glance at Pia, as if wanting to make sure she'd noticed what effect he had on the opposite sex.

Stupid fool, she thought, giving him a smile.

"What led to the disagreement between you and Dr. Kaltensee?" Bodenstein asked.

"There was no disagreement," Ritter insisted. "But after eighteen years, even the most interesting job eventually loses its appeal. I simply wanted to do something else."

"I see." Bodenstein acted as if he believed the man. "What line of work are you in now, if I may ask?"

"You may." Ritter smiled and crossed his arms. "I'm the editor of a weekly lifestyle magazine, and I write books, as well."

"Oh, is that so? I've never met a real writer before." Pia gave him an admiring look, which he registered with unmistakable satisfaction. "What sort of things do you write?"

"Novels, mainly," he replied vaguely. He had crossed his legs and tried in vain to give an impression of nonchalance. His eyes kept straying to his cell phone, which was lying next to the ashtray on the table.

"We've heard that your parting with Mrs. Kaltensee was not quite as amicable as you want us to believe," Bodenstein said. "Why, exactly, were you let go after the accident at the mill?"

Ritter didn't reply. His Adam's apple twitched up and down. Did he honestly think the police were so clueless?

"In the dispute that led to your termination without notice, apparently a trunk with unknown contents was involved. What can you tell us about that?"

"That's all nonsense." Ritter made a dismissive gesture. "The whole family was jealous of my good relationship with Vera. I was a thorn in their side because they were afraid I might have too much influence on her. We parted on completely friendly terms."

He sounded so convincing that Pia wouldn't have doubted him if it hadn't been for Anja Moormann's account.

"Then what's all the fuss about this missing trunk?" Bodenstein sipped at his coffee. Pia saw a flash of anger in Ritter's eyes. He kept toying with the cigarette pack. She would have preferred to take it away from him; he was infecting her with his nervousness.

"I have no idea," he replied. "It's true that a trunk was supposedly missing from the storeroom at the mill. But I never saw it and I don't know what happened to it."

Suddenly, the young woman behind the buffet dropped a stack of plates, which shattered with a crash on the granite floor. Ritter jumped as if he'd been shot, and his face went snow-white. His nerves seemed to be in a bad way.

"So do you have any idea what might have been in this trunk?" Bodenstein asked. Ritter took a deep breath, then shook his head. He was obviously lying—but why? Was he ashamed? Or was he trying to avoid giving them any cause to suspect him? Without a doubt, he had been treated badly by Vera Kaltensee. The humiliation of his dismissal without notice, done so publicly, had to be hard to bear for any man with a shred of self-respect.

"What kind of car do you drive, by the way?" Pia asked, changing the subject abruptly.

"Why?" Ritter gave her an annoyed look. He went to get another cigarette out of the pack but found it empty.

"Pure curiosity." Pia reached in her purse and set an unopened pack of Marlboros on the table. "Please, help yourself."

Ritter hesitated for a moment but then took one.

"My wife has a Z three. That's what I'm driving."

"Also last Thursday?"

"Possibly." Ritter snapped open his lighter, lit the cigarette, and sucked the smoke deep into his lungs. "Why do you ask?"

Pia exchanged a quick glance with Bodenstein and decided to take a wild shot. Maybe Ritter was the guy with the sports car.

"You were seen together with Robert Watkowiak," she said, hoping she wasn't wrong. "What did you discuss with him?"

Ritter's almost imperceptible flinch signaled to Pia that she was on the right track.

"Why do you want to know?" he asked irritably, confirming her suspicion.

"You may have been one of the last people to speak with Watkowiak," she said. "At the moment, we're working on the assumption that he was the murderer of Goldberg, Schneider, and Anita Frings. Maybe you know that last weekend he took his own life with an overdose of prescription drugs."

She noticed the relief that passed briefly over Ritter's face.

"I heard that." He let smoke escape from his nostrils. "But I had nothing to do with it. Robert called me. Once again, he had a problem. At Vera's request, I've helped him out of a jam often enough, so he probably thought I could help him this time, too. But I couldn't."

"And it took you two hours with him in the ice-cream parlor to tell him that? I don't believe you."

"But it's true," Ritter insisted.

"You visited Goldberg in Kelkheim the day before he was shot. Why?"

Ritter glibly lied, looking Pia straight in the eye. "I used to visit him often. I don't remember what we talked about that evening."

"You've been lying to us for the past fifteen minutes," Pia said. "Why? Do you have something to hide?"

"I'm not lying," Ritter replied. "And I have nothing to hide."

"Then why don't you simply tell us what you really wanted at Goldberg's house and what you talked about with Watkowiak?"

"Because I can hardly remember," Ritter said, trying to talk his way out of it. "It must have been something trivial."

"By the way, do you know Marcus Nowak?" Bodenstein interjected.

"Nowak? The guy who restores buildings? Not really. I met him once. Why do you want to know?"

"That's odd." Pia took her notebook out of her pocket. "Nobody in this case seems to know the others very well."

She leafed a few pages back.

"Ah yes, here it is: His wife told us that you and Professor Kaltensee met several times with Marcus Nowak at his office after the accident in the mill and your termination without notice. And for hours at a time." She fixed Ritter with her gaze, and he was visibly uncomfortable. With the arrogance of a man who considers himself smarter than the majority of his fellow human beings, especially the police, he had completely underestimated Pia, as he was now forced to realize. He glanced at his watch and decided on an orderly retreat.

"Unfortunately, I have to go," he said with a forced smile. "An important appointment in the editorial office."

Pia nodded. "Please don't let us keep you. We'll ask Mrs. Kaltensee about the real reason for your termination. Maybe she also has some idea what you discussed with Mr. Watkowiak and Mr. Goldberg."

The smile froze on Ritter's face, but he said nothing. Pia handed him her business card.

"Call us if the truth happens to occur to you."

"How did you get the idea that the man in the ice-cream parlor might be Ritter?" Bodenstein asked as they walked through the palm garden on the way back to their car.

"Intuition." Pia shrugged. "Ritter looks like the type who would drive a sports car."

For a while, they walked side by side without speaking.

"Why do you think he was lying to us? I can't imagine that Vera Kaltensee would fire her longtime assistant, who knows so much about her after eighteen years, all because of a missing trunk. There must be more to it."

"But who would know?" Bodenstein said.

"Elard Kaltensee," Pia suggested. "We ought to visit him again anyway. The missing trunk is in his bedroom, right next to the bed."

"How do you know what's in Elard Kaltensee's bedroom?" Bodenstein stopped and looked at Pia with a frown. "And why didn't you mention this earlier?"

"I didn't think about it until we were in the workshop at Mühlenhof," Pia replied, defending herself. "But I'm telling you now."

They left the palm garden and crossed Siesmayerstrasse. Bodenstein unlocked his car with a press of the remote. Pia already had her hand on the door handle when her gaze fell on the building across the street. It was one of those elegant apartment houses from the nineteenth century with a carefully restored facade from the industrial age. Those spacious classic apartments went for sky-high prices on the real estate market.

"Take a look over there. Isn't that our baron of lies?"

Bodenstein turned his head.

"It certainly is."

Ritter had clamped his cell phone between his ear and shoulder and was fumbling with a bunch of keys as he stood at the bank of mailboxes by the front door. Then he unlocked the door, still on the phone, and vanished inside the building. Bodenstein closed the car door. They crossed the street and examined the mailboxes.

"So, there's no magazine office here." Pia tapped on one of the brass nameplates. "But somebody named M. Kaltensee does live here. What could that mean?"

Bodenstein looked up at the facade. "We'll soon find out. First let's drive over and visit your favorite suspect."

Friedrich Müller-Mansfeld was a tall, slender man with a snow-white fringe of hair around a pate dotted with age spots. He had a long, furrowed face and red-rimmed eyes, which were unnaturally magnified by the thick lenses of his old-fashioned glasses. He had traveled to visit his daughter on Lake Constance and returned only last night. His name was one of those on the long list of residents and staff of Taunusblick, and Kathrin Fachinger harbored no great hope that she'd learn more from him than from the residents she'd already questioned. She politely asked the elderly gentleman the usual routine questions. For seven years, he had lived next door to Anita Frings, and he displayed the appropriate sorrow when he learned about the violent death of his neighbor.

"I did see her on the evening before I left," he said in a hoarse, shaky voice. "She was in very good spirits."

He grasped his right wrist with his left hand, but the tremor could not be overlooked.

"Parkinson's," he explained. "Most of the time I do well, you know, but the trip was a bit exhausting."

"I won't bother you for long," said Fachinger kindly.

"Oh, go ahead and bother me as long as you want." Old gentlemanly charm flashed in his blue eyes. "It's a nice change of pace to speak with such a pretty young lady, you see. Otherwise, there are only old bags here."

Fachinger smiled. "Good. So you saw Mrs. Frings on the evening of May third. Was she alone or accompanied by someone?"

"She could hardly move on her own. There was a lot going on here, including an open-air performance in the park. I saw her with the man who visited her regularly."

Fachinger listened carefully.

"Can you remember about what time that was?"

"Of course. I have Parkinson's, you know, not Alzheimer's."

It was supposed to be a joke, but since his expression didn't change, the officer didn't realize that at first.

"You know, I'm from East Berlin," said the old gentleman. "I was a professor of applied physics at Humboldt University. In the Third Reich, I wasn't allowed to practice my profession because I sympathized with the Communists. So I spent years abroad, but later in the German Democratic Republic, my family and I had a good life."

"I see," said Fachinger politely. She wasn't quite sure what he was driving at.

"Naturally, I knew the whole ruling Socialist Unity Party leadership personally, even though I can't really claim that they were particularly congenial. But as long as I was allowed to do research, the rest didn't matter to me. Anita's husband, Alexander, was in the Ministry of State Security; he was an officer in a special unit and responsible for covert operations in foreign-exchange management."

Fachinger sat up and stared at the man.

"So you knew Mrs. Frings from before?"

"Yes. Didn't I mention that?" The old man thought for a moment, then shrugged his shoulders. "Actually, I knew her husband. Alexander Frings was a counterintelligence officer during the war in the Foreign Armies East department, and a close colleague of General Reinhard Gehlen. Perhaps that name means something to you?"

Fachinger shook her head. She was taking notes feverishly, sorry that she'd left her tape recorder sitting on her desk.

"In his capacity as counterintelligence officer in the Abwehr, Frings had an intimate knowledge of the Russians, you see. And after Gehlen and his whole department surrendered to the Americans in May 1945, they were attached to the OSS, the predecessor of the CIA. Later Gehlen founded, with the express approval of the United States, the Gehlen Organization, from which the West German Federal Intelligence Service was formed." Fritz Müller-Mansfeld gave a hoarse laugh, which quickly changed to a cough. It took a while before he could speak again. "Within a very short time, dedicated Nazis became dedicated democrats. Frings didn't go with them to the United States preferring to remain in the Soviet Occupation Zone. Also with the approval and knowledge of the Americans, he infiltrated the Stasi and was responsible for foreign-exchange procurement for the GDR, but he remained in contact with the CIC, later the CIA, and Gehlen in West Germany."

"How do you know all this?" Fachinger asked, astounded.

"I'm eighty-nine years old," replied Müller-Mansfeld amiably. "In my lifetime, I have seen and heard a great deal, and forgotten almost as much. But Alexander Frings impressed me, you see. He spoke six or seven languages fluently, was very intelligent and cultivated, and he played along with the game on both sides. He was the control for numerous Eastern Bloc spies, and was allowed to travel in the West at will. He knew high-ranking Western politicians and all the important industrial leaders. The arms lobbyists in particular were his friends."

Müller-Mansfeld paused to rub his bony wrist.

"Why Frings was attracted to Anita—other than because of her looks—is to this day hard for me to understand."

"Why's that?"

"She was an ice-cold woman," replied Müller-Mansfeld. "There was a rumor going around that she'd been an overseer at KZ Ravensbrück, you see. She had no intention of going to the West, where she would have risked being identified by former concentration camp inmates. She met Frings in Dresden in 1945. When they married, he was able to protect her from further criminal prosecution because by then he had contacts with both the Americans and the Russians. With her new name, she had also shed her Nazi views and made a career for herself with the Stasi. Although . . ." Müller-Mansfeld snickered maliciously. "Her weakness for Western consumer goods earned her the secret nickname 'Miss America,' which annoyed her no end."

"What can you tell me about the man who was with her that evening?" Fachinger asked.

"Anita had visitors fairly often. Her childhood friend Vera was often here, and sometimes the professor, as well."

Fachinger patiently waited as the old man rummaged through his memory and lifted his water glass to his lips with a trembling hand.

"They called themselves 'the Four Musketeers.'" He laughed again, the sound hoarse and derisive. "Twice a year, they would meet in Zürich, even after Anita and Vera had buried their husbands."

"Who called themselves the Four Musketeers?" asked Fachinger in bewilderment.

"The four old friends from before. They'd all known one another since childhood—Anita, Vera, Oskar, and Hans."

"Oskar and Hans?"

"The arms dealer and his adjutant from the finance board."

"Goldberg and Schneider?" Fachinger leaned forward excitedly. "Did you know them, too?"

Fritz Müller-Mansfeld's eyes sparkled with amusement.

"You have no idea how long the days in an old folks home can be, even when it's as luxurious and comfortable as this one. Anita liked to tell stories. She had no relatives anymore, and she trusted me. Anyway, I'm also one of those from Eastern Germany. She was cunning, but not nearly as crafty as her friend Vera. She's a sly one. She's done well for a simple girl from East Prussia, don't you think?"

He rubbed his knuckles again, lost in thought for a moment.

"Anita was very excited last week. Why, she never told me. But she had a lot of visitors. Vera's son was here several times, the bald one, and also his sister, the politician. They sat with Anita in the cafeteria for hours. And the Little Tomcat, who came regularly. Used to push her wheelchair around in the park."

"The Little Tomcat?"

"That's what she called him, the young man."

Fachinger wondered what "young" meant from the point of view of an eighty-nine-year-old.

"What did he look like?" she asked.

"Hmm. Brown eyes. Slim. Medium height, average-looking face. The ideal spy, right?" Müller-Mansfeld smiled. "Or a Swiss banker."

"And he was also with her on Thursday evening?" Fachinger asked patiently, although she was quivering with excitement inside. Bodenstein was going to love this.

"Yes." Fritz Müller-Mansfeld nodded. Fachinger took her cell phone out of her pocket and searched for the photo of Marcus Nowak that Ostermann had sent her half an hour ago.

"Could it have been this man here?" She handed him the phone. He shoved his glasses onto his forehead and held the display very close to his eyes.

"No, that's not the man," he said. "But I've seen him, too. I think it might have even been that same evening." Müller-Mansfeld frowned. "Yes, I remember now," he said at last. "It was on Thursday, around eleven-thirty. The theater performance had just ended, and I went to the elevator. He was standing in the foyer, as if waiting for somebody. I noticed how nervous he was. He kept looking at his watch."

"And you're quite certain that it was the same man?" Fachinger asked, verifying this before taking back her phone.

"One hundred percent. I have a good memory for faces."

When they didn't find Professor Kaltensee at the Kunsthaus, Bodenstein and Kirchhoff drove back to the station in Hofheim. Ostermann greeted them with the news that the DA considered the grounds too flimsy to warrant a forensic examination of Nowak's vehicles.

"But Nowak was seen at the location where a body was found, and he was there at the approximate time the crime was committed!" Pia exclaimed, getting worked up. "And one of his vehicles was sighted in front of Schneider's house."

Bodenstein poured himself a cup of coffee.

"Anything new from the hospital?" he asked. Since early that morning, an officer had been assigned to sit outside Nowak's room and make a note of each visitor and the time of the visit.

"This morning, his wife was there," replied Ostermann. "At noon, his grandmother visited and one of his colleagues."

"That's all?" Pia was disappointed. The case was not moving forward.

"But I've found out plenty about KMF." Ostermann looked through his documents until he found the right folder, then gave his colleagues a report. In the thirties, Eugen Kaltensee, in a somewhat crass but at the time not unusual manner, had seized the company of a Jewish business owner who had discerned what was happening in Germany and left with his family. Kaltensee had used the inventions of the previous owner for the arms industry, expanded his business in the East, and made a fortune. As a supplier to the Wehrmacht, he had been a member of the Nazi Party and one of the biggest war profiteers.

"How do you know this?" Pia asked Ostermann in amazement.

"There was a trial," he replied. "The Jewish former owner, Josef Stein, sued to get his company back after the war. Supposedly, Kaltensee had signed a statement saying that in the event Stein returned to Germany, he would have to give back the company. Naturally, this document could not be found, a compromise was reached, and Stein received shares in the firm. It was a big story in the press at the time, because although there was clear evidence that Kaltensee had exploited KZ prisoners in his factories in the East, he was classified as 'exonerated' and did not face prosecution."

Ostermann gave a satisfied smile.

"I've traced the former general manager of KMF," he said. "He retired five years ago and does not have anything particularly good to say about Vera and Siegbert Kaltensee, because they booted him out in a rather nasty way. The man is familiar with the entire operation to the smallest detail, and he told me everything.

"In the early eighties, the company suffered a serious crash. Vera and Siegbert wanted more influence, so they hatched intrigues against Eugen Kaltensee, and as a result he restructured the firm. He set up a new shareholder agreement and divided the voting rights at his own discretion among family members and friends. A fatal decision, which to this day guarantees that there will be discord within the family. Siegbert and Vera each received twenty percent; Elard, Jutta, Schneider, and Anita Frings ten percent each; Goldberg eleven percent; Robert Watkowiak five percent; and a woman named Katharina Schmunck four percent. Before Kaltensee could change this agreement again, he fell down the cellar stairs and broke his neck."

At that moment, Bodenstein's cell rang. It was Fachinger. "Boss, I've hit the jackpot!" she shouted. Bodenstein motioned to Ostermann to wait a moment as he listened to the excited voice of his youngest colleague.

"Very good, Ms. Fachinger," he said at last, and ended the call. He looked up with a satisfied grin on his face.

"Now we can get an arrest warrant for Nowak and a search warrant for his company and residence."

23. August 1942. I'll never forget this day as long as I live, when I became an aunt! At 10:15 this evening, Vicky gave birth to a healthy baby boy—and I was there. It went so quickly, especially since the whole time I'd been thinking that something like this could take hours and hours. The war is so far away and yet so near. Elard has gotten leave from the front—he's in Russia—and Mama has been praying all day long that nothing will happen to him, not today. This afternoon Vicky's labor pains started. Papa sent Schwinderke to Doben to fetch Mrs. Wermin, but she couldn't get away. The wife of farmer Krupski in Rosengarten has been in labor for two days, and she's almost forty. Vicky was very brave. I admire her courage. It was terrible and wonderful at the same time. Mama, Edda, and I, with help from Mrs. Endrikat, got it done without Mrs. Wermin. Papa opened a bottle of champagne and finished it off with Endrikat—the two grandfathers. They were pretty tipsy when Mama showed them the baby. I also got to hold him in my arms. Incredible to think that this creature with the tiny hands and feet will one day turn into a big strong man. Vicky named him after our papa, Heinrich Arno Elard—even though Edda said he should at least have Adolf as his middle name—and then the two grandfathers shed a few tears and cracked open another bottle of champagne. When Mrs. Wermin finally arrived, Vicky had already soothed the baby, and Mrs. Endrikat had washed and swaddled him. And I will be the godmother! Oh, life is so exciting. Little Heinrich

Arno Elard was totally unimpressed when Papa explained to him quite solemnly that one day he would be the lord of Lauenburg Manor, and then the boy threw up on his shoulder. How we laughed! A marvelous day, almost like before the war. As soon as Elard comes home on leave, there'll be a christening. And soon a wedding! Then Vicky will really be my sister, although we're already the best friends that anyone can imagine. . . .

Thomas Ritter stuck a yellow Post-it in the pages of the diary and rubbed his burning eyes. It was unbelievable. Reading the entries immersed him in a long-vanished world—the world of a young girl who led a sheltered life on the huge estate belonging to her parents in Masuria. These diaries alone would have provided enough material for a splendid novel, a requiem for the doomed world of East Prussia. Almost as good as Arno Surminski or Siegfried Lenz. In great detail, the very observant young Vera had depicted not only the country and people but also the political situation. She wrote from the point of view of the daughter of a lord of the manor whose parents had lost two sons in World War I and then had retreated to the East Prussian estate. They had been critical of Hitler and the Nazis but did not stop Vera and her friends Edda and Vicky from joining the Bund Deutscher Mädel, the League of German Girls. Also fascinating was the depiction of the travels of the young girls with their BDM group to the Olympic Games in Berlin and Vera's sojourns at a Swiss boarding school for girls, where she'd missed her friend Vicky terribly. When the war broke out, Vera's older brother Elard went into the Luftwaffe and there quickly made a name for himself through his achievements. Especially moving was the development of the love story between Elard and Vicky, the daughter of the estate steward Endrikat.

Why had Vera objected so vehemently to portraying her youth in East Prussia in the early chapters of her biography? After all, she hadn't done anything to be ashamed of, except maybe for her membership in the BDM. But out in the country, where everyone knew everybody else, back then it would have been almost impossible not to join without getting into difficulties. Ritter kept on reading, and gradually he had understood why it would have been better for these memories from Vera's point of view to be thrown into the fire than fall into the hands of strangers. Considering what he had learned last

Friday, these diaries were truly explosive. As he read the entries, he'd taken copious notes, which had caused him to reorder the first chapters of his manuscript. In the diary from 1942, he'd then found the proof. After he'd read the description of August 23, 1942—the day that Hitler had ordered his bombers to attack Stalingrad for the first time—he went straight to the Internet and looked up the brief bio of Elard Kaltensee.

"That can't be," muttered Ritter, staring at the screen of his laptop. Elard was born on August 23, 1943, it said. Was it possible that Vera had given birth to a son exactly one year after the birth of her nephew? Ritter looked for the diary from 1943 and leafed through the pages to August.

Heini is one year old. What a sweet little guy—he looks good enough to eat. And he is already walking. . . . He went back a couple of pages, then flipped a couple of pages ahead. In July, Vera had returned from Switzerland to her parents' estate and spent the summer there, a summer that was overshadowed by the death of Walter, her friend Vicky Endrikat's eldest brother, who had fallen at Stalingrad. No word of a man in Vera's life, not to mention a pregnancy. There was no doubt that Elard Kaltensee was in reality Heinrich Arno Elard, who was born on August 23, 1942. Then why did it say in his biography that he was born in 1943? Had Elard made himself a year younger out of vanity?

Ritter jumped in alarm when his cell phone rang. Marleen asked where he was. It was already past ten. Thoughts were whirling around in Ritter's head, and he simply couldn't stop now.

"I'm going to be even later, I'm afraid, sweetheart," he said, trying to sound apologetic. "You know I have a deadline tomorrow. I'll be there as soon as I can, but don't wait up for me. Just go to bed."

She had scarcely hung up when he pulled over his laptop and started typing the sentences he'd formulated while he was reading. He smiled as he worked. If he could substantiate his suspicion with solid proof, then Katharina and her publishing colleagues would definitely have the sensational story they wanted.

"Nowak was also at Taunusblick on Thursday evening," said Bodenstein after he had told Ostermann and Pia about Kathrin Fachinger's conversation with Anita Frings's neighbor.

"And I doubt it was because of the theater performance," Pia remarked.

"Tell me more about KMF," Bodenstein said to Ostermann.

Vera Kaltensee had been furious when the new shareholder agreement was revealed during the reading of her husband's will after his death. In vain, she had attempted to contest the agreement. Then she attempted to buy out Goldberg, Schneider, and Frings's shares, but that was not permitted according to the agreement.

"By the way, Elard Kaltensee was suspected at the time of having shoved his stepfather down the stairs. The two of them had never gotten along," said Ostermann. "Later, it was judged an accident, and the matter was dropped." He looked at his notebook. "Vera Kaltensee was not at all happy that she now had to ask permission from her old friends, her stepson, Robert, and a friend of her daughter's for every deal she planned to make. But with Goldberg's help, she managed to be appointed honorary consul of Suriname. That enabled her to secure the rights to bauxite deposits in Suriname, which gave her an automatic entry into the aluminum business. She was no longer content to be merely a supplier. A few years later, she sold these rights to the American firm Alcoa, and KMF became the world leader in rolling mills for aluminum processing. The subsidiaries that administer the actual capital are located in Switzerland, Liechtenstein, the British Virgin Islands, Gibraltar, Monaco, and who knows where else. They pay next to nothing in taxes."

"Was Herrmann Schneider involved with these deals?" asked Pia. Like pieces in a puzzle, little by little the whole story seemed to be fitting together with her own theories. Everything had a meaning that would become clear as the total picture emerged.

Ostermann nodded. "Yes. He was a consultant to KMF Suisse."

"What's happening with the company shares now?" Bodenstein inquired.

"That's the thing." Ostermann straightened up. "Here it comes: According to the shareholder agreement, no shares could be bequeathed or sold. On the death of the shareholder, they pass to the executive shareholder. And this clause could be a real motive for four of our murders."

"How do you mean?" asked Bodenstein.

"According to the estimates, KMF is worth about four hundred million euros," said Ostermann. "There is an offer from a British leveraged-buyout firm for more than twice the present market value. You can do the math and see what that means for the individual shares."

Bodenstein and Pia exchanged a brief glance.

"The CEO of KMF is Siegbert Kaltensee," said Bodenstein. "So he acquires the shares of Goldberg, Schneider, Watkowiak, and Mrs. Frings upon their death."

"Apparently, that's right." Ostermann set his notebook on the desk and gave his colleagues a triumphant look. "And if eight hundred million euros isn't a motive for murder, then I can't imagine what is."

For a moment, no one spoke.

"I agree with you," remarked Bodenstein drily.

"Siegbert Kaltensee could neither sell nor take the firm public before that because he didn't hold a majority share. Now things look completely different. If my calculations are correct, he holds fifty-five percent of the stock, including his own twenty."

"Even ten percent of eight hundred million is nothing to sneeze at," mused Pia. "Any one of them could have benefited if Siegbert acquired the controlling shares and then converted their own shares into some serious dough."

"I just don't think that's the motive for the murders," said Bodenstein, drinking the rest of his coffee and shaking his head. "I think it's much more likely that our perp—without intending it—has done the Kaltensees a big favor."

Pia had taken the files from Ostermann's desk and was studying his notes.

"Who is this Katharina Schmunck, anyway?" she asked. "What does she have to do with the Kaltensees?"

"Katharina Schmunck's name today is Katharina Ehrmann," explained Ostermann. "She's Jutta Kaltensee's best friend."

Bodenstein frowned, thinking hard; then his face lit up. He remembered the photos he'd seen at Mühlenhof. But before he could say anything, Pia jumped up and rummaged in her pocket until she found the business card on which the real estate agent had written the name of the house owner.

"That can't be true," she said when she found the card. "Katharina Ehrmann owns the building in Königstein where we found Watkowiak's body. How does all this fit together?"

"It's obvious," said Ostermann, who seemed to be holding out the greed of the Kaltensee family as the most plausible motive. "They killed Watkowiak and wanted to throw suspicion onto Katharina Ehrmann. That way, they'd kill two birds with one stone."

Ritter's eyes burned and his head was roaring. The letters on the monitor started to blur together. In the past two hours, he'd written twenty-five pages. He was dead tired and at the same time in high spirits from sheer adrenaline. With a mouse click, he saved the file and went into his e-mail program. He wanted Katharina to read first thing in the morning what he'd done with her material. With a yawn, he stood up and went to the window. He had to put the diaries into the ATM-accessed safe-deposit box before he went home. Marleen might be naïve, but if she got her hands on this, she'd understand everything. And in the worst case, she'd turn to the page about her family. Ritter's gaze fell on the empty parking lot. The only other vehicle was a dark panel truck next to his convertible. He was about to turn away, when for a fraction of a second a light in the front seat of the truck went on and he saw the faces of two men. He heart began to pound frantically. Katharina had said that the files were explosive, maybe even dangerous. In the light of day, that hadn't bothered him. But now, at 10:30 at night in a lonely back court-yard of an industrial area in Fechenheim, this idea definitely had more menace to it. He grabbed his cell and punched in Katharina's number. She picked up after the tenth ring.

"Kati," said Ritter, trying to sound calm, "I think I'm being watched. I'm still at the office, working on the manuscript. Down in the parking lot there's a panel truck with two guys sitting in it. What should I do? Who could it be?"

"Calm down," replied Katharina in a low voice. Ritter could hear in the background the buzz of voices and a piano playing. "You're probably imagin-ing things. I—"

"I'm not imagining things, damn it!" Ritter snapped. "They're down there and they might be waiting for me. You said yourself that these files could be dangerous!"

"That's not how I meant it," Katharina assured him. "I wasn't thinking of bodily danger. Nobody knows about the material. Now go home and get some sleep."

Ritter went to the door and turned off the ceiling light. Then he went over to the window again. The panel truck was still there.

"Okay," he said. "But I still have to get the diaries to the bank. Do you think something could happen to me there?"

"No, that's nonsense," he heard Katharina say.

"All right, then." Ritter felt somewhat relieved. If there really was a danger, she would react differently. After all, he was her golden goose; she wouldn't put his life on the line. Suddenly, he felt silly. Katharina must think he was being ridiculous.

"By the way, I sent you the manuscript," he said.

"That's great," said Katharina. "I'll read through it first thing tomorrow morning. Now I've got to go."

"All right. Good night." Ritter ended the call; then he put the diaries in a plastic bag and his laptop in his backpack. His knees were shaking as he walked down the hall. "Just my imagination," he muttered.

Wednesday, May 9

"You're not going to believe who called me yesterday," said Cosima from the bathroom. "I tell you, I was totally flabbergasted!"

Bodenstein lay in bed, playing with the baby, who reached for his finger with a gurgle and held it with astounding strength. It was about time they solved this complex case—he wasn't getting any time to spend with his youngest daughter.

"So who was it?" he asked, tickling Sophia's tummy. She shrieked with delight and thrashed her little legs.

Cosima appeared in the doorway, only a towel wrapped around her, a toothbrush in her hand.

"Jutta Kaltensee."

Bodenstein stiffened. He hadn't told Cosima that Jutta Kaltensee had called him at least ten times in the past few days. At first, he'd felt flattered, but the conversations rapidly became too familiar for his taste. Not until yesterday, when she finally asked quite bluntly if they could have dinner together some time, did he realize what she was trying to do. Jutta Kaltensee was clearly putting the moves on him, and he didn't know how to react.

"Oh really? What did she want?" Bodenstein forced himself to keep his tone casual and continued to play with the baby.

"She's looking for people to work on her new image campaign." Cosima went into the bathroom and came back wearing a dressing gown. "She said she thought of me after she met you at her mother's house."

"Is that right?" Bodenstein didn't like the idea that Jutta had been gathering information about him and his family behind his back. Anyway, Cosima didn't do advertising films; she produced documentaries. The line about the image campaign was a lie. But why?

"We're meeting for lunch today, so I'll hear what she has to say." Cosima sat down on the edge of the bed and applied lotion to her legs.

"That sounds nice." Bodenstein turned his head and looked at his wife with a guileless expression. "Make sure to let her pick up the tab. The Kaltensees are loaded."

"Do you mind if I go?"

Bodenstein didn't know exactly what Cosima was getting at.

"Why should I?" he asked, instantly resolving to ignore Jutta Kaltensee's calls in the future. At the same time, it dawned on him how much he'd allowed himself to daydream about her. Too much. The mere thought of that shrewd and excitingly attractive woman aroused fantasies in him that weren't proper for a married man.

"Well, her family is the focus of your investigations," said Cosima.

"Just listen to what she has to offer," he suggested against his will. An unpleasant feeling came over him. What had been a harmless flirtation with Jutta Kaltensee could easily become an incalculable risk, and he certainly didn't need anything like that. It was time to put her in her place in a friendly but firm manner. No matter how sorry he was to do so.

Although she'd had only a few hours' sleep, Pia was already at her desk at a quarter to seven the next morning. It was essential to talk with Siegbert

Kaltensee as soon as possible; that much was clear. She sipped at her coffee, stared at the screen, and thought about Ostermann's report and conclusions from yesterday. Sure, it was conceivable that the Kaltensee siblings had hired someone to commit the murders. But there were too many things that didn't fit: What was the purpose of the numbers that the murderer had left behind at all three crime scenes? Why were the murders done with an ancient weapon and sixty-year-old ammunition? A hit man would probably have used a weapon with a suppressor and not taken the trouble to roll Anita Frings in her wheelchair from the retirement home into the forest. There was something personal behind the murders of Goldberg, Schneider, and Anita Frings. Pia was sure of it. But how did Robert Watkowiak fit into the picture? And why had his girlfriend had to die? The answer was hidden in a maze of phony sidetracks and possible motives. Revenge was a strong motive. Thomas Ritter knew the Kaltensees' family history; he had been deeply humiliated and hurt.

And what about Elard Kaltensee? Had he shot his mother's three friends—or ordered them shot—because they wouldn't tell him anything about his true origins? After all, he had admitted that he hated them and even felt a desire to kill them. Finally, there was Marcus Nowak, whose role seemed quite dubious. His van had not only been seen at Schneider's house at the time of the murder; he had also been at the house in Königstein when Watkowiak died and at Taunusblick on the evening Anita Frings was murdered. It couldn't be mere coincidence. For Nowak, it was always about a lot of money, as well. Nowak and Elard Kaltensee were much better friends than Kaltensee had wanted to admit to the police. Maybe they had committed the three murders together and might have been seen by Watkowiak . . . or was this all wrong, and the Kaltensees were really behind everything? Or was the perp someone else entirely? Pia had to admit that she was going in circles.

The door opened and Ostermann and Behnke came into the office. At the same moment, the fax machine beeped next to Ostermann's desk and began to hum. He set down his bag, took out the first page, and studied it.

"Well, finally," he said. "The lab has results."

"Let's see." Together, they read the six pages that the crime lab had sent. The weapon used to shoot Anita Frings was the same one that had fired the deadly shots at Goldberg and Schneider. Even the ammunition was the same.

The DNA that was found on a glass and on several cigarette butts in Schneider's home movie theater belonged to a man whose data were stored in the
computer at National Crime Police headquarters. A single hair found beside
Herrmann Schneider's body was confirmed in DNA analysis to be from an
unknown female. On the mirror at Goldberg's house was a clear fingerprint,
which, unfortunately, could not be matched. Ostermann logged on to the
database and discovered that the name of the man who'd been in the theater
in Schneider's basement was Kurt Frenzel, who had a police record for several
assaults and hit-and-run charges.

"The knife that was found next to Watkowiak was clearly the weapon
that killed Monika Krämer," said Pia. "His prints were on the hilt of the knife.
But the semen in her mouth was not from Watkowiak; it was from some unknown man. The deed was committed by a right-handed person. The evidence
in the apartment came mostly from Monika Krämer and Robert Watkowiak,
except for some fibers under her fingernails that could not be matched, and a
hair that's still being analyzed. The blood on Watkowiak's shirt also came
from Ms. Krämer."

"All of it sounds very unequivocal," said Behnke. "Watkowiak bumped
off his old lady. She was driving him crazy, after all."

Pia gave her colleague a dirty look.

"It couldn't have been him," Ostermann reminded them. "We have the
tapes from the surveillance cameras from the branches of Taunus Savings and
Nassau Savings which show Watkowiak trying to cash the checks. I'd have to
confirm the exact times, but I think it was between eleven-thirty and twelve.
According to the autopsy report, Monika Krämer died between eleven and
twelve o'clock."

"You don't really believe all this hit man shit that the boss dreamed up,
do you?" Behnke moaned. "What hit man would bother to bump off such a
stupid old woman, and why?"

"To shift the suspicion onto Watkowiak," said Pia. "The same perp also
killed Watkowiak, stuck the gun and the cell phone in his backpack, and put
the blood-smeared shirt on him."

At that moment, she decided to throw out her Nowak and Kaltensee
theories. She couldn't believe that either of them would commit such a brutal

murder, after first demanding a blow job. They were dealing with two perps; that much was certain.

"That does seem plausible," Ostermann conceded, reading aloud the part of the lab report about the shirt. It was buttoned wrong, it wasn't Watkowiak's size, and it was so new that there was still a pin in one of the sleeves, evidently overlooked when the shirt was removed from its plastic wrapping.

"We have to find out where the shirt was purchased," Pia said.

Ostermann nodded. "I'll check it out."

"Oh, that reminds me." Behnke looked through the stacks of paper on his desk and handed a page to Ostermann, who glanced at it and frowned.

"When did this arrive?"

"Yesterday sometime." Behnke turned on his computer. "I forgot all about it."

"What is it?" Pia asked.

"The movement profile of the cell phone that was in Watkowiak's backpack," replied Ostermann in annoyance, looking at his colleague, who always had an excuse for his carelessness. This time, Ostermann was really pissed off.

"Damn it, Frank," he snapped. "This is important; you know that. I've been waiting days for this."

"Don't make a federal case out of it," Behnke shot back. "Haven't you ever forgotten something?"

"When it comes to a homicide case—no. What the hell is wrong with you, man?"

Instead of answering, Behnke got up and left the office.

"Now what?" Pia asked, without commenting on Behnke's behavior. If Ostermann was also finally noticing that there was something wrong with Behnke, maybe he'd do something about it and clear up the matter, man-to-man.

"The cell phone was only used once, to send this text to Monika Krämer," said Ostermann after a thorough study of the page. "There were no numbers stored in it."

"Does it list which cell tower?" Pia asked curiously.

"Eschborn and vicinity." Ostermann snorted. "A radius of about three kilometers around the tower. Doesn't help us much."

•   •   •

Bodenstein stood at his desk, looking at the daily newspapers spread out in front of him. He had the first unpleasant encounter of the day, a meeting with Chief Commissioner Nierhoff, behind him. The chief had threatened to set up a special commission if Bodenstein didn't deliver some tangible results soon. The police spokesman was being bombarded with calls, and not only from the press. The Interior Ministry had also lodged an official inquiry, wanting to know how the investigations were progressing. The whole team was feeling irritable. They weren't even close to a breakthrough in any of the five homicides. The fact that Goldberg, Schneider, Anita Frings, and Vera Kaltensee had been friends since their youth didn't really help. The murderer had not left any identifiable traces at the three crime scenes, so it was impossible to construct a perp profile. For the time being, the Kaltensee siblings had the best motive, but Bodenstein was reluctant to endorse Ostermann's theories.

He folded up the newspapers and sat down, resting his forehead in his hand. Something was going on right before their eyes that they weren't seeing. He just couldn't figure out any way to connect the murders to the Kaltensee family and their circle that made sense. If there was, in fact, any sort of connection. Had he lost his ability to ask the right questions? There was a knock on the door, and Pia Kirchhoff came in.

"What's up?" he asked, hoping that his colleague wouldn't notice how insecure and helpless he was feeling.

"Behnke went over to see Frenzel, Watkowiak's pal, the guy whose DNA we found at Schneider's house," she said. "He brought Frenzel's cell phone back with him. Watkowiak had left him a voice mail on Thursday."

"And?"

"We wanted to listen to it now. By the way, we saw Ritter go inside a building on Siesmayerstrasse. A woman named Marleen Kaltensee lives there." She gave him a quizzical look. "What's the matter with you, boss?"

Once more, Bodenstein had the feeling that she was able to read his mind.

"We're not getting anywhere," he said. "Too many riddles, too many unknown individuals, too many useless leads."

"That's how it always is." Pia sat down on the chair facing him. "We've asked a lot of people a lot of questions and that has stirred things up. The case is now developing its own dynamic; we may not have any influence on it at the moment, but it's working for us. I have a strong feeling that something is going to happen very soon—something that'll put us back on the right track."

"You really are an optimist. What if your famous dynamic provides us with another corpse? Nierhoff and the Interior Ministry are putting enormous pressure on me."

"What do they expect from us?" Pia shook her head. "We aren't TV detectives. So stop looking so discouraged. Let's drive to Frankfurt and see Ritter and Elard Kaltensee. We'll ask them about the missing trunk."

She stood up and looked at him impatiently. Her energy was infectious. Bodenstein realized how indispensable Pia Kirchhoff had become in the past two years. Together, they made a perfect team. She was the one who occasionally offered bold conjectures and energetically drove things forward. He was the one who did everything by the book and reined her in when she got too emotional.

"Come on, boss," she said. "Forget the self-doubt. We have to show our new boss what we're made of!"

Bodenstein couldn't help smiling.

"Right," he said, and stood up.

"*—call me back, man!*" came the voice of Robert Watkowiak from the loud-speaker. He sounded frantic. "*They're after me. The cops think I bumped some-body off, and my stepmother's gorillas have been laying in wait for me at Moni's place. I gotta get out of here for a while. I'll call you again.*"

There was a click. Ostermann rewound the tape.

"When did Watkowiak leave this on the voice mail?" asked Bodenstein, who had recovered from his dejected mood.

"Last Thursday afternoon, at two thirty-five," said Ostermann. "The call came from a public phone in Kelkheim. A day later, he was dead."

"*. . . my stepmother's gorillas have been laying in wait for me at Moni's place . . .*" Robert Watkowiak's voice repeated. Ostermann worked the controls and let the message run again.

"All right, that's enough," said Bodenstein. "What's the news on Nowak?"

"Still lying in bed," replied Ostermann. "This morning from eight until a little after ten, his Oma and Papa were there."

"Nowak's father was visiting his son at the hospital?" Pia asked in amazement. "For two hours?"

"Yes." Ostermann nodded. "That's what a colleague told me."

"Okay." Bodenstein cleared his throat and looked around the table. Nicola Engel was absent today. "We're going to have another talk with Vera Kaltensee and her son Siegbert. I also want saliva samples from Marcus Nowak, Elard Kaltensee, and Thomas Ritter. We'll also pay another visit to Ritter today. And I want to talk to Katharina Ehrmann. Frank, find out where we can meet the lady."

Behnke nodded but made no comment.

"Hasse, get the lab moving on the paint traces from the car that rammed the concrete planter in front of Nowak's company. Ostermann, I want more information on Thomas Ritter."

"All that today?" asked Ostermann.

"By this afternoon, if you can." Bodenstein got up. "We'll meet here again at five to hear what you've found out."

Half an hour later, Pia rang Marleen Kaltensee's doorbell on Siesmayerstrasse, and after she held her ID up to the camera above the intercom, the door buzzed open. A few moments later, she and Bodenstein entered the apartment belonging to a woman in her mid-thirties with an unremarkable, somewhat puffy-looking face with bluish circles under her eyes. Her stocky figure, short legs, and a broad backside made her seem fatter than she actually was.

"I thought you'd be here much sooner," she began the conversation.

"Why?" asked Pia.

"Well"—Marleen Kaltensee shrugged—"the murders of my grandmother's friends and Robert . . ."

"That's not why we're here." Pia let her gaze wander over the tastefully furnished apartment. "Yesterday, we spoke with Dr. Ritter. You do know him, don't you?"

To her surprise, the woman giggled like a teenager and actually blushed.

"We saw him enter this building. All we want to know from you is what he wanted," Pia went on, a bit irritated.

"He lives here." Marleen Kaltensee leaned against the door frame. "We're married. I'm not Kaltensee anymore, but Ritter."

Bodenstein and Pia exchanged an amazed glance. It was true that yesterday Ritter had spoken of his wife in connection with the convertible, but he hadn't mentioned that she was the granddaughter of his former boss.

"We're newlyweds," she explained. "I haven't quite gotten used to my new name. But my family also doesn't know about our marriage yet. My husband wants to wait until a suitable moment, after all the uproar has died down."

"You mean the uproar about the murders of your ... grandmother's friends?"

"Yes, exactly. Vera Kaltensee is my Oma."

"And you are whose daughter?" Pia wanted to know.

"My father is Siegbert Kaltensee."

At that moment, Pia's gaze fell on the tight-fitting T-shirt of the young woman, and she deduced correctly.

"Do your parents know that you're expecting?"

Marleen Ritter first turned red, then beamed with pride. She stuck out her clearly swelling stomach and placed both hands on it. Pia managed a smile in spite of herself. After all these years, she still felt a pang in the presence of a happily pregnant woman.

"No," said Marleen Ritter. "As I said, my father has a lot on his mind right now."

Only now did she seem to remember her good manners. "May I offer you something to drink?"

"No thanks," Bodenstein said politely. "We really wanted to speak with ... your husband. Do you know where he is at the moment?"

"I can give you his cell number and the address of the editorial office."

"That would be very kind." Pia pulled out her notebook.

"Your husband told us yesterday that your grandmother had let him go because of a disagreement," said Bodenstein. "After eighteen years."

"Yes, that's true." Marleen Ritter nodded with concern. "I don't know exactly what happened. Thomas never says a bad word about Oma. I'm quite sure that everything will sort itself out once she hears that we're married and expecting a baby."

Pia was astounded at the naïve optimism of this woman. She doubted very much that Vera Kaltensee would ever take in the man whom she had chased from the estate in disgrace just because he had married her grand-daughter. On the contrary.

Elard Kaltensee's whole body was shaking as he drove his car toward Frank-furt. Could what he had just learned really be true? If so—what did they ex-pect from him? What should he do? He kept having to wipe his sweaty hands on his pants because it was hard to hold on to the wheel. For a moment, he was tempted to ram the car straight into a concrete pillar and simply end it all. But the thought that he might survive as a cripple kept him from doing that. He felt in the center console for the little tin box, then recalled that two days ago, full of euphoria and good intentions, he had tossed it out the win-dow. How could he have assumed that he'd suddenly be able to get along without lorazepam? His mental equilibrium had been shaky for months, but now he felt as if someone had pulled the ground out from under his feet. He didn't know what he had hoped to learn in all those years of searching, but it certainly wasn't this.

"Good God in heaven," he gasped with alarm as he fought against the conflicting emotions that, without the drug, were raging inside him. Every-thing was suddenly unbearably clear and painful to see. This was real life, and he didn't know whether he could or even wanted to confront it. His body and his mind emphatically demanded the relaxing effect of the benzodiazepine. When he had promised himself to give it up, he hadn't known what he knew now. His whole life, his whole existence, his identity were all a gigantic lie! But why? That was the question that kept hammering painfully in his head. Elard Kaltensee wished in despair that he had the courage to ask the right person about this. But the very thought of doing so filled him with a deep longing to run far away. For now, he could at least act as if he knew nothing.

Suddenly red brake lights went on in front of him, and he stomped so hard on the brake that the antilock braking system of his heavy Mercedes juddered. The driver behind him was honking wildly and veered off onto the shoulder just in time to avoid smashing into the trunk of his car. The fright snapped Elard Kaltensee out of it. No, he couldn't live like this. Nor did he care if the whole world knew what a pathetic coward was hiding behind the smooth facade of the worldly-wise professor. He still had a prescription in his suitcase. One or two tablets with a couple of glasses of wine would make everything more bearable. After all, he hadn't committed himself to taking any specific action. The best thing would be to pack a few things, drive straight to the airport, and fly to America. For a few days—no, even better, for a few weeks. Maybe even for good.

"Editor of a lifestyle magazine," Pia repeated mockingly in the face of the ugly flat-roofed building in back of a furniture warehouse in the Fechenheim industrial area. She and Bodenstein climbed up the dirty stairs to the top floor, where Thomas Ritter had his office. It was clear that Marleen Ritter had never visited her husband here, because even at the door of what he'd euphemistically called the "editorial office," she would have had her doubts. Emblazoned on the cheap glass door covered with greasy fingerprints was a trendy multicolored sign that said WEEKEND. The reception area consisted of a desk mostly taken up by a telephone system and a huge old-fashioned computer monitor.

"May I help you?" The receptionist of *Weekend* looked like she'd once posed for the cover of the magazine. But even her makeup couldn't hide the fact that it must have been quite a while ago. About thirty years.

"Criminal Police," said Pia. "Where can we find Thomas Ritter?"

"Last office on the left. Shall I tell him you're here?"

"Not necessary." Bodenstein gave the woman a friendly smile. The walls of the corridor were plastered with framed covers of *Weekend*. The bare facts were presented by various girls who all had one thing in common: cup size at least double D. The last door on the left was closed. Pia knocked and went in. Ritter obviously found it embarrassing to have Bodenstein and Kirchhoff encounter him in this setting. His classic luxury apartment building in the Westend was worlds apart from this cramped, stuffy office with porno photos on the walls. And there were also worlds between the ordinary-looking wife who was expecting his child and the woman standing next to him who had left her bloodred lipstick all over his mouth. Everything about her was stylish and expensive-looking, from her clothes to her jewelry and shoes to her hairdo.

"Call me," she said, grabbing her purse. She gave Bodenstein and Kirchhoff a brief, disinterested look, then rushed out.

"Your boss?" Pia asked. Ritter leaned his elbows on the desk and ran all ten fingers through his hair. He seemed exhausted and years older, matching the dreary appearance of his surroundings.

"No. What do you want now? And how did you know that I was here?" He reached for his cigarettes and lit one.

"Your wife was kind enough to give us the address of the *editorial office*." Ritter didn't react to Pia's sarcasm.

"You've got lipstick on your face," she added. "If your wife ever sees you like that, she might draw the wrong conclusions."

Ritter wiped his mouth with the back of his hand. He hesitated a moment with his reply, but then he made a resigned gesture.

"She's an acquaintance," he said. "I still owe her money."

"Does your wife know about her?" Pia asked.

Ritter stared at her, almost defiant. "No. And she never will." He took a drag on his cigarette and let the smoke out through his nose. "I've got a lot to do. What do you want? I've already told you everything."

"Quite the contrary," replied Pia. "You've kept most of it secret from us."

Bodenstein kept silent in the background. Ritter's eyes shifted back and forth between him and Pia. Yesterday, he'd made the mistake of under-estimating her. That wasn't going to happen today.

"Oh, really?" He was trying to act nonchalant, but the nervous flickering in his eyes betrayed his true state of mind. "Like what, for instance?"

"Why were you at Mr. Goldberg's house on the evening of April twenty-six, one day before he was murdered?" Pia asked. "What did you discuss with Robert Watkowiak in the ice-cream parlor? And why did Vera Kaltensee really fire you?"

With an abrupt movement, Ritter stubbed out his cigarette. The cell phone lying next to his computer keyboard warbled the first chords of Beethoven's Ninth, but he didn't even glance at the display.

"What's this all about?" he said suddenly. "I visited Goldberg, Schneider, and old lady Frings because I wanted to talk to them. Two years ago, I came up with the idea of writing a biography of Vera. At first, she was very enthusiastic and dictated to me for hours what she wanted to read about herself. After a couple of chapters, I realized that it was boring as hell. Twenty sentences about her past, that was it. What people really wanted to read about was her past, her aristocratic background, the dramatic flight with a small child, the loss of her family and the castle—not about business deals and charity crap."

The cell phone rang again with a single beep.

"But she wouldn't hear of it. Either I wrote the story as she wanted it or not at all. Unwilling to compromise, as always, the old vulture." Ritter snorted with contempt. "I tried to convince her, suggested making a novel out of her life story. All the failures, victories, high points, and setbacks in the life of a woman who had personally experienced the events of world history. We ended up arguing about it. She forbade me categorically to do any research, she forbade me to write, and she became more and more suspicious. And then the incident with the trunk happened. I made the mistake of defending Nowak. That did it." Ritter sighed.

"I was pretty well screwed," he admitted. "I had no prospect of a decent job, a nice apartment, or any sort of future."

"Until you married Marleen. Then you got it all back."

"What are you trying to imply?" Ritter retorted, but his indignation didn't seem genuine.

"That you made advances to Marleen in order to get revenge on your former boss."

"Nonsense!" he countered. "We met each other purely by accident. I fell in love with her and she fell in love with me."

"Why didn't you tell us yesterday that you'd married Siegbert Kaltensee's daughter?" Pia didn't believe a word he was saying. Compared to the elegant brunette who was there when they came in, the mousy-looking Marleen clearly came off second best.

"Because I didn't think it was any of your business," replied Ritter aggressively.

Bodenstein intervened. "Your private life doesn't interest us. What about Goldberg and Watkowiak?"

"I wanted information from them." Ritter seemed relieved at the change of subject and gave Pia a hostile look before completely ignoring her. "A while ago, somebody asked me whether I would be interested in writing a biography—a *true* account of Vera Kaltensee's life, with all the dirty details. They offered me a lot of money, firsthand information, and the prospect of . . . revenge."

"Who was it?" Bodenstein asked.

Ritter shook his head. "I can't tell you," he replied. "But the material I received was first-class."

"In what way?"

"Vera's diaries from 1934 to 1943." Ritter smiled grimly. "Detailed background information about everything that Vera absolutely wanted to keep secret. When I read the diaries, I came across quite a few inconsistencies, but one thing was clear to me: There is no way Elard can be Vera's son. The writer of the diary had no fiancé or suitor until December 1943. And she hadn't had sexual relations, so there was no question of her having given birth to a child. But . . ." He paused for effect and looked at Bodenstein. "Vera's older brother Elard von Zeydlitz-Lauenburg was carrying on a love affair with a young woman named Vicky, the daughter of the estate steward, Endrikat. In August 1942, she gave birth to a son who was baptized Heinrich Arno Elard."

Bodenstein received this news without comment.

"And then?" was all he said. Ritter was oddly disappointed by his lack of enthusiasm.

"The diaries were written by a left-handed girl. Vera is right-handed," he concluded abruptly. "And that's the proof."

"The proof of what?" Bodenstein asked.

"The proof that Vera is not really who she pretends to be!" Ritter couldn't sit still any longer and sprang up. "Just like Goldberg, Schneider, and Frings. Those four have shared some dark secret, and I want to find out what it is."

"And that's why you went to see Goldberg?" Pia asked skeptically. "Did you really think he'd be willing to tell you everything he'd kept secret for over sixty years?"

Ritter ignored her objection.

"I went to Poland to do research there. Unfortunately, there are no witnesses left to consult. Then I went to see Schneider and Anita, too, but I kept getting the same answer."

He grimaced in disgust.

"All three of them acted dumb, those self-righteous, arrogant old Nazis with their comrade evenings and their old-fashioned adages. I couldn't stand them even before, any of them."

"And when those three didn't help you, you shot them," said Pia.

"Precisely. With the Kalashnikov I always carry around. So arrest me," Ritter challenged her sarcastically. He turned to Bodenstein. "Why would I have bothered to kill those three? They were ancient; time would do the job for me soon enough."

"And Robert Watkowiak? What did you want from him?"

"Information. I paid him to tell me more about Vera. Besides, I was able to tell him who his real father was."

"How did you know that?" Pia asked.

"I know quite a bit," replied Ritter condescendingly. "The story that Robert was the illegitimate son of Eugen Kaltensee is a fairy tale. Robert's mother was a seventeen-year-old Polish maid at Mühlenhof. Siegbert had repeatedly assaulted her, until the poor girl got pregnant. His parents sent him off at once to college in America and forced her to have the baby in secret in the basement. After that, she disappeared, never to be seen again. I presume that they bumped her off and buried her somewhere on the grounds."

Ritter was talking faster and faster, and his eyes shone as if from a fever. Bodenstein and Pia listened in silence.

"Vera could have given up Robert for adoption as an infant, but she preferred to let him suffer under the assumption that he was an unfortunate indiscretion. At the same time, she enjoyed the way he admired and worshiped her. She has always been arrogant, considering herself untouchable. That's why she never destroyed the trunk with all its explosive contents. Too bad for her that Elard happened to form a close friendship with a contractor who specialized in restorations and came up with the idea of having the mill renovated."

Ritter's voice sounded full of hatred, and Pia only now realized the full extent of his bitterness and desire for revenge.

He laughed maliciously. "Oh yes, and Vera has Robert on her conscience. When Marleen fell in love with Robert, of all people—her half-brother— then they were in dire straits. Marleen had just turned fourteen and Robert was already in his mid-twenties. After the accident in which Marleen lost her leg, Robert fled from Mühlenhof. Shortly thereafter, his criminal career began.

"Your wife lost a leg?" Pia asked, recalling that Marleen Ritter had actually dragged her left leg behind her when she walked.

"Yes. As I said."

For a while, it was totally quiet in the little office, except for the humming of the computer. Pia exchanged a quick glance with Bodenstein; as usual, she couldn't tell by looking at him what he was thinking. Even if Ritter's information was only half true, it was definitely dynamite. Had Watkowiak had to die because he had learned the truth of his origins from Ritter and had then confronted Vera Kaltensee?

"Will that also be a chapter in your book?" Pia inquired. "It sounds a little risky to me."

Ritter hesitated, then merely shrugged. "It certainly is," he said without looking at her. "But I need the money."

"What does your wife say about you writing something like that about her family and her father? I wouldn't think she'd be pleased."

Ritter pressed his lips together to a narrow line.

"The Kaltensees and I are at war," he replied histrionically. "And in every war, there are victims."

"The Kaltensee family won't take this lying down."

"They have already arrayed their troops against me," said Ritter with a forced smile. "There is a temporary restraining order. And an injunction has been filed against me and the publisher. In addition, Siegbert has issued numerous threats against me. He says that I'll have no more joy from any of my royalties if I ever make my claims public."

"Give us the diaries," said Bodenstein.

"They aren't here. Besides, the diaries are my life insurance. The only insurance I have."

"I hope you're not making a mistake." Pia took a test tube out of her shoulder bag. "You certainly don't have any objection to a little saliva test, do you?"

"No, I don't." Ritter stuck his hands in the seat pockets of his jeans and sized her up disparagingly. "Even though I can't imagine what use it will be."

"So that we can identify your corpse more rapidly," Pia replied coldly. "I'm afraid you're underestimating the danger you've gotten yourself into."

The look in Ritter's eyes turned hostile. He took the cotton swab from Pia's hand, opened his mouth, and drew the swab across the inside of his cheek.

"Thank you." Pia took the test swab and sealed the tube in accordance with regulations. "Tomorrow we'll send our colleagues by your place to pick up the diaries. And if you feel in any way threatened, call me. You have my card."

"I don't know if I believe everything Ritter told us," Pia said as they crossed the parking lot. "The man is obviously obsessed with revenge. Even his marriage is pure vengeance."

Suddenly, something occurred to her, and she stopped abruptly.

"What is it?" asked Bodenstein.

"That woman in his office," said Pia, trying to remember her conversation with Christina Nowak. "Beautiful, dark-haired, elegant—it could be the same woman that Nowak met in front of the house in Königstein!"

Bodenstein nodded. "You're right. She seemed familiar to me, too. I just couldn't place her."

He handed Pia the car keys. "I'll be right back."

He went back inside the building and ran up the stairs to the top floor. He waited for a moment outside the door until he was no longer snuffling like a walrus, then rang the bell. The receptionist batted her fake eyelashes in astonishment when she saw him.

"Do you know the woman who was in Dr. Ritter's office earlier?" he asked. She looked him up and down, tilted her head, and rubbed her right forefinger and thumb together.

"Could be."

Bodenstein got it. He took out his wallet and pulled out a twenty-euro bill. The woman's contemptuous frown changed to a smile when a fifty appeared.

"Katharina . . ." She snatched the bill and held out her hand again. Bodenstein sighed and handed her the twenty, too. She slipped both bills into her boot.

"Ehrmann." She leaned forward and lowered her voice confidentially. "From Switzerland. Lives somewhere in the Taunus when she's in Germany. Drives a black BMW five with Zürich plates. And if you happen to know anyone who's looking for an experienced secretary, think of me. I've had enough of this outfit."

"I'll ask around." Bodenstein, who took it as a joke, winked at her and stuck his business card in the keyboard of her computer. "Send me an e-mail with your CV and references."

Bodenstein hurried along the rows of parked cars as he checked his e-mail on his cell. He almost ran into a black panel truck. Pia was thumbing a text as Bodenstein returned to his BMW.

"Miriam is going to check whether what Ritter just told us is correct," she explained, fastening her seat belt. "Maybe there are still some church records in existence from 1942."

Bodenstein started the engine.

"The woman who was in Ritter's office before was Katharina Ehrmann," he said.

"Oh yeah? The one with four percent of the vote?" Pia was astonished. "What does she have to do with Ritter?"

"Ask me something easier." Bodenstein maneuvered the BMW out of the parking space and pressed the multifunction key on his steering wheel to activate the callback function. A moment later, Ostermann checked in.

"Boss, all hell is breaking loose here," his voice said over the loudspeaker. "Nierhoff and the new woman are planning to set up special investigations for the pensioners and for Monika Krämer."

Bodenstein, who had expected something like this to happen, but much earlier, remained calm. He glanced at the clock. One-thirty. From the Hanauer Landstrasse, it would take him about thirty minutes at this time of day if he took the road across the Riederwald and then the Alleenring.

"We're meeting in half an hour at Zaika in Liederbach for a situation meeting. The complete K-Eleven team," he told Ostermann. "Order me carpaccio and chicken curry if you get there before I do."

"And a pizza for me!" shouted Pia from the passenger seat.

"With extra tuna and anchovies," Ostermann said, completing her order. "Sure. See you."

For a long while, they drove in silence, both busy with their own thoughts. Bodenstein was thinking about the accusation that his former boss in Frankfurt had often made. Detective Superintendent Menzel had claimed, preferably in front of the whole team, that he was inflexible and not a team player. Without a doubt, he was right. Bodenstein hated wasting time in meetings, squabbles over credentials, and stupid power plays. That was one of the reasons he'd been glad to transfer to Hofheim, to a manageable department with only five people. He still believed that too many cooks definitely spoiled the broth.

"Would you agree to two special commissions?" Pia asked at that moment. Bodenstein glanced over at her.

"Depends who's leading them," he said. "But the situation is very confused. What's this really all about?"

"It's about the murders of three old people, a young woman, and a man," Pia said, thinking out loud.

Bodenstein stepped on the brake at the top of Berger Strasse to allow a group of young people to cross the street.

"We're asking the wrong questions," he said, considering what Katharina Ehrmann might have to do with Ritter. There was something going on between them; that was obvious. Maybe she knew him from before, when he was still working for Vera Kaltensee.

"I wonder if she's still friends with Jutta Kaltensee?" Bodenstein asked. Pia understood at once who he was talking about.

"Why is that important?"

"Where did Ritter get the information about Robert Watkowiak's biological father? That has to be a family secret that only very few people know about."

"Then why would Katharina Ehrmann know about it?"

"She was always so close to the family. Eugen Kaltensee even transferred some shares in the company to her."

"Let's go visit Vera Kaltensee one more time," Pia suggested. "We'll ask her what was in the trunk and why she lied to us about Watkowiak. What have we got to lose?"

Bodenstein said nothing, then shook his head.

"We have to be very careful," he said. "Even if she can't stand Ritter, I don't want to risk a sixth dead body just because we ask a few rash questions. You weren't altogether wrong about Ritter treading on thin ice."

"The guy thinks he's as invulnerable as Vera Kaltensee," Pia retorted. "He's blind with vindictiveness, and he seems to think that any means are justified to get back at the Kaltensees. What a repulsive creep. And he's cheating on his pregnant wife with this Katharina Ehrmann. I guarantee it."

"I think so, too," Bodenstein conceded. "Still, he won't do us any good as a corpse."

The big noon rush was over when Pia and Bodenstein walked into Zaika, and except for a few businesspeople, the restaurant was almost empty. The K-11 team had gathered around one of the big tables in a corner of the Mediterranean-themed room and were already eating. Only Behnke wore a peeved expression as he sat there sipping from a glass of water.

"I have some good news, boss," Ostermann began when they had seated themselves at the table. "From the DNA profile that was established from a hair found in the apartment where Monika Krämer and Watkowiak were shacking up, the computer has spewed out a trace-trace hit. Looking at older cases, our colleagues from the NCP have analyzed and stored trace evidence. This perp had something to do with a previously unsolved murder in Dessau on October seventeenth, 1990, and an aggravated assault in Halle on March twenty-fourth, 1991."

Pia noticed Behnke's hungry look. Why hadn't he ordered anything to eat?

"Anything else?" Bodenstein grabbed the pepper mill to season his carpaccio.

"Yes. I've found out something about Watkowiak's shirt," Ostermann continued. "Shirts of this brand are produced exclusively for a men's clothing store on Schillerstrasse in Frankfurt. The manager was very cooperative and provided me with copies of receipts. White shirts, size forty-one, were sold exactly twenty-four times between March first and May fourth." He made a dramatic pause in order to ensure the full attention of all those present. "And a certain Anja Moormann purchased five white shirts, size forty-one, on behalf of Vera Kaltensee on April twenty-sixth."

Bodenstein stopped chewing and straightened up.

"Well, she's going to have to show us those shirts." Pia pushed her plate over to Behnke. "Here, take it. I can't eat any more."

"Thanks," he muttered, polishing off the remaining half a pizza in less than sixty seconds, as if he hadn't eaten for days.

"What about the neighbors of Goldberg and Schneider?" Bodenstein looked at Behnke, who was still chewing.

"I showed the man who saw the vehicle at Schneider's three different logos," replied Behnke. "He didn't hesitate for a second and pointed to Nowak's. He also pinned down the time. He went out with his dog at ten minutes to one, after some movie on ARTE was over. At ten after one, he returned; the vehicle was gone and the gate to the driveway was closed."

"Nowak was stopped at a quarter to twelve by our colleagues in Kelkheim," said Pia. "He could have easily driven back to Eppenhain after that."

Bodenstein's cell rang. He glanced at the display and excused himself for a minute.

"If we haven't made any progress by tomorrow, we're going to be saddled with twenty more colleagues." Ostermann leaned back. "And I'm not looking forward to that."

"None of us is," said Behnke. "But we can't just pull a perp out of a hat."

"But now we have more leads and can ask more relevant questions." Pia watched her boss through the picture window. He was pacing up and down with his cell at his ear. Who could he be talking to? Normally, he never left the room to answer the phone. "And do we know any more about the knife that was used to kill Monika Krämer?"

"Yes, we do." Ostermann shoved his plate aside and searched through the files he'd brought along until he found a specific one among the colored plastic folders that were an important component of his filing system. As disheveled as he might seem with his ponytail, nickel-framed glasses, and casual clothes, Ostermann was an extremely organized person.

"The murder weapon was an Emerson karambit fixed blade with a skeletonized handle, a copy of an Indonesian design. It's a tactical combat knife used for self-defense. Emerson is an American manufacturer, but the knife can be ordered from various Internet shops, and this model has been on the market since 2003. The serial number had been filed off."

"That rules out Watkowiak as the perp," said Pia. "So it could be a hit man. I'm afraid the boss is right."

"What am I right about?" Bodenstein returned to the table and launched into the rest of his chicken curry, now only lukewarm. Ostermann repeated the info about the knife.

"Okay." Bodenstein wiped his lips with the napkin and gave his colleagues a somber look.

"Now listen up. Starting right now, I expect a hundred percent more effort from all of you! We got a reprieve of one more day from Nierhoff. So far, we've been more or less fishing in the dark, but now that we have a few concrete leads—"

His cell rang again. This time, he took the call and listened for a moment. His expression darkened.

"Nowak has disappeared from the hospital," he informed the team.

"He was supposed to have another operation this afternoon," said Hasse. "Maybe he got scared and took off."

"How do you know that?" Bodenstein asked.

"We took a saliva sample from him this morning."

"Did he have any visitors when you were with him?" Pia asked.

"Yes," Fachinger said. "His Oma and his father were there."

Pia was surprised once again that Nowak's father would have visited his son in the hospital.

"A big strong guy with a mustache?" she asked.

"No." Fachinger shook her head uncertainly. "He didn't have a mustache, just a three-day stubble. And gray hair, a little longer—"

"Okay, great." Bodenstein shoved his chair back and jumped up. "That was Elard Kaltensee. When were you going to tell me that?"

"There's no way I could have known," Fachinger said defensively. "Should I have asked for his ID?"

Bodenstein said nothing, but his look spoke volumes. He handed Ostermann a fifty-euro bill.

"Pay the bill, okay?" he said, pulling on his jacket. "Somebody drive out to Mühlenhof and get the housekeeper to show you the five shirts. Then I want to know when, where, and from whom the knife was purchased that was used to kill Monika Krämer. And everything about Nowak's father's bankruptcy, and whether there was really a connection with the Kaltensee family. Find Vera Kaltensee. If she's in some hospital, post two uniforms outside her door to check who comes to visit her. We're also going to stake out Mühlenhof round the clock. Oh, yes: Katharina Ehrmann, née Schmunck, lives somewhere in the Taunus and possibly has Swiss citizenship. Got it?"

"Yep, great." Even Ostermann, who normally never grumbled, was anything but thrilled about the workload he'd been given. "How much time do we have?"

"Two hours," replied Bodenstein without a trace of a smile. "But only if one hour isn't enough."

He had almost reached the door when he thought of something else.

"What about that search warrant for Nowak's company?"

"We're getting it today," said Ostermann. "And an arrest warrant."

"Good. Send the photo of Nowak to the press and get it shown on TV today. Don't give out any information about why we're looking for him. Make up something. Say that he needs medication urgently or something like that."

"Who called before?" Pia asked when they were in the car. Bodenstein considered for a moment whether to tell her or not.

"Jutta Kaltensee," he said at last. "She supposedly has something important to tell me and wants to meet me this evening."

"Did she say what it was about?"

Bodenstein was staring straight ahead and stepped on the gas when they passed the Hofheim city limits sign. He still hadn't reached Cosima to ask her how her lunch with Jutta Kaltensee had gone. What sort of game was this woman playing? He didn't feel good at the thought of being alone with her. But he urgently needed to ask her a few questions—about Katharina Ehrmann and about Thomas Ritter. Bodenstein rejected the idea of asking Pia to go along. He wanted to deal with Jutta by himself.

"Earth to Bodenstein!" shouted Pia at that moment, giving him a start.

"Excuse me?" he asked in annoyance. He noticed the strange look on his colleague's face, but he hadn't heard her question.

"I'm sorry, I was thinking about something. Jutta and Siegbert Kaltensee were playacting that evening when I spoke to them at Mühlenhof."

"Why would they do that?" Pia was astonished.

"Maybe to distract me from what Elard had said earlier."

"And what was that?"

"Yeah, that's the big question. I have no idea!" Bodenstein exclaimed with unaccustomed impatience, regretting his outburst at once. He wasn't giving the case a hundred percent of his attention. If he hadn't spent so much time on the phone with Jutta Kaltensee recently, he might have remembered more of the conversation at Mühlenhof. "It was something about Anita Frings. Elard Kaltensee told me that his mother was informed at seven-thirty about her disappearance and a couple of hours later about her death."

"You didn't mention that to me," said Pia, clear reproach in her voice.

"Yes, I did."

"No, you didn't. So that means that Vera Kaltensee had enough time to send her people to Taunusblick to clear out Anita Frings's room."

"But I did tell you," Bodenstein insisted. "I'm positive I did."

Pia said nothing, thinking hard about whether it was true.

At the hospital, Bodenstein parked the car in the driveway out front, ignoring the protests of the young man at the information desk. The officer who was supposed to be guarding Nowak confessed sheepishly that he'd let himself be duped twice. About an hour ago, a doctor had shown up and taken Nowak away for an examination. One of the station nurses had even helped him push the bed into the elevator. Since the doctor had assured him that Nowak would be back from radiology in twenty minutes, the officer had sat back down on the chair outside the room.

"I thought my instructions were crystal clear. You were not supposed to let him out of your sight," Bodenstein said, his voice icy. "Your mistake will have consequences for you, I promise you that."

"What about the visitors this morning?" Pia asked. "What made you think that the man was Nowak's father?"

"The Oma said he was her son," replied the officer sullenly. "That was good enough for me."

The hospitalist, whom Pia knew from her first visit, came down the hall and informed them that Nowak was in grave danger. In addition to the seriously injured hand, he had also suffered a stab wound to the liver, and that was nothing to joke about.

Unfortunately, the information supplied by the officer who was supposed to watch Nowak wasn't particularly helpful.

"The doctor was wearing one of those green outfits with a cap," he said lamely.

"Jesus! What did he look like? Old, young, fat, thin, bald, full beard— you must have noticed something!" Bodenstein was just about to lose it. He'd wanted to avoid a situation like this, especially since Nicola Engel now seemed to be lurking in the background, eager to see him fail.

"He was around forty or fifty, I would say," the officer finally recalled. "And I think he was wearing glasses."

"Forty? Fifty? Or sixty? Or maybe it was a woman?" Bodenstein asked sarcastically. They were standing in the lobby of the hospital, and the SWAT team had just arrived. In front of the elevators, the squad leader gave his officers their instructions. Radios were blaring and curious patients were squeezing between the policemen, who were now setting off to search the building floor by floor, looking for the vanished Marcus Nowak. The patrol that Pia had sent to Nowak's house called in to report that he hadn't showed up there.

"Stay near the company door and call in right before your shift ends so we can send over your relief," Pia told her colleagues.

Bodenstein's cell rang. They'd found the empty hospital bed in an examination room on the ground floor, right next to an emergency exit. All hope of finding Nowak somewhere in the building was gone. A trail of blood led out of the room, along the hall, and out the door.

"So that's it, then." In resignation, Bodenstein turned to Pia. "Come on, let's go see Siegbert Kaltensee."

Elard Kaltensee was a brilliant theoretician but not a man of action. In his lifetime, he had dodged making decisions, leaving that task to others around him, but this time the situation had called for his immediate action. It had been hard for him to put his plan into action: It was no longer just about him, and only he could put an end to this situation once and for all. At sixty-three—no, sixty-four, he corrected himself—he had finally found the courage to take matters into his own hands. He had gotten the confounded trunk out of his house, closed the Kunsthaus temporarily, and sent all the employees home. Then he'd booked his flight online and packed his bags. And strangely enough, he suddenly felt better than ever before, even without the pills. He felt years younger, decisive and energetic. Elard Kaltensee smiled. Maybe it was a plus that everyone took him for a coward and no one would believe him capable of something like this. Except for the lady cop, but even she had been lured onto a sidetrack. A patrol car was parked in front of the gate at Mühlenhof, but not even this unexpected obstacle could deter him. If he was lucky, the police wouldn't know about the shortcut to the estate via Lorsbach and through the Fischbach valley, so he'd be able to slip into the house unnoticed. One encounter with the police per day was plenty for him. Besides, he'd have a lot of explaining to do about the blood on the passenger seat of his car. Something caught his attention and he turned up the radio. "—and the police are asking for your help. Since this afternoon, Marcus Nowak, thirty-four, has been missing. He disappeared from the hospital in Hofheim and is in urgent need of vital medications. . . ." Elard Kaltensee turned off the radio and smiled with satisfaction. Let them look for him. He knew where Nowak was. Nobody would find him anytime soon; he had made sure of that.

•   •   •

The headquarters of KMF was located close to the tax office on the Nordring in Hofheim. Bodenstein had decided not to give Siegbert Kaltensee advance notice of their arrival, and he presented his ID to the guard without comment. A man in a dark uniform stared without expression into the car and then raised the barrier.

"I'll bet you a month's salary that we'll find the men who attacked Nowak over there," Pia remarked, pointing to an inconspicuous building with a discreet sign that read K-SECURE. In the fenced parking lot were several VW buses and Mercedes vans with tinted windows. Bodenstein slowed down and Pia read the text on several vehicles: *K-Secure—Protection for Valuables, Property, and Personnel—Transport of Money and Assets.* The scratches from the concrete planter in front of Auguste Nowak's house had certainly been long since repaired, but they were on the right track. The crime lab had definitively linked the paint traces to a product used on Mercedes-Benz vehicles.

Siegbert Kaltensee's secretary, who had made it effortlessly to the final round of *Germany's Next Top Model,* told them it would be a long wait—her boss was in an important business meeting with clients from overseas. Pia responded to her condescending look with a smile and wondered how anyone could walk around all day with heels that high.

Siegbert Kaltensee had apparently decided to leave his overseas clients, as he appeared within three minutes.

"We've heard that you're planning some changes with respect to the firm," said Bodenstein after the secretary had served them coffee and mineral water. "It's our understanding that you now want to sell what you couldn't sell before because some of the shareholders exercised their veto power."

"I don't know where you got this information," Siegbert Kaltensee replied calmly. "But the matter is more complex than it was probably portrayed."

"Yet it's true that you did not have a majority backing your plan. Am I right?"

Siegbert Kaltensee smiled and leaned his elbows on the desk. "What are you driving at? I hope you don't think that I had Goldberg, Schneider, and Anita Frings killed in order to acquire their shares as CEO of KMF."

Bodenstein also smiled. "Now you're the one who's oversimplifying the matter. But my question was leaning in that direction."

"Actually, we had the company appraised by an auditing firm a few months ago," said Siegbert Kaltensee. "Naturally, there are always investors interested in a healthy, well-established firm that is also the worldwide market leader in its field and possesses a hundred patents. The evaluation was done not because we want to sell, but because we plan to go public in the near future. KMF will be completely restructured in order to conform to the requirements of the market."

He leaned back.

"I'll turn sixty this fall. No one from the family shows any interest in the company, so sooner or later I'll have to turn over the helm to a stranger. I'd like to remove family ownership from the firm before that happens. I'm sure you know about the stipulation in my father's will. At the end of this year, its validity will lapse, and then we can finally alter the organizational structure of the business. From a limited company a corporation will be formed, and that will take place within the next two years. None of us will make millions from our shares. Naturally, I have personally and extensively informed all shareholders about these plans, including, of course, Mr. Goldberg, Mr. Schneider, and Mrs. Frings."

Siegbert Kaltensee smiled again.

"By the way, that was the reason for the conversation last week at my mother's house when you came and asked us about Robert."

It all sounded perfectly logical. Siegbert's and Jutta Kaltensee's motive for murder, which neither Bodenstein nor Pia had ever considered especially viable, now evaporated.

"Do you know Katharina Ehrmann?" Pia asked.

"Of course," Siegbert Kaltensee said with a nod. "Katharina and my sister Jutta are close friends."

"Why was Ms. Ehrmann given company shares by your father?"

"I don't really know. Katharina spent part of her childhood at Mühlenhof. I assume that my father wanted to annoy my mother."

"Did you know that Katharina Ehrmann has a relationship with Thomas Ritter, your mother's former assistant?"

A furrow of displeasure appeared on Kaltensee's face.

"No, I didn't know that," he admitted. "But it really doesn't matter to me what that man does. He's a bad egg. Regrettably, it took my mother a long time to realize that he had always tried to set her against the family."

"He's writing a biography about your mother," Bodenstein said.

Kaltensee coolly corrected him. "He *was* writing it. Our lawyers have stopped it. Besides, he signed a contract when his employment ended, agreeing to maintain silence about all internal family matters."

"What will happen if he contravenes it?" Pia asked, curious.

"The consequences for him will be exceedingly unpleasant."

"Why, exactly, are you opposed to a biography of your mother?" Bodenstein inquired. "She's a remarkable woman with a splendid record of achievement."

"We don't really have any objections," replied Kaltensee. "But my mother would like to choose her own biographer. Ritter has dug up all sorts of abstruse stuff, purely to take revenge on my mother for the supposed injustice he suffered."

"For example, that Goldberg and Schneider were former Nazis and had assumed false identities?" Pia asked.

Siegbert Kaltensee smiled again noncommittally. "In the lives of numerous successful entrepreneurs from the postwar period, you will find connections to the Nazi regime," he retorted. "Even my father doubtless profited from the war, because his firm was in the arms business. That's not what this is about."

"Then what is it about?" Bodenstein asked.

"Ritter is making wild accusations that meet the criminal definition of libel and defamation of character."

"How can you know that?" Pia inquired.

Siegbert Kaltensee shrugged and said nothing.

"It has come to our attention that at one time your brother, Elard, was suspected of having pushed your father down the stairs. Does Ritter also write about that in his book?"

"Ritter's not writing a book," replied Siegbert Kaltensee. "Apart from that, I believe to this day that Elard was responsible. He could never stand my father. The fact that he received shares in the firm is simply preposterous."

His smooth, self-confident facade was showing its first cracks. What was the reason for such blatant dislike of his older half brother? Was it jealousy over his looks and his success with women, or was there more to it?

"Elard's been profiting for decades from my work, as if it were the most natural thing in the world. Yet in his eyes, the business of this company is merely a contemptible, empty chase after base mammon." He laughed caustically. "I'd love to see my high-principled, sensitive brother try to live without money and have to depend solely on his own abilities. The art professor is not particularly well equipped to cope with real life."

"Like Robert Watkowiak?" asked Pia. "Doesn't his death affect you at all?"

Siegbert Kaltensee raised his eyebrows and retreated to his nonchalant attitude.

"To be honest, no, it doesn't. I've been ashamed often enough that he was my half brother. My mother was lenient with him for too long."

"Maybe because he was her grandson," Bodenstein remarked in passing.

"Pardon me?" Kaltensee straightened up.

"In the past several days, we've been hearing about various matters," said Bodenstein. "Including the fact that in reality it was *you* who was Watkowiak's father. His mother was your parents' maid, and when they got wind of this ill-advised relationship, you were sent off to America. Then your father took the blame upon himself."

Siegbert Kaltensee was left literally speechless by this accusation. He rubbed his hand nervously over his bald pate.

"My God," he muttered, and stood up. "I did actually have an affair with my parents' maid. Her name was Danuta. She was a couple of years older than I and very pretty."

He paced up and down in his office.

"I was serious about her, the way it is when you're fifteen or sixteen. My parents, naturally, were not thrilled and sent me to the States to take my mind off things."

All of a sudden, he stopped cold.

"By the time I returned nine years later with my degree, a wife, and a daughter, I had completely forgotten about Danuta."

He went over to the window and stared out. Was he thinking about all the rejections and failings that had driven his alleged half brother first into criminality and then to his death?

"How is your mother doing, by the way?" Bodenstein asked, changing the subject. "And where is she? Because we urgently need to speak with her."

With a pale face, Siegbert Kaltensee turned around and again sat down behind his desk. He began absentmindedly doodling with a ballpoint on a pad of paper.

"No one can talk to her right now," he said softly. "The events of the past few days have taken a terrible toll on her. The murders that Robert committed, and finally the news of his suicide, were simply too much for her to bear."

"Watkowiak didn't commit the murders," said Bodenstein. "And his death was not a suicide. The autopsy definitively concluded that he died as a result of actions by some unknown perpetrator."

"The actions of an unknown perpetrator?" Kaltensee said in disbelief. The hand holding the ballpoint pen was trembling. "But who . . . and why? Who would want to murder Robert?"

"That's what we're asking ourselves. Next to his body we found the weapon used to kill his girlfriend, but he didn't do it."

In the silence, the phone on the desk rang. Siegbert Kaltensee picked up the receiver, brusquely announced he was not to be disturbed, and hung up.

"Do you have any idea who might have killed your mother's three friends or what the number one one six four five might mean?"

"That number doesn't ring a bell," replied Kaltensee, and then he thought for a moment. "I don't want to cast suspicion on anyone unjustly, but I know that Elard was putting massive pressure on Goldberg in the past few weeks. My brother refused to accept that Goldberg didn't know anything about his past, or anything about his biological father. And Ritter also visited Goldberg numerous times. I could easily picture him committing the three murders without a second thought."

Pia had rarely heard anyone utter such a blatant accusation of murder. Did Siegbert Kaltensee see an opportunity to get rid of the two men he despised from the bottom of his heart, and with whom he had competed for the favor of his mother for so many years? What would happen if Kaltensee learned that Ritter was not only his son-in-law but also soon to be the father of his grandchild?

"Goldberg, Schneider, and Frings were shot with a World War Two weapon and old ammunition. Where would Ritter get those sorts of things?" she now asked. Kaltensee stared at her for a moment.

"You've probably also heard the story of the missing trunk," he said. "I've had my thoughts about what it may have contained. What if it held items belonging to my father? He was a member of the Nazi Party and also in the Wehrmacht. Maybe Ritter stole the trunk and there was a gun inside."

"How could he have done that? After the incident, he was forbidden to set foot at Mühlenhof," Pia said. Siegbert Kaltensee refused to be rattled.

"Ritter wouldn't let something like that stop him" was all he said.

"Did your mother know what was in the trunk?"

"I assume so. But she won't talk about it. And when my mother doesn't want to talk about something, she won't." Kaltensee gave a spiteful laugh. "Just take a look at my brother, who's been searching for his father in vain for years."

"All right." Bodenstein smiled and stood up. "Thank you for taking the time to talk with us. Oh, just one more question: On whose authority did the people from your security force torture Marcus Nowak and beat him up?"

"Excuse me?" Kaltensee shook his head, looking annoyed. "Who did you say?"

"Marcus Nowak. The contractor who carried out the renovation of the mill."

Kaltensee frowned in thought. Then he seemed to remember.

"Oh, him," he said. "We'd had big problems with his father in his day. His shoddy work on the construction of the administration building cost us a lot of money. But what is our security force supposed to have done to his son?"

"That's something we'd be very interested in learning," said Bodenstein. "Do you have anything against having our crime-scene technicians take a look at your vehicles?"

"No," replied Kaltensee without hesitation, apparently amused. "I'll call Mr. Améry, the head of K-Secure. He will put himself at your disposal."

• • •

Henri Améry was in his mid-thirties, a good-looking southern European type, slim and tan, his short black hair combed straight back. He wore a white shirt, dark suit, and Italian shoes. He could have been a stockbroker, lawyer, or banker. With an obliging smile he handed Bodenstein a list of their employees, thirty-four in all, including himself, and answered all their questions without hesitation. He had been the head of K-Secure for a year and a half. He had never heard the name Nowak and seemed genuinely surprised to hear about the alleged covert action of his men. He had no objection to allowing the police to examine his vehicles. He provided a list of all the company vehicles with license plate numbers, make and model, registration dates, and odometer readings.

As Bodenstein was talking to Améry, Miriam called on Pia's cell. She was on her way to Doba, the former Doben, which had jurisdiction over the village of Lauenburg and the estate.

"This morning I'll be meeting a man who until 1945 worked as a Polish forced laborer on the estate of the Zeydlitz-Lauenburgs," she reported. "The archivist knows him. He lives in a retirement home in Wegorzewo."

"That sounds good." Pia saw her boss come out of the K-Secure office. "Keep your ears peeled for the names Endrikat and Oskar, okay?"

"Got it; I will," said Miriam. "Talk to you later."

"So?" Bodenstein asked as she flipped her cell phone shut. "What do you think of Siegbert Kaltensee and this Améry?"

"Siegbert hates both his brother and Ritter," Pia replied. "In his eyes, they were competitors for the favor of his mother. Didn't your mother-in-law say that Vera had almost idolized her assistant? And Elard not only lives at Mühlenhof, he's way better-looking than Siegbert. And in the past, at least, he had one amorous adventure after another."

"Hmm." Bodenstein nodded pensively. "And this Améry?"

"Cute guy, a little too slick for my taste," Pia pronounced. "A bit too helpful, as well. Probably the vehicle his men took to Nowak's place isn't even on the list. I think we can spare the taxpayers the cost of the inspection."

Back at the station, Ostermann was waiting to share the latest news: Vera Kaltensee wasn't in the hospitals in either Hofheim or Bad Soden. There was no trace of Nowak, but at least the search warrant had finally arrived. Patrol cars were posted in front of Nowak's company and at the gate of Mühlenhof. The shirts that Behnke had shown him, bought by Mrs. Moormann, belonged to Elard Kaltensee. In the meantime, Behnke was in Frankfurt, searching for the professor, but the Kunsthaus was still closed. By checking with the tax office, the residents' registration office, and the police information database of the NCP, Ostermann had found out that Katharina Ehrmann, née Schmunck, had been born on July 19, 1964, in Königstein. She was a German citizen with permanent residence in Zürich, Switzerland, and had given an address in Königstein as her second residence. She was an independent publisher, subject to tax in Switzerland, and had no previous police record.

Bodenstein had listened to Ostermann without comment. He glanced at the clock. Quarter past six. At 7:30, Jutta Kaltensee would be waiting for him at the Gasthaus Rote Mühle, near Kelkheim.

"Publisher," he mused. "Could she be the one who commissioned Ritter to write the biography?"

"I'll check it out." Ostermann made a note.

"And send out an APB," Bodenstein added, "for Professor Elard Kaltensee and his car."

He noticed Pia's satisfied expression. Apparently, her hunch had been right.

"Tomorrow morning at six, we're going to search Nowak's business and home. I want you to organize it, Ms. Kirchhoff. With at least twenty people, the usual team."

Pia nodded. The phone rang and Bodenstein took the call. Behnke had located the caretaker of the Kunsthaus. Around noon, the man had helped Elard Kaltensee load a trunk and two suitcases into his car.

"I also found out that the professor still has an office at the university," Behnke said in conclusion. "On the Westend campus. I'm on my way over there now."

"What kind of car does he drive?" Bodenstein put the phone on speaker so Ostermann could listen in.

"Just a moment." Behnke talked to somebody, then came back to the phone. "A black Mercedes S-Class, license plate MTK-EK two two two."

"Thanks. Keep Ostermann and Ms. Kirchhoff informed. If you run into Kaltensee, arrest him and bring him here," Bodenstein said. "I want to talk to him today."

"But you still want to put out an APB on him?" Ostermann asked after Bodenstein hung up.

"Of course," he replied, and turned to go. "And don't let anyone go home today without calling me first."

Exhausted, Thomas Ritter looked over the finished first draft of the manuscript. After fourteen hours and two packs of Marlboros, interrupted only by the Kripo people and Katharina, he'd done it. Three hundred and ninety pages of dirty facts about the Kaltensee family and their hushed-up crimes. This book was going to shake things up for sure; it would break Vera's neck and might even send her to prison. He felt completely worn-out and at the same time as wired as if he'd snorted cocaine. After he saved the file, on impulse he also burned it onto a CD-ROM. He rummaged in his briefcase for a mini audio cassette and stuck both into a padded mailer, which he addressed with an indelible marker—a safety precaution in case they wanted to threaten him again. Thomas Ritter switched off his laptop, stuck it under his arm, and stood up.

"I'm out of here, you shitty office," he mumbled, and didn't look back as he left the place for good. Nothing like going home and taking a shower. Katharina was probably expecting to see him tonight, too, but maybe he could postpone that. He didn't feel like talking about the manuscript, sales prospects, marketing strategies, and his debts. He had even less desire to have sex with her. To his own surprise, he was honestly looking forward to seeing Marleen. He'd promised weeks ago to spend a quiet evening alone with her, a cozy dinner at a nice restaurant, then a nightcap at a bar and a long night of love.

"You've got such a satisfied look on your face," remarked his receptionist, Sina, as he passed her desk. "What's up?"

"I'm looking forward to a night off," replied Ritter. Suddenly, he had an idea. He handed her the padded mailer. "Be a dear and keep this for me, would you?"

"Okay, no problem." Sina stuck the envelope in her fake Louis Vuitton bag and winked at him conspiratorially. "Have fun on your night off."

The doorbell rang.

"Finally." She pressed the door buzzer. "That's probably the courier with the proofs. He sure took his time today."

Ritter winked back and stepped aside to let the bicycle messenger pass. But instead of the courier they were expecting, a bearded man in a dark suit entered. He stopped in front of Ritter and gave him a brief look.

"Are you Dr. Thomas Ritter?" he asked.

"Who wants to know?" Ritter replied suspiciously.

"If you are, I've got a package for you," the bearded man said. "From a Ms. Ehrmann. I'm supposed to deliver it to you personally."

"I see." Ritter was skeptical, although Katharina was always good for a surprise. He wouldn't have put it past her to send him some sort of sex toy, to get him in the mood for the evening she'd planned. "So where's the package?"

"If you'll wait just a minute, I'll go get it. It's still in the car."

"No, that's all right. I'm on my way out anyway." Ritter waved good-bye to Sina and followed the man down the stairs. He was happy to be leaving the office in the daytime. Even though it was hard to admit, the panel truck in the parking lot and the crazy remarks by that disagreeable blond Kripo woman had given him a scare. But now he would turn over responsibility for the manuscript to the publishing house, and once it was printed, they could shove all their threats up their ass. Ritter nodded to the man as he politely held the front door open for him. Suddenly, he felt a stab in the side of his neck.

"Ow!" he yelled, and dropped the briefcase holding his laptop. Ritter felt his legs give way under him, as if they were made of rubber. A black van stopped right in front of him, and two men jumped out the side door and grabbed his arms. He was shoved roughly into the vehicle, the side door slammed shut, and it was pitch-dark. Then the interior lights came on, but he couldn't seem to raise his head. Saliva dribbled from the corner of his mouth and everything went fuzzy before his eyes. Fear flooded through him. Then he blacked out.

Thursday, May 10

Pia stood shivering next to the evidence team's van and yawned so widely that her jaw cracked. It was cold and unpleasant; the May morning felt like a November day. Last night, she hadn't left the office until 11:30. One after the other, Behnke, Fachinger, and Hasse now showed up and poured themselves cups of raven black coffee from the team leader's thermos. It was 6:15 when Bodenstein finally arrived, unshaven and obviously bleary-eyed. The plainclothes officers crowded around him for a last-minute rundown of the situation. They had all participated in enough house searches to know what mattered. Cigarettes were put out and coffee dregs were poured into the bushes next to the Aral gas station, where they had assembled. Pia left her car and got in Bodenstein's. He was pale and seemed tense. In convoy, the officers followed Bodenstein's BMW down the street to Nowak's company.

"The receptionist from Ritter's office left me a voice mail last night," said Bodenstein. "I just listened to it a little while ago. Ritter left the office at around six-thirty last night; she stayed behind to wait for a courier delivery. He was accompanied downstairs by a man who was supposed to give him a package from Ms. Ehrmann. When she left the office at seven-thirty, Ritter's car was still in the parking lot."

"Down that way." Pia pointed to the right. "That sounds strange."

"It sure does."

"By the way, how did it go yesterday with Jutta Kaltensee? Did you learn anything interesting?" She was surprised to see Bodenstein clench his jaw.

"No. Nothing special. Waste of time," he replied laconically.

"You're not telling me something," Pia said.

Bodenstein sighed and pulled the car over to the side of the road a few yards from Nowak's building.

"God help me if there ever comes a day when you're on my tail," he said grimly. "I made a gigantic, stupid mistake. I don't really know how it got to that point, but on the way to the car she suddenly . . . well . . . touched me inappropriately."

"Excuse me?" Pia stared at her boss in disbelief, then laughed. "You're pulling my leg, aren't you?"

"No. It's the truth. It was all I could do to get away from her."

"But you succeeded, right?"

Bodenstein avoided looking at her.

"Not really," he admitted. Pia made an effort to decide how to formulate her next question as diplomatically as possible without offending her boss.

"Did you happen to leave your DNA on her?" she asked cautiously. Bodenstein didn't laugh and paused before he replied.

"I'm afraid so," he said, and got out of the car.

Christina Nowak was already dressed when Bodenstein handed her the search warrant. She had deep circles under her red-rimmed eyes and watched apathetically as the officers entered the second-floor apartment and began their work. Her two sons looked shocked as they sat in their pajamas in the kitchen. The younger one started to cry.

"Have you heard anything from my husband?" she asked softly. Pia was having trouble concentrating on the task at hand. She was still stunned by Bodenstein's confession. When Mrs. Nowak repeated her question, Pia pulled herself together.

"Sorry, no," she said. "And we had no response to our request in the media for information from the public."

Christina Nowak began to sob. Loud voices could be heard in the stairwell; Nowak senior was complaining vociferously, and Marcus Nowak's brother was staggering down the stairs, drunk with sleep.

"Don't worry. We'll find your husband," Pia said, although she wasn't at all convinced they would. She was secretly sure that Elard Kaltensee had disposed of yet another witness. Nowak had trusted him, and in his injured condition he wouldn't have been able to defend himself. Most likely, he was already dead.

The search of the apartment produced nothing. Christina Nowak opened the door to her husband's office for the police. Since Pia's last visit, it had been cleaned up. The document binders were back on the shelves, and the papers were sorted in filing trays. One officer pulled the plug of the computer;

another cleaned out the shelves. The squat figure of the elder Mrs. Nowak suddenly appeared. She had no word of consolation for her grandson's wife, who was standing petrified in the doorway; she wanted to enter the office, but two officers stopped her.

"Ms. Kirchhoff," she called out to Pia. "I have to speak with you right away!"

"Later, Mrs. Nowak," said Pia. "Please wait outside until we're finished."

"Well, what have we here?" she heard Behnke say. She turned around. Behind the document binders was a wall safe.

"So he was lying to us after all." Too bad, she'd found Marcus Nowak so appealing. "He claimed there was no company safe."

"Thirteen-twenty-four-oh eight," Christina Nowak recited without being asked, and Behnke entered the combination. With a beep and a clack, the door of the safe sprang open just as Bodenstein entered the office.

"Well?" he asked. Behnke leaned over, reached inside, and turned around with a triumphant grin. In his gloved right hand, he held a pistol, in his left a box of ammunition. Christina Nowak gasped.

"I predict that here we have the murder weapon." He sniffed at the barrel of the pistol. "It seems to have been fired fairly recently."

Bodenstein and Pia exchanged a glance.

"The search for Nowak will be expanded," said Bodenstein. "We'll get the media to run a story on radio and TV."

"What . . . what does all this mean?" Christina Nowak whispered. Her face was snow-white. "Why did my husband keep a pistol in his safe? I . . . I don't understand anything anymore."

"Please sit down." Bodenstein pulled over the desk chair for her. Hesitantly, she obeyed. Pia shut the office door, despite the protests of Grandmother Nowak.

"I know that it must be hard for you to comprehend," said Bodenstein. "But we suspect your husband of murder. This pistol is most likely the weapon used to shoot three individuals."

"That can't be true. . . ." Christina Nowak murmured in bewilderment.

"As his spouse, you don't have to make any statement," Bodenstein informed her. "But if you do say something, then it must be the truth, because otherwise you'll be charged with perjury."

They could hear the loud voice of Nowak senior talking to the officers outside.

Christina Nowak paid no attention and fixed her gaze on Bodenstein. "What do you want to know?"

"Can you remember where your husband was on the nights of April twenty-seventh, April thirtieth, and May third?"

Her eyes filled with tears and she hung her head.

"He wasn't at home," she said in a choked voice. "But I would never believe that he killed anyone. Why would he do that?"

"Where was he on those nights?"

She hesitated for a moment, her lips quivering. She passed the back of her hand over her eyes.

"I assume," she stammered, "that he was with that woman I'd seen him with. I know that he's . . . cheating on me."

"I hardly drank anything," Bodenstein said later in the car without looking at Pia. "Only a glass of wine. But I felt as though I'd had two bottles. I hardly registered what she told me. Even now I can't recall large parts of the evening."

He paused and rubbed his eyes.

"At some point, we were the only ones left in the place. Out in the fresh air, I felt a little better, but I had a hard time walking. We were standing by my car. The people from the restaurant were leaving and driving off. The last thing I can remember is that she kissed me and unzipped my—"

Pia hurried to interrupt. "That's enough!" The thought of what might have occurred less than eight hours ago in this very car was terribly embarrassing.

Bodenstein's voice sounded strained when he said, "I shouldn't have let it happen."

"Maybe nothing did happen," said Pia uncomfortably. Of course she realized that her boss was only human, but she never would have believed anything like this of him. Maybe it was also his unusual candor that was confusing her. Even though they worked together on a daily basis, intimate details of their private lives had always been off-limits until now.

"That's what Bill Clinton once claimed," Bodenstein said in frustration. "I keep asking myself why she did it."

"Oh, come on," replied Pia cautiously, "you're not exactly ugly, boss. Maybe she was just looking for an adventure."

"No. Jutta Kaltensee doesn't do anything without a reason. It was planned. She's called me at least twenty times in the past few days. And yesterday, she met Cosima for lunch under a flimsy pretext."

For the first time during their conversation, Bodenstein looked at Pia. "If I'm suspended for this, you're going to have to lead the investigations by yourself."

"I don't think we've reached that point yet," Pia reassured him.

"We will pretty soon." Bodenstein ran his hands through his hair. "To be exact, as soon as Dr. Engel gets wind of it. She's just been waiting for something like this."

"But how would she find out about it?"

"From Jutta Kaltensee personally."

Pia saw what he meant. Her boss had gotten it on with a woman whose family was at the center of multiple homicide investigations. If Jutta Kaltensee had acted in a calculating manner, then they definitely needed to consider that she would somehow turn this incident to her advantage.

"Listen, boss," Pia said. "You should get a blood test. She must have put something in your wine or your food to make sure you'd let yourself be seduced."

"How could she have done that?" Bodenstein shook his head. "I was sitting next to her the whole time."

"Maybe she knows the restaurant owner."

Bodenstein thought for a moment.

"You're right. I'm sure she does. She was on a first-name basis with him and made a big fuss about being a regular there."

"Then he could have slipped something into your glass," said Pia with more conviction than she actually felt. "Let's go right over and see Henning. He can take some of your blood and analyze it right away. And if he does find something, then you can use it as proof that the Kaltensee woman set a trap for you. She can't afford a scandal that would undermine her ambitions."

A glimmer of hope brightened Bodenstein's weary face. He turned on the ignition.

"Okay," he said to Pia. "You were right, by the way."

"About what?"

"That the case would develop its own dynamic."

It was 9:30 by the time the team gathered again at the station to discuss the situation. The confiscated pistol—a very well-preserved Mauser P08 S/42, made in 1938, with a serial number and purchase stamp—and the ammunition from the safe in Nowak's office were on the way to ballistics. Hasse and Fachinger had taken over answering the phone, which, after the call for assistance from the public on the radio, was ringing off the hook. Bodenstein sent Behnke to Frankfurt to see Marleen Ritter. A patrol had reported that Ritter's BMW was still in the parking lot in front of *Weekend*'s offices.

"Pia!" Kathrin Fachinger shouted. "Telephone for you. I'll transfer the call to your office."

Pia nodded and got up.

It was Miriam. "Yesterday, I visited this old man," she began without bothering to say hello. "Write down what I tell you. This is the clincher."

Pia grabbed a notepad and pen. When Ryszard Wielinski was twenty-two, he arrived as a forced laborer at the estate of the Zeydlitz-Lauenburg family. His short-term memory was no longer the best, but it was razor-sharp about events from more than sixty-five years ago. Vera von Zeydlitz had been at a boarding school in Switzerland, and her older brother Elard was a pilot in the Luftwaffe. During the war, neither of them visited their parents' estate very often, but Elard had a love affair with the steward's pretty daughter, Vicky. Their liaison produced a son in August 1942. Elard had wanted to marry Vicky, but every time the wedding date approached, he was arrested by the Gestapo—the last time in 1944. Presumably SS Sturmbahnführer Oskar Schwinderke, the son of the paymaster of the Lauenburg estate, had denounced him in order to prevent the marriage. Schwinderke's ambitious younger sister Edda was madly in love with the young count and insanely jealous of Vicky and her close friendship with Elard's sister. During the war, Schwinderke visited the estate often because he was a member of the

Leibstandarte SS Adolf Hitler division and had served in the nearby Wolf's Lair, Hitler's eastern headquarters. In November 1944, Elard came home with a serious injury. On January 15, 1945, the official retreat order was issued, and the entire population of Doben set off on the morning of January 16 in the direction of Bartenstein. Staying behind on the estate were the old Baron von Zeydlitz-Lauenburg, his wife, the wounded Elard, his sister Vera, Vicky Endrikat with three-year-old, Heinrich, Vicky's sick mother, her father, and her little sister Ida. They were planning to follow the others on the trek from Doben as soon as possible. In the vicinity of Mauerwald, those on the trek approached a jeep. SS Sturmbahnführer Oskar Schwinderke was at the wheel; next to him sat another SS man, whom Ryszard Wielinski had seen several times at the Lauenburg estate. In the backseat were Edda and her friend Maria, who had both been working since 1942 in a prison camp for women in Rastenburg, one as a guard, the other as secretary to the camp commander. They spoke briefly with Oskar's father, paymaster Schwinderke and then drove on. That was the last time Wielinski saw those four people.

On the evening of the following day, the Russian army ran down those on the trek from Doben. All the men were shot; the women were raped and some of them were carried off. Wielinski survived only because the Russians had believed him when he said he was a forced laborer from Poland. Several years after the war, Wielinski returned to the region. He had often wondered about the fate of the Zeydlitz-Lauenburg and Endrikat families, because they had treated him well, and Vicky Endrikat had regularly studied German with him.

Pia thanked Miriam and tried to collect her thoughts. In the account she had read about Vera Kaltensee, it said that her entire family had perished during the escape attempt in 1945 or was listed as missing. If what the former forced laborer had reported was true, then they hadn't left the estate at all on January 16, 1945. What had Oskar Schwinderke—who was doubtless the phony Goldberg—done there, along with his sister and his friends, so shortly before the Red Army moved in? The events of that day held the key to the murders. Was Vera really Vicky, the daughter of estate steward Endrikat? If so, was Elard Kaltensee the son of the pilot Elard? Pia took her notes with her to the conference room. Bodenstein called in Fachinger and Hasse, as well. In silence, they listened to Kirchhoff's story.

"So Vera Kaltensee might actually be Vicky Endrikat," Fachinger began. "The old man from Taunusblick told me that Vera had certainly come far for 'a simple girl from East Prussia.'"

"In what context did he say that?" Pia asked. Kathrin took out her notebook and found the correct page.

She read aloud: "'They called themselves "the Four Musketeers." Twice a year, they would meet in Zürich, even after Anita and Vera had buried their husbands.' When I asked him who the Four Musketeers were, he said, 'The four old friends from before. They'd all known one another since childhood—Anita, Vera, Oskar, and Hans.'"

For a moment, no one spoke. Bodenstein and Pia looked at each other. The pieces of the puzzle were suddenly falling into place.

"'A simple girl from East Prussia,'" said Bodenstein slowly. "Vera Kaltensee is Vicky Endrikat."

"Back then, she saw her chance to join the aristocracy virtually overnight, after her prince left her pregnant but didn't marry her," Pia added. "And she pulled it off. Until today."

"But who killed her three friends?" Ostermann asked, baffled. Bodenstein jumped up and grabbed his jacket.

"Ms. Kirchhoff is right," he said. "Elard Kaltensee must have found out what happened back in 1945. And he isn't finished with his campaign of revenge. We have to stop him."

The two magic words *imminent danger* convinced the presiding judge to sign three arrest and search warrants within half an hour. Meanwhile, Behnke had spoken with a completely desperate Marleen Ritter. The day before around 5:45, she had phoned her husband from her office to make a date to go out to eat that evening. When she arrived home at 7:30, she found her apartment ransacked, and no trace of Ritter. He didn't answer his cell phone, and from midnight on, it was turned off. Marleen Ritter had notified the police, but they'd told her that it was too early to file a missing person's report; her husband was a grown man, after all, and had been

gone for only six hours. In addition, Behnke reported that Elard Kaltensee's Mercedes had been found parked in front of the departure hall at the
Frankfurt airport. The passenger seat and inside of the door were covered
in blood—probably Marcus Nowak's. It was being analyzed right now in
the lab.

Bodenstein and Pia drove to Mühlenhof, again accompanied by a team
of officers as well as additional crime-scene techs with a ground-penetrating
radar device and corpse-sniffer dogs. To their surprise, they found Siegbert
and Jutta Kaltensee there, along with their lawyer, Dr. Rosenblatt. They were
sitting surrounded by stacks of documents at the big table in the salon. The
aroma of freshly brewed tea hung in the air.

"Where is your mother?" Bodenstein asked, skipping the usual pleasantries.

Kirchhoff discreetly looked at Jutta, but she gave no clue as to what had
happened the night before. She didn't act like a woman who would have sex
with a married man in a parking lot at night, but you never could tell about
people.

"I told you that she didn't—" Siegbert Kaltensee began, but Bodenstein
cut him off.

"Your mother is in great danger. We suspect that your brother, Elard,
shot your mother's friends and is now going to kill her, too."

Siegbert Kaltensee froze.

"We also have a search warrant for the house and grounds." Pia handed
Kaltensee the document, which he mechanically passed to his lawyer.

"Why do you want to search the house?" the lawyer asked.

"We're looking for Marcus Nowak," replied Kirchhoff. "He disappeared
from the hospital yesterday."

She and Bodenstein had agreed to say nothing at first to the Kaltensee
siblings about the arrest warrant for their mother.

"Why would Mr. Nowak be here?" Jutta Kaltensee took the warrant
from the lawyer's hand.

"Your brother's Mercedes was found at the airport," Pia explained. "It
was full of blood. As long as we haven't found either Marcus Nowak or your
mother, we have to assume that it might be her blood."

"Where are your mother and your brother?" Bodenstein repeated. When he got no answer, he turned to Siegbert Kaltensee.

"Your son-in-law also vanished without a trace last night."

"But I don't have a son-in-law anymore," replied Kaltensee in confusion. "You must be mistaken. I really don't understand what the point of all this is."

Glancing out the window, Siegbert Kaltensee saw the police officers with dogs and the unit with the ground-penetrating radar trudging across the manicured lawns in a broad phalanx.

"You know very well that your daughter married Thomas Ritter ten days ago, because she is expecting a child by him."

"Excuse me?" Siegbert Kaltensee's face drained of color. He stood there as if thunderstruck, utterly speechless. He glanced at his sister, who looked astonished.

"I have to make a phone call," he said suddenly, pulling out his cell phone.

"Later," said Bodenstein, taking the phone out of his hand. "First I want to know where your mother and brother are."

"My client has the right to make a phone call," protested the lawyer. "What you're doing here is an arbitrary act!"

"Keep out of this," Bodenstein snapped. "So, what's it going to be?"

Siegbert Kaltensee was shaking all over, and his pale moon face was gleaming with sweat.

"Let me make a phone call," he begged in a hoarse voice. "Please."

At Mühlenhof the police found no trace of Marcus Nowak, Elard, or Vera Kaltensee. Bodenstein still suspected that Elard Kaltensee had killed Nowak and hidden the body somewhere—if not here, then somewhere else. Thomas Ritter hadn't shown up, either. Bodenstein called his mother-in-law and learned from her where the Kaltensees owned houses and apartments.

"The most probable seem to me to be the houses in Zürich and in the Ticino," he told Pia as they drove back to the station. "We'll ask our Swiss colleagues for their interauthority cooperation. My God, what a mess this is!"

Pia said nothing because she didn't want to rub more salt in his wounds. If he'd listened to her, Elard Kaltensee would have long since been in custody and Nowak might still be alive. Her theory of events was as follows: Elard had had the trunk with the diaries and the Luger 08 brought to him. Since he was not a man to make quick decisions and it might have taken him a while to grasp the importance of the diaries, he had stalled for months before taking action. He had shot Goldberg, Schneider, and Anita Frings with the gun from the trunk because they wouldn't tell him anything about his past. January 16, 1945, was the day of the trek from Doben, the day on which something drastic had happened. And Elard Kaltensee might have remembered some of it, if only dimly, because at the time he was not one and a half, but already two and a half years old. And Marcus Nowak, who knew about the three murders or had even helped with them, had to disappear because he could be dangerous to Elard Kaltensee.

Ostermann checked in on the phone. Marcus Nowak's and Elard Kaltensee's fingerprints on the murder weapon did not surprise anyone. In addition, a woman from Königstein had called the police after seeing Nowak's picture in the paper. She recognized the contractor as the man who around noon on May 4, had spoken with a gray-haired man in a BMW convertible in the parking lot of Luxemburg Castle.

"Nowak talked to Ritter, but shortly before that he met with Katharina Ehrmann. How does that fit together?" Bodenstein asked, thinking out loud.

"I've been wondering about that, too," replied Pia. "But this woman's statement confirms that Christina Nowak wasn't lying. Her husband was in Königstein at about the time Watkowiak died."

"So he and Elard Kaltensee might be involved not only with the three murders of the old folks but also with the deaths of Watkowiak and Monika Krämer?"

"At this point, I wouldn't rule anything out," said Pia with a yawn. In the past few days, she definitely hadn't gotten enough sleep and was yearning for a peaceful night. But for now, it looked like she could expect exactly the opposite, because Ostermann called again. He told her that downstairs at the duty officer's desk someone named Auguste Nowak was waiting, and she wanted to talk to Pia urgently.

"Hello, Mrs. Nowak." Kirchhoff extended her hand to the old woman, who got up from the chair in the waiting room. "Can you tell us where your grandson is?"

"No, I can't. But I have to speak with you urgently."

"Unfortunately, we're very busy right now," said Kirchhoff. At that moment, her cell rang. She cast an apologetic look at Nowak's grandmother and took the call. Excited, Ostermann told her that they'd been able to pin down the location of Marcus Nowak's cell phone for a few minutes. Pia felt adrenaline surging through her body. Maybe the man was still alive.

"In Frankfurt, between Hansaallee and Fürstenbergerstrasse," said Ostermann. "We don't have a more precise fix, as the phone was only turned on briefly."

Pia instructed him to get in touch with their colleagues in Frankfurt and have a wide area blocked off.

"Boss," she said, turning to Bodenstein, "Nowak's cell was located in Frankfurt on Hansaallee. Are you thinking what I'm thinking?"

Bodenstein nodded. "I certainly am. Kaltensee's office at the university."

"Please excuse me." Auguste Nowak put her hand on Pia's arm. "I really have to—"

"I just don't have time right now, Mrs. Nowak," said Pia. "We may find your grandson still alive. We'll talk later. I'll call you. Do you want someone to drive you home?"

"No thanks." The old woman shook her head.

"It might take a while. I'm sorry." Pia raised her hands in a gesture of regret and followed Bodenstein, who was already at his car. They had no time to lose, and so they didn't notice the black Maybach limousine. The engine started up as soon as Auguste Nowak came out the door of the Regional Criminal Unit.

When Bodenstein and Kirchhoff arrived at the former IG-Farben Building at Grüneburgplatz, where the new Westend Campus of Frankfurt University was located, uniformed officers had already sealed off the area around the entrance. The unavoidable rubberneckers had gathered at the police tape. Inside the building, angry students, professors, and university employees were arguing with the police, but the instructions they'd been given were unequivocal: No one could enter or leave the building until Nowak's cell phone had been found—in the best-case scenario, with its owner.

"There's Frank," said Pia, whose heart sank at the sight of the nine-story building, which was over seven hundred feet long. How was she going to find a cell phone that had been shut off again and could very well be anywhere on the thirty-five-acre campus, on the grounds or in a parked car? Behnke was standing with the squad leader of the Frankfurt Police between the four pillars in front of the imposing main entrance of the IG-Farben Building. When he saw Bodenstein and Pia, he went over to them.

"Let's start with Kaltensee's office," he suggested. They went inside the magnificent lobby, but none of them paid any attention to the bronze plaques and artistic copper friezes that decorated the walls and elevator doors. Behnke led Bodenstein, Kirchhoff, and a group of martial-looking SWAT team officers up to the fifth floor. Then he turned right and strode purposefully down the long, slightly curved corridor. Pia's cell rang and she took the call.

"The cell is on again!" Ostermann said excitedly.

"Is it in the building?" Pia stopped and covered her other ear so she could hear her colleague better.

"Yes, definitely."

The door to Kaltensee's office was locked. Another delay ensued until someone finally located the head janitor, who had a pass key. The elderly gentleman with a snow-white mustache fumbled with his key ring. When the door finally opened, Behnke and Bodenstein stormed past him impatiently.

"Shit," said Behnke. "Nobody here."

The janitor stood in a corner of the office, watching with big eyes the enormous efforts of the police.

"What's going on here anyway?" he asked after a moment. "Is it something to do with Professor Kaltensee?"

"Do you think we'd show up here with a hundred officers and the SWAT team otherwise? Of course it has to do with him!" Pia leaned over the desk and studied the desk blotter, which was covered with scribbles. She was hoping to find a name, a phone number, or some clue to the whereabouts of Nowak, but it seemed that Kaltensee had just enjoyed doodling while he was on the phone. Bodenstein rummaged through the wastebasket and Behnke searched the desk drawers while the SWAT team waited in the hall.

"He was acting strange yesterday," said the head janitor thoughtfully. "He seemed somehow . . . excited."

Bodenstein, Behnke, and Kirchhoff stopped at once and stared at him.

Behnke reproached the man angrily. "You saw Professor Kaltensee yesterday? Why didn't you tell us that right away?"

"Because you didn't ask me," he replied with dignity. The SWAT team leader's radio hissed and crackled; then a voice came through, barely understandable through the atmospheric static caused by the thick concrete ceilings in the building. The janitor pensively twirled one end of his mustache.

"He seemed elated," he recalled. "Which is generally never the case. He came out of the basement in the west wing. I wondered about that, since his office is—"

"Could you take us there?" Pia asked impatiently.

"Of course," the janitor said with a nod. "But what did he do, the professor?"

"Nothing much," Behnke replied sarcastically. "He just may have killed a few people."

The janitor's mouth fell open.

"My men are holding several individuals in detention who gained unauthorized access to the building," the SWAT team leader now reported in official police lingo.

"Where?" Bodenstein asked impatiently.

"In the basement. In the west wing."

"All right, let's go," Bodenstein barked.

The six men wearing black K-Secure uniforms were standing with their backs to the police officers, legs spread, hands on the wall.

"Turn around!" Bodenstein commanded. The men obeyed. Pia recognized Henri Améry, the leader of the Kaltensee security force, even without his suit and patent-leather shoes.

"What are you and your men doing here?" Pia asked.

Améry said nothing and smiled.

"You're under arrest." She turned to one of the SWAT team officers. "Get them out of here. And find out how they knew we were here."

The man nodded. Handcuffs snapped shut and the six men in black were escorted out. Bodenstein, Kirchhoff, and Behnke got the janitor to open every room—document archives, storerooms, electrical and heating equipment rooms, empty cellars. In the next-to-last room, they finally hit the jackpot. A person was lying on a mattress on the floor. Next to him were water bottles, food, medications, and a steamer trunk. Pia turned on the light. Her heart leaped into her throat as the fluorescent lights on the ceiling hummed softly and flickered on.

"Hello, Mr. Nowak." She went over to the mattress and squatted down. The dazed man blinked in the bright light. He was unshaven and deep furrows of exhaustion had become etched into his badly beaten face. With his good hand, he was clutching a cell phone. He looked very ill, but he was alive. Pia put her hand on his feverish brow and saw that his T-shirt was soaked in blood. She turned to Bodenstein and Behnke.

"Call an ambulance right away."

Then she turned back to the injured man. No matter what he might have done, she felt sorry for him. He must have endured incredible pain.

"You belong in a hospital," she said. "Why are you here?"

"Elard . . ." Nowak murmured. "Please . . . Elard . . ."

"What about Professor Kaltensee?" she asked. "Where is he?"

With an effort, Nowak turned to look at her, but then he closed his eyes.

"Mr. Nowak, you have to help us," Pia pleaded. "We found Professor Kaltensee's car at the airport. He and his mother seem to have vanished from the face of the earth. And in the safe in your office, we found the pistol that was used to shoot three people. We assume that Elard Kaltensee committed the murders, after he found the pistol in the trunk."

Marcus Nowak opened his eyes. His nostrils quivered and he was gasping for breath, as if he wanted to say something, but only a moan escaped from his split lips.

"Unfortunately, I have to arrest you, Mr. Nowak," said Pia with a certain amount of regret. "You have no alibis for the nights of the murders. Your wife has told us that you were not at home on any of those nights. Do you have anything to say about that?"

Nowak didn't answer; instead, he let go of his cell phone and reached for

Pia's hand. Desperately, he struggled to find the words. Sweat was pouring down his face, but an attack of chills made him shiver. Pia remembered the warning of the doctor at the Hofheim Hospital; he'd said that Nowak had suffered a wound to his liver in the attack. Apparently, being transported here had aggravated the internal injury.

"Take it easy," she said, patting his hand. "First we're taking you to the hospital. When you're feeling better, we'll talk."

He looked at her like a drowning man, his dark eyes wide with panic. If Marcus Nowak didn't get help soon, he was going to die. Had that been Elard Kaltensee's plan? Was that why he'd brought him here, where no one would find him? But why hadn't he taken away his cell phone?

A voice interrupted her thoughts. "The ambulance is here." Two EMTs shoved a gurney into the basement room, and a doctor wearing an orange vest and carrying an emergency medical bag followed them. Pia wanted to get up to make room for the doctor, but Marcus Nowak wouldn't let go of her hand.

"Please..." he whispered desperately. "Please...not Elard...my Oma..."

His voice trailed off.

"My colleagues will take care of you," said Pia softly. "Don't worry. Professor Kaltensee won't do anything else to you, I promise."

She detached herself from Nowak's grip and stood up.

"He has a liver injury," she informed the emergency doctor. Then she turned to her colleagues, who in the meantime had searched the trunk. "So, what did you find?"

"Among other things, the SS uniform of Oskar Schwinderke," Bodenstein replied. "We'll take a look at the rest back at the station."

"I knew the whole time that Elard Kaltensee was a murderer," Pia told Bodenstein. "He would have left Nowak to rot in that cellar hole, just to keep from getting his own hands dirty."

They were on their way back to Hofheim. Katharina Ehrmann was waiting at the station, and the six K-Secure men were in the holding cells.

"Who did Nowak call last?" Bodenstein asked.

"No idea. We have to request the itemized call listing."

"Why didn't Kaltensee take the phone away from him? He must have figured that Nowak would call somebody."

"Yes, I wondered that myself. Probably he didn't know that we could get a fix on the phone." Pia jumped at the shrill ring of the car phone. "Or maybe he just didn't think about it."

"Hello," a female voice came from the loudspeaker. "Mr. Bodenstein?"

"Yes," said Bodenstein, glancing at Pia and then shrugging. "Who is this?"

"Sina. I'm the secretary at *Weekend*."

"Oh yes. What can I do for you?"

"Mr. Ritter gave me an envelope last night," she said. "I was supposed to keep it for him. But now that he's disappeared, I thought it might be important. Your name is on it."

"Really? Where are you now?"

"Still here, at the office."

Bodenstein hesitated.

"I'll send a colleague over to pick up the envelope. Please wait until he arrives."

Pia was already calling Behnke on her cell and telling him to drive over to the editorial office in Fechenheim. She ignored his angry curse at the prospect of driving all the way across town at this time of day.

"Yes, that's right," Katharina Ehrmann said. "My company wants to publish the biography of Vera Kaltensee. I found Thomas's idea tremendously interesting, and I've supported him in his endeavor."

"You know that he's been missing since last night, don't you?" Pia observed the woman sitting across from her. Katharina Ehrmann was a little too beautiful to be real. Her expressionless face testified either to a lack of emotion or too much Botox.

"We had an appointment yesterday evening," she replied. "When he didn't show up, I tried to call him, but he didn't answer. Later, his cell phone was turned off."

That matched what Marleen Ritter had told the police.

"Why did you meet with Marcus Nowak in Königstein last Friday?"

Bodenstein asked. "Nowak's wife saw you get into her husband's car, and then you drove off together. Are you having an affair with him?"

"I really don't work that fast." Katharina Ehrmann seemed genuinely amused. "That was the first day I met him. He had brought the diaries and other documents I'd requested from Elard, and then he was nice enough to give me a ride before he met with Thomas."

Pia and Bodenstein exchanged a surprised look. That was interesting news. So that's how Ritter had gotten hold of the information. Elard had thrown his own mother under the bus, so to speak.

"The house where you met Nowak and in which Watkowiak's body was found belongs to you," said Pia. "What do you have to say to that?"

"What should I say?" Katharina Ehrmann didn't seem particularly bothered. "It was my parents' house, and I've wanted to sell it for years. The real estate agent called me last Saturday to reproach me. As if I could do anything about Robert deciding to take his own life in precisely that location!"

"How did Watkowiak get into the house?"

"With a key, I presume," Katharina Ehrmann replied, to Pia's astonishment. "I let him use the house when he needed a place to stay. We were once good friends, Robert, Jutta, and I. I felt sorry for him at the time."

Pia highly doubted that. Katharina Ehrmann didn't make an especially compassionate impression.

"By the way, he didn't take his own life," she said. "He was murdered."

"Oh, really?" Even this information did not disconcert the woman.

"When was the last time you spoke with him?"

"It wasn't that long ago." She thought about it. "I think it was last week. He called and told me that the police were looking for him for the murders of Goldberg and Schneider. But he said he didn't do it. I told him the smartest thing to do would be to turn himself in to the police."

"Unfortunately, he didn't do that. Otherwise, he might still be alive today," said Pia. "Do you think that Ritter's disappearance might have something to do with this biography he's writing?"

"It's possible." Katharina gave a shrug. "What we've discovered about Vera's past could put her in prison. And probably for the rest of her life."

"You mean that the death of Eugen Kaltensee was no accident? It was murder?" Pia asked.

"Among other things," said Katharina. "But primarily it's the fact that Vera and her brother were said to have shot several people back in East Prussia."

January 16, 1945. The Four Musketeers in the jeep on their way to the Lauenburg estate. The Zeydlitz-Lauenburg family, which since then had been presumed dead or missing.

"How did Ritter find out about it?" Pia inquired.

"From an eyewitness, a woman."

An eyewitness who knew the secret of the four old friends. Who was she, and whom had she told about it? Pia felt electrified. They were only millimeters away from solving the three murders.

"Do you think it's possible that somebody from the Kaltensee family has kidnapped Ritter in order to prevent the publication of the book?"

"I would believe anything of them," said Katharina Ehrmann. "Vera would stop at nothing. And Jutta isn't much better."

Pia glanced at her boss, but he was feigning indifference.

"But how did the Kaltensees learn that Elard had passed this information to Thomas Ritter?" she now asked. "Who knew about it?"

"Really only Elard, Thomas, Elard's friend Nowak, and myself," replied Katharina after a moment's thought.

"Did you ever talk on the phone about it?" Bodenstein asked.

"Yes," said Katharina hesitantly. "Not about details, but about the fact that Elard would put the contents of this trunk at our disposal."

"When was that?"

"On Friday."

The following Monday Nowak had been attacked. That fit.

"I just remembered that Thomas called me the night before last from the office. He was worried because there was a panel truck in the parking lot with two men in it. I didn't take it very seriously, but maybe . . ." Katharina fell silent. "Good God! Do you think they may have tapped into our phone conversation?"

Bodenstein nodded with concern. "It's possible, I think." The people from K-Secure were well equipped. They had been listening to the police band on their radios and learned where Nowak's cell phone had been traced to. For them, it was probably an easy task to listen in on other phone conversations.

There was a knock on the door, and Behnke came in and handed Pia the padded mailer, which she opened at once.

"A CD-ROM," she said. "And a cassette."

She reached over for her dictation machine, put in the cassette, and pressed PLAY. Seconds later, they heard Ritter's voice.

"Today is Friday, May fourth. My name is Thomas Ritter, and facing me is Mrs. Auguste Nowak. Mrs. Nowak, you would like to tell us something. Please go ahead."

"Stop!" Bodenstein ordered. "Thank you, Ms. Ehrmann. You may go now. Please inform us if you hear anything from Thomas Ritter."

The dark-haired woman understood and got up.

"What a shame," she said. "Just as it was getting exciting."

"Aren't you worried about Thomas Ritter at all?" Bodenstein asked. "He's still your author, who's going to deliver a best-seller."

"And your lover," Pia added.

Katharina Ehrmann smiled coolly.

"Believe me," she said. "He knew what he was getting into. Almost nobody knew Vera better than he did. Besides, I warned him."

"One more question," said Bodenstein, holding her back before she left. "Why did Eugen Kaltensee sign over company shares to you?"

Her smile vanished.

"Read the biography," she said. "Then you'll find out."

The voice of Auguste Nowak came from the loudspeaker of the cassette player that stood in the middle of the table. *"My father was a great admirer of the Kaiser. That's why he had me named after the empress, Auguste Viktoria. People used to call me Vicky, but that was a long time ago."*

Bodenstein and Pia glanced at each other. The whole K-11 team had gathered around the big table in the conference room. Next to Bodenstein sat Nicola Engel, a blank expression on her face. According to the clock, it was 8:45, and not even Behnke was thinking about going home.

"I was born on March seventeenth, 1922, in Lauenburg. My father, Arno, was the steward at the estate of the Zeydlitz-Lauenburg family. There were three of us girls living there: Vera, the daughter of the baron, Edda Schwinderke, the daughter of the paymaster, and me. All three of us were the same age and grew up almost as sisters. As young girls, Edda and I were wild about Elard, Vera's older brother, but he couldn't stand Edda. Even as a young girl, she was terribly ambitious and secretly envisioned herself as the mistress of Lauenburg Manor. When Elard fell in love with me, Edda was utterly furious. She thought Elard would be impressed because at sixteen she was already the leader of the girls' group in the BDM, but the opposite was the case. He hated the Nazis, even if he never said it out loud. Edda didn't notice, but she was always showing off with her brother Oskar because he was in the Leibstandarte SS Adolf Hitler."

Auguste Nowak paused. Nobody around the table said a word, waiting for her to go on.

"In 1936, the young girls in the BDM went to Berlin to the Olympiad. Elard was studying in Berlin. He took Vera and me out to dinner, and Edda almost exploded with jealousy. She castigated us for leaving the group without permission, and there was a lot of trouble because of it. After that day, she harassed me every chance she got, ridiculing me in front of the other girls at the weekly social evenings. Once she even claimed that my father was a Bolshevik. When I was nineteen, I got pregnant. Nobody had any objections to a marriage, even Elard's parents, but the war was on and Elard was at the front. When the wedding date approached, he was arrested by the Gestapo, although he was an officer in the Luftwaffe. The second wedding date also had to be postponed, because Elard was arrested again. By the way, it was Oskar who denounced Elard to the Gestapo."

Pia nodded. This account confirmed what the former Polish forced laborer had told Miriam.

"On August twenty-third, 1942, our son came into the world. In the meantime, Edda had left Lauenburg Manor. She and Maria Willumat, the daughter of the local Nazi Party group leader from Doben, had reported for duty at a women's prison camp. Because she was away and could no longer sniff around, Elard and Vera secretly smuggled money, jewelry, and valuables over into the West and into Switzerland. Elard was convinced that the war was lost, and he

wanted at least Vera, Heini, and me to go to the West. His mother's family owned an estate near Frankfurt, and he was going to settle us there."

"Mühlenhof," Pia said softly.

"But it never happened. In November 1944, Elard was shot down and came back to Lauenburg Manor with serious wounds. Vera had secretly left her Swiss boarding school and was back at home over Christmas. We helped Elard plan our escape, but we didn't receive the 'trek' permit until January fifteenth, which was much too late. The Russians were only twenty kilometers away. Those on the trek set off at dawn the morning of January sixteenth. I didn't want to leave without Elard and my parents, and because I stayed, Vera stayed, too. We thought that there would be an opportunity later to make it to the West."

They heard Auguste Nowak heave a deep sigh.

"Elard's parents would rather have died than leave the estate. They were both well past sixty and had lost their eldest sons in World War One. My parents were seriously ill with tuberculosis. And my younger sister Ida was in bed with a fever of one hundred and four. We hid in the cellar of the castle, provided with food and bedding, and hoped that the Russians wouldn't discover us and just move on. It was around noon when a vehicle drove into the courtyard, a jeep. Vera's father thought that somebody had sent Schwinderke to transport those who were sick, but it wasn't true."

At that point, Ritter asked her who had come.

"Edda and Maria, Oskar and his SS comrade Hans."

Once again, Auguste Nowak's account corresponded with the statement of the former forced laborer. Pia held her breath and leaned forward tensely.

"They came into the castle and found us in the cellar. Oskar threatened us with a pistol and forced Vera and me to dig a pit. The ground was sandy, but it was so hard that we couldn't manage it, so Edda and Hans took over shoveling. Nobody said a word. The baron and baroness knelt down and . . ."

The voice of Auguste Nowak, until then calm and involved, began to tremble.

". . . began to pray. Heini was screaming the whole time. My little sister Ida just stood there, tears running down her cheeks. I can still picture her today. We had to line up facing the wall. Maria tore Heini from my arms and dragged him away. The boy screamed and screamed. . . ."

It was so still in the conference room that they could have heard a pin drop.

"*First Oskar killed the baron and baroness with shots to the back of the head. Then came my sister Ida. She was only nine years old. Then he gave the pistol to Maria, who shot my mother in both knees and then in the head, and then she shot my father. Elard and I were holding hands. Edda took the pistol from Maria. I looked her in the eye, and she was full of hate. She laughed when she shot first Elard in the head, then Vera. Finally, she shot me. I can still hear her laughing. . . .*"

Pia could hardly believe it. What power it must have cost the old woman to speak so soberly and objectively about this massacre of her whole family! How could anyone live with such memories without going crazy? Pia thought about what Miriam had told her about the fates of the women in the East after World War II, the ones she had interviewed as part of her research project. These women had experienced unspeakable things and never talked about them for the rest of their lives. Like Auguste Nowak.

"*It was a miracle that I survived being shot in the head. The bullet came out through my mouth. I don't know how long I was unconscious, but somehow I managed to get out of the pit under my own power. They had shoveled sand on top of us, and the only reason I could breathe was that I lay halfway underneath Elard's body. I dragged myself up, searching for Heini. The castle was ablaze, and I ran straight into the arms of four Russian soldiers, who raped me in spite of my wounds and then took me to a field hospital later. When I had somewhat regained my strength, I was crammed with other girls and women into a cattle car. It was too crowded to sit down, and only when the guards occasionally were in a good mood was there a bucket of water for forty people. We came to Karelia and had to work by Lake Onega laying rails, felling trees, and digging trenches, at a temperature of forty below zero. All around me they were dying like flies, and some girls were only fourteen or fifteen. I survived five years in the work camp only because the camp commander seemed to like me and gave me more to eat than the others. I didn't come back from Russia until 1950, with a baby in my arms, a going-away present from the camp commander.*"

"The father of Marcus," Pia said. "Manfred Nowak."

"*I met my husband in the Friedland camp. We got work on a farm in*

Sauerland. I had long since given up hope of finding my eldest son. I never spoke about it. Even later, I never had the faintest idea that the famous Vera Kaltensee, whom we were always hearing and reading about, could possibly be Edda. Not until my grandson Marcus and I took a summer trip to East Prussia two years ago, and we met Elard Kaltensee in Gizycko, the former Lötzen. That's when I realized who he was and who had been living very close to me after I moved to Fischbach."

Auguste Nowak took another pause.

"I kept my knowledge to myself. A year later, Marcus was working at Mühlenhof, and one day he and Elard brought home an old steamer trunk. It was a shock when I saw all those things: the SS uniform, the books, the newspapers from the war. And the pistol. I knew right away that it must have been the exact same pistol used to shoot my whole family. Sixty years it had lain in that trunk, and Vera had never gotten rid of it. And when you, Dr. Ritter, Marcus, and Elard told me about Vera and her three old friends, I knew at once who they really were. Elard kept the trunk, but Marcus put the pistol and the ammunition in his safe. I found out where they lived, the murderers, and when Marcus was out one evening, I took the pistol and went to Oskar's place. To think that he, of all people, had disguised himself as a Jew all these years! He recognized me immediately and begged for his life, but I shot him the way he had shot Elard's parents. Then I got the idea to leave Edda a message. I knew that she would understand at once what those five numbers meant, and I was sure they would put the fear of death in her because she would have no idea who could know about it. Three days later, I shot Hans."

At the point, Ritter interrupted Auguste Nowak's narrative to ask, *"How did you get to where Goldberg and Schneider lived?"* She then explained what she had done.

"I took one of my grandson's vans. That was also the biggest problem with Maria. I had found out that there was going to be a theater performance at the old folks home, with fireworks afterward. But that evening I had no car, so I went there on the bus and had to ask my grandson to pick me up later. The boy never wondered what I was doing at the elegant Taunusblick; he was too wrapped up in himself and his problems. I gagged Maria in her apartment with a stocking and then pushed her in the wheelchair through the park and into the

woods. *Nobody paid us any mind, and during the fireworks no one heard the three shots."*

Auguste Nowak fell silent. It was deathly quiet in the room. The tragic life story of the old woman and her confession had shaken even the most experienced Criminal Police officers.

"I know that the Bible says 'Thou shalt not kill.' Then Auguste Nowak resumed her story, her voice all at once sounding brittle. *But the Bible also says 'An eye for an eye, a tooth for a tooth.' When I realized who they were, Vera and her friends, then I knew that I couldn't let this injustice go unavenged. My little sister Ida would have been seventy-one today; she could still have been alive. I had to keep that in mind the whole time."*

Thomas Ritter then inquired, *"So Professor Elard Kaltensee is your son?"*

"Yes. He's the son I had with my beloved Elard. He is the baron of Zeydlitz-Lauenburg, because Elard and I were married on Christmas Day, 1944, by Pastor Kunisch in the library at Lauenburg Manor."

The K-11 team sat for a while in silence around the table when the tape ended.

"She was here today and wanted to talk to me," Pia said, breaking the silence. "I'm positive she wanted to tell me this same story, so that we wouldn't suspect her grandson anymore."

"And her son," Bodenstein added. "Professor Kaltensee."

"And you let her go?" asked Nicola Engel, uncomprehending.

"How was I to know that she's our murderer?" Pia retorted. "Nowak's cell phone had just been located, and we had to go to Frankfurt."

"She probably went home," said Bodenstein. "We'll go pick her up. And it's likely that she knows where Elard is now."

"It's much more likely that first she's going to kill Vera Kaltensee," Ostermann ventured. "If she hasn't done it already."

Bodenstein and Behnke drove to Fischbach to arrest Auguste Nowak, while Pia read the biography of Vera Kaltensee on the screen, searching for an explanation for Katharina Ehrmann's relationship to Eugen Kaltensee. The life story of Auguste Nowak had shaken her deeply, and although as a police officer and the ex-wife of a pathologist she knew plenty about the dark side of humanity, she was stunned by the ice-cold cruelty of the four murderers. This crime could not be justified by the will to survive in an extreme situation; rather, they had even put themselves in mortal danger in order to commit their atrocity. How could they repress something like that and live with such a bloody deed on their consciences?

And Auguste Nowak, what she had been through! Her husband, her parents, her best friend, and her little sister had all been shot before her eyes. Then her son had been abducted, and she herself had been taken away by the Russians. Pia couldn't comprehend how the woman could have summoned the will to survive labor camps, humiliation, rape, hunger, and illness. Was it the hope of finding her son again that had kept her alive, or the thought of revenge? At the age of eighty-five, Auguste Nowak would have to accept responsibility for a triple murder before the court, as the penal code demanded. And now, when she had finally found the son she'd thought was lost, she would have to go to prison. There was no proof that could justify her actions in any way.

Pia stopped reading. But maybe there was. The idea at first seemed crazy, but the more she thought about it, the more plausible it seemed. Just as she dialed the number of Henning's private line, Bodenstein came into the office with a glum look on his face.

"We have to instigate a search for Auguste Nowak," he announced.

Pia put a finger to her lips, because Henning had just picked up on the other end.

"What's up?" he asked, clearly in a bad mood. Pia didn't pay any attention to that as she briefly gave him a summary of Auguste Nowak's story. Bodenstein shot Pia a quizzical look. She put the phone on speaker and informed Henning that her boss was listening in.

"Can you still extract DNA out of bones that are over sixty years old?" she asked.

"Under the right circumstances, sure." The irritated tone was gone from Henning's voice; he sounded curious. "What have you got in mind?"

"I haven't talked with my boss about it yet," replied Pia, looking over at Bodenstein. "But you and I need to go to Poland. Flying would be best, of course. Miriam can pick us up."

"What? Right away?"

"That would be best. No need to waste any time."

"I don't have anything left to do tonight," said Henning, lowering his voice. "On the contrary. You'd be doing me a favor."

Pia understood the reference and grinned. DA Löblich was on his back.

"By car, it would take about eighteen hours to Masuria."

"I was thinking of Bernd. He still has his Cessna, doesn't he?"

Bodenstein shook his head, but Pia paid no attention.

"I'll call him," said Henning. "I'll call you back soon. Oh—Bodenstein?" "The stat analysis of your blood sample showed traces of gamma-hydroxybutyric acid, GHB for short. It's also called liquid ecstasy. According to my calculations, last night around nine o'clock, you must have ingested a dose of about two milligrams."

Bodenstein looked at Pia.

"A dose of this size produces a restriction of motor control, similar to alcohol intoxication. Occasionally, an aphrodisiac effect is also noted."

Pia noticed that her boss was actually blushing.

"What do you make of it, then?" he asked, turning his back to Pia.

"If you didn't take it yourself, someone must have slipped it to you. Probably in a drink. Liquid ecstasy is colorless."

"Now I understand," said Bodenstein. "Thank you very much, Dr. Kirchhoff."

"Don't mention it. I'll call you back soon."

"So," said Pia, satisfied. "Jutta set a trap for you."

"You can't go to Poland," said Bodenstein, changing the subject. "You don't even know if this castle still exists. Besides, the Polish authorities won't be happy if we ask for their cooperation in the middle of the night."

"Then we won't. Henning and I are flying there as tourists."

"You make it sound so simple."

"It *is* simple," Pia said. "If Henning's friend has time, he can fly us to Poland tomorrow morning. He flies businesspeople to the East all the time and knows the regulations."

Bodenstein frowned. There was a knock on the door, and Nicola Engel came in.

"Congratulations," she said. "You've solved three homicides."

"Thanks," said Bodenstein.

"How do you intend to proceed? Why haven't you arrested the woman?"

"Because she wasn't home," said Bodenstein. "I'm sending out an APB now."

Nicola Engel raised her eyebrows and looked suspiciously from Bodenstein to Pia.

"You're up to something," she said.

"That's right." Bodenstein took a deep breath. "I'm sending Ms. Kirchhoff and a forensic anthropologist to Poland to that castle. If possible, they are going to recover bones so that we can then analyze them here. If it turns out that Auguste Nowak is telling the truth—which I'm positive she is—we'll have enough evidence to charge Vera Kaltensee with murder in a court of law."

"That's out of the question. We don't have anything to do with this woman's horror story." Nicola Engel shook her head energetically. "There is absolutely no need for Ms. Kirchhoff to drive to Poland."

"But then we could—" Pia began.

"You have two more homicides to clear up here," said Engel, cutting off any further objections. "Besides, Professor Kaltensee is still at large, and now Mrs. Nowak is as well, a confessed murderer. And where are the diaries that Ritter received from Nowak? Where is Ritter? Why are six men sitting downstairs in the detention cells? You'd better talk to them before you drive off to Poland on a wild-goose chase."

"But it'll take only one day," Pia argued, but her future boss proved intransigent.

"Dr. Nierhoff has authorized me to make decisions on his behalf, and that's what I'm doing now. You will *not* drive to Poland. That's an order." Engel held a file in her carefully manicured hand. "Here are some new problems you have to deal with."

"I see." Bodenstein showed little interest.

"The lawyer for the Kaltensee family has filed an official complaint with the Interior Ministry regarding your interrogation methods. At present, he is preparing a lawsuit against both of you."

"What nonsense." Bodenstein snorted contemptuously. "They want to scare us off by any means possible because they know that we're on their heels."

"You have another much more serious problem right now, Mr. von Bodenstein. Mrs. Kaltensee's lawyer has described it merely as coercion. If he wants to get nasty, it will soon turn into an accusation of rape." She opened the file and held it out to Bodenstein. He turned beet red.

"Ms. Kaltensee led me into a trap, so that—"

Engel cut him off. "Don't make a fool of yourself, Chief Inspector. You invited State Representative Kaltensee to a tête-à-tête and then forced her into sexual intercourse."

The veins visible at Bodenstein's temples showed Pia that it was costing him a great effort to avoid losing his self-control.

"If this matter in any way becomes public," said Engel, "I will have no alternative but to put you on suspension."

Bodenstein stared at her furiously. She stood her ground.

"Whose side are you on anyway?" he asked. Clearly, he had forgotten that Pia was present. Nicola Engel had also stopped paying attention to anyone else.

"Mine," she replied coldly. "You should have realized that by now."

It was 11:15 P.M. when Henning showed up at Birkenhof with his suitcase and complete equipment. Bodenstein and Pia were sitting at the kitchen table, eating tuna pizza from Pia's deep-freeze reserves.

"We can take off tomorrow morning at four-thirty," Henning announced, leaning over the table. "I can't believe that you still eat this junk."

Only then did he notice the oppressive mood.

"What's wrong?"

"How do you commit the perfect murder?" Bodenstein asked glumly. "You probably have a few good tips for me."

Henning gave Pia a quizzical look.

"Oh, I'm sure I could think of something. Above all, you have to avoid having your victim land on my table," he said lightly. "Who are we talking about?"

"Our future boss, Nicola Engel," said Pia. Bodenstein had told her in strictest confidence why Engel disliked him so much. "She's forbidden me to drive to Poland."

"Well, to be precise, we're not driving; we're flying."

Bodenstein looked up. "That's right." He grinned hesitantly.

"That clears that up." Henning took a glass from the shelf and poured himself some water. "Now bring me up to speed on the latest developments."

Bodenstein and Pia took turns relating the events of the past twenty-four hours.

"We definitely need proof of what happened on January sixteenth, 1945," Pia concluded. "Otherwise, we can forget about a murder charge against Vera Kaltensee. On the other hand, she will try to bury us under legal proceedings and complaints. And no court in the world would convict her on the basis of Auguste Nowak's testimony. In the end, she would simply claim that she did not personally fire any shots. Besides, we don't know where the diaries are, and Ritter hasn't surfaced yet."

"Vera and Elard Kaltensee have disappeared, as well as Auguste Nowak," Bodenstein added. With effort, he stifled a yawn and glanced at the clock.

"If you fly to Poland tomorrow morning, please leave your service weapon here," he told Pia. "Not that there won't be other difficulties."

"Check." Pia nodded. Unlike her boss, she was wide awake. Bodenstein's cell phone rang. He took the call as Pia put the dirty plates in the dishwasher.

"A female skeleton has been found on the grounds of Mühlenhof," he said in a weary voice once the call had ended. "And our Swiss colleagues called. Vera Kaltensee is not at either of her houses, not in Zürich or in Ticino."

"I hope it's not too late," said Pia. "I'd give anything to bring her to trial."

Bodenstein got up from his chair.

"I'm going home," he said. "Tomorrow is another day."

"Wait and I'll close the gate behind you." Pia followed him out, accompanied by her four dogs, who'd been waiting by the front door for the signal for their late-night walk. Bodenstein stopped by his car.

"What are you going to tell Engel tomorrow when she wants to know where I am?" Pia asked. She had a bad feeling that Bodenstein was still on the brink of being suspended.

"I'll think of something," he said with a shrug. "Don't worry about it."

"Just say that I simply got on a plane."

Bodenstein looked at her for a moment, then shook his head.

"I know you mean well, but I'm not going to do that. Whatever you do, you'll be doing it with my full backing. I'm your boss, after all."

They stood there looking at each other in the floodlit courtyard.

"Take care of yourself," said Bodenstein in a hoarse voice. "I really don't know what I'd do without you, Pia."

It was the first time he'd ever called her by her first name. Pia didn't know quite what to think of it, but something had changed between them in the past couple of weeks. Bodenstein was no longer keeping his distance.

"Nothing's going to happen to us," she assured him. He opened the car door but didn't get in.

"The conflicts over those investigations are not the only things between Nicola Engel and me," he finally admitted. "We met in law school in Hamburg and were together for two years. Until Cosima crossed my path."

Pia was holding her breath. Where had this sudden need to confide in her come from?

"Nicola never forgave me for breaking up with her and marrying Cosima only three months later." He grimaced. "She's still holding a grudge. Idiot that I am, I've now given her another chance to score against me."

Pia understood for the first time what her boss feared most.

"You mean she might tell your wife about the . . . uh . . . incident?"

Bodenstein heaved a sigh and nodded.

"Then tell her yourself what happened, before she finds out from Engel," Pia advised him. "You do have the lab results as proof that the Kaltensee woman lured you into a trap. Your wife will understand; I'm sure she will."

"I'm not," replied Bodenstein, climbing into his car. "So, take good care of yourself. Don't take any unnecessary risks. And check in regularly."

"I will," Pia promised, and waved as he drove away.

Bodenstein was sitting at his laptop, in which he had shoved a copy of the CD-ROM with the manuscript of the biography of Vera Kaltensee. He was trying to concentrate. Half a pack of aspirin hadn't done anything to alleviate his pounding headache. The text swam before his eyes, and his thoughts were somewhere else entirely. He had lied when he'd told Cosima earlier that he had to read the manuscript before he went to bed because it was important to his investigations. She had believed him without question. After wasting two hours, he was now deliberating whether he should tell her about the incident, and, if so, how to begin. He wasn't used to keeping secrets from Cosima, and he felt utterly miserable about it. With each minute that passed, his courage sank. What if she didn't believe him? What if in the future she would always distrust him whenever he was away for any length of time?

"Damn it," he muttered, and closed the laptop. He turned off the desk lamp and went upstairs with a heavy heart. Cosima was in bed, reading. When he came in, she put the book aside and looked at him. How beautiful she was, how familiar the sight of her! It was impossible to keep such a secret from her. Mutely, he looked at his wife, searching for the right words.

"Cosi," he said, trembling inside, his mouth as dry as paper, "I . . . I . . . have to tell you something. . . ."

"Well, it's about time," she said.

He stared at her as if struck by lightning. To his surprise, she was even smiling a little.

"Your guilty conscience is written all over your face, my dear," Cosima said. "I just hope it's nothing to do with your old flame Nicola. Now tell me."

Friday, May 11

Siegbert Kaltensee was sitting at his desk in the workroom of his house, staring at the telephone as his daughter cried her eyes out in the kitchen. It was now thirty-six hours since Thomas Ritter had vanished, as if swallowed up by the earth, and in her despair Marleen had seen no option but to confide in her father. Siegbert hadn't let on that he already knew about everything. She had begged him for help, but there was nothing he could do. In the meantime, he had learned that he wasn't the one pulling the strings as he had assumed the whole time. The police, using the ground-penetrating radar at Mühlenhof, had found the remains of a human skeleton. Siegbert couldn't get what the police had told him out of his head—that he was Robert's biological father, and that Vera had killed the maid Danuta shortly after her child was born. Could that be true? And where was his mother anyway? He had talked to her around noon. She had decided to have Moormann drive her to the house in Ticino, but so far, she hadn't called him back. Siegbert Kaltensee grabbed the phone and dialed his sister's number. Jutta hadn't wasted any thought on her mother or on Elard, who had also disappeared, like Ritter. Her only concern was for her career, which might be damaged by all these unfortunate events.

"Have you even looked at the clock?" she asked him indignantly.

"Where is Ritter?" Siegbert asked his sister. "What have you done with him?"

"Me? Are you nuts?" she said, incensed. "You were the one who latched onto Mother's suggestion so eagerly."

"I had him taken out of circulation for a while, that's all. Have you heard anything from Mother?"

Siegbert admired and adored his mother. All his life he had fought for her love and recognition, and he had always complied with her orders and requests, even when he wasn't convinced he was doing the right thing. She was his mother, the great Vera Kaltensee, and if he obeyed her, then she would one day love him the way she loved Jutta. Or Elard, who had burrowed his way in at Mühlenhof like a tick.

"No," said Jutta. "I would have told you already if I had."

"She must have arrived long ago. Moormann hasn't called from his cell phone, either. I'm worried."

"Listen, Berti," said Jutta, lowering her voice. "Mother will be all right. Don't believe the crap the cops are telling you that Elard is after her. You know Elard. He's probably flown the coop, that coward, along with his little friend."

"Who's that?" Siegbert asked, sounding worried.

"Don't tell me you don't know." Jutta gave a venomous laugh. "Lately, Elard has been inclined toward pretty young men."

"What nonsense!" Siegbert despised his older brother with all his heart, but Jutta was really going too far.

"How typical." Jutta's voice turned cold. "I wonder whether all of you are doing this just to hurt me. Mother and her Nazi pals, a gay brother, and a skeleton at Mühlenhof! If the press gets wind of this, I've had it."

Bewildered, Siegbert Kaltensee said nothing. In the past few days, he'd gotten to know a whole different side of his sister, one that had been utterly foreign to him before. He now realized that everything she did was determined by an ironclad calculation. She didn't give a shit where Vera was hiding, whether Elard had shot three people, or whose skeleton the police had found—as long as they didn't connect her name with any of it.

"Now don't lose your nerve, you hear me, Berti?" she cajoled him. "It doesn't matter what the police ask us about; we don't know a thing. And that's actually the truth. Mother has made mistakes in her life, and I'm certainly not going to take the blame for them."

"You don't give a damn what's happening to her," Siegbert asserted tonelessly. "But she's still our mother, after all. . . ."

"Don't get sentimental on me, Berti. Mother is an old woman who has lived her life. I still have plans, and I won't let them be ruined by her. Or by Elard or Thomas or—"

Siegbert Kaltensee hung up. He heard in the distance his daughter sobbing and the soothing voice of his wife. He stared unseeing into space. Where did these doubts come from all of a sudden? Doubts that had been gnawing at him ever since the conversation with those two Kripo officers? He had been forced to do what he could to protect the family. Family was everything, after all—that was his mother's credo. Then why did he suddenly feel that she'd left him in the lurch? Why didn't she call?

Miriam was waiting for them, as agreed, at eight-thirty in front of the regional airport near Szczytno-Szymany. It was the only airport in the region of Warmia-Masuria, and its days were numbered anyway. The flight in the surprisingly comfortable Cessna CE-500 Citation had taken just four hours, the passport control three minutes.

"Ah, Dr. Frankenstein." Miriam offered her hand to Henning Kirchhoff after she had warmly hugged Pia. "Welcome to Poland."

"You are really unforgiving," said Henning, grinning. Miriam took off her sunglasses and scrutinized him; then she grinned, too.

"I have the memory of an elephant," she told him, grabbing one of Kirchhoff's bags. "Come with me. It's about a hundred-kilometer drive to Doba."

In a rented Ford Focus, they buzzed along the highways, heading north-east into the heart of Masuria. Miriam and Henning talked about the castle ruins and speculated about whether the cellar would even be accessible after sixty-plus years of neglect. Pia sat in the backseat, listening with one ear and staring silently out the window. She had no connection to this countryside and its tumultuous and unhappy past. For her, East Prussia had been merely an abstract concept, nothing more than a recurrent theme of TV documenta-ries and theatrical films. Her family had never had to flee or suffer expulsion. Looking out the windows in the misty light of morning, she saw hills, woods, and fields flitting by, while cottony swaths of fog still hovered over the many large and small lakes. The haze only gradually dissolved under the warm rays of the May sun.

Pia's thoughts shifted to Bodenstein. The trust he had shown her moved her deeply. He didn't have to confide in her, but he obviously wanted to be honest with her. Nicola Engel had it in for Bodenstein for purely personal reasons; it was unfair, but there was no changing the situation. The only way to help him was to make no mistakes here today. At Mragowo, Miriam turned onto a narrow, rougher road that led them past sleepy farms and little villages as they drove along idyllic old tree-lined avenues. They kept catching glimpses of blue water through the dark woods. Masuria, Miriam had ex-plained, was the largest lake plateau in Europe. A while later, they drove past Lake Kisajno and through the tiny hamlets of Kamionki and Doba. Pia called Bodenstein on her cell.

"We're almost there," she reported. "What's the mood like at headquar-ters?"

"So far so good," he said. "I haven't seen Dr. Engel. Anyway, Auguste Nowak hasn't turned up yet, and the others are also . . . afford . . . morning . . . talk . . . with Améry . . . with . . . nothing . . . got . . . they . . ."

"Boss, I can't hear you. You're breaking up," Pia shouted; then she lost the connection completely. In huge tracts of the former East Prussia, there weren't many cellular towers, and the mobile phone network was erratic, as Miriam had already told them. "Crap," Pia said.

Miriam stopped at a crossroads and turned right onto a paved road. They drove a few hundred yards through a sunlit deciduous forest, and the car bumped from one pothole to the next, so that Pia whacked her head against the side window.

"Wait till you see this," said Miriam. "It's going to take your breath away."

Pia leaned forward and peered between the seat backs as they left the woods behind. To the right lay Doben Lake, dark and glittering; to the left stretched an expanse of hills, broken here and there by groves of trees and woods.

"See those ruins on the left? That used to be the village of Lauenburg," Miriam explained. "Almost all the residents worked at the estate. There was a school, a store, a church, and, naturally, a village pub."

Almost all that was left of Lauenburg was the church. Perched atop the half-collapsed spire of red brick was a stork's nest.

"They've used the village as a sort of quarry," Miriam said. "Most of the working quarters at the estate and even the walls surrounding the castle have vanished the same way. On the other hand, much of the castle itself is still standing."

From a distance, they could see the symmetry of the manor courtyard: the castle in the middle right on the shore of the lake, surrounded in a U- shape by buildings that were mostly gone, only their foundations shimmering through shining green foliage. In the past, a carefully laid out avenue of trees must have led to the main portal of the castle, but now trees grew in wild abandon in places where they surely never would have been permitted before.

Miriam steered through the arch of the portal, which, unlike the rest of the wall, was still intact, and pulled up in front of the castle ruin. Pia looked around. Birds twittered in the branches of the mighty trees. Seen from up close, the remains of the former manor looked depressing. The brilliant green turned out to be weeds and underbrush, stinging nettles grew a yard high, and ivy covered almost every free surface. What a feeling it must have been for Auguste Nowak to come back here after sixty years of repressed memories and find the site of both the happiest and most horrible moments in her life in this condition. Maybe she had decided on this very spot to take revenge for what they had done to her.

"If only these walls could talk," murmured Pia as she trudged across the sprawling area that after decades of neglect had been almost completely re-conquered by nature. Beyond the fire-blackened ruins of the castle, the lake glistened silver. High above in the deep blue sky, storks were flying, and on the shattered steps of the castle, a fat cat was lolling in the sun, probably feel-ing like the legitimate heir to the Zeydlitz-Lauenburgs. In Pia's mind, she could see the manor as it once must have looked. The castle in the middle, steward's house, smithy, stables. All at once, she could understand why the people who were driven out of this beautiful place were to this day unable to accept the final loss of their homeland.

"Pia!" Henning shouted impatiently. "Could you come over here?"

"All right, I'm coming." She turned around. Out of the corner of her eye she noticed a flash of light. Sunlight glinting off metal. Curious, she rounded a pile of rubble overgrown by nettles and stopped abruptly. Fright raced through her all the way to her fingertips. Before her stood the black Maybach limousine belonging to Vera Kaltensee, dusty from a long drive, the wind-shield sticky with insects. Pia put her hand on the hood. It was still warm.

"Katharina Ehrmann was the only friend Jutta Kaltensee ever had. She spent her vacations working in the office with Eugen Kaltensee, and he liked her." Ostermann looked tired from lack of sleep, which was no wonder, because he'd read through Ritter's entire manuscript the night before. "On the evening that Jutta's father died, she was at Mühlenhof and accidentally became an eyewitness to the murder."

"Murder? Really?" Bodenstein asked to make sure. When Ostermann came in, he had been sitting at his desk and looking through the files for the report that Kathrin Fachinger had written after her conversation with Anita Frings's neighbor from Taunusblick. To his infinite relief, Cosima had not made a scene last night, and she believed that he had been innocently lured into a trap. She had also noticed when she had lunch with Jutta Kaltensee that the purported image campaign was only a lame pretext. Bodenstein could cope with everything else, even Nicola's attempts to get rid of him. Viewed soberly, allowing Pia Kirchhoff to travel to Poland against Nicola En-gel's express orders was, in his present position, tantamount to career suicide. But in the cellar of the castle in Masuria lay the key to the events that had saddled them with five bodies in eight days. Bodenstein fervently hoped that Pia's efforts would be crowned with success; otherwise, he might as well pack up his things.

"Yes, it was undoubtedly murder," Ostermann now replied. "Wait a second, I'll read you the passage from the manuscript: "'Vera shoved him down the steep cellar stairs and then ran down as if she wanted to help him. She knelt down next to him, put her ear to his lips, and, when she noticed that he was still breathing, smothered him with his own sweater. Then she went upstairs, unmoved, and sat down at her desk. The body wasn't discovered until two hours later. A suspect was soon identified: After a vehement fight with his stepfather, Elard had left Mühlenhof in the late afternoon in a great hurry, and took the night train back to Paris that same evening.'"

Bodenstein nodded. Thomas Ritter must either be very naïve or truly blind with the desire for revenge to write such a book, he thought. It was clever of Katharina Ehrmann to make her knowledge public in this way. He didn't know why Katharina hated the Kaltensees, but it was impossible to ignore the fact that she did. One thing was certain: If this book were ever published, the scandal would drag some members of the Kaltensee family into the abyss.

The phone rang. He was hoping it was Pia, but it was Behnke. The description of the man who had accompanied Ritter the night before last as he left the editorial office might match an employee of K-Secure. But Améry and his five colleagues were being as closemouthed as the Sicilian Mafia.

"I want to speak to Siegbert Kaltensee," said Bodenstein, at the risk of being reported again for acting with arbitrary high-handedness. "Bring him here. And the receptionist from *Weekend,* too. We'll do a lineup with the K-Secure men. Maybe she'll recognize the messenger."

Where was Vera Kaltensee? Where was Elard? Were they still alive? Why had Elard Kaltensee locked Nowak in the basement of the university building? Marcus Nowak had been operated on last night, and he was now in the ICU of the Bethanien Hospital. The doctors still couldn't say whether he would survive. Bodenstein closed his eyes and rested his head on his hand. Elard had been in possession of the trunk and the diaries. At the request of Katharina Ehrmann, he had given the diaries to Ritter, and somehow the

Kaltensees must have found out about it. Absentmindedly, he leafed through the transcript. Suddenly, he stopped.

"*The Little Tomcat, who came regularly,*" he read. "*Used to push her wheelchair around in the park.*" ... "*The Little Tomcat?*" ... "*That's what she called him, the young man.*" ... "*What did he look like?*" ... "*Brown eyes. Slim. Medium height, average-looking face. The ideal spy, right? Or a Swiss banker.*"

Something stirred in Bodenstein's memory. Spy, spy ... Then it dawned on him. "Terrible, that Moormann," Jutta Kaltensee had said, and turned all pale when her mother's chauffeur suddenly appeared behind her. "Creeping all over soundlessly and scaring me half to death each time, that old spy."

That had been on the day when he'd met Jutta for the first time at Mühlenhof. Bodenstein thought about the shirt that Watkowiak had been wearing. Moormann could have easily worn one of Elard Kaltensee's shirts to lay a false trail.

"Good God," Bodenstein muttered. Why hadn't he thought of this before? Moormann, the servant, whose constant unobtrusive presence in the house was so taken for granted. He must know about everything that happened in the family. Did he know about the transfer of the diaries to Ritter, and had he perhaps listened in on Elard's phone call? Undoubtedly, the man was loyal to his employer. At the very least, he had lied for her. Had he also murdered for her? Bodenstein banged the folder shut and took his service weapon out of his desk drawer. He had to drive to Mühlenhof at once. Just as he was about to leave his office, Chief Commissioner Nierhoff appeared in his doorway with an ominous expression, accompanied by a rather smug-looking Nicola Engel. Bodenstein put on his jacket.

"Dr. Engel," he said before either of them could open their mouths, "I urgently need your help."

"Where is Ms. Kirchhoff?" Nierhoff asked sharply.

"In Poland." Bodenstein looked at Nicola Engel. "I know that I have disregarded regulations, but I had my reasons."

"What do you need help for?" Commissioner Engel ignored his explanation and returned his look with an unfathomable expression in her eyes.

"I've just realized that we've been overlooking someone this whole time," said Bodenstein. "I believe that Vera Kaltensee's chauffeur, Moormann, is the one who killed Monika Krämer and Robert Watkowiak." He hurriedly explained the suspicious circumstances.

"We have one trace-trace hit that we haven't been able to account for. I need Moormann's DNA, and I'd like you to accompany me to Mühlenhof. In addition, we need a lineup to show Ritter's secretary the K-Secure men. I can only keep them detained until this evening."

"But that's not procedure..." Nierhoff protested, but Nicola Engel nodded.

"I'll come with you," she said decisively. "Let's go."

Pia slowly went around the black limousine that had been parked carelessly between the thistles and a pile of rubble. The doors weren't locked. Whoever had come here in the vehicle had been in a hurry. Quietly, she moved away and went to tell Henning and Miriam about her find. None of their cell phones was working, but Bodenstein wouldn't have been able to help her now anyway.

"Maybe we'd better ask the Polish police to intervene," Pia suggested.

"Nonsense." Henning shook his head. "What do you want to tell them? 'There's a car over here. Could you please come out and take a look?' They'll have a good laugh at you."

"But who knows what might be going on down there in the cellar?" Pia said.

"We'll soon see," replied Henning, and marched off resolutely. Pia had a bad feeling about this, but it was silly to turn back when they were so close to their goal. Who could have driven the Maybach here all the way from Germany, and why? After a brief hesitation, she followed Miriam and her ex-husband.

The once-magnificent castle had almost completely caved in. The outer walls were still standing, but the ground floor was covered in rubble and offered no access to the cellar.

"Here," Miriam called in a low voice. "Somebody has gone this way, and fairly recently."

The three of them followed a narrow path through nettles and underbrush in the direction of the lake. Downtrodden grass told them that the

path had been used not long before. They made their way through head-high
reeds that rustled softly in the wind. Their feet squelched in the mire. Henning cursed, startled, when right next to them two wild ducks took off with a
loud quacking. Pia's nerves were stretched to the breaking point. The weather
had turned hot, and sweat ran into her eyes. What awaited them in the cellar
of the castle? How should they act if they actually ran into Vera or Elard
Kaltensee? They had promised Bodenstein not to take any risks. Wouldn't it
be smarter to notify the Polish police?

"Ah yes," said Miriam. "Here are the stairs."

The crumbling steps seemed to lead down into nothingness, since the
rear portion of the castle lay in rubble and ashes. The marble flagstones of the
former terrace with its spectacular lake view had long since vanished. Miriam
stopped and wiped the sweat from her face with her forearm. She pointed to
a gaping hole at her feet. Pia gulped and struggled with herself for a moment
before she was the first to climb down. She wanted to reach for her pistol,
when she remembered that she had left it back in Germany, at Bodenstein's
request. Cursing silently, she felt her way over a mountain of rubble down
into the darkness.

The cellar of Lauenburg Manor had survived fire, war, and the tooth of
time astoundingly well; most of the rooms were still intact. Pia tried to ori-
ent herself. She had no idea in which part of the extensive cellar they were
standing.

"Let me go first," said Henning, who had switched on a flashlight. A rat
scurried across the rubbish and paused for a moment in the beam of light. Pia
grimaced in disgust. After a few yards, Henning stopped suddenly and turned
off the flashlight. Pia bumped into him hard and staggered.

"What is it?" she whispered tensely.

"Somebody's talking," he said softly. They stood very still and listened,
but except for their breathing, they heard nothing for quite a while. Pia
jumped in fright when almost directly beside her an imperious female voice
resounded.

"Untie me, now! What's gotten into you, treating me like this?"

"Tell me what I want to know; then I'll release you," said a man.

"I'm not saying anything. And stop waving that thing around!"

"Tell me what happened here on January sixteenth, 1945. Tell me what you did, you and your friends, and I'll let you go immediately."

Pia squeezed past Henning, her heart pounding, and looked around the corner, holding her breath. A portable floodlight threw a glaring beam on the ceiling, illuminating the low cellar room. Elard Kaltensee was standing behind the woman he had always thought was his mother, pressing the barrel of a pistol into the back of her neck. She was kneeling on the ground, her hands tied behind her back. There was nothing left of the elegant, worldly woman. Her white hair stood out wildly from her head, she wore no makeup, and her clothes were dirty and rumpled. Pia could see the tension in Elard Kaltensee's face. He was blinking his eyes, licking his lips nervously. One wrong word or false move and he might fire.

When Bodenstein and Dr. Engel returned from Mühlenhof, having achieved nothing because everyone had already cleared out, Siegbert Kaltensee was waiting at the station.

"What do you actually want from him?" Nicola Engel asked as they went up the stairs to Bodenstein's office.

"I want to know where Moormann and Ritter are," he replied with grim determination. He'd been concentrating for far too long on the obvious and overlooking what was just below the surface. Siegbert, who had stood in the shadow of Elard his whole life, had been used by his mother exactly as she had used every other person who came near her.

"Why would he know that?"

"He's his mother's gofer, and she was the one who gave the orders for everything."

Nicola Engel stopped and held him back.

"How do you actually know that Jutta Kaltensee wanted to lure you into a trap?" she asked in earnest. Bodenstein looked at her. In her eyes he saw genuine interest.

"Jutta Kaltensee is a very ambitious woman," he said. "She realized that the murders, which were so closely connected to her family, could be extremely damaging for her career. And a biography that attracted attention, that produced negative headlines, was the last thing she needed. I still don't know who actually ordered the murders of Robert Watkowiak and his girl-friend, but both of them had to die to put us off the scent. The evidence pointing to Elard Kaltensee was also planted in order to make him seem un-trustworthy. When we dug even deeper, she decided on a desperate move to compromise me. The chief investigator forces a member of the Kaltensee family into a sexual liaison—what could be better?"

Nicola Engel looked at him thoughtfully.

"She made an appointment with me, ostensibly to tell me something re-lated to the case," Bodenstein continued. "I can hardly remember that eve-ning, although I drank only one glass of wine. Everything got very hazy. That's why I had a blood sample taken yesterday. Dr. Kirchhoff determined that someone had given me liquid ecstasy. Do you understand now? She planned the whole thing."

"To get you out of the way?" Nicola Engel asked.

"I can't come up with any other explanation," said Bodenstein. "She wants to be prime minister, but she could hardly manage it with a murderer for a mother and a skeleton discovered on the grounds of the family estate. Jutta will distance herself from the family in order to survive. And she'll make use of what she did to me, resorting to blackmail if necessary."

"But she doesn't have any proof, does she?"

"Of course she does," Bodenstein replied bitterly. "She's clever enough to produce something on which my DNA is detectable."

"You might actually be right," Nicola Engel conceded after thinking it over.

"I *am* right," Bodenstein insisted. "You'll see."

For a while, it was completely still in the vaulted space. Pia took a deep breath and moved forward a step.

"You might as well tell me, Edda Schwinderke," she said loudly, stepping into the light with her hands raised. "We know what happened here."

Elard Kaltensee spun around and stared at her as if he'd seen a ghost. Even Vera, aka Edda, gave a start in fright, but she quickly recovered from her surprise.

"Ms. Kirchhoff!" she cried in the sugar-sweet voice that Pia knew so well. "You're heaven-sent. Please help me."

Pia didn't look at her, going over to Elard Kaltensee instead.

"Don't do anything stupid. Give me the gun." She held out her hand. "We know the truth, and we know what she did."

Elard Kaltensee looked back at the woman kneeling in front of him.

"I don't care." He shook his head emphatically. "I didn't come all this way to give up now. I want a confession from this murderous old witch. Now."

"I've brought along a specialist who will search for the remains of the people who were shot to death here," Pia said. "Even after sixty years, DNA samples can be taken and the individuals identified. We can bring Vera Kaltensee to trial in Germany for multiple homicides. The truth will come out in any event."

Kaltensee didn't take his eyes off Vera.

"Go, Ms. Kirchhoff. This is none of your business."

Suddenly a small, stocky figure emerged from the shadow of the wall. Pia gave a start because she hadn't noticed that anyone else was in the room. In astonishment, she recognized Auguste Nowak.

"Mrs. Nowak! What are you doing here?"

"Elard is right," she said. "It's none of your business. This woman inflicted deep wounds on my boy that have not healed in sixty years. She stole his life from him. It's his right to hear from her what happened in this place."

"We've heard the story that you told to Thomas Ritter," said Pia in a low voice. "And we believe you. Nevertheless, I do have to arrest you. You shot three people to death, and without evidence for your motives, you will be sent to prison for the rest of your life. Even if that doesn't matter to you, then at least keep your son from doing something stupid and committing another murder. This woman is not worth it."

Auguste Nowak looked thoughtfully at the gun in Elard's hands.

"By the way, we've found your grandson," said Pia. "And in the nick of time, too. A few more hours and he would have bled to death internally."

Elard Kaltensee raised his head and looked at her with a flickering gaze. "What do you mean, 'bled to death'?" he asked hoarsely.

"He sustained internal injuries from the attack," Pia replied. "Because you dragged him into that basement, he's in critical condition. Why did you do that? Did you want him to die?"

Elard Kaltensee suddenly lowered the pistol, and his eyes went to Auguste Nowak, then to Pia. He shook his head.

"My God, no!" he exclaimed, deeply upset. "I wanted to make sure that Marcus was safe until I got back. I would never do anything to harm him."

His consternation surprised Pia. Then she remembered her encounter with Elard Kaltensee in the hospital and thought she understood.

"You and Nowak are more than acquaintances. Am I right?" she asked.

"Yes," he admitted. "We're very good friends. Actually . . . much more than that . . ."

"That's right," said Pia with a nod. "You're related. Marcus Nowak is your nephew, if I'm not mistaken."

Elard Kaltensee gave her the pistol and then ran both hands through his hair. In the beam from the floodlight, she could see that he'd turned deathly pale.

"I have to go to him at once," he muttered. "I didn't mean to hurt him, really I didn't. I only wanted to make sure nobody did anything to him before I got back. I . . . I had no idea that he . . . Good God! Is he going to recover?"

He looked up. His desire for revenge all at once seemed utterly pointless, and naked fear shone in his eyes. That was when Pia realized what sort of relationship there was between Elard Kaltensee and Marcus Nowak. She remembered the photos on the walls of his residence at the Kunsthaus. The rear view of a naked man, the dark eyes in close-up. The jeans on the bathroom floor. Marcus Nowak had indeed cheated on his wife. Not with another woman, but with Elard Kaltensee.

Siegbert Kaltensee sat slumped in a chair in one of the interrogation rooms, staring into space. Overnight, he seemed to have aged terribly. All the rosiness and joviality were gone; his face was gray and sunken.

"Have you heard anything from your mother in the meantime?" Bodenstein began. Kaltensee shook his head mutely.

"We've learned some very interesting things recently. For instance, we know that your brother Elard is not really your brother."

"Pardon me?" Siegbert Kaltensee raised his head and stared at Bodenstein.

"We've caught the murderer of Goldberg, Schneider, and Mrs. Frings, and she confessed," Bodenstein continued. "The real names of those three are Oskar Schwinderke, Hans Kallweit, and Maria Willumat. Schwinderke was your mother's brother. Her real name is Edda Schwinderke, the daughter of the former paymaster at Lauenburg Manor."

Kaltensee shook his head in disbelief, and his face revealed bewilderment when Bodenstein now told him in detail about Auguste Nowak's confession.

"No," he murmured. "No, that can't be."

"Unfortunately, it's true. Your mother has been lying to you all your life. The rightful owner of Mühlenhof is Baron Elard von Zeydlitz-Lauenburg, whose father was shot to death by your mother on January sixteenth, 1945. The mysterious number that we found at all the murder scenes referred to that day."

Siegbert Kaltensee hid his face in his hands.

"Did you know that Moormann, your mother's chauffeur, used to be in the Stasi?"

"Yes," said Kaltensee dully. "I knew that."

"We presume that he was the one who killed your son, Robert, and his girlfriend, Monika Krämer."

Siegbert Kaltensee looked up.

"What an idiot I am!" he exclaimed with sudden bitterness.

"How do you mean?" Bodenstein asked.

"I had no idea." The lost expression on Siegbert Kaltensee's face showed that his whole world was falling apart. "I had absolutely no idea what was going on the whole time. My God. What have I done?"

Bodenstein involuntarily tensed every muscle, like a hunter who unexpectedly sees his prey standing in front of him. He almost held his breath. But he was disappointed.

"I want to talk to my lawyer." Siegbert Kaltensee squared his shoulders.

"Where is Moormann?"

No reply.

"What happened to your son-in-law? We know that Thomas Ritter was abducted by people from your security firm. Where is he now?"

"I want to talk to my lawyer," Kaltensee repeated hoarsely, and his eyes seemed to be popping out of his head. "Right away."

"Mr. Kaltensee," said Bodenstein, pretending he hadn't heard him, "you gave the men of K-Secure orders to attack Marcus Nowak in order to get hold of the diaries. And you also had Ritter kidnapped so that he couldn't write the biography. As always, you've been doing your mother's dirty work, right?"

"My lawyer," Kaltensee murmured. "I want to talk to my lawyer."

"Is Ritter still alive?" Bodenstein asked insistently. "Or don't you care that your daughter is almost losing her mind out of worry over him? Bodenstein registered how the man flinched. "Incitement to murder is a felony offense. You will go to prison for it. Your daughter and your wife will never forgive you. You will lose *everything*, Mr. Kaltensee, if you don't answer me right now!"

"I want to—" Kaltensee began again.

Bodenstein did not back off. "Did your mother ask you to take care of these things? Was this a favor you did for her? If this is true, you should say so now. Your mother is going to prison anyway; we have proof of what she did, as well as eyewitness testimony that reveals the alleged accidental death of your father was, in fact, murder. Don't you get what this is about? If you tell us at once where Thomas Ritter is, you still have a chance of getting out of this whole mess with a relatively light sentence."

Siegbert Kaltensee gasped for breath. A hounded look appeared on his face.

"Do you really want to go to prison for your mother, who did nothing but lie to you and exploit you all your life?"

Bodenstein let his words take effect and waited another minute. Then he stood up.

"You stay here," he told Kaltensee. "Think everything over in peace and quiet. I'll be right back."

●　　●　　●

While Henning and Miriam went about searching the floor of the room inch by inch for human remains, Pia left the cellar with Elard, Vera, and Auguste Nowak.

"I hope you weren't exaggerating," said Elard Kaltensee as they emerged into daylight and crossed the former terrace. Auguste Nowak didn't seem especially strained, but Vera Kaltensee needed a pause. Her hands still tied, she sat down on a pile of rocks, exhausted.

"No, it's true." Pia had put the safety on Elard Kaltensee's pistol and stuck it in her waistband. "We know what happened here in 1945. And if we find any bones and can extract DNA from them, then we'll have proof."

"I mean what you said about Marcus," Elard said with concern. "Is he really in such bad shape?"

"Last night, his condition was critical," Pia replied. "But they'll take good care of him at the hospital."

"It's all my fault." Elard put both hands over his face and shook his head a few times. "If only I'd left that trunk alone. Then none of this would have happened."

He was undoubtedly right about that. Some people would still be alive, and all the Kaltensees' family secrets would still be well guarded. Pia's eyes moved to Vera, whose face had assumed a blank expression. How could a person live with such guilt and act so cold and indifferent?

"Why didn't you shoot the boy, too, back then?" Pia asked. The old woman raised her head and stared at Pia. Even after sixty years, her eyes blazed with naked hate.

"It was my triumph over that woman," she hissed, and nodded in Auguste's direction. "If she hadn't existed, then he would have married *me*!"

"Never," Auguste Nowak interjected. "Elard couldn't stand you. He was just too well brought up to let you see it."

"Well brought up!" Vera Kaltensee snorted. "That's a laugh. I didn't want him anymore anyway. How could he impregnate the daughter of Jewish Bolsheviks? He had already forfeited his life; anyone who had sex with a non-Aryan received the death penalty."

Elard Kaltensce, stunned, stared at the woman he'd called "Mother" his whole life. Auguste Nowak, on the other hand, remained amazingly calm.

"Just imagine how amused Elard would have been, Edda," she retorted derisively, "if he'd known that your brother, of all people, the Obersturmbahnführer, disguised himself as a Jew for more than sixty years to save his own skin. The staunchest Nazi of all had married a Jewish *mamme* and had to speak Yiddish!"

Vera Kaltensee's eyes were shooting daggers.

"It's a shame you couldn't hear how pathetically he begged for his life," Auguste Nowak went on. "He died the way he'd lived, a poor, cowardly worm! My family, on the other hand, faced death bravely, without whining. They were no cowards hiding behind a phony name."

"Your *family*? Don't make me laugh," Vera Kaltensee said poisonously.

"Yes, my family. Pastor Kunisch married Elard and me on Christmas Day, 1944, in the library of the castle. Oskar could do nothing to prevent it."

"That's not true!" Vera shook her bound hands.

"Yes, it is." Auguste Nowak nodded and grabbed Elard's hand. "My Heinrich, whom you passed off as your son, is the baron of Zeydlitz-Lauenburg."

"And Mühlenhof also belongs to him," Pia said. "Even KMF doesn't rightfully belong to you. You have stolen everything in your life, Edda. Anyone who was in the way was eliminated. Your husband, Eugen—it was you who pushed him down the basement stairs, wasn't it? And the mother of Robert Watkowiak, that poor maid, also had to die. By the way, we found her remains on the grounds of Mühlenhof."

"What else could I have done?" In her fury, Vera Kaltensee didn't realize that with these words she was offering a confession. "Siegbert would never marry such a common person!"

"Maybe he would have been happier with her than he is now. But you put an end to the relationship and thought you could get away with all those murders," Pia said. "But you didn't count on Vicky Endrikat surviving the massacre. Were you scared when you heard about the number that was found next to the bodies of your brother, Hans Kallweit, and Maria Willumat?"

Vera was shaking all over with rage. There was nothing left of the elegant, friendly lady for whom Pia had once felt sympathy.

"Whose plan was it back then to shoot the Endrikats and the Zeydlitz-Lauenburgs?"

"Mine." Vera Kaltensee smiled coldly and with obvious satisfaction, fully revealing the ice queen that had always lurked underneath her polished demeanor.

"You saw your big chance, didn't you?" Pia continued. "Your ascent to the aristocracy. But the price of it was a life lived in constant fear of exposure. For more than sixty years, everything went well, but then the past finally caught up with you. And you *were* afraid. Not for your life, but for your social standing, which was always more important to you than anything else. That's why you had your grandson Robert and his girlfriend murdered, leaving evidence behind that pointed to Elard. You and your daughter, Jutta, who is equally dependent on your high social status. The biography will be published. And with a first chapter that will shock everyone who reads it. The husband of your granddaughter Marleen refused to be intimidated by you."

"Marleen is divorced," Vera Kaltensee countered in a condescending tone of voice.

"That's possible. But less than two weeks ago, Thomas Ritter married her. In secret. And she's expecting a baby by him." Pia enjoyed the impotent rage that appeared in the woman's eyes. "So, this is the second man who has chosen someone else over you. First Elard von Zeydlitz-Lauenburg, who chose to marry Vicky Endrikat, and now Thomas Ritter."

Before Vera could say anything, Miriam emerged from the cellar.

"We found something!" she cried breathlessly. "A whole bunch of bones!"

Pia met Elard Kaltensee's eyes and smiled. Then she turned to Vera.

"I am placing you under provisional arrest," she said. "For suspicion of instigating seven counts of murder."

Sina, the receptionist, had unambiguously identified Henri Améry as the man who had come to the editorial office of *weekend* on Wednesday evening. Nicola Engel now offered him a choice: Tell everything or face charges of unlawful deprivation of personal liberty, obstruction of justice, and suspicion

of homicide. The head of K-Secure was no fool, and after ten seconds he decided on option one. Améry had visited Marcus Nowak with Moormann
and a colleague and kept Dr. Ritter under surveillance for a few days, on instructions from Siegbert Kaltensee. He discovered that Ritter was married to
Siegbert's daughter, Marleen. Jutta had insisted on keeping this fact from her
brother. The order to "pick up Ritter for a little talk," as Améry expressed it,
had come from Siegbert.

"What was the exact wording of the assignment?" Bodenstein inquired.

"I was told to bring Ritter to a certain location without a lot of fuss."

"Where to?"

"To the Frankfurt Kunsthaus. At Römerberg Square. And that's what
we did."

"And then?"

"We put him in one of the basement rooms and left him there. What
happened to him after that, I have no idea."

To the Kunsthaus. A clever idea, because if a body was found in the basement of the Kunsthaus, Elard Kaltensee would immediately be linked to the
murder.

"What did Siegbert Kaltensee want from Ritter?"

"No idea. I don't ask questions when I get an assignment."

"What about Marcus Nowak? You tortured him to find out something.
What was it?"

"Moormann was asking the questions. It was something about a trunk."

"What does Moormann have to do with K-Secure?"

"Actually, nothing. But he knows how to make people talk."

"From his years with the Stasi." Bodenstein nodded. "But Nowak didn't
talk, did he?"

"No," said Améry. "He didn't say a word."

"What about Robert Watkowiak?" Bodenstein asked.

"I took him to Mühlenhof on Siegbert Kaltensee's instructions. On
Wednesday, May second. My men had looked for him everywhere, and
then he happened to walk across the street right in front of me in Fischbach."

Bodenstein recalled the message that Watkowiak had left on Kurt Frenzel's answering machine: "My stepmother's gorillas have been laying in wait for me . . ."

"Have you ever received any assignments from Jutta Kaltensee?" Nicola Engel now inquired. Améry hesitated, then nodded.

"What were they?"

The self-confident and slippery security leader actually seemed embarrassed. He hemmed and hawed.

"We're waiting." Nicola Engel impatiently rapped her knuckle on the table.

"I was supposed to take photos," Améry finally admitted, looking at Bodenstein. "Of you and Ms. Kaltensee."

Bodenstein felt the blood rush to his face, and at the same time he was filled with relief. He caught a glance from Nicola Engel, but she concealed whatever thoughts she might have behind a blank expression.

"What was the exact nature of the assignment?"

"She told me to stay available and to come to the Rote Mühle later and take some pictures," Améry replied uncomfortably. "At ten-thirty, I got a text that I needed to be on hand in twenty minutes."

He cast Bodenstein a brief glance and smiled ruefully. "Sorry. It was nothing personal."

"Did you take pictures?" Engel asked.

"Yes."

"Where are they?"

"In my cell and on my computer at the office."

"We'll have to confiscate those."

"Be my guest." Améry shrugged again.

"What instructions did Jutta Kaltensee give you?"

"She paid me extra for special tasks." Henri Améry was a mercenary and knew no loyalty, especially since the Kaltensee family wouldn't be paying him anymore in the future. "Occasionally, I was her bodyguard, and now and then her lover."

Nicola Engel nodded with satisfaction. Exactly what she'd wanted to hear.

•   •   •

"How did you actually get Vera across the border?" Pia inquired.

"In the trunk." Elard Kaltensee smiled grimly. "The Maybach has diplomatic plates. I had counted on the border guards simply waving us through, and they did."

Pia thought about the statement by Bodenstein's mother-in-law that Elard was no man of action. What had led him to seize the initiative at last?

"I might have doped myself up with lorazepam so I wouldn't have to face reality," explained Kaltensee. "If she hadn't done what she did to Marcus. When I found out from you that Vera had never paid him for his work, and then when I saw him lying there, so . . . beat-up and suffering, something happened to me. I was suddenly so furious at her—the way she treats people, with such contempt and indifference. And I knew that I had to stop her. I had to prevent her by any means necessary from hushing it all up again."

He stopped, shaking his head.

"I had learned that she secretly planned to go to Italy and from there to South America, so I couldn't wait any longer. There was a police car at the gate, so I left the house another way. All day long, there was no opportunity, but then Jutta drove off with Moormann, and a little later Siegbert left, too; then I was able to overpower my mo—I mean . . . that *woman*. The rest was child's play."

"Why did you leave your Mercedes at the airport?"

"To leave a phony trail," he explained. "That way, I could concentrate less on the police and more on my brother's security men, who were hot on the trail of Marcus and me. Unfortunately, *she* had to wait in the trunk of the Maybach until I came back."

"When you visited Nowak at the hospital, you claimed to be his father." Pia looked at him. He seemed more relaxed now, finally at peace with himself and his past. His personal nightmare was over after he freed himself from the burden of uncertainty.

"No," Auguste Nowak interjected. "I said that he was my son. And that wasn't a lie."

"Right." Pia nodded and looked at Elard Kaltensee. "The whole time, I thought you were the murderer. You and Marcus Nowak."

"I can't blame you," replied Elard. "We were behaving pretty suspiciously without meaning to. I wasn't really aware of the murders; I was too wrapped up in myself. Marcus and I, we were both utterly confused. For a long time we didn't want to admit what was going on. It was . . . it was somehow unthinkable. I mean, neither he nor I had ever had anything to do with a . . . man before."

He gave a deep sigh.

"The nights for which we had no alibis, Marcus and I spent together at my Frankfurt apartment."

"He's your nephew. You're blood relations," Pia noted.

"Well, yes," said Elard Kaltensee, a smile flashing across his face, "but it's not as if we can have children together."

Pia also had to smile at that.

"It's a shame that you didn't tell me all this earlier," she said. "You would have saved us a lot of work. What are you going to do now when you get home?"

"Well," said Baron von Zeydlitz-Lauenburg, taking a deep breath, "the time for playing hide-and-seek is over. Marcus and I have decided to tell our families the truth about our relationship. We don't want to stay in the closet. For me, it's not so bad—my reputation is dubious anyway—but for Marcus, it will be a difficult step to take."

Pia took him at his word. Marcus Nowak's family and friends would never display even a spark of understanding for this sort of relationship. His father and the whole family would probably commit collective hara-kiri if it became known in Fischbach that their son, husband, and brother had left his wife for a man thirty years older.

"I'd like to come back here sometime with Marcus." Elard Kaltensee let his gaze sweep over the lake glinting in the sun. "Maybe we could restore the castle once the ownership claims are settled. Marcus would be a better judge of that than I am. But it would be a wonderful hotel, right on the lakeshore."

Pia smiled and glanced at her watch. It was high time to call Bodenstein.

"I suggest we take Mrs. Kaltensee to the limousine," she said. "And then we'll all drive back together. . . ."

"Nobody's going anywhere," a voice suddenly said from behind her. Pia spun around in alarm and looked straight into the barrel of a gun. Three figures clad in black and wearing balaclavas over their heads, pistols drawn, had come up the stairs.

"Well, finally, Moormann," she heard Vera Kaltensee say. "It's about time."

"Where's Moormann?" Bodenstein asked the head of K-Secure.

"If he's on his way somewhere in the car, I can find out." Henri Améry wasn't keen on having a police record, so he was helpfulness personified. "All vehicles of the Kaltensee family and K-Secure are equipped with a chip, which allows them to be located by means of computer software."

"How does it work?"

"If you'll let me use a computer, I'll show you."

Bodenstein immediately escorted the man from the interview room to Ostermann's office on the second floor.

"Go ahead." He pointed to the computer on the desk. Bodenstein, Ostermann, Behnke, and Nicola Engel watched with interest as Améry entered the name of a Web site called Minor Planet. He waited until the page displayed completely, then logged in with user name and password. A map of Europe appeared. The vehicles were listed on it, along with their license numbers.

"We introduced this monitoring system so that I can see at a glance at any time where my employees are," Améry explained. "And in case any vehicle should be stolen."

"Which car might Moormann be driving?" Bodenstein asked.

"I don't know. I'll try one after the other."

Nicola Engel signaled Bodenstein to follow her out to the hall.

"I'm preparing an arrest warrant for Siegbert Kaltensee," she said in a low voice. "There will be problems with Jutta Kaltensee, because as a representative in the state parliament, she has diplomatic immunity, but I'd like to bring her in for a talk at any rate."

"Okay." Bodenstein nodded. "I'll drive with Améry over to the Kunst-haus. Maybe we'll find Ritter there."

"I think Siegbert Kaltensee knows what happened," Nicola Engel said. "He has a guilty conscience because of his daughter."

"I think so, too."

"I've got it," Améry reported from the office. "He must have taken the M-Class Mercedes from Mühlenhof, because it's in a place where it shouldn't be. In Poland, in a place called . . . Doba. The vehicle has been stationary for forty-three minutes."

Bodenstein felt himself go ice-cold. Moormann, the presumed murderer of Robert Watkowiak and Monika Krämer, was in Poland! On the phone, Pia had told him a couple of hours ago that they had almost reached their destination, and that Dr. Kirchhoff was going to search the cellar thoroughly. So that meant they probably hadn't left the castle. What was Moorman doing in Poland? All of a sudden, he realized where Elard Kaltensee was. He turned to the head of K-Secure.

"Check on the Maybach," he said in a hoarse voice. "Where is it right now?"

Améry clicked on the license number of the limousine.

"It's there, too," he said a moment later. "No, hold on. The Maybach started moving one minute ago."

Bodenstein looked at Nicola Engel. She understood at once.

"Ostermann, you keep track of both vehicles," said Engel decisively. "I'll inform our colleagues in Poland. And then I'm going to Wiesbaden."

One of the black-clad men who had appeared so unexpectedly had driven off with Vera Kaltensee. Her last order was clear: Tie the hands of Elard Kaltensee, Auguste Nowak, and Pia Kirchhoff and shoot them in the cellar. Pia desperately thought of how she could get out of this hopeless situation and warn Miriam and Henning. There was no mercy to be expected from these men; they would simply carry out their assignment and then drive back to Germany as if nothing had happened. Pia knew that she bore the responsibility for Henning and Miriam. She was the one who'd gotten both of them into this terrible situation. All at once, wild rage overcame her. She had no desire to be led like a lamb to the slaughter. It couldn't be true that she would die without ever seeing Christoph again. Christoph! She had promised to pick him up at the airport when he came back from South Africa tonight. Pia stopped in front of the opening that led down to the cellar.

"What do you intend to do with us?" she asked to gain time.

"You heard it," said the man. His voice sounded muffled through his ski mask.

"But why—" Pia began. The man gave her a hard shove in the back. She lost her balance and tumbled down the side of the pile of rubble. Because her hands were tied, she couldn't break her fall. Something hard rammed painfully into her diaphragm, and, wheezing, she turned over on her back and gasped for air. She hoped she hadn't broken anything. The other man shoved Elard Kaltensee and Auguste Nowak ahead of him. They had their hands tied behind their backs, too.

"Get up!" The disguised man was standing over her, yanking at her arm. "Come on, go!"

At that moment Pia realized what had almost broken her ribs: Elard's pistol, which was stuck in her waistband. She had to warn Henning and Miriam.

"Ow!" she screamed as loudly as she could. "My arm! I think it's broken!"

One of the killers cursed softly, pulling Pia to her feet with the help of his pal, and shoved her down the passageway. If only Henning and Miriam had heard her cry and would find a hiding place. The two of them were her only hope, because Vera Kaltensee hadn't remembered to tell the men about them. As she stumbled along the passage, Pia tried in vain to loosen the cord around her wrists. Then they reached the cellar. The floodlight was still on, but there was no sign of Henning and Miriam. Pia's mouth was dry as dust, and her heart hammered against her ribs. The man who had pushed her down the hole now took the mask off, and Pia recognized who it was.

"Mrs. Moormann!" she exclaimed, stunned. "I thought . . . you . . . I mean . . . your husband . . ."

"You should have stayed in Germany," said the housekeeper from Mühlenhof, who obviously was more than a housekeeper. She pointed the pistol with a suppressor directly at Pia's head. "It's your own fault that you're in trouble."

"But you can't just simply shoot us. My colleagues know where we are and—"

"Shut your trap." Anja Moormann's face was expressionless; her eyes seemed as cold as glass marbles. "Now line up."

Auguste Nowak and Elard Kaltensee didn't move.

Pia ventured one last try. "The Polish police have been informed and will be here any minute if I don't call them back." Behind her back, her hands wriggled desperately with the cord. Her fingers were already numb, but she thought she could feel the bonds loosening. She had to gain some time.

"Your boss will be arrested at the border," she gasped. "Why are you doing this? It doesn't make any sense."

Anja Moormann paid no attention. "Get moving, Professor," she said, aiming her pistol at Elard Kaltensee. "Down on your knees."

"How can you do this, Anja?" Elard Kaltensee said with astounding calm. "I'm very disappointed in you, really I am."

"On your knees!" commanded the woman who was supposedly a housekeeper.

Sweat was breaking out all over Pia's body as the cord finally gave way. She balled her hands into fists and opened them again to get some feeling back in her fingers. Her only chance was the element of surprise. With a resigned expression, Elard Kaltensee took a step toward the pit that Henning and Miriam had dug in the ground and knelt down obediently. Before Anja Moormann or her accomplice could react, Pia pulled the pistol out of her waistband, flicked off the safety, and fired. The shot was earsplitting and shredded the upper thigh of the second figure in black. Anja Moormann didn't hesitate one second. Her gun was still aimed at Elard Kaltensee's head, and she fired. At the same instant, Auguste Nowak made a lunge forward and threw herself in front of her son, who was kneeling on the ground. The suppressor meant that only a dull plop was heard as the bullet struck the old woman in the chest and hurled her backward. Before Anja Moormann could fire a second time, Pia dived forward and slammed into her with all her might. Both of them fell to the ground.

Pia was sprawled on her back and Anja Moormann was kneeling on top of her, her hands closing around Pia's neck. Pia fought back, trying to remember tricks from her self-defense courses, but she had never really had to defend herself against a trained professional killer. In the dimming beam of the battery-operated floodlight, she was aware of Anja Moormann's face, which was contorted with exertion. Pia wasn't getting any air and had the feeling that her eyes were going to pop out of her head any second. If the oxygen supply to her brain was cut off, she would lose consciousness in about ten seconds, and after another five seconds all her brain functions would irreversibly cease. In the autopsy, the pathologist would confirm point hemorrhages in her conjunctiva, a fracture of the hyoid bone, and congestion hemorrhages in the oral and pharyngeal mucous membranes. But she didn't want to die, not now and not here in this cellar. She wasn't even forty yet! Pia got a hand free and dug her fingers into Anja Moormann's face, the fear of death giving her more strength than she could have imagined. The woman gasped, bared her teeth, and growled like a pit bull, but her grip loosened at once. Then Pia felt something hard strike her temple, and she lost consciousness.

Jutta Kaltensee was sitting at her place among her party colleagues in the third row of the chamber of the Hesse State Parliament, across from the government bench. She was listening halfheartedly to the eternal battle of words that the prime minister and the chair of the joint Green/Bündnis 90 were waging regarding Item 66 of the daily agenda on the topic of airport expansion. But in her mind, she was somewhere else entirely. It didn't matter how often Dr. Rosenblatt assured her that the police had no evidence against her, and that all suspicions and accusations were directed solely at Siegbert and her mother. She was still worried. The incident with the inspector and the photos had been a mistake—that much she had realized. She should have stayed out of the whole thing. But Berti, that weakling, had suddenly started getting nervous, even though for years he had carried out Vera's instructions without a trace of remorse and without asking questions. At this point in her career, Jutta couldn't afford to be associated in any way with murder investigations and dark family secrets. Soon her party would nominate her as their lead candidate for the state parliamentary election next January. Until then, she had to get a handle on the situation somehow.

She kept glancing at the display of her cell, which was on vibrate. That was why she didn't notice at once the commotion that was spreading throughout the chamber. Not until the prime minister broke off his speech did she raise her head and see two uniformed police officers and a red-haired woman standing in front of the government bench. They were speaking softly to the prime minister and the president of the parliament, who seemed scandalized and were looking all around the chamber. Jutta Kaltensee felt the first prickle of genuine panic at the back of her neck. There was no evidence that could incriminate her. Impossible. Henri would sooner let himself be drawn and quartered as open his mouth. Now the redhead was walking toward her with a determined stride. Even though fear was creeping like ice water through her veins, Jutta Kaltensee forced herself to remain calm. She had diplomatic immunity, and they couldn't simply arrest her.

The basement room smelled damp and musty. Bodenstein felt for the light switch and was deeply relieved to see Thomas Ritter in the flickering light of the fluorescent tubes, lying there tied up on a metal table smeared with blobs of paint. A young Japanese woman had opened the door of the Kunsthaus to the police after repeated rings. She was one of the artists being sponsored by the Eugen Kaltensee Foundation, and she'd been living and working in the Kunsthaus for half a year. Confused, she had watched mutely as Bodenstein, Behnke, Henri Améry, and four officers of the Frankfurt police streamed past her and headed for the basement door.

"Hello, Dr. Ritter," Bodenstein said as he stepped over to the table. But it took a few seconds for his brain to accept what his eyes had already registered. Thomas Ritter lay there with eyes wide open, but he was dead. Somebody had shoved a cannula into his jugular vein, and with each beat his heart had pumped the blood out of his body into a bucket under the table.

Bodenstein grimaced in disgust and turned away. He was fed up with death and blood and murder. He was especially fed up with always chasing a half step behind the criminals and not being able to prevent any more bad things from happening. Why hadn't Ritter listened to their warnings? Why had he been so dismissive about the threats issued by the Kaltensee family? Why hadn't he taken them more seriously? For Bodenstein, it was inconceivable that the desire for revenge could be stronger than all reason. If Thomas Ritter had kept his fingers off this ill-fated biography and the diaries, he would have been a father in a few months and could have had a long, happy life ahead of him. The ringing of his cell tore Bodenstein away from his musings.

"The M-Class Mercedes has also left Doba," Ostermann informed him. "But I still can't reach Pia."

"Damn." Bodenstein felt more miserable than he'd ever felt in his life. He had really screwed up this time. If only he'd forbidden Pia to go to Poland. Nicola was right: It was none of her concern what had happened there more than sixty years ago. Her only task was to solve the current series of murders.

"What's the story on Ritter?" Ostermann asked. "Did you find him?"

"Yes. He's dead."

"Oh shit. His wife is waiting downstairs and won't leave until she talks to you or Pia."

Bodenstein stared at the body and the bucket full of coagulated blood. His stomach contracted into a knot. What if something had happened to Pia? He pushed the thought aside.

"Try one more time to get hold of Pia, and try Henning Kirchhoff's cell, too," he told Ostermann, then ended the call.

"Are you going to let me go now?" asked Henri Améry.

"No." Bodenstein did not deign to look at him. "For the time being, you're under arrest for suspicion of murder."

Paying no attention to Améry's protests, he left the basement. What had happened in Poland? Why were both cars on the move? Why the hell didn't Pia check in as promised? Pain settled around his head like an iron ring, and he had a nasty taste in his mouth. He suddenly remembered that today he hadn't eaten a thing but had had way too much coffee. He took a deep breath when he got outside onto Römerberg Square. The whole situation had spiraled out of control, and he longed to go for a walk alone in order to sort out the thoughts whirling around in his head. Instead, he now had to find a way to tell Marleen Ritter gently that he'd found her husband dead.

When Pia came to, her neck was aching, and she couldn't swallow. She opened her eyes and saw in the dim light that she was still in the cellar. Out of the corner of her eye, she discerned a movement, someone coming up behind her. She heard labored breathing, and abruptly the memory came back. Anja Moormann, the pistol, the shot that struck Auguste Nowak in the chest! How long had she been unconscious? Her blood froze in her veins when behind her she heard the click of the safety on a pistol. Pia wanted to scream, but only a hoarse gurgle came out of her throat. Her insides clenched up, and she closed her eyes. How would it be when the bullet smashed through her skull? Would she feel it? Would it hurt? Would . . .

"Pia!" Somebody grabbed her shoulder and her eyes flew open. A wave of relief flowed through her body when she looked into the face of her ex-husband. She coughed and grabbed her throat.

"How . . . what . . ." she croaked in confusion. Henning was as pale as a corpse. To her surprise, he started sobbing and took her into his arms.

"I was so worried about you," he murmured into her hair. "Oh God, your head is bleeding."

Pia's whole body was trembling and her throat hurt, but the knowledge that she'd escaped death at the last second filled her with an almost mystical feeling of happiness. Then she remembered Elard Kaltensee and Auguste Nowak. She freed herself from Henning's arms and sat up in a daze. Kaltensee was sitting in the sand among the bones of his murdered ancestors, holding his mother in his arms. The tears were streaming down his face.

"Mama," he whispered. "Mama, you can't die . . . please!"

"Where's Anja Moormann?" Pia whispered hoarsely. "And the guy I shot?"

"He's lying over there," said Henning. "I clobbered him with the flash-light when he was about to shoot you. And then the woman took off."

"Where's Miriam?" Pia turned and looked into her friend's eyes, which were wide with terror.

"I'm all right," she whispered. "But we're going to need an ambulance for Mrs. Nowak."

On all fours, Pia crawled over to Auguste Nowak and her son. An ambu-lance would be too late. Auguste Nowak was dying. A thin line of blood trickled out of the corner of her mouth. She had closed her eyes but was still breathing.

"Mrs. Nowak," said Pia, her voice still raw, "can you hear me?"

Auguste Nowak opened her eyes. Her gaze was astoundingly clear as she reached for the hand of her son, whom she had lost in this exact spot so long ago. Elard Kaltensee gripped her hand and she sighed deeply. After more than sixty years, a circle had finally closed.

"Heini?"

"I'm here, Mama," said Elard, making an effort to keep his voice under control. "I'm here with you. You're going to get better. Everything is going to be fine."

"No, my boy," she murmured, and smiled. "I'm dying. . . . But . . . you shouldn't . . . cry, Heini. Do you hear? Don't cry. It's . . . good like this. Here . . . I am . . . with him . . . with my . . . husband, Elard."

Elard Kaltensee stroked his mother's face.

"Take . . . take care of Marcus . . ." she whispered, and coughed. Bloody foam oozed from her lips, and tears filled her eyes. "My dear boy . . ."

She took one more deep breath and then she sighed. Her head sank to the side.

"No!" Elard raised her head and clasped the body of the old woman tighter in his arms. "No, Mama, no! You can't die now!"

He sobbed like a child. Pia felt herself close to tears, as well. In sympathy, she put her hand on Elard Kaltensee's shoulder. He looked up without letting go of his mother, his face wet with tears and contorted by pain.

"She died in peace," said Pia softly. "In the arms of her son and in the presence of her family."

Marleen Ritter was pacing up and down in the small room like a predator in the zoo. Now and then, she would look over at her father, separated from her by a glass pane and sitting in the next room motionless, a blank stare on his face. He looked years older. He seemed like a marionette whose strings had been cut. Badly shaken, Marleen had now comprehended what she hadn't been willing to recognize all these years. Her grandmother was not the generous old lady she had always taken her to be—on the contrary. Vera had lied and cheated as she pleased. Marleen stopped in front of the glass pane, staring at the man who was her father. His whole life, he had obeyed the whims of his mother, had done everything to please her in an attempt to win her praise. But in vain. For him, the knowledge that he had been shamelessly exploited must be terribly bitter. And yet Marleen could summon up no sympathy for him.

"Sit down for a moment," said Katharina, standing behind her.

Marleen shook her head. "Then I'd go crazy," she said. Katharina had told her everything: all about the trunk, Thomas's disastrous idea concerning the biography and how she had brought him the diaries, and the fact that Vera wasn't the person she pretended to be.

"If anything has happened to Thomas, I'll never forgive my father," she said dully. Katharina didn't reply, because at that moment Jutta Kaltensee, formerly her best friend, was led into the interview room. Siegbert Kaltensee raised his head when his sister came in.

His voice came through the loudspeaker. "You knew about everything, am I right?" Marleen clenched her fists.

"What am I supposed to have known?" replied Jutta Kaltensee coolly on the other side of the window.

"That she had Robert murdered to keep his mouth shut. And his girlfriend, too. And you wanted the same thing she did, for Ritter to disappear, because both of you were afraid of what he was going to write about you in his book."

"I don't know what you're talking about, Berti." Jutta sat down on a chair and crossed her legs nonchalantly, self-confident and firmly believing that she was invincible.

"Just like her mother," Katharina murmured.

"You knew that Marleen had married Thomas," Siegbert Kaltensee asserted, reproaching his sister. "You also knew that Marleen is pregnant!"

"So what?" Jutta Kaltensee shrugged. "There was no way I could have known that you'd go so far as to kidnap him!"

"I wouldn't have allowed it if I'd known all the details."

"Oh, come off it, Berti." Jutta gave a scornful laugh. "Everybody knows that you hate Thomas like the plague. He's always been a thorn in your side."

Marleen was standing at the window as if paralyzed. There was a knock on the door, and Bodenstein came in.

"They had my husband kidnapped!" yelled Marleen. "My father and my aunt! They . . ."

She froze when she saw Bodenstein's face. Even before he could say a word, she knew. Her legs gave way under her and she sank to her knees. And then she began to wail.

Pia felt like someone who had been freed from a long hostage situation as she climbed the stairs to the station in the late evening. Not twenty minutes after the death of Auguste Nowak, their Polish colleagues had shown up. They had taken Henning, Miriam, Elard Kaltensee, and Pia to the police station in Gizycko. It took a few phone calls to Nicola Engel in Germany to explain things enough that the Polish police were willing to let Pia and Elard Kaltensee go. Henning and Miriam stayed in Gizycko to recover the bones in the cellar of the castle ruins early the next morning with the help of Polish specialists. At the airport, Behnke was waiting for her, and then they both drove the professor to the hospital in Frankfurt to visit Marcus Nowak. Now it was ten o'clock at night. Pia walked along the deserted corridor and knocked on Bodenstein's door. He came out from behind his desk and, to her surprise, gave her a big hug. Then he took her by the shoulders and looked at her in a way that made her feel embarrassed.

"Thank God," he said in a hoarse voice. "I'm so happy you're back."

"You couldn't have missed me that badly. I've only been gone for less than twenty-four hours," Pia attempted sarcasm to get the awkwardness she was feeling under control. "You can let go of me now, boss. I'm all right."

To her relief, Bodenstein decided to match her tone of voice.

"Twenty-four hours was clearly too long," he said with a grin, and let her go. "I was afraid I'd have to write all these reports by myself."

Pia grinned, too, and pushed a stray lock of hair out of her face.

"So all the cases are wrapped up, right?"

"Looks that way." He nodded and gestured for her to take a seat. "Thanks to this vehicle-tracking software, our colleagues were able to arrest Vera Kaltensee and also Anja Moormann at the Polish-German border. Anja Moormann has already confessed. She killed not only Monika Krämer and Watkowiak but also Thomas Ritter."

"She confessed just like that?" Pia rubbed the sore bump on her temple that the barrel of Anja Moormann's automatic had left, and thought with a shudder of the coldness in that woman's eyes.

"She was one of the best spies in the GDR and has quite a long record," Bodenstein explained. "With her statement, she has incriminated Siegbert Kaltensee. He was namely the one who gave her the kill orders."

"Really? I would have bet that Jutta was behind it."

"Jutta was too sly for that. Siegbert has already confessed to everything. We were able to uncover the personal possessions of Anita Frings at Mühlenhof, including the items they palmed off on Watkowiak to throw suspicion onto him. And Mrs. Moormann also described how she killed Watkowiak. In the kitchen of her house, by the way."

"My God, what an ice-cold monster." Pia realized how easily her encounter with Anja Moormann could have turned out deadly for her, too. "But who put the body in that house? It looked like the work of a dilettante. If they hadn't swept up and put him on top of a mattress, I probably wouldn't have been suspicious."

"It was Améry's men," replied Bodenstein. "They don't have a lot of brains."

Pia suppressed a yawn with difficulty. She was longing for a hot shower and twenty-four hours of uninterrupted sleep. "I still don't understand why Monika Krämer had to die."

"It's simple: to make Watkowiak look even more suspicious. The cash that we found on him was from Anita Frings's safe."

"What about Vera Kaltensee? Wasn't Siegbert just acting on her behalf?"

"We can't pin the murders on her. And even if we could, it wouldn't do him any good. But the DA's office is going to reexamine Eugen Kaltensee's death and also investigate the murder of Danuta Watkowiak, with Vera Kaltensee as the prime suspect. The girl was in Germany illegally at the time, and that's why nobody reported her missing."

"I wonder if Moormann knew what his wife was up to," said Pia. "Where was he the whole time, anyway?"

"His wife locked him in the cold storage, where the trunks were kept," Bodenstein replied. "Naturally, he knew about his wife's past; he was in the Stasi, too. Like his parents."

"His parents?" Pia rubbed her sore temple in confusion.

"Anita Frings was his mother," Bodenstein explained. "Moormann was the Little Tomcat, the man who visited her so often and pushed her wheelchair around the grounds."

"You've got to be kidding."

For a while, they sat there in silence.

"What about the trace-trace hit?" Pia asked with a pensive frown. "The unsolved cases in the East. That was male DNA. How could it have come from Anja Moormann?"

"She's a real pro," said Bodenstein. "On her hits, she wore a wig of real hair and deliberately left a hair at each scene. As a red herring."

"Unbelievable." Pia shook her head. "By the way, Dr. Engel had my back with the Polish colleagues. They were definitely not happy about our unauthorized action."

"Right," said Bodenstein. "She behaved very fairly. Maybe she's going to be a decent boss after all."

Pia hesitated a moment and looked at him. "And the . . . um . . . other problem?"

"It's over," Bodenstein said lightly. He got up, went to his cabinet, and took out a bottle of cognac and two glasses.

"If Nowak and Elard Kaltensee had been honest from the beginning, things wouldn't have gotten so out of hand." Pia watched as her boss poured exactly two fingers of cognac into each glass. "But I never in my life would have figured out that those two were lovers. My suspicions were really miles off."

"Mine, too." Bodenstein handed her a glass.

"So what are we drinking to?" Pia gave him a crooked smile.

"If you're keeping count, we've solved at least ... hmm ... fifteen murders, including the two cases from Dessau and Halle. I think we've done pretty well."

"All right, then." Pia raised her glass.

Bodenstein stopped her. "Just a minute. I think it's about time we behave like the rest of our colleagues all over Germany. What would you think if we were on a first-name basis from now on? My name is Oliver, by the way."

Pia tilted her head and grinned. "But you don't want to drink to brotherhood with kisses and everything, do you?"

"God forbid!" Bodenstein grinned, too; then he clinked glasses with her and took a sip. "Your zoo director would probably wring my neck."

"Oh shit!" Pia lowered her glass in shock. "I forgot about Christoph! I was supposed to pick him up at the airport at eight-thirty. What time is it?"

"Quarter to eleven."

"Damn! I don't know his number, and my cell is probably somewhere in a Masurian lake."

"If you ask me nicely, I'll lend you mine, Ms. Kirchhoff," Bodenstein offered magnanimously. "I happen to have his number."

"Hey, I thought we were on a first-name basis now," Pia said.

"You haven't drunk anything yet," Bodenstein reminded her. Pia looked at him, knocked back the cognac in one gulp, and grimaced in disgust.

"So, Oliver," she said, "would you be so kind as to hand me your cell phone?"

•　　•　　•

Christoph's daughters looked surprised when Pia rang the doorbell at eleven-thirty at night. They hadn't heard from their father and assumed that Pia had picked him up. Annika tried to call his cell, but it was still turned off.

"Maybe the plane was late," said Christoph's second-eldest daughter, who didn't seem too worried about her father. "He'll call soon enough."

"Thanks." Pia felt miserable and deeply depressed. She got into her Nissan and drove from Bad Soden to Birkenhof. Bodenstein was now with Cosima, who had forgiven him for his slipup. Henning and Miriam were together in a hotel in Gizycko; she couldn't overlook the fact that during the whole episode sparks had flown between them. Elard Kaltensee was at the hospital, holding Marcus Nowak's hand. Only she was alone. Her vague hope that Christoph would have come straight to her house from the airport was not fulfilled. Birkenhof was dark, and there was no car parked in front. Pia fought back tears as she said hello to her dogs and opened the front door. He had probably waited, searched in vain, tried to call her on her cell, and then gone to have a drink with his attractive colleague from Berlin. Damn! How could she have forgotten? She turned on the light and let her shoulder bag drop to the floor. Suddenly, her heart skipped a beat. The table in the kitchen was set with wineglasses and the good china. A bottle of champagne stood in a champagne cooler with half-melted ice; on the stove were covered pots and pans. Pia smiled, feeling touched. In the living room, she found Christoph sound asleep on the couch. A warm surge wave of happiness flowed through her body.

"Hey," she whispered, squatting down next to the sofa. Christoph opened his eyes and blinked sleepily in the light.

"Hey," he murmured. "Sorry, the food is probably cold."

"I'm sorry I forgot to pick you up. My cell phone got lost and I couldn't call you. But we did solve all the cases."

"That sounds good." Christoph reached out his hand and stroked her cheek affectionately. "You look pretty beat."

"I've been under a little stress the past few days."

"I see." He studied her attentively. "What happened? Your voice sounds kind of funny."

"Not worth mentioning." She shrugged. "The Kaltensees' housekeeper tried to strangle me in a ruined castle in Poland."

"Oh, right." Christoph seemed to think it was a joke and grinned. "But otherwise everything's okay?"

"Sure." Pia nodded.

He sat up and opened his arms wide.

"You wouldn't believe how much I've missed you."

"Really? Did you miss me in South Africa?"

"Oh yeah." He wrapped her tightly in his arms and kissed her. "I sure did."

Epilogue

Marcus Nowak looked at the soot-blackened remains of the brick facade, the empty window frames, and the caved-in roof. But he didn't see the sorry state of the ruins; in his mind, the castle appeared as it once had looked. The neo-classic facade, wonderful in its simple symmetry, the narrow center risalit flanked by two-story side wings, which were again flanked by huge pavilions with hood roofs and little openwork towers. Slim Doric columns in front of the main portal, a shady avenue leading to the castle, an extensive park with grand hundred-year-old red beech and maple trees. The expanse of the East Prussian landscape, the harmony of water and woods, had deeply moved him on his first visit two years before. This was the land of his and Elard's ancestors, and the events that had occurred in the cellar of this castle almost sixty-three years ago had had a long-lasting effect on both their lives.

In the past four months, much had changed. Marcus Nowak had told his wife and his family the truth and had moved in with Elard at Mühlenhof. After two additional operations, his hand was almost as flexible as it had been before. Elard had changed completely. The ghosts of the past no longer tormented him, and the woman that he had believed was his mother was in prison, as were her son, Siegbert, and Anja Moormann, the professional killer. Elard had received his aunt Vera's diaries back from Marleen Ritter. In a few weeks, coinciding with the annual Frankfurt Book Fair, the biography would appear—the book that had caused the death of its author and the downfall of the Kaltensee family. It had been making headlines weeks in advance.

In spite of all this, Jutta Kaltensee had been nominated as the lead candidate of her party for the state parliamentary election, which would take place in January, and had a good chance of winning. Marleen Ritter had taken over as CEO of KMF and was now busy converting the company into a corporation with the support of the company board. In the trunks from Mühlenhof they'd found documents in which Josef Stein, the Jewish former owner of the company, had provided for the reconveyance of the firm in the event of his return to Germany. In her arrogance, Vera—or rather, Edda—had never destroyed anything.

But that was all in the past. Marcus Nowak smiled as he saw Elard, the baron of Zeydlitz-Lauenburg, coming toward him. Everything had turned out better in the end. He even had in his pocket the contract for his company to restore the Old Town in Frankfurt. In addition, together they would realize their dream of a lifetime in Masuria. The mayor of Gizycko had already given verbal consent to the sale of the castle to Elard; not much more stood in the way of their plans. As soon as the purchase contract was signed, the mortal remains of Auguste Nowak, together with the bones from the cellar that had been partially identified by DNA comparisons, would be buried in the old family cemetery by the shore of the lake. So Auguste, together with her dear Elard, her parents, and her sister, would find her last resting place in her homeland.

"And?" Elard stood next to him. "What do you think?"

"It's doable." Marcus Nowak frowned in thought. "But I'm afraid it's going to be insanely expensive and will take years."

"So what?" Elard grinned and put an arm around Marcus's shoulder. "We've got all the time in the world."

Marcus leaned against him and looked over at the castle once more. "Hotel Auguste Viktoria by the Lake," he said, smiling dreamily. "I can picture it already."

Acknowledgments

I would like to thank Claudia and Caroline Cohen, Camilla Altvater, Susanne Hecker, Peter Hillebrecht, Simone Schreiber, Catrin Runge, and Anne Pfenninger for reading excerpts and offering feedback on the manuscript.

Very hearty thanks to Professor Hansjürgen Bratzke, director of the Institute of Forensic Medicine in Frankfurt, for detailed answers to my numerous questions about forensic medical details. For any errors of a technical nature, I take sole responsibility.

Thanks also to Chief Detective Inspector Peter Deppe of K-11 in the Regional Criminal Unit in Hofheim, who provided detailed answers to all my questions about the sequence of investigations and the work of the criminal police. Among other things, he drew my attention to the fact that Criminal Police officers are on a first-name basis all over Germany.

I owe a very special thank you to my editor Marion Vazquez. I have thoroughly enjoyed our work together on *The Ice Queen*.

Thanks to my American translator, Steven T. Murray, and his wife, Tiina Nunnally, who have done such a great job for the third time.

Also, thanks to my publisher, St. Martin's Press, and my editor, Daniela Rapp, for their trust and support.

naive, and deeply satisfying. I devoured it. This is one that's going to stay with me for a long time."

—Sarah Gailey, author of *Magic for Liars*

"A deeply satisfying and darkly funny feminist fairy tale . . . The plot snaps along as quickly as a good joke, and beneath the whimsy, there's an underlying sympathy and sincerity that enables Kingfisher to handle tricky issues like domestic violence with great compassion and care. At its heart a story of good people doing their best to make the unjust world a fairer place, this marvelous romp will delight Kingfisher's fans and fairy tale lovers alike."

—*Publishers Weekly* (starred review)

"Somehow, Kingfisher writes stories that put you at your ease and make you want to crawl out of your skin at the same time. I loved the way this horrified me—and, in the end, gave me hope. Marra's journey is a memorable and entertaining one filled with bone dogs, demon chickens, godmothers, and conversations with the dead."

—Kevin Hearne, *New York Times* bestselling author of the Iron Druid Chronicles

"Charming and macabre—often both at the same time—*Nettle & Bone* has bite, proper jokes, effortlessly good storytelling, and a really wonderful tomb labyrinth. I finished it and had to go read three more of T. Kingfisher's books because I was sad it was over. *Nettle & Bone* is so good! I loved it."

—A. K. Larkwood, author of *The Unspoken Name*

"This book is so exciting, deeply wise, sad, brutal, and compassionate all at once. And beautifully written, with a plot as cunning as fine embroidery. I can tell that this is a story that will linger with me. I hope it does. When I finished I could hardly bear to tear myself away from this eerie, vivid world, with its struggling, flawed, wonderful characters. I will miss Bonedog in particular."

—Catriona Ward, author of *The Last House on Needless Street*

"*Nettle & Bone* leans into the macabre and evokes the Grimm-est of stories . . . but the characters of the main party are lovable and easy to root for, and seeing how the next happily-ever-after trope will be subverted is a big part of the fun. Highly recommended for fans of fractured fables like Naomi Novik's *Uprooted* and Helen Oyeyemi's *Gingerbread*." —*Booklist* (starred review)

"There are known fantasy tropes here—but Kingfisher always comes at them from a direction you don't anticipate. . . . *Nettle & Bone* is full of delights and surprises—and proves that Kingfisher has more than a few tricks left up her sleeve." —*Locus*

"Blending fairy-tale familiarity and common-sense characters, Kingfisher's prose balances grim circumstances with humor and heart. Readers of Alix E. Harrow's *A Spindle Splintered* and Melissa Albert's Hazel Wood series should pick this up immediately." —*Library Journal*

TOR BOOKS BY T. KINGFISHER

A House With Good Bones
What Moves the Dead
Nettle & Bone

NETTLE & BONE

BONE

T. Kingfisher

Tor Publishing Group

New York

NETTLE & BONE

Endpaper art by Ursula Vernon

A Tor Book
Published by Tom Doherty Associates/Tor Publishing Group
120 Broadway
New York, NY 10271

www.tor-forge.com

Tor® is a registered trademark of Macmillan Publishing Group, LLC.

The Library of Congress has cataloged the hardcover edition as follows:

Names: Kingfisher, T., author.
Title: Nettle & Bone / T. Kingfisher.
Other titles: Nettle and Bone
Description: First Edition. | New York : Tor/Tom Doherty Associates Book, 2021. |
Identifiers: LCCN 2021041767 (print) | LCCN 2021041768 (ebook) |
ISBN 9781250244048 (hardcover) | ISBN 9781250244031 (ebook)
Classification: LCC PS3611.I597 N48 2021 (print) |
LCC PS3611.I597 (ebook) | DDC 813/.6—dc23
LC record available at https://lccn.loc.gov/2021041767
LC ebook record available at https://lccn.loc.gov/2021041768

ISBN 978-1-250-24400-0 (trade paperback)

Our books may be purchased in bulk for promotional, educational, or business use. Please contact your local bookseller or the Macmillan Corporate and Premium Sales Department at 1-800-221-7945, extension 5442, or by email at MacmillanSpecialMarkets@macmillan.com.

First Tor Paperback Edition: 2023

Printed in the United States of America

0   9   8

dedicated to Strong Independent Chicken,
a bird in a million

NETTLE

&

BONE

Chapter 1

The trees were full of crows and the woods were full of madmen. The pit was full of bones and her hands were full of wires.

Her fingers bled where the wire ends cut her. The earliest cuts were no longer bleeding, but the edges had gone red and hot, with angry streaks running backward over her skin. The tips of her fingers were becoming puffy and less nimble.

Marra was aware that this was not a good thing, but the odds of living long enough for infection to kill her were so small that she could not feel much concern.

She picked up a bone, a long, thin one, from the legs, and wrapped the ends with wire. It fit alongside another long bone—not from the same animal, but close enough—and she bound them together and fit them into the framework she was creating.

The charnel pit was full, but she did not need to dig too deeply. She could track the progression of starvation backward through the layers. They had eaten deer and they had eaten cattle. When the cattle ran out and the deer were gone, they ate the horses, and when the horses were gone, they ate the dogs.

When the dogs were gone, they ate each other.

It was the dogs she wanted. Perhaps she might have built a man out of bones, but she had no great love of men any longer.

Dogs, though . . . dogs were always true.

"He made harp pegs of her fingers fair," Marra sang softly, tunelessly, under her breath. "And strung the bones with her golden hair . . ."

The crows called to each other from the trees in solemn voices. She wondered about the harper in the song, and what he had thought when he was building the harp of a dead woman's bones. He was probably the only person in the world who would understand what she was doing.

Assuming he even existed in the first place. And if he did, what kind of life do you lead where you find yourself building a harp out of corpses?

For that matter, what kind of life do you lead where you find yourself building a dog out of bones?

Many of the bones had been cracked open for marrow. If she could find two that went together, she could bind them back to wholeness, but often the breaks were jagged. She had to splint them together with the wires, leaving bloody fingerprints across the surface of the bones.

That was fine. That was part of the magic.

Besides, when the great hero Mordecai slew the poisoned worm, did he complain about his fingers hurting? No, of course not.

At least, not where anyone could hear him and write it down.

"The only song the harp would play," she crooned, "was O! The dreadful wind and rain . . ."

She was fully aware of how wild she sounded. Part of her recoiled from it. Another, larger part said that she was kneeling on the edge of a pit full of bones, in a land so bloated with horrors that her feet sank into the earth as if she were walking on the surface of a gigantic blister. A little wildness would not be out of place at all.

The skulls were easy. She had found a fine, broad one, with powerful jaws and soulful eye sockets. She could have had dozens, but she could only use one.

It hurt her in a way that she had not expected. The joy of finding one was crushed easily under the sorrow of so many that would go unused.

I could sit here for the rest of my life, with my hands full of wire, building dogs out of bone. And then the crows will eat me and I will fall into the pit and we shall all be bones together . . .

A sob caught in her throat and she had to stop. She fumbled in her pack for her waterskin and took a sip.

The bone dog was half-completed. She had the skull and the beautiful sweep of vertebrae, two legs and the long, elegant ribs. There would be at least a dozen dogs in this one, truly—but the skull was the important thing.

Marra caressed the hollow orbits, delicately winged in wire. Everyone said that the heart was where the soul lived, but she no longer believed it. She was building from the skull downward. She had discarded several bones already because they did not seem to fit with the skull. The long, impossibly fine ankles of gazehounds would not serve to carry her skull forward. She needed something stronger and more solid, boarhounds or elkhounds, something with *weight*.

There was a jump rope rhyme about a bone dog, wasn't there? Where had she heard it? Not in the palace, certainly. Princesses did not jump rope. It must have been later, in the village near the convent. How did it go? *Bone dog, stone dog . . .*

The crows called a warning.

She looked up. The crows yammered in the trees to her left. Something was coming, blundering through the trees.

She pulled the hood of her cloak up over her head and slid partway down into the pit, cradling the dog skeleton to her chest.

Her cloak was made of owlcloth tatters and spun-nettle cord. The magic was imperfect, but it was the best she had been able to make in the time that she had been given.

From dawn to dusk and back again, with an awl made of thorns— yes, I'd like to see anyone do better. Even the dust-wife said that I had done well, and she hands out praise like water in a dry land.

The cloak of tatters left long gaps bare, but she had found that this did not matter. It broke up her outline so that people looked through her. If they found some of the bands of light and shadow lay a little strangely, they never stayed long enough to puzzle out why.

People were remarkably willing to dismiss their own sight. Marra thought perhaps that the world was so strange and vision so flawed that you soon realized that anything and everything could be a trick of the light.

The man came out of the trees. She heard him muttering but could not make out the words. She only knew it was a man because his voice was so deep, and even that was guesswork.

Most of the people of the blistered land were harmless. They had eaten the wrong flesh and been punished for it. Some saw things that were not there. Some of them could not walk and their fellows helped them. Two had shared a fire with her, some nights ago, although she was careful not to eat their food, even though they offered.

It was a cruel spirit that would punish starving people for what they had been forced to eat, but the spirits had never pretended to be kind.

Her companions at the fire had warned her, though. "Be careful," said one. "Be quick, quick, quiet. There's a few to watch for. They were bad before and they're worse now."

"Bad," said the second one. His breathing was very labored and he had to stop between each word. She could tell that it frustrated him, trying to speak between the pauses. "Not . . . right. All . . . of us . . . now"—he shook his head ruefully—"but them . . . *angry.*"

"It doesn't do any good to be angry," said the first one. "But they won't listen. Ate too much. Got to like the taste." She cracked a laugh, too high, looking down at her hands. "We stopped as soon as there was something else, but they kept eating it."

The second one shook his head. "No," he said. "More . . . than that. Always . . . angry. Born."

"Some are born that way," Marra agreed, nodding to him. She knew too well.

Some of those people are men. Some of those men are princes. Yes, I know. It is a different kind of anger. Something darker and more deliberate.

He looked relieved that she had understood. "Yes. Angrier . . . now. Much."

All three of them sat in silence around the fire. She stretched her hands toward the flames and exhaled slowly.

"Mostly they kill us," said the first one abruptly. "We can't always run. Things get confused—" She sketched a gesture in the air above her eyes that Marra could not begin to understand, although her companion nodded when he saw it. "We're easy to catch if it's like that. But if they see you, they'll try for you, too."

The fire crackled. This land was very damp, and she was grateful for the heat, and yet— "Aren't you worried that they'll see the fire?"

The woman shook her head. "They hate it," she said. "It's the punishment. The more they eat, the more they fear it—they do not cook the flesh, you see . . ." She rubbed her face, obviously distressed.

"Safer," said the man. "But . . . can't burn . . . all the time."

They leaned against one another. She bent her head down against his shoulder and he reached his arm across his body to hold her close.

A few days ago, Marra would have wondered why they did not leave this terrible land. She no longer did. They might not be sane, as the outside world understood it, but they were not fools. If they felt that they were safer here than they were outside it, it was not her place to tell them otherwise.

If I had to explain to everyone I met what had happened to me, have them judge me for what I'd had to do—no, I might think a land with a few roving cannibals was a small price to pay, myself. At least here, everyone understands what's happened, and they are as kind to each other as they can be.

As a girl, she would not have understood that, but Marra was not the girl that she had been. She was thirty years old, and all that was left of that girl now were the bones.

For a moment she had envied them, two people punished through no fault of their own, because they had each other.

Now, as she sat in the pit of bones, the skeleton cradled against her chest twitched.

"Shhhh . . ." whispered Marra into the skull's openings. "Shhhhh . . ."

Bone dog, stone dog . . . black dog, white dog . . .

She heard the footsteps as he approached. Had he seen her?

If he had, then he, too, dismissed it as a trick of the light. The footfalls skirted the edge of the pit, and the sound of breathing faded away.

"Probably harmless," she murmured to the skull. Even if he were not, she would be a difficult target.

The other, gentler folk in here were uniquely vulnerable. If you had learned not to trust your own senses, you might wait too long to run from an enemy.

Marra was no longer as sure of her own perceptions as she had once been, but the edges of her mind were only slightly frayed, not blasted open by furious spirits.

When the footsteps had been gone for many minutes and the crows had settled, she sat up again. Fog lined the edges of the wood, hanging in low swirls over the meadow. The crows cawed together like a disjointed heartbeat. Nothing else moved.

She bent back over the bone dog again, fingers moving on the wires, hoping to finish her task before darkness fell.

* * *

The bone dog came alive at dusk. It was not quite completed, but it was close. She was bent over the left front paw when the skull's jaws yawned open and it stretched as if waking from a long slumber.

"Hush," she told it. "I'm nearly done—"

It sat up. Its mouth opened and the ghost of a wet tongue touched her face like fog.

She scratched the skull where the base of the ears would be. Her nails made a soft scraping sound on the pale surface.

The bone dog wagged its tail, its pelvis, and most of its spine with delight.

"Sit still," she told it, picking up the front paw. "Sit, and let me finish."

It sat politely. The hollow eye sockets gazed up at her. Her heart contracted painfully.

The love of a bone dog, she thought, bending her head down over the paw again. *All that I am worth these days.*

Then again, few humans were truly worth the love of a living dog. Some gifts you could never deserve.

She had to wrap each tiny foot bone in a single twist of wire and bind it to the others, then wrap the entire paw several times, to keep it stable. It should not have held together, and yet it did.

The cloak had gone together the same way. Nettle cords and tattered cloth should have fallen apart, and yet it was far more solid than it looked.

The dog's claws were ridiculously large without flesh to cloak them. She wrapped each one as if it were an amulet and joined them to the basket of thin wires.

"Bone dog, stone dog," she whispered. She could see the children in her head, three little girls, chanting to each other. *Bone dog, stone dog . . . black dog, white dog . . . live dog, dead dog . . . yellow dog, run!*

At *run*, the little girl in the middle of the rope had jumped out and begun to run back and forth through the swinging rope, the only sound her feet and the slap of the rope in the dust. When she finally tripped up, the two girls on the ends had dropped the rope and they had all begun giggling together.

The bone dog rested his muzzle on her forearm. He had neither ears nor eyebrows, and yet she could practically feel the look he was giving her, tragic and hopeful as dogs often were.

"There," she said, finally. Her knife was dulled from cutting wire and it took her several tries to hack the last bit apart. She tucked the sharp end underneath the joint where it would not catch on anything. "There you are. I hope that's enough."

The bone dog put its paw down and tested it. It stood for a moment, then turned and sprinted into the fog.

Marra's fist clenched against her stomach. *No! It ran—I should have tied it. I should have thought it might run—*

The clatter of its paws faded into the whiteness.

I suppose it had another master somewhere, before it died. Perhaps it's gone to find them.

Her hands ached. Her heart ached. Poor foolish dog. Its first death had not been enough to teach it that not all masters were worthy.

Marra had learned that too late herself.

She looked into the pit of bones. Her fingers throbbed—not in the horrible stinging way they had when she pieced together the nettle cloak, but deeper, in time to her heartbeat. There was redness working its way up her hands. One long line was already snaking through her wrist.

She could not bear the thought of sitting down and sculpting another dog.

She dropped her head into her aching hands. Three tasks the dust-wife had given her. Sew a cloak of owlcloth and nettles, build a dog of cursed bones, and catch moonlight in a jar of clay. She'd failed on the second one, before she'd even had a chance to start the third.

Three tasks, and then the dust-wife would give her the tools to kill a prince.

"Typical," she said into her hands. "Typical. Of course I'd manage the impossible thing, then not think that sometimes dogs run off." For all she knew, the bone dog had caught the wisp of a scent and now it would end up a hundred miles away, chasing bone rabbits or bone foxes or bone deer.

She laughed into her swollen hands, misery twisting around, as it so often did, into weary humor. *Well. Isn't that just the way?*

This is what I get for expecting bones to be loyal, just because I brought them back and wired them up. What does a dog know about resurrection?

"I should have brought it a bone," she said, dropping her hands, and the crows in the trees took up the sound of her laughter.

Well.

If the dust-wife had failed her—or if she had failed the dust-wife—then she would make her own way. She'd had a godmother at her christening who had given her a single gift and smoothed her path not at all. Perhaps there was a debt owing there.

She turned and began to make her way, step by dragging step, out of the blistered land.

Chapter 2

Marra had grown up sullen, the sort of child who is always standing in exactly the wrong place so that adults tell her to get out of the way. She was not slow, exactly, but she seemed younger than her age, and very little interested her for long.

She had two sisters, and she was the youngest. She loved her oldest sister, Damia, very much. Damia was six years older, which seemed a lifetime. She was tall and poised and very pale, a child of Marra's father's first wife.

The middle sister, Kania, was only two years older than Marra. They shared a mother but no goodwill.

"I hate you," said twelve-year-old Kania, through gritted teeth, to ten-year-old Marra. "I hate you and I hope you *die*."

Marra carried the knowledge that her sister hated her snugged up under her ribs. It did not touch her heart, but it seemed to fill her lungs, and sometimes when she tried to take a deep breath, it caught on her sister's words and left her breathless.

She did not talk to anyone about it. There was no point. Her father was not unkind, but he was mostly absent, even if he was physically present. At best he would have patted her awkwardly on the back and sent her to the kitchen for a treat, as if she were very small. And her mother, the queen, would have said, "Don't be absurd, your sister loves you," in a distracted voice, opening the latest dispatch from her spymasters, making the political decisions to keep the kingdom from falling into ruin.

When Prince Vorling was betrothed to Damia, the household rejoiced. Marra's family ruled a small city-state with the misfortune to house the only deep harbor along the coast of two rival kingdoms.

Both those kingdoms wanted that harbor, and either one could have rolled over the city and taken it with hardly a moment's effort. Marra's mother had kept them balancing between two knives for a long time.

But now Prince Vorling, of the Northern Kingdom, would marry Damia and thus cement an alliance between them. If the Southern Kingdom tried to take the harbor, the Northern Kingdom would defend it. Damia's first son would sit someday upon the Northern throne, and her second (if she had one) would rule the harbor city.

It was, perhaps, a trifle odd to expend a firstborn son on so small a thing as the Harbor Kingdom, but it was said that the royal family of the North had grown thin blooded and had married too many close cousins over the centuries. They were protected by powerful magic, but magic could not fix blood, so the kings looked to marry outside their borders. By sealing the Harbor Kingdom and its shipping port to them by marriage, the Northern Kingdom enriched their blood and their coffers at a single stroke.

"At last," said Marra's father. "At last, we will be safe." Her mother nodded. Now the Southern Kingdom would not dare to attack them, and the Northern Kingdom would no longer need to.

It was only Marra who cried. "But I don't want you to go!" she sobbed, clinging to Damia's waist. "You're going *away!*"

Damia laughed. "It will be all right," she said. "I'll come visit. Or you'll come visit me."

"But you won't be *here!*"

"Stop it," said her mother, thin lipped, pulling her daughter away from her stepdaughter. "Don't be selfish, Marra."

"Marra's just bitter because she doesn't have a prince," said Kania, taunting.

The unfairness of this made Marra cry harder. She was twelve and she knew that she was too old to throw a tantrum, but she felt one coming on anyway.

The nurse was fetched to take her away, and that meant that Marra did not see Damia leave, with all the pomp and ceremony of a bride going to her bridegroom's kingdom.

She was watching five months later, though, when Damia's body was brought home in state.

There was a black wagon pulled by six black horses, flanked by riders dressed in mourning bands. There were three black carriages before and after the wagon, the curtains drawn. Their horses, too, were black. They had black bridles and black saddles and black barding.

It struck Marra, watching, as an extravagance of grief. Someone wanted the world to know how sad he could afford to be.

"A fall," said the whispers. "The prince is heartbroken. They say she was carrying his child."

Marra shook her head. It was not possible. The world could not be so poorly ordered that Damia could be allowed to die.

She did not cry, because she did not believe that Damia was dead.

It seemed very strange that everyone else did believe it. They ran back and forth, sometimes weeping, more often planning the details of the funeral.

Marra crept into the chapel that night. If she could prove that the body lying there was not Damia, then all the foolishness of funerals could be set aside.

The shrouded figure smelled strongly of camphor. There was a death mask atop the shroud. It was Damia, her face composed.

Marra stared at the figure for a little while and thought that it had been several days since they had heard of Damia's death. They had been cool days, but not cold. The camphor could not quite chase out the scent of decay.

If she tried to push aside the death mask and tear off the shroud, she would see a rotting corpse. Who knew what it would look like?

I was thinking like a little child, she thought angrily. *Thinking that I would be able to tell if it was Damia. It could be anyone under there at all.*

Even her.

She crept away and left the shroud undisturbed.

The funeral was lavish but rushed. The riders that the prince had sent were better dressed than Marra's mother and father. Marra resented her parents for being shabby and resented the prince for making it obvious.

They lowered the body into the ground. It could have been Damia. It could have been anyone. Marra's father wept, and Marra's mother stared straight ahead, her knuckles white where they gripped her cane.

Days followed, one after another, chasing each other into weeks. Marra came to believe that it had been Damia, mostly because everyone else seemed to believe it, but by then it seemed too late to mourn, and anyway, how could such a thing be possible?

She tried, once, to say something to Kania.

"Of course she's dead," said her sister shortly. "She's been dead for months."

"Has she?" asked Marra. "I mean—she has. But . . . dead! Really? Does it make any sense to you?"

Kania stared at her. "Don't be ridiculous," she said. "It doesn't have to make sense. People just die, that's all."

"I guess," said Marra. She sat down on the edge of the bed. "I mean . . . everybody says she is."

"They wouldn't lie about it," said Kania. "Marrying the prince meant that we were going to be safe. If Damia's dead, then the prince will marry someone else and we'll be in danger again."

Marra said nothing. She had not thought of that, either.

I must start to think like a grown-up. Kania is doing it better than I am.

The two years between them seemed suddenly vast, full of things that Marra knew but had never thought about.

Kania sighed. She reached over and hugged Marra with one arm. "I miss her, too," she said.

Marra accepted the hug, though she knew her sister hated her. Hate, like love, was apparently complicated.

* * *

The edge of the blistered land was before her. Marra looked at it for nearly a minute, thinking.

It was strange how clear the edge was. It looked like the shadow cast by a cloud. This bit here was dark and that bit was bright. It took a moment or two for wind blowing from one side to reach the other.

She could hear the crows calling back and forth. The ones on the outside sounded like normal crows—*Awk! Awk! Awk!*

The ones over her head sounded like *Gah-ha-hawk! Gah-ha-hawk!*

She wondered if the outside crows hated the crows of the blistered land the way that the villagers outside hated the people inside. They had warned her against going inside.

"They'll kill you soon as look at you," one man had said, leaning against the fence. A second man—his friend or his brother, Marra wasn't sure—nodded in time. "It's creeping," the second man said. "Gets a little bigger every year."

The first one nodded. "There's trees that used to be on this side that are on that side now." He spat. "Full of cannibals. You go in there, they'll eat you and lick out your bones."

"Ain't no reason to go in," said the second one. "Not for canny folk."

They looked at her suspiciously. The first one spat again, near her feet.

Marra had found that the people inside were much more welcoming. They had shared their fire and given her the best directions they could offer.

I was worried about the wrong things.

As usual.

It had taken her a day and a half to get to the blistered land from the dust-wife's home. In the back of her head, Marra had a notion that it should have taken longer. She'd never heard of the blistered land before and it shouldn't have just been there, right there, practically on the doorstep.

Magic, maybe. Magic or worse. That a land like this existed at all. That the gods had destroyed it. That if you picked a direction and walked, holding the thought in your mind, you would come to it, no matter which way you went.

She did not like the thought. It meant that the blistered land might touch her own kingdom, that the gods that would punish starving people might someday reach out and touch her own. It was too close and too real and too hungry.

Marra pulled the owlcloth cloak around her shoulders and stepped out of the blistered land.

The curse tugged at her as she went, an itch like mosquito bites across her skin. She slapped at her arms instinctively, even knowing that there was nothing there.

The ground felt strangely hard underfoot, as if she had just stepped off carpets and onto stone. She looked around, blinking in the bright light.

She made ten steps, more or less, holding her hands against her chest, before someone shouted, "Stop!"

* * *

It was barely a season after Damia's funeral when word came down that the prince was willing to marry Kania.

"Not yet," said Marra's mother. "Not for a year or two. It wouldn't be seemly. But after that, to keep the alliance going."

Kania nodded. Her skin was darker than Damia's had been and she was at least six inches shorter, but at that moment, Marra thought they looked very much alike—resolute and strong and a little bit afraid.

"No . . ." said Marra, but she said it quietly, and no one heard.

It was absurd to think that Kania would die because Damia had. Damia's death had been an accident—that was all. It had been a tragedy. It was no one's fault.

Marra knew all these things. They did not shake the gnawing dread that had lodged itself under her breastbone. She felt as if the dread must be visible to other people, like a growth, and it seemed strange that no one ever commented on it.

"Be careful," she said to Kania one day. "Please. Don't . . ."

She stopped. She didn't know how to finish that. Don't get married? Don't walk down any stairs?

Kania gave her a sharp look. "Careful how?"

Marra shook her head miserably. "I don't know," she said. "I just feel like something's going to go wrong."

"Nothing will go wrong," said Kania. "What happened to Damia was an accident. It won't happen to *me!*"

Her voice rose sharply on the last word, and she turned and stalked away.

I've made a mess of it again. I can't say anything until I know more.

A year passed, and Kania went away to the north, with slightly less pomp than Damia had. Marra dug her nails into her palms and watched her go. Her sister was much too young, and no one was saying anything about it.

Before Damia died, Marra would have spoken up and demanded answers and explanations. Now she bowed her head and said nothing.

Everyone else knows. They must know. They are not talking about it for a reason. Why is no one talking about it?

"Don't cry," her nurse said, as she stood on the castle wall, watching the prince's horses take Kania away. "Try to be happy for her. You'll have a prince of your own someday."

Marra shook her head. "I don't think I want one," she said.

"Of course you do," said her nurse. She was hired to see that the princesses were dressed and fed and learned to walk and talk and smile politely, not to unravel the strands of their thoughts. Marra knew this and knew that she was asking for too much, so she said nothing more and simply watched the horses take her sister farther and farther away.

* * *

Marra went to the convent eight months later. She was fifteen. It made no sense that she would go to a convent, when she might conceivably marry a prince and bear sons, but Prince Vorling did not want that. Kania had not yet had a child. If Marra married and bore a son before Kania did, then that child might be a challenge to the throne of the little Harbor Kingdom.

Prince Vorling got what he wanted. The Northern Kingdom's knife was still at the little kingdom's throat, and now he had Kania as a hostage.

The queen explained this to her, although she did not use the word *hostage*. She used words like *expediency* and *diplomacy*, but Marra knew very well that *hostage* was lurking somewhere in the background. Kania was hostage to the prince. Marra's future children, if any, were hostage to Kania's fertility.

"You'll like the convent," said the queen. "More than you like it here, at any rate." She and Marra looked very much alike, round and broad-faced, indistinguishable from any number of peasants working the fields outside the castle. The queen's mind was as brittle-sharp as an iron dagger, and she spent her days delicately threading the web of alliances and trade agreements that allowed their kingdom to exist without being swallowed up. She had apparently decided that Marra could be withdrawn from the game of merchants and princes and safely set aside. Marra both resented her mother for being so clear-eyed and was grateful to be free of the game, and she added this to the store of complicated things piled up beneath her heart.

And she did like the convent. The house of Our Lady of Grackles was quiet and dull, and the things that people expected of her were clear-cut and not shrouded behind diplomatic words. She was not exactly a novice, but she worked in the garden with them and knit bandages and shrouds. She liked knitting and cloth and fibers. Her hands could work and she could think anything she wanted and no one asked to know what it was. If she said something foolish, it reflected only on her, and not on the entire royal family. When she shut the door to her room, it stayed shut. In the royal palace, the doors were always opening, servants coming and going, nurses coming and going, ladies-in-waiting coming and going. Princesses were public property.

She had not realized that a nun had more power than a princess, that she could close a door.

No one but the abbess knew that she was a princess, but everyone knew that she somehow was of noble rank, so they did not expect her to shovel the stable where the goats and the donkey lived. When Marra realized this, a few months after she had arrived, something like anger flared up inside her. She had been proud of the work she was doing. It was something that belonged to *her*, to Marra, not to the princess of the realm, and she did it well. Her stitches were small and fine and exact, her weaving uniform and careful. That she was still living under the shadow of the princess woke the stubbornness in her. She went to the stables and picked up a pitchfork and set, inexpertly, to work.

She was very bad at it, but she did not stop, and the next day she went back to it, even though her back ached and blisters formed on her palms. *It is no worse than when you first fell off a horse. Keep shoveling.*

The goats watched her suspiciously, but that did not mean anything, because goats watched everyone suspiciously. She suspected that they didn't think much of her shoveling technique.

"No one expects you to do this," said the mistress of novices, standing in the doorway of the stable. Her shadow fell down the central aisle of the stable, like a standing stone.

"They should," said Marra, gripping the pitchfork's handle while her blisters shrieked. She edged the tip of the tines under a clot of manure and lifted it cautiously.

The mistress sighed. "Sometimes we get novices who have never worked," she said, almost absently. "Some of them fear hard work. Then you get some who do not feel work should apply to them. And then again, some who wallow in it, who treat it like mortification of the flesh."

Marra flipped the manure into the waiting wheelbarrow and straightened up. Her back asked if she really, truly wanted to be doing this. "Which do you think I am?"

The mistress shrugged. "Eventually, everyone winds up in the same place. You do the work because it needs to be done, and it is satisfying to have it done for a little while." She took the pitchfork away and cleared a bit of stall with two or three expert strokes.

"Hold it like this. You are holding too close to the fork, you lose the leverage."

Marra took the pitchfork back and tried, cautiously. It was easier that way and seemed to weigh less. The goats, less amused now that she was doing it correctly, wandered off.

"I will add you to the rota," said the mistress of novices, flicking a bit of dirt from her robe. "When you have finished this stall, be done for the day. And speak to the Sister Apothecary about those blisters."

"Thank you," said Marra, almost inaudibly, and bowed her head. She felt as if she had passed some test, even if it was only in her mind, and she did not know what, if anything, she had learned.

Chapter 3

On the edge of the blistered land, Marra stood and looked around for the source of the voice. It was too bright here. She had gotten used to the dimness of the blistered land. Her eyes ached as if she were staring at a snowfield instead of a dusty road and a line of fences.

"I saw you," said the voice. She squinted against the light and saw the speaker. A man. Perfectly ordinary looking, in the gray-brown garb that everyone wore, here on the edge of the desert. There was nothing that stood out about him, except that he was shouting at her.

"Hello?" she croaked. Her voice sounded as harsh as the crows overhead.

"I saw you come out of there," growled the man. "You're one of them. One of the bad ones."

Marra shook her head. This was absurd. She'd broken bread with cursed souls, and of course it was a supposedly sane man who was going to try to stop her. It was ridiculous. It was . . .

Typical. The prince is sane, too, as men judge these things. I should probably have seen it coming.

"I'm not from there," she said, fighting the urge to defend the people inside. "I got lost. I'm from the Harbor Kingdom."

"The Harbor Kingdom is nowhere near here."

Despite herself, Marra felt a pang of relief. Good. The blistered land did not touch her own kingdom—not yet.

Her relief was short-lived. The man was carrying a shovel. Marra eyed it warily. Shovels were good for burying dead bodies, and also for making bodies dead in the first place.

"I traveled for a long time," said Marra. "To get here. Well, not here specifically. To the dust-wife." She wondered if the dust-wife's name would help. Surely everyone respected dust-wives?

The man spat on the ground. "Trying to raise the dead?" he asked. "The bad dead in there?" He took a step forward.

"No, I . . ." Marra retreated, darting a glance over her shoulder. Could she make it to the safety of the fog?

This is completely ridiculous. Did the hero Mordecai have to stop and explain about the poison worm to the locals? Did they try to chase him back into the swamps? Bad enough that Marra had failed in the task, but now this?

He took another step forward and lifted his shovel. "You go back in," he said. "You go back in or I'll kill you. You stay where you belong."

"But—"

She tried to explain. She really did. The words spilled out of her like blood from a wound, a jumble of explanations about the dust-wife and the bone dog and three impossible tasks and traveling on the coaches from the Harbor Kingdom, and after about thirty seconds, she realized that he wasn't listening to her at all. He was staring past her, into the fog.

Marra turned and saw shadows moving in the murky edge of the blistered land.

"Oh god," the man whispered, clutching his shovel. "Something's coming."

Marra froze, trapped between the shadow and the shovel, not daring to move. She could hear footsteps pounding on the earth, a rattling sound, and then . . .

It galloped out of the fog, an articulated ghost, bouncing on its forelegs. Briefly it rose up and swiped at her face with its nonexistent tongue, then dropped back down again.

"Dog," she said. Tears began to spill down her face. "Dog. You came back."

The bone dog gazed up at her from empty sockets, mouth open in a fleshless grin.

"M-monster!" shouted the farmer, scrambling backward. *"Monster!"*

Monster? Where?

Marra looked behind her, wondering if something terrible had come out of the blistered land. The skeleton dog barked soundlessly, bouncing on his paws, and Marra heard the rattle-bone click of vertebrae and wire.

She grabbed the dog by the backbone, trying to find a convenient way to hold him. You couldn't very well scruff an animal with no scruff. "Hush!" she begged him. "Settle down! Be quiet!"

The edge of the blistered land was calm. A crow cawed and it echoed in a space neither here nor there. The man was long gone and had left his shovel behind.

Monster?

And then she looked down and realized that her assailant had been talking about the skeleton of the dog.

Oh. Right. I suppose . . . yes.

She scowled. He was a *good* dog. He had excellent bones and even if she had used too much wire and gotten it a bit muddled around the toes and one of the bones of the tail, she'd think that a decent person would stop and admire the craftsmanship *before* they screamed and ran away.

"No accounting for taste," she muttered. She was still crying a little, but her tears felt as ghostly as the bone dog's tongue. "All right. Let's go back to the dust-wife and show her you exist."

* * *

Because she was a novice but would never take orders as a nun, Marra was not expected to attend services three times a day. Sometimes she did anyway. The services for Our Lady of Grackles were short. The goddess—or saint, no one was quite sure—did not care for complex theology. No one knew what she wanted, only that she was generally kindly disposed toward humans. "We're a mystery religion," said the abbess, when she'd had a bit more wine than usual, "for people who have too much work to do to bother with mysteries.

So we simply get along as best we can. Occasionally someone has a vision, but she doesn't seem to want anything much, and so we try to return the favor."

The statue of Our Lady of Grackles was a woman with a hood that fell in folds over her face to the lips. She had a small, wry smile, and four birds perched on her arms. Her altar cloths were embroidered with depictions of lesser saints. Since the goddess did not seem to want anything, the nuns offered prayers to saints that had no worshippers of their own. "Some of them probably aren't alive," said the abbess, lighting candles, "but a few prayers for the dead won't go amiss, either."

The convent shared a wall with a monastery, and if she had a chaperone, Marra could go to their library. She had never been terribly easy with reading, but there were books on everything, not merely religion, and she found books on weaving and knitting. It was worth puzzling out the longest words to learn new patterns. She pieced bits together on scraps and sometimes things worked and sometimes they didn't, but the burn of curiosity to see if the next thing would work, and the next thing, and the next, kept her forging ahead.

She could not remember ever feeling such a thing before. There was no call to nurture intellectual curiosity among princesses. She did not even quite know what to call it. It felt like a light shining in her chest and she could see just a little way ahead, and that was enough to keep her going forward. There was no one to tell her what she wanted to know or whether the information even existed. She had no one to share her excitement with, but she did not mind, because it did not occur to her that anyone else might care.

Because she was royal, and not quite a nun, Marra was allowed to keep going forward. When, once a season, the abbess wrote to the royal house and requested the payment to keep a princess, she mentioned that her charge was very fond of knitting and embroidery, and so fine wool and dyed thread found its way to the convent alongside the coin.

Her mother, the queen, sent careful, precise letters once a month.

There was nothing in them that a spy could have found interesting. The king had a cold. The apple trees in the courtyard were flowering. The queen missed her. (Marra did not know whether or not she believed this bit.) And one line, the same every month, "Your sister says that she is well."

When she was eighteen, Marra fell passionately in love with a young acolyte from the monastery who was apprenticed to the Brother Cellarer. He had beautiful eyes and skilled hands and she was utterly lost. They had four or five frantic, awkward couplings, and then Marra overheard him boasting to the other acolytes that he had bedded one of the king's by-blows. It did not matter that they jeered at him and didn't believe him. She went to her room and curled into a ball of misery and decided that she would die of a broken heart. Minstrels would write sad songs about how she had turned her face to the wall and died of the false-heartedness of men.

She could not quite make up her mind whether she wanted to be a ghost who would haunt the convent or not. It would be very satisfying to be a sad-eyed, beautiful ghost who drifted through the halls, gazing up at the moon and weeping silently, as a warning to other young women. On the other hand, she was still short and round-faced and sturdy, and there were very few ghost stories about short, sturdy women. Marra had not managed to be pale and willowy and consumptive at any point in eighteen years of life and did not think she could achieve it before she died. Possibly it would be better to just have songs made about her.

The Sister Apothecary came to her, the nun who doctored all the residents of the convent for various ailments, and who compounded medicines and salves and treatments for the farmer's wives who lived nearby. She studied Marra intensely for a few minutes. "It's a man, is it?" she said finally.

Marra grunted. It had occurred to her about an hour earlier that she did not know how the minstrels would find out that she existed in order to write the sad songs in the first place, and her mind was somewhat occupied with this problem. Did you write them letters?

The Sister Apothecary poured out two small measures of cordial and handed Marra one. "Drink with me," she said, "and I'll tell you about the first boy I ever loved."

It took three more measures of cordial and two more tales of woe, but Marra uncurled and told the Sister Apothecary everything. The Sister gave her a tea to bring her courses on, just in case, and went to the abbess, and the young man was reassigned to another monastery a week later. Marra was left feeling raw and hollow, and brooding over the fact that somehow "unknown noblewoman" had translated into "king's bastard daughter" in the minds of the monks.

Well. It was safer than being a princess. She was outside the hierarchy and so she had been assigned a story that made sense of her position. Marra felt embarrassed for her mother, because now everyone thought that the king had been unfaithful, and then suddenly it occurred to her that maybe he had been unfaithful and she did have half sisters out in the world and that was too large and staggering a thought, so she buried it immediately.

But her heart healed, as hearts almost always do. She brooded for a little time and then she stopped brooding. She had a powerful and thoroughly unrequited love for a visiting scholar with fiery red hair and soulful eyes, which left her in pleasant agonies. Rather than ghosts or minstrels, this time she fantasized about growing old in the convent and telling young novices about the great lost love of her life.

And time went on, and even that great passion became a fond memory, and the letters from the queen arrived, month after month, to tell her that her sister Kania was well.

* * *

When she was twenty and had spent five years in the little room with whitewashed walls and baskets of yarn and thread, she was summoned to the Northern Kingdom. Her sister Kania was about to bear a child at last.

It was strange to travel in the queen's carriage again. Marra was not confined to the convent and traveled often enough to the nearby village, but she walked or rode on the donkey cart with one of the sisters. To be in a well-sprung carriage with velvet seats, drawn by swift gray horses, was a forgotten luxury.

She stared out the window and thought how odd it all was, how very odd.

"You look very well," said the queen.

"Thank you," said Marra. She ran an appraising eye over her mother. It was like looking in a mirror, twenty-odd years into the future. The queen's hair was still black, though henna played a part, and her clothing was as carefully layered as armor, creating a shape with which enemy eyes could find no fault.

"Mostly corsets," said the queen, amused, watching Marra's gaze. "There's a trick to it, at my age. You must have a good figure for having born two children, but not so girlish that people suspect artifice and not so ripe that people think you are trying to be seductive."

"It matters that much?" asked Marra, looking down at her own plain robes. The material was very fine and there were grackles embroidered around the sleeves, but no one would mistake her as being from anywhere but a convent.

"For a queen? Yes."

Marra sighed. It seemed absurd. The abbess was stout as a barrel, and the Sister Apothecary had narrow shoulders and wide hips, like a pear, and both of them wore layered robes like Marra, except that the abbess also had vestments and the Sister Apothecary tied her sleeves back to keep from trailing them in the herbs.

"Clothing can be arranged for you," said the queen. "If you would like dresses instead of robes for the week." Her voice was carefully neutral, as if she did not wish to prejudice Marra's decision.

Marra looked at the queen's clothing and remembered how long it had taken her in the mornings to get ready, even at age fifteen. At the time it had seemed exciting. Now it seemed like so much work, and the eyes on her would be far less indulgent than the ones when she had been a teenage princess in her own family's castle.

I have forgotten whatever I knew. There would be maids and ladies-in-waiting to tend me and do my hair and powder my face, but I would have to sit for hours while they dressed me like a doll, and then for the rest of the day I would be afraid to eat or drink for fear of ruining all their handiwork.

"I would rather appear as a nun," she said.

Her mother nodded. "More robes, then," she said. "It is easily done. But you will be treated as a nun, not as a princess, you know."

"I think," said Marra, folding her hands to hide the calluses from shoveling manure, "that I would prefer it."

* * *

The Northern Kingdom's capitol was set on a hill above a cold, flat plain. There were few trees. The mountains in the background loomed like swords, but the city loomed higher, as if it had been made to stand against the mountains.

The first city had been walled, then had outgrown the walls, so a second set had been built, then a third, until there were five sets of high white walls and a main road spiraling up the hill between them to the palace.

The white stone glowed against the brown earth, but it was a chilly glow, like moonlight on snow. Marra felt very small compared to that immense white city, very small and insignificant, and yet she had the feeling that the effect was deliberate, as if the city was designed to make visitors feel insignificant in comparison.

Perhaps it makes it safer against invasion, she thought. *But it does not seem like a friendly place.*

The carriage passed through the gates, under portcullises edged like saws. Marra pulled the lap quilt more tightly around herself, as if the cold were seeping in. Then came the long, winding way up to the palace, through streets that wrapped in a circle, over and over, as if they were climbing the body of a coiled eel. There were eels in the river near the convent and sometimes people tithed them to the nuns. Marra had eaten a great many eels. She suspected that this one would stick in her throat if she tried.

At the palace, hardly anyone waited to meet them. Marra'd had a vague notion that there should have been a great show of pomp and royal favor and she had been braced to withstand it. When it failed to materialize, she felt off balance. "Not many people," she murmured.

"We are being put in our place," said the queen calmly. "We are here as Kania's family, not as royal envoys, and so we are being reminded that we are poor relations."

"What do we do?"

"We ignore it." And she proceeded to alight from the carriage as if she were the queen of this kingdom, not a poor relation at all.

Two footmen in livery flanked a woman who reminded Marra of the Sister Apothecary. "She's gone into labor," said the midwife bluntly. "Your majesty. It'll be hours yet, but it's been hours already, and the first time's always hard."

"Take me to her."

The palace was a blaze of color and hallways and tapestries. Marra was swept along in her mother's wake, following the midwife. She had also expected to go to a room and perhaps be able to rest or eat, but it seemed there was no time.

Am I going to be there? Am I actually going to see it?

Well, perhaps she was.

The midwife opened a door and there it was, a bedroom the size of a great hall, with a fireplace at one end. Whatever the failings of their reception, the Northern Kingdom did not stint the midwives for their princess. It looked like half an army had encamped in the room, and in the middle of it, in a bed like a battlefield, was the dim brown circle of Kania's face.

"You look radiant," said the queen, taking her daughter's hands. Marra lurked behind her shoulder, unsure what to say.

Kania did not look radiant. She looked exhausted and wan and her eyes were dark wells in her face. "Mother," she said, clutching the queen's hands. "Mother." She closed her eyes and swallowed. It sounded like a click in her throat.

"It will be over soon," promised the queen. "It hurts, but then it's over."

"I don't care how much it hurts," said Kania hoarsely. "I want this child out of me. *Now.*"

"That's every woman, when the time comes," said the queen. She stooped and kissed Kania's forehead. "Soon enough. I promise." She rose. "I'll get you something to drink," she said, and turned to demand tea of the ladies-in-waiting.

Marra looked after her mother nervously, then back to Kania. She had not seen any woman deliver before and she did not know what to expect, but the knowledge of Kania's hatred was tucked up under her heart. Would her sister even want to see her here?

"Marra?" whispered Kania.

"I'm here," she said, taking her sister's hand. "I'm here."

"You're here," Kania repeated. She looked past Marra's shoulder. "Where is Mother?"

"She went to get a drink for you," said Marra. "She'll be back soon."

"No time, then," said Kania softly. She beckoned Marra closer, until her lips were nearly beside Marra's ear.

"Kania . . . ?"

"Listen," hissed Kania. "Listen! If I die, don't let her marry you off to the prince. Run away. Ruin yourself. Whatever it takes. Don't let her drag you into this hell along with us."

Marra blinked. Kania clutched at her shoulder and might have said something more, but a contraction ripped through her and she shrieked, her swollen body bucking on the bed.

What is that? What was that? Marra looked around, panicking, because such a thing could not be normal, but the midwives were calm and acted as if it were every day that a woman's body writhed like a dying snake on the bed.

The queen returned. Kania gave Marra a last, searching look before dropping her hand. The queen tipped water into her daughter's mouth and made soothing noises, and the midwives circled like jackals, waiting for the babe to come.

Chapter 4

The babe, when it came, was a girl. Kania took this news with her lips white and set. She had screamed terribly through labor, but she was strong and healthy and the babe was strong and healthy and perhaps only Marra thought it strange that her sister took this news like a blow.

The queen lifted her granddaughter and smiled down at her, the broadest smile that Marra had ever seen. The prince did not come to visit. Marra had still never seen him. In her mind, he had become something other than human, a creature like a dragon, something large and powerful and uncertain.

The Northern Kingdom's palace certainly seemed as much like a dragon's domain as a human's. It was huge and rich and there were a hundred corridors and a hundred tapestries on every corridor and a hundred courtiers lurking, watching for signs of weakness. Even after Kania's babe was delivered, there was no privacy. She could not ask Kania what she had meant, or if she had meant anything at all.

Marra did not like the courtiers. She was, in truth, a little intimidated by them. The Northern palace was so much larger than the small, shabby one that she had grown up in, and that palace itself was so much larger than the convent. Had it truly only been five years since she had walked among them? It seemed like far longer, like an entire life had passed. She was glad that she had not chosen to wear the dresses that her mother had offered.

The courtiers bothered Marra, but for the most part, they did not bother *with* her. She was too minor a player to be worth cultivating. When they spoke to her, they were polite and careful, and after two days, she realized they thought she was simple.

Well, as far as they are concerned, I might as well be. These machinations are beyond me. I would rather look at tapestries and try to work out the stitches.

She met the king, who was very old. He had false teeth made of walrus ivory, and his mind wandered. Sometimes he was very sharp and sometimes very vague. When he had vague days, he wandered the halls of the palace and called Marra by her grandmother's name. The guards with him pretended that nothing strange was happening, and Marra pretended as well.

They stayed for a week, until the christening. The palace seemed very cold to Marra, even with all the tapestries on the walls. There were drafts in unexpected places, even in her room, and no matter how she tried, she could not seem to find out where they were coming from.

"That's the dead kings, I expect," said her maid matter-of-factly.

"Dead kings?" Marra sought her eyes in the mirror.

The maid nodded. She was younger than Marra, but she had lived in the Northern palace for most of her life and had taken pity on the princess's sister for her lack of worldliness. Marra rather liked her. She never stopped talking, but her chatter was a combination of harmless gossip and acute political commentary. When she told Marra, on the first day after the birth, that she must wear her hair in a particular arrangement, Marra bowed her head and allowed the maid to braid it as she saw fit. She was glad of it later, too, when she saw the way that the other women wore theirs. A simpler style would have called attention to itself by its very simplicity, and Marra preferred to simply fade from notice.

She had not, however, realized that the maid might be superstitious. "What dead kings?" she asked.

"Under the palace," said the maid. "That's where the crypts are. You have to keep them down there deep so that the frost doesn't heave them back up, but it means they're all cold and dry and they don't really go to bones as quick as they should. Tuck your chin, ma'am, so I can get this bit here . . ."

Marra tucked her chin obediently. In the mirror, her neck vanished into a plump roll. She wondered if the maid was going to continue on her own or if she needed to ask for more information. Fortunately, this was apparently a favored topic.

"All the dead kings are down there, and the dead princes, too. They say it's a whole palace of the dead down there. Each king got a room, you see, and the queen got her room next to his. If she had any babies who died, they put them in her room, and in his room . . ." She gave a small, pleased shudder. "In his room, they'd put the royal concubines, back in the days when they had them, yes? And if the concubines weren't dead when they buried him, why, they'd strangle them with a silken cord and put them down there beside him."

Marra watched her own eyes go wide in the mirror. "Goodness! What did the queens think of that?"

"I expect they were just glad to get their own room," said the maid practically. "But of course, some of the kings had more than one queen. If she died before she had any babies, they sent her back to her people, but otherwise, they buried her here, so sometimes the kings have three or four rooms branching off their room, and then the princes would also have rooms nested in there, so now it's like a maze down under the palace, and nobody knows how far back it goes. Sometimes people try to explore it, but they have to take a family tree in one hand and a map in the other, and they don't always come back." She wrinkled her nose. "The dead don't always lie easy, particularly kings, and they don't always approve of the way their descendants are running things, so they come up and walk around and disapprove. That's why there's so many drafts."

"Goodness," said Marra again. She would have liked to swear rather more strongly, but it did not seem appropriate for the princess's sister, who was also mostly a nun. "Are there so many kings as that?"

"They don't last that long," said the maid, matter-of-fact about the royal family's mortality. "It's hard to be a king, and the ones who don't die in battles waste away young. You've seen His Majesty, of course."

"He's very old," said Marra, thinking of the ivory teeth and the wandering mind.

"He's barely fifty."

"What?"

The maid laughed, but kindly. "Oh, aye, it's in the blood. My mother served his father *and* his grandfather, and she only retired last year. Some say there's a terrible magic over the kingdom and it's the godmother's blessing that keeps it all at bay, but the strain of it wears on them, poor souls. My mother, she said they burn themselves out keeping us all safe. Who knows, though? Anyway, that's why the palace under the palace is so large."

"Oh . . ." said Marra faintly, wondering what her sister had married into.

"There's some who say that it's not just the kings," added the maid. "You can't have a great big palace of the dead like that without grave robbers, can you? So it's all laid about with curses that rip the souls out of the robbers and wad them all up together, and they say that goes waddling and wiggling through the halls of the dead palace, looking for more souls to eat."

"Oh my."

"Makes you fair shiver, doesn't it?" said the maid cheerfully. She patted Marra's shoulder as if she were a horse. "You're all ready to go, ma'am. Best not be late for the christening."

* * *

It was at the christening, for the first time, that Marra saw Prince Vorling.

He was small. That surprised her the most. Her whole family had ordered their lives around his whims, and he had loomed very large in her mind. But he was barely taller than Kania, slim-hipped, with a narrow, angular face. He stood behind the golden cradle and smiled and smiled, his eyes as flat as river stones. He did not look as if he were aging out faster than a normal man, but perhaps it came on the kings all at once, or perhaps it was only a maid's gossip.

Still. She looked over at the king, his hair as soft and thin as that of the infant in the cradle. Could he really only be fifty?

The christening itself was dull. Courtiers stood around and pretended to be fascinated by the sight of a cradle that presumably held a child somewhere in the pile of lace and linen. As a family member, Marra was closer than she might have been, but as a very unimportant person in the family, her primary view was over her mother's left shoulder.

The cradle had golden ribbons on it. The king mumbled a name and then Vorling shouted his daughter's name in a carrying voice. Marra caught that the first name was Virian and then it dissolved into a welter of names that slipped out of her mind as soon as it went in. *Surely they cannot be saddling this child with all those names?* she thought. She wanted to give her sister a bemused look, but she could only see the side of Kania's face.

And now there will probably be speeches, she thought, and steeled herself to stand looking calm and composed and politely interested.

But there were not speeches. Instead, Vorling stepped back and said, "The godmother's blessing," and was silent. The courtiers, too, fell instantly quiet. The double door at the side of the great audience hall opened.

"The godmother of the royal house," said the herald in the doorway, and then he, too, stepped aside and a figure in gray came through the door.

The godmother was old, very old, older than Marra knew a person could be. She did not have wrinkles any longer. Her skin had drawn tight across her skull, almost translucent. Marra could see the shadow of bones in her face, as if there were light streaming through her like stained glass and the bones were the lead between panes of skin.

She moved very slowly. Her spine was curved, but in a way that gave the impression of a scimitar blade rather than old age. She leaned on a black cane and her progress toward the cradle took many minutes, but not one of the courtiers, nor even the prince, showed the slightest trace of impatience.

It occurred to Marra that the king was not treated with half as much deference as the godmother.

She wore dove gray, but her skin was so pale that it looked almost black by contrast. She made her slow way to the cradle, and it was not until she lifted her hand that Marra noticed the exquisite layers of lace that draped her sleeves.

Marra herself had tried making lace once and never again. It was ruinously expensive. Even the prince and the highest ranked lords only had it at their cuffs and hems, and here was the godmother wearing enough to buy a palace.

The lace swayed as she pushed the curtains of the cradle open, and one shadow-bone hand rested on the air over the child's head.

"This is my gift," said the godmother. Her voice was not loud, but it was so silent that it carried to the far corners of the room. "I shall serve her as I have served all her line, my life bound to theirs. No foreign magic shall harm them. No enemy shall topple their throne. As it has been for all the children of the royal house, so shall it be for her, as long as I draw breath."

The king bowed his head. The prince did as well. As the godmother turned and began to make her slow way to the door, the new princess of the Northern Kingdom began to cry.

Kania half turned as if to go to her, but the prince caught her arm and held it fast. A nursemaid hurried from the sidelines, her footsteps muffled on the carpet, and caught up the infant, hushing her with soft, frantic whispers.

Even at her own christening, she is not allowed to cry. Marra bowed her head so that no one would see her lips twitch. She, too, had been a princess once. *And I do not know that I would wish it on you, niece, but I am only a youngest daughter dressed up as a nun, and no one cares what I think either way.*

* * *

Returning to the convent was a relief. The white walls were restful and cool after the opulence of color. Marra had a head full of stitches and mangled a few bits of fabric trying to duplicate them all.

Several of the novices, still thinking her a bastard daughter, wanted to know all about the palace and the christening and the princess. Marra tried to answer but found herself with very little to say. Had the men all been very dashing? She didn't think so. Had the women all been very beautiful? She remembered the dark circles under Kania's eyes and the tightness of her lips. Had the prince been handsome? She truly had no idea. She tried to describe him and the only word she could come up with was *short*.

This was nothing the novices wanted to hear, and all the other things Marra could tell them were nothing she wanted to say aloud. Eventually they gave up asking, and both parties went away mutually disappointed.

The abbess had her own questions, which Marra was also mostly unable to answer. She was interested in Prince Vorling's fairy godmother, but much more so in the priests and clerics that had attended. "Did you see Archbishop Lydean?"

Marra spread her hands helplessly. "I don't know. Did I?"

"A young person," said the abbess. "The youngest ever named archbishop. They would have been with the Archimandrite, a very old man in blue robes."

Marra vaguely remembered the old man, who had been a blaze of cerulean in the crowd. Yes, she had seen him. He had coughed and coughed and looked like a shaking bit of sky.

"Ah!" said the abbess. "We have heard his health is not good. When he dies, Lydean will take the mitre and become Archimandrite, but there will be resistance because they are so young."

"All right," said Marra, conscious of politics swirling around her that had little to do with princesses.

The abbess patted her hand and went away again, and Marra tackled her new stitches and weeded the garden and let the convent's quiet settle over her like a blanket against the cold.

Six months later, a letter from the queen mentioned that Kania was pregnant again, which troubled Marra more than she would admit. It seemed very fast, and of course, the queen would not have mentioned it unless she was several months along. Marra had not really thought you could get pregnant so swiftly after giving birth, but the Sister Apothecary said that it was possible.

Months slid by, Marra expecting to be summoned at any moment for the birth and christening, until one day she counted on her fingers and realized that Kania would be eleven months pregnant at the very least. *She must have lost the child,* Marra thought, *or perhaps there never was one.*

She knew more about miscarriages now than a princess probably should. Her friendship with the Sister Apothecary had continued, and because she could read and research and wrote with a steady hand, she found herself doing small chores for the other woman. And then one day a farmhand was hauled in on a door, screaming from the pain of his broken leg, and Marra found herself holding the lamp and handing the Sister bandages, acting as a second set of hands.

Long after midnight, the Sister washed her hands in a bucket of bloody water and said, "You did well," to Marra.

The praise warmed her down to her bones because it was true and it was not for the princess.

It was a few days later when there was a knock on her door near midnight. Marra opened the door, puzzled—no one ever knocked so late, and Our Lady of Grackles only held midnight services on the solstices and equinoxes—and saw the Sister Apothecary there, holding a cracked leather satchel. "It's a birth," she said shortly. "You've seen one, haven't you?"

"One . . . ?" said Marra. "Only one."

"Then you're ahead of the Brother Infirmarian. He hasn't touched that end of a woman since he slid out of one. My assistant's down with the flux and I need someone to hold a lamp."

Marra gulped. She waited to see what she would do next, half-convinced that she would curl up in a ball and whimper, but instead she straightened up and said, "All right. Let me get on my shoes."

* * *

The labor went very much the same way that Kania's had, which seemed strange to Marra. *Then again, peasants and princesses all shit the same and have their courses the same, so I suppose it's no surprise that babies all come out the same way, too.* Having thus accidentally anticipated a few centuries' worth of revolutionary political thought, Marra got down to the business of boiling water and making tea.

It went more quickly than Kania's, at least, but it was still a long, tense, tedious stretch. Marra nodded off more than once and sometimes came to with the lamp in her hand and the Sister Apothecary crouching between the mother's legs, wondering if she was really awake or if she was having a strange sort of dream.

Dawn had passed and it was most of the way to morning when the baby emerged into the world, looked around, and burst into tears.

"You get used to it," the Sister told the infant, and handed the child to Marra, who stared at it with intense horror. It was bloody and wrinkly and reddish gray and looked like the sort of thing you would drive back to hell with holy water. "Um," said Marra.

"Is it . . . Is . . . " The mother was panting and could hardly breathe. "It cried. It's alive, right?"

"Oh yes," said Marra hurriedly. "Very alive." She stared at it, trying to find something else to say. "Has arms and legs. And, uh . . . a head . . ."

"That's good," said the mother, and began giggling with high, hysterical laughter. "Oh, that's good. You want them to have heads."

"Lady of Grackles have mercy," muttered the Sister Apothecary, but as she was saying this directly into the birth canal, no one but Marra heard.

Fortunately the afterbirth arrived immediately and the Sister swapped burdens with her. "Go and give that to her husband," she said. "He'll know what to do."

Marra bowed her head and fled.

The husband was a farmer with a young face and gnarled, ancient hands. He took the afterbirth as reverently as if it had been a child itself. "Will you help me then, sister?"

Marra swallowed. "I'm . . . I'm not a sister. Not all the way."

He smiled a little. "Don't have to be. Not for this."

She walked with him and picked up the spade he pointed to. They buried the strange, muscleless piece of birth meat under a hickory tree, down among the roots. "Oak's usual," said the farmer, sitting back, as Marra patted the earth into place. "Oak's strong. But hickory's lucky. We've got two strong children already, and the third could use a little luck to make their way."

Marra stifled a sigh, thinking of her own godmother, who had given them gifts of health and princes. A little luck might have smoothed the way for all of them.

She went with the Sister the next time she was called out as midwife, and she was called out often at night because the town midwife was old and slept soundly. Once or twice a month, there would come a tap on Marra's door and it would be the Sister going out to tend to a woman laboring.

She was never asked to do more than hold hands and bring water, but she learned nevertheless. Among other lessons, she learned to pretend not to hear the terrible threats uttered by women in labor. Strange as it was, this set her mind at ease. Kania could not have meant what she had whispered in Marra's ear.

It was the labor—that was all it was. When the miller was brought to her bed, she threatened to put her husband's balls on the millstone and grind them fine if he ever so much as looked at her again.

She saw babies born and mothers die. She saw mothers have an easy birth and then the bleeding simply never stopped, until they died white and bloodless against the pillow. She saw a birthing hook and how it was used to extract babies who had not survived long enough to emerge.

It was the fifth or sixth or tenth labor, as they walked back to the convent, that Marra could no longer keep silent. "It's so *stupid*!" she said.

The Sister glanced at her mildly. "They both lived," she said. "That's a good outcome, in my book."

"Not that," said Marra. Both mother and child had lived, although it had been a harder labor than anyone was happy with. "Just . . . Lady of Grackles! We lie on our backs or sit in a chair and push out a thing that's too big to fit so that everything's torn bloody! What a stupid, *stupid* way to bear!"

"Oh, that," said the Sister. "Yes. I've often thought so. Cows have a much better time of it. Goats and sheep, too. Granted the legs are a bit harder to untangle, but it's not half the mess of humans."

"I won't do it," said Marra.

"Nobody's asking you to," said the Sister. She paused. Marra was fairly certain that the Sister knew exactly who and what she was, and who her parents were, and was trying to find a way to phrase her next sentence. "Well, not at the moment, anyway. And if someone should . . . ah . . . well. There are ways."

Run away. Ruin yourself. Whatever it takes. Don't let her drag you into this hell along with us.

Marra licked her lips. Had they used a birthing hook on Kania, for the child who had gone much too long without being born?

"Ways?"

The Sister glanced around, as if someone might really be eavesdropping in a remote hedgerow in the hour before dawn. "Ways," she said. "Herbs, mostly. Sponges soaked in lemon juice. None of them work perfectly, and anyone who says they do is lying to you. Most of them are dangerous. Sometimes everyone dies anyway, and there's nothing to be done. But there are things that can make pregnancy less likely."

Marra's heart leapt. Could she find out? Could she tell Kania? The entire point of queens and princesses was to act as broodmares for royalty, but if there were ways to prevent it . . .

"I want to know," she said. "All of them."

The Sister Apothecary sighed. "It can be done," she said. "But not tonight."

*   *   *

The Sister was as good as her word. It was all rather abstract at the moment for Marra, but she memorized the methods and even brewed an entire vial of extract, with the Sister standing over her to make certain she did it correctly.

"You care very much about this," said the Sister.

Marra shrugged. She did not want to care. She did not want to think that her time in the convent might come to an end, that she would be dragged back out onto the game board with all the other pawns and princes.

But if I am, I will not go unarmed. I won't. I have to learn. And maybe I can tell Kania. She had already seen women wearing themselves out from too much bearing.

There was a letter in her room now, another polite, correct letter from her mother, and at the end, her mother had written that Kania was pregnant again.

This is too much. Surely it is too much. She is wearing herself out to bear an heir, and if she dies . . .

Marra told herself that it was fear for her sister that drove her on, not fear for herself. She clamped down on the traitorous little whisper that said that she would have to take her sister's place as broodmare to the prince.

I will not. I will not. *But it will not come to that. I will learn . . .*

Chapter 5

In the spring of Marra's fifteenth year at the convent, a fever went through the kingdom. It laid Marra low for many days, and when she struggled to her feet at last, it was to discover that the abbess was near death. For nearly a week, it was touch and go. Because she had recovered, Marra was allowed to tend to the older woman. In truth, there was not much to be done except to sit in the room and practice her needlework and listen to the rattle of breathing that would not quite be still.

The abbess recovered, but there was white in her iron-gray hair, and she moved more cautiously than she had done. She needed a cane to go up stairs and it clearly infuriated her. The abbess had never been patient with her own weakness.

Marra herself recovered well, though there were days when she only dozed at the window and could not will herself to move. Even the view from the window reminded her of plague. They lost two novices, and the old man who sold goat milk was replaced by his son, who told them quietly that his father would not be coming back.

She was gazing out the window, not quite awake, thinking long unraveling thoughts, when there was a tap on the door and the Sister Apothecary was waiting.

"It's bad news," she said, holding out a letter. "The abbess asked me to bring it to you. She would have done it but she can't handle the stairs. I don't know what it is, but it's not good."

Marra broke the seal. If the Sister said something else, she didn't hear. Her heart was pounding too hard in her ears. If the abbess had been informed of the contents, then it must be bad; it must be . . .

I regret to inform you that the fever took your niece, Virian. The funeral will be held as soon as the family can travel to the Northern Kingdom. If you are well enough to travel, a carriage will be sent to fetch you.

"Oh," said Marra. She was horrified to find that the sensation she felt was relief. It was not her mother, not her sister, not her father. Her heart ached for Kania's grief, but part of her said, *It is only a child you saw for a few minutes at her christening and never again,* and she hated herself for feeling that way, but the loss was at a remove and her love was an abstract love, not one born of close familiarity.

"My niece," she said, realizing that the Sister was waiting for an answer. "My niece has died of the fever. There's a funeral. I have to go. I . . . someone should be told . . . I don't know what I do next, but they're supposed to come and fetch me . . ."

Someone did. Two days later, she was in a carriage traveling north. The horses were black, the bridles were black, the coachman clad in charcoal gray. The Northern Kingdom was showing off its wealth again, and Marra found herself crying, not for her niece but for Damia. *Late again,* she thought. *That was so many years ago. You're being slow again, only mourning now. Probably you'll actually get around to crying for your niece in a decade or so.* Which was comforting, in a foolish way, because maybe that meant that she was not a complete monster. She had been wondering since her first instinctive relief.

She was met by a footman who led her to Kania's chambers. It was all so much like the first time that she half expected Kania to be in labor again. But her sister was not. She was standing at a window, with her mother's arm around her, and the first thing that Marra saw was the roundness of her sister's belly.

"You're pregnant again," she blurted. There had been other letters over the years, announcing pregnancies, but never births. Eventually they had stopped coming, and Marra had thought that perhaps Kania had stopped trying. *Perhaps she has only stopped telling people.*

Kania and the queen both looked at her. Kania had blue circles under her eyes and her face was swollen, but she was still so clearly her mother's daughter that it was like being studied by the queen and her reflection. Marra managed a stammering apology, or perhaps it was only a stammer and Kania took pity on her instead. "I am," she said.

"You . . . um. Felicitations. I'm sure you must be very . . ." *Oh hell. How can she be happy? She just lost her daughter, the one that was already born.* Marra looked around the room wildly, hoping that the right words would come but they didn't, and eventually the silence stretched out so long that no words could have fixed it.

The queen sighed, but Kania gave a strangled laugh and came across the room to embrace Marra. "I'm glad you're here, Sister," she said.

"I'm sorry," said Marra miserably. "I'm sorry for Virian, for you, or— I'm so sorry. I'm not good at this."

"It's all right," said Kania. "I'm not, either." She wiped her eyes and stepped back. Marra thought perhaps she wasn't very far along, but her clothes were cut to show her belly, or perhaps she was one of those women who began to show almost immediately.

"Can I do anything?" asked Marra. "Anything at all?"

"There is nothing to be done," said Kania. "Sit with me. The funeral's tomorrow." Marra nodded and they sat at the window and she tried not to say anything too horribly foolish, with the result that they mostly sat in silence.

There was a family dinner that night. It was strained and everyone picked at their food. There were too many courses, all of them far too rich, and the servants took them away again, barely tasted. Marra watched turtles go by, cooked in their shells, and quail stewed with apricots, and venison in lingonberry and truffles and trifles and wondered who in their right mind served such a thing to mourners.

The old king was having a vague sort of day, intercut with moments of lucidity. Vorling's smooth, handsome face was smoother and colder than Marra remembered. She wondered if he was beginning to age like the old king had. She had no idea how old he was. Forty? Forty-five? He did not look old. He did not look young. He looked like carved marble. Kania, beside him, was all too clearly flesh. Her wrists and ankles were swollen and her skin was puffy.

Marra wanted to grab her hands and beg her not to get pregnant again, to dump everything she'd learned about preventing conception into her sister's lap.

She did not, because even she was not so far gone as to do that at dinner, particularly not with the husband who had bought her sister to give him sons. She fiddled with the stem of her wineglass and waited for the endless courses of food to just go away. Finally they did. The last plate was removed and the king stood and everyone else got to their feet as well.

"Tomorrow," said Vorling. His eyes flicked over Kania. "Clean yourself up for it. You look a fright."

Marra inhaled sharply. Had he really said that? Had she misheard? Why was no one else reacting? That was shockingly cruel. She couldn't really have heard it.

She glanced at her mother's face, seeking confirmation, but the queen's face was utterly calm, the same calm that she wore when speaking to enemies and diplomats. The two attendants who helped the king began to lead the monarch gently toward the door, and Vorling followed.

"I would like to stand vigil for my daughter tonight," said Kania to Vorling's back. "In the chapel."

Vorling turned. Marra saw his lips thin, saw them start to form a denial, but the old king looked at her and smiled blearily and said, "Yes, yes, right and proper . . ."

Rage flashed across Vorling's face. It was so strange and unexpected that Marra almost didn't recognize it. For a moment she thought that the prince was in pain or about to have some kind of fit. Then it passed and his face resumed that flat, smooth tranquility.

"I will send guards," he said.

"I would prefer to keep vigil alone," said Kania. Her voice shook a little, as if she were asking for some enormous favor. "But I will take my sister with me for comfort."

Vorling's face turned toward Marra. There was something masklike about his expression, and Marra wanted to take a step back, but Kania was also looking at her, and so was the old king.

"Yes, of course," she murmured, folding her hands inside her sleeves. "I would be honored."

"You must keep a guard," said Vorling.

"I must mourn," she said. "A nun is chaperone enough, I think."

Marra wanted to say that she was not really a nun, but she knew that her sister knew that, and if her sister thought it was important enough to lie, she would not be the one to expose her.

A tear slid down the old king's face, and he wiped it away. His wispy hair seemed to float as he nodded. "It's proper," he said. He nudged his son's shoulder. "You have to let the ladies weep in their own way."

Vorling's lips tightened over his teeth. "My guards will escort you," he said in a clipped voice, and he turned on his heel and walked away.

* * *

The guards came for Marra that night after dinner. She had sent the maid away and was staring at the tapestries in her room, pacing from one to another. They mostly showed treaties being signed and were remarkably tedious, but she had to admire the craftsmanship that suggested writing on pages without actually spelling out the letters. *That is a fair bit of design. I wonder if I could do that . . .*

One of the tapestries billowed in a draft, perhaps from the palace of dust underfoot. Tomorrow her niece would go to join the ancient kings. It seemed like a cold and lonely place to send a child.

Someone knocked on the door, then opened it immediately. Two guards came in, wearing the white cloaks of the prince's personal guard. "You are sent for," said the taller of the two.

Marra nodded. It occurred to her, somewhat belatedly, that guards might address a princess with a little more respect, but here in this place built on dead kings, perhaps there was no great worth to a princess. She walked behind them, her head bowed, and concentrated on looking as much like a nun as she could.

Lady of Grackles, forgive me for this deception. It seems like it must be important.

The chapel where her niece's body lay in state seemed larger at night, with candles flickering and the shadows looming in the corners. Kania stood just inside the door, her face blank, as if she had stepped away from her own face for a little while and retreated somewhere deep inside.

There were two more guards with her, also clad in white. The four of them went through the chapel, looking in each pew and each shadow. It struck Marra as almost a parody of watchfulness. There were no places to hide in the chapel. Were they trying to impress her with their care? Seeking assassins under the pews?

She was half-surprised that they did not look inside the closed sarcophagus, but they left it alone. When they had scoured the room, the leader of the four nodded curtly to Kania and they left the chapel. Marra heard a bar grinding into a socket as they were locked inside.

"That was . . . thorough . . ." she murmured.

Kania snorted. "The prince fears that I keep lovers under every bush," she said. "If the king had not thought that it was *sweet*"—she rolled the word on her tongue and spat it out with scorn—"I would not have been allowed even this much solitude."

"Oh," said Marra faintly. She swallowed. Kania? Keeping lovers? She understood all the words, but they did not seem to line up in her head. "Oh."

They knelt together at the rail before the coffin. Kania settled heavily, her belly swollen against her legs. Marra wanted to tell her that it was too many pregnancies, ask her if she knew about the ways to stop from conceiving, but how could you do that in a room with a dead child? Instead she bowed her head and tried to pray. *Our Lady of Grackles, please . . . please . . .* She could not think of anything to pray for. What did you ask for when a child was dead? *Please make this as easy on my sister as you can,* she thought finally. That seemed like the only thing worth asking for.

She stared at the stone coffin and thought again of how she had felt relief that it was only her niece who had died. Shame washed through her. She dropped her eyes to her hands.

"You learned to pray in the convent," said Kania quietly.

"I suppose," Marra said. "Mostly I learned about ways to weave and embroider. And how to shovel a stable. And lately, how to deliver a baby." She glanced over at Kania, wondering if this was an opening, but her sister said nothing.

They continued to kneel. The candles burned down slowly, a drop of wax sliding down the pale pillars.

After what seemed like an hour, Kania said, "My daughter is in this coffin, and I do not feel anything." She gazed at the small sarcophagus, dry-eyed. "Did your convent teach you what to do about that?"

Marra swallowed hard and shook her head.

"They took her from me as soon as she was born," Kania said. "You remember? I did not hold her, not even for a moment. They took her to her father, and then to the wet nurse. She had an army of nursemaids and tutors. I saw her for a few minutes a day at most." She shook her head slowly. "There were so many things I missed, and I did not even know that I was missing them. She took her first step and spoke her first words, and I heard from the nursemaids."

"Perhaps you mourned then," said Marra, hoping desperately that it was true. *I didn't mourn her, either, and now it seems like no one is, not really, and that's not right.*

"Perhaps. But I should be mourning now," Kania said, sounding thoughtful. "I should be destroyed. This should be the greatest pain that a mother could know. And yet it is as if a stranger's child had died. I feel badly for that stranger, but it does not seem as if it has anything to do with me."

"I'm sorry," croaked Marra. *Our Lady of Grackles, please tell me what to say. Our Lady of Grackles, please fix this because I can't.*

"I am, too." Kania shifted her pregnant bulk, grimacing. She put a hand to the small of her back and winced, then stretched her arms out along the prayer rail. "They took my daughter and now they have taken even my ability to mourn her. The children I lost before they were born—they felt more real than this."

It would have been an opening to talk to her about the lost pregnancies. It would have been the time. But Marra's gaze was transfixed on her sister's wrist, on a line of livid purple marks there.

She held out her hand, trembling a little, and the marks matched. Fingerprints. A man's hand, larger than hers, but fingerprints nonetheless.

"Kania," she said hoarsely.

Kania looked down at her arm and pulled the sleeve to hide the marks. "Ah," she said.

"Were those . . . how did you . . . ?" Her throat closed up. They could not be what it looked like. *It was an accident—surely it was an accident. She fell and he caught her . . .*

"Normally he's careful not to leave them where they show," said Kania in a voice so weary that the carvings on the walls should have come to life and wept. "But since I'm pregnant, his ability is limited. And he was very angry that I would keep a vigil alone."

Marra stared at her. The words fell into her like stones into a well, and she could hear them rattling down into her mind, but they did not seem to make any sense. They could not *possibly* make sense.

"He . . ." She had to stop and swallow. Her throat was suddenly dry. "He . . . he hurts you?"

Kania gave her one of those quick, sharp looks she remembered from childhood, when she had been too slow to realize something. It was the same look that she had worn when Marra had refused to believe Damia was dead. Marra flinched back as if it were a blow.

"Of course he does," said Kania. "Though he mostly stops when I'm pregnant. He doesn't want any more miscarriages. He gets them anyway." She smiled sourly. "Although it's not much of a respite, because he saves up a great deal of anger in those months. You'd think he'd have whores to take it out on, but the man's got a horror of bastards and bastardy, so it's me or nothing."

"The prince," said Marra, feeling as if she were still half a step behind the conversation. "The *prince* is doing this?"

Kania gave her another sharp look. "Of course. Who else?"

"But someone has to stop him," said Marra. "The king . . . or . . ."

She trailed off, because who could stop a prince? Did you call the guard on them? You couldn't do that, could you?

"The king is in his dotage," said Kania. "You saw. He shows up at ceremonies and mumbles and waves, then goes back to bed. Vorling is the true ruler here. Has been for years."

"How long has this been going on?" whispered Marra.

"Since the beginning."

"Oh." Marra swallowed. No king. No guards. No help. "Come home, then. Leave him and come home where he can't get to you."

Kania's look was almost pitying. "And he will declare war on our country for breach of contract. Do you think I haven't asked? I haven't even been allowed home for a visit. I told you he's terrified of bastards. It goes both ways. If I'm allowed out of his sight for a day, he's sure that I'll be pregnant by some other man. He tells me he'll have no bastards on the throne. It's the spell, you know. The godmother's blessing. No enemy shall take the throne—but only as long as the bloodline continues. A bastard on the throne means the Northern Kingdom falls. Or so he believes."

Each word rang out ugly, like the chop of an axe into heartwood. Marra shook her head slowly. It was baffling. Appalling. It made no sense. "But you wouldn't do that!"

Kania gave a short, hoarse laugh. "In a heartbeat," she whispered, dropping her voice. "In an instant. If I thought I could have a child that did not carry that monster's blood . . ."

Marra stared at the coffin, because she could not look at her sister's eyes any longer.

"He was away on a military campaign early on," said Kania. "It lasted for years. When he came back, he would not touch me for nine months. To be sure, he said. To be absolutely sure." She gave another hoarse laugh. "Those were the best years of my marriage. Except that I was still young and fool enough to think that he might change."

Marra took a deep breath. "Then you must kill him," she said, her own voice barely above a whisper. Could the guards on the door hear her? She dropped it even lower. "Stab him when he's asleep."

Kania looked at her with pity and despair. "He does not sleep with me."

"Then . . . when he . . . you know . . ." Marra felt herself turning bright scarlet.

Kania's face softened as she looked at her sister. "His guards are with him, even then," she said very gently. "I think it excites him to know they watch."

The whole world seemed to slew sideways. Marra had never thought . . . never even dreamed . . . "Oh," she said.

She couldn't deal with that. There was no place in her head to put that piece of information. She tried to think of something else, something that would fix things. Kania sat in silence, her hands folded, looking at the coffin of the daughter she had not been allowed to love.

"If . . . if you had an heir," said Marra, "if you bore him an heir, would he let go? You could go away. Somewhere else. A separate estate, or back home? Something. He wouldn't need you anymore."

"He would not need me anymore," agreed her sister. "And the moment he does not need me, the moment that he has a son that will rule both our kingdom and his, then my life will be worth less than the lowest peasant. I will not die quickly, but I will die."

"Then you can't have any more children!" said Marra hopelessly. Her mind was full of horses with black bridles, a funeral procession of mourners, the wrapped body that must be Damia's. "You can't! One could be a boy!"

And if she does not bear children, she will no longer be useful to him. He will kill her and marry the next sister in line, to get that son.

The next sister.

Kania gazed at her steadily and Marra realized that her knowledge must be written across her face.

"You see how it must be," said Kania softly. "If there is a way out, I cannot find it." She drew herself up, every inch a queen. "But I endure. For the sake of our people, I will endure."

* * *

The next three days were nauseating in the dullness of their horror. Marra did not dare speak to anyone about what she had learned. The prince would hear. He must. Kania had not dared to speak of it except in the chapel, to her sister and the body of her daughter. *I do not dare speak of it to anyone. He will know. He will know.*

But just as there was no speaking, there was no way to stop thinking about it. There was no moment, waking or sleeping, when it was not burning in Marra's brain. She choked down dry toast and dreamed about the marks on Kania's arms, and the only mercy was that everyone took her horror for grief.

Her niece's coffin was interred in the crypts below the palace. All Marra could remember was great iron doors opening, then a procession through a maze of cold stone corridors. She walked behind Kania with her hands tucked into her sleeves and watched Vorling's face and realized that she had never hated before now. This must be what this new feeling was. It took up so much space in her chest that she did not know if she could breathe around it.

When she and her mother left the Northern Kingdom, relief took her so strongly that it felt like joy, as if she might fling herself out of the carriage and dance in the road. *I cannot be relieved. Kania is still trapped. I was never the one in danger. I do not deserve to feel this way.* But she felt it anyway and the shame of it struck her in waves, but when they ebbed, the wild joy of being away from Vorling's palace was still there.

She stayed only one night in her father's palace. Her old room was still kept for her. Even a small, poor kingdom can usually afford to keep a princess's room for her. It was much too young, filled with stuffed toys, and Marra was thirty years old now. *But I can hardly ask them to change it, for a room I use one night in a decade. That would be wasteful.* The abbess would have looked down her nose at the extravagance, which might have gone to feed the poor, and the Sister Apothecary would have shaken her head and laughed.

There was one thing that she could do, though, in her father's house, and one thing only. Marra took her courage in both hands. It had not occurred to her that living as a nun might have robbed her of bravery, and yet facing her mother seemed far more alarming than it ever had when she was a child. She was too aware that the other woman was the queen first and her mother second, and that Marra herself was a small, insignificant piece in the game.

"I need to talk to you," she said, when her mother looked up at her. "Uh, Your Majesty. Mother. Please."

Well, that was even worse than I expected, she thought. She had never been terribly clever with words, but apparently she had lost what little skill she'd ever possessed.

A line formed between the queen's eyebrows. "Leave us," she commanded the waiting women, and they filed out, glancing curiously back over their shoulders.

"Kania's in trouble," said Marra, as soon as the door closed behind them.

The queen cocked her head to one side. "How so?"

"It's the prince." Marra swallowed. Her throat felt very dry. *She's listening—that's something.* "Prince Vorling. She's scared. She's very scared. I think . . . I'm pretty sure . . ."

She could not say the words. They were right there in her head. *He's hurting her.* And yet she couldn't seem to get them out. *I can't say it. Why can't I say it?*

It felt as if she were about to say something horrible and shameful. Her throat wanted to close up, to prevent her from saying such awful things, even if they were true, even if it wasn't Kania's fault, it was Vorling, but for some reason even just saying the words seemed impossible. She swallowed. Her face felt hot.

Say it. Say it. She thought of the line of violet fingerprints again and tried to focus. Why was this so hard? Kania hadn't asked for her help, but she had to get the words out. Their mother would fix it. The queen fixed things—it was why their father had married her. She understood politics and expediency and she would fix it somehow.

"He's . . . he's doing . . ." Marra took a deep breath. *Say it. You have to say it.* "He's hurting her. There were marks. We have to get her away."

"Ah," said the queen.

Does she believe me? What if she doesn't believe me? All the memories of childhood reared up in her head, all the childish lies, Kania saying that she was just jealous because she didn't have a prince . . . *Oh, Lady of Grackles! What do I do? Do I drag her back to the Northern Kingdom and show her Kania's arm with the marks?*

The thought was absolutely shattering. She watched as the queen bent her head over the bit of embroidery in her hands. Marra could identify the stitch from where she stood, a cranefly knot, and thought that she would have done it better and more neatly. That gave her a tiny shred of courage, that she was more skilled at something than the queen, and she had so little courage left.

"Prince Vorling is a monster," said the queen crisply. "He is undoubtedly hurting her in all manner of ways, although he has learned not to do anything that might cause a miscarriage. We shall hope the next child is a son, so that your sister has some chance of retiring from his immediate attention."

Marra's mouth hung open, but there were no words in her throat. *But he won't let her go. He'll kill her, then.*

"Until she has a son, however, she is at his mercy. And so are we."

"But . . ." croaked Marra.

The queen yanked the needle through the fabric with an impatient flick. "Think, Marra! We are a very small kingdom and his knife is at our throat. If the protection of the Northern Kingdom is withdrawn, then the Southern Kingdom marches on us to seize our harbor."

"But . . . but they didn't before . . ." Marra felt as if she were stumbling through the steps of a dance that was far more intricate than she had believed.

"They did not, because the Northern Kingdom would have stopped them. If not for our sakes, so that the South did not control the harbor. But if the Northern Kingdom let it be publically known that we had fallen out of favor and they were no longer interested in defending us, then we will have Southern troops surrounding the castle in a fortnight."

Marra tried to imagine the fields around the castle sprouting with tents and swords and pikes and could not.

Another stab of the needle into the cloth. The stitch would be too tight and would pucker the fabric. "Or," said her mother, "if we defy Vorling before he has an heir that might conceivably inherit our throne, he well might decide to march on us himself and raze this entire city to the ground in a single bloody day."

Marra swallowed. "But Kania . . ."

"Is threading a very dangerous needle right now. Did she ask you to get her out?"

"No . . ." Marra felt as if she were standing a few paces behind herself, completely outside the world that could be so strange and cruel and complicated. "No, I . . . no."

The queen nodded.

She wanted to say so much more. She wanted to say that Kania thought that a son would be the death of her, but maybe Kania was wrong or perhaps the queen was wrong or perhaps everyone was wrong and nothing could be made right. But another thought was beating at her skull like a moth against a windowpane.

"Did you know?" asked Marra. "Before?"

"I knew that he had questionable appetites," said the queen. There was nothing in her face or her tone that asked forgiveness. "I had hoped he was wise enough to keep them quiet. I did not think he would be fool enough to torment his wife to miscarriage and death." She shook her head, her lips a grim line.

Death? But . . . It took far too long before it finally occurred to Marra that her mother was talking about Damia, not Kania.

Oh.

Oh.

So he did kill her.

And Mother knew.

She did not know how to feel. It was too huge, too strange. She did not know if she wanted to weep or rage or throw herself from the castle wall. There was nothing in her heart or her history that told her what to do with this new knowledge. It was too big. She had to shove it aside and focus on Kania or else she would be lost completely.

"We could get her away," said Marra hopelessly. "She could come and stay with me. Take orders with the sisters. He couldn't get her, then."

"Marra," said the queen, her voice softening. "Marra, love, do you think a man who tortures his wife and would wipe out a kingdom on a whim would be stopped by an abbey's walls?"

She was still standing too far back from herself, trapped in amber. She watched herself bow her head and say, "No. Of course not."

The fury rising inside her was doused at once. Her mother had known, and she had also known that there was nothing she could do. It was too late. Perhaps it had been too late since Vorling came courting Damia, many years before.

Don't let her drag you into this hell along with us, Kania had said, her eyes dull with agony, clutching at her sister's robes. *Run away.*

The knowledge bloomed inside her like blood soaking through a bandage. Prince Vorling had picked a tiny, vulnerable kingdom who could not fight back. He had done it deliberately. He had married their daughters, knowing that he could torment them at a whim, and they would have to take whatever he gave, to keep their people safe.

. . . Oh.

"Don't do anything foolish," said the queen. "Don't talk to anyone about this. If word gets back to the prince, it will go badly for your sister." She set her embroidery aside. "I don't talk about it, either, for the same reason."

"Will she be all right?" asked Marra. She knew that the answer was no, but she wanted the queen to comfort her, to tell her that everything would come out for the best, the way that she had when Marra was very young.

"She's managed this long," said the queen. "She is riding a dragon, and all of us in the kingdom are riding along with her."

Chapter 6

Marra had spent fifteen years in the convent all told. Half her life, barring a few months. She could embroider and sew and knit, and she knew, perhaps, a little more of politics than an ordinary nun might. But she could do nothing to save her sister.

She had thought that returning to the familiar routine of the convent would soothe her, but it did not. Days after her return from the Northern Kingdom, Marra still could not settle. She went back and forth, her fingers itching with inactivity, unable to bear the stillness of the convent. What could she do? She had to help Kania, but she could not, but she had to but she could not but . . .

"Are you in love or pregnant?" asked the Sister Apothecary.

"Neither," said Marra, somewhat horrified.

"Don't look so appalled. You're as jittery as a grasshopper, and those are the two ailments I know of that start that way."

"No," said Marra. She trusted the Sister Apothecary a great deal, but she remembered what the queen had said about word getting back to the prince . . . "No. I'm worried about my sister. She's . . . she's had a lot of pregnancies. Very quickly. And she lost a few and . . . you know."

"I know," said the Sister Apothecary heavily. "I see it all the time. 'One child, one tooth,' as the peasant women say, and half these poor women have no teeth left to spare. They wear themselves out bearing. But your sister is a princess, and princesses get better care than the rest of us. She is in good hands."

It's the prince's hands I worry about. Pinching and grabbing and bruising . . . She remembered the line of violet fingerprints on Kania's wrist.

"I have to do something," she muttered, pacing back and forth, worrying at her own wrists with her fingers.

"It's not yours to fix," said the Sister Apothecary. "You think I wouldn't stop women from catching pregnant until they die? But you don't get that choice. You can't go around kicking their husbands out of bed. I can mix up bushels of special tea, but I can't force them to drink it."

Marra stared down at her hands. "I have to do something," she said.

"Good luck," said the Sister Apothecary, saluting her with a glass of cordial. "If you find a way, let me know."

* * *

Days stretched into weeks, while Marra fretted and dug her nails into her skin. The abbess was worried, but the Sister Apothecary mixed up a salve for her scratches and simply said, "You're kicking against the world, that's all."

This was true, so far as it went, but Marra resented it. It was the sort of thing you were supposed to get out of the way when you were sixteen, not thirty. *I have always been slow for my age, but this is too much.*

Weeks became a month, then another month, then another, while Marra did nothing but pace and worry and feel increasingly useless. *I should do something. I should be able to do something. I should be able to fix this somehow.*

She could not think of a way. It was a job for heroes, perhaps, and Marra did not know how to be a hero. She lay awake at night, chasing phantoms behind her eyes, reliving the moments in the chapel over and over, the moments with her mother over and over. She made dramatic plans in the darkness and discarded them in daylight. She would go and ask for an audience with Vorling and stab him. (No, the guards would stop her.) She would attempt to seduce Vorling on condition of the guards being sent away and *then* stab him. (She was nearly a nun—what did she know of seduction?) She would take plants from the Sister Apothecary's store and poison

him. (How would she even get close to his food?) She would . . . she
would . . .

Apparently she would do nothing. Every course of action ended
with Marra dead and her sister or her kingdom destroyed. The plans
played out in her head night after night, all of them useless.

Worthless plans. Worthless Marra. What good am I to anyone?

It occurred to her that Kania's pregnancy was well advanced by
now. *If she's showing, maybe she's safe. She said he leaves her alone when
she's pregnant. Mostly.* She thought of her sister's clothes, the way
that she had seemed to be showing so very early. It did happen that
way, sometimes, but Kania was no fool, and perhaps her dressmak-
ers had cut her clothing so that her pregnancy was obvious.

Assuming she hasn't lost this one, too.

But it was not the baby that she lost next. Instead the word came
down, not from letters but from gossip, that the king had died and
Prince Vorling was now King Vorling of the North.

Is this better?

Is this worse?

Are more people watching him?

But he is the king and no one can stop him now.

She had no answers. She did not know whether this was good or
bad or terrible, whether Kania had been thrown a lifeline or given
a death sentence. She could not even get her mind around it. *King
Vorling* made no sense. He was still *Prince Vorling* in her head. She
remembered that flash of rage when Kania had asked to hold a vigil
for her daughter. How could a man like that be a king and hold a
whole kingdom at his fingertips?

She took to weeding the garden with savage intensity, ripping out
dock and plantain and rabbit tobacco, her teeth grinding in her jaw.

If I were a man, I would fight him.

*If she were a man, no one would force Kania to try to bear child after
child. If I were a man, I would not be the next in line to be married if
he kills her. If we were men . . .* She stared at her fingers curled in the
dirt. It did not matter. They were not and the history of the world

was written in women's wombs and women's blood and she would never be allowed to change it.

Rage shivered through her, a rage that seemed like it could topple the halls of heaven, then vanished under the knowledge of her own helplessness. Rage was only useful if you were allowed to do anything with it.

She was still staring at her hands when she heard two of the lay sisters talking. "I don't know what to do," said one. "I'm out of ideas."

"Go to the dust-wife," advised the other. "She knows things."

"What sort of things?"

"You know. Magic."

Marra looked up sharply. Too sharply as it turned out. They saw her and moved away hurriedly, lowering their voices, but the seed was planted.

The dust-wife.

In this part of the kingdom, every graveyard of any size had its dust-wife. Marra was vaguely aware of their existence, but she came from the western side of the kingdom, and there was a definite difference. On the seacoast side, churchyards buried a dog to guide and guard the dead—church grims they were called. On the eastern mountain side, there were dust-wives. (In one or two places in the middle, there was both a dust-wife and a church grim. "They're no trouble," said one dust-wife of the grim, "and it's good to have a dog about the place.")

Dust-wives lived in little houses by the cemeteries. They operated as combination witches and gravediggers, digging the holes and laying out the dead. Even when a dust-wife got too old and frail to dig the graves herself, she would totter out with a spade and move the first spadeful of earth before hired hands did the rest. Otherwise, there was a chance that the dead might think the diggers were graverobbers, and their curses would be upon them, if not for the dust-wife's blessing.

It was said that the dust-wives could speak the language of the dead and that they knew all the secrets that lay beneath the earth. When a dust-wife died, she was cremated and her ashes were spread across her graveyard, so that each dust-wife who came after might keep the wisdom of her predecessors near at hand.

Marra pulled her cloak's hood up over her hair and went out to find the dust-wife. The convent had its own tiny cemetery, but those souls belonged to Our Lady of Grackles. She had to go into the town to the big church, consecrated to Our Lady of the Harvest, to the graveyard there.

The dust-wife was working outside, tending the graves. She was a fat, sturdy woman with a pink face. "Good afternoon," she said, smiling. "Can I help you, lass?"

"I need a spell," blurted Marra, then stood there, unsure if she had committed some dreadful social error. Were you supposed to make small talk with a dust-wife? Beg? Offer money? "I'm sorry. I don't . . ." She put her hands to her cheeks. They felt hot.

The dust-wife pushed herself to her feet and patted her hand gently. "Let's start at the beginning. My name's Elspeth. What's yours?"

"Marra," said Marra, before it occurred to her to lie.

"Good, solid name. Like our princess. Come sit down and tell me what's wrong."

Marra took a deep breath. Her mother's warning hung heavy in her mind. How much could she say? "My sister is married," she said, sitting down on the wall beside the dust-wife. "He's . . . he's not good. She stays pregnant so he won't beat her. But it's hard on her. She loses them sometimes, and then it's worse. I can't . . . I have to help her. But he's . . . um. Not going to let her go." She stared at her hands.

"Poor girl. That's hard. Does he have the rank to get away with it?"

Bursting into hysterical laughter would not help anyone, so Marra simply said, "Yes."

Elspeth leaned back, face grave. "What would you have me do, child? It does not sound like barrenness will help her. I could give you a charm to make childbearing easier, but I tell you true, it's little enough and it cannot save a babe that does not wish to come into the world."

Marra closed her eyes and thought about treason and regicide and whispered, "Can you give me a spell that kills him?"

The dust-wife was silent for a long time. Marra opened her eyes, expecting to see horror, but Elspeth's eyes were full of sorrow and understanding. "No," she said. "If I could, I might, though I'm not an executioner and I'd need to know more before I bloody my hands. But the sort of magic you're asking for is far beyond me. That's real power, not charms and knowing and listening to the dead." She looked away, apparently measuring her words carefully, then said, "If you go to the capital, there is a woman, I am told, who knows much of poison."

Marra shook her head. The prince employed a food taster, of course, but she could not very well explain that. "If he was poisoned, they would think of her immediately," she said instead.

Elspeth reached out and took her hand. Marra thought for a moment that the woman was offering her comfort, but the grip was too tight. She looked up, startled, and the dust-wife's eyes had gone strange and slack, the pupils huge, the irises nearly gone.

The eyes of the dead, Marra thought, and then, *Damia's eyes must have looked like this.*

Then Elspeth blinked and her eyes were normal again. She dropped Marra's hand and rubbed at her face. "Well," she said, almost to herself. "*Well* then. So that's how it is."

"I'm sorry?" said Marra.

"The dead could help you," said Elspeth. "But you need a real dust-wife, one married to clay and bone and grave dirt, not an old herb witch good at digging holes." She squinted and winced, as if the brightness of the day pained her. Marra watched a tear leak from the corner of her eye and run down her cheek.

"Where do I find someone like that?" asked Marra.

"South," said Elspeth. "South and east. Not here. Go around the south side of the mountains. The dry plains, you know?"

Marra nodded. Her father had taken the princesses there once, part of a royal procession, the whole land bone-dry, stone-dry, kicking up vast clouds of white dust as they traveled. "I know it."

"There's a great necropolis there, but you don't want that. Stop before you get there. The mountainside and the carved caves, the abandoned dwelling and the skulls of bulls. There. There's a dust-wife who's worth the name. The dead would crawl on their knees to give her their secrets."

Marra nodded again. "Thank you," she said, sliding off the wall.

"Don't thank me," said Elspeth. "Come back to tell me, after it's over."

Thinking of the long journey southeast, Marra shook her head. "I may not live to do it," she admitted.

"I know," said the dust-wife gently. "But I'll still be able to hear you."

* * *

It was a long road. The only person she told was the Sister Apothecary, who looked at her with steady eyes and then handed her a purse full of coins and a bag full of tea leaves. "Magic," she said. "Magic is beyond my skills. Come back as you can, and if you can't, I hope fate is kind to you."

Marra no longer had much faith in fate. She had been born a princess, which should have been lucky, but the price for never going hungry was to be caught in a struggle between people too powerful to call to justice.

She also rather wished that the Sister Apothecary would tell her not to go, because then she would have something to push back against. She was used to being stubborn, but having people agree with her was off-putting and didn't give her much to work with.

With the Sister Apothecary covering her absence, she pulled up her cloak and went into town again. The dust-wife directed her to a shepherd taking fleeces to market in Low Bandai to the south, and Marra rode with him clear to the city. The shepherd seemed to like company but did not talk a great deal, and that suited Marra, who had little to say that wasn't *Oh god oh god what am I doing oh god . . .*

From Low Bandai, there were coaches that traveled in all directions. She parted ways with the shepherd and took one southeast as far as it went, then another. She hoarded her coins for food and slept either in the coach or on benches while waiting for coaches. She was tired and snarly and often the hood of her cloak was to cover the wreckage of her hair, but her stock of coins did not go down as quickly as they would have if she demanded rooms at an inn.

No one would have mistaken her for a princess.

It was frightening the first time she had to go and request a seat on a coach. She had never done it, and she was afraid that she would say something so foolish that the driver would laugh at her and refuse her a seat. But she screwed up her courage and said, "I need to go to Essemque," and the driver named a price. She handed up a coin and he nodded and told her that the coach left in twenty minutes and to be on board.

The next time was easier, and the next after that. She got used to the coaches and she learned that being crammed inside was a recipe for rattle-bone nausea, but it was the cheapest way. She was not certain where this sudden frugality had come from, but something in the back of her mind whispered that there was no help coming and if she ran out of money, she had no real way to earn more. Her only skills were embroidery and weeding gardens. *I suppose I could sell my body, but I'm not sure how one does that, either.* It seemed like it would be a lot more complicated than getting a seat on a coach. Did you approach people, or did they approach you, and how did you start a conversation that ended in money for sex? Was there an etiquette?

This was not the sort of thing one was taught at convents. It was easier just to sleep in the coaches.

Sleep by bone-jarring sleep, she made her way south and east around the tail of the mountains. It occurred to her that the abbess had probably had to tell the queen that she was missing. Had she run away? Could you really run away when you were thirty years old?

She was lucky, as such things went. No one bothered her—much. Only once did a man try to engage her in conversation that proved dangerous.

"Where are you going?" he asked her, sitting opposite inside the coach. He had all his teeth and she could see each one in his smile.

"South," she said.

"Which city?"

Marra shrugged. "South," she said again, trying to hide the way her pulse jumped. Had he recognized her? Why was he asking?

He asked her name and she looked at him in silence. He asked more questions—where she was going and did she have family there—and when she did not answer him, his tone turned ugly. He spit an insult at her, heedless of the other passengers listening.

It was a middle-aged woman who saved her, leaning over and snapping her fingers in front of the man's face. "You rude young fool," she growled. "Can't you see she's a nun? Why are you taking your temper out on a nun on pilgrimage?"

The man was in the middle of cursing the woman when her words sank in. He stopped in midobscenity, the consonants getting lost on his tongue, and stared at Marra in her travel-stained robes as if seeing her for the first time. "A nun?" he said.

Marra seized the opening. "I serve Our Lady of Grackles," she said to the woman. It was not as much of a lie as it might have been. "Thank you." *Lady, forgive me.*

The man mumbled something, flushing, and did not bother her any longer. He left at the next stop. The middle-aged woman sat with Marra until the next coach came, though, her eyes weak and watery and sharp as flint behind the weakness. "Tell them you're a nun right away," she advised. "There's many a man who'll not think twice to mistreat a woman but who lives in fear of a habit and a holy symbol. Might save you some trouble along the way."

Marra nodded. After that she tried to walk like the abbess, to fold her hands into her sleeves as the sisters did. She had a carved grackle-feather necklace that her mother had sent her, which she had thought to sell, but she wore it on the outside of her clothing instead. It looked enough like a clerical medal to buy her a little more space on the coaches, a little more distance around her. People who would jostle Marra the woman would step aside for Marra the nun.

And Marra the princess? she thought, bemused. *Would they stand aside for her?*

The issue would never arise, of course. A princess did not ride on common coaches. She did not sit on the benches of common coach yards, or fall asleep with her head against the wall. The princess she had been was dead now, as dead as Damia in her grave, as dead as the children that Kania tried and failed to bear.

* * *

At the last town before the great necropolis, she made her way to the churchyard, where she found the local dust-wife, a woman so old that she could barely hold the spade to turn the earth.

"I am looking for the dust-wife," Marra said. "The . . . the powerful one."

"Ah," said the old woman. "I know who you mean. Walk out of town toward the rising sun until you see two walls, a little higher than a man's head. There's a gap between them, and lots of loose stones. Walk across them, and you'll see a flat place full of graves, and a little stone ridge. Her house is built into the ridge."

"Thank you," said Marra.

"Be careful," said the old woman. The dead looked out through her eyes, and Marra wondered who exactly was issuing the warning. "Be polite. She's not like a devil—she won't try to trap you in words—but she knows too many things."

It was on Marra's tongue to ask how you could ever know too many things, but then she thought of all the things she had learned about Prince Vorling and Damia's death. She bowed to the dust-wife, as a princess never bowed to anyone, and the dust-wife sighed and watched her trudge away to the east.

* * *

The walls were not so high as a man any longer. Perhaps they had been taller in the old woman's youth, or perhaps memory had increased them. Marra walked between two shoulder-high walls and looked across hundreds of loose, flat stones, each the size of her hand, with writing in some language she did not know.

Set within the sea of stones were little oval buildings, like beehives without openings. Marra knew at once that they were graves. You saw such markers sometimes, even in the north, usually where a family had their own plot.

The flat stones made for uneven footing. She set her feet carefully. If she had to run, she would risk breaking an ankle or worse. They rattled and slid underfoot, talking to each other in stone language, saying all the words they had been saving up until the next time a human walked across them.

Marra was watching her feet and so not looking up much, when she heard a sound that surprised her, not for its strangeness but for its familiarity. It was not a sound she expected, here in a strange, stony plain on the edge of ancient graves. She looked up.

Bok, said the chicken again, turning its head to look at her more closely.

Marra let out a gasp of laughter. There was a stony rise and a round house built into the side of it. In the yard in front of the house, a small flock of chickens scratched and wallowed in the dust. As she watched, one hen leaned over and pecked one of her fellows, who squawked and ran off into the stones.

The house was very like the beehive graves in construction, layers of stacked flat stones but with a dark, yawning mouth. It would have been alarming if the chickens weren't out in front of it, being so relentlessly chicken-like. It was hard to be frightened of the unknown when the unknown kept chickens.

"Yes, yes," she heard someone say inside. The voice was not thin or querulous, and yet something about it suggested great age. "Yes, I hear you. We've a visitor, I suppose."

Marra froze, unsure whether she should approach the house or knock or call out. One of the hens decided that a human standing still was an extreme threat to chickens everywhere and ran away, cackling in alarm.

"Well, come on," said the voice. "I'm not getting any younger." And then, almost as an afterthought, "Mind the brown hen. There's a demon in her."

Marra looked around but saw no brown hens in the immediate vicinity. She took a deep breath, squared her shoulders, and stepped forward to meet her destiny and win the tools to kill a prince.

Chapter 7

The first task was the easiest one, in a way. "It's straightforward, anyway," said the dust-wife. "This is owlcloth." She ran her hand down the fabric. It did not shimmer or shine in the light, but there was something about it that confused the eye. There were a half dozen ragged pieces laid out across the flat roof of the dust-wife's home. "Make a cloak of it. You must spin the thread yourself." She gestured to a wooden drop spindle and a distaff and a coarse mass of something only slightly more substantial than smoke. "With that."

Marra frowned. It seemed too easy and she was suspicious of things that seemed easy. She had spun thread before—everyone in the convent spun on drop spindles all the time while talking or sitting or even praying. It was the only way to keep the weavers supplied with thread. You needed six sisters with spindles for even one sister weaving.

She reached out and touched the smoky mass and snatched her finger back at once. It smarted as if she'd been stung. She stuck it in her mouth to cool it.

"Nettle wool." The dust-wife did not look smug, which was the only thing that made it bearable. "You must spin it into thread to sew the owlcloth together. It will hurt you if it can."

"They used to make cloth of nettle thread," said Marra. "It can't have been like this."

"Oh, no. You let the stems stand in the field for a few months and it acts like anything else. This is the wool of a ram who was trapped in brambles for a hundred years, while the thorns grew into his blood and his eyes." The dust-wife nudged the wool with her boot.

"Is that true?" asked Marra skeptically.

"Probably not. But it's evil, enchanted stuff, nonetheless." She straightened. "You have from dawn to dusk and back again. There's water in the jug." She swung herself down on the ladder and left Marra alone on the roof with the wool that could not be spun.

* * *

She did it in the end, of course. She had the same bitter feeling as when she had shoveled the stable—*I will do this. You will not stop me.* She tried a half-dozen different ways to cover her hands, only to find the fabric too clumsy to work with or too thin to offer any protection. Finally she stared at the mass of smoke and thought, *I am doing a heroic task and heroic tasks are not done by half measures. It's only pain. Kania's pain is so much worse than mine.* And she plunged her left hand into the mass of smoke and nettles and began to spin.

It burned and stung and blazed against her flesh. She hissed and cursed and bent over her hand. *No. Keep going. You can't stop once you've started.* She thought of every birth she had ever seen. Those women had been in far worse pain and they had done it, because once you started, you couldn't stop. She would do this. *Left hand only. I will need the right to thread the cord.* She could protect her right hand with fabric for this bit but she needed her left to pull the wool onto the distaff and there was no protecting it.

She was clumsy with her left hand, but it did not have to be done well, only done. Her fingertips turned angry red and her knuckles began to swell, but that did not matter. She only had to keep her fingers in position and let the angry smoke flow through them. The sun crawled overhead. The web of skin between thumb and forefinger hurt and hurt until it stopped being pain and became something else entirely.

It was hard to keep the drop spindle going slowly enough. She wanted to rush through it. But a faster spin meant finer thread and she wanted coarse, heavy stuff to hold her cloak, so that she need not use so much of it. She bit the inside of her cheek bloody and stared at her clawlike left hand and wondered if she'd ever do anything much with it again.

At last she had enough. Probably. The nettle wool was nearly gone, leaving only a great sharp thorn as long as a sheep's foreleg, with a point that could have pierced a man's heart. She dropped the spindle and clutched her ruined hand to her chest. It was red and violet and the joints were swollen thick. When Marra tried to open her fingers, she could feel the tendons grating against bones and could not contain her scream.

She looked up. The sun was on the far horizon and the shadows were turning blue. She drank water, holding the jug with her right hand. She tried to pour a little over her left. It didn't do anything. She cried a little, and that didn't do anything, either.

Marra had saved her right hand for the delicate work. She took a deep breath and then worked the thread loose from the spindle while her flesh blazed as if it had caught fire. The thread came off lumpy and ugly and uneven, but there was nothing to be done. She had no more nettle wool to spin anyway. She wished that she could ply it, but she did not have enough time and she did not know how much more pain she could endure.

There was no needle. She stared at the owlcloth scraps and the thread in her hand and could not believe that she had missed that. *There's always a needle,* she thought wearily. *I am an embroiderer; I always have a needle.* She started laughing softly to herself, the broken laughter of a mortal wound. All her needles were in her room at the convent, carefully jabbed into a pincushion shaped like a little white rat. It had been a gift from the Sister Apothecary.

She looked over the rooftop, looking for a shape she had missed, the wink of bone or metal in the moonlight. When had the moon come up? Had it been that long already?

Marra did not find a needle. Instead she saw the dull gleam of light on the bitter thorn at the heart of the nettle wool.

She picked it up in her swollen fingers and looked at the point. It was sharp enough to serve as an awl. She would have to push the thread through with her fingers and then grab it on the other side and pull it through and it would burn and burn and her fingers would stop working and then, Lady of Grackles help her, perhaps she would have to use her teeth.

Did you think impossible tasks were so easily done?

She looked at her sad, misshapen pile of thread and the soft, shifting owlcloth, and she cried a little more, and then she bent her head over the fabric and set to work.

* * *

"God's balls," said the dust-wife a week later, looking at the bone dog. "You did it." She did not sound happy about it. She hadn't sounded happy about the cloak of nettles, either, when Marra had come down with her ruined hands and her swollen lips and dropped the owlcloth garment at her feet.

"I did," said Marra. "Where do I begin the next task? Moonlight in a jar of clay?"

The dust-wife groaned. She got up without answering and went to rummage in her pantry. Eventually she found a pile of chicken bones and tossed them to the bone dog.

Marra had a vague notion that chicken bones were bad for dogs, but she also wasn't sure that there was anything in the bone dog to be injured. He lay down happily and began to gnaw. Bits of splintered bone rained out of his neck as he swallowed.

The dust-wife pulled out a chair at the table and slumped into it. She was tall and bony and stoop shouldered where Marra was short and round. "Do you know why you set someone an impossible task?" she asked.

Marra scowled. This was the sort of question that she hated, the kind that made her think that the other person was trying to be clever at her expense. But the dust-wife had dealt fairly with her, so she tried to think of an answer. "To see if they can do it?" She racked her brain, thinking of all the old legends: Mordecai and the worm; the white deer who loved a human and her terrible quest to save her lover; Little Mouse who killed the dragon on her wedding day. "To see if they are heroes?"

"Heroes," said the dust-wife with an explosive snort. "The gods save us all from heroes." She gazed at Marra, her normally expressionless face lined with sorrow. "But perhaps that's the fate in store for you after all. No, child, you give someone an impossible task *so that they won't be able to do it.*"

Marra examined this statement carefully from all directions. "But I did it," she said. "Twice."

"I had noticed," said the dust-wife grimly. "And quite likely you will do the third task and then I will be obligated to help you kill your prince."

"He isn't *my* prince," said Marra acidly.

"If you plan to kill him, he is. Your victim. Your prince. All the same. You sink a knife in someone's guts, you're bound to them in that moment. Watch a murderer go through the world and you'll see all his victims trailing behind him on black cords, shades of ghosts waiting for their chance." She drummed her nails on the table. "You sure you want that?"

"He killed Damia," said Marra. "He's torturing Kania. He deserves to die."

The dust-wife said nothing. For a little time, the only sound was the crunch of bones and the patter of splinters on the floor.

"Lots of people deserve to die," said the dust-wife finally. "Not everybody deserves to be a killer." She sighed heavily. "I can't change your mind, can I?"

"No."

"Right." The dust-wife scooted her chair back, reached up one long arm, and hooked a jar from the shelf. "Here," she said, passing it to Marra. "Open it."

The jar was heavy earthenware, squat, completely unremarkable. Marra opened the lid cautiously. Moonlight bathed her face, a streaming blue-white radiance.

"Close it again," ordered the dust-wife. "There. The moon in a jar of clay. Give it back to me, please."

Marra, by now thoroughly bewildered, closed it and passed it back to the dust-wife. Her eyes felt dazzled by the moon that had shown at midday inside the house.

"There," said the dust-wife. "You have given me moonlight in a jar of clay. Well done. That's the third task."

"But . . ." Marra stared at her and the little clay jar with the moonlight inside. "But I didn't earn it. I didn't do anything."

"It was an impossible task," said the dust-wife. "The other two should have been impossible, but here you are with a bone dog and a cloak made of owlcloth and nettles. Catching the moon would have broken you, though. That's not a task for mortals who want to keep their hearts."

"But . . ."

"I didn't want to do this," said the dust-wife. "That's why I gave you the impossible tasks, so you'd fail and go away and not ask any more. I don't like travel and I don't like going places and I'm going to have to find someone to watch the chickens. And also this is a fool's errand and we'll probably all die."

"But . . . ?" A hope began to bloom in Marra's heart. She fought it down, telling herself that she must be mistaken.

The dust-wife shook her head. "You want a weapon against a prince. Well, I haven't got a magic sword or an enchanted arrow or anything nicely portable." She leaned back in her chair. "So. Your weapon against the prince. That's me."

* * *

Setting out from the dust-wife's home took longer than Marra liked. "Three days," said the dust-wife. "I've got things to pack and things to settle." In the yard, the brown hen stared down the bone dog, apparently unfazed by his lack of eyes.

"Kania could be dead in three days," said Marra.

"Then she will die," said the dust-wife implacably. "Because it will take us weeks to walk to the capital of the Northern Kingdom, particularly given the stops we must make along the way."

Marra took a deep breath and schooled herself to patience. Even a princess learned patience in a convent, and what the nuns had not taught her, she had learned from knitting and weaving. Haste led to dropped threads and mangled socks. They could not afford haste with Kania's life.

Besides, she thought bleakly, *you have waited many years already. If you had noticed her bruises five years earlier, or ten, it would all be done already.* The bone dog, tired of being stalked by a chicken, flopped down on his side in the yard. It was impossible to tell when he was sleeping, but there was a sense of relaxation in the slow up-and-down movement of his rib cage.

"What's his name?" asked the dust-wife.

Marra blinked at her. "Who?"

"The dog, child! Dogs have human names. It's what keeps them from being wolves."

"Uh . . . uh . . . Bonedog?"

"Are you asking me or telling me?"

"His name is Bonedog," said Marra more firmly. In the yard, Bonedog rolled over and wiggled his backbone in the dust.

"Imagination is not your strong suit, is it?" asked the dust-wife. A smile cracked the planes of her face. "That's not an insult, child— don't look so surly. For this sort of work, you want feet on the ground, not castles in the air."

The brown hen came around the side of the house, saw Bonedog, and advanced like a general leading a host. She pecked Bonedog's tail and was rewarded with a ghostly yelp. Bonedog rolled to his feet, puzzled, and the hen ran off cackling in triumph.

The dust-wife took out a cloak made of bottles and pockets and tabs, like a walking cupboard, and spun it around her shoulders. Marra was surprised that she didn't rattle when she walked. Then she took it off again and began filling the pockets and bottles from the jars on the wall, decanting drops of liquid and placing odd packets. Marra watched her pack up feathers and mouse skulls and bits of lint and finally said, "What is the good of all that?"

Hummingbird feathers gleamed as the dust wife slipped a tiny bird skin into her pocket. "No idea," she said. "Most of it probably won't do us any good at all. But I agreed to help and that means you get the best I can do." She licked her fingers and placed three small black beads into a wax paper envelope, then paused. "Show me your hands."

"Eh?"

"Your hands. You're favoring them."

Marra held out her hands. The joints were stiff and the red puffiness where she had gouged herself with wires had gotten worse.

"Saints and devils," said the dust-wife. "Open wounds in the blistered land. Hold still." She got down a jar from the shelf.

"Is it bad?" asked Marra.

"It would probably kill you in a week or so," said the dust-wife, bending over her hands. "You'd get a taste for human flesh first, though, which would be exciting for everyone . . . Oh, don't look so stricken." She unstoppered the jar. Marra smelled honey, but the liquid that the dust-wife dabbed onto her wounds was red as fire.

"What is it?"

"Rust honey. Made by clockwork bees." The dust-wife rubbed it into the joints of Marra's fingers, muttering words that Marra couldn't quite make out. Eventually she sat back. "That should do it. Tell me if you get the urge to take a bite out of someone, though."

"There's a long list of people I'd like to bite," said Marra, a bit dryly.

The dust-wife snorted. "Fair enough. Just tell me if you get the urge to chew afterward, then."

Marra cradled her hands together, flexing her fingers. Already her knuckles seemed less stiff. She wondered if the words that the dust-wife had said had been magic, or if it was all the work of the honey.

She drifted to sleep in the corner, still wondering, soothed by the sound of the dust-wife moving around the room, the jars rattling, as the old woman packed away bits of magic inside the folds of her coat.

* * *

The brown hen rode on top of the dust-wife's staff, on the bone crosspiece. Her body moved as the staff moved, but her head stayed level in that peculiar way of chickens. Marra was first incredulous, then amused.

"You're bringing the hen?"

"She's got a demon in her," said the dust-wife. "It'd be rude to leave her for the neighbors to deal with."

The hen rode until midmorning, whereupon she would stretch, walk down the dust-wife's outstretched arm, and climb into her pack. The top flap was left open for just this reason. The hen would sit there for about a quarter of an hour, give a single pleased cluck, and then saunter back down the arm and onto the staff again. The dust-wife would pause, retrieve a single large brown egg from her pack, and tuck it into a safe pocket. In the morning, she would cook the egg, divide it in exact halves, and share it with Marra.

Half an egg did not make a terribly satisfying breakfast, but it was a great deal better than nothing. Sometimes Bonedog would flush a rabbit and kill it and they would stop and roast the rabbit. Sometimes a farmer would sell them eggs or a loaf of bread, although the dust-wife had to go alone to ask, because if the farmer saw Bonedog, there would be questions.

For the same reason, they could not take coaches, or even beg rides on farm wagons. They could not ask to sleep in barns where it might be warmer. There was no way to disguise Bonedog. Their progress back to the northwest slowed to a crawl.

"This won't do," said the dust-wife, the third or fourth day. "Your sister will have died of old age before we reach her, and I'll be so bent over from sleeping on the ground that I'll be cursing your prince's kneecaps."

"What do we do?" asked Marra. They had put a collar on Bonedog, although it was more like a knot with a loop tied around his neck bones. She slid a hand through the loop protectively. She could not leave him. She'd brought him back to life and that felt like a bargain to her, even stronger than the bargain that humans made with living dogs who loved them.

But I cannot let Kania down, either.

"No need to look so downcast," said the dust-wife. "The moon is full and the goblin market's still in season."

"Eh?"

"The goblin market," repeated the dust-wife. "Lords of Earth! What do they teach you in a convent, anyway?"

"Not much about goblins," said Marra. "I could tell you a great deal about knitting bandages and drying herbs and the feast days of lesser saints."

"Well," muttered the dust-wife, in the tone of one determined to be fair. "That's not completely useless, anyway. Whose feast is it today, then?"

Marra had to stop and work out the date. "Saint Ebbe," she said finally. "Patron of boar hunters."

"Hmm. Well, boar are cunning and fierce and hard to kill, much like your prince, though I respect the boars rather more. We could do worse than to offer prayers to such."

Marra bowed her head dutifully and offered a prayer. So little was known of Saint Ebbe that there was no specific form, so she used the standard invocation that could be applied to any saint—"Saint Ebbe, watch over us. Saint Ebbe, protect us and keep us from harm. Saint Ebbe, intercede for us . . ."

She was surprised when the dust-wife joined in on the final "May it be so." The old woman had not struck her as religious.

But I could easily imagine someone making a saint out of her, a hundred years hence. Maybe some of the saints were like that, too—cranky, old women with strange gifts. She remembered the one icon she had seen of Saint Ebbe, a gray-haired woman with her foot on a boar's snout, holding it pinned. Both she and the boar had been grinning. She'd thought at the time that perhaps the icon painter hadn't been very good. *But if I were going to paint the dust-wife as a saint, she'd have a brown hen with her, and that hen grins—I am nearly certain of it.*

She realized that she had gotten distracted. "The goblin market?"

"What it sounds like," said the dust-wife. "The marketplace of the goblins and the fair folk, and whatever humans go wiggling and wandering in. Curses and treasures in equal measure. And ordinary things as well, of course."

"The fair folk?" Marra licked her lips. "Is it dangerous?"

"Deeply," said the dust-wife. "But everywhere's dangerous if you're foolish about it. The goblin market has rules, and if you obey the rules, it's no worse than anywhere else." She considered for a moment. "At least if you're there outside the dark of the moon. The rules change in the dark, and sometimes they change minute to minute. Full and waxing are more forgiving. We'll go tonight."

"Where is it?"

"Doesn't matter." The dust-wife's mouth crooked up at the corner. "If we can find a stream, it's easier to get there. If not, we'll go by fire."

Marra had to be content with that, because no further information was forthcoming. She added the goblin market to things that she had to worry about, and felt anxiety gnawing inside her rib cage.

In the end, it was frightening but not difficult. There was a broad, shallow stream washing across the stones a few miles away. They walked along it in the growing dusk and eventually came to a shallow ford, full of round gray pebbles that glinted black where the water rushed over them.

"Hmm," said the dust-wife, sounding distracted. "Hmm . . ." She held out a hand to stop Marra moving. "Yes. There's one here. There usually is at a ford."

Bonedog, bored, sat down and began trying to lick his nether regions. Since he had neither tongue nor anything to lick, this accomplished nothing but seemed to please him.

The dust-wife drew a line in the pebbles with the tip of her staff, while her hen, half-asleep, muttered in annoyance. "Don't talk to it," she said.

"Talk to what?" said Marra, and then the dust-wife called up the dead.

Chapter 8

Marra's first indication was that the crickets fell silent. In the distance, a bird sang *oh-die-will, oh-die-will*, and as the crickets stopped, it sang more loudly. The river's hiss and roil seemed to slow, and then, very distantly, Marra heard splashing as something approached.

"There's something coming," she said. Bonedog quivered with alertness.

"Hush," said the dust-wife. "The drowned ones are tricky."

Marra closed her mouth on whatever she was about to say, but something else answered the dust-wife, a burbling liquid sound that might have been a laugh or a sob.

A shape was coming upstream. The moon was just high enough to throw cold, glittery light over it. At first Marra thought of beavers, otters, swimming creatures, but no otter had ever been so large, nor had a face like that.

The dead boy swam upstream, quick as a fish, and rose to his feet. Water streamed from his mouth and his empty eye sockets. His skin had swollen and split his clothes, a pale, bloated thing with flesh puffing out between strands of waterweed.

I will not be sick, thought Marra. *I will not. There is no blood. It is not as bad as that time the farmhand broke his leg and the bones stuck out. It isn't.*

Whatever the dust-wife said, Marra missed it. She was only vaguely aware of the other woman speaking at all. Then the dead boy replied, a hard gurgling as if wires were piercing his drowned throat, and Marra stopped hoping not to be sick and began hoping that she wouldn't faint instead.

"Good," said the dust-wife. "Which way?"

The drowned boy lifted his arm. His fingers had swollen together into a white mitten. He pointed upstream and gargled an answer.

The dust-wife nodded. "Do you wish ending?" she asked as brusquely as if she were negotiating with a farmer for a loaf of bread.

Another gargle. His face turned toward Marra and she knew that she should feel pity, not horror, but there was something strange and leering about the way he moved, as if he knew that she was frightened and delighted in it. He made a beckoning gesture with his swollen hand and then gulped with laughter when she shrank back.

"Enough of that," said the dust-wife. "She's not for drowning."

More laughter. He took a step forward, the water hilling up around his legs as if it were sand, then another.

The brown hen made a low, hostile noise. The boy froze, looking up. For a long moment he stared eyelessly at the bird; then he lowered his head.

"Cock's crow and demon's heart," said the dust-wife. "Don't test me, boy."

He gurgled sullenly but retreated.

She reached into a pocket and pulled something out. Marra couldn't make out the shape in the dimness. She tossed it over the stream and the drowned boy caught it with his bloated white hands.

"Go on, then," said the dust-wife, flicking her fingers dismissively. "Back to the water, and mind you don't pull down a traveler unless they break the covenants."

The drowned boy hunched his shoulders and turned away. The moon dripped light over him as he walked down the riverbed, sinking deeper with each step, until he dove like an otter and was gone.

"Bleah," said the dust-wife. "The ones who die by water go bad as often as not. Something about the water turns them dark. Give me bones in the ground any day."

Marra held her hand over her mouth and concentrated on breathing until her stomach stopped lurching. "Why did you summon that?" she asked finally. *What kind of monster is walking with me? What am I about to unleash? She's not just an old woman with a chicken . . .*

You knew that already, she answered herself. *You knew that, which is why you came to her. You want to kill a prince. Don't get squeamish now.*

"Directions," said the dust-wife. "Which he gave, although he would have liked to pull a much higher price than I was willing to pay."

"Directions?"

"Indeed. Now, follow me, and let's see what they were worth."

Apparently, they were worth a great deal, because within twenty minutes they reached a gnarled tree that overhung the bank.

"There," said the dust-wife. One of the tree roots stuck out over the water. "Earth and wood and water." She reached into a pocket and pulled out a cord with a stone tied to the bottom, then tied it to the root so that the cord fell down into the water. "Hold your breath," she said, almost as an afterthought, then ducked into the arch formed by the cord and the root and the overhung bank.

She took two steps, splashing, and passed through the arch. She came out the other side, looking just the same to Marra, and yet the sound of her footsteps in the water seemed to come from much farther away.

Bonedog cocked his leg meditatively on the tree root. Nothing happened, but it seemed to satisfy him. Marra supposed that he was already holding his breath, insomuch as he didn't breathe at all. She took a deep gulp of air and walked through the root archway.

Nothing obvious happened. It wasn't like the gluey sensation when she walked out of the blistered land. But a few steps later, her ears popped, and when she turned her head, everything seemed to move a fraction of a second slower than it should have, as if her eyes were struggling to catch up.

She scrambled up the riverbank. The dust-wife stood impatiently, tapping her staff. The brown hen grumbled.

"Does the chicken hold her breath?" asked Marra.

"She's got a demon; she doesn't have to." The dust-wife turned and began to walk back the way they had come.

Wait—that wasn't just a figure of speech?

"Do you mean that your chicken has a *literal* demon in her? Not that she's just a . . . a bad chicken?"

The words sounded incredibly foolish as she said them, and the dust-wife's look indicated that they did not improve upon hearing.

"Girl, have I given you any indication in the last week that I joke about *anything*?"

"How did you get a *demon* in your chicken?"

"The usual way. Couldn't put it in the rooster. That's how you get basilisks."

Marra opened her mouth to ask what the usual way was, then stopped because there was an enormous staircase in the ground that had most definitely not been there when they had walked by earlier.

It had broad stone steps, easily wide enough for two horses to pass abreast. Marra could not possibly have missed it. The steps ran straight down into the ground, ignoring the existence of the nearby river that should have turned them into a waterfall. The dust-wife walked down them without pausing, not even ducking her head.

It was dim for the first few steps but green light illuminated the lower stairs. Marra looked around for the source, then wished she hadn't. In alcoves on each side of the stairs, a firefly the size of a house cat blazed with light.

"Where does this go?" she whispered, hurrying to catch up with the dust-wife. The fireflies ignored her, but their antennae moved slowly in the air. "Who made this?"

"To the goblin market," said the dust-wife. "But in answer to your second question, I don't know. I'm not entirely sure it was made, in truth. Some things come into being once it's inevitable that they will exist."

Marra was still trying to parse that one when the stairs ended at a landing above a sunken room, and Marra gazed down into the goblin market.

* * *

It looked like a market, but such a market as Marra had never seen. There were jeweled pavilions crowded next to mud huts and hide tents and things that looked like upside-down bird nests. The aisles between were crowded, but the people within them did not move like a crowd. They moved like dancers, some light, some heavy, some in circling, solitary waltzes. They reminded Marra far more of the courtiers in the prince's palace than of the town on market day.

She had been a little afraid of the courtiers, and now she was more than a little afraid of the people here. The courtiers, for all their cloth and starch and politics, had been human, and some of the crowd here were obviously . . . not.

And I am here with a dog skeleton at my heels and a woman with a chicken on her staff, so what must they think of me?

"Don't stare," murmured the dust-wife, "but don't look away if someone looks at you. Show as little weakness as you can. Agree to nothing and accept nothing until you know the price."

With that, she stepped forward into the crowd, and Marra hurried after her.

The majority of the crowd had looked human from a distance, but once she was among them, she had her doubts. Some were human shaped but had green or blue skin. A number had horns rising from their foreheads, short and pointed as antelopes'. One woman walked by with a rack of antlers that would do any stag proud, and small black birds seated on each tine, wearing silver collars around their necks.

Others were not even human shaped. A trio of boars in starched collars, walking on their hind legs, went grunting past. Six white rats, each nearly three feet tall, carried a palanquin on their shoulders. And who could guess what lay beneath the pale braids that covered that figure from head to toe?

Where did they all come from? Are they from other parts of the world or are they all from here? But how could they be from here?

You heard stories, of course. Stories of the Fair Folk, of little people that lived behind the world. Stories of old gods that had never learned how to die. But Marra had never imagined that there might be so many or that they might be *right here,* on the other side of a tree root, not far away under the hills.

Even the blistered land had not prepared her for that.

"Hmm," said the dust-wife. She had stopped at a table that held a little wooden tray divided into squares. In each square lay a moth, apparently dead. "Hmm. That one." She pointed.

"Shows you what you need," said the woman behind the table, sounding bored. She was old and wrinkled, with thin gray braids coiled around her head. "You sure you don't want the one that shows you your heart's desire? It's much better."

"Also a lot more expensive, I suspect."

The woman grinned. She had no teeth. Instead her tongue was banded with red and black and had a snake's golden eyes. "Five years of your life. But you get the rest to spend with your heart's desire, so it's worth the price."

"I'll stick to needs, thank you." The dust-wife tapped the moth. It flicked its wings, startling Marra. It was white, but there were broken black lines all over, like writing.

"Ugh. Six weeks of your life."

"Six days."

"One month."

"One week."

"A fortnight, and that's my final offer. And don't blame me when it lands on a bucket because what you need is to drink more water."

"A fortnight's fair." The dust-wife beckoned Marra. "Two weeks of your life, child."

"Uh," said Marra. "What?"

"That's the price in this place, unless you've something to barter."

"What if I'm going to die in a week?"

"Doesn't work like that. It's off the time you *could* live. If you get hit by a beer wagon tomorrow, everyone still gets paid."

Marra felt a shiver crawl down her spine and fought it back. *You wouldn't give up two weeks of your life for your sister? To save her from losing all the weeks of hers?* "All right."

"Half a moment," said the snake-tongued woman. She pulled out a silver abacus and moved the beads back and forth. "There. Fortnight." The dust-wife looked over and nodded approval.

The abacus had a little dish at the bottom filled with what looked like plant stems. The woman picked one up and Marra saw that it was a caterpillar. "Hold out your hand."

Marra held her hand out worriedly. Would it hurt? What did losing two weeks of your life feel like?

The snake-tongued woman dropped the caterpillar into her palm. It unrolled itself and crawled over the side of her hand. Marra noticed, unsurprised, that her hand was trembling.

The caterpillar attached a thread of silk to her thumbnail and let itself down. It curled itself up and began a rapid wiggle, spinning silk across itself. Marra stood frozen, watching it build a cocoon far faster than any normal caterpillar she had ever seen.

In less than a minute, it was wrapped up and had turned a bright shade of green. "Ah . . . I . . . What am I supposed to do?" she whispered to the dust-wife.

"Won't be long," said the dust-wife, watching the caterpillar. Bonedog realized that Marra wasn't moving and sat on her foot, pelvis digging into her ankle.

The cocoon split open. A crumple-winged moth emerged, velvety brown in color, stretching wet wings. "There we go," said the snake-tongued woman. She caught Marra's wrist and pulled it toward her, plucking both moth and spent cocoon from her hand. The moth went into one of the little wooden boxes, and then she popped the empty cocoon into her mouth. Marra caught a glimpse of the snake tongue opening, and she turned away, feeling vaguely queasy.

"Take your moth," said the dust-wife, pointing to the white one still in the tray. Marra reached out and fumbled the white moth free. "Now, blow on it and tell it to find you what you need."

Marra had an increasing sense that she was in a dream, even more so than she had in the blistered lands. Only Bonedog's solid, uncomfortable weight convinced her that it was all really happening.

She lifted the moth level with her face. It was very fuzzy and had big black eyes. *Don't think of it like an insect. Think of it like a . . . a mouse. A mouse with feathers for ears.*

She blew across the moth's back. "Please," she whispered to the moth, "find me what I need to help my sister."

Its wings shivered. For a moment the black lines seemed to rearrange themselves, forming letters, words, sentences. Then it spread its wings and flew.

The brown hen took a snap as the moth went by but missed as the dust-wife flicked the staff aside. "Shame!" she said to the hen. The hen looked unrepentant.

"Now what?" asked Marra.

"Now follow that moth!"

* * *

They threaded their way through the goblin market, through the strange sea of people. The moth stayed fluttering a little way overhead, swooping to avoid antlers or banners or wings.

They had moved across two aisles and turned down the third when the crowd shifted around them. The people of the goblin market drew back, leaving a long avenue open between them. Conversation hushed, not in awe but in annoyance. Marra was reminded of the way that crowds moved to avoid a leper with a bell.

The woman who came down the center of the aisle moved as stately as a queen. Marra's impression was that she was very tall, and yet when the woman drew near, Marra could have met her eyes without looking up. Perhaps her apparent height was because of the light.

For she did not glow—not precisely—but she moved through a cloud of light as if it were dust. Her footsteps kicked up motes of brilliance. The light roiled around her feet and trailed behind her, refusing to settle. She carried a severed hand in her right hand. Her left wrist ended in a stump, not bloody, simply there. The motes of light seemed to gather near it, briefly forming fingers, then falling back to the ground again.

"Saint," muttered someone behind Marra in a tone of disgust.

Perhaps Marra and the dust-wife had not pulled back far enough in the crowd. Perhaps it was simply the brown hen, who refused to be intimidated by anyone, who let out a grumpy *errk* and fluffed her neck feathers. The saint turned her head.

Her face was as serene as the statues of the convent. She was not Our Lady of Grackles—Marra was almost certain of that—and yet it seemed perhaps the two might know each other. Did saints communicate? Was there some place that they all went and spoke together, putting their feet up and shaking their heads over mortal foibles?

For a moment the eyes of the saint looked into hers, as deep and wise as a good dog's eyes.

The sisters at the convent had never prepared her for what to do if you met a saint. It was not assumed that the issue would ever come up. Marra sank down to one knee, almost genuflecting, as she looked into the saint's eyes.

Did the serene lips curve up a little? Marra could not say. It took an effort to drag her gaze away. The world was dark and seemed to throb in the corners of her vision, as if she had been staring into a fire. She blinked away tears.

The dust-wife said something that Marra couldn't quite make out and pulled her to her feet as the crowd closed up behind the saint. The brown hen *errk*ed again.

"Where did the moth go?" asked Marra. She rubbed her eyes, trying to clear the dazzlement from them.

"Not sure . . . there! End of the aisle." She plunged ahead. Marra hurried after. The strangeness of the market seemed less somehow after the saint's passage, or perhaps strangeness did not quite measure up to glory.

The moth circled overhead, spun too close to a light—Marra held her breath—and then dropped down into a stall. Marra inched closer to it and saw velvet cloth laid out with dozens of small white objects. Jewels? Ivory? Shells?

Teeth.

Of course it would be teeth, her mind said, while her skin tried to crawl off her body and run away screaming. *It was never not going to be horrible. Teeth. Yes.*

The apparent owner of the stall had brilliant yellow eyes like a lizard. He lounged against one of the poles holding up the awning, watching the crowd. Ivory clicked softly on his chest from a necklace made of teeth.

I can't possibly need a tooth. Where is the moth?

The white moth had landed on the arm of a broad-shouldered man wearing the remains of a coat and tabard. There was a delicate silver collar around his neck, more like lace than metal. He was stacking boxes near the back of the stall, his face expressionless.

Marra didn't know what to do. Did she just go up to the man and say, "Excuse me, I need you"? That seemed like it could be misinterpreted in a great many ways. She tried to catch his eye, but he did not look in her direction, or at anything but his work.

The dust-wife bent over the teeth, making occasional appreciative noises. Eventually the yellow-eyed man drifted over, keeping a wary eye on the chicken. "You looking to buy, mistress?"

"Maybe. Not quite seeing what I need."

"What do you need?"

"I don't know, but I'll know it when I see it." She prodded a particularly large molar, the size of a shoe. "Hmm. Maybe."

"Cyclops. You won't find another like it."

"I will if I check in an elephant's mouth." She gave him a narrow look. "I wasn't birthed yesterday, my lad."

The yellow-eyed man grinned. "Ah, well, can't blame a man for trying."

The dust-wife's expression indicated that she could indeed blame him. She leaned back, eyes sweeping over the stall.

"The big one back there," she said, sounding bored. "Is he sound?"

"Sound enough. Fool enough to sleep in a fairy fort. I pulled him out before something worse got him."

"He available?"

"Might be. Not sure you want him." He leaned back against the pole again. "He's a killer. Had blood on his hands when I found him."

The man had stopped and was looking toward them. His eyes were too shadowed to make out their color.

"What do you want for him?"

Are . . . are they talking about buying him? No, surely not. Even here in the goblin market where all the rules were different, you shouldn't be able to buy people. Even the awful Northern Kingdom with its awful new king didn't let you buy people. That was barbarism.

"Ten years," said the yellow-eyed man.

"Not a chance. He won't last ten years."

Marra spoke up. "Is he a hireling?"

The yellow-eyed man rolled his eyes. "Anybody who sleeps in a fairy fort is fair game. What you do with them once you've got them is your problem. Eat them, wed them, set them free—it's all the same. He moves boxes for me."

The man who had slept in a fairy fort reached a hand up to the silver collar and touched it, as if picking at a scab.

The dust-wife eyed the necklace around the man-seller's neck and said, "Forget years. I'll give you a nun's tooth."

His yellow eyes narrowed, going sharp as needles. "A nun's tooth?"

"Pulled, not dropped," said the dust-wife. "Eh?"

"Reeeeeally . . ." He glanced at Marra.

Marra had a sudden bad feeling. "Um . . ."

"Smell the convent on her," suggested the dust-wife.

"But—"

"Hush," said the dust-wife. And to the seller, "Go on."

The seller approached Marra, nose working. Marra's skin crawled. *My tooth? What? Is he going to snatch one out of my head?*

"Yessss . . ." said the seller, his nostrils flared so wide that Marra could see an edge of pink inside them, like seashells. "Yes, yes! I taste it. Faith and straw. A hint of vespers. Yes! I'll take it. A tooth for him."

"Wait a minute," said Marra, starting to realize that this was really happening and they were talking about her actual teeth. "Wait. You can't—"

The seller turned his head and shouted, "Eh! Toothdancer! Get over here!"

"The moth says we need him," said the dust-wife. "And one of your teeth has been bothering you, hasn't it?"

"Well, yes, but—"

"I thought so. You wince a little when you chew."

"Eh! Toothdancer! Stir your stumps!"

"But you're going to have someone pull my tooth? Right now? Because a bug landed on him?" She flailed her hand at the man who had been moving boxes. He watched her emotionlessly. She wondered if he was under some spell, or if he simply no longer cared. Then she saw the Toothdancer emerge from behind a curtain in back of the stall and stopped worrying about the other man at all.

The Toothdancer looked like a stork or a heron, with a long hard bill and a curved, mobile neck. He wore a tattered black suit, with feathers sticking out of the holes, and his hands were very human. When he turned his head, Marra saw half a man's face below the beak, as if it were a mask, and yet his eyes were clearly a heron's, the color of new-minted coins, and set back from the beak like a bird's.

She gulped.

"This one," said the seller. The dust-wife took hold of Marra's elbow.

"Will it hurt?" whispered Marra, suddenly six years old again, with a baby tooth that pained her.

"No," said the Toothdancer in a kindly voice. He sounded like a friend, not like a monster with a living mask. "I know my work." He tapped her chin with a blunt finger. "Open, please."

Marra opened her mouth and closed her eyes. It was all completely ridiculous, and she didn't want to do it any more than she had when she was six, and yet you had to—that was how life went when a tooth went bad. You opened your mouth . . .

Something pressed against her lips. She opened her eyes, realized that the Toothdancer's beak was actually inside her mouth, and hastily squeezed them closed again.

Tap . . . tap . . . tap . . . The beak was tapping against her teeth, surprisingly delicate, the end much smaller than it looked. *Oh, sweet gods. Lady of Grackles, let this not be happening!*

Tap . . . tap . . .

The dust-wife held her elbow steady. She didn't tell Marra to relax, which was good because she was so far from relaxed that she thought she might scream.

Tap-ta-tap-tap. The Toothdancer had found the bad tooth. Lower molar on the right side. It had been twinging when Marra ate sometimes, and she had taken to chewing on the other side to prevent a bolt of pain from lancing through her jaw.

The beak withdrew. Marra clamped her lips shut, breathing heavily through her nose. She poked frantically with her tongue and found that the offending tooth was still there.

Maybe it's like magic maybe he's just taking a ghost tooth maybe it will be okay—

The Toothdancer took a pennywhistle from his coat pocket and began to play a spritely tune on it, using the human lips that Marra had seen before. She wondered if the beak opened at all, and then she stopped wondering because her teeth had begun to dance.

They twitched in her jaw like living things. She shrieked, not in pain but in horror, her mouth suddenly full of wiggling bone, as if she were in one of those nightmares where all her teeth fell out at once. It was like chewing and squirming and wiggling a loose tooth, wrapped all together, in time to the pennywhistle's tune.

She tried to bite down hard, hoping to still the awful dance, but it was worse, much worse, all the teeth rattling against each other, her skull filling up with the sounds of chattering. *Oh god oh god no no no no NO!*

If most of her teeth were dancing, the one bad molar was kicking. It felt as if it were battering against her cheek and the rest of her teeth, like a bird at a window, slam, slam, slam.

The Toothdancer leaned in closer and played more quickly. Marra wanted to scream a denial, but if she opened her mouth, all her teeth would dance out. *Oh god this was worse than anything worse than the blistered land, that had been outside, and this was inside her skin inside her face—*

With a popping sensation, the bad tooth pulled itself free of her jaw. It landed on her tongue, bouncing like an insect, and began to batter against the backs of her lips. Marra yelped at the sensation of hard, crawling life loose inside her mouth. She tried frantically to spit.

The Toothdancer dropped the pennywhistle, leaned in, and plucked the tooth neatly from the surface of her tongue with his beak. He turned and dropped the tooth, wet and glistening, into the tooth seller's palm.

Then he bowed very politely to Marra, patted her arm, and walked away.

Marra wrapped her arms around her ribs and sank to her knees, gasping. It hadn't hurt. She would have preferred that it hurt. She would prefer that she had never felt the sensation of all her teeth leaping and bounding in their sockets. She touched her tongue to the gap, hesitantly, and tasted blood.

"Oh god," she said hoarsely.

She thought she might start crying, but that would be to show weakness in front of the goblin market. For all she knew, there was a creature who would pull the tears out of her skull like teeth and sell them. She squeezed her eyes closed and thought fixedly about the pit of bones, the wires in her hands, silver looped over silver, building Bonedog, building calm.

An arm went around her, warm and solid. The dust-wife? No, surely not. Who, then?

For a wild instant she thought it was the Toothdancer, who had a kind voice, and the sudden horror of the thought made Marra open her eyes.

The white moth was just visible on his opposite shoulder. He knelt beside her, arm around her shoulders, the muscles in his jaw tense under the line of blue-gray stubble. "Enough," he said to the tooth seller or the dust-wife or both. "Stop this. I'm not worth it."

"Done is done," said the stall owner, licking Marra's tooth. "No taking it back now."

Bonedog had realized that something was wrong and was trying to get to her. The man she had sold a tooth for half turned, throwing his body between them. *No, no, it's all right; he doesn't know . . .* Bonedog must have looked like a monster to him, in this place already full of monsters. "It's all right," she said against the man's shoulder. "The dog is mine. My friend."

She didn't know if she spoke loudly enough, but he must have heard. He moved, one arm still around her, and Bonedog jumped in to wash her face with a nonexistent tongue. Bone and wire claws on her knee pricked through her clothes and she took a deep breath and said, "It's fine, boy. I'm fine."

"Here," said the dust-wife, handing her a tiny square of fabric. "Felted cobweb tobacco. Put that in the hole. It'll keep it from going bad."

She pushed the fabric into the gap in her teeth and nodded.

"Better?" asked the large man holding her. He spoke quietly, almost under his breath. Perhaps he, too, had learned not to show weakness.

"Better," she said.

He got to his feet and helped her up. The corded, effortless strength of his arm might have been alarming under other circumstances, but in the goblin market, she was glad of it.

"You want the collar?" asked the yellow-eyed man.

The dust-wife sniffed haughtily. "Take it off."

"As you wish." He reached toward the man's neck, and Marra watched the man very obviously not flinch away and wondered what not flinching cost him. The yellow-eyed man flicked the collar three times with his thumbnail, and it fell apart into cobwebs and dust.

The man inhaled sharply. The yellow-eyed man said, "Your problem now," and turned back to his wares, fondling Marra's tooth.

The dust-wife walked away and turned a corner. The man waited for Marra to move before he followed. His eyes were brown in the twisting light of the market, but there were still shadows on them.

"There," said the dust-wife. "We'll talk later, young man. Stay close, and we'll get out of here in a few moments yet."

"Are you human?" he asked, looking from the dust-wife to Marra.

Marra nodded. The dust-wife shrugged. "My parents were, anyway. You able to walk out of here under your own power?"

He swallowed. "Yes."

"One more thing we need," said the dust-wife, patting Bonedog's skull. "Then we're done."

"Not another tooth," croaked Marra. The dust-wife shrugged again.

She walked away through the crowd, one hand on Bonedog's collar. Marra moved to follow.

"May I take your arm?" asked the man.

Marra blinked at him. The formality of the gesture seemed to come from a world a long way off, a world where she was a princess instead of a nun. Did he think that she needed his support?

You did just collapse in front of him . . .

Then it occurred to her that he had been a prisoner in the market while she walked free. Perhaps he wanted to be sure that no one tried to imprison him again. "Yes, of course," she said, slipping her arm through his. She tugged him forward, following after the dust-wife.

The dust-wife backtracked down one of the aisles they had passed, and stopped before a stall that seemed to be divided in half. One side groaned under the weight of gems and gold, piled up and carelessly spilling over a silken runner. A bird with feathers made of fire watched over them, in a cage with bars that shone like moonlight.

The other side of the table barely registered to the eye. River stones and dried leaves, on an old burlap feed sack. There was a birdcage there, too, with a little gray finch perched inside it. As Marra watched, the finch opened its beak and sang two small, twittering notes, then pecked at a scatter of seed on the floor of the cage.

She looked at the caged phoenix on the pile of treasure, then back to the finch and the burlap and the stones, and began to realize what sort of stall this might be.

"I need a glamour," said the dust-wife. She picked up a river stone and set it down in the pile of treasure. It acquired facets and blazed like a ruby under her hands. She picked up a coin, stamped with the face of an ancient king, and moved it to the other side of the table, where it was a dried leaf with the edges turning to powder.

The person behind the stall nodded. Their appearance shifted every few seconds—old and young, short and tall, male, female, neither, both. "What do you wish disguised?"

The dust-wife clicked her tongue to Bonedog, tugging him forward.

"Nice work," said the glamour seller, coming out from behind the table. Their appearance settled somewhat, into a nondescript person with enormous donkey's ears. "Yours?"

"Mine," said Marra.

The glamour seller's ears swiveled in her direction and they nodded. "What would you like?"

"Sight and touch," said the dust-wife, "so that bystanders don't notice her dog is lacking in the flesh department." She thought for a moment, then added, "I suppose sound is expensive?"

"Sound's expensive," agreed the glamour seller. "People expect to see or feel certain things. Their minds do half the work. Play with sound and you have to convince the world, too, or else the echoes don't come out right. And don't ask me for something that will fool other dogs. I'm good but not that good."

"If it fools human onlookers, that's enough," said the dust-wife. "What does it cost me?"

The long gray ears flicked. "Is your demon for sale?"

Everyone looked at the brown hen. The hen said, *Errrrrrk,* in much the same tone that the Sister Apothecary used to pronounce someone dead.

"No," said the dust-wife. "She's my best layer. Could give you a demon's egg, though."

"Done," said the glamour seller. The dust-wife fished the day's egg out of her pocket, and the glamour seller went back behind the table and began digging through a basket. The contents of the basket looked like so much junk to Marra, but then, so did the contents of the dust-wife's pockets. She poked the hole in her jaw with her tongue and found that the bleeding had stopped and the little square of felt had settled into the empty socket as if it belonged there.

The man at her side stood like a palace guard. He had the same erect posture, the same air of watchfulness. Marra wanted to ask him how he came to be a prisoner in the goblin market and what a fairy fort was, but surely this was not the time, not when they were surrounded by creatures alert for weakness . . . She poked her tongue at the hole again.

The glamour seller took a ball of twine and a handful of snail shells and began measuring Bonedog and muttering.

"Are you all right?" whispered Marra, when she couldn't stand it any longer.

The man looked down at her. "I don't know. Are you planning on killing me?" he asked. He sounded as if he were commenting on the weather.

"No! I need your help, but I wouldn't . . ." It occurred to her suddenly that killing a prince was a very dangerous thing to do, and perhaps the moth had landed on him because someone was going to have to die, and that was what she had needed after all. *Oh gods! That can't be it, can it?* "That is, I don't know if I . . . I . . ." She stared up at him, having run out of words and wanting very much to not have said anything.

One corner of his mouth crooked just slightly. Marra stared at it wonderingly, that anyone could maintain a sense of humor in this dreadful place. He bent his head toward hers. "This is not the time or the place," he murmured. "We can sort everything else later."

"Right," mumbled Marra. "Right. Yes."

"Twine and snail shells, wires and bones," sang the glamour seller, half to themself, while their ears flicked and swiveled. "There!" The twine was a grid, then a net, then they flung it over Bonedog, who bounced on his feet as if he were being given a treat.

The glamour settled around him and left a smell like burning dust. Marra saw the outlines of flesh, a shadow of fur, and then Bonedog shook himself and he was a great gray dog with a skull like a battering ram and a blaze of white across his chest. His tail was still a narrow, bony whip but there was fur across it. He had immense jowls and when he looked up at Marra, they all sagged into a gigantic smile.

"Oh, Bonedog," she said. He licked her hand and she could feel his tongue, not quite substantial but more than it had been.

"Enough of this place," said the dust-wife. "Everyone have their souls still? Shadows still attached? Then let's go before that changes."

They went up the stairs very slowly. The staircase seemed much longer going up than coming down. Perhaps that was always the way in a fairy world. The man she had ransomed, the man she needed, had his arm locked around hers. They leaned against each other, shoulder against shoulder, two humans in a place where no humans should ever have come. When Marra looked over at him in the sickly firefly light, she could see a silvery terror in his eyes, mastered but very much alive. Bonedog walked beside them, Marra's hand wrapped around the rope collar. She felt the illusion of fur against her fingers, except when she didn't and he briefly felt like bones.

The square at the top of the stairs became deep blue instead of black. It grew closer one agonized step at a time, bisected by the dark figure of the dust-wife. Stars began to appear in it, but the outline seemed restless, as if there were a shadow laid across it that should not have fallen just there.

There is something waiting at the top, Marra thought. *How many teeth will it take to get past? How many years off my life to buy our way free?* She exhaled on a long, shuddery breath and the man beside her half carried her up the next step, until she found her strength again.

It will take as many as it takes.

There was something at the top. She never saw what it was. The dust-wife reached the opening first and a shadow reared up, but the hen threw back her head and crowed like a rooster at dawn.

The shadow fled. The hen settled, making an indignant *errrk.* "I know," said the dust-wife soothingly, "I know. Crowing is always so embarrassing for a lady."

Rrr-rr-rrrk, muttered the hen, shaking out her neck feathers.

They emerged, stumbling, into the starlight. The man at Marra's side gasped in air as if he had never breathed before. "Free," he said. "Am I free of that place?"

"Almost," said the dust-wife. "Not quite yet. We've got one foot in the other world, and it isn't safe to linger." She led them back along the river, toward the tree root. The man still held Marra's elbow. She did not know whether to feel trapped or to be glad of the touch.

The drowned boy was waiting on the other side of the roots, chin-deep in the water. He gargled at them and the dust-wife made a noise of annoyance and gestured at him, swift and rude and backed by magic. The drowned boy sank down into the water and swam away, fast as an otter. "Now," said the dust-wife, leaning on her staff. "Now we're all the way back. Now you're free."

Chapter 9

I am Fenris," said the man. He started to say something more, to
add another name or a rank, perhaps, but cut himself short. "Fenris," he repeated instead.

"Marra."

"Fenris," said the dust-wife. She snorted, looking over at Marra.
"So you built yourself a dog and found yourself a wolf. If a fox shows
up looking for you, we'll have a proper fairy tale and I'll start to
worry."

"Why?" asked Marra. "If I'm in a fairy tale, I might actually have
a chance."

"Fairy tales," said the dust-wife heavily, "are very hard on bystanders. Particularly old women. I'd rather not dance myself to death in
iron shoes, if it's all the same to you."

"Perhaps you're the fox," said Marra.

"Ha!" The dust-wife's laugh really did have a bit of a fox's bark to
it. "I deserved that."

"Do you have a name, Lady Fox?" asked Fenris. Marra could not
tell if he was amused or irked by the conversation.

"Yes," said the dust-wife.

The silence stretched out. Marra picked at a thread of the nettle
cloak, waiting.

If there was a battle of wills, the dust-wife won. Fenris's laugh
was not terribly unlike the dust-wife's, the short, self-deprecating
sound of a man who could still recognize absurdity. "What do you
wish me to call you, then, ma'am?"

"*Ma'am* will work very well indeed. I am a dust-wife."

"Ah." He nodded. "One of those who live among the dead? We do not have them in my country, but we know of them."

The silence grew again. Marra wondered what he was thinking and what he made of them. *A shy nun and an old woman who communes with the dead. I don't know if I even know what I think of us . . .*

He's a killer, the yellow-eyed man had said. The thought was alarming. Fenris was large enough to break her in half with his bare hands, and however imperious the dust-wife was, she was still fundamentally an old woman with a chicken. Did he think he was still a prisoner? They'd ransomed him from the tooth seller, but they hadn't exactly set him free, had they? She'd gabbled something about needing him in the market. If he decided to escape his supposed captivity, their only defense would be a dog who was currently bouncing in the water to make it splash.

"You don't have to stay with us," she said.

Fenris looked over at her, his eyes unreadable. "Beg pardon?"

"I mean . . ." *No, don't explain about the moth—the moth is too complicated and sounds ridiculous if you say it out loud.* "Uh, there was magic that took us to a thing we needed. And it picked you. But you aren't a prisoner anymore."

"Magic said that you needed me?" He was smiling now, but it was a smile like his laugh, not so much humorous as incredulous at the shape of the world.

"Don't get any ideas," said the dust-wife. "Might turn out that our fate is sealed inside a jar and we need someone to loosen the lid."

His laugh that time had genuine humor in it, which seemed to surprise Fenris as much as it surprised Marra.

"Do we have time for me to wash?" he asked, as they left the river. "It has been a long time . . ."

The dust-wife shook her head. "Not here. The dead are restless and won't settle for a day or two. We'll find you a pond where no one's drowned."

"Well, I do like not drowning."

It took them perhaps half an hour. Even though Marra felt as if an age of the earth had passed in the goblin market, the moon had barely moved in the sky. It splashed a white reflection across a stock pond. Several sleeping cows stood on the other side of a fence, black shapes on the moonlit grass.

"How did you end up in the goblin market?" asked Marra, as Fenris sat down by the edge of the pond and began to unlace his boots.

"I was a fool," said Fenris. "I slept in a fairy fort. I knew better, but I . . ." He looked away.

"What's a fairy fort?" asked Marra.

"A ring of earth. Trees grow up the sides, but the centers are usually clear. Ruins, some say, of an old people. Dwellings of the hidden ones. Uncanny places. I should not have been there."

"You were on the run from something," said the dust-wife crisply, "or you were trying to kill yourself but didn't have the nerve to hold the knife. You're from Hardack, by your accent, and no Hardishman would sleep in a fairy fort, not dead drunk with two broken legs."

Fenris's lips twitched. He inclined his head to the dust-wife. "As you say."

"Well?" The dust-wife plunked herself down. The brown hen regarded Fenris with a baleful eye. "Which was it?"

"Both," said Fenris. He rubbed his forehead. "I am . . . was . . . a knight. In Hardack, as you say. I served the Fathers, not any particular clan. The Fathers rule the clans, but their rule is not absolute. Those who serve them work as diplomats as much as enforcers."

"And?" said the dust-wife, merciless.

"And I was a fool." He said it with no particular intonation, less flagellation than fact. "I did not recognize what was under my nose, and the day came that I had to kill a man because of it. A clan lord."

Marra pricked up her ears, suddenly intent. Was a clan lord as well protected as a prince?

"There was nothing I could do, within the law," Fenris said. "A lord's word is law in the clan's keep. The Fathers could censure him, but they could do no more. So I could let him walk free with blood on his hands, or deal justice with blood on mine." He shrugged. "I murdered three men who had committed no crime except defending their liege, and killed the lord, and left my sword atop him so that they would know who did the deed. And then I walked away and spent the night in a fairy fort."

"Deliberately," said the dust-wife thoughtfully. "You wanted to die, but not by human hands."

Fenris gave her a quick, wry glance. "For all that we say that we are servants of the Fathers, everyone knows what clan we hail from originally. I am a criminal, but whoever killed me would make an enemy of my clan. But if I was not killed, then the clan of the lord I had killed would lose face as long as I walked free." He tossed a pebble into the water. "It was not their fault that their lord was a monster. They suffered under his hands more than any of the rest of us."

"And Hardishmen consider suicide shameful," said the dust-wife.

Fenris shrugged. "I do not much care for my honor, but to fall on my sword would be to say that I believed what I had done was wrong." He sighed, and a little emotion crept at last into his voice. It sounded like weariness. "So here I am. I was in the goblin market for a long time and I am very tired."

* * *

Marra looked toward the pond. Fenris had requested a little privacy to bathe. She wondered if he was really doing so, or if he was running off into the woods to put as much distance between them as he could.

I did not tie the bone dog, and he came back. She rubbed Bonedog's skull, feeling the ghost of fur under her fingers as they pushed through the glamour.

"That was a sad story," she said aloud. "Poor man."

"If it's true, yes," said the dust-wife.

"You don't believe him?"

"Mm." The dust-wife shrugged. "He doesn't feel like a liar, but that only means he believes himself. I imagine most of it's true, more or less. But there's men that would kill a rival and convince themselves they'd done it for noble reasons." She laced her fingers behind her head, lying back on her bedroll. "Everybody makes up a story about their sins. Sometimes to make them less, sometimes to make them the worst thing a mortal's ever done. Really depends on the person. I'd wager this one's more martyr than apologist, but you never can tell."

"Do you think he'll try to leave?"

The dust-wife shrugged again. "If he comes back tonight, I doubt it. But if he has any sense, he'll take his freedom and go and we'll never see him again."

Marra bit her lip. "The moth said we needed him."

"We needed him *then*, yes." The dust-wife tilted her head. "It is possible that he has already done what he needed to do."

"What?" Marra frowned. "That was an hour ago!"

"Yes. And perhaps we would have been attacked in the goblin market if we had not had a large bodyguard walking with us, and his purpose is over and done."

Marra blinked. "Do you . . . do you think that's likely?"

The dust-wife shrugged yet again.

"But if it isn't, we still need him!"

"Indeed. But just because you need someone doesn't mean that they are under any obligation to provide. He may leave to take his chances elsewhere."

"I have not left," said Fenris from the shadows. Marra jumped. How could a man walk so silently? And how much had he heard?

She looked up, and Fenris walked out of the shadows, his tread slow and heavy as a draft horse. "I have little enough sense, Lady Fox," he said. Again that bemused smile. He turned his gaze to Marra. "We ransom prisoners often in my land, and usually it is only with gold. But you have bought my freedom with your own blood and bone. What little honor I have left is yours, and if I can be of service, I will."

* * *

Breakfast the next morning was dry bread without even one third of an egg apiece. Fenris snapped his up in three bites but did not complain about the scanty rations. Marra wondered how on earth they were all going to feed themselves on the way to the Northern Kingdom.

Fenris walked much more quickly than either of them at first, a ground-eating stride that would probably have him in the Northern Kingdom before Marra and the dust-wife had even left the Southern. He had to stop and check himself several times, almost apologetically.

Marra was having a difficult time herself. She had become used to ducking away from travelers, to making sure that Bonedog was out of sight. The first time that a farm wagon passed them, she grabbed his collar and almost dove into a hedgerow before she remembered.

The wagon driver did stare at them, but not at Bonedog. Instead he was looking at the hen on top of the dust-wife's staff and grinning hugely. "How'd you teach her to do that?" he called.

"Teach her, nothing," said the dust-wife. "Couldn't get her to stop." The driver laughed loudly and tapped his cap, then drove on, while Marra tried to calm her racing heart.

"Easy," murmured Fenris.

It was on the tip of Marra's tongue to be annoyed, but then she looked over at him and realized that he was talking to himself as much as to her.

How long was he in the goblin market? Does this seem strange to him as well?

She turned it over in her mind for a few moments, and then she simply asked.

"Too long." Fenris looked up at the sky, which had lost the pale gray-gold notes of dawn and was turning to blue. "It was hard to keep track of the days. They say that people who go into a fairy fort will dance for a night and come back to find that years have passed. I don't know if that's true. I don't know if the goblin market is always running. It seemed like I was always there in the stall, but sometimes I'd sleep and it felt like a long, long time had passed. And sometimes it was . . . different."

"Different how?" asked the dust-wife sharply.

"Colder. Darker. Different . . . things."

"Things? Do you mean people?" asked the dust-wife.

"I mean that when my captor sold a tooth, the *thing* he sold it to looked like a woman, right up until it bit the tooth in half like an apple." His voice was very calm, and he did not look at either of them as he spoke. "Then it pounced on the first person that walked by and left them dead on the floor of the market. And that yellow-eyed bastard only complained about the mess and called someone to haul the body away."

For the first time that Marra could remember, the dust-wife looked very slightly abashed. "Ah. Dark of the moon. The goblin market is at its worst then."

"I'm sorry," said Marra.

Fenris looked at her then. His eyes were bleak, but he forced half a smile. "I was, too. For all of us. There were a few other humans, I think, working in other stalls. It's hard to say. We would nod to each other, but we did not get a chance to speak." He drew a deep breath and straightened his back. "Well. If that was the dark of the moon, then I suppose I was there for three months. I would have guessed it was more like a few weeks. The days seemed very long, but not like that."

"What did you do?" asked Marra.

He shrugged. "Thought, mostly. Turned over all the ways that I had failed, and all the places I could have turned aside from my path. Thought about escaping." He shook his head. "I wasn't able to talk to anyone else but the Toothdancer. He was not so bad, for all his looks. But it was a cruel place." He exhaled slowly through his nose. "And I, being a selfish bastard, thought only of getting free. Perhaps I should have told you to take someone else in my place. I deserved my captivity."

"You're the one we needed. Or that the moth said we needed."

He shrugged again.

"Perhaps when this is all over," said Marra recklessly, "perhaps we could go back. Find the others there."

The look he gave her this time was surprise. "Will you sacrifice a tooth for each of them, then?"

Her skin crawled at the thought, but what was a tooth compared to someone's life? "If I have to."

The silence went on too long, and then he offered her his hand, not to hold but to shake. Marra did. His fingers were callused against her skin.

"So," said Fenris. "Now that we have pledged to one another's hopeless quests, may I ask where we are going on yours?"

"The Northern Kingdom," said Marra.

"I have not been there," Fenris said. "You must warn me if there are any customs that I do not know that will lead us all into difficulty."

"I don't think there are any," said Marra. She racked her brain, trying to think of anything useful. "But I don't know if I'd know. I grew up very near there, so my people would do the same thing, I suppose. Um. Don't hit anyone in the face with a glove?"

Fenris's expression was indescribable. "Is this a thing your people do often?"

"No, not unless we want to fight duels. Which we don't. I mean, I don't."

"Might save time," said the dust-wife. "We send him to duel the prince and get it over with."

Marra considered this. Fenris was a little older than the prince but a great deal larger. Did that matter? "Hmm . . ."

"A prince, eh?" Fenris glanced at her for acknowledgment. "And you want him dead?"

"Is that a problem?" *What if he leaves and tells the prince? No, we didn't say a name, and he's never even been to the Northern Kingdom. He can't know it's Vorling, and anyway, Vorling's the king now . . .*

"Does he deserve to die?" asked Fenris, as if they were talking about the weather.

"Very much so."

"Then it's not a problem. Do your rulers accept challenges from strangers, though?"

"No . . ." said Marra. Of course it wouldn't be that easy. "No, I'm pretty sure they don't."

"Good. It's a foolish way to choose rulers, even if it does make things less convenient for us now."

"They allow it in Hardack, as I recall," said the dust-wife.

"They do," said Fenris. "It's foolish there, too. You get a competent, judicial man who knows the names of each of his vassals, who can balance the needs of the clan against the needs of individuals . . . and then you get a brute whose only skill is swinging an axe. And like as not, the man with the axe wins, and then it's his boot on the clan's neck until someone sends to the Fathers to sort matters out, which half the time we can't."

"I'm beginning to suspect you've dealt with this before," said Marra.

"However did you guess?" He gave her a wry glance. "Yes. I've seen four clans ruined by it. One saved as well, but we could have found other ways. What did this prince do?"

The question was delivered in the exact same tone as the rest, and it caught her by surprise, like a blow. She missed a step and Fenris moved to catch her, then stepped back when she caught herself on her own.

"He killed my sister," she said. "And my other sister . . . his now wife . . . he . . ." Her throat tried to close up again and she forced the words out. "He hurts her. He leaves marks and she . . . she stays pregnant so that he will not beat her, but she will die of it eventually. Then he'll take another wife and do it to her again."

Fenris nodded, as if what she had said was perfectly comprehensible, even though she could barely comprehend it herself. If the fact that a nun was kin to a prince's wife surprised him, he gave no sign. "I understand. Men like that never stop. If they can be isolated or thrown at the enemy, it is for the best, and then the clan gets some good of them in the end. But often they cannot be, and then we must find other solutions."

"That's what we're trying to do," said Marra. "Other solutions. Whatever that may be."

"It's a fool's errand and we'll probably all die," said the dust-wife.

"Oh, well then," said Fenris. "I always enjoy those."

"What now?" Marra asked the dust-wife. "You had the ideas before. Or do we simply walk north until we get there?"

The dust-wife scratched her hen's keel bone thoughtfully. The bird looked annoyed, but then, it always did. "I can almost see my way forward," she said. "If it were only mortals we faced, then you and I and your large friend there might be enough. But the godmother is where everything falls down."

"The prince's fairy godmother?"

The dust-wife nodded. "They've had the same one for a long time. Bound to the royal family and kept alive long past when a sensible person would die. Her protection will lie over the prince." She gnawed on her lower lip. "The dead I may command, but that is a different power."

"Stronger?" asked Marra.

"Different." The dust-wife paused, then smiled ruefully. "Probably stronger. I speak with the dead and for the dead. Our two powers have nothing to say to one another. We might pass each other in the street without speaking or she might blast me into nothingness."

"I suppose you can't blast her into nothingness first?" asked Fenris.

"I've never tried," admitted the dust-wife, "but it doesn't seem very likely."

Marra sighed. "So what do we need to fight a power like that? My fairy godmother was nearly useless."

The dust-wife raised an eyebrow. "You had a fairy godmother?"

"Yes, of course. Princesses, you know . . ."

"Not all of them," said the dust-wife, "not even most of them, come to that. And the ones who do tend to be in much larger kingdoms, not little nations poised between dangerous neighbors. Power calls to power."

Marra snorted. "Well, she wasn't worth much, so you're not far wrong."

"Oh?" said the dust-wife.

"She blessed us all with good health," said Marra grimly. "And

Damia she said would marry a prince. Which wasn't much of a blessing, given he killed her."

"Health's not so little a thing," said the dust-wife. "Compared to the alternative, anyway."

Marra's lip curled. "She might have wished us *safe*," she growled. "Or at least that we wouldn't marry someone who'd murder us."

"She might have," said the dust-wife. "But parents object to people making pronouncements like that at christenings, for some odd reason."

"You'd think they'd be grateful."

"No accounting for human nature."

Marra did not know Fenris well enough to read his expressions, but she would have sworn that he wanted to say something. He kept glancing at the dust-wife. A line formed between his eyes with each glance, growing deeper, until finally he apparently gave up and said, "Lady Fox?"

The dust-wife snorted. "Yes?"

"You claim to speak with the dead?"

"I don't claim it," said the dust-wife calmly. "I do it. Although most days it's less speaking and more listening. People who won't shut up in life rarely shut up in death."

Fenris shook his head. After a moment he said, picking his words carefully, "I do not know that I believe in ghosts."

"Yet you believe in fairies," said the dust-wife, sounding amused rather than offended. "Enough that you offered yourself to a fairy fort."

"And now I suppose that I should say that is different," said Fenris. "But the truth is that I did not believe in fairies, either. No one I know does." He rubbed a hand through his hair, and Marra saw threads of white salted through the dark length.

"You did not believe in fairies, but you were afraid of a fairy fort?" said Marra, puzzled.

"Well . . . yes." Fenris gave her another of his bemused how-am-I-here smiles. "We do not believe, but you still wouldn't cut trees

from a fairy mound or spend the night in one. Just in case there is
something there, whether you believe in it or not."

"There you are, then," said the dust-wife. "The dead are there,
whether you believe in them or not."

"Mm."

Marra felt an urge to jump in and try to smooth the conversation
over, but she did not know how she would manage that. She had
never liked disagreements, but they both seemed amused, anyway,
rather than heated. She studied Fenris under her lashes, trying not
to be too obvious.

In daylight, he was even larger than she had thought in the goblin market. Broad shoulders, barrel chest. Even if he was older than
the prince and had thickened around the middle with age, no one
would mistake him for anything but a warrior. His hands were covered in dozens of small, healed scars and his forearms were corded
with muscle. You did not get muscle like that simply from lifting
boxes. *If he wanted to, he could probably throttle me one-handed.* Marra
licked suddenly dry lips. *The spell said we needed him. Surely we couldn't
need someone who was going to try to kill us. Unless the world is very
strange indeed, and maybe I should be dead and the dust-wife should raise
me up and send me after Vorling as a vengeful shade.*

This seemed like a lot.

The dust-wife clearly had no fear of Fenris, even if he was twice
her size. "You do not believe in ghosts, Hardishman," she said, "yet
would you desecrate a grave?"

Fenris's eyes went wide in clear dismay. "No! Of course not."

"Well then."

They walked along in silence for nearly half an hour. Bonedog
nosed at something in a hedge and snapped his jaws closed. Whatever it was fell out through the bottom of his jaw and ran off into
the grass. He came back, grinning hugely, very proud of himself.

Finally Fenris broke the silence, saying, "You may be right, Lady
Fox. But I find that I feel differently about the fairy forts than a
grave. Even when I did not believe, the forts were . . . uncanny. There
was always a little dread, under the surface. Dread of the unknown.

But when I think of desecrating a grave, I do not feel dread but re-vulsion. I am not afraid of what lies in the grave, but it would be dishonorable. Disgusting, even. I do not fear retribution; I fear what sort of person I would become by doing it."

The dust-wife slowed then and gave Fenris a sharp, appraising look. The brown hen gave an indignant squawk and rocked on top of the staff.

One of her rare smiles crooked her lips. "You are still wrong, Hardishman," she said. "But you are wrong in an interesting way."

Fenris bowed his head, a knight accepting praise from a queen, and Bonedog wagged his tail and barked silently at them both.

Chapter 10

Traveling on the road with Fenris was different than traveling solely with the dust-wife. Different and also, Marra had to admit, easier.

He was clearly used to camping roughly. He could build a fire while Marra was still fumbling with flint, and keep it going longer. He had no gear of his own after his time in the goblin market, so the dust-wife sacrificed a metal measuring cup and Marra handed over the smaller of her two knives so he could eat and drink.

After two days, Marra no longer seriously believed that Fenris would turn on them. He was calm and judicious and the dust-wife needled him more or less constantly, which he took in good humor. Occasionally Marra would share a glance with him, a bemused one that said, *Can you believe that two sensible people such as us are in this situation?*

The look warmed her. She had not shared that look of fellow feeling since she had left the Sister Apothecary at the monastery.

Nevertheless, there were times when he stood up too quickly, or loomed too large, and some shadow on her mind whispered that no one had thought Vorling would turn on his wives, either. *Am I being too cautious? Or not nearly cautious enough?* And she remembered the farmer who had tried to kill her, the one who likely thought that he was a decent man but had seen only a monster from the blistered land, and she would put a few more steps between them and try not to make it too obvious.

If he noticed, he gave no sign.

He did eat more than the dust-wife and Marra put together. She could tell that he was trying not to, but she could also hear his stomach growling. They stopped at farmhouses whenever they could. One night all they had was tea, but the next afternoon Bonedog rousted a rabbit and Fenris cleaned and spitted it and they ate better than they had in days.

As they went farther north, travel became easier. Everyone needed firewood split and Fenris could use an axe with the ease of long practice. They went up to doors and asked if he could chop wood in return for a bit of food for the road, and generally people were happy to see them. Occasionally they'd even point to someone farther along the road that would also need work. Fenris's stomach stopped growling, and they no longer had nights where there was nothing but tea.

With the north, however, came cold. Since Fenris had no gear, he had no blankets, either. They slept in barns when they could, but that was not always possible. Marra woke one morning to find frost on the ground and Fenris crouched so close to the fire that his beard was in danger of going up in flame.

"Uh," she said that night. "It's cold. If you'd like to share my blanket . . ."

The dust-wife snorted. Fenris's eyebrows went up. Marra wondered if that was a euphemism in Hardack, too. "Not like that," she said hastily. "I mean, if you're cold. It's cold. That is to say, you can have part of mine. I'm not suggesting anything more than that."

The dust-wife was having a coughing fit. Fenris, however, bowed his head gravely to her and said, "It is probably not the path of honor to deprive a young woman of half her blanket, but my bones are old enough that I thank you."

"I'm not that young," said Marra.

"And don't even talk to me about old bones until you're over seventy, youngster," said the dust-wife.

Fenris gave her a mild look. "That's about thirty years hence, at which point you will undoubtedly tell me that I cannot complain until I am over a hundred."

The brown hen cackled and the dust-wife thumped the staff until the bird flapped. "Don't get smart," she muttered, although whether she meant the hen or Fenris, she didn't say, and no one tried to find out.

Marra unwrapped her bedroll. The dust-wife had given it to her, one long blanket, enough to wrap one person comfortably, even if, like Marra, she tended to stretch out in her sleep.

It was very small for two. They lay down back-to-back, the blanket over both of them, although Marra was quite certain that Fenris was giving her the lion's share. She could feel his back against hers like a wall, though they were both wearing too many layers for her to catch his breathing.

Bonedog usually slept humped over her feet, his rib bones gouging into her ankle. Finding two sets of feet, he did not seem to know what to do. He circled, whined briefly, and then draped himself over her shins. The glamour tried to soften the hard points of his pelvis but failed.

Marra could not seem to get comfortable, either. It was hard enough to sleep on the ground, but had the ground been this hard last night? Was that a rock under her? Her arms were pulled inside her robes for warmth, but had the sleeves always been so constricting?

She shifted position, trying to get comfortable, then wondered if she was waking Fenris up, or if he was still awake and she was annoying him. She didn't squirm this much when there wasn't another person there, did she? Or did she, but she didn't worry about it and didn't notice she was doing it?

How many years had it been since she'd slept near another human being? She tried to remember. In smaller houses, with fewer beds, people bundled up two and three to a bed, but princesses slept alone.

When she had been very young, she had sometimes crept from her bed to Damia's. *I had a bad dream,* she would say. Her older sister had been very patient, had pulled the blankets aside and helped her climb up onto the tall bed. Marra remembered it all with sudden vividness, the scent of dried lavender under the pillow and the crispness of the sheets. She hadn't thought of that in years.

I can't remember Damia's face, she thought, gazing dry-eyed into the dark, *but I remember the lavender.*

Her back was beginning to warm up. Unfortunately one side of her sinuses was starting to clog. Normally she would have rolled over, but if she did that, she'd have her face squashed into Fenris's spine. She wished she could sleep on her back, but it always made her feel short of breath. (Women in her family did not sleep on their stomachs after puberty. She hadn't even tried since she was fourteen.)

She fidgeted again, located a rock under her hip, and tried to get it out of the way without squirming too much. Bonedog got up, circled three times, and collapsed again in exactly the same position.

Fenris is probably regretting agreeing to this. He is probably thinking he got better sleep with his face an inch from the coals.

It was foolish to even try . . . she thought, and then it was morning and the warmth against her back was gone and the brown hen was clucking irritably for her breakfast.

* * *

The day they crossed back into Marra's own kingdom felt strange, because it didn't feel like anything at all.

The borders were porous and no one particularly cared, and they were on a back road that lacked even a guard post. There was a faded wooden marker with an approximation of the royal crest burned into it, recognizable even if the dragon looked more like a snake and the hare looked like a blobby dog. Marra paused at the line, then stepped over as if stepping into cold water.

I should feel something, she thought. *This is my land. I'm a daughter of the royal house.*

She didn't.

She'd been asleep on the coach when she had crossed the other way, and she'd been so anxious about finding the dust-wife that she hadn't given it much thought. But this time she knew where she was and she was walking into her own kingdom and it seemed as if she should feel . . . something.

"Problem?" asked Fenris.

"I live here," said Marra. She nudged the dirt with her boot. "I'm home, I guess. Except it doesn't feel like much of anything."

"Ah."

"The poet Tarus said that when he came home, the land itself sang under his feet, and his heart sang with it."

"That may be unique to poets." Fenris started to rest his hand on a nonexistent sword hilt, caught himself, and shoved his hands in his pockets instead. "I came back from my first campaign and I'd been in my own clan's lands for half an hour before I noticed."

She glanced up at his face, surprised.

"I was cold and wet and very tired," he said. "When I did feel something, it was because I realized we were only about twenty minutes from the keep and I might get warm again." He shrugged. "And then again, other times I have come home and felt as if I had finally woken up after a long illness. I suspect these things say more about us than they do about the land itself."

Marra was watching his face, and so she saw the sudden flash of pain across it, quickly stifled, the deepening of the lines between his eyebrows.

"Will you be able to go back to your clan's lands again?" she asked.

"No." He lifted his head, looking around them. This part of the countryside did not go red and orange with autumn, only dun and yellow. Wind rustled through the dry stems of broom straw at the edges of the road. "No. I can go anywhere in the wide world that I wish, but the borders of Hardack are closed to me."

"There is no appeal?" asked Marra. "You can't . . . um . . . wait for someone to die? Or forget?"

His smile was acknowledgment that she was trying, not happiness—a quick flicker, then gone. "No. My return would start a senseless war of vengeance. I will not sentence so many people to die merely because I am homesick."

"I'm sorry."

"As am I." The flicker of a smile lasted longer this time. "But I am told that this is a fool's errand and we will all probably die, so I do not let it trouble me overmuch."

They trudged onward, into her kingdom, Bonedog weaving in and out between them. Marra thought of all the stories of exiles returning home, and wondered how many, like Fenris, simply never returned at all because the price was too high.

And what will I do, if we succeed? Will I go back to my little room at the convent and hope to be left alone again?

It was because of Prince Vorling that she had never married. He did not want any competing claims to the little kingdom's throne. If he was dead, would that change?

Lady of Grackles, please, no. Let me stay insignificant. Let me be a weaver and a midwife, not a princess.

She took a deep breath, then set the thought aside. *This is still a fool's errand, and probably we will all die.* A familiar thought. It was strange to take such comfort in it.

"Marra?" The dust-wife looked over at her. "Where does your godmother live?"

"My godmother?" Marra frowned. "I don't know. No, wait . . ." She rubbed her forehead, trying to dredge up old memories. Had her mother said something once? Nothing important. The godmother had not been important, had just been one more actor in the drama of childbirth. But they had gone out in a carriage years ago, passing through the countryside on the way to somewhere else, and the queen had said something about the godmother living over that way . . .

"I think near Trexel," she said finally. "We went out for hawking and Trexel is where they have goshawks."

"You're a falconer?" asked Fenris.

"Not even remotely," said Marra. "But there's an absurd tradition that only the royal family is allowed to hunt with goshawks, so we have to go out and there's a whole ridiculous ceremony where the falconers gift you the birds and then you ask them to hold the bird in trust, so that they can hunt with them. There's probably still a bird or two out there that are technically my property, but what am I going to do with one?" She remembered the ceremony more clearly now, the pale bird with its mad red eyes and the heavy glove weighing down her arm. "So the falconers get to fly goshawks and put food on the table for the house that trains them—I've forgotten the name, one of the distaff branches—but if anyone asks, the birds belong to the royal house."

The dust-wife had paused while the hen climbed down her arm and made her way to the pack to lay her daily egg, but snorted at this. "Not the worst system I've ever heard of. The godmother lived near there?"

"I think so." Marra had a vague memory of her mother trying to entertain her and her sister, pointing out the window and saying, "Your fairy godmother lives over that way. Isn't that interesting?"

"Then let us make for Trexel," said the dust-wife.

Marra grimaced. She didn't want to see the woman who had sent her sisters out in the world so ill prepared. *But if I must, I suppose I can demand to know why she wasted such a chance. She could have stopped all of this long before it happened. Why didn't she?*

"Yes," said Marra, feeling anger stir in the pit of her stomach, anger that for once had little to do with Vorling. "Yes, let's."

* * *

It was one of life's ironies, thought Marra, that they had left the Southern Kingdom unmolested, only to be attacked as soon as they returned to her own lands.

Marra and the dust-wife were sitting by a well in a little gray town on a little gray road, surrounded by little gray fields. There was nothing to make anyone think it was dangerous. Fenris had negotiated a meal with the innkeeper in return for splitting yet more firewood. Marra was sitting on the edge of the well, thinking nothing in particular, when a shadow fell over her feet.

"The hell are you supposed to be?" said a thick, wet voice.

Marra jerked upright, panic firing her nerves. She had to grab for the stone to keep from pitching backward into the well.

The owner of the voice was not looking at her. He was a big, lanky, rawboned man and he was swaying slightly. *Day-drunk,* thought Marra. *Oh, Lady of Grackles.*

He was looming over the dust-wife.

The dust-wife was deeply unimpressed. Under normal circumstances, Marra would have applauded her calm, but she'd encountered a few drunks in her time with the Sister Apothecary and very few of them liked to be ignored. It made them angrier. The Sister Apothecary had been good at talking them down, usually by saying that there was a birth going on and suggesting they go have a toast to celebrate. Unfortunately that didn't seem like it would apply here.

"You a witch?" asked the drunk, stabbing a finger at the dust-wife. "That your *familiar*?" He snickered.

Marra looked around wildly. Where was Fenris? Behind the inn, probably, chopping wood. *Dammit.* Two or three bystanders had stopped and were watching, but no one was intervening.

"Go back to the bottle, man," said the dust-wife. "Leave an old woman alone."

He made a grab for the brown hen. He was in no danger of succeeding, but the dust-wife stepped back anyway. Marra was very sure that the dust-wife could protect herself, and also that if she did, they might have to leave the village in a hurry.

Do something! Stop this! Think! *How are you going to fight a prince if you can't even handle one drunk?*

"*There's many a man who'll not think twice to mistreat a woman but who lives in fear of a habit and a holy symbol.*" Remembering these words, Marra stepped in front of the dust-wife, running her fingers down the cord that held the carved grackle feather. "We mean no harm, my son," she said, trying to sound like the abbess.

The drunk blinked at her. "The hell are you?"

"I serve Our Lady of Grackles." She sent a silent prayer to the Lady to add it to her tab for these frequent impersonations.

Glory be, he took a step back. Marra had a moment to think that she'd pulled it off, that it was all going to work, and then Bonedog began to bark at him.

Perhaps if he had a voice like a normal dog, it might not have mattered. But the working throat and snapping jaws of a silent bark caught the man's attention and he aimed a kick at Bonedog, with predictable results.

"Ow! Goddamn beast bit me!"

Oh hell. She snatched for Bonedog's collar and took a step back.

"It bit me!" he shouted to the growing crowd. "You all saw it!"

From what Marra could see, Bonedog had barely scraped the man's boot leather. She took another step back, dragging the dog with her. The dust-wife muttered something under her breath and dipped a hand into a pocket. Marra hoped she was grabbing something that would calm the man down, not something that would strike him dead and leave them with a corpse to explain.

A shadow fell between them.

"Excuse me," said Fenris.

Relief flooded Marra. At least if they had to make a break for it, they wouldn't get separated. And possibly the drunk would listen to another man, if not a nun.

The drunk turned. He had to look up to meet Fenris's eyes. "This isn't your problem, old man," he said.

"Friend," said Fenris in a just-between-us voice, "you're frightening the nuns. Let them go on their way in peace. The gods look out for them and so should we, eh?"

"Their dog bit me," muttered the drunk man.

"Ah well, even nuns have protectors, eh? Come now. I'm new in town, and you look like the sort of man who can tell me where I might find something . . ."

Fenris had a sort of matter-of-fact air that made it seem like the easiest thing in the world to go along. The drunk allowed himself to be escorted to the inn door, telling Fenris very seriously about blacksmiths and horse collars, and it should have worked, except that a bystander snickered and said, "Running from a nun, eh?"

"Oh hell," said the dust-wife.

The drunk wheeled around. Everything happened very fast and all at once and Marra had to grab for Bonedog's collar and then the drunk man was *right there* and something glittered in his hands and somebody shouted and Marra yelled, "Fenris, he has a knife!" and then, almost apologetically, Fenris stepped in close and punched the drunk in the head twice.

The man shook his head as if to clear it and Fenris punched him again. This time he fell down.

"And now I believe we should be going," said Fenris. "Quickly."

The three of them did not quite run out of the town, but they weren't slow. Bonedog wanted to go back and bite the man and Marra's shoulders ached from holding him.

When, after about twenty minutes, no one appeared to be chasing them, she relaxed enough to feel some other emotion, and it felt too much like anger for her liking. "Fenris!"

"Yes?"

"You could have died!" hissed Marra. "He had a knife!"

"But you would have gotten away," said Fenris.

"But—" Marra gaped at him, not sure if she wanted to throw herself into his arms or shake him until his teeth rattled. "But you would have been dead!"

He shrugged.

Marra took a deep breath. Why was she angry? It didn't make any sense to be angry, except that she'd been afraid and the fear didn't know what to do with itself. *It was just a drunk. You're fighting a prince. You'll face worse dangers than this.*

"Enough," said the dust-wife. "No one is dead, and let us get out of here while that's still true."

Chapter 11

It was easy to find the godmother, once they got to Trexel. Marra had visions of the dust-wife using magic or asking the dead, but what she actually did was lean over a fence and say, to a woman with three children and a harried expression, "Is there a godmother who blesses children about?"

The woman's face briefly turned cheerful. "Oh yes— Don't put that in your mouth! The godmother. She's very kind— I swear to the saints, Owen, I will take you to market and sell you for a three-legged goat!—Five miles down the road, turn where it crosses the stream and go along the bank until— Owen, I've had about enough!—You'll find a little house with a garden and a signpost out front. The sign's fallen down, but the post is still there. There's usually trumpet flower up the post and I don't think we've had a hard enough frost yet— *Owen! You leave that cat alone!*"

These directions proved quite good, unlike Owen. They found the garden, the house, and a post with a wooden crosspiece and two rusted iron links that had probably held a sign at some point. The trumpet flower had gone up the pole and flowered extravagantly scarlet.

"Hello?" said Marra's fairy godmother, looking up from her work in the garden. Marra knew her at once, though she had not seen her since she was in the cradle. Something inside her snapped toward the woman, like an iron filing snapping to a magnet. *Her. There. That's the one.*

The garden was just slightly out of control. It was nothing that a week or two of work couldn't fix, but the weeds were flourishing around the base of the plants and Marra could see the dried stems of last season's beans still twined around the poles, despite the new growth covering them. None of the preparations for winter had been made, although the first frost would hit any day now. *A little too much for one person.*

Her godmother had the kind but faintly anxious look of someone who was permanently in just a little over her head. She smiled at Marra, a smile with a little worry at the edges, and started to say, "How can I hel—" and then a line formed between her eyes and in midsentence, she switched to "Oh! You're one of mine, aren't you?"

She dropped the stake that she had been trying, without success, to slide into the already rampant tomatoes. She was round and flushed and there were sweat drops on her forehead. As Marra watched the woman push to her feet, wiping at her face and leaving a streak of dirt across her cheek, it was hard not to compare her to the ancient aquiline majesty of Prince Vorling's godmother. It was not a kind comparison. Marra felt a pang of something like despair.

"I can always tell," said the godmother happily. "I'm Agnes!" She reached out to take Marra's hand with her own. There was dirt on her fingers and a dead tomato leaf adhered to her hair. "It's so good to see one of mine all grown up!"

She hasn't got the faintest idea who I am, does she?

"I'm Marra." The dust-wife stepped through the garden gate, with Bonedog and Fenris hard on her heels. "*Princess* Marra."

The dust-wife walked forward. There was a run in the corner of the garden with a half dozen hens. The brown hen looked down at them imperiously, then away, profoundly uninterested in her fellows.

Agnes's mouth fell open. "Oh," she said in a much different voice. "Oh. You're . . . oh." She looked down at Bonedog, and her eyes widened. "Oh." She wiped her hands on her skirt, leaving stains. "I see. You . . . ah. You should come in. Maybe tea?"

"Tea would be a kindness," said the dust-wife, inclining her head.

They all followed the godmother into the cottage. It was cluttered but not dirty, the windows large and streaming with light. Agnes hurried to put the kettle on.

The uselessness of it all struck Marra like a blow. This was the woman who had given them all a gift of health and said that Damia would marry a prince. And meanwhile Vorling's godmother kept the entire kingdom wrapped in immortal magic, warding off enemy curses and usurpers to the throne. "We should go," said Marra in an undertone. "She won't be able to help us."

The dust-wife gave her a quelling look. Agnes, who must have heard, continued making tea. "It's good tea," she said. "The horse trader brings it, you know, when he's gone to sell a string of yearlings. I blessed his youngest and he brings me tea every time. I tell him he doesn't need to, but it's such good tea, and he's such a sweet man to do it."

"What did you bless her with?" asked the dust-wife.

"Health, of course. I always give them—"

"*Health!*" exploded Marra. She had not thought that she could feel rage toward this small, foolish woman but there it was, coiled around her heart, and suddenly it had found an outlet. "You gave Damia health and marriage to a prince and she was healthy enough, yes, right up until the day the prince killed her! And Kania is healthy now, too, and so she survives the beatings he gives her and the pregnancies she's forced to bear one after another. Health! What were you *thinking*?"

The fairy godmother stopped moving. Her hands locked over the edge of the little washbasin and her back sagged. After a moment she reached slowly for the tea.

The cottage was utterly silent as she made the tea and brought the teapot slowly to the table. She put out mismatched mugs. Her eyes were full of tears, and Marra began to feel ashamed of herself, as angry as she still was. Agnes's hands were shaking. The dust-wife took the teapot away from her and poured it.

"I always give them health," said Agnes, wrapping her fingers around her mug. "It's a good gift. You lose so many children to fevers, you know, every year. Not one of mine ever died of fever."

A suspicion began to form in Marra's mind, but the dust-wife got there first. "Health is the only gift you can give, isn't it?"

Agnes nodded. "The only one that anyone would want."

"But you said that Damia would marry a prince . . ." Marra let her voice trail off.

"It seemed like a safe bet," said Agnes, gazing into her mug. "She was the oldest daughter of the king and queen. I thought it was likely she would." She wiped the back of her hand across her eyes. Her voice shook. "Health's a *good* gift."

"It is a very good gift," said the dust-wife in a voice that left no room for doubt. "You have saved many lives."

The godmother smiled a little, and another tear fell and landed, unheeded, on the table.

Marra began to feel like a monster.

This isn't some great power who could have saved you. She did her best. And you've never been really ill in your life, have you? You recovered from that fever. And if it weren't for her, perhaps Kania would not still be alive to save.

"I'm sorry," she said. She was still angry, at the universe if not at Agnes, and it came out clipped. She tried again. "I shouldn't blame you. I didn't realize . . ." She gestured aimlessly.

"It's all right," said Agnes. She reached out and patted the air near Marra. "I didn't know that your sisters . . ." Another tear slid down her face. "I'm so sorry, my dear. I wish I could have given them something better. I would have, if I could." She smiled, though her lips were trembling.

"I mean no offense," said Fenris, speaking for the first time. His voice sounded like a growl of thunder in the small space, after the voices of the women. "But why would a godmother with such a specific talent—however useful—be chosen to stand for the royal family of the kingdom?"

Marra admired his diplomacy. When he had said that he was a warrior and a diplomat, she'd given more weight to the part with swords than words.

"Ah," said Agnes. She wiped at her eyes again. "Did no one tell you, Marra?"

"Tell me what?"

"The reason I'm the royal godmother." Her smile this time was stronger, if self-deprecating. "I'm your great-aunt Agnes."

* * *

Of course we would be related, thought Marra wearily. *Of course the godmother who is terribly outmatched would be family. All of us are small and in too far over our heads. Perhaps it's simply in our blood.* It did make a kind of sense, though. Why the Harbor Kingdom would have a fairy godmother at all. *Power calls to power*, the dust-wife had said. *And we have so little power that all we could call up was a relative, and not even a powerful one.*

"I didn't think there was any magic in the royal family," said Marra.

"Oh, there isn't. And my father—your great-grandfather—the king," said Agnes, "for the most part was very faithful. That's what made it so odd, you see. He was out hunting one day and met a woman and she enchanted him. They'd made love twice already before he realized that she had cow hooves and tore himself away. Eleven months later, she came to the palace. It was . . . oh, not a scandal, exactly. She was very discreet."

Unprompted, the dust-wife poured more tea into Agnes's mug, who took another swallow, her voice growing stronger. "Obviously your grandmother knew. But the woman came with the cow's hooves obvious, so she didn't blame the king for it, because she knew he had to have been enchanted. I think he would probably have had me killed, to try and make it up to her somehow, but she said that I was part of the family, even if I was a bastard, and nobody was killing anybody." Agnes took another sip of tea. "Not at the palace, of course. The king's old nurse had retired in comfort, and I was sent to her. I don't have cow hooves myself." She grinned, a brief flash across her round face. "I'm sure all of you are suddenly wondering what's inside my shoes! No hooves. But there's enough fairy blood in me that I was a godmother." She sighed, the grin fading. "I've always wondered if my mother would have kept me, if I was more powerful. I suspect she had a plan, and probably I wasn't right for it after all. But I don't want you to think anyone was ever unkind to me! Not at all. And of course when I could be a godmother, the queen insisted I come out and do the blessings. I think it was her way of trying to acknowledge me as part of the family, you know. She was very gracious. She didn't have to be, but she was."

Marra looked at the earnest, hopeful face of the godmother and felt as if she had been unspeakably cruel.

Why did I think she must have slighted me? Why didn't it occur to me that she might just be doing the best she could?

She answered her own question almost immediately. Because of Prince Vorling. Because the one godmother she had seen as an adult was a terrifying power, so she had assumed that all godmothers fit the same mold. *Vorling and his kingdom get proof against malign magic, and we have a witch who is simply grateful that she wasn't murdered by her own father and received the barest acknowledgment from her family. Saint's teeth.*

The anger that had simmered inside her shifted and found a different target. How dare they dump Agnes in the middle of nowhere? If she had not had so much else to deal with, she would have brought her great-aunt to the palace herself and demanded that she be treated like family.

Which means . . . what? That she is dragged off to live in a palace she does not know? That she is watched by courtiers every moment? That she has no privacy to herself?

That she gets married off to a monster to forge an alliance?

Marra put her head in her hands and heard herself give a brief, choking laugh. Over her head, she could hear the dust-wife quietly explaining what they planned to do to Vorling, and the godmother saying, "Oh. Oh my!"

Someone squeezed her shoulder. Fenris. His hand was warm and she leaned toward it a little, drawing strength from the grip. Perhaps she could ask him about how to help Agnes. He had experience with diplomacy the way that she did not. She was almost a nun and barely a princess and she had never felt the lack more keenly than these last few weeks.

Bonedog rolled over and wiggled on his back. Agnes looked at him thoughtfully. "He's magic, isn't he?" she asked. "I don't mean like a familiar. I don't quite know what I mean. But something."

"There's a glamour on him," said the dust-wife. "Look sideways a bit."

Agnes frowned. "I don't . . . wait . . ." She turned her head and squinted, then said, "Oh! He's all bones, poor thing!"

"I don't think it bothers him much," said Marra.

"Well, he's a dog. They don't have an idea how the world's supposed to be, so it doesn't bother them when it isn't." Agnes frowned. "Except herding dogs, I think. They have a pretty clear idea in their heads, so they're always nipping and worrying and trying to get it to fit. Of course, there's people like that, too."

"A great many of them," rumbled Fenris. "They are either excellent organizers or terrible zealots. There doesn't seem to be a great deal of middle ground."

"Right." Agnes nodded. "All right. Well, I see there's no hope for it. I'll come with you, then, shall I?"

Marra stared at her.

"Kania's my niece," said Agnes. "And her child is my grand-niece. Or grand-nephew." She rubbed her face. "Or perhaps it's my great-grand-niece and my great-grand-nephew. I can never keep track. But anyway, they're in danger, so I'll come."

No, thought Marra. *No, this is absurd. She'll die.*

. . . Haven't you been saying this is a fool's errand and you'll all die?

Yes, but I didn't mean . . . not like . . .

"Good," said the dust-wife. "I'm glad to have a godmother along. There's magic and then there's magic and there's the dead and then the living and I'm only skilled with one."

"I don't know how skilled I am," said Agnes. "But I'll do my very best to help."

"But . . ." Marra felt as if she should put a stop to this, but she didn't know how to say, *Agnes is useless—can't you see?*

As useless as a princess who only knows embroidery?

She stared into her tea.

Marra knew just how useless she felt, and yet somehow she had pulled together the dust-wife and Bonedog and Fenris. Perhaps . . . perhaps this was more of the same. Her hand crept to the carved grackle feather. Perhaps the saint was leading her.

"All right," she said, not looking at Agnes. "All right. Thank you."

"Five of us," said Fenris, looking over at the others approvingly. Marra leaned down and scratched Bonedog's spine until his jaws clattered with pleasure. "Five is a fist. Five is a hand on the enemy's throat."

"I suppose that makes us each fingers," said Marra. She curled her own around Bonedog's spine, taking comfort from the hard ridges. "You're the thumb," she told the dog. Bonedog wagged his tail.

* * *

They slept that night on the godmother's floor, near the hearth. Agnes took down blankets and so Fenris had his own and they no longer had to sleep back-to-back.

It should have been a relief. She had her own blankets again and no longer had to worry about keeping him awake with her fidgeting.

Of course, I am contrary as ever and nothing goes easily.

Her back felt cold and unprotected. She felt as if something might grab her. Her mind conjured all manner of demons in the dark: the drowned boy, the Toothdancer, all reaching out to grab her.

You are being ridiculous. You are much safer in here than you ever were on the road. And you shared a blanket less than a fortnight. You haven't had time to get used to sleeping next to someone. This is absurd.

Anyway, he's . . .

He's what?

Bonedog rolled over on his back, wired paws paddling at the air. She could hear the even sound of Fenris breathing.

Grow up, Marra. You're trying to save your sister and kill a monster. This is not the time to feel anything else. You're too busy.

There was a large basket to one side of the hearth, full of yarn.

Marra shifted around, scooting the blankets until she could set her back to it. Immediately she felt better.

There. You see? It's not him after all. It's just being nervous. It doesn't mean anything. He's only a companion on the way. That's all . . .

The relief that she felt was too great to be anything but a lie, but Marra took comfort from it nonetheless and drifted to sleep, listening to the sound of Fenris breathe.

Chapter 12

Intellectually, Marra knew that there had never been any chance of getting an early start. *And I shouldn't worry about it. One more day, more or less, is not going to change anything. If I wanted to be done sooner, I should have started sooner.*

Nevertheless, she felt a pang as the sun crawled up the sky and noon passed with no sign of getting on the road at all. Agnes had cooked an enormous breakfast to use up all the food in the larder, then had packed, unpacked, repacked, and was about to start on a third round when Fenris gently stepped in and offered to carry the extra.

"Are you certain?" asked Agnes, blinking up at him.

"Yes, of course. Though I will beg a blanket or two from you as well, for the road." Which sent Agnes off in a flutter to locate blankets for him, leaving her gear strewn across the kitchen table.

"She seems . . . easily distracted," said Marra, determined not to say anything harsher after she had made such an ass of herself the day before.

The dust-wife also looked distracted, gazing after Agnes. A line had formed between her eyes.

"Something wrong?" Marra asked.

"Mmmm." The dust-wife shook her head. "Wrong, no. Interesting. I'll sort it out, I expect."

Marra wrinkled her nose. "*Interesting* interesting, or *dangerous* interesting?"

The dust-wife peered down the hall. Agnes's voice floated back to them. "Oh dear, this one has a hole in it . . ."

"Interesting," said the dust-wife finally. "I can't tell you more than that yet."

* * *

Eventually they did get on the road. Marra thought, somewhat despairingly, that they'd be lucky to make five miles before they had to stop, but she kept her mouth shut. At least they were moving. *And anyway, you just uprooted the woman's entire life and yelled at her about being a lousy godmother. Half a day isn't much at all.* She flushed and stared at the road in front of her, embarrassed by her own frustration.

It's because you're too much alike. What did the abbess used to say? That our own flaws infuriate us in other people? How long did it take you to leave the convent?

Blissfully unaware of Marra's thoughts, Agnes was walking alongside the dust-wife. Occasionally the godmother reached up to chuck the brown hen under the chin. The hen seemed deeply appalled but was apparently too surprised to resist.

"How does one become a godmother, then?" asked the dust-wife. "Is there training?"

"Oh dear. I wish there was! Maybe there is, if you know the right people. But I didn't. Don't." Agnes waved her hands. "I knew that a godmother was a thing that people like me could be, you understand. So I practiced."

"How does one practice something like that?" asked the dust-wife.

"On kittens, mostly," Agnes said. "I think I blessed every barn cat from the time I was nine or ten on. Ducklings, too. And once I ran out of those, mice." She bit her lower lip. "I tried everything I could think of. That they would live for many years, that they would find love, that they would never know hunger. Nothing took. You can feel it when it takes, you understand—it's like stamping your foot down and then you see the footprint. I can see the print after the blessing. Marra's still got it. And Fenris . . ." She screwed up her face thoughtfully. "There was a godmother at your christening, wasn't there?"

"We don't call them that in Hardack," said Fenris, "but I believe our erl-wives perform the same function. Can you see it?"

"Oh yes. You will live with honor and never waver. Your shield will not break."

Something about the solemnity of the words, delivered in Agnes's thin but cheerful voice, made Marra want to laugh. Fenris smiled broadly. "That is correct," he said. "And my shields never broke in battle, either. Mind you, I dropped a fair number of them over the years . . ."

"What about curses?" the dust-wife asked. "There are many stories about the wicked fairy at the christening."

Agnes shook her head. "I'm not sure," she admitted. "I always wondered if maybe those godmothers could only give bad gifts. And then you have to wonder if maybe there are lots of godmothers out there who don't do anything because the only gifts they could give would be curses."

"Have you ever tried to curse?" asked the dust-wife.

Agnes ducked her head, failing to hide a guilty expression. The dust-wife pounced like a chicken on a worm. "You did. And you found you could, couldn't you?"

"I shouldn't have," whispered Agnes. "It was on a mouse. I . . . I said it would die before its seventeenth birthday. I'd read a story with a princess who was cursed and . . . well, I shouldn't have, but I did. And it took. I felt it. It was like a black stain on that poor little thing's future." She dabbed at her eyes. "I tried to tell myself that mice hardly ever live past two anyway. Most of them don't live anywhere near that long. But what if it *would* have been a particularly long-lived mouse and I cursed it?"

Sweet Lady of Grackles, thought Marra. *She's genuinely upset that she might have stopped a mouse from becoming ancient. Because of course she is.*

"You said before that health was the only gift you could give that anyone would want," said the dust-wife. "Were there other gifts? Ones that you think no one would want?"

Agnes, wilting beneath the inquisition, hung her head. "Yes. Keen whiskers. I'm good at keen whiskers. It isn't much good for anything but kittens and mice, though. You can't give a human baby keen whiskers. It wouldn't work—or what if it *did*?"

Marra pictured a child in the cradle suddenly growing a full set of cat whiskers and put her hand over her mouth.

"Now, that would be an interesting experiment," said the dust-wife.

"No," said Agnes, with surprising firmness. "No, I wouldn't do it. It's not fair to the child. It's not *decent*."

"I suppose." The dust-wife didn't sound entirely convinced. "Any others you managed?"

"Well, I blessed a whole litter of mice that cats wouldn't eat them. But I don't think that's very useful for a child, either. And then once I said a kitten would have many fine sons."

All three of them looked at her sharply. Bonedog, sensing something, whined.

"I'd just been reading a book, you see, and it had a king and a queen and she bore him . . . I was *twelve*! I didn't think!"

"What happened?" asked Marra. In her head, her mother's words echoed around and around, like a coin in a begging bowl. *We shall hope the next child is a son. Kania is riding a dragon, and all of us in the kingdom are riding along with her . . . hope the next child is a son, hope the next child is a son . . .*

"It was awful," said Agnes. "She had six litters and every kitten was a tom. The barn was overrun. Nothing but fighting and pissing everywhere, and yowling when they weren't pissing."

"Just like the barracks," said Fenris nostalgically.

"Interesting," said the dust-wife slowly. "So you are rather more versatile than you claim, but health is the only gift that you're willing to give."

"Health can't go wrong," said Agnes. "Most of the rest can. If you bless a mouse that they'll always be happy, they run right out in front of a cat and get happily eaten. But health always works. No one regrets being healthy."

"What did the prince's godmother say?" asked the dust-wife, turning to Marra. "Her exact words?"

Marra wracked her brain, drawing up the image of the ancient godmother, the stained-glass skin stretched over bone. "'I shall serve her as I have served all her line, my life bound to theirs. No foreign magic shall harm them. No enemy shall topple their throne. As it has been for all the children of the royal house, so shall it be for her, as long as I draw breath.'"

Agnes sighed. "That's a good one," she said. "A big one. I couldn't do that."

"That's what we're up against," said Marra. "Vorling can't be harmed by foreign magic. Supposedly the Northern Kingdom's enemies are always throwing spells at them, but they don't take." She remembered the king, aged and infirm before he had turned fifty. "But it burns them out. I wish it would burn Vorling out faster."

"Can his guards be harmed by magic?" asked Fenris.

"Eh?"

"Well, if Lady Fox here can arrange to put his guards to sleep, I can just stab him."

The dust-wife snorted. Agnes's eyes were very round.

"What?" said Fenris. "Simple plans are best."

"You're not wrong, but I doubt I can put an entire palace to sleep," said the dust-wife. "Particularly since I've never put even one person to sleep. I have a great many talents, including raising the dead, but if you want lullabies, that's someone else."

"Can you distract them somehow? At least long enough for me to stab him?"

"Probably not long enough for you to get away again, no."

Fenris raised his eyebrows. "That's not really a requirement, is it?"

"Yes," said Marra, annoyed. "It *is*."

"Fine, fine." He lifted his hands. "No death-and-glory final stands unless we have no other options. Hmm. Can you raise up an army of the dead to fight the guards?"

The dust-wife rolled her eyes. "Armies of the dead *seem* like a good idea," she said. "Until you're standing in front of a thousand blind, withered husks who only know how to kill and kill and keep on killing. We might as well just drop plague corpses in the town well at that point."

"I would have to object to that," admitted Fenris. "All right. No armies of the dead, then."

"*Could* you do that?" asked Marra tentatively.

The dust-wife shrugged. "I don't know. It's never really come up."

"Yes, but if it did, would you know how?"

Feathers and movement announced the brown hen's emergence from the pack. The chicken walked up the dust-wife's arm and settled back on the staff, her comb at a decidedly jaunty angle.

"I know how I'd start," said the dust-wife finally. "Some things I expect you don't know until you're doing them. But it's been done before." She leveled a glare at Marra. "But don't get any ideas. We're here for a straightforward regicide, not to level the city."

"Yes, ma'am," said Marra meekly, and dropped her head.

* * *

They stayed that night in a barn, courtesy of Fenris's firewood-splitting skills. The farmer even threw in a meal of salted potatoes and gave them apples for the road.

"I promise I did not bring you along to make you split firewood," said Marra.

Fenris laughed. The two older women had gone inside to sleep, and it was only the two of them and a very small fire, well away from the barn.

"It's all right," he said. "I've done many things that were terribly important, lives hanging in the balance and so on and so forth. There is something pleasant about chopping wood. If I miss a stroke, nothing awful happens. If a piece of wood is not quite right, it will still burn. If I stack it and it isn't perfect, clans will not fall."

"It sounds very difficult."

"Mm. Sometimes." He fixed her with a thoughtful look, and it occurred to her that his eyes were the color of sun-warmed earth, and she did not quite know what to do about it. "But you know, don't you? You are the daughter and the sister of queens, so there must have been many times in your life when things hung on your actions."

Marra inhaled sharply. Fenris poked at the fire with a stick. "I'm sorry," he said. "I did not mean to distress you."

"No. No, it's not your fault. I . . . yes. I have too much power for who I am. My mother sent me away, finally, and I know it was partly because I was not . . . not good at these things. But none of it is *my* power. It is only other people, moving me on a game board. It was a relief when I went to the convent. When I have to come out, for the christenings or the funerals . . ." She wrapped the nettle cloak more tightly around herself. "It's why I like needlework," she added.

Fenris lifted an eyebrow.

"Like splitting wood. Like you said. Embroidery doesn't *do* anything. It isn't anything but what it is, and I don't have to worry that I'm doing something terribly wrong and my tutors will get sent away or that I slighted someone important and they'll want to close down trade with my kingdom. I can just make pictures and patterns, and if I make a mistake, I can tear it out again and no one dies." She took a deep breath. "It doesn't matter that I'm a princess. The thread doesn't care."

She was looking at the fire and did not expect the hand that came out of the dark and took hers and squeezed.

"And yet here we are," he said. His thumb lay like a warm bar across her palm. His hands were very large compared to hers, and the calluses from the sword and the axe were much thicker than the ones she had developed from shoveling stables. "Freed of all our duties, we charge headlong to take on another responsibility."

"I have to save my sister," said Marra. "I lost one already." She laughed and heard the bitterness in it. "Kania doesn't even like me very much, I don't think. But I still have to do it."

"And very likely we will not survive." He rubbed her palm absently. She wouldn't swear that he even knew he was doing it.

"We will," she said. She caught his hand in both of hers, gripping hard enough to hurt. "Fenris, we *will* survive."

He gave a half smile and a small nod. She could tell that he was humoring her, and she recalled the look in his eyes when she had yelled at him that he might die when that drunk had pulled a knife. *He doesn't want to die, I don't believe he does, but . . . it's like he expects to. Like it's inevitable.*

Like he doesn't mind.

"Suppose we do survive. What happens then?"

"I don't know." Marra looked at the fire. "I suppose I go back to my convent and work on my embroidery."

"Mm." He squeezed her hand again, then released her and began to put out the fire. "Well, if you find that your convent needs someone to split firewood, it happens that I know a fellow . . ."

* * *

Two days later, they reached the capital of the Northern Kingdom.

She had been keeping her head down, hoping not to be recognized, and mostly watching the dust-wife's feet. When they topped a small rise and the dust-wife stopped, Marra looked up for the first time in what felt like hours.

The prince's city shone savagely before her, high walls leading in an endless spiral to the Northern palace. People streamed through the gates, vanishing into the maw of the city, and all she could think was that there were so many people, hundreds, thousands, all of them living in the prince's city and loyal to him and what was she? What were five against so many? What could they do?

It is too much, she thought bleakly. *We have grand plans, but in reality? Most likely we'll get into the city, and look up at the palace, and talk and plan and talk some more, and eventually realize there's nothing we can actually do, and leave again. That's the way it happens outside of the stories.*

The weight of this thought was suddenly very real, more than a feeling, a physical burden, heavy in her stomach and tight in her chest, and before she realized, she staggered unsteadily to the side of the road and went to her knees, out of the way of the crowd of traders and pilgrims. None of them looked at her. A dusty, weeping woman meant nothing, not with the sight of the city so bright and cold and hard before them.

It was Bonedog who noticed first. He put his paws on her shoulders and licked her face frantically. There was enough of the glamour for his tongue to feel wet, but he could not actually touch her tears.

"Good boy," Marra whispered. "Good dog." He was a good dog. Even if his master failed to save her sister or her kingdom, she had done one good thing—giving Bonedog a second chance.

Then Fenris was beside her, putting his arm around her as he had in the goblin market. He half lifted her, his great strength no longer shocking, and moved her farther out of the way of the crowd.

Fenris. Yes. There are good men in the world, and I have met one. And he is my friend, whatever else happens.

"Easy," said Fenris. "Easy. Are you hurt?"

It was such a decent, obvious, ridiculous question that she found herself laughing, the quiet, gulping laughter that comes with tears. "No," she said. "No, I just . . ." She waved her hand toward the city. "We'll never do this, will we? This is all completely absurd. We can't do this. It's impossible."

"You wove a cloak with nettle thread," said the dust-wife, standing over her, "and built your own dog out of bones, and *now* you are concerned about what is impossible?" She shook herself and all the jars and bottles in her pockets rattled like a porcupine's quills.

Marra began to feel embarrassed, not just for having dragged the others with her on this absurd mission, but also for having had the poor taste to have a breakdown in the middle of the road. "I'm sorry," she said. Fenris helped her to her feet. His hand against her back was warm and strong. Bonedog lashed her shins with his tail.

"Oh, my dear," said Agnes, sliding her arm through Marra's. "It's all right. It's all just a little overwhelming, isn't it?" She found a slightly crumpled handkerchief and passed it over to Marra. "You've done so much and here we are and now it feels like there's so much left to do, doesn't it?"

Marra accepted the handkerchief. If she'd had more energy, she'd be alarmed at how well the woman had read her. Yes. It did feel exactly like that. She had done so much and was so tired and how could it only be the beginning?

She wiped at her eyes and, arm in arm with her godmother, she passed through the gates that guarded the city of the prince they had come to kill.

Chapter 13

W ell," said the dust-wife. "Now what?"

All three of them looked at Marra, who looked away, at the narrow street, the buildings close overhead. They had made it through the gate unnoticed. No one cared. No one had pointed at her and shouted, "Princess!" or "Runaway!" And now they were inside, standing in a small alley off the main street, and there was the next thing to do.

Bonedog came and sat on her foot. She closed her fingers around his collar and thought, *My dog trusts me,* and then, *My dog is witless and also dead,* but things loosened a little in her chest nevertheless.

"We'll have to find somewhere to stay," she said. "I don't have much money left. But I can't . . . I don't think I should just . . ." She waved her hand vaguely toward the top of the hill and the shining white palace. *Yes, that would go well. I just waltz in unannounced and then the prince turns up dead. I don't see any way that would end with the Northern Kingdom declaring war on my homeland and grinding us all into dust.*

"I suppose we'll have to figure out how to get up to the palace without being noticed," she said, looking down at Bonedog, whose illusionary tongue was lolling out. "And then . . . er . . . well. I don't think we're going to do this tonight, are we?"

She looked back at her trio of—followers? Weapons? Friends? She had been so narrowly focused for so long that she had not thought very much about what to do once she arrived at the city, except that she should stay out of Prince Vorling's sight.

"Definitely not," said the dust-wife.

"Where should we stay?" asked Fenris.

"Um . . ." Marra shook her head. "I've never been here. Down here, I mean. I was always up there."

Fortunately he took this in stride. "Then we will have to learn if there is a curfew and what parts of the city to avoid. I do know that any inn near the front gate is likely going to prey terribly on travelers, so we would be wise to seek accommodations elsewhere."

"Er . . ." Agnes cleared her throat. It was a very small noise, nearly lost in the sound of movement past the mouth of the alley, but everyone turned to look at her nonetheless. It had been a hopeful sound.

"Oh dear," she said, twining her fingers together. "I had a thought. It's not much, but you know how you talked about the moth? The moth that found what you need? I was thinking . . . Well, it seems unlikely. But I might be able to do something like that."

The dust-wife leaned forward, eyes intent. "What do you need?"

"A baby," said Agnes.

"I'm not kidnapping children," said Fenris. "I realize we're working for a higher cause here, but I have to draw the line."

"Oh, goodness no!" Agnes waved her hands, agitated, like a bird trapped against a wall. "No, no! Not a human child! No, of course not! Just a baby something. Anything. And we can bring it back to its mother afterward."

The dust-wife rubbed her forehead. On her staff, the hen cackled.

"What about a chick?" asked Marra, gazing up at the hen. "Would that work?"

"Oh yes," said Agnes. "That would be perfect!"

Buying a live chick in a strange city was surprisingly easy, although Marra imagined it would have been very difficult indeed if it were just her. *I'd have to get my nerve up to talk to a stranger and ask them if anyone sold chickens and where, and if they didn't know, I'd have to ask the next person . . .*

Fenris, apparently untroubled by such complicated matters, simply walked out of the alley and addressed the first local he saw, a man selling pickles out of a large barrel on a cart. "You, sir! Do you know where I might find a place selling live fowls?"

"You sure you don't want a pickle instead? Much less trouble than fowl."

"Sadly, I do not. Not even such fine pickles." Fenris put a hand over his heart, somehow managing to indicate a profound sense of loss at his inability to eat the pickle in question. "But I've need of live fowl at once."

Marra didn't know how he did it, but two minutes later, Fenris was in possession of directions to the market and the location of the least crooked poultry seller in the place. Five minutes after that, they were standing in front of a stall full of assorted chickens. Full-grown hens sat in cages, clucking to each other, and there was an entire box filled with small, fluffy chicks.

The dust-wife's hen drew herself up very tall and glared down at her imprisoned sisters with something very like scorn.

"We need to buy a chick," said the dust-wife.

The chicken seller was a large man with even larger eyebrows. He gazed up at the hen on her perch and raised one eyebrow very slowly. "The crate," he said.

Agnes leaned over the edge of the crate and cooed at the chicks. "Oh, they're always so adorable at this age . . ."

"Focus," said the dust-wife.

"Oh yes, of course. I suppose we'll have to keep it, won't we? He won't just let us borrow a chicken . . ."

The chicken seller did not look like a man who routinely let customers borrow chickens.

Marra shoved her hands in her pockets and tried to look like someone who was possibly a nun and definitely not the queen's runaway sister. After a minute or two, though, it became obvious that she didn't need to bother. The chicken seller gazed at Agnes, who was picking up each chick and whispering to it, then slowly turned to Fenris. He didn't say anything, but his eyebrows were eloquent.

"She's very particular about her chickens," said Fenris. "Very particular."

"It's not taking," Agnes whispered to the dust-wife, just loud enough for Marra to make out the words. "It won't take. Oh, it was a silly idea. I don't know why I thought it would ever work . . ."

"Keep trying," ordered the dust-wife.

The chicken seller looked back at Agnes, then to Fenris again. His eyebrows inched higher up his skull.

Fenris remained absolutely deadpan, as if it were perfectly normal for women to whisper to chicks before buying them. Marra didn't dare look at Agnes, because if she did, she was going to burst into hysterical laughter.

"*Fine,*" said Agnes in the tone of someone reaching her limits. Marra's ears popped. "There!"

"*That* took," observed the dust-wife dispassionately.

"Not well at all and I have to keep . . . I'm pushing it . . . It doesn't want to stick; it's like jelly sliding down a bowl!"

"Keep pushing," said the dust-wife. "Keep blessing it over and over if you have to."

"Oh dear . . ."

Marra darted a glance at the chick in question. It was a dark, fuzzy little lump with a bright yellow bill and, for a chicken, a remarkably phlegmatic expression.

The chicken seller's eyebrows did a complex dance across his forehead. He named a price that was frankly ridiculous for a day-old chick.

"Don't be absurd," said Marra, stung out of her silence. "It's a chicken, not a phoenix."

The chicken seller's eyes drifted back over to Agnes, followed by his eyebrows.

"The sooner we pay," rumbled Fenris, "the sooner we will go away."

The price mysteriously plummeted.

Agnes fumbled with her belt pouch and handed over a coin, cupping the chick against her bosom with one hand. "Who's a good chicken?" she said, looking down.

They left the chicken seller and his dancing eyebrows behind and made it into a nearby courtyard without Marra losing her composure completely.

"What did you do?" asked the dust-wife. "There's magic on it, but I can't read it."

"I told it that it would find us somewhere safe," said Agnes. "Like the moth that found what you need. I don't know if it'll work. Maybe it could only take us someplace that it would feel safe or that was safe for chickens. But it's there—I just have to keep pushing . . ."

"That's a curse," said the dust-wife. "That's why it finally took."

"No!" Agnes looked upset, cradling the chicken. "It's not! It's . . . Okay, it's not exactly a blessing, but it's not really a curse. Nothing bad will happen."

"Well, let's see if it works," said the dust-wife. "Go on."

"Okay," said Agnes. "Go on, little chick! Find us a safe place!" She set the chick down on the ground and made flapping motions.

The chick looked around, then cheeped and began to run down the alley with Agnes and the dust-wife in hot pursuit.

"See, this would take much longer with a baby," said Fenris.

Marra jammed her elbow into his side, which was rather like elbowing a stone wall. He grunted, possibly to be polite.

They followed the chick to a staircase, which it could not climb on its own. Agnes swooped it up in her hands. The chick cheeped.

"Magic's fading again," said the dust-wife.

"Oh . . . Well—" Agnes looked around as if she were doing something illicit, then something happened and Agnes looked at least a foot taller and the alley was suddenly full of shadows and her eyes flashed and she said, "You will find us a safe place to stay or . . ." in a voice like the tolling of a great bronze bell.

Cheep, said the chicken. The shadows fled. Marra's ears popped again. Bonedog let out a threadlike whine and put his nose behind Marra's knee.

Agnes started up the steps, holding the chick. It seemed content to ride until they reached the second landing, and then it began to struggle. Agnes set it down and chased after it again, followed by the dust-wife, Marra, and Fenris. Bonedog, who would ordinarily enjoy a good run after a small animal, did not seem inclined to leave Marra's side.

The chick led them, after a few false starts, to a narrow alley that opened into a cul-de-sac. It reached the steps of the building at the farthest end and began to bounce determinedly against them.

"Well," said Agnes, scooping up the chick in her hands. "Is this a rooming house, do you think?"

All four of them looked up at the house. It was small and shabby but very clean, with the kind of cleanliness that spoke of poverty. Marra had seen babies delivered in homes like these and could practically hear a voice saying, "We may be poor, but we're *not* dirty!"

There was a girl sitting on the steps of one of the buildings nearby. She, too, was neat and clean, though her clothes were much too thin and so was she. She looked over at them solemnly. "Are you going to Miss Margaret's?"

"Possibly," said Agnes. "Does she own the house at the end?"

The girl nodded.

"Does she ever take boarders?"

Another, slower nod. The girl thought this over for a moment, then said, "Most people don't stay, though. Only locals. There's no harm in her, Da says, but people don't like it."

"What don't they like?" asked Marra.

The girl frowned. The brown hen shifted her feet and let out a low, worried *errrrk*.

"*Him,*" said the girl, eyeing the hen doubtfully. "You'll see him. It's no secret. He can be awful. She's nice, though, Miss Margaret. I run her errands sometimes."

Fenris and Marra traded a brief glance. "A husband, do you think?" whispered Marra.

"Or a brother or a father. Hard to say."

"Dangerous?"

Fenris shrugged. Marra remembered him handling the drunk at the well and felt a stab of envy for anyone who could go through life so unconcerned about possible physical violence.

"Thank you," said Agnes to the girl. She put the chick under her arm and walked to the door of the boardinghouse.

Marra was close enough behind her to hear the godmother whisper to the chick. "Is this right? Are you sure?" The chick peeped. "Was that a yes?"

"That means your chicken is hungry," said the dust-wife dryly.

"Oh dear . . ."

Fenris reached past her while Agnes tried to settle the chicken, and knocked on the door.

They waited for so long that Marra began to doubt whether anyone was coming, and then the door creaked open on darkness.

* * *

Miss Margaret was a tall, stoop-shouldered woman with bony hands and a bony face. She stood in the shadows, at right angles to the door, so that Marra could only make out her profile.

"May I . . . may I help you?" she asked. Her voice sounded as if she was forcing words out around a lump in her throat.

"We need somewhere to stay," said Agnes cheerfully, holding up the chick. "And you're safe. Well, supposed to be safe. The chicken said—"

"Do you have rooms to let?" asked Marra, hastily trying to stem the flow of words.

Miss Margaret looked at her sideways, like a bird. "Yes," she rasped. "Two."

"How much?"

She named a price so low that for a moment Marra thought that she must mean for each of them individually. She stopped herself just before she said *That's all?* and said, "May we look at the rooms?" instead.

The woman nodded again, stepping back down the hall to let them inside the door. Then she shuddered and turned to face them full-on.

Marra's first thought was that there was some kind of animal on her shoulder—a weasel, perhaps, or a particularly long-bodied cat. Then she got a clearer look and she put a hand to her mouth. Even Fenris took a step back.

Him. Of course.

He was a wooden puppet. Some kind of marionette, Marra thought, the kind that traveling performers used to entertain very young children. He had the carved hands and the clacking jaw, the articulated arms and legs. But the only string on him was a black cord that looped Miss Margaret's throat, and the puppet held it in one hand.

He moved as they watched. It was a slow, considered movement, like a tortoise turning its head in the sun, and it set Marra's nerves crawling.

"Oh, *interesting*," said Agnes in a tone of professional curiosity. "That's a curse-child, isn't it?"

The puppet scowled. Bits of wood dragged down across his face. He yanked tightly on the string. The woman nodded, her eyes large and alarmed and clearly begging her visitors not to say more.

"Oh dear! I'm sorry," said Agnes. "No offense meant. That was insensitive of me, wasn't it?" She smiled gently at the woman, as if having a horrible piece of living wood on your shoulder was a perfectly normal sort of thing.

The puppet grudgingly loosened the string. Miss Margaret's throat worked as she swallowed.

"Don't worry," said Agnes. "These things happen. I won'ttttt . . ."

Marra was close enough to see the color suddenly drain out of her face, as if she were a bottle that had been upended. Agnes blinked several times, looking very surprised. Then she said, eyes straight ahead, "Please take the chick, Marra. If I fall on it, I might hurt it."

Marra snatched the handful of fluff out of Agnes's hands, alarmed by the mortal calm in the godmother's voice.

"Good," said Agnes, and fainted.

She collapsed against the wall, rattling the boards, and then slid down into a neat heap. Fenris let out an oath and tried to grab her, but between Marra and Miss Margaret, there was no room in the hallway for another person, let alone one of his size. The chick peeped. Miss Margaret's eyes were enormous.

"What did you do?!" cried Marra. "What did that thing do to her?"

"Nothing . . . nothing . . . I can't . . . he can't . . ." said the land-lady, and then the cord at her throat was yanked tight and she choked.

"It's not the curse-child," said the dust-wife. "All of you, get out of the way! It's the magic. She poured it right out to keep the bless-ing going and pushed herself right to fainting, the little fool."

She looked up at Miss Margaret, ignoring the puppet entirely. "Take us to the rooms. She needs rest and tea and quiet."

Miss Margaret nodded. The puppet's eyes were fixed on the brown hen, whose red comb brushed the ceiling atop the staff. The hen glared down at the puppet and snapped her beak.

Their landlady turned slowly. The puppet shifted, keeping his balance. She led them up the stairs, the dust-wife following, Fenris behind her with Agnes in his arms, Bonedog at his heels, while Marra carried the chick and waited for the puppet to launch himself at someone's face.

He didn't. They climbed the stairs to a whitewashed hallway lined with doors. Miss Margaret stopped in front of one and gestured in-side, eyes downcast. They crowded in.

"The next one, too," rasped the landlady, opening another door. "There is one meal . . . one m-meal—" The puppet yanked on the cord. She stopped, putting a hand to her throat, and gave Marra a pleading look.

"One meal included?" asked Marra. *Listen to how normal I sound. I am having a normal conversation with a woman being strangled by a wooden puppet and we are all acting as if the important thing is meals being included with the price of the room.*

The landlady nodded and fled. Marra inched farther into the room and closed the door. Fenris had arranged Agnes on one of the beds and stepped back out of the way. The dust-wife sat on the other bed, managing to look both annoyed and concerned.

"We can't stay here!" hissed Marra. "That puppet thing—you can't tell me it won't do something awful!"

"It's done something awful to the landlady, certainly," said the dust-wife. "But it won't do anything to the rest of us. It can't. It's just a curse-child."

"Just?" Marra had a hard time imagining that clacking puppet as *just* anything.

"Probably a sad story," said the dust-wife. "They usually are. Somebody gives a lonely child a toy and they pour all their hopes and fears and problems into it. Do it long enough and intensely enough, and then it just needs a stray bit of bad luck and the toy wakes up. Of course, it knows that the only reason it's alive is because of the child. A tiny personal god with one worshipper. It latches on and . . . well." She clucked her tongue. "Normally you get them pried off and burned long before adolescence. Impressive that it lasted this long."

"We can burn it," said Marra. "Burning is fine. I'll get the kindling."

"Not without her permission. You don't go tearing off an adult woman's god and setting it on fire." The dust-wife gave her a sharp look, as if she were suggesting something rude.

"It was choking her!"

"It's her neck, not yours. We can ask before we leave, if you like."

"But it could be wandering the halls at night!"

"No, it would stay attached to her. They really don't have power over anyone else. I suppose it could tell her to murder us in our beds, but any innkeeper could decide to do that, too, so I wouldn't worry about it. It won't risk losing its worshipper if we fight back."

Marra opened and closed her mouth several times, completely unable to form words. How could the dust-wife be so calm?

"This works very much in our favor," said the dust-wife. "She can't tell anyone who or what we are. Nobody trusts a curse-child, and it'll choke her if it thinks she's paying too much attention to something else." She nodded down to Agnes. "Her magic worked. Unorthodox and somewhat inefficient, but it worked."

"Is the chick all right?" asked Agnes from the bed. Her voice was very weak.

Marra looked down at her hands. The chick's fluff was a bit damp from the sweat on her palms, but it seemed fine. "Yes?"

"Oh good . . . I was afraid I'd . . ." Agnes closed her eyes. She was still very pale, almost shockingly white against the pillow. "I'm sorry to be so much trouble."

"You drained yourself down to nothing on that bird," said the dust-wife.

"Did I?" Agnes sounded bemused. "It's never happened before . . . Normally the magic just takes or it doesn't. But I kept redoing it in my head to make it stick . . ."

"Yes, and knocked yourself out in the process." The dust-wife's voice thawed a bit, and she patted Agnes's pillow. "It's fine. It worked. We're here now. Now, you get some rest."

"Wait!" said Marra as the dust-wife began to shoo her out the door. "What about—"

"We're staying," said the dust-wife. "This place is safe. Cheap, too."

"No, I meant the chick."

"What?"

"I don't know how to take care of a chicken."

The dust-wife's angular face drew into tight triangles. "It's a *chicken*. Didn't they teach you at the convent?"

"No! Chickens were someone else's problem. I knit bandages and helped deliver babies." She wedged her foot in the door to keep from being left in the hall in care of the chick.

"Babies happen occasionally. Chickens happen all the time." The dust-wife plucked the chick out of Marra's fingers, shaking her head. As the door was closing in her face, Marra heard, "I know you aren't broody, demon, but you're going to make an exception or so help me . . ."

The door shut with a click.

Chapter 14

The other room had two narrow beds with a small table and basin between them and a shuttered window. Marra collapsed onto one with a groan and put her head in her hands.

"Are you all right?" asked Fenris.

"Horrible puppet," she said, "demon chicken, fairy godmother."

"And it's a fool's errand and we're all going to die," said Fenris. He patted her shoulder. "Still, I have to admit I didn't see the chicken or the puppet coming."

"Nothing's ever easy," said Marra, too tired to yell at him for taking her fatalism to heart. She remembered suddenly that she had cried in front of everyone earlier in the day and felt herself flush with embarrassment. To hide it, she turned away, pulling back a corner of the blanket and investigating the mattress.

It was stuffed with horsehair and the blankets were coarse but clean. The room itself was shabby but painfully neat, much like the rest of the house. She did not see fleas jumping anywhere. "Well, it's not a bad room." It reminded her of her room in the convent.

"I've slept in far worse," agreed Fenris. The small bed looked even smaller when he sat on it. Marra was fairly certain that his feet were going to hang over the edges. He gave her an apologetic look. "I, uh . . . realize it's awkward that you have to share a room with me. If there were a stable, I'd offer, but there isn't one. And honestly, I'd rather be close at hand, in case . . ."

He trailed off, but Marra knew that he was thinking about the curse-child. "I'd prefer you were close, too," she said. "It's fine. No worse than the road."

Fenris made a noncommittal noise. Marra knew perfectly well

what he meant. Once you added walls and a door, things became . . . complicated.

It's not complicated. It doesn't have to be. He's your friend and you're here to kill a prince and that's all you need to know or think about. She forced a smile. "I suppose beds like this aren't quite what you're used to."

Fenris shrugged. "I'm not really used to anything. I slept in barracks for a long time. When I was traveling, I'd sleep on the ground. Sometimes I'd go from sleeping on dirt to sleeping in the best guest chamber in the castle."

"And sometimes in fairy forts," she added.

His face changed. She felt as if a shutter had closed in his eyes. *You fool, why did you say that?* "I'm— I'm sorry," she said, stammering a little. "I'm sorry, I shouldn't have joked about it—"

"It's all right." He reached out and took her hands in his. The room was so small that he could do so easily. "Marra . . . *Princess* Marra . . ."

She winced. "Don't. I'm not. I mean, I am, but I'm really a nun, except I'm barely even that."

"You are the princess of the Harbor Kingdom," he said. "I learned that at the first inn we stopped at in your homeland. Your sister Kania is married to Vorling of the Northern Kingdom."

Of course he'd learn that. You should have guessed. It's not like it was much of a secret. She told herself this firmly, trying to ignore the sudden clawing in her chest that screamed that he would tell Vorling, he would betray them all, he knew too much and it would all be used against them . . .

No. This is Fenris. He is a friend, and he has never been anything but decent. She stared down at their joined hands, trying not to feel trapped, wondering what price she would have to pay for his silence.

"People love to gossip about the royal family," he said. His voice was very gentle. "They told me why you were sent to the nunnery. A few people thought there had been some scandal, but most of them said that you would be Vorling's third wife if your sister died. You were being held in reserve, they said."

*no no my mother said that I was out of the game I was set free I was
sent away because I did not have to stay at court because I hated it and
I was free*

She looked at her own thoughts and they seemed to belong to a
much younger Marra, one who had never been to the goblin market, one who had never built a dog out of bones. One who could
afford to be innocent and ignorant. *I can no longer afford to be that
person.*

"It's probably true," Marra said, marveling at how steady her voice
was. "My mother never said as much, but Vorling is obsessed with
having his own blood sitting on my father's throne. And, of course,
our harbor was worth controlling anyway. A good, deep harbor is a
kingdom's wealth. I could never have been allowed to marry anyone
else and produce a son that might challenge that. And there was
always the chance that my sister might die, like our older sister did,
and that I would need to be pulled out of the convent and sent to
the altar."

Fenris nodded. His hands were warm. He turned them gently and
caught both of her hands between his palms. "I suspected as much.
So do many of your people. They know that Vorling is ambitious."
He paused, as if weighing his words, and then said, almost hesitantly,
"They still remember your sister Damia fondly."

"She was so beautiful," said Marra. "And so kind."

He squeezed her hands tightly. She took a deep breath, wondering if she was going to cry again. No, it seemed not. The pain had
softened over the years, the edges worn down by time. She gazed
dry-eyed at their hands. Her left hand had never quite recovered
from spinning the nettle thread. One of the knuckles was more swollen than the others, and there was a numb band along the side of
her little finger.

"After the second or third inn, I felt like I knew too much," Fenris said. "You know hardly anything about me, and I had heard so
much about you and your family." He took a deep breath. "So. Yes. I
slept in a fairy fort. There was a battle, you see. One clan overthrew
another. It happens, though the Fathers try to keep it from coming

to that. The clan that was destroyed had been fostering a young lad as a squire, and the lady of the conquering clan said that her people would not make war on children, so he was spared by her command. He was handed over to us, who served the Fathers. He could not have been more than thirteen, and a young thirteen at that. His voice was as high as a novice nun's."

"Fenris," said Marra, looking up at him, "you don't have to tell me this."

"I know. I want to. Then we'll be even and . . ." He smiled down at her, with an edge of pain that cut her heart. "And I find that it's important to me that we be even." Marra bowed her head. The edge of one of his thumbnails had a nick in it. She could feel the heat of his skin across hers, crossing the numb band of skin, heat and then vague pressure and then heat again.

"So. This squire was afraid to go home. Afraid that his father would think that he had failed by being captured alive. By not dying like a hero." Fenris's lip curled. "I spent a week convincing him that his father would be so glad that his son was alive that there would be no talk of failure. I could see myself in him. I had been his age once and terrified of failing to live up to my father's example. And I saw myself so clearly that I did not see him at all."

She had a sense of the story to come and she did not want to hear it, as if not hearing the words could erase them. "Fenris . . ."

"You brought me out of the goblin market, and I fear this tale is a part of me. It follows wherever I go." Marra was not certain if that was bitterness or duty speaking, or perhaps both. *Duty and love and hate are complicated . . .*

"I thought there was something odd when we delivered him to his father. 'Hiding behind a woman's skirts?' the lord said. It was odd, and the manner he said it was odd. But I had duties and I went about them and left the son with the father. But it nagged at me."

"And?" said Marra, who knew her duty as the listener.

"And a week later, I returned. I could not get the way that the father had spoken out of my head, or the look in his eye. It wasn't right for a father. I don't have children, so far as I know, but that look . . ." He shook his head. "I went back. But I waited too long, fool that I am."

"He was dead," said Marra. She wondered if the Sister Apothecary felt this way when someone told her of an ailment that she had diagnosed from the first word.

"Flogged to death. His father had branded him a traitor and a coward. He was hanging by his wrists from a pole in the courtyard. I cut him down myself." His voice was flat and utterly emotionless. Marra was reminded of Kania prepared to marry her prince, the same flatness. *This is happening and I am part of it but that is all.* "He had taken at least a day to die."

"I'm sorry," said Marra, feeling the inadequacy of the words. She turned her hands to squeeze his, and he looked down at them, seeming almost puzzled.

"And that is why I could not kill myself, after I had killed his father and his guards. I would not shame that young man's memory any further."

"You were right to kill his father," said Marra fiercely. "That wasn't wrong."

"Everything else I did was wrong," said Fenris, "from first to last." He sighed. "I failed to listen and failed to understand, and a child died a tortured death of my failures. Because my father was a good man, and I was so full of my own foolishness that I could not see why this boy was frightened."

"My father is a good man, too," said Marra. "That's probably why it took me so long to see what was happening to Kania. I knew something was wrong but I suspected all the wrong things. I knew she was pregnant too often, but I never knew why." She tugged at her hands and he released her immediately. "And my mother was my mother, and I knew she loved me, so it took me a long time to realize that she would also move me as a game piece to save the kingdom."

Fenris nodded. "Sometimes that was my job as a servant of the Fathers," he said. "To move people and alliances like pieces on a board. It would have been much harder if I had loved them."

Marra exhaled. Had it been hard for her mother? She wanted to believe that it had been. Life would be easier. But that was her sorrow and Fenris had his own. "You're stronger than I am," she said. "You did it all yourself. I couldn't stop Vorling. I had to go find someone powerful who could. I'm scared all the time and don't tell me that courage is going forward when you're scared because it's not like that. I was scared of the carriages and the people at the inns. The only thing I did right was find the dust-wife."

"Ah, Lady Fox." He shook his head. "I think finding her makes up for anything else you did wrong."

"Maybe, but you . . . you did what you could to make it right." She didn't know how to say what was in her head, that Fenris was a good man and maybe the weakness of being good was that evil didn't occur to you. That never in a thousand years would she have dreamed that Vorling was intentionally hurting her sister. It had never even crossed her mind. "And then you did your best to make sure no one else suffered."

He snorted. "By jumping into a fairy fort. Not the best idea I've ever had."

Marra clasped her hands together. They seemed much colder now that Fenris had released them. "Well, if you hadn't, we never would have met."

"No, we wouldn't have." His eyes held hers for just a moment too long, and in the end, Marra's dropped first.

* * *

"So you *do* curse things," said the dust-wife.

Marra woke, startled. It sounded as if the dust-wife were talking directly to her. *A curse? What was a curse?*

"I don't," said Agnes. "I'm not like that."

"You couldn't bless any of those chicks, could you? Until you gave up and cursed the last one."

Marra propped herself up on her elbows and realized that the walls were so thin that she could hear the conversation.

"Fine." Agnes sounded defeated. "A small curse. Only a small one."

"Not so small. The only reason the magic took was because you cursed the chick, wasn't it?"

"All right, yes. I've never been much good at blessing people, not really. But I didn't hurt the chick. It was fine."

"What was the curse portion? There had to be something."

Agnes mumbled something.

"What?"

"I *said,* if the chick didn't find us a safe place, it would die."

Marra's eyes widened in the dark.

"But it found it," Agnes continued, "so it worked out all right." She sounded worried, even through the muffling plaster, and Marra could picture her fretful expression.

"You're skilled at cursing. Genuinely skilled. More than that, you've got a talent for it. I saw the way the world slipped sideways in the alley. It wasn't just the one mouse that time, was it? You've done it before."

Another mumble.

"Who was your mother, really? Or what? Not just a random maiden with hooved feet, was she?"

Marra glanced across the room. Could Fenris hear this? No, he was asleep, hands folded neatly next to his head, breathing slow and even.

"You're a poor liar, Agnes. Tell me the truth."

Marra had been feeling a slight pang of guilt over eavesdropping, which immediately vanished. She wedged her ear against the wall, just in time to hear Agnes say, "What good is it? I'm not going to go around punishing children for being born. That's a terrible thing to do. People really don't like that."

"So you are giving up your power in order to be liked," said the dust-wife heavily.

"No." That was loud enough that Marra winced. "I am giving up my power in order to be *decent*. If warriors are allowed to stop killing people and bang their swords into plowshares, I ought to be allowed to keep chickens and give children good health and not curse them."

The dust-wife said something else, too low to hear.

"The world can go *hang*," said Agnes, sounding perilously close to tears, and as long as Marra listened, she heard no more from the next room.

Chapter 15

I was thinking," said Agnes the next morning. "Maybe I should go talk to this godmother."

"Eh?" said Marra.

"Eh?" said the dust-wife.

"Is that wise?" said Fenris.

Peep, said the chick.

They were all sitting around a table in a little whitewashed room. The surface of the table was scarred from years of use, but everything was very clean. Miss Margaret's breakfasts were very plain—coarse bread, cooked eggs, and little fish dried whole—but she was not stingy on the portions, which was good because Fenris ate as much as the other three humans put together.

"Well, we don't know exactly what the blessing is, do we?" said Agnes. "We know what the words are. But maybe there's a loophole. It's not always words. You figure that she had to make a good speech to the court, but she might have said something simpler to the baby."

"And you think she'll tell you?" asked Marra.

"She might. Professional courtesy, you know."

Marra nodded, though she had trouble picturing that grim figure with the stained-glass skull extending any professional courtesy to anyone.

Surprisingly, Fenris agreed. "She might," he said. "Very unlikely people, you know, will share confidences with each other if they think the other person understands. A prisoner who won't tell a guard anything will thaw immediately if he's put in a cell with another man in for the same crime. And doctors who would bite off their tongues before showing indecision to a patient will tell another doctor about how little they know and how frightened they are. I've seen it happen many times. It's how spies work."

"There is something to what you say," said the dust-wife. "But if the prince turns up dead, then I would assume that this godmother would be suspicious."

"Why?" asked Agnes. "I'm a godmother. I can't do anything to an adult. And I've got a perfectly good reason to be here. The queen's about to bear another child. As the godmother for the royal family, I've got an interest."

"I'll go with you," said Marra. She could just imagine sweet, cheerful Agnes running into the prince's godmother, in much the same way that Bonedog might run headlong into an unexpected wall. *I wouldn't go see her by myself, either. Maybe the dust-wife could hold her own, but the rest of us mortals . . .*

"She's seen you before," said the dust-wife.

"Not really." Marra shrugged. "I was a long way off and there was a king and a queen and a prince in the room. I wasn't on the dais. I don't think she even glanced in my direction."

"So that's settled," said Agnes. "Will you look after Finder?"

"Finder," said the dust-wife in a tone that did not invite further comment.

"The chick. I named him Finder."

The dust-wife looked at her, then at the little black chick, then back at Agnes. "Finder," she said again.

"Because that was the blessing. That he'd help us find somewhere safe."

"You named the chicken."

"Well, of course! Doesn't your chicken have a name?"

The dust-wife looked at the brown hen, who glared back. "First of all, no, and second of all, she's got a demon in her, so I would be naming the demon, which already has a true name. I am not going to go around naming demons. It gives them ideas."

"I name all my chickens," said Agnes. "Specky and Buff and Milady and Jonquil and Shadow. Don't you name any of your chickens?"

"No. They're chickens. They don't come when they're called."

"Well, no, but it's easier if you're going to talk about them to other people. You can't always be saying 'the big tan one with the feathered feet' and whatnot."

"I do not talk about my chickens to other people," said the dust-wife with an air of finality.

"I've heard you talk about other people to your chicken, though," put in Fenris. Agnes giggled.

"For the first time," said the dust-wife, mostly to the ceiling, "I am beginning to question the sense of this entire enterprise."

"I've been questioning it since day one," said Marra.

"I have not," said Fenris. "I have faith in all of you."

"You *would*," muttered the dust-wife. "Fine. I'll watch . . . Finder."

Agnes beamed at her. "Be a good chick," she instructed Finder, and handed him over to the dust-wife. Finder peeped. The brown hen made a low, reptilian noise of disdain.

Agnes dusted off her hands. "Let's go," she said. "I can't wait to meet another godmother."

* * *

Finding where the prince's godmother lived was easier than it should have been. Agnes simply asked the landlady.

"I don't know," she rasped, while the puppet glared at them and tapped his wooden nails together. "But someone like that will live rich, and the houses get richer as you climb the spiral. Go up the spiral road and ask again."

"Right, then!" said Agnes happily, and off they went, Marra in her drabbest robes with no medal, a servant or a poor relation.

"Won't she live in the palace?" asked Marra.

"Would she?" asked Agnes. "I don't."

"Yes, but . . ." Marra identified a conversational pit trap and carefully stepped around it. *Yes, but you're you. Yes, but in the Northern*

Kingdom, the godmother is terrifying and respected, not a poor relation. Yes, but . . .

And an hour later, *Yes, but you were right.*

The godmother did not live in the palace. She lived in the temple district, among the tall, narrow houses of the gods and saints, as if she were a priest.

"Near the top of the city, of course," said Agnes. While the city was arranged in a spiral of roads, steps had been cut as short cuts. They worked. They were also extremely steep. "Why do gods always want you to walk to them? You'd think they'd do more good if they were near where most of the people live."

"I suppose it depends on what people want in a god," said Marra. "But the abbess always said that most people want gods to be close enough to get them if you want them, but not have them breathing down your neck all the time."

Agnes grunted, waving for a halt. They sat down on a bench halfway up the steep flight of stairs. Both of them were panting.

"So," said Agnes.

"Unnnh?"

"Fenris?"

"Fenris what?"

Agnes nudged her in the ribs. "*Fenris,*" she said, lifting her eyebrows.

"Oh gods," said Marra. She rested her elbows on her knees and dropped her head. *Please do not make me have this conversation with my great-aunt. Please.*

"Eh? Eh?" Another nudge. "Handsome lad, isn't he?"

"He's not a lad; he's nearly forty. And I haven't been thinking about it, Aunt Agnes. I've had other things on my mind."

"You watched him chop firewood the other day."

"What does that . . . ?" Marra had to pause. Yes, she had. He'd taken off his shirt. There had been a lot of muscle on display. Even the dust-wife had paused for a look. Her hen had cackled so loudly it had set off the others in the nearby barnyard. "Oh. That. All right. I'm not *dead.*"

An elderly woman, older than Agnes, went by. She was bent double under the weight of a basket and she went up the stairs twice as fast as either of them. Marra didn't know if that was inspiring or depressing.

"So you *have* noticed," said Agnes, pleased. "And he's quite a gentleman, too."

"He's wanted for murder in his home country."

If she'd been expecting that would stop Agnes, she was sadly disappointed.

"I'm sure he had his reasons."

"Well, yes."

"Good with chickens, too. Finder likes him."

Marra put her face in her hands. *Lady of Grackles, if you would like to open the earth and let it swallow me whole, now would be an excellent time.* "Aunt Agnes, we have—" No, she couldn't very well say that they had an assassination to plan, could she? Not where people might be listening. Blast. "—a lot going on right now."

"All right, all right. I'll stop. Just, you know, keep it in mind. Not every day a man like that comes along, eh?"

"I am very suspicious of men right now," muttered Marra through her fingers.

"A little moth told me he's what you need."

"He's *not*—" Marra dropped her hands, realized the exact words that Agnes had used, and glared at her great-aunt. Agnes looked smug.

"Besides, I'm sure he doesn't think that about me," said Marra. "So it's all moot anyway."

"You're sure about that, are you?"

Fenris's hand on hers, absently stroking her palm. Fenris's wry smile. His solid presence against her back. The mutual awkwardness of finding themselves in a bedroom together. The way he had held her hands, then let her go the moment she pulled away. "Completely sure," grated Marra. "Now, come on. We're supposed to be meeting a terrifying godmother, or have you forgotten?"

"Yes, yes." Agnes got to her feet. "More stairs. Joy."

"Humph."

Both of them were red-faced and gasping by the time they reached the temple district. A tall woman with close-cropped hair, wearing the medals of the Unconquered Sun, gave them directions. "For all the good it will do," she said. "She sees no visitors."

"Oh, it's all right," said Agnes cheerfully. "She'll see me. Probably."

Marra expected a cynical look, but the woman's eyes softened as she looked down at Agnes. "Then good luck to you, grandmother."

The godmother's house looked like a temple. It shared walls with the buildings on either side, one a priest's home and one a shrine to the Saint of Dust. There was a guard standing outside the door, armed and armored, holding a halberd before him.

"Hello," said Agnes, walking up. "I'd like to see the godmother, please."

The guard tilted his head almost imperceptibly. "She does not see any visitors."

"It's important," said Agnes.

"You waste your time. She does not bless anyone but the royal family."

"Oh, that's all right." Agnes reached out and patted his arm as if he were a small child. "I don't need a blessing. I'm a godmother."

Marra braced herself to grab Agnes and roll out of the way if the guard took offense to being touched, but he only looked bemused. "Another godmother?"

"Yes. Can you go tell her I'm here?"

"Is she expecting you?"

Agnes shrugged. "Well, I don't really know, do I? If she's an extremely powerful godmother, she might be able to see the future, in which case yes. But if she's like the rest of us, then probably not. Or she might be very powerful, but not good at seeing the future, which happens, too. Futures are very muddy. You can't really get much out of them, you know."

He was beginning to get the look that most people dealing with Agnes got. Marra wondered if that was something a person could learn, or if you were born with it. *Or perhaps it only works if you're obviously older and seem a bit silly and so obviously devoid of malice . . .*

"How do I know you're a godmother?"

Agnes searched his face. Little strands of white hair had escaped from the pins and gave her a wispy halo. "You . . . did not have a godmother," she said slowly, "but your mother did, and the blessing was . . . was . . . Oh dear, I'm afraid I can't tell exactly. That her children be born strong or born healthy, one of the two." She patted at the air with her hands. "It was a good blessing," she said. "I think it worked."

The guard's eyes widened. He looked over his shoulder at the door, as if expecting to find someone looking at him.

"Wait here," he said, pulling the door open, and stepped inside.

"You could really see that blessing?" whispered Marra.

"Oh yes. Normally you can't go too far back, but the ones about what kind of children you have leave marks on the child. They have to or they wouldn't work. It doesn't last forever, though. I tried with mice." She shook her head. "By the third or fourth generation, even if you wish that all their descendants be healthy, it's just too faint. Magic spreads itself thin after a while. It has to, I think. To keep itself going past that, it'd be constantly drawing on the person who cast the spell, and that's no good. One litter of mice isn't much, but a hundred or so, having litter after litter? You saw what happened making the magic stick to Finder. I don't want to find out how many healthy baby mice it takes to make me drop dead of exhaustion."

The guard opened the door again. "The royal godmother will see you," he said, his face impassive once more.

"Thank you," said Agnes, beaming at him. Marra gave him a wry look as she passed, aware of the effect that dealing with magic could have on ordinary souls. She thought that she caught the trace of a smile around his eyes, but perhaps that was only her imagination.

The godmother's dwelling was also a temple.

It was strange to see. Marra had expected doors, apartments, the trappings of normal living. Instead it was a long, narrow hall, hung with tapestries. The godmother sat on a dais at the far end, her robe forming a triangle with her pale skull at the apex. Bowl candles with a dozen wicks flickered, casting deep shadows on the ceiling, and the room smelled of scented wax.

Does she sit here all day? Marra wondered. *Is this how she receives visitors, or does she simply sit here and wait to be called to the palace?*

It was somehow easy to believe the latter. There was an immobility to the godmother in this pose, as if she had been crafted from leather and layered fabric, a doll that had never been made to move. She looked like the god of the temple, not like a person in her own home.

When she moved, it was a visceral shock. Marra took a step back as if she'd suffered a blow. It seemed as if that ancient skin should crack apart instead of stretching.

"Come closer," said the godmother in a voice like an echo from the bottom of the bone pit.

"Hello!" said Agnes. "I'm a godmother, too."

"Yessss . . ." The sibilants drew out and faded away. The godmother's eyes flicked over Marra, dismissed her, and settled on Agnes. Marra wondered if, having said that, the godmother was about to throw them out again.

And then the godmother smiled, her almost lipless mouth pulling tight across bone. "Come in and have some tea."

* * *

Marra's hands ached, and the little numb patch of skin had flared as if brushed with the ghosts of nettles. Nothing bad had happened, though. Had it? The godmother had made tea. Hadn't she? Marra couldn't quite summon the memory of the water boiling, only the long, withered hands on a black iron teapot, pouring it into little lacquer cups.

Marra concentrated on breathing in and out. The room was not spinning or anything so dramatic, but something was happening inside her ears, a queasy, dizzy feeling. She felt as if she were standing just behind her own shoulder, watching herself breathe.

The godmothers seemed very far away. She could hear them

talking and understand the words, but only if she concentrated. It was as if they spoke in a language that she was not fluent in, and had to focus on every word.

". . . a curse? Heh. Yes, of course there is a curse . . ."

Is there something in the tea? Or the candles? No, Agnes was obviously unbothered, and Marra had barely drunk the tea.

She stood up. Neither Agnes nor the godmother seemed to notice. When Marra glanced over at them, she was struck by how similar they looked, which made no sense. The godmother was very tall, wasn't she? But Agnes was as well, somehow. Had she been wearing black? Marra couldn't remember. *Of course she must have been. It's not like she could have changed clothes without you noticing.*

". . . that's very clever. I couldn't have done that . . ."

The godmothers did not seem very interesting. The hangings, though—the hangings were very strange. *Tapestry weave,* Marra thought absently, *but what on earth was the weaver doing?* It seemed as if they were switching back and forth between styles with no sense of pattern or structure.

She drifted over to one of them while Agnes and the godmother continued talking. Up close, it was even more complicated and less aesthetic. Blocks of color interlocked or failed utterly to do so. Marra had never been much of a weaver, preferring embroidery. Tapestry weaving required a great deal of advance planning, and she could never get her head around it well. Still, even her worst efforts were neater and more regular than these.

This bit is a weft lock . . . and this is split weaving here . . . but why? Weft locks interwove two threads; split weaves left a small but perceptible gap between them. Neither was terribly unusual, but weavers usually picked a style and stuck to it. This followed no discernable pattern. Six splits would be close together, followed by a run of weft locks and then straight runs of a single color. The effect was disorientating. At the bottom right corner, for no apparent reason, the weaver had used golden embroidery thread to make a kind of knot, as if tying off the tapestry, except that was certainly not how you did it—you'd need to tie off the warp ends and this looked more like a child had stabbed thread into the weaving, over and over, leaving ugly loops. *Is this a signature?*

Agnes laughed, and her voice sounded deeper and somehow older. Marra glanced up, but they were only two women sitting together, cloaked in darkness. What mattered was the tapestry, the strange irregular weavings . . .

"Are you a weaver?" asked the godmother.

Marra had been leaning so close to the tapestry that she hadn't registered that conversation had stopped. "No," she said, pulling back. "I mean . . . I have. I'm not good at it. I embroider, mostly."

"I have been working on these for many years," said the godmother in that strange, flat voice that seemed to echo in some other space. "You might find them of interest."

"Ah . . . yes, of course," said Marra. She schooled her face into a polite smile. You did not tell anyone that they had produced a muddled lump of ugliness. She would not have insulted a novice that way, let alone an undying creature of terrible power.

She went to the next tapestry and found that the bottom third was identical to the first one she had looked at, but then it wandered off into other colors, other patterns, other erratic joinings of warp and weft. The next one also shared the same bottom third as the others, and the next.

Is this supposed to look like something? Regardless of how she squinted or turned her head, she could not make it resolve into anything. There was a blob of red that might have been a sword, but it might also have been a lizard or the head of a rabbit with particularly stiff ears.

She was sufficiently engrossed that she only half heard the two godmothers finishing their pleasantries. "A moment before you leave," said the godmother. "I will give you something."

Marra's pulse leapt, as if the offer of a gift was a threat. *Which possibly it is . . .*

The godmother rose to her feet. Marra took a step back, ready to flee.

Agnes gave her a sharp look and offered the godmother her arm. Marra half expected the woman to shun the offer, but the godmother leaned heavily on her colleague, then picked up her cane.

"As I said," she said, moving slowly to the second tapestry, "I have worked on these for some time." She stood before it, but her eyes were on Marra. "Do you know what they represent?"

"No?" said Marra. The blocks of color did not look like anything. They were not even enough to be a map or a floor plan, not varied enough to be writing.

The godmother nodded. "Then I may give it to you." She reached into her sleeves. Metal flashed and Marra thought, *Oh god it's a knife she's going to stab Agnes*, and then, *Why am I so frightened? She has never offered us so much as an unkind word.*

She knew why, of course. Vorling feared the godmother and Marra feared Vorling, links in a chain from predator to prey. *I am a worm and Vorling is a starling. The worm has nothing to fear from the hawk, but I cannot quite convince myself of that . . .*

Shears. They were shears that the godmother carried. She caught hold of the tapestry and closed the blades over a spot not quite half-way up. Marra cried out in surprise. Even as ugly as the weavings were, they represented hours and days of work.

The godmother was ruthless. She chopped off the bottom of the weaving and held it out to Marra. Her hands shook and the stray threads, unraveling from the top, swayed back and forth. Marra was suddenly reminded of the silk threads of the cocoon in the goblin market, the moth that had taken days of her life away, and what would this strange, violent gift take away from her?

"Take it," said the godmother. "You may find it useful. Or you may not." Her eyes bored into Marra as she spoke.

The worm has nothing to fear from the hawk. She took the piece of tapestry and their hands touched for an instant. The godmother's skin should have been cold, but it was the same temperature as the air, as if she had no heat of her own.

Marra noticed that her hands were shaking as badly as the god-mother's. She stared down at the ragged-edged bit of weaving. "I . . .

I . . . Thank you," she said finally, as if she were a small child and her nursemaid was prompting her to remember her manners.

The godmother made a noise somewhere between a hiss and a grunt. She nodded to Agnes, and then Agnes took Marra's arm and led her out of the strange little temple.

The light outside was shockingly bright. Her eyes watered. She blinked, looking down at the strange, butchered weaving in her hands.

Wait . . . wait—what just happened? Did I really leave Agnes talking to the godmother and go wander around the room?

"Agnes?" she said, surprised at the volume of her own voice. "Agnes, did something just happen? I was sitting with you, and I was paying attention, but then I wasn't . . ."

Agnes chuckled softly. "She's good," she said. "As powerful as the dust-wife and ten times as old."

"Was there something in the tea?"

"No, not at all. She just wanted to talk without anyone listening. Including you." Agnes patted her arm. "It'll wear off in a minute. It wasn't anything harmful, just misdirection."

The dust-wife is going to have my head. I went along to keep Agnes safe, and instead I get caught by a spell. "Do you think she knew who I was?"

"I don't think she cared," said Agnes. "I don't think she cares about very much anymore." She chewed on her lower lip. "It seems like it would be lonely, to be that old and not care, but maybe she doesn't care about being lonely, either."

Her step was light as they went down the stairs, almost dancing. Marra's head throbbed and everything seemed very bright. She tried not to be curt. "Did we learn anything?"

"Oh yes, a great deal," said Agnes. "For one thing, she's not blessing those babies. She's cursing them. And has been for centuries now."

Chapter 16

"A curse?" asked the dust-wife, sitting in the little parlor room in Miss Margaret's house. The innkeeper brought them a pot of tea and the curse-child stared balefully over her shoulder. "A protection from malign magic. How is it a curse?"

"Because we're listening to the wrong part," said Agnes. She waited until landlady and puppet had left the room and dolloped honey into her tea. "We all were obsessing about the foreign magic and enemies taking the throne. That bit's mostly theater. But the actual curse is that she will serve them as she served the family, her life bound to theirs, as long the godmother still draws breath." She beamed at the other three people at the table.

". . . I don't get it," said Fenris. Underneath the table, Bonedog gnawed happily on a soup bone, which felt vaguely like cannibalism to Marra.

"She'll serve them as she served the rest of their family, and she bound their life to hers. How do we know that's a good thing?"

The dust-wife sat back, suddenly thoughtful. Marra frowned. "Do you mean she's hurting them?"

"The royal family of the Northern Kingdom has been dying young for centuries, haven't they?" Agnes tapped the tabletop. "It's not even gossip anymore. Everybody just knows."

"A maid told me there was a curse on the kingdom and the kings burned out from it," said Marra slowly. "And it was the godmother who protected them from it."

"It's the godmother who's doing it," said Agnes. "She got immortality from somewhere, and that's how. Their life is bound to hers. She's pulling it out of them to keep herself alive." She paused.

"You know, I don't think she likes it at all. One of the kings—the very old kings, way back when, the one who built the first palace, I think—bound her to the royal family. She has to serve them. It's not something she chose to do. But she has to stay alive to serve them, so she's draining the life out of them. It's awful for everybody, when you think about it."

A terrible thought struck Marra. "Is that why my niece died? Did the godmother kill her?" Fenris inhaled sharply.

"No, no." Agnes waved her hands. "Probably not. Not when she's got Vorling, and the king was still alive to work on then, too. But she's also keeping any magic from helping them. That means that if I went in and tried to give a baby a blessing of health, it'd fall right off. The royal family can't so much as get a wart removed by a witch. Magic can't touch them. Which means magic can't break the spell, either."

The dust-wife grunted. After a moment she said, "But that doesn't help us, does it? It's the same as it ever was. We can't enchant Vorling."

"Not while the godmother draws breath," said Agnes. "That's the other half." She looked up at the trio of puzzled faces. "Oh dear. Look, it's like Finder, right?"

Marra rubbed her forehead. The chick was currently snuggled under the brown hen's body. The hen didn't look terribly happy about it. "What about Finder?"

"The spell—" Agnes caught the dust-wife's eyes. "Fine, the *curse* on Finder was that he'd find us a safe place to stay or . . . well, it'd be bad," said Agnes. "Most curses are like that. They come in two halves. This curse is that the royal family is bound to her, isn't touched by any other magic as long as they live, *and as long as the godmother draws breath.*"

"That's not promising," said Fenris. "Do we have to kill her?"

Agnes's eyes went round. "I don't think we could. I mean, she might want to let us, but if she could die that easily, she would have just done it already. I don't think she can be killed in the normal sense."

"This is getting worse and worse," muttered Marra. Agnes had seemed so excited earlier, but when she tried to explain things, they sounded terrible to Marra. What happened to the next of Kania's children? She was probably due to give birth soon—she'd already been round at the funeral . . . What if they did kill Vorling somehow and the child grew up and was drained of life to fuel a curse?

"But she's only doing this because she has to!"

"Does she resent them?" asked Fenris.

Agnes gnawed on her lower lip. "I don't think so," she said. "I think maybe she would have, a long time ago. I'm sure she hated them once. But now she just doesn't care. She's been alive too long. She outlived any real feelings. She can't die. She just goes and curses a child and then she goes away and sits in her temple and just . . . exists."

"What a dreadful fate," said Fenris.

"She should at least keep chickens," said the dust-wife. "Or take up gardening. Immortality is wretched, but you can always make the best of it."

"Do you think she'll help us?" asked Marra.

Agnes gave her a worried look. "I don't think the spell would let her. I think she already did as much as she could."

Marra took out the butchered chunk of tapestry. Another few strands had come loose. It was agonizing to look at, like an open wound. "She said she could give me this, because I didn't know what it was."

The dust-wife looked it over but shook her head. "It doesn't mean anything to me. It isn't any kind of magic, or if it is, I can't sense it. I don't know why she gave it to you, but presumably she had a reason."

Marra stared at it, trying to make sense of the pattern. Nothing came to her. She leaned her head back against the wall. Fenris had sat down opposite her, trying to minimize the amount of space he took up in the tiny room. Bonedog was half under the table, his illusionary tongue hanging out. Finder the chick had wandered down to sit between his paws, apparently napping.

Bonedog freed from the pit of bones. Fenris freed from the goblin market. Finder freed from a pen in the market. *Everywhere we go, we set things free, and we're trying to free Kania from Vorling . . .*

"Could we free her?" asked Marra. "The godmother?"

"The king who bound her is long dead," said Agnes. "I don't—"

She stopped. Her eyes went round. She looked at Marra and Marra felt the same idea strike her all at once, a shared moment of realization. *The king is dead.*

Slowly, holding the thought in her head as delicately as an egg, Marra turned to the dust-wife. "The dead kings live in a palace of dust below the living palace," she said. She remembered the billow of tapestries, and the maid telling her about the maze beneath the palace. She'd seen it herself, however briefly, hadn't she? She remembered the stone underfoot and staring at the back of Kania's dress, trying not to get lost in the dark. "They're all there. Can you find the king who bound the godmother? Find him and make him let her go?"

The dust-wife drummed her fingers on her knee. "I don't know," she said. "Let's find out."

* * *

"Three sets of iron doors and a portcullis, each of which requires teams of draft horses to move," said Fenris grimly. "That's leaving aside the honor guard and the fact that it's on the main square opposite the living palace, where anybody can see us trying to get in."

Fenris had spent two days lurking outside the palace, scouting the main entrance to the palace of dust, occasionally with help from Agnes and the dust-wife, sans chicken. Marra couldn't go in case she was recognized, but she remembered the place well enough. When members of the royal family were interred, the horses wore black caparisons and were blessed by the priests of seven temples. Marra remembered the solemn pacing of the great beasts as her niece's coffin was carried through the iron doors, the thudding of drums.

"There must be a way in that doesn't require horses," said Marra. "People have to go in first to prep the tomb. You couldn't get a bunch of horses in every single time."

"It's theater," said Agnes.

Fenris looked puzzled, but Marra nodded. "Yes, exactly. A royal funeral is like a wedding. And the christening is the same way. You need set dressing and staging and schedules. Horses don't just show up spontaneously in the right outfits and march."

Fenris considered this. "I suppose you're correct. Though it is not work I had considered. The coronations I have overseen mostly involved getting someone to a point of being crowned. Actually setting up the feasts and the clothes and the priests was someone else's problem."

Marra thought privately that it was probably mostly a woman's problem, but at least Fenris was acknowledging it was work.

"So there must be a way to get in and out of the tomb," said Agnes. "Without all the horses."

"It might be inside the palace, though," said Marra. While she was reasonably confident that no one would recognize her in the city, going into the palace itself seemed like tempting fate.

"It's a tomb," said the dust-wife. "There are always entrances. If they are hollowing out new areas, or building new rooms, there must be an entrance for masons that does not involve tracking brick dust through the palace."

"Do the dead know?" asked Fenris.

The dust-wife rolled her eyes. "The dead are already there. They don't worry about how to get in and out. They're corpses, not cat burglars."

Fenris leaned back, tapping his thumb against his lower lip. "Bricks. Hmm. Could there be a quarry? Or an entrance from a quarry? How can we find out?"

"Put out that you want work as a stonemason," said Agnes.

"A stonemason?" He raised his eyebrows. "I don't know the first thing about stone."

"Take off your shirt," said the dust-wife, poking Fenris with her staff, "and I suspect you won't have nearly as much trouble as you think."

* * *

In the end, Fenris did not have to take off his shirt. Apparently he was sufficiently well muscled that no one questioned a history of chiseling stones into shape. (Marra tried not to act disappointed. Agnes didn't even bother to try.) He came back from his first day, drenched in sweat and covered in white dust, and went immediately to the well to dump water over his head. ("Almost as good," said Agnes, elbowing Marra. The dust-wife's chicken cackled.)

"It's not terrible," he said. "I'm the low man on staff, so nobody's handing me a chisel. I'm just moving things around and trying to memorize the jargon. I don't know how long I can keep it up before they realize I'm a complete novice, though. They may fire me tomorrow."

"Hopefully it won't matter," said Marra. A knot of excitement was forming in her chest. *This is it. We're on the way. We're actually doing something.* "You just have to last long enough to find the way in."

Fenris was a quick learner, and apparently he picked up the specialized speech of the trade at a good enough pace that he wasn't sacked the next day, or the day after that. But there were also a number of connected quarries and no way to know which one might lead to the palace of the dead unless the dust-wife went along and asked the dead, and so for about five days, she and Fenris wandered through the quarries at night, dodging guards and talking to spirits, while Agnes made friends with the neighbors and Marra bit her nails down to the quick.

This was exactly what she had always feared. They would get to the city and then no one would know what to do and they would talk and talk and talk and nothing would get done and whatever they tried would fail and eventually they would run out of money and Fenris would probably get a job cutting firewood and Agnes would want to go home and check on her chickens and Kania would take a mysterious fall just as Damia had and eventually Vorling would die of old age and all of Marra's efforts would have come to nothing. Except now that she knew that if Kania had a living child, that child would also be cursed and grow old before its time.

She sat in the tiny, dilapidated courtyard of the boarding house and tried not to scream. *I did three impossible tasks—well, two—and went to the goblin market and now I am just sitting here while my friends break into quarries. Oh, Lady of Grackles, this is hard.*

Maybe skipping the third task was where I went wrong. Maybe that was the one that makes you a hero. The first two were just gritting my teeth and beating up my hands. She rubbed her thumb over the numb line of skin along her little finger.

She wondered if all the old stories of heroes slaying monsters and maidens locked in towers had involved long, tedious stretches of trying to find the monsters or build the towers in the first place. *Probably. No, almost certainly. Who wants to hear the dull practical bits?*

Me. I do. It would make me feel less like I am failing.

She sighed and sat back on the bench. It was midafternoon, just barely warm enough to sit outside. The view in the courtyard wasn't much. One bench, three walls, one door. A half dozen pots that had probably held flowers once but now held sticks. There was a climbing rose that had died back for winter and shed curled greenish-brown leaves across the bricks. It looked like it had seen better days and was only holding on out of habit. Marra found herself identifying a little too much with the rosebush.

Agnes had befriended a woman next door and was doing laundry with her. Marra could hear her laugh drifting over the wall from time to time. *And did the great heroes do laundry? I don't remember hearing about it. You'd think after slaying a hundred men, they'd need a good wash.*

Bonedog watched a bird hopping through the dead rosebush, his illusory ears twitching. Marra started to stand up and then Agnes burst through the door and gasped on one breath, "*Thequeenhasgivenbirthtoaboy.*"

* * *

"She can't have," said Marra blankly. "It can't have been that long. Surely."

Agnes shrugged. Her face was pink with exertion. Finder was tucked into her generous cleavage, presumably dreaming the dreams of small warm chickens. "It's all anyone is talking about. There are criers in the marketplace, announcing that Vorling's heir has been born."

Early? thought Marra. And then she remembered Kania kneeling uncomfortably, her belly on her knees, and it had been months after that that she left the convent and another month before she came back to the Northern Kingdom. *It could easily have been nine months. You never asked how far along she was.*

"Kania?" she croaked. "Have they said anything about Kania?" She snatched up her cloak and grabbed Bonedog's leash. *It's not as if they'd send out criers if they weren't sure. The babe must be expected to live. But Kania—how is Kania? How is my sister?*

They were halfway down the corridor when the innkeeper stepped in front of Marra. She gestured to the outside and rasped, "Have you heard? The queen . . . the queen—" Her eyes were wide with delight. The puppet on her shoulder chattered its jaw and glared. "A boy, they say. A b—" The puppet decided that this was enough words and yanked the cord. Miss Margaret hung her head, but her eyes still danced.

"We heard," said Marra. "Going to get more details."

"It's so exciting!" bubbled Agnes. "A royal baby!"

Miss Margaret got her finger under the puppet's leash and pulled a little slack. "And after . . . after the last . . ." She beamed.

Marra considered screaming but settled for turning sideways to pass the innkeeper and her rider.

"Relax," said Agnes, as they emerged into the alley. "It's normal. Gossip about the royal family is the only real benefit to having one. You have to let people enjoy it."

"They're gossiping about my sister," grated Marra. "And my niece. My *dead* niece."

"Who is also my great-great-niece," said Agnes calmly. "But it doesn't feel that way to them. And if you go around listening to this news with a face like thunder, people will think you're not happy, and that will seem suspicious."

Marra took a deep breath. That much, at least, was true. She schooled her expression to one of polite interest and followed Agnes through the alley, Bonedog tugging on the leash.

"This is hopeless," said Marra, after ten minutes and as many stories. The queen was dead. The queen was alive but dying. The queen had died and her dying wish was that the prince take religious orders. The queen was alive but the baby was drinking her blood mixed with breast milk and would not survive. The queen was fine but tired. The baby was alive. The baby was dead. There were two babies. There was one baby. The queen had given birth to a school of fish.

At last, they found a crier in the market, surrounded by a crowd. The crier wore the livery of the palace and shouted, "Rejoice! Rejoice for the heir is born! The queen has borne an heir to the throne!"

"And the queen?" called Marra, jostling through the crowd. "How does the queen fare?"

"She has borne an heir," bellowed the crier. "A son to take the Northern throne!" Scattered cheers erupted from the crowd.

"But is she alive? Is she well?" The crowd surged and Marra could not be certain that the crier had even heard her. He didn't answer. She looked around at the crowd and saw only mouths, opening and closing, as if they were biting off pieces of her sister's story and devouring it.

You have to let people enjoy it, Agnes had said. This did not feel like enjoyment. This felt wicked and terrible and strange.

She started to push forward again, but Agnes took her arm. "Let it lie," the godmother said. "We'll find out soon enough. There's nothing we can do either way."

"I can fret," snapped Marra. "And I intend to!"

"And I won't stop you." Agnes patted her arm. "A good fret is balm for the soul. Just don't overdo it."

Marra ground her teeth. *If I go to the palace and demand to see the queen . . . No, no, I can't. My mother might be here, and if she's here, she'll see me. And this is all far too much to explain.* She took a deep breath and let it out again. She walked back to the boardinghouse, with the woman who had a puppet at her throat and the girl sitting on the steps who missed more meals than she ate and who was crowing about babies that weren't quite right.

You have to let people enjoy it.

This is not right. This is not fair.

And what is fair? Marra snarled to herself. *How is it fair that you grew up and ate meat at every meal and were never expected to shovel a stable because your mother married a king? How is it fair that Vorling cannot be brought to justice? How is it fair that some women wear themselves out in bearing and others cannot have a child? How is it fair that Fenris can never go home again because he killed a terrible man? How is it fair that gods punish starving people in the blistered land?*

Nothing is fair. Nothing is right.

She took a deep breath and stared at the wall, dry-eyed. Agnes touched her arm, concerned.

Nothing is fair, except that we try to make it so. That's the point of humans, maybe, to fix things the gods haven't managed.

The front door opened. The brown hen squawked.

"We know how to get in," said Fenris.

Chapter 17

T here's always a haunted quarry," the dust-wife explained. "People moving giant blocks of stone around like they do there, someone's bound to get crushed sooner or later." She waved her hand dismissively. "I don't know how long it's been abandoned, but there's definitely an opening to the catacombs there. There are a couple of curses and some bars on the entrance. The ghost who told me said that the bars have been there as long as he could remember, and he's been dead longer than he was ever alive." She sniffed. "Nice fellow. Chief stonemason once upon a time, one of those people who has to keep checking up on everything. That sort never lets death stop them."

"What sort of curses?" asked Marra.

"Oh, they're all ostentatious ones. Very impressive looking but nothing that will stick." She scowled. "Once we're inside, there may be real ones."

"Do you think we can get to the old king's tomb from there? The one who bound the godmother?"

"It's as good a chance as any."

"We have to go soon," said Agnes. "Tomorrow night at the latest. They'll be holding the christening in a few days, as soon as they're sure the child will live. Three days is usual. She has to be unbound before that. Then I can go and . . . well, I have an idea."

Marra barely heard her. A christening. A few days. It was happening. It was happening *right now*. All the talking and fretting and standing around and everything was suddenly falling together.

"How will we get into the palace itself?" asked Fenris. "The christening will be full of nobles and nobles come with guards. Are they just going to let us walk in, because we've got the queen's sister with us?"

"Maybe," said Marra. She looked over the other three, wondering if a princess, even a princess who was sister to the queen, would be able to sweep inside with a large dog and a woman with a chicken on her staff. *After they treated us as poor relations the last time . . . No, it might not be that easy.*

Agnes cleared her throat.

"I can get in," she said.

"What?"

"How?"

"I'm a godmother," said Agnes.

All three of them looked at her blankly.

"I know I wasn't invited," said Agnes. "That's the point."

"Eh?"

She smiled gently, that tiny, frazzled woman. "There's only one story about godmothers that's always true. Bad things happen if you don't invite us to the christening."

* * *

"Try to sleep," said the dust-wife. "I don't know what's going to happen, but I suspect we'll be glad to be well rested for it. We'll go tomorrow night."

"What about Miss Margaret?" asked Marra. "Don't we have to . . . ?" She trailed off, gesturing at her throat.

"Oh, that. Yes. We'll offer before we go."

Marra tried to sleep that night and couldn't. She tossed and turned, her mind roiling. Agnes thought that she could do . . . something . . . at the christening. The dust-wife seemed to agree. Marra would have been much happier if she knew what, but Agnes had waved her hands and said that if it didn't work, it would be better if nobody worried, and the dust-wife just folded her arms and said that Marra had come to her for help, not an education in magic.

"Free the godmother and the protections go away," she said. "That's all you need to know. And once the protections are gone, there are a thousand magics that can . . . rectify . . . the situation."

"You can't tell me more?"

"The less you know, the less you can spill when you talk to your sister about getting us into the palace. You're a terrible liar, Marra. You look as if you're afraid the universe is ashamed of you."

Marra didn't want to accept this, but the dust-wife locked the door to the bedroom and left her to toss in bed and fail to sleep. Her sister had given birth. They were going to the palace of the dead. Her sister had given birth to a boy. Kania's life was in terrible danger and if she died, she would be buried in one of the tombs underground, next to Vorling's tomb, and she would have to stand next to him for eternity. Could ghosts torment one another? Would Vorling's bones creep from his sarcophagus and hammer on the lid of Kania's coffin?

Oh gods and saints, she thought, rolling over and burying her face in the pillow. *Oh. Let them only be empty bones.*

"I never could sleep the night before a battle," said Fenris.

Marra turned to face him, even though she couldn't see. "Is this going to be a battle?"

"I don't have the slightest idea what to expect. It might be. Or maybe we'll just wander around in the dark for a while and the dust-wife will wave her hands and it will all be over."

Marra shook her head, forgetting he couldn't see her in the dark. "I doubt it. Whenever I go anywhere with her, something terrible and magical happens and then I wish it hadn't."

"I had noticed something of the sort, yes."

"I suppose that's still better than a battle."

"Mm." She could picture his expression, the way his lips would be twisting at one corner as he considered this. "Battles are terrible, but they're also comprehensible. You know what you're doing. Well . . . all right, that's not entirely true. You know what you're *supposed* to be doing. There's a lot of yelling and hitting things and then you look up and it's over. But once you've been through a few of them, you know more or less how things go. Magic, though . . . I don't know how it's supposed to work or why."

Fenris paused for so long that Marra wondered if he had fallen asleep. Then he said, "I was never so frightened as when we were leaving the goblin market. If you had not led me out, I would still be hiding in a corner there, hoping that everything would go away."

Marra blinked up at the darkness. "I didn't lead you out. We went together. I leaned on you for half of it."

He chuckled softly. "That's not how I remember it. I remember you holding my arm. You were very calm and very brave, even though you'd just had someone yank your tooth out."

The Toothdancer. Marra shuddered. "I didn't feel calm *or* brave."

"You hid it well."

It was easier to talk in the dark, somehow. Marra took a deep breath. "I don't feel brave now. I feel frustrated. I want to run in and drag Kania away from that monster, but I can't. If you hadn't found the way into the tombs tonight, I would probably have done something foolish."

"So long as you take me with you."

"I'd rather you didn't get killed for my foolishness."

"I have been resigned to dying for a long time."

"Fenris . . ."

"No, no, don't sound stricken. What else am I good for now? You gave me something useful to do with my death. I will be grateful forever."

"No dying," said Marra angrily. "I don't want you to die! I want you to live to a ripe, old age so that I can say, 'Hey, Fenris, remember the time we went into a horrible catacomb and the dust-wife said something cryptic and Agnes waved a baby chicken at us,' and you say, 'Of course I remember,' and I don't have to try to explain to someone who wasn't there."

The silence from the other side of the room was suddenly deeper and more textured. Marra bit her lip. "Besides," she said, after a moment, "someone has to chop all my firewood. I've gotten spoiled."

"Hmm."

She rolled over again. She could not seem to get comfortable.

If I ask, he'll think I'm propositioning him.

. . . Am I?

No. Definitely not. Not while all this is going on. It'll just make things terrible and complicated, and they're already terrible and complicated enough.

I might never get another chance.

But if I do and it's awkward and weird, then we'll probably die with things being awkward and weird and I cannot handle that.

Marra thumped the pillow and then gave up. "Fenris?"

"Yes?"

"I don't know how to ask this without giving you completely the wrong idea."

"All right?"

"Do you remember on the road, when we slept back-to-back?"

He did not answer, but she heard the bed creak, and then the indignant snuffle of Bonedog being nudged out of the way. Her own bed sagged as Fenris sat on the edge of it. Marra scooted up against the wall to give him room.

His back was as solid and warm as she remembered. She sighed and felt something unclench, although whether it was in her jaw or her gut or her soul, she couldn't say.

"You're a saint," she mumbled, tugging the blanket up around her shoulder.

"You have no idea," muttered Fenris.

* * *

They slept as late as they could, and then got up and stared at the walls. They ate. Marra threw the nettle cloak over her clothes, watching the owlcloth break up the outlines. Fenris went out for an hour and came back with his pack full of food. "God knows how long it'll take us down there," he said. "I'd rather we didn't starve."

Marra had been doing frantic math in her head. If the child had been born before midnight, they had two days to the christening. If the child had been born after midnight, they had three days. Neither of these options were good.

The only kindness was that darkness fell early. The moment the shadows began to stretch, she was up and pacing.

"For the love of the gods," said the dust-wife. "Let's go. I'd rather fight with the dead than watch Marra wear holes in the floor."

"Will we have to fight the dead?"

"Anything's possible."

Marra paused. "There are stories about graverobbers having their souls ripped out and haunting the catacombs."

"These things happen." The dust-wife stood up, held out her staff, and let the chicken settle herself. Agnes tucked Finder under her scarf.

They made their way down the stairs in a grand procession, only to encounter the innkeeper in the hallway.

"Miss Margaret," said the dust-wife. "We thank you for your hospitality." Her words rolled out with the air of a dread pronouncement, as if she were sentencing the innkeeper to be thanked, perhaps for all eternity.

Miss Margaret looked bewildered, then dropped a curtsy. The puppet glared from her shoulder.

Quick as a striking snake, the dust-wife reached out and grabbed the puppet's head. As soon as her fingers locked around it, it went limp. The cord at the woman's throat went slack and she gasped, clutching at her neck. Raw furrows had been etched against the sides of her throat, the skin abraded so many times that it had left patches as red and scaled as a dragon.

"It cannot hurt you now," said the dust-wife.

"Don't hurt him!" cried Miss Margaret, voice suddenly loud. "Don't!"

"I have not hurt . . . him. If I release him, everything will be exactly as it was. But you have been kind to us, so I offer you a choice." She loomed over the innkeeper, a tall, rattle-bone creature of deserts and dust, shockingly out of place in the little hallway. "Say the word and you can be free. He will be destroyed and never trouble you again."

The choice was so obvious that Marra never doubted, and so the innkeeper's words were doubly shocking.

"*Put him back!*" she shrieked, tugging on the dust-wife's wrist. "Let him go! He never hurt you; he never hurt anybody!"

. . . What?

"You are certain?" asked the dust-wife, implacable as death.

"Let him go! Don't hurt him!"

"Very well." The dust-wife released the puppet and stepped back.

The gnarled wooden face gave her a savage glare, and then the innkeeper gathered the puppet to her like a child, holding him against her breast. "It's all right," she crooned. "It's all right." And to the dust-wife, furious, "You'd better go."

"Very well," said the dust-wife again, and the four of them walked out of the boardinghouse forever, with Bonedog hushed and silent at their heels.

* * *

"What just happened?" hissed Marra. "What— Why didn't she— Was it still controlling her?"

The dust-wife shrugged. "She didn't want to lose it. People get to choose."

"But she's choosing *wrong*! I don't understand! And . . . and . . ." Marra ran out of words and waved her hands.

"I know," said the dust-wife. "I know."

"She can't have realized—she must not have understood!"

"She understood."

"Was she scared? Did she not believe us?"

"Maybe," said the dust-wife. "But more likely she simply did not want him destroyed."

"You cannot help people who do not want help," rumbled Fenris. "You can't force someone to do what you think is best for them." He paused, then added, somewhat reluctantly, "Well, you can. But they don't appreciate it and most of the time it turns out that you were wrong."

"But—"

"We can only save people who want to be saved," said the dust-wife. "If it's still bothering you, we'll come back afterward, assuming any of us are alive to do so. But we are out of time."

Marra clutched Bonedog's collar and shut up.

It was a long way to the quarry. The shadows got longer and then pooled together, deep blue on the white walls of the city. Marra kept looking up, to the palace, where her sister and her newborn nephew waited.

She bore an heir. After the christening, Kania's life will mean nothing to the prince.

No, no, surely not. Children die too easily; he'll wait until he has another one, won't he? Surely? It would be the sensible thing to do.

Why do you expect a man who tortures his wife to be sensible?

Marra gripped her temples. Concerned, Fenris reached over and took Bonedog's leash. "Are you all right?"

"No, but I'll manage."

It was dark when they left the city. No guards stopped them. This was the poorest quarter, where you lived because you could not afford better. No one cared who went in or out. Rats and alley cats watched them, and children with eyes like alley cats, but no one else.

For a moment, looking down into the quarry, Marra thought that she was looking back into the bone pit in the blistered land. The white stone was the color of moonlit bones and the chunks of abandoned rock looked unpleasantly like skulls. Her brain sang that it had all been a long, impossible dream and now she was back at the beginning with everything still to do again. Her foot slipped on the edge of the slope and Fenris reached out to steady her.

"I'm fine," she muttered. "It's nothing." Her head was still full of Miss Margaret clinging to the puppet and probably it was no wonder that she was a bit vague right now. *Also you're about to enter the cursed palace of the dead. That tends to have an impact on your nerves.*

She wondered what Mordecai had thought, standing at the swamps at last, and whether the poison worm had been right there in front of him or if he'd had to go wandering through the swamp trying to locate it. They still didn't have a map. She had the ruined fragment of the godmother's tapestry, but unless it started glowing or talking, it didn't seem like it was going to do any good. Another of life's little intelligence tests, and as usual, Marra had failed to even learn the question.

The entry to the palace was halfway down the slope, but a good road had been built to it once. Even though it was long abandoned and had corrugated with neglect, it was still stable underfoot. They approached the entryway three abreast, while Fenris walked behind with his hand on Bonedog's leash.

The paleness of the stone continued inside the passage, which meant that the iron bars stood out like bands of shadow. Marra wondered how they were supposed to break them down. There were no keys or gates. No one had expected this way to come into use again.

The dust-wife tapped her nail against each of the bars in turn, then grunted. She muttered a few words under her breath, lifted her staff, and cracked the end across the iron, which promptly shattered.

Marra gasped. The dust-wife cackled. So did the hen. She smacked the next bar and the next, and each one shattered like a black icicle.

"Is that magic?" breathed Marra. "Can you do that to the guards' swords?"

"Of a sort," said the dust-wife. "And I suppose I could, if you can get me the swords at least a day beforehand."

"She did something to them last night," murmured Fenris. "Rubbed them with grit and then poured a little vial over them." Marra stifled a sigh. Magic never seemed to be much use at doing the things you wanted done in a reasonable time frame.

They stepped over the broken teeth of the bars and into the passageway. Fenris wrapped Bonedog's leash around his wrist and took a candle from his pack. The dust-wife pulled something from her many pockets, said two sharp words, and moonlight blossomed under her hands.

"Is that the moon in a jar?" asked Marra, feeling a pang of recognition.

"Only a little of it. It won't mind. The moon loves things like this." She hung the little vial of moonlight from her staff. The brown hen cast a molten shadow on the ceiling, crowned with horns.

"So that bird really is a demon," said Fenris, eyeing the shadow.

"Of course she is. Why would I lie about something that ridiculous?"

The light revealed carved words overhead. Marra pointed upward. "What do those say?"

"Curses against graverobbers. Threats to tear your soul out and sentence you to wander for all eternity—that sort of thing."

"Should we be worried?"

"No, it's the usual grandstanding." The dust-wife sniffed. "Although I wouldn't rob any graves, just in case."

They set out. The passageway was rough, the kind of tunnel built for service instead of ceremony. Bits of broken stone littered the ground. Bonedog snuffled but clearly didn't smell anything of interest.

"Do we know where we're going?" asked Agnes. "We want the first king, the one who bound the godmother."

"Was it the first king, then?" asked the dust-wife.

"Oh yes. It was the godmother's power that let him keep his dynasty going. Before that, all these little Northern witch-kings were cursing each other constantly, knocking down any clan that looked like they were getting too powerful. The godmother tipped the balance. Imagine, a godmother changing everything like that!" Agnes beamed with pride, the way she did when Finder did something clever.

"The tombs are laid out by family," said Marra. "So presumably we'd need to just go back and back until we find the oldest one." Her voice echoed down the passageway and sent back words: ". . . one . . . one . . . one . . ."

"Easier said than done," muttered the dust-wife. Her chicken flapped its wings, leaving demon shadows on the wall.

The passage opened up into a larger room, littered with broken pick handles and old logs that had probably been used as rollers. Bonedog was very interested in the smells and had to poke them all.

There were three corridors leading off from the room. Marra looked from one to the next in dismay. "We need the oldest one," she muttered. "But which one is that?"

For lack of any better ideas, they took the smallest. The ceiling was low enough that Fenris had to duck his head and the dust-wife had to hold her staff at an angle, much to the brown hen's annoyance.

The roughness underfoot gave way suddenly to a smooth floor, and the hallway flared out. The dust-wife paused, looking around. "I believe we are entering the tomb proper," she said.

Marra stepped out behind her and said, "Whoa." She had seen the carved and vaulted room where her niece had been laid to rest but had not really considered the implications for the rest of the catacombs.

This was truly a palace of the dead. The ceilings vanished into darkness. The entire boardinghouse where they had spent the last week could have fit within the walls. Carvings circled the room, an endless procession of warriors and great beasts chasing each other for eternity. Racks of weapons stood against the walls, pole arms bristling like wheat, swords still gleaming dully after who knew how many years.

The center of the room held a single slab of stone, and on it, inlaid with metal, a sarcophagus. The slab had been worked into the shape of a great bear, holding the coffin on its back, its teeth buried in the belly of some unfortunate animal.

Fenris whistled softly, and the sound woke echoes like a flight of birds in the far reaches of the ceiling.

"Ostentatious," muttered the dust-wife. She laid her hands on the sarcophagus and scowled. Marra was struck by the incongruity of it, the thin woman with her robes full of packets and string, presuming to command the sort of person that could be laid to rest in such a room as this.

"Nothing." The dust-wife stepped back. "This ghost is long gone."

Marra bit her lip. "What if the king we're after is gone?"

"If he was gone, he couldn't still compel the godmother. No, he's around. Probably mad as hell, too."

"That was comforting," said Fenris. "I am comforted." He shared a bemused look with Marra, who smiled in spite of herself.

Two doorways led in opposite directions. Fenris and Marra took one side and the dust-wife and Agnes took the other. Bonedog trotted between them, bored by the lack of new smells or motion.

"Oh," said Marra softly, taking in the next room. "Oh, I see." The room was much smaller, the walls holding touches of red paint. There were neither weapons nor carved warriors, only small jars ornamented with gold. The death mask on the sarcophagus was of a woman younger than Marra. Perhaps it was only the shadows, but she thought the woman's eyes looked sad.

"His wife," said Fenris. There were two more rooms branching off, barely more than niches. He stepped forward and looked into each one, then turned back, shaking his head to Marra. "I don't think what we're looking for is in there."

"It's her children, isn't it?"

"Yes." He took her hand. Marra could picture the small coffins and wondered if they were more or less ornate than her niece's. She was glad of the hand in hers. He was very much alive—him and Bonedog, who wasn't alive but didn't know it.

"Over here," called Agnes. "We've got a hallway."

The hallway was as broad as the wife's room had been. It vanished in both directions, with branchings off on the same side as the tomb they stood in. "Lady Fox?" said Fenris. "I think you likely have more experience here than the rest of us. Which way?"

"Huh!" She lifted the light on her staff. "My dead were all sensible people in the ground. Not these great frozen tombs. Your ghost would rattle around like a pea in a dish in here. I've no idea."

Bonedog solved the problem by straining at his leash in toward one of the branchings, although it turned out that he only wanted to pee against a wall, which he did, meditatively, while everyone else pretended to be interested in the bas-reliefs on the walls.

The branching, newly anointed, led to another room like the last one, but with no hallways leading away from it. "Unmarried?" hazarded Marra. "So there are no other rooms for his bloodline?"

"Makes sense." Fenris nodded to the grave mask, which was young but bore the lines of pain. There were fewer weapons here. They backed out of that room, and the next. At the end of the hall was an ornate threshold with carvings that stretched out five feet from the doorway itself—screaming faces, reaching hands, broken swords.

"That's a little disturbing," said Marra, poking the toe of her boot at one of the carvings.

"Enemies defeated in battle?" asked Agnes.

"Or sinners cast into hell."

"Do they believe in hell, up here?"

"They do," Marra said. "You freeze in eternal cold." She shook her head. The concept had seemed foreign to her when she heard it. The Harbor Kingdom, sensibly, believed that the dead went into the sea, and the good were reborn from it, while the damned sank to the bottom and were devoured by crabs. Still, she couldn't blame the Northern Kingdom for their confusion. There probably weren't very many crabs up here.

"I hate to walk on them," she muttered.

"They're only stone," said the dust-wife. "They were never alive." She walked across the screaming carvings, the hem of her robes brushing over their faces. One by one, the others followed.

This tomb was as large and ostentatious as the wife's tomb had been plain. The walls were ribbed with statues, each one of a stern-faced Northern god, and yet despite their faces, the impression was of a great throat waiting to swallow the unwary.

There were shadowy figures flanking the sarcophagus. Marra paused in the threshold, trying to make sense of the number of legs, the shapes . . .

"Oh," she said softly. "Oh, I see."

The cold air of the palace of dust had preserved the dead horses far better than she would ever have guessed. They had sagged and withered, but they were still identifiable. Poles thrust up into the bodies held them in place, standing at attention around their dead master. The proud arch of their necks had sunken in, but Marra could still recognize the marks of breeding and the richness of the golden bridles.

"A wealthy man," said Fenris. "To be buried with his warhorses like this."

"The father?" muttered the dust-wife, gazing up at the sarcophagus. "Or the son? Are we going forward or back?"

"If we go long enough in one direction, the weaponry should change," offered Fenris, studying the carvings on the walls. "These saddles have stirrups. If we find a tomb without them . . ."

"If I could find a damn ghost, I could just ask," said the dust-wife, annoyed. She smacked the sarcophagus lid and a hollow ringing filled the crypt, then died away. "But these are too quiet and too long dead. We need younger corpses. Or at least angrier ones."

Marra did not have much time to worry about that, because the next corpse they found was positively furious.

Chapter 18

It was a small tomb off the grand one. A concubine's room, perhaps. The materials were costly and exquisite, gold and jade and rosewood, and the death mask was beautiful and painted with lapis. Despite the materials, though, it seemed . . . hasty. As if everything had been slapped together swiftly and in fear. Jade tiles crunched under their feet, having fallen from the coffin, and there were no carvings, only faded paintings. The threshold was plain and uncarved and the doorway was hidden in the shadow of one of the scowling statues.

"This one," said the dust-wife, with professional satisfaction. "This one here. This one is old, but she has *grudges.*"

She pulled something out of a pocket—Marra got a glimpse of orange red, like cinnabar—and dusted it over her hands, then knocked on the coffin lid as if it were a door.

Marra expected it to take a few minutes, as the drowned boy had, a slow swelling of horror as the ghost manifested itself, but she barely had time to brace herself before the room erupted.

Dust exploded up from the coffin. Broken tiles flew around the room. Fenris flung himself over Agnes and Marra, while Bonedog yapped silently, trying to catch one in his mouth. Only the dust-wife was unmoved, standing in the center of the chaos, with the light of the moon and her familiar's shadow falling over her like a shield.

"Calm yourself," she said. "Or I'll lay you back down and find another spirit to work with. Your rage does not impress me."

The entire sarcophagus twisted as it came alive, bouncing on the slab, and then it rolled to one side so that the death mask faced them.

The beautiful face was still and calm but the eyes were alive and smoldering with fury.

you wake me!

The voice was made of echoes, of small green tiles falling from the badly mortared sarcophagus, of golden ornaments rattling together like metal cobwebs.

you dare to wake me!

peasant! commoner! you come into the tomb of the great . . . the great . . . the consort of kings, the great . . .

"Forgotten your name, have you?" asked the dust-wife. "Well, it happens, kings and commoners alike." She thumped her staff on the floor of the tomb. "So what kept you furious all this time?"

replaced replaced replaced! The wind went around the room again. *set aside! how dare they, how dare they. do they not know who I am? the great . . . the great . . .* Again the stirring wind, the sense of a shriek somewhere beyond human hearing, like bats hunting overhead.

"Poor thing," murmured Agnes, having freed herself from Fenris's attempt to protect her. "Set aside, were you? Were you the king's mistress?"

mistress! I was his wife of seven years! but I bore him no child so he took another and when her brats were murdered with a scarlet cord, they put the blame on me! me!

"Did you murder them?" asked the dust-wife, sounding interested rather than horrified.

no.

I wish I had.

if they would blame me and send me home to my parents to die, at least I might have done the crime.

I did not love them.

but no.

Marra was starting to think that Vorling had come by his wickedness honestly, at least.

"It seems we've stumbled on an ancient scandal," said Agnes. "A daughter of the king sent home in disgrace."

disgrace.

oh yes.

they could not kill me, you know, so they locked me up in here.

I was buried alive to hide their shame.

Fenris inhaled sharply.

does that shock you, peasant?

it shocked me down here in the dark.

I screamed and no one came and eventually I died and still no one came.

"So they buried you alive . . ." The dust-wife frowned. "Do you know the layout of the catacombs?"

no.

why would I?

I am a queen, not a crawler of tombs.

The dust-wife narrowed her eyes. "What did you see when they brought you here to bury you? They must have already begun your father's tomb, but what did your grandfather's tomb look like?"

The death mask rolled its painted eyes.

I don't care.

he is long dead and he was dull.

I am a queen and the consort of kings. I am the great . . .

The dust-wife slapped her red-tinted palm against the sarcophagus and the spirit yelped as if it had been struck.

aah!

how dare you, peasant.

do you not know who I am?

"No, and at the moment, neither do you."

The spirit went raging around the room, tiles flying. The dust-wife lifted her hand again and it quieted. When it spoke next, the voice was sullen, the distant keening of resentful birds.

he was buried with his boat.

he always talked of it until I wanted to scream.

the raids up the rivers when he was young.

dull dull dull.

"Thank you," said the dust-wife gravely. "That is very helpful."

I do not care about helping you.

you are also dull.

the thief-wheel will catch you soon enough and you will go wailing through the dark forever.

do not think that I will acknowledge you, peasant.

"Thief-wheel?" said the dust-wife, but the ghost only laughed. One last, weak sweep around the crypt, stirring the broken jade fragments to knee height, and then the death mask closed its eyes and the sarcophagus was only a coffin knocked off its plinth, and the gold ornaments fell silent.

"Is she gone?" asked Marra.

The dust-wife shrugged. "More or less. She's still in there, but she doesn't want to come out, and it would take more power than I'm willing to spend to compel her."

"Imagine being here all this time," murmured Agnes, "and still being so angry."

"Injustice and the desire for revenge age the body, but they keep the soul going halfway to forever," said the dust-wife practically. "And being buried alive for a crime you didn't commit will certainly keep you going for a while. I doubt she was a particularly nice person to begin with, but we don't bury people alive for being snobs."

"What do you think a thief-wheel is?" asked Marra.

"No idea."

"I have visited countries where they break criminals on cart wheels," said Fenris slowly. "They strap them across the wheel and lay them out to die of exposure. It's ugly business."

"They don't do that here," said Marra, "at least, not that I've ever heard of." She frowned. "Of course, in this ghost's time, maybe things were different."

"At least we know to look for a boat," said Agnes practically.

They found the boat about twenty minutes later, after a few hallways leading to minor royals and their various family members. The dust-wife reported no ghosts, or if there were, they were sleeping soundly.

"Well, that's a boat, all right," said Agnes.

It was about twenty feet long, with a prow carved in the shape of a snarling beast. Oars stuck out like centipede feet and the sarcophagus sat in the center of the longboat in a place of honor. The carvings all around the tomb were of waves and sea monsters and naval battles, and the mast of the ship still bore a sail, preserved by the cold dry air. Marra could look up at it and make out blue and white stripes on the fabric.

She rather wished that they had time for her to go up and look and see what it was made of. *No. Focus. We have to find the old king before the christening.*

"Which way from here?" asked Fenris.

"If we assume that one of the earliest kings bound the godmother," said Marra, "then we head toward his father, and then his father, and so forth."

"This direction, then," said the dust-wife. They crossed the tomb with its ancient ship and into the hallway beyond.

There were five openings off this hallway, but they ignored them all. The tomb at the end was less grand than the ones that came after, though the carvings were more realistic. Marra could have done without the image of the beast with its mouth full of entrails, each curl and twist lovingly detailed, crouched over the entryway.

The tomb was a crossroad, four openings on four walls. They looked at each other helplessly and went forward. Another three openings, another cross . . .

Marra began to feel an itch at the back of her brain, as if she'd seen something like this before.

Was there a map somewhere in the palace? Something about this seems familiar.

She did not have time to dwell on it. The next tomb had been robbed.

"Saint's teeth," muttered Agnes. The sarcophagus lid was smashed. The rows of weapons had clearly been plundered. A broken pike lay discarded on the floor where it had been used unsuccessfully as a lever. Someone had chiseled the gems from the plinth, leaving beasts with broken sockets for eyes.

"They didn't finish raiding it," said the dust-wife thoughtfully.

"How can you tell?"

"In my line of work, you get a feel for it. They may have been interrupted, or were too nervous to finish the job." She laid her hand on the sarcophagus and tilted her head. After a moment she said, "Whatever's in there, it's lost most of its personality. It's probably annoyed that it's been robbed, but there's just not enough left to work with."

Something whistled nearby. Everyone jumped. Bonedog jerked upright, straining against the leash. Fenris was holding him now, and the dog pulled so hard that he nearly jerked the warrior off his feet.

"The ghost?" asked Fenris, trying to hold Bonedog.

"Not this one," said the dust-wife. "Another one wandering the halls, perhaps." She turned in her tracks. "I can't quite find it . . ."

Bonedog subsided slowly, his illusionary hackles lowering. The whistle was not repeated.

Two tombs later, they heard it again. Bonedog actually bayed this time, his ghostly voice waking echoes like sibilant birds. "I don't like that," said Agnes to no one in particular.

"I can't get a grip on it," said the dust-wife. "It should have some attachment to a body somewhere, but there isn't one. The bodiless dead are much harder to grab. But they also can't hurt you, usually."

"Usually?"

"Never say never."

The last syllable of *never* echoed for much too long, *er . . . er . . . er . . .* And then Marra realized it wasn't an echo at all. She took a step back from the mouth of the hallway behind her.

. . . un . . . un . . . un . . . run . . . run . . . !

"Did an echo just tell us to run?" asked Agnes, adjusting Finder and looking rather calmer than Marra felt.

"Do ghostly echoes have our best interests at heart?" asked Fenris, also remarkably calm.

"Rarely," said the dust-wife.

Marra thought, *I'm surrounded by lunatics, and I love them all, but maybe we should be running anyway.* She took another step back.

. . . run . . . running . . . coming . . . coming . . . coming for you . . . run . . .

Erk, said the brown hen, with deep distrust.

Whistles erupted from the hallway they had just come down. The echoes sped up until they tripped over each other—*Run! Coming! Hide! Robbers! Run! Run!*

Bonedog went berserk. Fenris stopped trying to hold his leash and just picked him up bodily, hands slipping through the illusion to clutch at his spine. The dust-wife slammed the butt of her staff on the ground. The hen crowed.

The thief-wheel filled the passageway and came spilling out into the room.

* * *

At one point, it might indeed have been a wheel. When it was smaller, perhaps, when there were only five or ten souls jammed together, rolling over each other, ghostly faces screaming before being ground into the floor to move the bulk of the creature along. Now there were dozens of faces and the wheel had become a thick slug, elongating through the passageways, ten feet high and the gods only knew how long.

Run!

Hide!

It's coming!

Run, robbers, run!

It filled the doorway, heaving with screams as if breathing. The echoes rang through the room. Some of the faces had hands beside them, waving frantically, and Marra realized that the graverobbers trapped inside were trying to warn the living humans away. *They aren't threatening us. They're trying to tell us to get away before it gets us, too.*

The dust-wife never faltered. She stepped forward, directly into the thief-wheel's path. "Bodiless dead," she said. "We are not graverobbers. You have no power over us."

She was so calm and so confident that Marra believed her. Of course the dust-wife could fix it. She was the master of the dead. She could raise ghosts and lay them. Why had she ever doubted?

The thief-wheel screamed a warning from fifty mouths and ran the dust-wife down.

The moonlight vanished. The room went pitch-black.

Marra blundered away from the thief-wheel, staggering through the dark. She pitched over something and went down hard, skinning her palms on the ground. She could hear shrieks and shouting, the wails of the dead, and over it all, the furious clucking of the demon hen.

Something grabbed her. It didn't feel like a human. It felt like a great wall of glue that engulfed half her body. Marra screamed and slapped at it, which was a mistake. Her arm went in and got stuck. She retained enough presence of mind to throw her head back to try and keep her mouth free.

"Marra!" shouted Fenris.

Then the thief-wheel was moving with a sickening forward slide. She bashed the back of her head against the wall and saw pinpricks of white against the blackness.

Run!

Run!

Run! piped the faces around her in the dark. And then one, next to her ear, *I'm sorry, I'm sorry, I can't make it stop, it just keeps going . . .*

Were they going through another corridor? Stone scraped her back. She was being carried forward but also sliding inexorably toward the back of the thief-wheel in a queasy, seasick motion. *Oh god,* she thought very clearly. *I will be devoured and stay as a ghost forever under the palace.*

This seemed uniquely horrible. Not that she would die, but that she would be trapped here, in the palace, which she was beginning to hate with a fine and enduring passion. Her back scraped against more stone and she tried to lean closer into the thief-wheel but she couldn't, not without putting her face in it, and she'd rather not have any skin on her back at all than do that.

I'm so sorry I can't stop it, sobbed the voice next to her ear. *I keep trying but it won't stop . . .*

"It's all right," she said automatically. She was going to be ill and she was being dragged backward along the length of a creature made of lost souls and glue and still she was trying to reassure someone. Of course she was. That was how she was going to die, telling someone it was all right for stabbing her, really, she didn't mind . . .

The thief-wheel dropped her. Perhaps she had worked her way to the end. She struck the floor of the corridor and then, mercifully, she fainted.

Chapter 19

When Marra came to, she was freezing. She had curled up under the nettle cloak but had no idea how much time had passed. Long enough for the stone floor to leach all the warmth out of her, at least. She listened for the sound of the thief-wheel but could hear nothing. "Fenris?" she called. "Agnes? Dust-wife?"

Her voice echoed but brought no response. There was no spark of light anywhere.

She got to her feet and spread her arms wide, feeling for walls. A corridor. She yelled for her friends again to no avail.

"When you're lost in the woods, stay put," Marra muttered. "That way people can find you. But this isn't the woods, and I don't think we've got enough time . . ."

Which direction had the thief-wheel dragged her? How far had she gone? She had no idea.

She took a deep breath and pulled the nettle cloak tightly around her. "All right," she murmured. "All right." She picked a direction and began to walk.

Doorways to tombs opened under her fingers. She ignored them. The big tombs were always at the ends of the corridors. She walked forward until she reached some kind of threshold and then felt her way forward in the dark. The echoes sounded like a large room.

Smooth metal. Carved stone. Tiny square edges. Something that felt familiar, and then Marra realized she was touching a death mask. She jerked away and blundered toward the wall, only to realize that she had lost track of where her entryway was. How would she know if she was going in the right direction?

She fetched up against a wall and felt like weeping.

I'm lost. I'm lost in the dark and I will die down here. The dust-wife might already be dead. Oh, Lady of Grackles, help me, help me. I tried to help myself, but I don't think I can help this bit . . .

Silence. Cold. Dust.

And then, in the great darkness under the palace, Marra saw a light.

It was only a spark at first, more golden than torchlight. She thought perhaps it was not really there, because it looked like the gold sparks that came when she rubbed her eyelids. But it strengthened and came closer and closer still, illuminating the walls with their carvings of cold, dead kings.

It was a woman. Where she walked, she kicked up clouds of light, like dust.

Marra lifted her eyes and saw that the woman held a severed hand in her right hand and that her left wrist ended in a stump.

It was the saint from the goblin market.

A long time later, it would occur to Marra to wonder why the saint had been there, in the palace of dead kings. At the time, it did not. She was a saint. Saints walked where they would.

The saint lifted her severed hand so that the first finger lay across her lips in a gesture for silence. Marra crouched at her feet, gazing up, and nodded.

The saint beckoned, and Marra followed.

They went slowly but sure-footedly. The light of the saint's passage glittered off carvings of men and gods and stranger things. Marra watched whole histories unfold, as carved generals defeated armies of beasts misshapen and beautiful and strange.

Then, step by step, she began to fade.

Marra wanted to cry out, to beg her not to leave, but she bit her lower lip. The gods had intervened on her behalf. Surely they would not take her only halfway.

Wait. Wait and see. The world is not always cruel.

She followed the fading footsteps of the saint. It seemed to take a long time, shifting slowly from gold to silver, and finally Marra realized that the saint was gone and the silver light came from farther ahead, from a vial filled with moonlight trapped in a jar.

She broke into a run, not caring if the thief-wheel heard her now, half sobbing. "Fenris! Agnes! Dust-wife!"

"Marra?"

She broke into the room and before she could even focus, Fenris had thrown his arms around her and had his face pressed against her hair. "You're alive," he said. "I thought I'd lost you. You're alive."

"You're alive, too!" she said. She wanted to stop and think about what *I thought I'd lost you* might mean, but it didn't quite seem like the time. And he was very warm and she was very cold and it was very pleasant to be held in such a fashion. "You're alive."

"Yes, yes," said the dust-wife testily. "We're all alive. Please don't cry on me about it, though."

Fenris finally released her, although not without reluctance. Bonedog immediately leapt up on her, washing her face with his tongue.

"What happened to you?" asked Marra. "I got picked up by the thief-wheel . . ."

"So did I," said Agnes. "Didn't realize it got you, too."

"Bonedog ran after you," said Fenris. "Dragged me with him, and I thought he might have the best chance of following you. When he finally lost track, we were totally lost."

"How did you get back?" asked Marra.

"Oh, I had Finder do it," said Agnes. She patted her chest, where the exhausted chick was sleeping. "Asked him to take me somewhere safe. Then the dust-wife turned up."

"Bonedog found them," said Fenris. "I was going to suggest we start looking for you, but then you turned up. How did you find us?"

"A saint led me," said Marra. "The one from the goblin market."

All three of them stared at her.

"Huh," said the dust-wife.

"How fascinating!" said Agnes.

"A few months ago, I would have thought you were mad or lying," said Fenris. "Now I suppose I'm just surprised she didn't stay for tea."

"But how did you get away?" asked Marra. "The thief-wheel fell on you. I saw it."

The dust-wife sniffed haughtily. "It was nothing."

"It squashed you!"

"Fine, it was something." She looked annoyed. Marra noticed that her coat was rumpled and there were a few stains where the contents of the pockets had broken. The brown hen was missing a couple of tail feathers. "They were very disobedient dead."

"Bad dead. No treat," said Fenris, not quite under his breath.

Marra choked and spluttered and began, helplessly, to laugh. So did Agnes. The dust-wife folded her arms and the hen went *errrk* indignantly, which only made Marra laugh harder.

"I'm glad you're all amused," said the dust-wife when they had giggled themselves out.

"What *was* it, though?" asked Marra, torn between hilarity and renewed shudders.

"A tangle. A mangle. Graverobbers and a few unfortunate souls, probably lost builders. The curse ripped their spirits out and wadded them all up together, to roam the catacombs and find more. But it wasn't terribly well designed. They never put an upper limit on the souls, so it collected too many over the centuries and got muddled. That was the problem giving it orders. Nothing's in charge anymore; it's just blundering around in confusion." She grimaced. "I slapped it and it ran away. And you didn't steal anything, so it couldn't eat your souls, it just dragged you around. It's still out there, but it won't come anywhere near me again."

"Can you unmake it?" asked Fenris. "Set them free?"

"I could if we had a few days to spare. But we don't, so I sent it away." She looked down her nose, the lines drawing tight around her mouth. "We're running out of time."

"Are we?" asked Marra.

"What?" said Agnes.

"I fainted for a bit," Marra admitted. "How long has it been?"

Fenris's face was suddenly grave. "Almost a full day," he said. "We have to hurry. We're going to be late to the christening."

* * *

Four corridors and an intersection. Two intersections and three more corridors. Marra's mind tugged again at the sensation that she knew this pattern, that she had seen something like it, but it wouldn't surface. Perhaps it didn't matter.

They had found the tomb of the first king.

It was small. Marra had expected something huge and grand, vast archways framed by carved warriors, gold and jade and glory. Instead it was a little stone room with wooden beams holding up the ceiling. There was a single sword, tossed almost casually across the stone coffin lid. The king's death mask was very simple and had cracked across the forehead like a scar.

The walls were the most impressive part. Red and black paint glimmered in the captive moonlight. The murals were stark and strong and age had tinted the white pigment of the Northern faces to blue, so it seemed that an army of stylized blue-skinned warriors swept across the walls of the tomb. In the center, a blue king sat upon a throne, holding a sword across his knees.

The dust-wife laid her hands on the sarcophagus and gave a short, sharp little laugh, like a fox's bark. "Oh yes," she said. "Yes, he's in there."

"You can tell?"

"Gods, yes. Like having a sleeping bear in the room." She closed her eyes and leaned her weight on her palms. "Wake up, dead man. We have business with you."

Marra, insomuch as she expected anything, thought that perhaps the death mask might begin to speak, as it had for the daughter who had been buried alive. Instead the sword rattled on the lid, and on the wall, the painted king lifted his head and stared with pigmented eyes at the dust-wife.

Why have you come here?

The words had no sound, but the echoes rang through the room.

Marra felt as if they were being pounded into her skull with a metal hammer. There was weight to them and a mind like steel and stone. Bonedog yipped and tried to hide behind Fenris's knees.

Why do you intrude upon my grave?

"You must release the godmother from her service," said the dust-wife. "She has been held far too long and it is harming your descendants."

Godmother? What godmother do you speak of?

"The woman who blesses your children and who serves the royal line."

Oh. The witchskin. The contempt tasted like tin inside Marra's head. *I won; she lost. I could have slain her on the spot, but I gave her immortality. She should be grateful.*

The dust-wife's fingers curled into fists against the sarcophagus lid. "Eternal slavery is no gift."

The painted king narrowed his eyes. Behind the throne, the painted warriors moved and rippled, lifting their shields. An archer drew the charcoal line of his bowstring taut. *Who are you?*

"One who can talk to the dead."

What is the witchskin to you?

"Nothing. We've never even met. But I do not allow the living to serve the dead forever. Release her, and I will leave you to your rest."

Beg me, then. Perhaps I'll release her if you beg.

The dust-wife raised her eyebrows. "Do you think I wouldn't beg for another person's life? I will, if it would sway you."

The painted king looked away, the blue paint moving around the sour black slash of mouth. *It would amuse me.*

"Amusement is not enough. You must free her."

I will not.

The dust-wife took one hand off the sarcophagus and took up her staff, which had been leaning against it. The brown hen flapped her wings. "Then I will fight you," she said.

You? You who have lived a puny mortal lifetime would fight me for a witch who should have died a thousand years ago? The king began to laugh. It was a deep, roaring laugh, even more like a hammer on metal than his voice, and Marra started to feel like her skull was on the anvil. *Go away, little deadspeaker. I am older and greater than you.*

The dust-wife ran her fingertip across the crack in the death mask and the laughter in Marra's head stopped abruptly.

"There," said the dust-wife as calmly as if they were discussing where to place a stitch. "There, I think. Yes." She reached up to the brown hen, who stepped onto her hand. Marra had held goshawks on the wrist that did not look so proud as the demon hen in that moment. The dust-wife set her down on the sarcophagus and the hen stabbed her beak down into the crack in the mask.

The king's scream sounded like a sheet of iron being ripped in half, a long metallic shriek that made Marra's teeth rattle in her jaw. Her head pounded. Bonedog barked, not an alarm bark but the high, rapid bark of a dog in trouble and desperately calling his pack for backup. It was barely audible, but it hung in the air around them.

What are you doing, witch?!

"Fighting," said the dust-wife as if it should have been obvious. The hen began to hammer at the crack, occasionally pausing to lift her head and rake her claws across the death mask.

"There's something else happening," whispered Fenris. "Isn't there?" He slumped against the wall next to Marra, holding his temples. "It's not just a chicken and a mask. She's doing . . . something . . ."

"Oh yes," said Agnes. Alone of all of them, she seemed to be enjoying herself. Her eyes were bright with interest. "You can see it—oh dear, I suppose you can't see it! But it's very good. His magic is all laid out like swords on a rack and she's . . . no, that's a terrible analogy; it's not like that at all. But it's good, though!"

"Good?" said Marra weakly, her skull still ringing with the dead king's scream.

"Let go," said the dust-wife. "You tried to protect your descendants and instead you shortened their lives for generations. Their souls are feeding the spell that keeps the godmother alive. I can see it. Can't you?"

Her voice was so confident that Marra found herself looking at

the air over the sarcophagus as if there might be something that
mortal eyes could see. There was only dust and the brown hen busily
cracking open the death mask.

*The spell works. It has worked for a thousand years. My descendants
are strong and they have endured. I will not allow you to break it.*

"You are dead," said the dust-wife coldly. "Your time to control
your family is done." The demon hen cackled as chips flew from the
broken mask. "They cannot live in your shadow any longer."

The king gathered himself. It felt as if the tomb were breathing
in. The painted warriors lifted their swords and the archers let fly
their arrows, aimed at the dust-wife. They were trapped in the wall
and it should not have been possible for them to reach her, and yet
for a moment, it seemed as if she would be drawn into the wall, as
if the arrows must reach her . . .

Moonlight flashed as she held up her staff and the painted arrows fell apart into scattered pigment across the floor.

I will not bend! hissed the dead king, rising from his throne.

"Then you will break," said the dust-wife, and slammed her staff
across the painted wall.

It sounded like a thunderclap in that small room. The moonlight
went out. Something metallic hit the floor. For a second time, Marra
stood in complete and utter darkness. She heard Bonedog's ghostly
whimper and then Fenris fumbling with his tinderbox. "Candle . . ."
he muttered next to her. "Candle, candle. Where is the— Aha!"

Light flared. The dust-wife was lying half-sprawled across the
sarcophagus, her hair wild around her shoulders. She pushed herself up, looking annoyed. The brown hen stood on the death mask,
which had split in two, looking as serene as only a chicken can
look. As Marra watched, the hen lifted her tail, voided her bowels
on the king's broken face, and then strolled to the dust-wife's shoulder with a satisfied cluck.

Fenris lifted the candle. The sword had fallen to the floor. On
the wall, the king was back in his throne, the archers back in their
original positions, but there was a long, jagged mark across the paint,

like a lightning bolt, that cut across the king's face and broke the shield of the guard beside him.

"Is it over?" asked Marra. The air seemed very still and the room somehow smaller. "Is he gone?"

"Gone, no," said the dust-wife. "People like that hang about for ages. I pried his fingers loose from the world for a bit, though, and that should be enough for the godmother to slip her bonds."

"Just like that?" asked Marra wonderingly. "That's all it took?"

"That's all," said the dust-wife, striding confidently forward, and promptly crashed to the floor in a semiconscious heap.

Chapter 20

"Well, it was a little bit more than it looked," said Agnes, when they had rescued the indignant hen and made certain that no bones were broken. The dust-wife protested weakly as they propped her against the wall and poured water down her throat. "You don't just knock out a dead sorcerer-king and then go for breakfast after."

"I'm fine," grumbled the dust-wife. She tried to push herself to her feet and failed spectacularly.

"You poured yourself into the magic and knocked yourself to fainting, little fool," said Agnes in a remarkably good imitation of the dust-wife herself. "Isn't that what you said to me?"

The hen cackled. The dust-wife glared up at Agnes and snatched the leather bottle of water out of her fingers. "Fine. Possibly I deserved that. Possibly."

"Definitely."

"Can you walk?" asked Fenris. "I can carry you on my back if need be."

"I can walk," she growled. "Give me my staff. And give me a minute."

"I do not know how many more minutes we have," he said. "My sense of time is not working well, but I think that we are very close to running out of it."

"I might be able to still enchant the babe," said Agnes a bit doubtfully. "Even if we miss the christening. But it doesn't take as well, not with humans. You lay a name on them and suddenly their whole future is rolled out like dough in front of you, but it doesn't last. Life starts to bake it pretty quick."

"That," said the dust-wife witheringly, "was a *terrible* analogy. Someone give me my staff so that I can beat her about the head and shoulders." Agnes giggled.

Fenris went to pick up the staff and paused. The sword lay on the ground beneath it. "The sword fell," he said.

"Take it," said the dust-wife. "Mine by right of conquest. But I'll let you have it. You might need a sword, and not even the thief-wheel could think that was grave robbery." She took the staff from him and this time managed to get upright, with the help of Fenris under one arm and the questionable assistance of Bonedog bouncing around her feet.

"What happens now?" asked Marra. "Is the godmother dead?"

"I imagine so," said the dust-wife. "I wouldn't stick around if I were her." She took another limping step forward. "I'm most curious about all the other spells that people have cast over the years. If any of them are active, now that the godmother's gone, they might come home to roost."

They all shuffled to the door of the tomb and then stopped. The hallway stretched out before them. Three openings on one side, two on the other.

"Now what?" asked Agnes. "I got turned around when that screaming thing dragged me along."

"Going back to the source was one thing," said Fenris, holding up the candle. "We could follow so many dead ends . . . Can Finder help?"

Agnes frowned. "I don't think so. We're much safer here than we are in the palace, aren't we? Maybe once we run out of food and water, but Finder will just keep moving us around the tombs to avoid the wheel thingy."

Three openings on one side . . . two on the other . . . six openings on one side . . . five openings . . .

Do you know what they represent? . . . Then I may give it to you.

"I've got it," she said. She laughed incredulously. "We've had it this whole time—the tapestry."

She unrolled the frayed bit of tapestry in her pack, running her fingers along the weave. Three lines of thread. The middle one a single continuous line, the two flanking a combination of split weaves and weft locks. Six split weaves in a row. At the time she'd thought it was absurd, ugly, fiddly stuff, but it wasn't. It was marking the openings on the walls of the tombs. Six corridors, and then a weft lock to mark . . . *to mark the place where you go through? Yes! That's it!*

She laughed again. Fenris looked over her shoulder. "Is it a map? It doesn't look right."

"No, no, it's not a map. It's *directions*. The godmother couldn't help us, not really, because of the spell on her, so she couldn't have given me directions if I knew what they were. But I thought it was just an ugly tapestry, so she could." Possibly this was not the clearest explanation. Fenris looked baffled. She tried to explain about split weaves and weft locks and Fenris held up his hands. "Can you read it?"

"Yes."

"Then that's good enough for me. Lead the way."

"I have to figure out where we are," she said. "The gold knot . . . Is that the king or . . . No, no, the weave doesn't match. I think that's the way out. The palace, maybe, or another exit. I just have to find where we are on the tapestry." She ran her fingers over the thick threads, letting touch work where eyesight failed. Three split weaves on one side, two on the other, and a weft lock in the middle of the center row, indicating that you'd reached your destination—there it was, yes!

Marra flipped the ragged cloth around and walked forward. Fenris held the candle aloft. Bonedog bounced around Agnes, and the dust-wife grimly brought up the rear, her footsteps uneven on the stone.

"Weft lock . . ." she muttered to herself. "Split weave, split weave . . . weft lock here." She took the indicated turn, then the next.

"This is the way we came," said Fenris. "So far so good."

Suddenly confident, Marra hurried onward. The tapestry came alive under her fingertips and she knew where she was going. She did not realize that she was practically running until Fenris called ahead to her. "Wait a moment, Marra."

"Right." She stopped, letting the dust-wife and Agnes catch up. "Right. I'm sorry. I just . . ." She waved aimlessly overhead. *What time is it up there? It can't have started yet, surely? We must be close.* Time suddenly seemed physically present, rushing past her like air through the tunnels. *What happens now that the godmother's gone? Old spells? Agnes thinks she can use her powers if we get to the christening, or maybe the dust-wife was going to cast a spell on Vorling, or raise up the dead, but she can't do that now . . .* Could she get to her sister before the christening and warn her that something was going to happen? Was there time? Or would spells laid centuries ago, biding their time, already be exploding like fireworks over the palace?

They followed the tapestry path for another half dozen familiar turns, and then it diverged. Fenris looked up. "I think this is not the way we came," he said. "But I trust your directions."

"Don't mind us," called Agnes. "We're coming."

Marra took a deep breath and led them forward into the dark.

* * *

It was a much shorter route than the one from in the quarry, or perhaps that route had seemed longer because they had gotten turned around and gone so slowly and down so many dead ends. Once they reached a tomb that seemed to have no exits and Marra began to wonder if she had misread, until Bonedog ran snuffling to a tapestry that moved in an unseen breeze. Behind it, half-hidden, was the next door. And then, practically before she had time to comprehend it, there was a bright outline at the end of the hall and Fenris pushed open the door and stepped through, sword at the ready . . . into the godmother's temple.

It was a small room, but Marra could see the main hall through a carved screen. Perhaps priests had once prepared for their sermons here. The godmother sat on a little raised platform, still in that perfect dark triangle of skull and robe and shoulders. She did not move her head when she spoke. "Stay your sword, warrior," she said. "I suspect that I will die very soon in any event."

"I wasn't going to . . ." Fenris lowered his sword and looked abashed. "Forgive me, madam."

She laughed. "There is nothing to forgive. You did not free me, though. Nor did you." Her eyes moved to the door as Agnes came through. "And you are powerful, for all you try to hide it, but not in a way that could compel the dead. So it must be . . . ah. Of course. It must have been you."

The dust-wife inclined her head.

"I could have died when the spell broke," said the godmother. "I thought about it. But I was curious as to who had finally set me free." She searched the dust-wife's face, took in the coat full of pockets and the brown hen hunkered down on the staff. "Why? I have never done you a kindness. And we are a long, long way from your own beloved dead."

"A friend asked me to," said the dust-wife.

"Ah." The godmother smiled then, and cracks ran across her skin from the motion, like a plaster wall falling apart. As Marra watched in horror, a chip of skin fell from her cheekbone. There was no blood under it, nothing but cool, brown bone. "Yes. Agnes, will you pass me my teacup? It seems that I am about to die, and I would like a little more tea."

Agnes rushed forward and poured the tea with trembling hands. She tried to press it into the godmother's hands, but they were only bone, folded politely in a pile of dust. "Oh no," she said softly. "Oh dear." She knelt, held the teacup to the ancient lips and tipped it up.

"Thank you," said the godmother against the rim of the teacup, and then she fell apart. Marra took a step back but there was something oddly peaceful about it, about bones sinking down into the robes and the dust pattering down around them. There had been very little flesh left to the godmother, only skin and skeleton and iron will. Her robes stayed in their perfect triangle, stiff with gold brocade.

Agnes wiped her eyes. "Dammit," she whispered. "I have to go be impressive. I have to go be the wicked godmother. I can't cry."

"She's at peace now," said Fenris.

Agnes gave him an ironic glance. "She's been at peace for centuries, I think. I still get to cry about it."

She rose and wiped her hands on her dress. She looked small and bedraggled in her shapeless dress, scarf around her neck with a sleeping chicken in it. Her hair was in flyaway wisps and there were lines around her eyes from worried smiling.

And then she took a deep breath and shook herself and her eyes flickered green as poison. "All right," she said. "Let's go."

* * *

The front door of the godmother's temple was locked from the inside, but Marra could hear frantic pounding. *The guard. Yes, of course there was a guard.* A merely human guard seemed so banal now. The metal door rang like a gong, and when Fenris opened it, the guard was so shocked that he fell back a step, his mouth hanging open. "The godmother," he said. "They've summoned the godmother and she was supposed to come and she always does but she didn't. Where is she? She's going to be *late!*" His voice cracked on the word *late*, panic rendering him much younger than his years.

Agnes patted his hand kindly. Marra stayed well back in the shadow of the door, wondering if they were going to have to hit the guard over the head, but Agnes said, "She's coming. Don't worry."

"Yes," said the dust-wife. "We apologize. We were consulting her on a matter of wizardly importance."

The guard blinked at her, then at the staff and the chicken. "Oh. Uh. I . . . Is she ready?"

"Yes. You should go in. She's very tired, though."

He bolted past them, not even glancing in Marra's direction. They closed the door behind them and the dust wife took out a little jar from her pocket and dabbed something on her finger. She smeared it down the seam of the door and the metal knit together from either side, as high as she could reach, soft and malleable as clay.

"What is that?" asked Fenris.

"Slip from the potter's wheel of a great saint. He preached to statues and they came to life to praise the gods." She shrugged. "He's dead now, of course."

"He is?"

"You can't keep bringing statues to life for religion. Sooner or later they figure out they don't have souls, and then things go very badly for everyone." She tried to turn, then sat down heavily on the steps. "Oh hell."

"Lady Fox!"

"No, no," the dust-wife said. The hen clucked warily. "I'm done. Go on. I'll make sure our friend here doesn't bother anyone."

"Are you going to kill him?" asked Agnes, not sounding particularly appalled.

"No, losing his memory for a few days should be plenty. Hopefully he hasn't accepted any surprise offers of marriage or anything." She made shooing gestures. "Go, go. You heard him. The christening is about to start."

* * *

Marra had very little memory of the panicked rush through the streets. Bonedog galloped beside her. Just before they reached the palace gates, Fenris caught the dog's leash and Agnes waved Marra forward. "Go," she said. "I'll make my grand entrance just behind you."

She had no time to question. She ran to the guards. "My sister," she gasped. "My sister. The queen. I'm her sister. The nun." She lifted her necklace with the grackle feather. She was gasping for breath, but hopefully that made her story more plausible. She waved frantically toward the lower city. "My carriage. Horse. Threw a shoe. Please. My mother's already there. I have to be there!"

She didn't expect it to work. It probably shouldn't have worked. But the guards blinked at her and then at each other and she moved between them. Both of them clearly waited for the other one to say something but neither one did and by the time they had realized it, she had pushed past them.

Thank the Lady of Grackles, there was a footman that she recognized just beyond the guards. "Please!" she gasped to him. "Please, I'm late, I'm so late. Where is the christening?"

"Princess Marra?"

"Yes! My carriage— The horse—" She couldn't remember if she'd said the wheel broke or the horse threw a shoe, so she just waved her hands.

"You know her?" asked one of the guards. "She's the princess?"

"Yes, of course. But where is the godmother?" He peered over her shoulder. "She always comes." He sounded a bit lost.

"Didn't see her," said Marra. "Take me to my sister. I'm sure she'll show up."

The footman led her away through the hall, still occasionally turning to look behind them, which footmen never did. Marra's skin crawled. Was Agnes coming? Was Fenris? Had they gotten past the guards? Surely they could, but she would have felt much better if the dust-wife were with them.

I can do this, she thought grimly. *I can do this. I did two impossible tasks and found the way out of the palace of dust. I can finish this. I just have to find Kania.*

They reached the room full of courtiers. All eyes turned as the great doors opened and the room held its breath. "The godm— The princess Marra!" announced the majordomo at the door.

The silence broke. The courtiers looked away and began murmuring among themselves as Marra entered the room. They knew Princess Marra, and they knew that she was of no consequence.

"Marra?" said her mother, and did not ask *Where have you been?* or *How did you get here?* though her eyes were full of questions.

"Where is the godmother?" said Vorling. He, too, sounded lost and Marra hated him for it, the way that she had not hated the footman or the guard. *How dare you?* she thought. *How dare you pin the royal bloodline on a woman held captive so long that she turned to living dust? How dare you?* Which was unfair, and she knew it was unfair, but she did not feel any need to be just to the man who left bruises on her sister's arms.

"Marra?" said Kania. She stood back from the cradle, her eyes huge. "Marra, is that you?"

"I'm sorry I'm late . . ." Marra babbled, rushing across the vast room. She could feel eyes on her, but they were contemptuous and dismissive and that was good, that was all good—no one cared about her here, no one knew to be afraid of what storm might follow in her wake. She fetched up at Kania's side and clutched her sleeve. "Kania. Kania, I have to tell you— Kania—"

"Tell me what?"

Marra opened her mouth and realized she had no idea what to say next. She had always planned to speak to her alone, to warn her that there would be a different godmother, that something strange was probably going to happen, but Vorling was only a dozen feet away and her mother was right there. "It's . . . it's . . . I'm late . . ." she heard herself say.

"Where is the godmother?" said Vorling, turning toward her. He did not sound lost any longer. He sounded angry. "Was she behind you? Why am I being made a fool of in my own palace?"

Kania's hand crept to Marra's and squeezed in sudden fear.

Marra lifted her chin and met Vorling's eyes. *You are not so big. You are only a living king. I saw an old woman defeat a dead one. You cannot hurt me any worse than spinning thread of nettle wool, and you cannot confuse me any more than the palace of dust. Even your cruelty is small compared to the blistered land.*

Perhaps he saw some of that defiance in her. Men like him always had a sense for it, did they not? He took a step forward and his hands clenched at his sides.

"Everyone's asking about her," said Marra in a clear voice. "No one at the gates has seen her. They're saying she's dead."

"*What?*"

He took another step toward her and Kania took a step back. Marra pushed herself between them, wondering if decorum would hold him, knowing in her bones that if a king decided to beat his wife and her sister in front of the court, the court would stand there and watch. *Please, Lady of Grackles. Please.*

"I will stand as the child's godmother," cried Agnes from the doorway.

Chapter 21

Agnes, tall. Agnes with her eyes flashing green like beast eyes reflected in a fire. Agnes, a wicked godmother.

Vorling wheeled around and this time he was the one who took a step back.

She did not look like a tiny, fluttery woman who lived with chickens and a garden that had gotten out of control. She looked like a creature of magic and terror, the dark mirror of a saint, more at home in the goblin market than the throne room.

Despite everything, Marra's first instinct was to lunge for the cradle and throw herself over her nephew to protect him. Instead she grabbed Kania tighter.

Her sister tried to move forward. Marra clutched her arm. "Don't," she whispered. "Don't! It's our old godmother, the godmother's gone, the curse . . ." She was making no sense and she knew that she was making no sense, but it didn't matter. She didn't have to make sense. She just had to hold Kania until Agnes reached the cradle, and then it would be over quickly.

"The godmother of the Northern Kingdom has died at last," said Agnes, her voice ringing like steel in that great stone room. "The curse is broken. And so to this child, I give a new gift for a new age."

Marra looked at Vorling, surrounded by his little triangle of guards, and saw his lips moving. *Dead?* He looked astonished, as if this was not something he had ever considered, as if the sun had risen in the west and then fallen from the sky.

Agnes leaned down and laid her fingertips across the infant's skull. Kania tried to move again but Marra had her arm in a death grip.

"This gift I give you," said Agnes. "You shall grow up fatherless."

And then, in a voice much more like the old Agnes, she added, "And healthy."

For the length of a half dozen heartbeats, the room was absolutely still. Then everyone seemed to breathe in at once. Vorling shouted, "Stop her!" and the courtiers leapt forward or stepped back, depending on their nature, and the guards rushed Agnes, drawing their swords, and Agnes hiked up her skirts and ran for the door, no longer a towering figure of darkness but a little round woman with a flushed face and a half-grown chicken tucked into her scarf.

"Stop her!" shouted Vorling again. "This is an attack! Cut her down! Bring me her head! Find the real godmother!"

The two guards flanking the doorway stepped forward, halberds at the ready. Marra stuffed the side of her hand in her mouth. Agnes was going to get cut down and there was no way to save her. Pretending to be a nun wouldn't work—couldn't work—

A ghostly growl filled the hallway. Bonedog took the guard on the left from behind, his teeth sinking into the silks of the dress uniform and tearing out a great gash of thigh. The man screamed, his leg buckling, and he went down.

Bonedog snapped and snarled soundlessly at the second guard and Agnes got past him into the hallway. "Go, go!" yelled Vorling to the men surrounding him, "Go! Kill her familiar and bring me her head!"

They charged across the room. Vorling stood alone and then there were four of them going after Bonedog and he couldn't get all of them. *Oh, Bonedog, no, no, run—Fenris, where are you? You have to save him, Fenris!*

Fleeing had never been in Bonedog's nature. Marra dragged in one long breath and held it, and Bonedog's jaws closed on a man's knee. Then the halberd came down and the ghost of a yelp filled the room.

Bones exploded in every direction, no longer held together by wire. The tiny joints of paw and tail rattled across the floor like unstrung beads. Marra moaned and the only mercy was that the courtiers were gasping and shrieking in surprise so that no one noticed except her sister.

"Foul magic!" cried one of the courtiers, a big man with a fox-colored beard. "Sorcery!"

"Stop h—" Vorling shouted again, and then the last word went soft and wet and startled. Marra wrenched her eyes away from Bonedog, back to Vorling.

Fenris had his hand on the king's shoulder, almost a friendly gesture, except for the foot of steel protruding from Vorling's chest. Vorling stared down at the blade, his expression just as puzzled as before, and then Fenris pulled the sword out and blood came from the king's mouth and he died.

"He did it," said Marra in a very small voice. "He did it." *He must have been working his way along the wall while everyone was staring at Agnes and Bonedog. That was the right thing to do. That was why we came. Wasn't it?*

She would have traded victory in a heartbeat to have Bonedog whole again.

Kania turned her head. Her eyes swept over her dead husband and then to her living sister, and Marra could see everything snapping into place. But then, unlike Marra, Kania had never been a fool.

The guards who were trying to chase Agnes skidded to a halt. They ran back toward Fenris. There were five of them, four with swords, one with a halberd. Fenris had no armor and only the old iron sword stained with the king's blood.

He looked across the room and his eyes met hers. It was the same look he always had, the one that said, *Can you believe two sensible people like us are caught up in this?* And then he turned to meet the guards and Marra saw on his face the moment that he decided to die.

They circled him. He raised his sword. She was trapped in one of those nightmares where no matter how fast she ran or how loudly she yelled, she would be too slow, the air was like glue, and so she stood with her throat closed and her feet nailed to the floor, unable to look away.

Swords rose. They had only to attack him, all together, and it would be over. He could not defend from all directions, and all of them were young.

Into that terrible moment of waiting, the queen of the Northern Kingdom shouted, "*Hold!*"

* * *

The guards obeyed. It seemed impossible, but they all took a step back, widening the circle around Fenris. Their eyes flicked to Kania and then back to Fenris.

Kania spoke as clear and crackling cold as ice. "This man was sent by our enemies to kill our king. I want to know everything he knows before he dies." She walked forward and somehow the guards were listening and the courtiers were watching her as if she was truly the queen and not merely the king's beaten wife. She stood over the cradle. "My son has been cursed," she said, still in that cold, clear voice. "My husband is dead. I will know who did this. You will take him alive."

Another long, terrible waiting moment, but somehow the balance had shifted. The pivot point was no longer the blades of the guards but the queen standing over the cradle. The man with the fox-colored beard moved forward to stand a little behind her, as if lending her his presence, and all the courtiers saw it and Marra saw it register on many faces, although she did not know what it meant.

Please, thought Marra. *Please, Fenris, please.* She begged him with her eyes to surrender. If he lived, she could get him out of this. Probably. Or at least the dust-wife could, or Agnes, or someone.

Fenris laid down his sword.

The guards rushed him and they were not gentle. He went to his knees and they dragged his arms behind him. "Put him in a cell," said Kania. "He will be alive when I see him again, or all of your lives will be forfeit. Do I make myself clear?"

"Yes, my queen," said the guard with the halberd, and they dragged Fenris away.

Kania did not watch. She turned to Marra, and Marra recognized the look in her eyes. It was the look that she had as a child, when she had been doing something she should not have done. It said, *Don't you dare tell on me, or I will end you.*

It settled Marra's nerves as hardly anything else could. Suddenly they were both children, both in this together, and the awareness of her sister's hate, the one that had been under her breastbone since she was a child, fell away. She took a step forward.

"You tried to warn us, Sister," said Kania. Throwing her the lie, waiting for her to catch it.

"I did," she said in her best nun's voice. "I'm sorry. I was late and the . . . the false godmother was behind me. I could tell something was wrong. I only wish I'd realized what she had planned."

Kania nodded. "Your warning might have spared us much worse. This was a cunning trap, well laid," she said, and somehow, because she said it like a queen, it became true. All the courtiers had seen Agnes run away and Fenris was just one man with a sword, and yet Marra could practically hear the story shift inside their heads.

"My son is the rightful king," said Kania. "But he is not a week old and already he has been cursed by this kingdom's enemies." Her gaze swept the room. "I will stand as his regent, but I will not stand alone. I will require loyal advisors to stand with me, men who will put the kingdom first, above power or personal gain." She turned to the fox-bearded man. "Lord Marlin, I would have you be first among those. Will you accept?"

Lord Marlin inclined his head gravely. Marra suspected that he had begun planning the moment that the king had died, but he let the silence draw out, to give the question appropriate gravity. "Yes, my queen," he said. "For the young king."

"And General Takise," said Kania, sweeping in the other direction. "You were his grandfather's closest confidant. Will you stand with the young king, also?"

General Takise had iron hair and an iron bearing. He put his fist over his heart. "For the young king," he said gruffly.

"Then we are agreed," said Kania. She reached into the cradle and lifted her son. "We three shall serve as regents, until my son reaches his majority. And now . . ." For the first time, her voice filled with emotion, with sorrow so finely feigned that Marra marveled at it. "Now I must mourn my husband and make arrangements for his funeral. And his murderer. I beg you, my fellow regents, to bring me proposals for my son's safety. It seems that we are at war with someone, and we must learn who. And quickly."

And she swept out of the room, her head held high, carrying her son, while the courtiers erupted into amazement behind her.

* * *

"That was astoundingly well done," said Marra's mother, less than an hour later. "You got the two biggest rivals to the throne backing you."

"They had to back me, or risk the other one gaining ascendancy. Takise is a good sort, anyway. Marlin you can't trust any farther than you can throw him, but he is at least predictably power hungry." Kania held her son to her breast, gazing at him with a kind of baffled astonishment. "Mother . . . what the hell do I do now?"

"Exactly what you've been doing. You seized control at the moment when it was all up in the air. If one of the others had acted like they were in charge first, you would have lost everything, but you moved first and that matters."

Marra shook her head. She was beyond exhausted and she could hardly think. "Fenris . . ." she began.

Kania looked around. She had dismissed the servants and they were all in the tiny chapel again, ostensibly praying for the soul of Vorling. "I'll do what I can," she said, half in a whisper. "But I don't know if I can spare his life. He murdered the king in front of everyone. I don't know."

Marra's stomach clenched. She rested her forehead on the rail that separated mourners from coffins. There was no coffin yet. Would there be a coffin for Fenris?

I thought we had a better plan. I thought it was going to make more sense. I thought that Agnes would give the curse and then magic would make Vorling trip on the stairs or choke on a fish bone or something. I didn't realized Fenris would just . . . just . . .

But of course he had. He was a man who got things done. He had been willing to die and he had seen a way to end the matter. Agnes had gotten away. Kania was free. A tyrant was dead. Fenris would have thought it was a fair trade, his life for Vorling's death, but all Marra could think was that it was not fair, it was one more cruelty, as if Vorling had reached out from the grave and struck a final blow.

"We'll figure something out," Kania said. Marra lifted her head.

Her mother looked unconvinced. "Sometimes there are sacrifices that have to be made," she said. "It may not be possible without risking everything you have gained. Your position is not secure, not yet. It is only the lack of clear rules of succession that let you step into the regency as you have."

"Bless the paranoia of these Northern kings," muttered Kania. "None of them allow anyone with power to oppose him to flourish." She rubbed her forearm, and Marra wondered what bruises lay concealed beneath the sleeve.

"True. Nevertheless, if you are seen as soft on your husband's killer . . ."

Kania stared down at her son. It occurred to Marra that she did not even know the child's name. They had arrived too late to the christening for such niceties.

"I hated him so much," she said softly. "So much, and for so long. I thought if he died, it would feel like a great weight off my shoulders, and yet I am just as weighed down as I was. Is he really dead? Is this truly happening?"

"It is," said her mother.

Kania gave a single dry sob, startling the infant king, who began to cry.

"You did so good," said Marra. "You did. All that with the lords and the generals and you even convinced people I wasn't part of it. I couldn't believe it."

The sob had a laugh at the bottom this time. "Oh yes," Kania said. "Oh yes, *that* part I knew. I've been running it through in my head for years, what I'd do if he miraculously died. I had every possible scenario memorized. It's only now that I don't know what I'm doing."

"I'm sorry I couldn't do it sooner," said Marra helplessly. "I'm sorry. Everything took so long to do and . . . and . . ."

She tried to explain. She got as far as Bonedog and began to cry and Kania also began to cry and their mother put an arm around each of them and held her daughters as if they were all much younger.

"I'll help you," her mother said. "I'll help as much as I can. I can't stay for terribly long, but grandmothers are allowed some time to dote on their grandchildren, and we'll go through all the details while I'm here. There may be angles that you can find to keep the rest of the courtiers from seizing power."

Kania wiped her eyes. "I wish Damia were here," she said. "I wish she could have known that it got fixed. That there was justice."

Marra gulped. Her eyes and nose were streaming and she wiped them on her sleeve. Justice seemed so little, so late. Kania had suffered for long years and the godmother for long centuries. The Northern kings had left scars on time. Even the thief-wheel still roaming the halls, even the furious ghost daughter . . .

I was buried alive to hide their shame.

She looked up. An idea had come to her, as terrible in its way as the very first idea had been, the one that had set her on the road to kill a prince and curse a kingdom.

"I know how to save Fenris."

Chapter 22

The funeral of King Vorling was small by the Northern Kingdom's standards. He had reigned for less than half a year and barely any preparations had been made on his tomb. His wife, the new queen regent, said that her husband would have preferred the wealth be spent on strengthening the kingdom's defenses, as they were clearly targets of an enemy who might strike again, whatever ridiculous tale the Hardishman assassin had spun about a dust-wife and a goblin market and a geas. Diplomats had been dispatched to Hardack to demand answers, but no one was optimistic. There was sorcery afoot.

Perhaps the nobles might have been worried, with a foreign woman on the throne, but Queen Kania had already proven herself as ruthless as the kings of old. For at the foot of Vorling's sarcophagus, under a screaming death mask, the assassin had been interred alive, to die of thirst in the halls of the dead. The queen had stood at the head of the procession and watched the lid come down. "For what you did to my husband," she said, "for what you did to me." And then darkness had covered the face of the Hardishman and the procession had left the tomb behind, deep in the dark and the dust.

It was fourteen hours later that Marra and the dust-wife flung themselves at the stone lid, scrabbling with all their strength. For a horrible moment, she thought that it would not be enough, that they would have to come back with levers, but it began, inch by agonizing inch, to slide. They got it perhaps six inches and had to stop, panting.

Fingers slid out of the gap and caught the edge. Marra nearly wept with relief. Fenris shoved the lid aside and sat up, gasping for air.

"You're really here," he said, bending over so that his forehead touched his drawn-up knees. "I kept imagining voices, but you're really here this time."

"We're here," said Marra, the words *this time* jabbing her like pins.

He took a half dozen sobbing breaths. "It is very close in there," he said, "even with the holes." His face was slick, with sweat or tears, Marra did not know. "Close and cold."

"I'm sorry," said Marra. "I'm sorry. It was the only way I could think of." She pulled him out of the coffin, or he climbed out and she helped, and he wrapped his arms around her and they stood together, shaking.

"It worked," he said. "I would not want to do it again. How many days has it been?"

"A little over half a day," said the dust-wife.

"Only that? It seemed so much longer."

They slid the lid back in place and crept out of the tomb, through the tomb that had been cut for Kania, through the small, sad room where Marra's niece lay in her bed of stone. She had to help hold Fenris up. His muscles had cramped and knotted and he staggered as he walked. "Why are there no guards?" he whispered.

"Because of the queen," said the dust-wife.

"She could not pull the guards from the entrance without it looking peculiar," said Marra, "but she called on the others to escort her. She had gone to Vorling's mother's tomb. She said that no one thought of the mothers in this time and she wanted to commune with the shade who had lost a child and— Oh, it was amazing. It really was. She's so good at this. At being queen. Everyone was very impressed."

"I was certainly impressed," he said a bit dryly. "When she looked down on me in that stone box, I thought that she was going to let me die a slow death in the dark." One corner of his mouth crooked up. "And I found that I did not want to die. Not like that."

"I'm sorry," said Marra again.

"Don't be. I had faith. I thought if I could just hold out long enough . . . well, you and Lady Fox here would come for me."

The dust-wife snorted. "I would have," she said. "You might not have been alive at the time, though. Dead men are much less trouble."

He staggered again. Marra winced. "Did they torture you?"

"Very little, considering. General Takise is a good man, but more importantly, a good soldier, and he knows how little torture is worth for extracting usable information. I made up a tale that had truth scattered through it, and he decided that I was likely mad, but with the magic we had seen, he could not be sure. Torture only tells you what the victim thinks will save him, and they knew that. So they beat me a little, and when my story did not change to anything they could use, they stopped.

"Where are we going now?" asked Fenris.

"Away." The dust-wife glanced over her shoulder. "Agnes arranged for a cart."

"Agnes is walking around freely?"

Marra laughed. "Everyone remembers her as very tall," she said, "with bright green eyes. It's the damnedest thing."

"She was, though," said Fenris. He had to stop and lean against the wall for a moment, stretching his legs and bending his knee to work the kinks out. "When I saw her. Wasn't she? Was it an illusion, like the one on Bonedog?"

"It's not an illusion," said the dust-wife. "Not exactly. Your mind knows what certain things ought to look like, and when your eyes are wrong, your mind wins. Agnes's magic thinks she ought to be six feet tall with eyes like a starving wolf. That Agnes's body didn't comply is just an oversight, so far as the magic is concerned."

"She's a very wicked godmother, isn't she?" asked Marra.

"Evil magic could flow through her like a river in full flood. Fortunately for the rest of us, there's a lot of Agnes in the way. Whether that makes her wicked, I'll leave to philosophers. This turning here, I think."

They emerged into the gritty light that precedes dawn. Marra barely took note of their surroundings. Another quarry, it looked like. She was too busy helping to shore up Fenris. One step after another, one step, one step more, and then there was a wagon in front of them and Agnes was falling off the driver's seat and threw her arms around them. "You're alive!" she said. "But of course you are; I didn't think you were dead— I mean, Fenris, I thought there was a chance you were dead, I didn't know, but of course Marra wasn't dead—not to disparage the dead, obviously they serve their purposes and we'll all be dead eventually anyway, so you probably shouldn't speak ill of them, although I can't say that I'm sorry to see Vorling go—"

"How is Finder?" asked Fenris, stemming the flow of words.

Agnes rummaged around in her scarf and produced Finder, who was half asleep and clearly indignant at being awoken.

"You need to train him to sit somewhere else," said the dust-wife disapprovingly. "Otherwise you'll have a rooster who thinks he should dive headfirst into your cleavage when he wants to roost."

"It's been a while since any man wanted to dive into my cleavage," said Agnes. "It might be a nice change."

"Not when the spurs grow in."

"Oh, well, probably not."

They got Fenris into the wagon and Marra handed up the bag slung across her back. It rattled as he took it. "What's in here?"

"A friend."

His eyebrows went up. Marra climbed up beside him and she and the dust-wife arranged empty feed sacks to conceal him. He sneezed a few times but did not argue.

"I see you have much to tell me," he said. "Ah . . . not over the face unless it looks like we'll be stopped. I was in that box too long, and having things on my face . . ." He smiled up at her, but it was a thin layer over deeper horror. Marra found his hand under the layers of burlap and squeezed. *Another wound for Vorling's tally. But if we get away, then it is done. It is all done, at last.*

"No talking now," said the dust-wife. The wagon wheels creaked as they left the quarry, going away from the city. Marra pulled the nettle cloak tight around her shoulders, chilly in the predawn cold. Fenris's fingers were warm in hers.

By the time the sun had risen, the white city was behind them. She could still see it, like a canine tooth in the earth's jaw, but it was far away and had no more power to bite.

And I will never go back.

When she had taken leave of her sister for the last time, they had both known it. Kania had said as much. "I do not know how long I can keep you out of this. I can try, but . . ."

"I know," said Marra. "I know. Someone will remember seeing me. Someone will make a connection. As long as I'm here, there's the risk. It's better if I go."

"It's not quite that," said her sister. "Although that is certainly true. You are now the sister of the queen regent of the Northern Kingdom, and you are no longer staying unwed to appease Vorling's paranoia. Mother will begin thinking where to put you."

For a moment, Marra was too astonished to be appalled. "But I'm . . . I'm not a virgin and not a princess. I'm almost a nun!"

"*Almost* is the key," said Kania a bit dryly. "You could rush home and try to take orders, and I will bet you the finest horse in the kingdom that the abbess won't accept them."

Marra inhaled sharply. To be wed for politics. To be shipped off to a strange man's bed, while Fenris lay in a box in the palace of dust, waiting for rescue . . .

"She doesn't mean to be cruel," said Kania. "She isn't. She stopped a war by marrying our family into Vorling's. The Northern Kingdom would have rolled over us like a tide and our people would all be feeding the crabs by now. She had to choose the people over us, and use our bodies to seal the deal." She rubbed absently at her forearm, where the bruises were yellow and faded. "She saved thousands of lives."

"I know," said Marra. "I know."

Kania had given her two gifts before she left. One was a pouch full of money and one was a sack full of bones.

"They gathered them all up," her sister said. "Every one, down to the smallest claw. They were terrified that if they left any, it would give evil magic a way into the room. I told them that they needed to be disposed of properly and that my sister would take them to Our Lady of Grackles for the nuns to sanctify before they were burned."

Marra could not see through sudden tears, but Kania wrapped her arm around her sister's shoulder. "Go," she whispered in Marra's ear. "Run and be free. They cannot use what they cannot find."

And Marra hugged her back and went out through the god-mother's palace door with her hood over her head, then slipped away into the city to meet the dust-wife and save her friends.

* * *

They meandered south, day by day. The wagon was drawn by an exceedingly patient mule who tolerated the brown hen standing on his back. Marra sat in the back of the wagon and worked as well as she could with everything moving and rattling under her. At night, by the fire, she made much better progress, but then the light was bad and she jabbed her fingers bloody again. Agnes tutted and salved her fingertips. The dust-wife watched her, her long face expressionless.

"Will it work?" asked Marra, wrapping wires.

The dust-wife stood looking down at her and her skirt full of bones. "It would never work on a human," she said. "Humans know when they're dead. It might work on a dog. Dogs are simpler."

She slept back-to-back with Fenris at night. No one commented. Sometimes he moved and she knew that he was also awake in the darkness, but neither of them quite had the nerve to act on it, not with Agnes and the dust-wife there. *I could roll over. I could put my arm around his waist. I could . . .*

"I'm going home," said the dust-wife one morning. "Agnes, you should probably come with me. They'll sort out the godmother thing one of these days, and you'll be left trying to fend off the enemy with a chicken."

"I know," said Agnes. "I always expected I'd go with you."

"Oh?"

"Yes, of course." Agnes tapped Finder's beak. The young cockerel was growing in his adult feathers, though he was still half the size of the brown hen and had no wattles to speak of. "Finder, find me the safest place for me to be."

Finder cocked his head to one side, then turned and walked to the dust-wife's feet, where he began scratching in the dirt after an interesting worm.

"Ah," said the dust-wife.

"But we have to stop by my cottage. I want my good medicine chest and I'm not leaving all my chickens. And I want seeds of all my good plants. And . . ."

"Yes, yes." The dust-wife turned back to Fenris and Marra. "You two will be better off making your own way. By which I mean that all this poorly suppressed longing is giving me hives."

Fenris coughed. Marra put her hands over her face.

"Come see us," said Agnes. "Please. I'll want someone to talk to who isn't grumpy."

"I'm not grumpy."

"You are an absolute grump and so is your chicken." The two old women climbed into the wagon and drove away, still bickering. Marra felt a pang in her heart and a surge of relief, all at once.

They spent the day where they had made camp the night before, in a little shepherd's hut on a hillside, out of the wind. Fenris kept the fire up, and Marra threaded wire through bits of bone, rubbing her fingers across the broad, faithful skull and the long cage of ribs, the narrow whip of tail.

He sat beside her and handed her bones and wire as she asked, but he did not press her.

At sunset, just as the light from the fire became brighter than the light from the doorway, she finished. The skeleton lay across her lap, complete, claws wired to paws, vertebrae strung like beads.

"Wake," she whispered, while the light faded outside the door. "Wake. *Please.*"

The bones lay motionless in her lap. She bowed her head. *Please. Please, Bonedog. I'm never going to see my sister again, or my mother. I'm not going to see the Sister Apothecary or the abbess. I need one more friend. Please.*

It was too much like the first time. The second impossible task was also the third. She had always known that she had gotten off too lightly, being handed the moon in a jar.

Fenris took her free hand, careful of her sore fingertips, and held it between his palms, waiting with her.

"Please," she said again, and a single tear ran hotly down her cheek and splashed on the white expanse of skull.

Bonedog yawned and stretched and woke.

Marra let out a sob of relief and buried her head in Fenris's neck. He held her in the crook of his arm while Bonedog stood up and bounced and cavorted around the hut.

"We'll have to get him enchanted again," said Fenris, watching the dog trying to lick parts that had vanished along with the glamour.

"We'll figure something out."

"Mm. And what happens now? Are you going back to your convent?"

Marra thought about sitting up, but it was very warm against his side. "You said once that you couldn't go back," she said. "You said that homesickness wasn't worth a clan war."

Fenris nodded. "It's still true."

"If I go home now, I don't know what will happen. Maybe nothing. But they'll probably marry me off and I'll be back in that world and I . . . I'm not good at it. I'm so very bad at it. And there's always a chance that someone figures out what we did." Marra took a deep breath. "I think it's more trouble than it's worth."

"Very likely." He was looking at her with that grave, thoughtful look again, but there was a hint of humor in his eyes, which was encouraging or maddening or both together.

"And I already agreed to help you ransom the other humans in the goblin market."

"You did."

"So. Maybe you and I could . . . not go home together?"

The words hung in the air between them, as fine as spun glass and just as fragile. Marra waited for him to say something, to catch the words or shatter them, whichever he chose.

"I think I'd like that," said Fenris.

Marra sagged with relief.

She had been so focused on what he might say that she hadn't quite expected what he might do. So it came as a surprise when he wrapped both arms around her and put his lips against her hair. "I think I would like that very much," he murmured.

"Oh good," said Marra against his neck. And then she would have kissed him or he would have kissed her, but Bonedog decided that they were wrestling and jumped up and barked soundlessly at them both.

Black dog, white dog,
Live dog, dead dog,
Yellow dog, run!

Author's Note

This book started in a grocery store parking lot, with the line "with the dog made of bone at your side." I don't know why, but that line showed up in my head and started hammering away like a tuneless earworm.

It's always neat when something drops in your lap like that, but you generally spend the first hour trying to figure out if you thought of it or if it's a fragment of something you read once. Authors have minds like packrats and a lot of stuff gets squirreled away, some of which belongs to other people. Nevertheless, the line was insistent and didn't seem familiar.

By the time I reached the grocery store, it had grown to "You came to me in your cloak of nettles with the dog made of bone at your side." At the checkout line, I had most of a very short story called "Godmother." It had a lot of imagery in common with the book you just read, though the plot, such as it was, was very different. I put it on the internet and then in an anthology and then went on about my life.

Still, the images nagged at me. Why did she build her own dog out of bones? Why were her hands stained with a prince's blood? What does building your own dog feel like? Who was the godmother narrating the story? Judging by some of my reader mail, it nagged at them too. People wanted to know about the woman with the bone dog.

At the same time and unrelated, in my other life as a children's book author, an editor asked me if I could do a fairy tale retelling of "The Princess and the Pea," and I couldn't do it. I have always found that story . . . well . . . squicky. Why does a prince want a bride with skin that sensitive? If a pea under a dozen mattresses is enough to leave bruises, what would a human touch do? Why would you *want* that? What does it say about the prince? None of my thoughts were the sort of thing you want in an upbeat romp aimed at seven-year-olds. We compromised on "Little Red Riding Hood" and I took my squick elsewhere.

Somewhere between the bone dog and the prince obsessed with tender skin, I wound up with the opening chapters. It included someone called a "dust-wife" about which I knew nothing, and the blistered land and Kania and Damia being married off. And then, as often happens, the story sat fallow for a half dozen years, occasionally getting dusted off and poked and prodded, and then one day I sent about ten thousand words off to my editor with my usual note: "Hey, I got this thing, you want it?" (I have heard some authors write cover letters and synopses and so forth. Someday I will have to try that.)

Well, she did want the thing, as it turned out, and that meant that I had to come up with a lot more book, in relatively short order. What's a dust-wife? What do they do? Where's the godmother? Why are godmothers involved at all? Why is my deadline only two months away? What am I doing? Why did I not become a medical test subject, like Mom always wanted? Do I really need both these kidneys, when the black market for organs is so lucrative?

This is a standard part of the authorial process, and of course the questions got answered and the book got written eventually. I suspect that I would probably still be stuck in the grocery store parking lot if not for the aid of a couple of people, though. First, my fabulous editor, Lindsey Hall, who would get excited about certain bits and thus make me realize I had to actually do something with those bits instead of just leaving them dangling in the wind; my agent, Helen, who has made peace with my "you want this thing?" style of cover letter and makes sure that I actually remember to sign forms and get money for the thing; my beta reader, Shepherd, who explained patiently about spinning and drop spindles and weft locks and tapestries, and even demonstrated how a drop spindle worked, despite my refusal to add more sheep to the book; and my beloved husband, Kevin, who is endlessly supportive and also keeps chickens, several of which found their way into the story in one form or another.

I could probably write books without all these people, but they would be significantly worse books and I would be far more frazzled and possibly short a kidney. Any particularly good bits are probably their fault, and any errors were almost certainly mine, made despite their best efforts to stop me.

I hope your dogs are all loyal and goofy and good-natured and that your chickens remain free of demons.

T. Kingfisher
North Carolina
May 2020

**Turn the page for a sneak peek at
T. Kingfisher's bestselling horror novella**

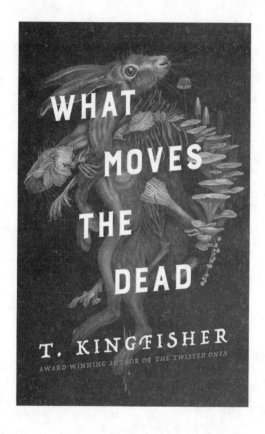

Available now from Tor Nightfire

CHAPTER 1

The mushroom's gills were the deep-red color of severed muscle, the almost-violet shade that contrasts so dreadfully with the pale pink of viscera. I had seen it any number of times in dead deer and dying soldiers, but it startled me to see it here.

Perhaps it would not have been so unsettling if the mushrooms had not looked so much like flesh. The caps were clammy, swollen beige, puffed up against the dark-red gills. They grew out of the gaps in the stones of the tarn like tumors growing from diseased skin. I had a strong urge to step back from them, and an even stronger urge to poke them with a stick.

I felt vaguely guilty about pausing in my trip to dismount and look at mushrooms, but I was tired. More importantly, my horse was tired. Madeline's letter had taken over a week to reach me, and no matter how urgently worded it had been, five minutes more or less would not matter.

Hob, my horse, was grateful for the rest, but seemed

annoyed by the surroundings. He looked at the grass and then up at me, indicating that this was not the quality to which he was accustomed.

"You could have a drink," I said. "A small one, perhaps."

We both looked into the water of the tarn. It lay dark and very still, reflecting the grotesque mushrooms and the limp gray sedges along the edge of the shore. It could have been five feet deep or fifty-five.

"Perhaps not," I said. I found that I didn't have much urge to drink the water either.

Hob sighed in the manner of horses who find the world not to their liking and gazed off into the distance.

I looked across the tarn to the house and sighed myself.

It was not a promising sight. It was an old gloomy manor house in the old gloomy style, a stone monstrosity that the richest man in Europe would be hard-pressed to keep up. One wing had collapsed into a pile of stone and jutting rafters. Madeline lived there with her twin brother, Roderick Usher, who was nothing like the richest man in Europe. Even by Ruravia's small, rather backward standards, the Ushers were genteelly impoverished. By the standards of the rest of Europe's nobility, they were as poor as church mice, and the house showed it.

There were no gardens that I could see. I could smell a faint sweetness in the air, probably from something flowering in the grass, but it wasn't enough to dispel the sense of gloom.

"I shouldn't touch that if I were you," called a voice behind me.

I turned. Hob lifted his head, found the visitor as disappointing as the grass and the tarn, and dropped it again.

She was, as my mother would say, "a woman of a certain

age." In this case, that age was about sixty. She was wearing men's boots and a tweed riding habit that may have predated the manor.

She was tall and broad and had a gigantic hat that made her even taller and broader. She was carrying a notebook and a large leather knapsack.

"Pardon?" I said.

"The mushroom," she said, stopping in front of me. Her accent was British but not London—somewhere off in the countryside, perhaps. "The mushroom, young . . ." Her gaze swept down, touched the military pins on my jacket collar, and I saw a flash of recognition across her face: *Aha!*

No, *recognition* is the wrong term. *Classification*, rather. I waited to see if she would cut the conversation short or carry on.

"I shouldn't touch it if I were you, officer," she said again, pointing to the mushroom.

I looked down at the stick in my hand, as if it belonged to someone else. "Ah—no? Are they poisonous?"

She had a rubbery, mobile face. Her lips pursed together dramatically. "They're stinking redgills. *A. foetida,* not to be confused with *A. foetidissima*—but that's not likely in this part of the world, is it?"

"No?" I guessed.

"No. The *foetidissima* are found in Africa. This one is endemic to this part of Europe. They aren't poisonous, exactly, but—well—"

She put out her hand. I set my stick in it, bemused. Clearly a naturalist. The feeling of being classified made more sense now. I had been categorized, placed into the correct clade, and the proper courtesies could now be deployed, while we went on to more critical matters like mushroom taxonomy.

"I suggest you hold your horse," she said. "And perhaps your nose." Reaching into her knapsack, she fished out a handkerchief, held it to her nose, and then flicked the stinking redgill mushroom with the very end of the stick.

It was a very light tap indeed, but the mushroom's cap immediately bruised the same visceral red-violet as the gills. A moment later, we were struck by an indescribable smell—rotting flesh with a tongue-coating glaze of spoiled milk and, rather horribly, an undertone of fresh-baked bread. It wiped out any sweetness to the air and made my stomach lurch.

Hob snorted and yanked at his reins. I didn't blame him. "Gahh!"

"That was a little one," said the woman of a certain age. "And not fully ripe yet, thank heavens. The big ones will knock your socks off and curl your hair." She set the stick down, keeping the handkerchief over her mouth with her free hand. "Hence the 'stinking' part of the common name. The 'redgill,' I trust, is self-explanatory."

"Vile!" I said, holding my arm over my face. "Are you a mycologist, then?"

I could not see her mouth through the handkerchief, but her eyebrows were wry. "An amateur only, I fear, as supposedly befits my sex."

She bit off each word, and we shared a look of wary understanding. England has no sworn soldiers, I am told, and even if it had, she might have chosen a different way. It was none of my business, as I was none of hers. We all make our own way in the world, or don't. Still, I could guess at the shape of some of the obstacles she had faced.

"Professionally, I am an illustrator," she said crisply. "But the study of fungi has intrigued me all my life."

"And it brought you here?"

"Ah!" She gestured with the handkerchief. "I do not know what you know of fungi, but this place is extraordinary! So many unusual forms! I have found boletes that previously were unknown outside of Italy, and one *Amanita* that appears to be entirely new. When I have finished my drawings, amateur or no, the Mycology Society will have no choice but to recognize it."

"And what will you call it?" I asked. I am delighted by obscure passions, no matter how unusual. During the war, I was once holed up in a shepherd's cottage, listening for the enemy to come up the hillside, when the shepherd launched into an impassioned diatribe on the finer points of sheep breeding that rivaled any sermon I have ever heard in my life. By the end, I was nodding along and willing to launch a crusade against all weak, overbred flocks, prone to scours and fly-strike, crowding out the honest sheep of the world.

"Maggots!" he'd said, shaking his finger at me. "Maggots 'n piss in t' flaps o' they hides!"

I think of him often.

"I shall call it *A. potteri*," said my new acquaintance, who fortunately did not know where my thoughts were trending. "I am Eugenia Potter, and I shall have my name writ in the books of the Mycology Society one way or another."

"I believe that you shall," I said gravely. "I am Alex Easton." I bowed.

She nodded. A lesser spirit might have been embarrassed to have blurted her passions aloud in such a fashion, but clearly Miss Potter was beyond such weaknesses—or perhaps she simply assumed that anyone would recognize the importance of leaving one's mark in the annals of mycology.

"These stinking redgills," I said, "they are not new to science?"

She shook her head. "Described years ago," she said. "From this very stretch of countryside, I believe, or one near to it. The Ushers were great supporters of the arts long ago, and one commissioned a botanical work. Mostly of *flowers*"—her contempt was a glorious thing to hear—"but a few mushrooms as well. And even a botanist could not overlook *A. foetida*. I fear that I cannot tell you its common name in Gallacian, though."

"It may not have one." If you have never met a Gallacian, the first thing you must know is that Gallacia is home to a stubborn, proud, fierce people who are also absolutely piss-poor warriors. My ancestors roamed Europe, picking fights and having the tar beaten out of them by virtually every other people they ran across. They finally settled in Gallacia, which is near Moldavia and even smaller. Presumably they settled there because nobody else wanted it. The Ottoman Empire didn't even bother to make us a vassal state, if that tells you anything. It's cold and poor and if you don't die from falling in a hole or starving to death, a wolf eats you. The one thing going for it is that we aren't invaded often, or at least we weren't, until the previous war.

In the course of all that wandering around losing fights, we developed our own language, Gallacian. I am told it is worse than Finnish, which is impressive. Every time we lost a fight, we made off with a few more loan words from our enemies. The upshot of all of this is that the Gallacian language is intensely idiosyncratic. (We have seven sets of pronouns, for example, one of which is for inanimate objects and one of which is used only for God. It's probably a miracle that we don't have one just for mushrooms.)

Miss Potter nodded. "That is the Usher house on the other side of the tarn, if you were curious."

"Indeed," I said, "it is where I am headed. Madeline Usher was a friend of my youth."

"Oh," said Miss Potter, sounding hesitant for the first time. She looked away. "I have heard she is very ill. I am sorry."

"It has been a number of years," I said, instinctively touching the pocket with Madeline's letter tucked into it.

"Perhaps it is not so bad as they say," she said, in what was undoubtedly meant to be a jollying tone. "You know how bad news grows in villages. Sneeze at noon and by sundown the gravedigger will be taking your measurements."

"We can but hope." I looked down again into the tarn. A faint wind stirred up ripples, which lapped at the edges. As we watched, a stone dropped from somewhere on the house and plummeted into the water. Even the splash seemed muted.

Eugenia Potter shook herself. "Well, I have sketching to do. Good luck to you, Officer Easton."

"And to you, Miss Potter. I shall look forward to word of your *Amanitas.*"

Her lips twitched. "If not the *Amanitas,* I have great hopes for some of these boletes." She waved to me and strode out across the field, leaving silver boot prints in the damp grass.

I led Hob back to the road, which skirted the edge of the lake. It was a joyless scene, even with the end of the journey in sight. There were more of the pale sedges and a few dead trees, too gray and decayed for me to identify. (Miss Potter presumably knew what they were, although I would never ask her to lower herself to identifying mere vegetation.) Mosses coated the edges of the stones and more of the stinking redgills pushed up in obscene little lumps. The house squatted over it like the largest mushroom of them all.

My tinnitus chose that moment to strike, a high-pitched

whine ringing through my ears and drowning out even the soft lapping of the tarn. I stopped and waited for it to pass. It's not dangerous, but sometimes my balance becomes a trifle questionable, and I had no desire to stumble into the lake. Hob is used to this and waited with the stoic air of a martyr undergoing torture.

Sadly, while my ears sorted themselves out, I had nothing to look at but the building. God, but it was a depressing scene.

It is a cliché to say that a building's windows look like eyes because humans will find faces in anything and of course the windows would be the eyes. The house of Usher had dozens of eyes, so either it was a great many faces lined up together or it was the face of some creature belonging to a different order of life—a spider, perhaps, with rows of eyes along its head.

I'm not, for the most part, an imaginative soul. Put me in the most haunted house in Europe for a night, and I shall sleep soundly and wake in the morning with a good appetite. I lack any psychic sensitivities whatsoever. Animals like me, but I occasionally think they must find me frustrating, as they stare and twitch at unknown spirits and I say inane things like "Who's a good fellow, then?" and "Does kitty want a treat?" (Look, if you don't make a fool of yourself over animals, at least in private, you aren't to be trusted. That was one of my father's maxims, and it's never failed me yet.)

Given that lack of imagination, perhaps you will forgive me when I say that the whole place felt like a hangover.

What was it about the house and the tarn that was so depressing? Battlefields are grim, of course, but no one questions why. This was just another gloomy lake, with a gloomy house and some gloomy plants. It shouldn't have affected my spirits so strongly.

Granted, the plants all looked dead or dying. Granted, the windows of the house stared down like eye sockets in a row of skulls, yes, but so what? Actual rows of skulls wouldn't affect me so strongly. I knew a collector in Paris . . . well, never mind the details. He was the gentlest of souls, though he did collect rather odd things. But he used to put festive hats on his skulls depending on the season, and they all looked rather jolly.

Usher's house was going to require more than festive hats. I mounted Hob and urged him into a trot, the sooner to get to the house and put the scene behind me.

About the Author

T. KINGFISHER writes fantasy, horror, and occasional oddities, most recently including *What Moves the Dead* and *A House With Good Bones*. Under a pen name, she also writes bestselling children's books. She lives in North Carolina with her husband, dogs, and chickens who may or may not be possessed.

Look out for T. Kingfisher's
next novel from Tor Publishing Group

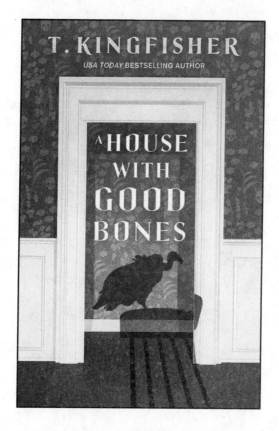

Available Spring 2023 from Tor Nightfire